THE LOSS OF INNOCENCE

A Bridge of Magic Novel
by Robert E Balsley, Jr.

Illustrations in Collaboration with
Jim Charles and Shelley Charles

COPYRIGHT

Copyright © 2020 by Trient Press

Trient Press
3375 S Rainbow Blvd
#81710, SMB 13135
Las Vegas,NV 89180

Ordering Information:
Quantity sales. Special discounts are available on quantity purchases by corporations, associations, and others. For details, contact the publisher at the address

above.
Orders by U.S. trade bookstores and wholesalers. Please
contact Trient Press: Tel: (775) 996-3844; or visit
www.trientpress.com.

Printed in the United States of America

Publisher's Cataloging-in-Publication data
Balsley, Jr., Robert E.
        A title of a book : The Loss of Innocence
        ISBN Hard Cover 978-1-953975-59-1
        Paperback 978-1-953975-57-7
        E-Book 978-1-953975-58-4

BRIDGE OF MAGIC

The Salvation of Innocence
The Struggle for Innocence
The Loss of Innocence

<u>DEDICATION</u>

During the writing of this book, my father passed away. He was a simple man who grew up in a simpler time… a time when faith in God, country, and family was much more commonplace. My father believed strongly in each of these facets of life, and those values he passed down to all his children. We never had all we wanted, but we always had all we needed.

For you, dad!

TABLE OF CONTENTS

Illustrated by Toby Briles

B'nai Elohim (Doom Warrior)

Illustrated by Toby Briles

Royal Mountain Saber Cat

Aster World Map

PREFACE

From the Book of the Unveiled:

Empath: An extraordinary group of healers unique to the elven city of Elanesse and believed to have the power to control the thoughts of another mortal being. As the empaths grew in prominence, fear of their rumored mind control abilities gave rise to suspicion and civil unrest. The elven lords of the city declared empaths outlaw and issued orders for their systematic capture and execution. Because the accepted truth was no magical spell could guard against the empath ability to control thoughts, the clerics of Elanesse devised powerful magic to ward against this talent. This magic also gave those who sought the empath the means through which the empath could be tracked. This magic, known as the Purge, was designed to be wielded by all willing rangers in Elanesse and the surrounding Forest of the Fey... for it was the rangers who were the enforcers of the law and the legal executioners. All empaths discovered within city limits were put to the sword. No quarter was given. Any empaths who escaped this slaughter were methodically hunted down by elven rangers and destroyed.

The goddess Aurora, to whom many rangers owed allegiance, did not favor her followers being used as executioners. Aurora, however, couldn't force her rangers to ignore the law of their mortal masters, nor could she stop the magic that allowed her rangers to be the instruments of this horrific slaughter. Other than making the participating rangers outcast, there was little she could do to prevent the carnage. Mortals had a right to govern their own affairs. Althaya, the goddess of healing and the immortal champion of all things magical, was just as helpless. She could only provide succor when possible and ensure the souls of the doomed empaths found eternal rest.

Unknown to the elven overlords of Elanesse, the empath ability often skipped multiple generations. Thus, while all known active empaths were murdered, the bloodline of the empath may not have been completely exterminated. This has never been proven, however, since there have been no reports of the existence of empaths for over three thousand years. The level of involvement, if any, played by the higher powers in this mystery is unknown.

The true power of an empath: Contrary to the belief at the time, the empath does not control thoughts. The empath is attuned to what people feel emotionally, love and hate being the two strongest. Hate can kill an empath. It was reported that many of the empaths killed in the Purge were so overwhelmed by the feeling of hatred emanating from their ranger executioners they died before suffering physical harm. While hate can kill, love can serve to protect the empath. For this reason, empaths were never alone during their childhood. To be so in the world would mean death. Their protection came from a bond that was forged with another who has a strong emotional attachment to the empath. This was usually the mother. It was only after the empath matured into an adult where they be able to thrive on their own, having by then developed sufficient internal coping mechanisms against pure emotions.

Empaths can also sense the state of the soul. They can feel good as well as evil. No evil deed or intent can escape the detection of the empath. But this ability made them a target of unnatural evil such as the undead and demonic forces.

The empaths greatest ability, however, is their natural aptitude for healing. They do this by accepting the injury or disease from their patient to their own body. Their empath power within would then heal the transferred injury. Empaths freely sacrifice themselves for others if the need is great. This healing ability has one significant benefit for the empath. It gives them an unusually long-life span. It has been rumored that the empath and the long-lived elf age at the same pace.

Author Unknown

<u>FORWARD</u>

From the Book of the Unveiled:

The Creation of Aster: The universe of which Aster is part is but one of many universes that make up the Nine Heavens. Like all the other planets in Aster's universe, the beginning was marked by bits and pieces of the 'stuff of creation' coalescing into a planet-sized sphere. Gravitational forces within the young planet of Aster formed and fused its multitude of different components into one.

For millions of years this barren, lifeless world roamed the universe until a young star captured it. The light from the star prompted the core of Aster to ignite into a swirling mass of molten metal — iron-nickel with smaller percentages of other elements. The liquid core gave in to the tremendous pressure that surrounded it and contracted. As a result, Aster became much denser. Its gravitational pull increased ten-fold. Smaller parts of matter in the surrounding space became trapped by this force and pulled into the planet. The addition of this new material resulted in a much larger planet... a planet large enough to generate an atmosphere from which life could spring and be sustained.

Several million years later the formation of a primordial atmosphere began to take place. Large volcanoes spewed thousands of tons of gases into the air. These gases combined to create the first hints of breathable air. They surrounded Aster and protected it from all the invisible dangers found in the void of space. It was also during this time that Aster was exposed to the corridors of magical energy, or ley lines, that intertwined and connected all the universes of the Nine Heavens. And thus, magic came to Aster.

As time drove relentlessly forward, the volcanic forces on Aster slowed and the planet cooled down. With this cooling came the first hints of water, another critical ingredient in the creation and sustainability of life. At this point Aster caught the attention of the gods and goddesses that ruled the Nine Heavens. To ensure the process of life would continue unhindered, they created the race of sylphs to act as guardians against any threat short of a natural catastrophe.

Generations of long-lived sylphs lived and died pursuing their calling. Every foot of Aster became known to the sylph as they patrolled – never resting – never compromising their duty. Only once during the guardianship of the sylph did a threat to Aster materialize. The threat came from the heavens above and lit the night in brilliant light as it streaked across the sky. As it drove through Aster's young atmosphere, it broke into two pieces and both landed on one of Aster's larger islands. The more massive piece landed in the north, turning that portion of the island into vapor. The smaller piece landed in the southeast. Though the damage from this piece was not as extensive, the resulting crater still measured several miles across. Earthquakes shook the entire island, and much of the northern half not destroyed broke into pieces. The sea rushed in to fill the void at both impact points.

The sylphs rushed through underground tunnels to inspect the damage, prepared to battle any threat that might present itself. Though they found the island topography had been significantly changed, there was no direct danger to Aster. When the sylph examined the impact point of the smaller piece, now under water, they discovered a large boulder of unknown makeup and origin. The heat from the stone's voyage through Aster's atmosphere still radiated and boiled the surrounding water. The sylphs carefully moved the boulder to the nearest shore. Tendrils of smoke swirled up as soon as the boulder was exposed to the air. Through a closer examination, the sylph's discovered this piece of stone was unlike any other on Aster. It was denser and so foreign to their experience it worried and frightened them. But even though the unknown composition was troublesome to the sylph, their high priest determined it was no threat. The sylph, reassured, returned to their guardianship of the planet entrusted to them. However the strange boulder was now constantly monitored.

Though the world of Aster was now primed for life, it didn't bear the fruit until several hundred thousand years later. By the time the first evidence appeared, the sylphs had become comfortable with Aster and thought of it as their own. Instead of being the guardian of the miracle of new life as their creators had intended, they became selfish and jealous of what they feared would be competition to their existence. They defied their ordained duty and sought to eliminate what they came to think of as parasites. Only one sylph remained true to her calling.

She was young. Like all sylphs, she was born from the magic of the gods. Unlike her fellow sylphs, however, she was untarnished by selfishness and jealousy. Within her the spark of righteousness — and loyalty to the gods and goddesses that gave her life — remained. Time after time she witnessed young life betrayed and snuffed out by her people. She asked why they would do this... why they would destroy the very life they were sworn to protect. She was told that the world of Aster belonged to no others... that only the sylph had the right to claim it as their own.

The young sylph was very troubled by the road of betrayal her people had taken. She went deep below the surface to consider the words and actions of her people. Though she understood why the sylph felt the way they did, she couldn't see how it justified what they did. With great sorrow, she prayed to the gods of creation. She told them of the sylph infidelity. She told them that new life — life that was to be cherished and protected — was instead being destroyed. She told them how her people had come to think of Aster as their own and wanted no interference from others. She scolded the gods for making this possible by abandoning the sylph instead of taking an interest in their progress. Finally, she asked the gods to show restraint when punishing her people.

The gods heard the young sylph's petition. They sentenced the sylph to eternal slumber with the promise that one day they might have a chance to prove themselves again worthy of trust. They collected the sylph and banished them into a deep underground cavern which had been newly prepared for that purpose. Only the young female sylph escaped this reprimand… though she would face a lifetime of loneliness wondering the tunnels and caverns beneath the surface of Aster. Each sylph, before drifting into the blackness of their own dreams, spoke the name of the sylph who had betrayed them — Elbedreth-Ahlasim.

Author Unknown

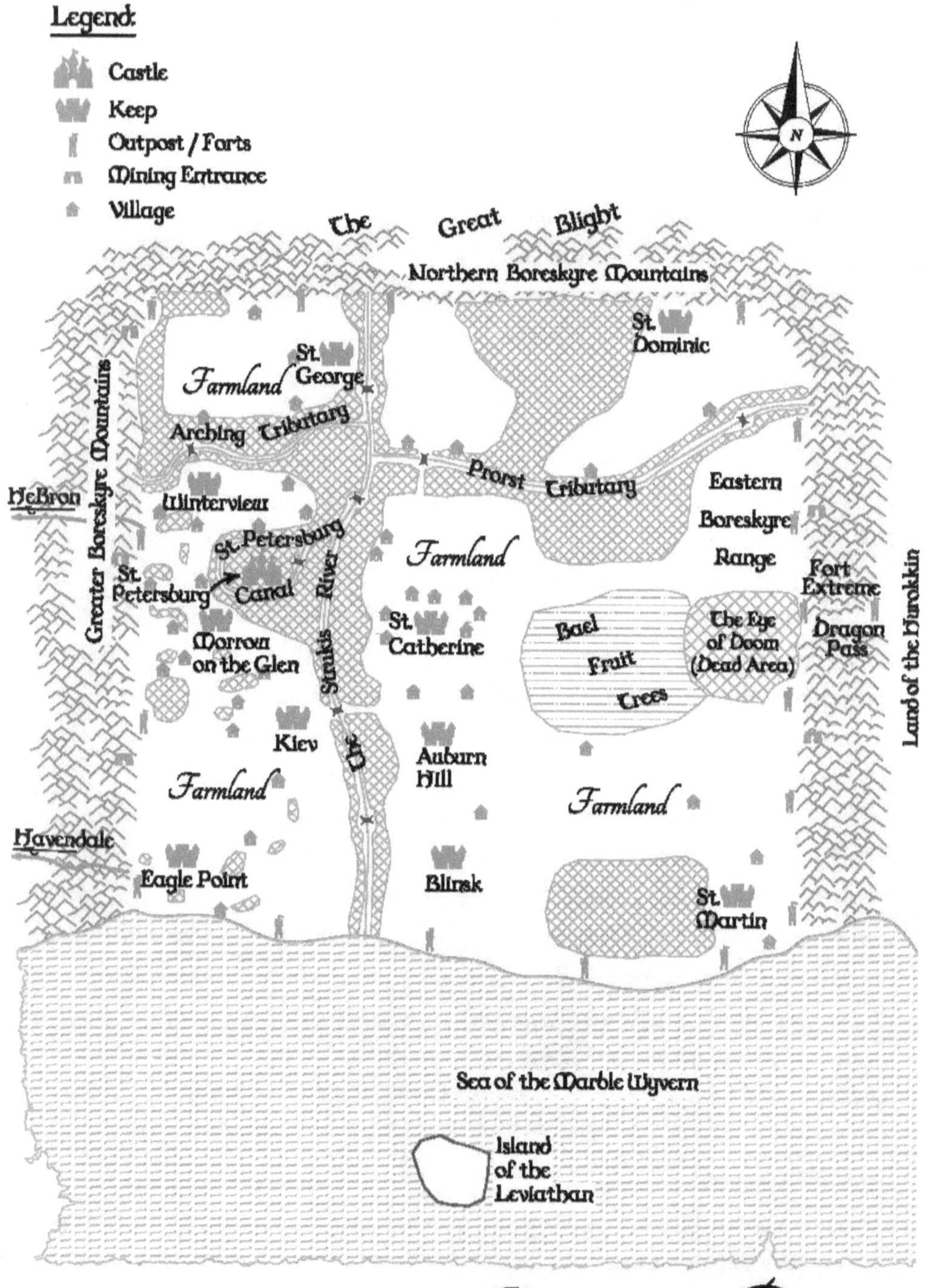

Legend:
Castle
Keep
Outpost / Forts
Mining Entrance
Village

The Great Blight
Northern Boreskyre Mountains
St. Dominic
Farmland
St. George
Arching Tributary
Eastern Boreskyre Range
Prorst Tributary
HeBron
Winterview
St. Petersburg
St. Petersburg Canal
Farmland
Greater Boreskyre Mountains
Fort Extreme
Dragon Pass
Morrow on the Glen
St. Catherine
Bael Fruit Trees
The Eye of Doom (Dead Area)
Strukis River
The
Kiev
Auburn Hill
Farmland
Farmland
Havendale
Eagle Point
Blinsk
St. Martin
Land of the Harokkin

Sea of the Marble Wyvern
Island of the Leviathan

Draugen Pesta

<u>PROLOGUE</u>

Land of the Draugen Pesta
(1000 Years Ago)

Mortal enemies — two or more factions which, because of political, religious, or racial disagreement, are in constant conflict. In some instances, however, there's no reason, foundation, or justification for this animosity. It just is. The Hyrokkin are our mortal enemies, and we are theirs. Typically, the only answer to this enmity is distance... or the complete destruction of one or the other. Since only a mountain range separates our two lands, distance isn't the solution.

-From the papers of Kir, Court Philosopher to His Majesty Lord Fedor, King of the Draugen Pasta

From the battlements of Fort Extreme Irinushka Abramovich looked to the east through Dragon Pass. The fort is on the eastern edge of Draugen Pesta lands and the first line of defense against the Hyrokkin. Several miles away on the other side of the pass was the Hyrokkin fort which marked the beginning of their hereditary lands. A long-standing agreement between the two races marked the pass itself as neutral territory.

"I still don't see what you hope to accomplish, myshka," Fort Extreme's commandant, General Pavel Garin, said. He wore black, as did all Draugen Pesta's military forces. His silver-trimmed, black cape bellowed in the wind.

Irinushka looked over at the fort commander before returning her gaze back to the pass. "It could avert another war with the

Hyrokkin, Pavel," she replied. "Maybe even put a truce in place that'll last more than a few weeks."

"Bah! We'll always be at war... at least until one of us figures out how to destroy the other."

Irinushka put a hand on Pavel's arm. "Don't say that. Both our peoples have a right to live in peace."

Pavel shook his head. "Irinushka, you're a priestess with a kind heart. But I think perhaps you have a naivety regarding the Hyrokkin that borders on insanity." Pavel took her hand. "They'll never honor a truce. They'll only use the time to get stronger and plot for our destruction. I've fought them. I know their butchering hearts. You don't."

"They honor the neutrality of the pass, Pavel. Maybe we can hope for something better?"

"I can give you a thousand reasons why those four-legged beasts honor the neutrality," Pavel replied hotly. His anger was growing by the minute because he knew she wouldn't listen... and that caused him to fear for her life. "But none of them have to do with honor!"

"It's the king's will," Irinushka said softly after a few moments of silence.

"Fedor was once a great warrior," Pavel replied. "Perhaps the finest our people had ever seen. But now he's old and weak... and not right in the head. He should have retired years ago. It still amazes me the people accept his leadership."

Irinushka sighed. She loved Pavel, but she was getting tired of constantly defending the king's position in this. "The people want peace," she said. "We've been at war with the Hyrokkin for centuries. Even warrior nations eventually tire of all the killing. Since they were the ones that asked for this meeting, maybe, just maybe, they feel the same. Lord Fedor simply wishes to explore the possibility."

Pavel brushed the side of Irinushka's face with the back of his hand. "Don't go, my love. If you're so certain about the Hyrokkin's intentions, then surely it can be handled by someone else. Send one of the king's lackeys."

"You know I can't do that," Irinushka replied as she wrapped her arm around his and laid her head on his shoulder.

"You're our High Priestess! As such you're far too valuable to our people... and to me personally... to be placed in such jeopardy."

Irinushka shook her head. "My position is irrelevant. I have my orders... as do you."

Pavel nodded. "My orders say nothing about how I'm to get you to the meeting... only that I do. I'm going with you. The High Priestess of the Draugen Pesta people should have a suitable escort."

"I was hoping you'd say that," Irinushka said as she smiled. "Come. Tomorrow will be here soon. We need to rest... among other things."

The Hyrokkin, a race of centaurs – half man, half horse – had no intention of pursuing or honoring peace with the Draugen Pesta. But a direct assault against the Draugen Pesta nation through the Dragon Pass, though tried many times in the distant past by both antagonists, was a campaign nightmare... a funnel through which many Hyrokkin had died. Crossing the Eastern Boreskyre Range was even more dangerous, however. Its mountains presented an almost impenetrable barrier between the two warrior nations.

All of that changed, however, when a band of dwarves stumbled into Hyrokkin lands. Captured after a brief fight, the dwarves were given one chance to prove their worth to the Hyrokkin people. The dwarves, fearing for their lives, demonstrated their natural ability as miners and successfully argued the potential wealth beneath their feet would allow the Hyrokkin to become a world power. There were also, they said upon learning of the animosity between the Hyrokkin and Draugen Pesta, other ways to win a conflict, or, as one dwarf said, "Lads, there's more than one way to skin a cat." While the enticement of wealth seduced the Hyrokkin, the potential to destroy the Draugen Pesta sealed the pact with the dwarves. Before long, the dwarves had mined into the Eastern Boreskyre Range and discovered several large veins of silver to prove their point. The dwarves volunteered to teach the Hyrokkin their mine-craft in exchange for their freedom. The Hyrokkin, however, never intended to honor their agreement. If they couldn't go over the Eastern Boreskyre Range, perhaps they could go under it and mine for precious metal at the same time. They kept the dwarves as slaves... and the 'great burrowing' began.

For over two centuries the dwarves and their centaur overseers excavated three separate tunnels under the Eastern Boreskyre Range. During that time, the Hyrokkin continued to make small raids into Draugen Pesta lands... but these raids were only for show. Any change in their behavior would raise the suspicions of their western enemies.

Ten years before the planned invasion, the Hyrokkin, hoping to lure their enemy into complacency, sent emissaries to Draugen Pesta. They believed the Draugen Pesta, though magnificent warriors with a large standing army, preferred the tranquility of peace to the chaos of war. They were right... and the neutrality of Dragon Pass was established and all Hyrokkin incursions into Draugen Pesta lands ceased.

A few days before the invasion, the Hyrokkin sent a message to the Draugen Pesta king, explaining they were interested in peace and the joint pursuit of common goals. Though the king was favorable to the idea, his advisors warned against accepting on face value something that went against Hyrokkin character. It was nothing other than a trap, they insisted. The king was adamant, however. He knew they were probably right, but he was desperate for a chance at peace. And if it was a trap, he felt they might as well spring it.

The king's advisors were right. It was a trap. A trap meant to direct Draugen Pesta's attention to the pass and away from the western slopes of the Eastern Boreskyre Range. Unfortunately for the Hyrokkin, though, was that the dwarves had set their own traps in the tunnels to reward the centaurs for more than two centuries of mistreatment and slavery.

On the day of the invasion, the Hyrokkin's ambush in Dragon Pass went as planned... at least in the beginning. But by nightfall of the day of the invasion, most of the Hyrokkin army lay dead and buried deep underneath the Eastern Boreskyre Range.

It stormed during the night, and the following morning was dreary. Light drizzle kept everything damp and everyone outside miserable. High Priestess Irinushka Abramovich, General Pavel Garin, and a small troop of twenty-four guards, twelve warrior monks of Irinushka's order and twelve of Pavel's security detail, made their way to the designated meeting place, the center of Dragon Pass. By the time they had arrived, the Hyrokkin contingent had just left their fort. The Hyrokkin had three times the number of guards.

"Now do you believe me?" Pavel said. "They're bringing a small army. We should turn back while we still can."

Irinushka didn't like the looks of the approaching Hyrokkin either... but wouldn't let that interfere with her objective. It was too important. "They're under a flag of truce in neutral territory," she replied. "Until we know for sure, we stay."

The Hyrokkin stopped one hundred yards away, dropped the flag of truce to the ground, and raised their attack standard. Scores of arrows filled the air from the back of the Hyrokkin column, while those in the front charged.

"Shields up!" Pavel screamed.

But it was too late. The overcast skies prevented him from spotting the arrows until they were already on their downward trajectory. Eleven of Irinushka's escort, including Pavel, went down, either dead or wounded. Irinushka dropped to her knees as she inspected Pavel's wound... but saw he had died instantly with an arrow in his right eye and another in his chest. As she cradled his head in her lap, she looked around. The Hyrokkin where closing rapidly while screaming their war cries as another volley of arrows took flight. All they hit this time were iron shields.

The Draugen Pesta charged forward to meet the Hyrokkin attack, but Irinushka knew it wouldn't be enough. She stood after gently placing Pavel's head on the hard, stone floor of the pass.

"I need time," she said to the two warrior monks who had remained behind to guard her. "Your sacrifice will be remembered in the words of poets... and the prayers of all those in your warrior order." Both monks knelt to receive Irinushka's blessing and, once they had it, darted off to join the battle.

Irinushka's anger took root as she watched the monk's run to their deaths. It was anger at the death of her one and only love, Pavel... anger at the Hyrokkin treachery... anger at the gullibility of the king to believe peace was possible with the centaurs... and anger at herself for believing the same thing. Looking up into the wet and dark sky, she raised a fist into the air and screamed. It was a primal scream full of hate and self-loathing.

The priestess looked down at the dead and decided enough was enough. "I don't care if you forgive me or not," she whispered to her goddess as she raised her hands and chanted:

> *"Spirit, wind, toxic fire.*
> *Read my soul, read my ire.*
>
> *Doom the ones who cause me pain.*
> *Feel the anger I can't refrain.*
>
> *Test my fortitude, test my mettle.*
> *See the claim I wish to settle.*
>
> *Heed my call, insidious beasts.*
> *Come to me, I grant you release."*

"ANIMA MEA REFERT SURGE!"

The drizzle turned into heavy rain which swallowed up the din of the battle taking place deeper into the pass. Lightning streaked across the sky and thunder shook the ground, knocking Irinushka off her feet. A great crack made its way across the pass in front of the priestess as the ground rose and then dropped back down. Enormous bluish bolts of electricity dropped from the sky and disappeared into the open ground before her, setting off a kaleidoscope of light deep in the depths of the fissure. Then, except for the heavy rain still beating down, silence prevailed, and the light died. Irinushka looked around. There was a feeling of anticipation in the water-drenched air.

The battle between her escort and the Hyrokkin seemed to be over. There were no sounds of swords clanging together, and the screams of the dying and the wounded abruptly ceased.

'The Hyrokkin have won and are dispatching the injured," Irinushka thought. *'They'll come for me soon."*

Irinushka pulled a knife from her cloak and lowered her body into a defensive fighting stance. She knew she was going to die... but she was determined to make her death as expensive to the Hyrokkin as possible.

The footfalls of the centaurs could now be differentiated from the rainfall, but another sound caught her attention. It came from the opening in the pass floor. Irinushka first heard a great tearing as if a bed sheet were being ripped in two but multiplied a thousand times. Then she heard the screams and cries of millions of inhuman voices.

As Irinushka stared, a wet fog of steam rose from the fractured pass and blocked her ability to see clearly. She closed her eyes and concentrated. After a few seconds, her mind separated and identified the different sounds. She heard the Hyrokkin come closer as their hooves clattered on the stone floor of the pass. She heard the rain sizzle as it went down into the breach in the earth. Whatever was down there must be incredibly hot. She heard inhuman voices —

voices that cried for release – voices that cried for the freedom to mangle, slaughter, and destroy. Finally, she heard movement deep within the fog. She knew at that moment her prayer had been answered. And it terrified her.

Forms rose from the great crevice and took shape in the mist. There were seven and they were monstrous. Each was twenty-seven feet tall. Atop their dragon torsos were large dog-like heads, but instead of two eyes, there were six, three to each side. The gold-colored eyes sparkled with intelligence, wisdom, and something else Irinushka couldn't quite put her finger on. Perhaps it was a great weariness. The scales on their bodies shimmered with a shiny black coloration which reflected light back at the observer. Four powerful arms protruded out of the torso... each ending with a three-talon hand. Four legs, each clawed, as thick as the trunk of a large tree, and as long as Irinushka's ten-foot height, secured these great beasts to the ground. Their tails extended another fifteen feet and ended in a three-talon tip. But the most significant part of these creatures... Irinushka thought the most beautiful part... were the wings. Each wing was twenty feet long with large claws protruding outward from the point where the delicate wing skeletal structure began. The membrane on each wing was flexible and nimble but also appeared to be very tough. Like the body, the wings shimmered a deep purple which faded about half-way down and turned to crimson. Gold flakes covered the wings and sparkled even in the dim light of the dreary day.

The charging Hyrokkin came to a sudden stop when the creatures came into their view. The world had never seen the like, and they were unsure how to proceed. As much as they wanted to take the head of the Draugen Pesta priestess back with them to prove their great victory, they weren't in any hurry to lose their lives in doing so... at least not until they had gauged the fighting prowess of the huge creatures standing before them.

Six of the creatures turned to face the Hyrokkin while the remaining one moved closer to Irinushka. Towering over her, it looked down.

"I am Michael," he said. "You've called upon us at a most inconvenient time, priestess. But we have vowed to answer. What is your pleasure?"

Irinushka stared. She had been expecting horrid creatures to do her bidding and not such an impressive exquisiteness.

Michael seemed to understand Irinushka's momentary delay. "Do not confuse splendor with weakness," he said. "My brethren and I spend our long lives battling demons... demons that would otherwise invade your world. You're lucky it is us who intercepted and answered your call. The demons your summoning was intended are impossible to control and would have ravaged you. Now, we're wasting time. What do you require of us?"

Irinushka, still staring, pointed at the waiting Hyrokkin.

"You wish them dead?" Michael asked. "They do not appear to be a threat at the present moment."

Irinushka finally found her voice. "They attacked under a flag of truce and murdered my people," she replied angrily. "They deserve the same consideration. I command you to kill them!"

Michael turned to look at the Hyrokkin, who by this time had read the situation and were beginning to retreat. "And?" he asked after turning his attention back to the priestess.

"And..." Irinushka dropped to her knees once again, cradled Pavel's head in her lap, and kissed his forehead. When she looked back up at Michael there were tears in her eyes.

"Ahh... I see," Michael said. "You want retribution."

"Yes!" Irinushka answered before shaking her head. "No! I want justice! I want them punished!"

Michael studied the priestess as she cradled the head of the one she loved. She continued to weep... her tears mixed with the rain as they fell. "Punishment is something I understand." Michael turned to his waiting comrades and nodded his head. The Hyrokkin tried to escape their doom, but it was impossible.

Irinushka heard their screams over the incessant pounding of the rainfall. She tried to push her feelings aside but found she couldn't. She now regretted dealing with the Hyrokkin in such a harsh manner.

Michael continued to study her. He understood the emotions he saw in her eyes... in her body language. "I see you comprehend the finality of your actions. It's a heavy burden to sentence one to death... even if that's what they deserve. It's an even greater burden to be the executioner."

Irinushka looked up. "I didn't..."

"You didn't what?" Michael interrupted. "You didn't end their lives? You've no blood on your hands?" Michael paused to let his words find meaning. "Accept your responsibility in this killing."

"I..." Irinushka stopped and looked back down. "You're right. It's no different than if I had run them through with a sword myself. But it's not what I was trained to do. As a priestess, I'm supposed to succor, not destroy. I feel... dirty... like I've betrayed my vows."

Michael nodded. "Yes, in this instance we were your sword. But we're not your conscience." Michael paused as he considered. "Priestess, I don't know if this helps, but those we killed were evil. We wouldn't have done it otherwise. Is it not your duty to protect the good from such evil? If so you have done well today."

Irinushka stood. "Thank you, but that's little consolation."

Michael shrugged his shoulders. "So be it. Listen closely, priestess. We intervened to save you and your world from a great mistake. Demons should never be used as a solution to a problem. Though we answered your call, that does not mean you commanded us. Nor does it mean we will always act upon your best interests... if those interests don't coincide with ours. Remember that for the future."

"I understand," Irinushka replied.

Michael picked up a stone and made a fist around it. The unmistakable gleam of magic surrounded his hand, and when he opened it, a small, chained locket had replaced the stone. He handed it to Irinushka. "As I mentioned, we only came here by mere happenstance since your summoning was intended to call a demon. That would have been most unfortunate. The next time you have need of us, use this."

Irinushka bowed. "My people are in your debt," she said.

Michael nodded. "We will be your Doom Warriors," he said before he turned to join his companions at the edge of the crevice. Without another word, each flapped their wings to gain altitude before diving back into its depths. As Irinushka watched them spread their wings to take flight, she thought they were the most beautiful creatures she'd ever seen. Shortly after the Doom Warriors disappeared, the crevice closed, leaving no sign it had ever existed. She put the locket around her neck and under her tunic next to her bare skin, turned, and began her walk back to Fort Extreme. She needed to coordinate retrieval of the bodies and report the day's happenings to her liege. As she made her way, she debated telling the king about her newly discovered allies. The more she thought about it, however, the more she felt Pavel was right. The king wasn't sane enough to use the locket wisely.

Irinushka passed the locket down to her successor after guaranteeing by solemn vow that the locket would be guarded as any other sacred relic of the faith... that it wouldn't be relinquished until a worthy king sat upon the throne. She also spread rumors about the Doom Warriors... turning them into the things that go bump into the night to ensure they wouldn't be called lightly. For several generations the locket stayed with the High Priestess of the Draugen Pesta people – for no king had been judged worthy – until Lord Ternborg's father, King Verasmus, sat upon the throne. King Verasmus, on his deathbed, surrendered responsibility for the locket to his son, Lord Ternborg.

During all that time, the locket was never used to call the Doom Warriors. For with the locket came the warning that it was a two-edged sword... a sword that could cut both ways. The legend of the Doom Warriors grew until it had spread across both the Draugen Pesta and Hyrokkin domains. Doom Warriors became the 'boogie man' by which parents in both realms scared their children to sleep. The myth of the Doom Warriors came to be such that both King Verasmus and his son, Lord Ternborg, feared using it. That is until Lord Ternborg met someone he feared even more... Nightshade.

CHAPTER ONE

Havendale, The Mainland
(Present Day)

"Magical energy is derived from both nature and the magical lines of energy which span the world. It's neither good nor evil. More specifically, the fundamental nature of sorcery is impartial. It follows the command of all who know how to use it to whatever ends they desire. But there ARE good sorcerers and evil sorcerers. What's the difference? It's simple. The difference lies in the heart of each of you. It lies in your realization there are consequences to every spell you cast. Never forget that! Consequences are real. I wouldn't use a fire spell in a hay-filled stable filled with horses. There'd be too much collateral damage. Too much pain and destruction. But the evil sorcerer? He wouldn't care. And that, my students, is the distinction."

-Taken from a lecture by the elven Master Sorcerer Rathal Arquen, Lord Paramount of Havendale, to students in the Academy of Sorcery.

"So you see, the teleportation spell seems easy enough… but like all spells, casting it is dangerous if you don't thoroughly understand it. You must know exactly where you wish to go. You have to…"

There was a knock on the door to the classroom.

"Not now!" Rathal Arquen called out irritably. "As I was saying, if the endpoint isn't within sight, you must visualize the destination in your mind and…"

The classroom door opened and Rathal's assistant, Shynaria D'Valmaris, stuck her head in. "Rathal, I'm sorry, but it's urgent. Amkissra needs to see you in the observation room."

Rathal frowned as he looked over, but saw she was clearly agitated which wasn't in her nature. Concerned, he switched back to his students. "Class dismissed until further notice. And don't try to teleport just yet," he said as they filed out of the room. "You might find yourselves stuck in a wall or something. And if you do, by the gods, I'll leave you there for all to see!"

Shynaria pushed her way through the throng of students. "Sorry," she said as she reached Rathal's side.

Rathal brushed her apology aside. "Shy, what's going on. I've never seen you look so worried."

"I don't really know for sure," she replied. "You know how much Amkissra likes to keep things to herself. But when she asked me... no, that's not correct... when she ordered me to get you, she looked scared. I could see it in her eyes. Rathal, she's seen something... something bad."

As the two walked down crowded hallways, Rathal asked, "The others?"

"Already on their way," Shynaria replied. "Oh, and Rhys will also be there."

"Rhys? What interest does our master of spies have in this?"

Shynaria chuckled. "He once told me all things mattered to him. That it's the only way to capture the big picture."

Rathal frowned. "I've never been comfortable around him."

"He's a person of many faces... many talents..."

"Most of which I don't approve!" Rathal retorted.

"His cadres of spies serve Havendale well," Shynaria replied. "And you know it."

"Yes, of course you're right. He's shown his loyalty many times over. Still..."

"We've had this discussion before, Rathal," Shynaria said. "He'd do anything for you."

Rathal glanced over at his assistant. "For me? Or for you?"

"My personal life..."

"Yes, yes... I know," Rathal said. "Your personal life is none of my business. But if you want to keep it that way, try to be less obvious."

Shynaria nodded. "Very well. He loves Havendale even more than he loves me. But love me he does. And I him. So get used to it, my lord."

Rathal laughed. "Only if you agree never to call me that again. Here we are."

Rathal and Shynaria climbed the stairs going up the north tower to the observation room and Amkissra's laboratory. They entered a large, domed room with part of the ceiling open to the sky. Around the room were shelves of maps, tomes, and observation notebooks, all arranged in either alphabetical order or, in the case of the observation notebooks, by date. Several mercury-filled scrying basins stood throughout the room. In the center was a large metal globe of Aster mounted on a base with several movable arms which could be placed anywhere on the sphere. The runes etched into each of the arms glowed with powerful magic. The sphere itself depicted the known landmass of Aster along with longitude, latitude, and ley lines etched into it. Off against a wall was an unmade portable cot. Amkissra had been withdrawn of late, but Rathal hadn't known she was spending her evenings here. Besides Amkrissa, standing around the globe was the entire Havendale ruling congress, as well as top military generals and, of course, Rhys, Havendale's chief spy.

Rathal stopped short as soon as he saw the globe. It had a small funnel-shaped formation over the island of InnisRos. From the funnel's apex, a sinister looking cloud expanded outward going nowhere. "That's not right!" he said before picking Amkissra out from the rest of the crowd and hurrying over to her. "What am I looking at?"

Amkissra was a female elf approaching middle-age who had all the characteristics of her race – beautiful with long dark hair, petite body structure, pale skin, dark expression-filled eyes, and several platinum rings pierced through each elongated ear. She acknowledged

Rathal with a nod and pointed at the funnel. "A corridor has been opened from InnisRos to... somewhere. It's not to the Alfheim, that much I know. Its characteristics are similar, but it's been... tainted... as if some type of malignancy has taken hold."

"And the cloud?" Rathal asked.

"Disturbing, my lord. And a threat." That answer came from Havendale's military commander, General Kelsia Húrön.

Rathal looked over at his general, then back to Amkissra. "Explain."

"You're familiar with the *Ak-Séregon Stone* and the *Ak-Samarië Shard*, and how they work together to form a stable corridor of passage between our world and the Alfheim?" Amkissra asked.

"I am," Rathal replied. "All sorcerers are... at least any worth their salt."

"The *Ak-Séregon Stone* has gone rogue and opened a corridor without the *Ak-Samarië Shard* acting in kind on the other end," Amkissra explained. "That's why it looks so malignant."

"And you don't know where the new corridor's going?"

Amkissra shook her head. "No, Rathal. But the problem extends beyond that. Watch closely."

As they did, the cloud vanished. The enchanted runes on the arms of the globe blazed with magic. The globe suddenly became vague, its sharp outline indistinct. This lasted for barely a second before the globe returned to normal. The corridor and the cloud emanating from it seemed to become darker... angrier... and didn't shift back when the globe did.

"What just happened?" Rathal asked.

Amkissra sighed. "Without being there to study it, I can only surmise that the new corridor created by the *Ak-Séregon Stone* on InnisRos is being forced. However, the stone itself isn't strong enough to maintain the necessary magical output without drawing additional power from somewhere."

"And that somewhere is?"

"From its surroundings." Amkissra paused and took a deep breath. "That's what the cloud is doing... drawing energy to feed the corridor. But it goes deeper than that. As you know, the corridor created by the *Ak-Séregon Stone* can punch holes through any number of universes. In this case, it's hard to tell how many since I don't know where it's going. But without the *Ak-Samarië Shard* on the other side to stabilize it, it's pulling what it needs from the universes it crosses."

"And this is bad how?"

"I think somehow this is causing Aster to begin a shift," Amkissra replied. "A shift from our position in this universe to another. As the *Ak-Séregon Stone* takes what it needs to stabilize itself, its hold on the other end solidifies." The sorceress looked hard at Rathal. "The power of the stone is dragging Aster behind it as it seeks to strengthen its grip on the endpoint, wherever that might be. But Aster resists this dragging, instead trying to maintain its place in this universe. All of this puts a tremendous amount of pressure on the portal. What we witnessed just a moment ago is Aster moving from its place in our universe. Granted, in relative terms, the movement is slight. But each time it happens, it lasts longer, and Aster moves farther. I believe our world is being pulled towards what I'll call the 'snap-point'. When this is reached, one of two things will happen. The corridor will break. Or it will hold. Either way, it'll sling Aster out of our universe."

Rathal looked around the room at all those gathered. He knew what that meant for Aster. And from the looks on their faces, they did to.

Amkissra continued her narrative. "If the corridor breaks, there'll be enough power to hurl Aster spinning through space. If the corridor holds, it will pull Aster through however many universes the corridor crosses until it reaches the endpoint. In either scenario, all life on our world will be destroyed."

There was complete silence in the observatory.

"This is inevitable?" Rathal asked.

Amkissra shook her head. "No... not if the corridor is shut down."

"How much time do we have?"

"Uncertain," Amkissra replied. "There's one other consideration."

Rathal looked up at the sky through the opening in the ceiling. It was clear and bright with no hint of the disaster rapidly approaching. "What would that be, Amkissra?"

"The Alfheim," she replied.

"Tell me."

"The *Ak-Samarië Shard* is a relic... created by the gods and given to the Alfheim. Even without the *Ak-Séregon Stone*, it's powerful enough to safely maintain the passageway between our two worlds." Amkissra shook her head. "But if they don't break that link, their world will suffer the same fate as ours."

Rathal frowned. "They should be warned."

"Yes," Amkissra agreed. "If they don't know already. But without the *Ak-Séregon Stone* connected to the shard on the Alfheim, communications are only one way. We can't get a message to them from this end."

"Rhys, do you have any contacts on InnisRos?" Rathal asked.

"InnisRos has gone dark, my lord," Rhys replied.

Rathal looked at the spymaster.

Rhys didn't flinch. "That's part of the reason I'm here," he said. "We need to talk. Alone."

Rathal knew better then to ask Rhys to explain in front of everyone. He nodded. "As soon as we're finished here."

"Is there any way at all you can better pin-point when?" This question came from Shynaria. "There has to be some way you can figure out a time-frame? We can't afford to be uncertain."

Amkissra looked at Rathal, who nodded. "I don't know," she replied. "I'll study the duration of time each shift lengthens and come up with an approximation, but the magic of the globe will only tell us so much. Nor can it predict the future."

"What can we expect from these 'shifts' you're talking about?" Rathal asked.

Amkissra looked at Rathal curiously before understanding. "Oh! You mean the physical manifestations of the shift." She shook her head. "Unknown until we've experienced them. But if I were to make a guess, I'd say strong weather fronts with storms more powerful than we've ever seen. There will probably be an increase in the intensity and number of tornados, hurricanes, and earthquakes… that type of thing. Most of us won't have to worry about the snap-point. The weather will have wiped us out long before we reach it."

The stunned silence that surrounded Rathal and his advisors was broken by Rhys. "Madam sorceress. Is it possible for these... shifts, as you call them... to expose part of Aster to another world? Or another universe?"

"What do you mean?" Rathal asked.

Rhys looked at Rathal as he tried to decide whether he should speak freely.

"I know what he means," Amkissra said, ending Rhys' conundrum.

Rathal saw a brief look of relief cross the face of his spymaster.

"In theory I suppose that's possible," Amkissra said. "But it'd probably be more accurate to say that Aster, or at least part of it, overlaps with other worlds or universes during the time of a shift. That's to say, they both momentarily occupy the same spot in time and space."

"What are you..." Rathal said before being stopped by the raised hand of Rhys.

"Then would it be possible for someone from this world to be left in another universe," the spy stated.

Amkissra nodded. "Assuming overlap actually occurs during a shift, then yes, I'd say very possible. The opposite would also be true."

This sudden line of questioning by Rhys took Rathal off guard. But now that it was out in the open, the implications were astounding.

Not only are the races of Aster in danger of being 'kidnapped'... they're also in danger of whatever might be left behind from another world or universe. One could only imagine the demons or beasts that could find themselves on Aster.

"How about land masses? Or structures?" Shynaria asked.

Rathal nodded. "Good question, Shy. Amkissra?"

"No, I don't think that's a possibility," the sorceress replied. "They're rooted to their world, whereas people are not."

"We need to get this threat relayed to the other city-states as soon as possible," Rathal said. "Rhys..."

Rhys nodded. "I'll get the word out, my lord. Everyone on the mainland west of the Greater Boreskyre Mountains will have the information within a day."

"Thank you," Rathal replied. "As soon as that's completed, please come to my quarters. Shy, if Rhys has no objection, you're free to go with him. I won't need you until later."

Shynaria looked at Rhys who smiled and nodded. They walked out of the observation room together.

Rathal then turned to General Húrön. "General, please put our military on full alert."

General Húrön, a husky female dwarf, smiled. "Aye, lad. I'll do exactly that," she said as she turned to her adjutant, a young male dwarf, who suddenly came to attention. "You heard the lord, ye daft knuckleheaded idjit. Get cracking!"

As the adjutant hurriedly left the room, General Húrön wheeled around on another of her staff, a human female. "Double up the patrols along the Merchant's Way up to Silverstone and over to Ordenskyr. Coordinate your efforts with the leaders of both those cities. And have a small contingent ride up to Saint Seton and put the Riders of the Elderdale on notice."

"Aye, General," the girl said as she saluted and ran off.

"You three," General Húrön addressed the last three in her staff. "Go and make yourselves useful!" Turning back to the others in the room with hands clasped behind her back, she looked at the globe of

Aster. "Right now, our greatest ally will be our ability to spot these otherworld critters as soon as they arrive, if they do. The gods help us all if something from another universe escapes and no one knows about it."

"I don't think we can prevent that from happening, General," Amkissra said.

"Perhaps not, lassie," General Húrön replied. "But by the beard on my father's chin I'm damn sure going to try!" She looked at Rathal. "With your permission, my lord."

Rathal nodded. "Go, Kelsia. See to your command."

The members of Havendale's congress followed General Húrön out the door with instructions from Rathal to keep quiet for the time being. The stark contrast between a filled observation room and a nearly empty one was clear... and welcomed. Rathal returned his gaze to the globe and frowned. "What else is there to do?" he asked himself.

Amkissra came up behind him and put her arms around his waist. "Talking to yourself again?" she said has she laid her head on his back.

Rathal was tall for an elf... close to seven feet. There were rumors among the people of Havendale that he might have giant blood running through his veins. He never gave those rumors much credence... but who ever really knew for sure. Compared to Amkissra, who stood at only five feet tall, he WAS a giant.

The two were an odd match. While the size difference certainly made this obvious, there was also stark dissimilarities in their personalities. Whereas Rathal was gregarious, Amkissra was timid and introverted. Though she was smarter and probably more suited to lead the Academy of Sorcery, and by extension rule Havendale, she preferred her solitary work in the observatory. The only person she truly felt comfortable around was Rathal.

Rathal and Amkissra had been childhood friends and had been in love with each other for a long time. When they reached marrying age, it seemed natural the two of them would take the lifelong plunge.

That all changed when Rathal accompanied a small caravan up to HeBron. Something terrible had happened. Only Rathal and an exotic female elf survived. Rathal never told Amkrissa what had occurred, or how the female elf was involved... only that they had saved each other's lives. Havendale's ruling congress investigated the incident and then sealed the records... ostensibly because it would've caused a diplomatic incident with HeBron.

The female elf, only known as Annessa, stayed in Havendale for a week and then quietly left, never to be seen or heard from again. Rathal was inconsolable and delved into his studies of the arcane arts with renewed vigor. He allowed no time for anything else and cut off all who were his friends, including Amkissra. But after ten years Rathal emerged from the wall he had built around himself. He had an epiphany of sorts. It was a discovery he could neither identify nor understand. But through it he now saw hope for the dreary life he had painted himself into. He remade who he was into something new... and as a result, became Havendale's ruler, resumed all the friendships he had discarded, and allowed Amkissra back into his heart. Though he still wouldn't tell her exactly what took place all those years ago, Amkissra felt confident Rathal had finally moved on.

Rathal suddenly wheeled on Amkissra, grabbed her by the shoulders and, setting her at arm's length, asked, "Is there any way we can develop some kind of early warning system? Something that will tell us when a shift is about to occur?"

Amkissra frowned... then shook her head. "Not from here," she replied. "I understand the properties of the corridor and could probably create a magical charm which would work... but it'd have to be placed in close proximity to the *Ak-Séregon Stone.*"

Rathal gazed off into the space. "No point in doing that," he said. "If we could get that close, we'd just shut the stone down. Besides, I have a feeling we don't have that much time. We need something we can use right now."

The master sorcerer released Amkissra and sat in a nearby chair, staring at the globe. Even as he stared, another shift occurred. "Damn!" he swore softly.

Amkissra also saw the shift... but her mind was racing far too fast to give it much notice. "No doubt InnisRos will take whatever action deemed necessary to shut down the *Ak-Séregon Stone*," she said. "Their sorcerers are well versed in its operation. I'm sure they'll have things under control soon enough. Rathal, there's nothing we can do about it from here."

"Maybe, maybe not," Rathal replied. "But let's give them the benefit of the doubt. Moving that aside, what's left? We need to protect our people from the potential aftereffects of each shift. That means figuring out a way to keep anyone from transitioning to another world... and to warn us if something from another world... something bad... comes here."

Amkissra took a chair facing Rathal. "The only way we'll keep people safe is to close the corridor. I mean, we can warn everybody, I suppose. But what good will that do? Besides the widespread panic it'd cause, how do you keep them safe? Ask them to cross their fingers?"

Rathal frowned.

"Look, Rathal," Amkissra continued, "as long as the unknown corridor remains in place, the shifts are going to happen. They'll occur randomly and will continue to lengthen. This will increase the time our world is exposed. There's no way to predict where, for how long, or for that matter what the consequences will actually be."

"So, you're of the opinion it's all a matter of luck?" Rathal replied. Amkissra was making sense and there was frustration in his voice. "That I tell the family of someone who's vanished that it was pure happenstance?"

"I'd prefer to use the term destiny," Amkissra replied. "On the bright side, it might save them if our world is destroyed."

Rathal shrugged his shoulders. "If the world they disappeared to is survivable. Guess it's better than nothing at all." He stood. "I need to get to my meeting with Rhys. I wonder what bad news HE has for me."

Amkissra stood also and kissed Rathal. "Do you want to talk about how we protect ourselves from whatever might be left behind after a shift?"

"I'm still working on it. Dinner tonight? Normal time?"

Amkissra smiled. "I'll have the kitchen send something up."

Rathal hugged Amkissra tightly. "Don't go outside unless absolutely necessary," he whispered.

Rathal found Rhys and Shynaria in his tower library drinking a glass of wine. A fire had already been stoked which made the room warm and comfortable. Though it was late spring, and temperatures were warming up, the stone walls of the tower kept a perpetual chill in the air. Rathal walked over to the liquor cabinet and poured his own glass of wine, then collapsed into his well-worn leather chair. As he settled into the chair's familiar softness, he took a sip of wine, closed his eyes, and allowed it to warm his body.

"Well, what's the verdict?" Shynaria asked.

"Huh?" Rathal grunted.

Shynaria sighed. "What brilliant plan did you and Amkissra come up with to protect our people?"

Rathal rubbed his eyes. "There's no plan… unless you want to call providence a plan." Rathal took another sip of wine. "I had hoped we could develop a warning system which would allow us to predict when these shifts were going to occur. Amkissra nixed that idea. She said she could create a charm which would do the trick, but it would require getting close to the *Ak-Séregon Stone*. That's not going to happen. We don't have enough time to get there and we don't know what the situation on InnisRos is. And forecasting when a shift might occur is damn near impossible. They're coming at random intervals."

"So, we're helpless?" Shynaria asked.

Rathal snorted. "Now you know why there's no plan. That's not to say we just sit on our thumbs and pass our future off to a hope and a prayer. We can still take steps to protect our people from any... oh, shall we say dangerous unfortunates... who happen to shift our way."

"How?"

"I don't know, Shy," Rathal replied as he got up to pour himself another glass of wine. "But if either of you have any suggestions, I'm more than willing to hear you out. But until then we need to get on with business. Rhys, you requested this meeting. Speak."

"There's several things that concern me, my lord," Rhys said. "As I mentioned, I've lost all contact with my operatives on InnisRos."

"The entire island?" Rathal asked.

Rhys shook his head. ""I only had them in the capital city of Taranthi. That's where the flow of information is usually concentrated. Everything important begins there."

Rathal frowned. "You might want to revise your operating procedures just a bit."

"I'm already doing that," Rhys replied.

Rathal nodded. "Any idea at all about why? I mean, could our people have been neutralized in some way?"

"Highly unlikely, my lord. I've several implanted in the government and none of them know who the others are. I could have lost one, or maybe two, but not all of them."

"And yet your precautions don't seem to have done us any good," Rathal replied. "So, what does that tell you?"

Rhys frowned. "It could only mean one thing. The entire city has somehow been cut off."

Rathal leaned forward. "You mentioned before there's been rumors of war... something about a struggle for power between the Queen and her First Councilor. Could the city be under martial law?"

"Martial law probably wouldn't have put a magical net over the city," Rhys said as he shook his head. "I should still be able to get information via communication crystals. No, something bigger is going on."

Rathal sighed. "Do we have any other options?"

"None that I'm aware of," Rhys answered. "I've reached out to my colleagues in the other cities to see if they had any more information. So far, everything I've told you is all any of us know."

Rathal looked at Rhys. "Your colleagues?"

"Every city has spies, my lord. I thought you knew that."

"Well yes, of course I knew," Rathal said. "I just didn't know you actually communicated with them. Are we being spied upon?"

"Certainly," Rhys replied dismissively. "And I know who they are. Occasionally I feed them bits and pieces of real information just to keep them interested."

Rathal shook his head. "If they're as good as you are, then they no doubt have spies you've yet to root out. Be careful how you play your game."

Rhys didn't answer.

"What's next?" Rathal asked.

"The armies of HeBron and Madeira are in the field," Rhys said without preamble.

Rathal choked on his wine. "What!" he exclaimed. "It takes days to mobilize an army. How come I'm just hearing about this now?"

"Well, obviously because I didn't hear about it until this morning," Rhys replied defensively. "Three good men died getting this information to me. The secret police for both cities are quite thorough."

"I'm sorry, Rhys," Rathal said.

Rhys waved Rathal's apology off. "Some things are worth dying for. Their families are being well taken care of."

"Are they moving against each other?" Rathal asked. "There's certainly no love lost between the two ruling families. Border skirmishes occur all the time."

Rhys shook head. "No, my lord. They've combined their armies and moved to the northeast."

"That makes little sense," Rathal said. He stood and walked over to the window on the east tower wall and looked out. To the north he could barely make out the southernmost foothills to the Greater Boreskyre Mountains. Though he couldn't see it from where he stood, the large inland Sea of the Marble Wyvern lay a few miles away to the east and northeast. North of the sea and west of the mountains marked the territory of the Draugen Pesta... the Ghosts of the 'Black Death'... a race of ferocious black-clad giants. Fortunately for all, they weren't aggressive and stayed in their lands, though they were known to trade with the mainland, particularly with Elanesse. But that was centuries ago when Elanesse was a vibrant and powerful elven city. More recently he'd heard one had actually traveled to InnisRos and joined their Navy. But most attempts to initiate contact with the Draugen Pesta was turned away by a mysterious fog filled with shadows. Rathal always felt the fog was nothing but a magical ruse to scare away intruders... not real ghosts... and probably not even dangerous.

As dangerous as the giants appeared to be, the Sea of the Marble Wyvern was even more so. Somewhere in those murky waters a creature, or creatures, of unbelievable size lurked. Every attempt to explore the sea by ship failed with only a small number of survivors to tell of their fate. Even attempts to settle on the shores of the sea had resulted in disaster... usually destroyed in the dead of night. The creature was by some estimates over four hundred feet long and fifty to sixty feet wide. Despite its huge size, it moved with speed and grace in both the water and on the land. It's body was elongated like that of a snake... or worm... and its massive head had several rows of tentacles surrounding the huge maw. Each tentacle had eye-like protrusions on the end. All along the body these same eye-like protrusions ran down its length.

Rathal shivered. "Rhys, what's your assessment?"

"Frankly, I don't know," Rhys replied.

"That's a first," he said as he turned away from the window. "Then speculate."

"Well, there's no way they'll turn north and go into the Great Blight. Few people can live in that wasteland... and the few expeditions that went there saw no sign of anything other than desolation."

"If anyone did, they'd have to be a hardy bunch of souls," Shynaria commented. "Even if they could endure the weather, what would they live on. There's no plants to cultivate or animals to hunt."

"Or they could be living underground," Rathal remarked. "What we consider inhospitable isn't necessarily proof that it is. There's so little we know about that area of Aster." Rathal suddenly had another thought. "Rhys, do you think they got it in their minds to conquer the Draugen Pesta?"

Rhys nodded. "It's possible. But they wouldn't do it on their own... unless they somehow reached a deal with the Hyrokkin. It's common knowledge the Draugen Pesta and the Hyrokkin have been enemies for centuries. A coordinated attack by Madeira and HeBron on one side and the Hyrokkin on the other just might cause considerable problems for the giants."

"But you don't really think so," Rathal observed.

"No," Rhys replied. "For two reasons. It would be extremely difficult to form an alliance involving three nation-states without alarming intelligence services all over the mainland, particularly since two of the three are constantly at each other's throats."

"With three of your spies murdered, it seems both Madeira and HeBron have been brutally efficient doing just that," Rathal pointedly remarked.

Rhys winced. "Point taken. No, you're right, we can't rule out an alliance between the three. But the other reason I don't believe that's happened is the nature of the Hyrokkin. They're... well, they just don't like anyone, if reports I have on them are correct. A warrior race by nature and arrogant to the point they feel all other races are beneath them. The only two things that keep their domination tendencies at bay are the Draugen Pesta, who have them bottled up in that valley of theirs, and geography."

"How do you know all of this?" Rathal asked as he moved away from the window.

"I'm your intelligence chief," Rhys replied with a smile. "You pay me to know. How I do it is my business."

Rathal sat back down. "What other possibilities are there? Surely Madeira and HeBron aren't going to invade the Draugen Pesta by themselves?" Rathal shook his head. "No, they wouldn't do that. I know little about the Hyrokkin, but I have a fair understanding of the Draugen Pesta. It'd be suicide to move against them. And I'm sure both those city-states know it as well. Perhaps they've allied with the Draugen Pesta to attack the Hyrokkin?"

Rhys scowled. "What would the Draugen Pesta offer that would bring those two cities together? Gold? Certainly not land. Unless…?" Whatever Rhys was going to say remained unspoken. He shrugged. "I don't know. We're blind, my lord. I'm not used to that. And I hate speculation. That's like a dog chasing its tail round and round. All you get is dizzy."

There was a sudden silence in the room. Rhys closed his eyes and rubbed his temples, thinking. Rathal appeared to be transfixed by the dying fire. A blank look crossed his face and sweat appeared on his brow. Shynaria, who knew Rathal as well as anyone except for Amkissra, saw Rathal and immediately understood what was happening. She reached over and laid a hand on Rhys' leg.

"Look," she said after she had his attention, tilting her head towards Rathal.

"What…"

Shynaria hushed Rhys. "Shhh. He's having a premonition," she whispered.

Rhys looked at Rathal and then at Shynaria. "He can do that?" he whispered back.

"It happens only rarely, but when it does, he's never been wrong," Shynaria replied. "What he sees will most assuredly come to pass. He guards this secret most closely, so mention it to no one." Shynaria looked at Rhys who nodded.

"The talent is said to have vanished among mortals," Rhys remarked. "If it ever existed at all."

Shynaria frowned. "It exists, though it's true that precognition has been very rare throughout our history. But there are documented instances of elves, and some humans, having the talent... though I've read of none who were correct more than fifty percent of the time."

"Come on, Shy! Those are all stories."

"No!" Shynaria exclaimed softly. "They're real! And he has the gift!"

"I'll be damned!" Rhys looked at Rathal who looked like he was coming out of the vision. "I'm beginning to think I'm not a very good spy," he lamented. "It appears there's a lot I don't know."

Rathal shook his head, stood, and darted to a nearby washbasin to retch. Both Shynaria and Rhys helped him back to his chair. Shynaria poured some water on a linen washcloth and wiped his face. Rhys handed him a glass of wine to rinse the taste of vomit out of his mouth. Rathal gratefully accepted it and, after spitting the first mouthful into the fireplace, took a deep swallow.

"Thank you," Rathal said as he leaned over to control his breathing.

"Your ears!" Rhys said with concern. Both were bleeding.

"I'll be fine," Rathal said, though he made no move to wipe the blood that trickled down his neck.

Rhys looked at Shynaria who sighed. "Tell him, Rathal."

Rathal looked up at Shynaria.

"Tell me what?" Rhys asked... but both were focused upon each other and didn't seem to hear him.

"If you don't, I will," Shynaria scolded her sorcerer friend.

Rathal shook his head. "Can't you just leave it, Shy."

"No, I can't," she replied. "You won't tell anyone in the congress. You won't tell General Húrön. You won't even tell Amkissra."

Rathal wasn't moved. He stared at Shynaria.

The sorcerer's assistant didn't back down. "Someone needs to know!" she pleaded. Rathal finally nodded.

Shynaria hesitated, suddenly unsure of herself.

"Tell me what, Shynaria?" Rhys asked again.

"Rhys... Rathal is dying."

The spymaster gaped at Havendale's ruler. "You're dying..."

Rathal waved the spy's comment aside. "Everyone dies eventually. We have more important things to discuss."

"But healers? Clerics?"

"They can do nothing for me," Rathal said. "Rhys, it's a consequence of my precognitive talent. There's nothing anyone can do for me. Now, let's move on."

Rhys nodded. "What did you see?"

Rathal closed his eyes. "I saw troops in the Elderdale. They wore the livery of Madeira and HeBron. Giants accompanied them..."

"You mean the Draugen Pesta," Shynaria said.

Rathal nodded. "Yes, the Draugen Pesta. The Black Death. But despite their reputation, the known ruthlessness of both Madeira and HeBron was being held in check by the giants. They were not allowing rape, pillage, or mass slaughter. Any Elderdale inhabitants resisting were only restrained. Killing was only a last resort."

Rhys shook his head. "I don't understand why the Draugen Pesta would move west and into our lands. Even with Madeira and HeBron allied with them, they must know they're no match for the combined armies of the mainland."

"They feel no pleasure in what they do," Rathal said. "Look to another motivation before you judge the Draugen Pesta."

"What else did you see, Rathal?" Shynaria asked.

Rathal, his eyes still closed, grimaced. "I saw dragons over the dead and haunted city of Elanesse and the Forest of the Fey. Huge, evil dragons led by an even larger five-headed monster. Only Elanesse was no longer dead... and... someone familiar... someone I should know but do not... was in grave danger. By the gods the dragon-breath was taking a terrible toll. I can still hear the cries of the trees... the animals... Elanesse and her guardian."

Rathal collapsed, unconscious. Though he was breathing easy and didn't appear to be in immediate danger, fresh blood streamed out of his ears.

CHAPTER TWO

Deep Under Elanesse

"Two sylphs and a ghost walk into a cavern..."

*-Dwarven pub bouncer Charlie (Chuckles) Granitesmasher had a very short
career as a standup comedian.*

"Lassie, I had no idea there were so many tunnels and passages this
deep!" Azriel-Ahlasim remarked. "And I was a dwarf!"

Azriel-Ahlasim and Elbedreth-Ahlasim were deep underground
beneath Elanesse... traveling the myriad of tunnels, passageways, and
corridors as they journeyed to the place where Elbedreth-Ahlasim's
people had been imprisoned by the gods. Azriel-Ahlasim was in
constant awe at the spectacles that seemed to reveal themselves
around every corner... in every cavern.

Elbedreth-Ahlasim smiled in the sylph way. "It is a most
wondrous place," she replied as she nudged him gently... the sylph
method of showing affection. "I had forgotten how beautiful it is...
and how natural it feels to be so far under the surface. Perhaps...
but..." Elbedreth-Ahlasim's thought faltered.

It was Azriel-Ahlasim's turn to nudge his love. "Speak your mind,
lassie," he said. "There should never be secrets between us."

Elbedreth-Ahlasim studied the sylph she had grown to love. She
trusted him with her life. But because his 'conversion' had only
recently occurred, there were things he must be taught, especially if
he would go amongst her people... and more importantly, if he was
to survive that encounter. With so much to do, the future seemed

very far away, yet she felt compelled to speak honestly as he said she should.

"I was just wishing we could make this our permanent home," she said.

But Azriel-Ahlasim didn't reply. Instead, he stopped and became silent. They had just entered a large cavern... and the wall along one side was solid gold. "I... I..." he stuttered.

"What's wrong?" Elbedreth-Ahlasim asked.

"What's wrong?!" Azriel-Ahlasim cried out incredulously. "Lassie, can ye not see the gold wall?"

Elbedreth-Ahlasim was confused. "Is that something special?" she asked as she walked over to it. Using one of her blades, she cut a shallow, thin, horizontal line along a portion of the wall. "What purpose does soft metal like this serve? Stone is much harder."

"But..."

"Would you like some?" Elbedreth-Ahlasim asked. "I can cut out a chunk for you. Maybe you could make it into a trinket or something."

"But..."

"Though I think you should wait, Azriel-Ahlasim," Elbedreth-Ahlasim said as she cut an image into the gold. "Farther below are caverns lined with much harder substances of many colors... purple, red, white, and green. Perhaps you could make me a trinket from one of those. It would be much more beautiful than this awful color. And like our love, it would last as long as eternity itself."

"But you don't understand, my wee lassie," Azriel-Ahlasim stammered. "In my world..."

Azriel-Ahlasim caught himself. He wasn't in his world, was he? At least not his old world. Nor was he still a dwarf. He was a sylph. Perhaps it was time to consider himself as such. He had once vowed to discover the reason behind his sudden change... but now he wasn't so sure it was still important to him. All that mattered was Elbedreth-Ahlasim and his friends on the surface. Perhaps his change wasn't a fulfillment of his own destiny... but rather a fulfillment of Elbedreth-

Ahlasim's. Would that be so bad? Besides, if that much gold were to be brought up to the surface, it would flood the market and its value would be worthless. The dwarf that remained in Azriel-Ahlasim still understood supply-side economics.

"You're correct, my bonnie love," Azriel-Ahlasim said. "This metal is useless. And perhaps I WILL make that trinket for you. A trinket of diamonds and emeralds to serve as a physical reminder of my vow to never leave you."

Elbedreth-Ahlasim nodded. "I would like that."

Azriel-Ahlasim went over to the wall where Elbedreth-Ahlasim had been cutting on the surface. Etched into the gold was an outline of two sylphs side-by-side... one had cutting blades while another had a great battleaxe and a staff.

He took his ax and etched a heart surrounding the two images. "On the surface, this is the symbol for love and devotion," he remarked as he nudged Elbedreth-Ahlasim.

Nothing else needed to be said.

Azriel-Ahlasim and Elbedreth-Ahlasim heard water falling in the next cavern long before they entered. The cavern was huge – several hundred feet wide and at least half a mile long. The sound of water came from the other side. And though they couldn't yet see it, they could tell the amount of water falling was significant. All around the cavern multi-colored mosses grew... on the walls, the stalagmites that rose from the floor, and the stalactites that hung from the ceiling. The mosses, besides being dazzlingly multihued, also radiated light from chemical reactions within their leaves. The sylphs found that they could see easily enough. As they approached the opposite end of the cavern, they saw that the water didn't bottom out in a pool at its base as expected, but instead continued through a crevice and into the darkness below the floor.

Azriel-Ahlasim noted that there didn't appear to be an obvious way out of the cavern. *"There has to be a way out,"* he thought. As he looked around, he spied what appeared to be a shimmering line going down the wall to his left roughly ten yards from the waterfall. Curious, he took one of Elbedreth-Ahlasim's appendages and led her in that direction, determined to identify this new discovery. Drawing near, Azriel-Ahlasim saw a liquid-like material move down natural channels in the wall and collect in a deep hole at the base. The liquid had a thick constitution with characteristics closer to syrup than water.

"I know what this is," he suddenly exclaimed. "But that can't be! It's not even warm!"

"What concerns you so?" Elbedreth-Ahlasim asked.

"That!" Azriel-Ahlasim said as he pointed at the liquid. "That's liquid silver... in a natural state. Not heated, but natural. That's unheard of!"

"Unheard of on the surface," Elbedreth-Ahlasim said. "But many things down here are unheard of on the surface. This, for example. We call it quicksilver. Its properties are far different from the metal you call silver."

Azriel-Ahlasim bent down and cupped a bit of the quicksilver in the palm of an appendage. It dropped away, leaving no trace of any kind.

"Listen to me, Azriel-Ahlasim. Though many the wonders of the underground are, we must be ever alert. We must not let things like this distract us from our mission or cause us to linger long. They are of little consequence. We must reach our people to convince them to set aside their animosity towards those on the surface."

Azriel-Ahlasim, still looking at the quicksilver, nodded. "I hear you, lassie... and I'm trying. It's just that some things will take more time than others. Precious metals and gems are a couple of those things. Ale being another."

"What is ale?"

"Ah, lassie," Azriel-Ahlasim replied with a chuckle. "A smooth, heady drink with bristling foam that puts a fire in your belly and then kicks you in the arse. Ale is the life-blood of a...". But he didn't finish.

Elbedreth-Ahlasim smiled. "You were going to say 'dwarf', were you not?"

Azriel-Ahlasim nodded. "Instincts, my love. Most damning."

Elbedreth-Ahlasim waved off his admission. "We have similar drinks... though I was never old enough to partake. We didn't want much when we were on the surface world. But one of the things we did want was strong drink."

"On the surface?"

"Yes, on the surface. Some of the males became quite good at making the drink. So good, in fact, that's all they really did."

"You had brewmaisters?" Azriel-Ahlasim said incredulously.

Elbedreth-Ahlasim smiled. "Makers of drink? Of course. But if a non-sylph drank it, that person would probably not survive the experience. And if they did, it was because they didn't consume much. Even so, their insides would be scarred for life."

Azriel-Ahlasim rubbed two appendages together. "I just HAVE to try some of that, lassie!" he said excitedly.

"It'll have to wait until we get back closer to the surface," Elbedreth-Ahlasim replied. "I'll show you where we stored it. But when you do, let none of the drink spill on your magnificent great-axe or staff. It'll dissolve the metal."

Azriel-Ahlasim let out a full-throated, hearty laugh. "Now that sounds like an ale I can appreciate!"

Both sylphs turned away from the small river of quicksilver... though Azriel-Ahlasim didn't do so without a sigh. "I don't see a way out," he said. "Do you?"

Elbedreth-Ahlasim shook her head. "No... what was that!" she suddenly exclaimed. Her blades suddenly appeared, and she took a defensive posture to guard against attack.

Azriel-Ahlasim's looked around as his own weapons also appeared. "What did you see?"

"Movement. A shadow between those two stalagmites," Elbedreth-Ahlasim said as she pointed.

"Could it be your... our people coming up from their imprisonment?"

"No," Elbedreth-Ahlasim replied with certainty. "It didn't move right. Besides, our people would never send just one... but instead waves of twenty or thirty at a time."

Just the thought of even one wave sent shivers down Azriel-Ahlasim's spine... or whatever he had for a spine. "Let's go see what we're dealing with," he said as he glided towards the stalagmites Elbedreth-Ahlasim had pointed out.

"ooooOOOOOooooo!"

Azriel-Ahlasim stopped. "That had to be the worse moan I've ever heard in my life," he said out loud.

"Is that a... ghost?" Elbedreth-Ahlasim asked. "It's dark like me. I've never seen one... but on the occasion I've happened upon humans who ventured into my home, they'd always run away screaming that word."

"I shouldn't wonder," Azriel-Ahlasim said. Then he suddenly laughed. "Humans also have a tendency to piss in their pants when they're frightened."

"Piss in their pants?"

"Never mind, lassie. Something about that moan did sound familiar, though."

Elbedreth-Ahlasim tilted her head. "You know a ghost?"

"I do... or did," Azriel-Ahlasim replied. "Her name was Angela, and she was a very protective mother... the mother of young Emmy. She wouldn't pass on to the next life until she was sure her daughter was safe."

"Well now you know two ghosts, you cantankerous, old belly-scratching, cavern-dwelling, dung beetle!" a voice called out from behind a stalagmite.

Elbedreth-Ahlasim bristled with anger. "Show yourself!" she called out. "Ghost or no ghost, you shan't call Azriel-Ahlasim such names without answering to me!"

"It's okay," Azriel-Ahlasim said as he took a step forward and in front of his companion. "As hard as it is to believe, I think I know this ghost."

"Of course, you do," Max the ghost said as he stepped from behind the stalagmite. "I'm just having as hard a time believing what I'm seeing... though I'd know that voice anywhere! We have a lot to discuss, Azriel."

"His name is Azriel-Ahlasim," Elbedreth-Ahlasim said. She was annoyed. "He is sylph now."

"Calm down, my bonnie lass. He's my friend... and yours, though you know it not." Azriel-Ahlasim approached Max with Elbedreth-Ahlasim trailing behind. "I didn't think I'd ever see you again."

"This is the last place I expected to be," Max agreed. "After I helped Elrond become a tree, I thought, 'Now it's time to enjoy an afterlife of beautiful women, wine, gold, and all the other trappings of wealth a former person like me deserves.' But no! It would appear the gods have more hero things planned for me. Instead, I flickered away from Elrond... he made a damn fine-looking tree, by the way... and into absolute darkness. I knew I was in an underground tunnel, so I just wandered around until I ended up here. Then you and your... what was it you called her... your bonnie lass? You dwarves. Sometimes I wish you'd speak like a normal person. Anyway, I knew it was you as soon as I heard you speak. I thought, 'Well, Elrond's a tree, why can't Azriel be a... a... black darkie thing'. But just to make sure, I hid behind a couple of stalagmites for a while to scope things out."

"Max..."

"But as I was moving to the stalagmites, your bonnie lass spotted me. I thought ghosts could become invisible if they wanted. Guess not... or at least I haven't figured it out yet."

"Max..."

"Then again, maybe one advantage of being a black, darkie thing means you can see ghosts. Who's to say."

"Max, will you..."

"Well, since the jig was up, I thought, 'Damn, I sure do hope you were you, because I know ghosts can be banished.' Then I thought, 'Even if it is you, what if you don't know who I am?' When I saw your axe I thought, 'By the gods, I'm in for it now!' Then I thought I'd try a moan... mostly to see if I could do it... but also to scare you a little. Did it scare you? So, I..."

"Max, will you take a breath and be quiet!" Azriel-Ahlasim exclaimed.

Max frowned. "Now that you mention it, I don't think ghosts actually breathe. Instead..."

"Max, shut ye piehole!" Azriel-Ahlasim roared.

There was complete silence... for about five seconds.

"What's wrong with your bonnie lass?" Max asked.

"Her name's Elbedreth..." Azriel-Ahlasim replied before he stopped himself. He turned and saw that there did appear to be something wrong with his companion. She had fallen back and looked pensive... and he suspected why. She was Max's killer.

"Max, what do you remember about your death?" Azriel-Ahlasim asked.

The ghost of Max shook his head. "Nothing much. It was awfully dark. Something grabbed me by the leg and pulled me into a tunnel. Then there was a sudden terrible stabbing pain in my chest and then nothing. Until I came back to help Elrond. And now you, it would seem."

Azriel-Ahlasim looked back at Elbedreth-Ahlasim. She had heard and started to move forward tentatively. "Now is not the time to confess," Azriel-Ahlasim whispered.

Elbedreth-Ahlasim understood and nodded. But the guilty look on her face could not be hidden. Though she had her reasons for killing Max at the time, her relationship with Azriel-Ahlasim and his other friends had taught her much. She now understood not all conflicts, or fear of the unknown, need be handled with the blades of violence. Still, it hurt her heart that she had been so brutal with her mate's friend.

"Why do you ask?" Max said, bringing both sylphs back to the here and now.

Azriel-Ahlasim shook his head. "No reason, I was just curious. Now, what's all this about Elrond being a tree?"

Max smiled. "Do I have a story for you!" he said with enthusiasm. "You see, it all started when I found myself under Elanesse. You know, under the branches of the tree Elanesse, not the city Elanesse. Elrond was sitting there, sulking and talking to a squirrel... or was it a chipmunk... I didn't get a close enough look at it before it scurried away. Anyway..."

Azriel-Ahlasim rolled his eyes as Max prattled on. He'd reached the salient point of Azriel-Ahlasim's original question ten minutes ago... but continued to talk as they searched the cavern for a passage out.

"I can find nothing," Elbedreth-Ahlasim said. Frustration tainted her voice. "We've not lost our way, for I know our course is correct. And yet nothing's here."

"Think, lassie. I know it's been a long time since you traveled these tunnels, but you have the answer locked away, I'm sure of it."

Elbedreth-Ahlasim shook her head. "I've gone over the way a hundred times in my head. I can think of nothing I've missed."

Max, suddenly quiet, was sitting on the floor, his legs crossed, watching the waterfall. The small stream of quicksilver hadn't piqued his curiosity. Though it was certainly an anomaly, and probably worth a fortune on the surface, he discovered he had no real interest. After all, what was he going to do with it? He's dead.

As Max continued to study the waterfall, he had a thought. "Bonnie lass," he called.

Azriel sighed. "Max, her name is..."

Max held up his hand. "Bonnie lass is easier to remember, Azriel," he said.

"I'm here, Max, friend of Azriel-Ahlasim," Elbedreth-Ahlasim replied.

"Do you remember this cavern?" Max asked.

Elbedreth-Ahlasim shook her head. "There's hundreds of caverns between the surface and where my people are being held... many including waterfalls and quicksilver."

"What're you getting at, Max?" Azriel-Ahlasim asked.

Max looked at him. "Look at the problem like a dwarf, you big dunderhead. Sure, you look different, but you still have the heart of one. How would a dwarven miner approach this problem?"

Azriel-Ahlasim smiled. "By anvil and hammer, he'd beat a passage out, that's what he'd do!" Then he paused to re-consider. "But not before ruling out all other possibilities."

"What do you mean, Azriel-Ahlasim?" Elbedreth-Ahlasim inquired.

"He means there's still one area of the cave that hasn't been investigated," Max said.

"Aye, lassie... one area," Azriel-Ahlasim agreed, suddenly understanding Max's point.

Max nodded. "One area."

Azriel-Ahlasim moved closer to inspect the falling water. "I should've seen it earlier. See how the edges of the crevice are almost sharp? There are no signs of the natural erosion that occurs when rock is exposed to water for thousands of years. That can only mean this crevice in the floor is more recent than the cavern itself." Azriel-Ahlasim pointed to the other side. "Over there, on the other side of the crevice. See Max? Next to the base of the wall? It looks like irregularly shaped stones... as if they were part of a larger piece of stone that broke apart when it hit the floor."

Azriel-Ahlasim looked up. "It's too dark. I wish I could see where the water comes out. It doesn't really matter, though." Azriel-Ahlasim looked over at Max. "I'd bet the hair off my... well, never mind. Max, there's a passageway back behind the water. There must've been an earthquake which caused cracks both here and up there, releasing water from an underground spring, river, or lake. That's why we can't find the exit... it's hidden by the water."

Max nodded. "You want me to reconnoiter?"

"If you please."

"Almost seems like the old times, doesn't it, Azriel," he said as he stood.

"Be careful, Max, friend of Azriel-Ahlasim," Elbedreth-Ahlasim called out as Max floated through the waterfall.

Somewhere along their march downward, Max convinced Elbedreth and Azriel to drop the sylph honorific of 'Ahlasim'. He successfully reasoned that it took too much time to say, and quick communications during an emergency might be the difference between life and death. Whether it was the logic Max used in his argument, the constant prattle about it until the two sylphs gave up and agreed, or the fact that Max would stop calling Elbedreth 'bonnie lass', was uncertain.

As they moved deeper into the bowels of Aster, the temperature rose, and all hints of water disappeared. The fungi, moss, algae, and lichen that had been their constant companion gave way to a landscape of barren stone. Even the stalagmites and stalactites in the few caverns they came across had abandoned them. The great myriad of tunnels they traveled didn't seem to confuse or deter Elbedreth, who appeared to recognize the way to an almost instinctive exactitude. She didn't know how she knew, but once Max learned about the nature of the sylph and why the gods created them, he speculated they implanted the information in her... like birds flying south for the winter. This led to three hours of speculation about what birds who are already living in the south do. Do they have the same instinct and fly further south? Is it a regional thing? Why do southern birds not fly north in the spring like northern birds?

Many memories returned to Azriel as he listened – pleasant memories of adventures – of Max, Elrond, Lester, and himself on the road, sitting around campfires and enjoying cigars. It was becoming more and more obvious that the ghost of Max had changed little, and that the death of Max hadn't left a traumatic scar on his soul. Azriel couldn't have been more wrong.

The sylph race awoke from their forced slumber deep, deep beneath the surface. They sensed the millions and millions of parasites that now inhabited their world. This could not stand! It represented an insult to their existence! They broke through the weakened bonds of their imprisonment and the first wave of many began the long ascent to the surface. There was bloodlust in their eyes and hate in their hearts. They were all quite mad.

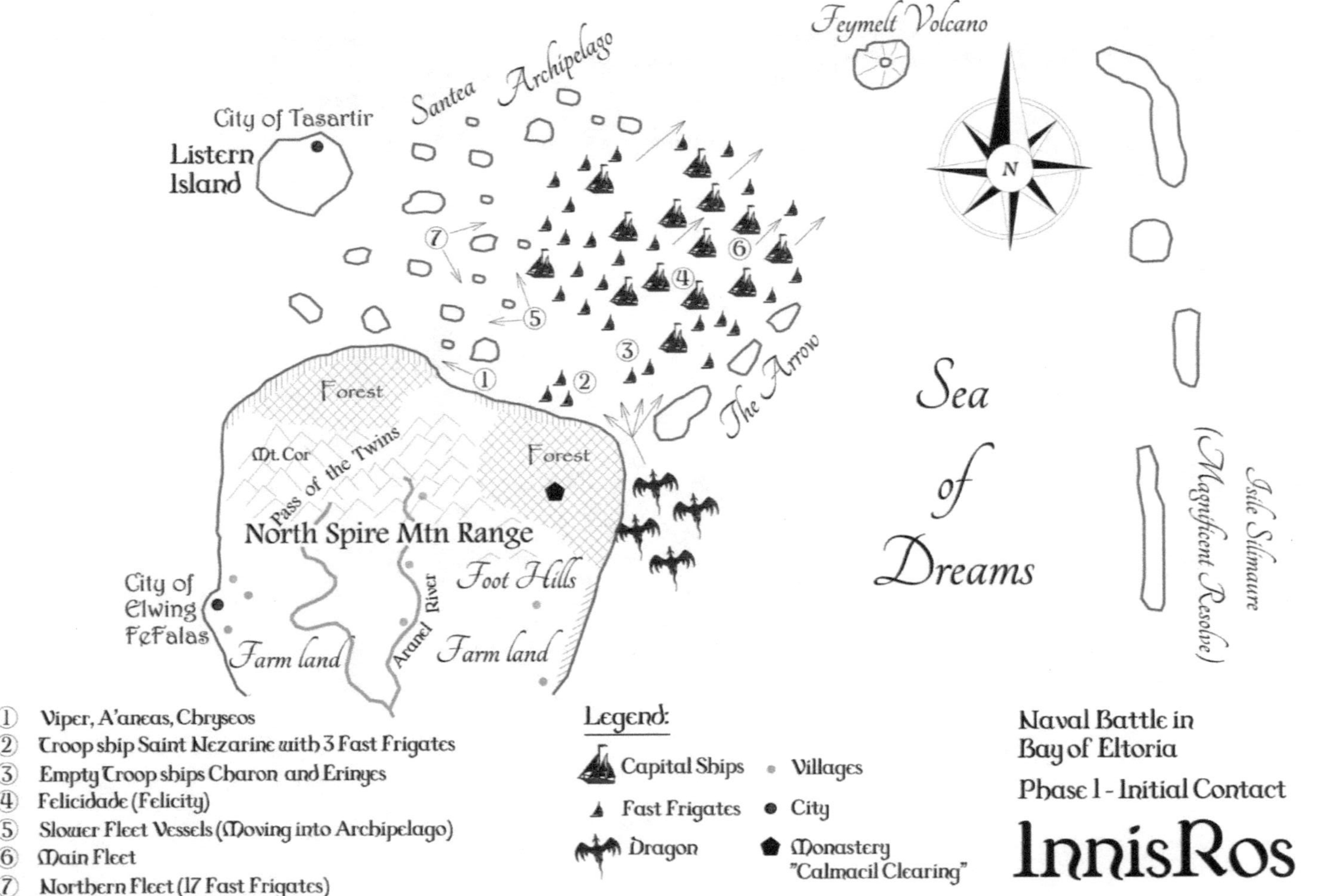

Feymelt Volcano
Isile Silimaure
(Magnificent Resolve)
Sea
of
Dreams
Naval Battle in
Bay of Eltoria
Phase 1 - Initial Contact
InnisRos
Santea Archipelago
The Arrow
City of Tasartir
Listern Island
Forest
Forest
North Spire Mtn Range
Mt Cor
Pass of the Twins
Foot Hills
Arand River
Farm land
Farm land
Farm land
City of Elwing
FeFalas
Legend:
Capital Ships
Villages
Fast Frigates
City
Dragon
Monastery
"Calmacil Clearing"
1 Viper, A'aneas, Chryseos
2 Troopship Saint Nezarine with 3 Fast Frigates
3 Empty Troopships Charon and Erinyes
4 Felicidade (Felicity)
5 Slower Fleet Vessels (Moving into Archipelago)
6 Main Fleet
7 Northern Fleet (17 Fast Frigates)

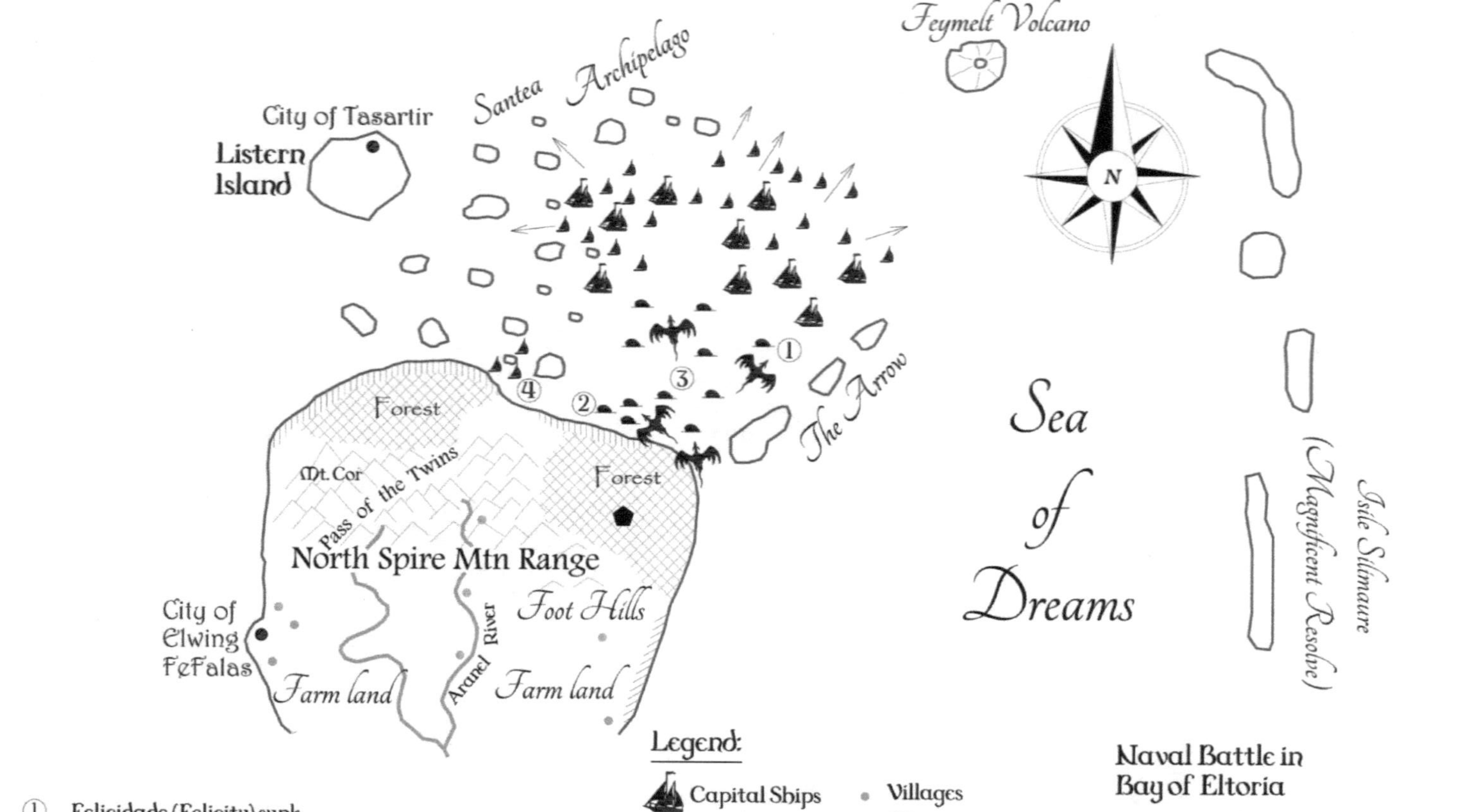
Isile Silimaure
(Magnificent Resolve)

Feymelt Volcano

N

Sea

of

Dreams

Naval Battle in
Bay of Eltoria

Phase 2 – First Attack

InnisRos

Santea Archipelago

The Arrow

City of Tasartir

Listern
Island

Forest

Forest

Mt. Cor

Pass of the Twins

North Spire Mtn Range

Foot Hills

Farm land

Aranel River

Farm land

Farm land

City of
Elwing
Fefalas

Legend:

Capital Ships

Fast Frigates

Dragon

Villages

City

Monastery

"Calmacil Clearing"

Sunken Ships

Felicidade (Felicity) sunk

Troop ship Saint Nezarine with 3 Fast Frigates
(Grounded or sunk)

Empty Troop ships Charon and Erinyes (Sunk)

Viper, A'aneas, Chryseos

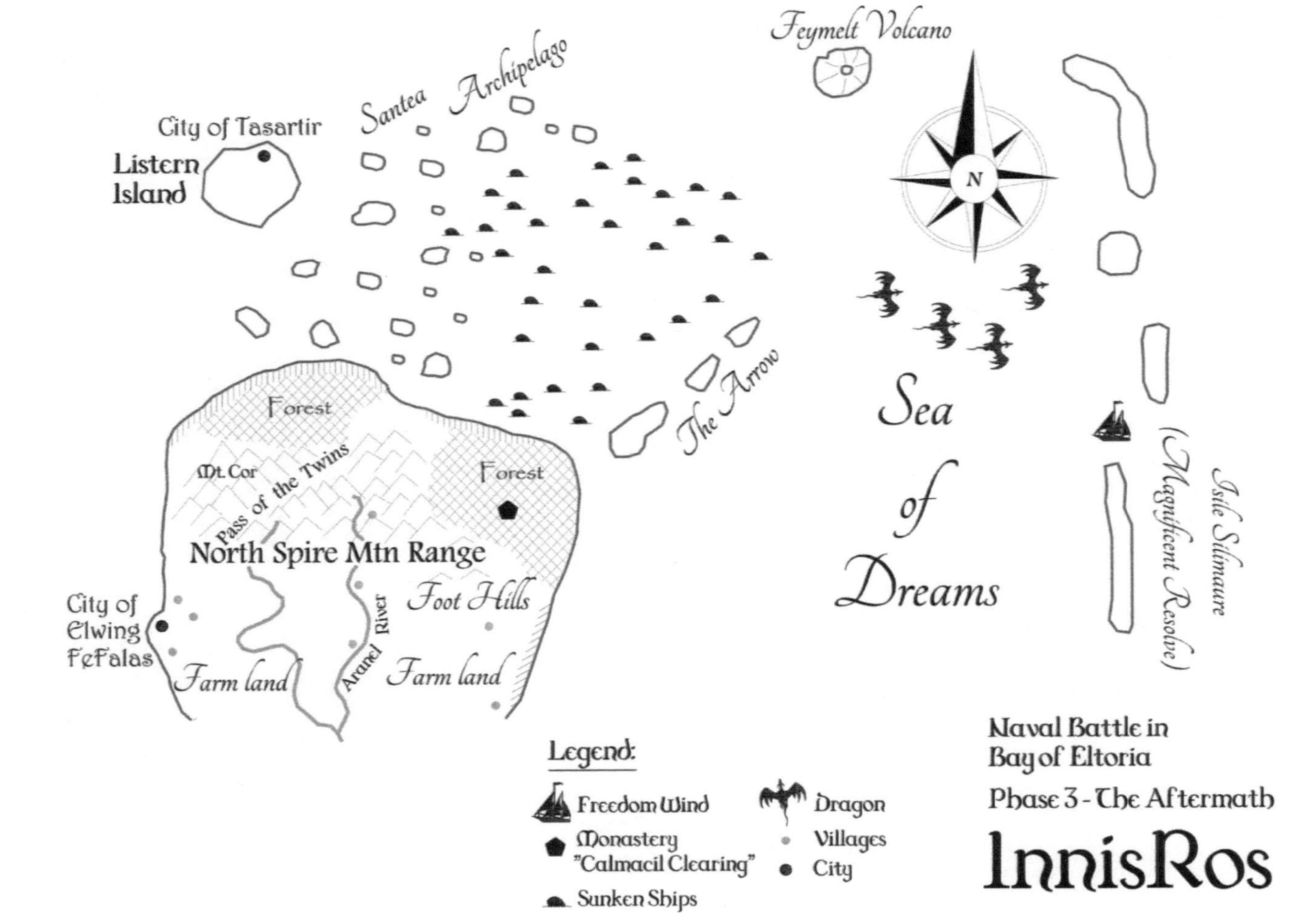

Feymelt Volcano
Santea Archipelago
City of Tasartir
Listern Island
The Arrow
N
Sea
of
Dreams
Forest
Mt. Cor
Pass of the Twins
Forest
North Spire Mtn Range
City of Elwing FeFalas
Foot Hills
Aranel River
Farm land
Farm land
Isile Silimaure
(Magnificent Resolve)
Legend:
Freedom Wind
Monastery "Calmacil Clearing"
Sunken Ships
Dragon
Villages
City
Naval Battle in
Bay of Eltoria
Phase 3 - The Aftermath
InnisRos

CHAPTER THREE

InnisRos (Bay of Eltoria)

No war has ever been fought without sacrifice... without loss. I understand that. However, the magnitude of the loss following the battle in the Bay of Eltoria was unfathomable to me at the time. I wanted nothing more than to curl into a ball and wish the world away.

-From the letters of Queen Lessien Arntuile to her sister, StarSinger Nefertari.

Admiral Tári Shilannia stood on the quarterdeck of her flagship, the *Felicidade*, and studied the maneuvers her fleet was making to avoid the incoming dragon onslaught. She watched as the four dragons cleared the base of the Arrow, split away from each other and began their descent to attack her ships. The fast frigates *Viper*, *A'aneas*, and *Chryseos* were already underway and moving along InnisRos' northern shore into the Santea Archipelago. If all went according to plan, they'll hide until the dragon threat was over. Their mission was to get the Queen to the mainland, so their survival was important, though all three captains bristled at their orders to run.

The troop ship *Saint Nezerine* had been grounded and her Marines were disembarking. Admiral Shilannia hoped the three fast frigates used to cover the unloading would be enough to keep the dragons occupied long enough to get the Marines ashore.

The empty troop ships *Charon* and *Erinyes* were anchored one thousand yards to the southeast of the Marine landing. They wouldn't draw all four dragons off... but at least one, two if the fleet was lucky. *"I suspect luck will be in short supply today,"* Admiral Shilannia thought.

Admiral Shilannia turned to her adjutant. "Contact Admiral Brúnor of the Northern Fleet and tell him to change course and scatter into the archipelago. He'll be of no help today."

"Aye, Admiral!"

Admiral Shilannia leaned over the front railing of the quarterdeck to address the *Felicidad's* captain, who was directly below in the wheelhouse. "Are the battle sorcerers in place?" she shouted over the commotion created as the crew ran to their battle stations, ready to defend the ship at all costs.

"Yes, ma'am," he replied. "Ballista's as well. We'll not go down without a fight."

"Captain Thanis, I don't plan on the *Felicity* going under," Admiral Shilannia admonished. "Now fight your ship!"

Admiral Shilannia looked up at the sails. They were catching little wind, and the *Felicidade* was only making three knots. The frigates, smaller, lighter, and carrying more sail compared to mass, went twice as fast, but instead of making their run out to sea as ordered, they were providing cover for the slower, heavier ships. She raised her spyglass and directed her gaze at the fast approaching dragons. One dived on the two abandoned troop ships, one headed for the Marine landing, while another attacked the rest of the fleet. The larger, five-headed dragon flew toward the *Felicidade*.

"The bitch knows my flag!" she said aloud, referencing the command flag that flew over the *Felicidade*. Admiral Shilannia had no way of knowing if the dragon was female... but it felt right to her. She frowned. "These aren't ordinary dragons," she said in a much lower voice.

Admiral Shilannia turned back to her adjutant, who had just finished speaking with the Northern Fleet through a communications crystal. "Too little wind. We're not all going to make open water... and even if we did, I fear we'll be sitting ducks. Signal all ships... *Evade and find safe harbor at earliest. My compliments, Admiral Shilannia.*" Admiral Shilannia watched as the signal flags went up. Her command message released each captain to do what he or she could to save their ship and crew. They were on their own. Several magical lightning bolts conjured by the *Felicidade's* sorcerers struck the attacking dragon... but it brushed the bolts off. The ballistae had even less affect... their massive arrows hitting some type of invisible barrier surrounding the beast, snapping on contact and falling into the water below. As the dragon came closer, one of the heads stared directly at Admiral Shilannia while the other four spewed their terrible breath weapon upon her ship. She pulled her magical sword and stood ready. She'd done all she could for the fleet and the *Felicidade*. Now she needed to save herself... or die a warriors death.

Dragon breath from four of the heads raked the *Felicidade*. All three masts were turned to char and dropped to the deck, their sails, now ash, floated in the air. The crew manning the sails were turned into melted pieces of bone and teeth. Liquefied flesh formed crimson pools on the deck and seeped into the wood. The top deck of the ship was riddled with long scorch lines that penetrated below decks and into the water. The agonized screams of the crew who had survived being touched by the breath echoed throughout the ship. The arms and legs of many had melted away, leaving only exposed bone. Others had the whole lower part of their body melted. The shrieks of those unfortunates quickly faded as death overtook them.

Admiral Shilannia, sword raised, watched helplessly as her ship was destroyed by invisible dragon's breath. She heard the continued shrieks of her crew as they died or suffered terrible wounds. She felt the ship as it listed to starboard and knew this was the beginning of its roll and plunge to the bottom. The last thing she remembered was a horrible impact as one of the dragon's talon-tipped claws grabbed her, sending her sword flying from her grasp and into the bay.

Admiral Shilannia was only unconscious for a few moments. When she awoke, she found herself clutched in the claw of the gigantic five-headed dragon. It was lumbering on a circular course around the bay. One thousand feet below, the battle between her fleet and the dragons was playing itself out. A massive head – the one that had looked at her – lowered to face Admiral Shilannia. Its exhaled breath washed over her, and the stink of which caused her to vomit.

"I have spared you, for now, so you can watch as we destroy your ships," the dragon said.

Admiral Shilannia remained perfectly still. She knew one squeeze of the claw would end her life. She very much wanted to live so she could exact her revenge on this evil.

"How did you know?" Admiral Shilannia asked. She wouldn't deny her position or rank... for if the dragon thought she was of no importance she knew it would get rid of her.

"I did not," the dragon answered. "You told me by the way you were giving orders to others on your vessel. I saw the many different flags hoisted and followed the reactions by the all the other ships. I noticed the look of defiance in your eyes as I drew closer." The dragon laughed. "You yourself told me you were the leader... and now I have you."

"Why didn't you just kill me?"

The dragon's black eyes studied the Admiral. "I see your heart. Death for a leader such as you, particularly under these circumstances, has little meaning. You don't fear it... and you're willing to welcome it into your embrace if it's honorable and for something significant... something important to your miserable life. Noble, I suppose. But for one such as me, foolish and inexplicable. I live for my personal wellbeing. I follow orders only if they benefit me. No cause is greater than my self-interest. True death to a leader like you, however, is being forced to observe all you hold dear... in this case your navy... being ripped apart and destroyed. True death to a leader like you is knowing your righteous cause cannot be victorious... that the people you sacrifice will have died in vain."

The dragon's head rose back up. Admiral Shilannia looked down at the ongoing battle. The *Felicidade* had just began her death roll. She only saw a few of her crew jump off the condemned ship. She turned away, not willing to witness its end... but dutifully watched as the rest of her fleet was being obliterated. At that moment, she understood exactly how true the dragon's words had been.

As the five-headed dragon circled, the other three dragons attacked. Multiple magic attacks from fleet sorcerers, such as lightning, fire, and magic missile spells, exploded on the dragons with little impact. Physical attacks from ballistae, bow and arrow, as well as any other range weapon thrown against them, also had no effect. The same invisible barrier that guarded the five-headed dragon also protected her smaller cohorts.

The three frigates covering the Marine landing were scorched, charred, and sinking after just one pass of the first dragon. Their destruction occurred so quickly that most of the surviving crew below decks had no time to abandon the ships as they sank.

The empty troop ships *Charon* and *Erinyes* suffered the same fate. However, because their size is significantly larger than a frigate, they sank much more slowly. The attacking dragon made several passes with its breath weapon to insure the fate of both ships.

The third dragon attacked the scattering fleet, sinking several larger ships that couldn't maneuver fast enough to get out of the line of attack. All of the frigates, though they had little room to evade in the ship-crowded bay, still managed to elude the touch of the deadly dragon breath weapon... although two of them accidently smashed into one another, leaving both dead in the water.

As Admiral Shilannia viewed the action from high above, she understood her fleet had no chance of success against these monsters. Already, a dozen ships had gone under with a terrible loss of life.

Magic attacks against the dragons didn't work... and physical attacks such as those by the ballistae also had no effect because of a magical defensive shield surrounding each dragon.

"STOP!" she screamed.

One of the dragon heads lowered and faced her. "Save your breath, little admiral. My dragons will destroy every ship. You'll watch knowing you're powerless to do anything about it. Then you'll understand the true meaning of a soul filled with desolation before you die." The dragon head appeared to smile. "I bask in your despair. Your hopelessness fills me like a swallow of fresh meat soaked and brimming with steamy blood."

Admiral Shilannia looked away and down. By now the destruction of her fleet was almost complete. Only those ships that could make the archipelago would have any chance of survival.

"WHAT DO YOU WANT!" Admiral Shilannia shouted in frustration.

The dragon head snorted. "What do I want?" it replied. "You're witnessing it! First your fleet. Then every other fleet on this gods-forsaken world. I want death and destruction. I want suffering. I want to rule the skies and oceans of Aster. And that is what the demon Aikanáro has promised me."

Admiral Shilannia watched as the dragons delivered the *coup de grâce* to the ships that didn't make it to archipelago. "*And I thought open water was where they'd have a better chance for survival,*" she thought.

Suddenly the five-headed dragon released her. She felt relieved, and a deep sadness as the water rushed to meet her.

Cincinnatus Lafayette, the ranking sorcerer assigned to the four-masted *Prometheus*, was struggling to keep his head above water as he clung to a charred piece of deck planking. Swimming had never been his strong suit. His ship, along with most of the fleet, had just been sunk by several dragons. The Bay of Eltoria was filled with crew using whatever they could find in the water to stay afloat until help arrived. Among the survivors floated lifeless bodies. For the moment the living outnumbered the dead.

"That won't last long," Cincinnatus thought. Even as he watched, bodies, and some of those still alive, sank into the depths.

As he continued to struggle, he looked skyward towards the retreating dragons and saw a figure drop from the claws of the five-headed behemoth. Even from a distance he recognized the purple cloak of the falling figure. "The Admiral!" he bellowed.

Without hesitation, the master sorcerer hooked his arms over the planking and began to craft a spell. Though the distance was extreme, Cincinnatus recognized his magic was the Admiral's only chance of survival. It crossed his mind that, considering the current state of the fleet, she might not be so thankful... warriors had such a strange sense of honor... but he quickly disregarded the thought. As he concentrated on his spell, whispering incantations and using his fingers and arms to create precise symbols in the air before him, he started to lose his precarious grip on the plank. He ignored it.

"Warrior's plight, oh so sure.
Plummeting from the sky with no true cure.

Cruel hearted intentions will be her death.
And when she lands, she'll not draw breath.

Wind and water break her fall.
One gets thicker, one gets tall.

Wrap her in your billowing embrace.
Bring her home with all due haste."

"AUDI SERMONEM MEUM!"

The air surrounding Admiral Shilannia became thicker as she fell, and the velocity of her fall decreased considerably... but not enough to save her. This was never Cincinnatus' intent. If he had made the air even just a fraction thicker to stop the fall altogether, the Admiral wouldn't be able to breathe. As delicate as the spell was, the air pressure was still enough to cause unconsciousness. While the air slowed the Admiral's descent, the water rose like a gigantic blue-green titan to grab hold of the falling figure.

Cincinnatus felt the plank slip away as he guided the spell, but his concentration was such he didn't notice it until he had slipped beneath the waves. Drowning will break even the most absorbed state of mind. Cincinnatus thrashed about wildly, certain he would never see the light of day again. As the first painful inhalation of water entered his lungs, a strong hand grabbed the sorcerer by the scruff of his cloak and pulled him out of the water and into a lifeboat.

"Spit it out, my friend," a deep, unfamiliar voice said while pounding the back of Cincinnatus with an open hand.

Water flew out and then Cincinnatus coughed uncontrollably. It took a few minutes of violent coughing before he could breathe deeply again.

Cincinnatus undid the amulet to his drenched cloak and let it drop to the bottom of the lifeboat. It felt good to have that weight lifted. He turned to thank his rescuer... but stopped and backed away.

"You're..." Cincinnatus said. His words died before being uttered. For a moment he considered jumping back into the water. Cincinnatus had been told one of his rescuer's kind was a sailor in the fleet, but he never envisioned meeting him face to face.

"You were going to say a giant, weren't you?" the huge sailor laughed. "I prefer Draugen Pesta."

Cincinnatus shook his head as if to clear cobwebs stuck in the back of his mind. "No, I was going to say Black Death."

"That's a bit harsh, don't you think?" the sailor responded. "My people are very misunderstood." The sailor extended his hand. "I'm

Yury Petrenko, Master at Arms and chief cook on the *Cassiopeia*... or what used to be the *Cassiopeia*."

"Cincinnatus Lafayette," Cincinnatus replied. "Master sorcerer from the..."

"From the *Prometheus*," Yury interrupted. "Maybe it's I who should shrink away. Your reputation throughout the fleet as a no-nonsense sorcerer who can turn a sailor into a beetle is quite legendary."

"Yes. Well, I've never actually done that," Cincinnatus replied.

"But you could," Yury countered. "Though I'd say my size would be more suited for a... oh, I don't know... a cat?"

Cincinnatus smiled. "More like a medium-sized dog," he said before changing the subject. "Grab the oars. The Admiral is about a quarter mile away. We need to get to her before she goes under for the last time."

Ten minutes later Yury was dragging a sputtering admiral from out of the water.

Admiral Shilannia recognized the sorcerer's cloak lying on the bottom of the lifeboat. "You saved me?" she asked.

Cincinnatus nodded. "Cincinnatus Lafayette at your service, Admiral," he said. "My companion here is Master at Arms Yury Petrenko."

"From the *Cassiopeia*, ma'am," Yury added.

Admiral Shilannia shook hands with each. "I heard we had a Draugen Pesta crewman in the fleet, though I believe you're the only giant west of the Greater Boreskyre Mountains."

Yury looked embarrassed. "As far as I know, I am. There was a situation that... required me to leave my homeland," he said somewhat sheepishly.

"Nothing illegal, I trust," Admiral Shilannia said.

"Certainly not, madam," Yury exclaimed. "But a certain young lady got it in her mind that I... that I... well... let's just say the whole thing was nothing but a big misunderstanding. She finally came to her senses. But her brothers..." Yury sighed. "I suppose one could surmise they weren't looking for me to share a mug of ale. It was all quite disturbing."

Admiral Shilannia stared at the giant sailor for a few moments before turning her glance away. Yury looked down as his face tuned red. Cincinnatus laughed. He owed Yury his life, that was true, but he had discovered he also genuinely liked him.

"Very good," the Admiral said. She'd heard similar stories from sailors her whole career. "Let's see if we can find any other survivors. Then it's important I get to shore. I need to report to the Queen. And there's still a small fleet scattered in the archipelago that needs to be gathered up."

"Dragons on the starboard bow!" the *Freedom Wind's* main mast lookout called.

Captain Jasmine Dubois and her First Officer, Thomas Krist, directed their spyglasses to the spot in the sky the lookout pointed. The sky had clouded up over the last half hour, and now large, billowy clouds covered much of it. However, the black dragons served as a stark contrast to the whiteness of the clouds which made them easily recognizable.

"I'm not familiar with black dragons, Captain," Mr. Krist said as he studied the four figures flying several miles to starboard. "And the larger one has five heads!"

"Hydra, Mr. Krist," Captain Dubois replied. "I've heard stories... myths actually... of one up north past the Crystal Wasteland. It's said a magnificent silver hydra lives at the base of the Crystal Death Mountain." She turned to Mr. Krist. "Let's go to general quarters, Thomas. It doesn't look like they've noticed us... but you never know."

Mr. Krist saluted. "Aye, Captain," he said before turning to carry out her orders.

Captain Dubois returned her attention to the black dragons. They were now almost directly parallel to the *Freedom Wind*... but still four or five miles away by her estimation. "What the blazes is going on?" she whispered.

"Fogbank ahead!" another lookout reported.

Captain Dubois looked at the fogbank which was still several miles distant. As she watched, it grew larger. It was unnatural. Suddenly a huge waterspout appeared in the fog and grew upwards. As it reached into the sky, blue bolts of lightning came down and traveled the length of the waterspout and into the fog. She swore.

In Havendale, thousands of miles away, the globe flashed close to the island of InnisRos. Amkissra noted the length and location of the shift and added it to the information she had already recorded. Even though she'd been developing strong empirical data about the shift, she was still at a loss trying to figure out how much time Aster had before it was thrown out of the universe.

Amkissra rubbed her forehead and sighed. "This can wait a couple of hours," she thought as she closed her notebook. "Rathal will be here soon for dinner."

Admiral Shilannia, Cincinnatus, and Yury had only just begun the hunt for survivors when a strange fogbank materialized. The fog, besides coming upon them unnaturally quick, was dry instead of moist, and extremely dense. So much so that visibility shrank from unlimited to only a few feet. A waterspout, intertwined with lightning, developed in front of their lifeboat and headed toward them. Yury's strength and his ability to work the lifeboat oars gave them a few valuable minutes. With life comes hope. However, as the waterspout gained in size, the outcome became more and more apparent.

"This isn't right," Admiral Shilannia observed. "Cincinnatus, is there any magical explanation?"

"Well, Admiral, the fog's certainly not normal," Cincinnatus replied as he looked around. He whispered an incantation while he made precise movements with his fingers, drawing magic from the air around him. Using the magic he'd just conjured to identify the makeup of the fog, he found it was infused with powerful enchantments. However, it was a bit off, as if it didn't belong. "Yes, Admiral. Quite a bit of magic. This isn't just magical, however. It's unworldly."

Yury snorted. "I could have told you that much without using a spell, my friend," he said before directing his gaze to the admiral. "Admiral, we need to get out of the way of that waterspout before..."

Yury stopped talking as the fog suddenly lifted and the waterspout disappeared. They knew immediately they were no longer on Aster. The water around them had become tranquil... as if they sat upon a vast sea of glass. The light of three moons reflected off the surface and brightened the night. And the stars...

"Admiral, that's not our sky!" Yury exclaimed. "The constellations are all wrong... too many stars!"

Admiral Shilannia nodded. "I see that Mr. Petrenko," she said as she scanned the horizon. "There's a landmass to port. Let's go get some answers."

As Yury rowed the skiff towards land, both Admiral Shilannia and Cincinnatus looked in wonder as a huge object moved across the alien sky, blotting out one of the three moons.

"That's a strange looking cloud," Cincinnatus said. "As big as a small city, I'd say. Are those tentacles hanging down from it?"

Without warning, it disappeared.

In the monastery at Calmacil Clearing, Eric the Black choked on his light mid-day meal. Landross beat him on the back to clear the obstruction. Not uncharacteristically, the big knight underestimated his strength and sent Eric the Black head-first into the table.

"Oh, sorry there, Eric," Landross apologized.

"Never mind that," Eric the Black replied as he stood. "Something strange just happened. I need to talk with the Queen and Father Goram."

Landross stood as well. "I'll come along in case you need help getting through those Marine guards she surrounds herself with."

"What about her wolves?"

"I can't be expected to do everything," Landross chuckled good-naturedly.

CHAPTER FOUR

The Mainland

A mother will move heaven and earth to protect her young. This is a universal truth. It's a trait built into her soul. Many wise scholars have postulated the reason behind this devotion, with most concluding its nothing more than nature's way of ensuring the survival of the species. But a mother, upon hearing this, will shake her head and laugh. How can love be so simply defined?

-The Book of the Unveiled

Tangus lay with his back against a tree stump, dozing. Loki, his three-legged Royal Mountain Saber Cat, and Kevik, Romulus' adopted son, were playing, something they seemed to do nonstop. It'd only been two days since they returned from their battle with the Purge, and he was still feeling its aftereffects. Kristen, Emmy, Jennifer, and Mariko were quietly conversing with Elrond and Elanesse. Emmy acted as interpreter since she could communicate with them through their thoughts. This saved Elrond from forming words with branches and leaves — a slow and inefficient process. Though each of the gigantic and powerful trees had true names, they both insisted their friends address them as they always did. "Hell, what kind of name is *Elendrel-Telperiën*, anyway?" Elrond exclaimed at the time, exasperated. "I'm not even sure I'M saying it right!"

Lester and Safire, true to their word, left the previous day to get married, make a home in Saint Seton, and join the Riders of the Elderdale. Tangus already missed them both terribly, even though they were only two days ride away. They seemed happy as they said their farewells, mounted their horses and rode off. Tangus had been thinking about asking some of those living in the Elderdale to pick up roots and come to Elanesse. It was time to make that city a home. Perhaps the two would return in the future.

As the banter between his friends droned on, the sleep-induced state of Tangus' mind barely noted the words. For the moment, all seemed well as the sounds of the forest and the voices of his people played in the background. Then Tangus heard a well-known voice that caused him to come awake and sit up. It was Elrond. Then another, unfamiliar melodious female voice caught his ear. That could only be Elanesse. Tangus got up and walked over to his wife. He looked at the two trees. In between those massive trunks was the grave of Charity.

"Am I hearing right?" he asked. "Are Elrond and Elanesse actually talking in my head?"

"Brilliant observation," Elrond said. "Who else sounds like me, you big dope?"

"What the *Elendrel-Telperiën* is saying..." Elanesse said before being cut short.

"Stop calling me that!"

Elanesse sighed. It sounded like wind rustling through her leaves. "What Elrond is saying is that your wife has performed a spell that allows you to understand us."

"I didn't know you could do that," Tangus said to Kristen.

Kristen gave Tangus a quick peck on the cheek. "Emmy has once again shown me a different path for a magical spell I already knew. It's a different way of looking at things."

Tangus looked at Emmy and frowned.

"Oh, father, don't look so grim," Emmy said. Her eyes were sparkling. "Some spells are more than just three-dimensional. Depending on the subject, they have the potential to do so much more. In this case, I showed mother a way to change her spell so that it specifically focused on Elrond and Elanesse. It wouldn't have worked on just an ordinary tree. Besides, it makes things easier if you can talk to Elrond and Elanesse directly, don't you think?"

Tangus nodded. "If you say so."

"I'm sorry we disturbed you, honey," Kristen said. "I wanted to give you a few more hours of rest before updating you."

Tangus recognized apprehension in Kristen's voice. "Bad news from InnisRos?"

"Father tells me the Army and Navy belong to the Queen once again," Kristen replied.

"That's a relief," Tangus said. "Maybe now we can rest easy since your father has the manpower to stop Mordecai."

Kristen shook her head. "Something strange is happening in Taranthi. They lost all contact with the capital city."

"Probably Mordecai playing his games," Tangus remarked.

"Strange animals are showing up," Mariko said. "Creatures of legend. Father Goram called them wyverns... and they come from the Svartalfheim. It appears the dark elves have crossed time and space to invade our world."

This time it was Elrond who spoke. "There was also a battle between the navy of InnisRos and dragons... black dragons. The fleet was virtually destroyed."

"I've heard of black dragons under the earth, but only very rarely on the surface," Tangus said. His concern now matched his wife's. "The Svartalfheim?" he asked.

Kristen nodded. "So my father believes. Survivors of the battle reported that one dragon had five heads and was as big as a small mountain. Their breath is invisible and hot enough to melt skin from bone."

Tangus looked at Kristen. "So now your father has to deal with an invasion, strange dragons, and Mordecai? That's not coincidental."

Kristen looked away.

"What is it, dear?" Tangus asked.

"The *Freedom Wind* turned up and anchored offshore at the base of the Arrow," Kristen said.

Tangus smiled. "How are our friends Captain Dubois and Mr. Krist?"

"They're fine... father didn't go into specifics," Kristen replied. "My communications crystal was about powered out. But they too saw the black dragons."

Kristen paused.

Tangus frowned. "Well?"

"Jasmine said the dragons were heading east," Kristen answered. "There were four of them and they were last seen crossing the Isile Silimaure and flying over the Ocean of the Heavens."

Tangus sighed. "It's a good bet those dragons are coming for us."

"We have about a week if that's the case, providing they don't catch a decent tailwind," Mariko said. "But that's not all."

"That's not all?" Tangus said as he shook his head. "What else?"

Kristen looked at the huge tree. "Tell him, Elrond."

Elrond cleared his throat. "It would appear I'm sort of a king... well, to everyone except that oak down south..."

"Please stay on point, dear," Elanesse gently chided.

"We have issues, that oak and I..."

Elanesse interrupted more forcibly this time. "Elrond stop! You're being petulant!"

"Okay! Okay!" Elrond snapped. "But I'm going to settle that score, you can mark my words!"

"I'm sure you will, dear."

Elrond's leaves abruptly shook as he sighed. "Anyway, as I was saying, trees and shrubs in the area seem to feel it necessary to report every little thing they experience to me. I'm constantly hearing 'Oh, the wind blew off some of my leaves!', or 'One of my branches snapped!', and my personal favorite, 'How do I get this bird nest off!' It's enough to drive a tree..."

"Elrond! Please!" Elanesse once again reminded him.

"There's a small shrub northeast of here living at the base of the Greater Boreskyre Mountains..."

Tangus shook his head in amazement. "I'm sorry, but a shrub that knows where it's planted in the earth?"

"C'mon, Tangus!" Elrond exclaimed. "I'm filling in the blanks. Shrubs don't know anything, but they got eyes... well, whatever it is a plant uses to see things."

Elanesse suddenly blurted, "We don't actually see things, sweetheart, we..." A rustle of Elrond's leaves stopped her. "Sorry, please continue," Elanesse said after a slight pause.

"Harrumph!" Elrond commented impatiently. "Are you sure?"

Elanesse sighed and bobbed a few branches in agreement.

Elrond swished his leaves in apology. "Perhaps I overreacted a bit. Sorry. Anyway, the shrub reports two small, encamped armies. They're just sitting there waiting for something."

"Hmm... that has to be Hebron and Madeira," Mariko said. "They're the only two city-states with standing armies in the area. But they don't get along. So, if they're not fighting each other, they must have a mutual objective."

"Perhaps that objective has something to do with the giants that came out of the mountains," Elrond said. "It would appear the Black Death is on the march."

Tangus shook his head. "The Draugen Pesta haven't come across the mountains in hundreds of years. And even then, the history books and legends say it was for trade only."

"You're correct," Elanesse said. "I have memories of giants trading in the marketplace. Only rarely did they ever come to our side of the mountain, but most assuredly they did. Occasionally one would decide to go west rather than return to their homeland. But never did any of them ever cause problems... always polite and, though hard bargainers, they always treated the merchants fairly. They never used their size to intimidate."

Tangus picked up Loki who had decided pawing at his boots was the thing to do. The cub had sharp claws. "It doesn't sound like they're here to trade," he said as he stroked the head of the saber cat.

"Why invade?" Kristen wondered. "Other than land, what's their motive for bringing their army across the Greater Boreskyre?"

"Sometimes land is motivation enough," Mariko said.

"There are other reasons," Emmy remarked. She'd been so quiet they forgot she was there. But each person present took her counsel seriously. "While I can't be sure, I doubt the prospect of land is the only thing that motivates the Draugen Pesta. It goes against their nature. Except for their dealings with the Hyrokkin, they're a peaceful and noble people."

"What are Hyrokkin?" Kristen asked.

"Centaurs, dear," Tangus replied. "They're the hereditary enemy of the Draugen Pesta."

"It has to be Nightshade!" Mariko brusquely exclaimed. "I never met anyone... or anything... as devious as her. I've always suspected she was up to something other than the capture of Emmy and Kristen. She wasn't working for Mordecai, but rather was playing him for a fool. And it could explain the dragons. She's a very powerful demon and would have access to the supernatural... or the unworldly. They might be from the Abyss."

"Or maybe the Svartalfheim," Emmy remarked.

Mariko nodded. "Perhaps... particularly since a portal has been opened to that world. But, though she can summon other demons from the underworld, I'm pretty sure she's not strong enough to pull off the connection between our world and the Svartalfheim."

"Yet that connection has been made and InnisRos is being invaded by the Elves of Dark," Tangus said. "And more than likely she and Mordecai are responsible."

"There's only one other explanation," Kristen said. "She used the power of the *Ak-Séregon Stone* for her own purpose. And as long as she controls that..."

"She controls what worlds have access to ours." Tangus gently placed Loki next to a sleeping Kevik. Romulus and Sakkara were lying close by. "I don't believe InnisRos will stand long against the armies of the dark elves. But InnisRos is only one island. Surely they've bigger prey in mind... like perhaps the city-states over here?"

"I see where you're going with this," Mariko said.

Kristen frowned. "Then enlighten me, please. The humans have large standing armies themselves. How would the dark elves even be able to get a foothold?"

"Probably use a diversion to attract the bulk of the human armies east so they can invade from the west," Tangus said. "But there's something else... something I'm missing." Tangus clasped his arms behind his back and started to pace.

"I know that walk," Elrond said. "Tangus is perplexed."

"No, not quite," Kristen observed. "He's biting his bottom lip. That's his 'I'm thinking' look."

Elrond's leaves shivered in tree laughter. "He always looks so serious when he's deep in thought. I often wondered if..."

Tangus stopped and stared at the huge tree. "Don't you have some shrubs to order around?" he asked. "My thinking is just... of course! Havendale!"

"Eureka!" Elrond exclaimed. His leaves were shimmering between bronze and green. "Interesting... I didn't know I could do that."

"Elrond!"

"The Academy of Sorcery," Elrond said.

Tangus nodded. "They're the largest concentration of sorcerers in the world... at least in our portion of it. Take that city... or at least keep them occupied... and the few sorcerers employed by the city-states wouldn't be enough to stop an invasion." Tangus turned to Kristen. "We need to get word to them."

"Master Sorcerer Rathal Arquen, the Lord Paramount of Havendale, already knows," Emmy said. No one wondered how she knew that... they just accepted it as fact.

Lord Viktor Ternborg, King of the Draugen Pesta, looked at the Hebron and Madeiran leaders and sighed. They were to be his allies during this affair, but the more he listened to them prattle on, as if they had anything important to say, the more disgusted he became with the whole situation.

Major Konstantin Timoshenko leaned over and whispered into Lord Ternborg's ear. "Do you want me to throw them out?"

Lord Ternborg shook his head. "No, let them have their say. I can't afford to give Nightshade reasons to doubt our sincerity."

"Eventually you'll need to call the Doom Warriors, Viktor," Major Timoshenko said, changing the subject. "Nightshade demands it. But if stories you've told me about them are true, they're not the evil demons my grandmother warned me about. They're just as likely to attack our so-called allies as they are our enemies. That's not going to sit well with that demon bitch."

Lord Ternborg nodded at the HeBron general who was outlining his battle plan for the upcoming campaign with a stick, making crude caricatures in the soft earth. It had captivated all the human generals and their staff, and they weren't paying much attention to him. "You're right, Konnie. When I call the Doom Warriors, I'll be able to exercise little control over them... and I've no doubt they'll attack these wretches from HeBron and Madeira if so much as a hair on an innocent head is harmed. I don't want Nightshade to see that yet. If she does, I'll never see Daphnia again. Besides, I won't need them until the rest of the human armies arrive to kick us out of Havendale once we've taken it. That gives us some time."

Major Timoshenko shook his head. "She'll want a demonstration before then."

"Perhaps." Lord Ternborg leaned further towards his second-in-command. "I suddenly have a need to keep the locket closer. By the gods, I hate wearing that thing! It feels as if it's cursed or haunted... like it wants to strangle me. But the stakes are too high. Go back to my tent and retrieve it. You know the small chest it's in, right?"

Major Timoshenko nodded and left.

"Lord Ternborg?"

The Draugen Pesta king turned his attention to the general who had spoken. "You are General...?" he asked.

"Pallis, my lord. Rouvin Pallis."

"Very well, General Pallis. You will be the spokesman for both HeBron and Madeira," Lord Ternborg said.

"Now just a minute..." a Madeiran general began before Lord Ternborg's raised hand stopped him.

"You'll have equal input, but I only want one liaison," Lord Ternborg said. "I've chosen General Pallis."

"You can't just arbitrarily decide to..."

"CAN I NOT?!" Lord Ternborg roared. "DO YOU WANT TO TAKE THE MATTER UP WITH NIGHTSHADE?!"

At the mention of the name, each of the gathered humans recoiled. The Madeiran general backed down. "As you wish, Lord Ternborg."

"I so wish it," Lord Ternborg said as he walked over to study the makeshift map outlined in the earth. The human soldiers looked like children compared to the giant stature of the Draugen Pesta king. "We're not to go past the Olympus Mountains."

General Pallis nodded. "That too is my understanding... at least for the time being."

Lord Ternborg nodded. "When the city-states west of the mountains realize what's happening, they'll come east to drive us away. This land doesn't have one king... but it does have plenty of alliances between city-states."

"We know that," the Madeiran general said.

Lord Ternborg looked at him for a few moments before getting back to business. "We need to hold the entrances into this valley here,

here, and here," he said as he used his sword to point north and south of the mountains as well as the center pass through them.

"You intend to take the Hammer?" the Madeiran general asked. The tone of his voice was barely civil. "Any child knows you don't attack the Hammer!"

Lord Ternborg sighed. "General, what's your name?"

The general looked back defiantly. "General Edric Ujarak... my lord."

"Be forewarned, general. Any future impertinence and I can have you, or anyone else, either whipped, hanged, or both. So tread lightly." The Draugen Pesta king paused to let his meaning sink in. "In answer to your question, no, I don't intend to take the Hammer. We'll stop at Ascension. From there we should be able to bottle up any force coming through the pass."

"Plague's been reported in Ascension," General Pallis remarked. He stood a little taller after hearing Ujarak reprimanded.

That brought Lord Ternborg to a stop. Plague was the last thing he needed. It'd turn even the most powerful army into bed-bound wretches – those that survived, that is – in a matter of weeks. "How recent are these reports?" he asked.

"Two weeks, my lord," General Pallis replied.

"Then if it hasn't run its course, they'll stay behind their walls. If it has, their warriors won't be in any shape to resist. Either way, we win." Lord Ternborg spent a few moments thinking. "General Ujarak, does Madeira have enough resources left to guard the north?"

"Madeira would never leave itself undefended," the general replied. "We..."

Lord Ternborg's attention drifted away from General Ujarak when he saw Major Timoshenko return with the ornate platinum box that held the locket. He didn't look happy.

Turning his gaze back to General Ujarak, he saw everyone looking at him. "So, you think Madeira has the wherewithal to defend the north without additional help," he said, recovering quickly. He wanted nothing more than to end this discussion and find out what worried Major Timoshenko so much.

"Without a doubt, my lord."

"Let's hope, if the time comes, your opinion is more than just mere braggadocio," Lord Ternborg replied.

General Ujarak shook his head. "It's not."

"HeBron will be more than willing to come to Madeira's defense should they so need," General Pallis snickered. "Since they only have old men, women, and children defending the city."

"I'll kill you, you dirty, sniveling little coward!" General Ujarak yelled as he drew his sword. Men from both sides drew their weapons as well and were within a few seconds of ending the truce.

"STOP!" Lord Ternborg bellowed. His deep voice brought everyone to a standstill. At a raise of his hand, his own bowmen aimed arrows at the humans. "If you do not put away those swords THIS INSTANT, I'll have all of you killed!"

The two warring sides looked at each other suspiciously as they slowly put swords back into scabbards.

Lord Ternborg looked at Major Timoshenko who was signaling with a flat hand across his throat. *'It's time to end this farce,"* he thought.

"What other resistance will we face?" Lord Ternborg asked.

"The Riders of the Elderdale patrol the Alpine between Saint Seton and Silverstone," General Ujarak replied.

General Pallis interrupted. "They're nothing but mounted farmers pretending to be knights."

General Ujarak shook his head. "Lord Ternborg, my esteemed colleague is only partially correct. The farmlands between Saint Seton and Silverstone are rich and highly productive. The people are happy and giving. Many a retired knight, as well as some in their prime, have settled there to live out their remaining days. These same knights ARE the Riders. I wouldn't take them lightly."

Lord Ternborg frowned at General Pallis, who backed away, giving General Ujarak the stage. He knew he had just lost favor and now wanted to prevent getting his neck stretched... or worse.

Whereas the Madeiran general showed little fear of the 'Black Death' and fearlessly stood up for himself, the Draugen Pesta king frightened General Pallis.

"It's never wise to underestimate an adversary," Lord Ternborg said. "What else, General Ujarak?"

"Havendale, my lord."

Lord Ternborg nodded. "I have my own intelligence on Havendale. A large standing army and many sorcerers. Did I miss anything?"

General Ujarak shook his head.

"Very well." Lord Ternborg looked at General Pallis and motioned him to come closer. "I have something to attend to. Both of you get together and draw up a battle plan to take Havendale."

"Take the city, my lord?" General Pallis squeaked. "Wouldn't it be easier to just lay siege and keep them bottled up?"

Lord Ternborg shook his head. "Not with all those sorcerers it wouldn't. We need to neutralize the city. It's imperative if we're to hold the valley. I can't afford a hostile city at my back when defending the southern route."

Both generals worriedly looked at each other, which didn't go unnoticed by the Draugen Pesta king.

"Come, gentlemen," Lord Ternborg said. "When it's all said and done, I'm sure Nightshade will be extremely happy with your work at Havendale... perhaps enough to add to your blood money. And it's not like you'll be joining your men to attack the city. I mean, from everything I know about humans, their general's like to plant themselves well away from the fighting and run the battle from a safe distance."

General Ujarak snorted and walked away... his men following. General Pallis' face had drained of all color. But he was still mindful enough of his surroundings to bow and back away.

Major Timoshenko approached his king as soon as the humans had left. "Some allies Nightshade's given us," he mocked.

Lord Ternborg was still watching the retreating backs of the men as he answered. "Pallis is a conniving little bastard who owes his position to his name rather than his ability. But Ujarak... Ujarak is someone I think we can count upon." He looked at Major Timoshenko. "Show me the locket."

Major Timoshenko presented the box and opened it. The locket was gone. In its place was a note addressed to him. He recognized the handwriting.

Sofia Ternborg, Queen of the Draugen Pesta and mother to Daphnia, had her attendants and guards clear the huge marble and stone receiving room of all petitioners. What she needed to do must remain a closely guarded secret.

She wore a black leather jerkin over a silk white top with large, billowing sleeves, black leather pants, and knee-high boots. A row of six throwing knives, attached to her belt, circled her waist. The only thing that marked her as the queen was the large emerald ring she wore on her right hand and the simple, platinum circlet surrounding her head. Her long, black hair draped down to the middle of her back, which she kept controlled with several long braids during the day. Her expressive, dark violet eyes communicated her opinion to those who knew her well, particularly the one true love of her life, Viktor, and their mischievous daughter, Daphnia. From a pocket in her jerkin, she withdrew a locket and held it up to the light. This was the locket entrusted to her husband many years ago by a dying High Priestess to the goddess Dennitsa. That same priestess was her great aunt. The stone inside the locket was onyx carved to resemble a six-legged, winged dragon. But it sparkled with magic and spoke to her of its power. The legends say this is the locket that will summon the Doom Warriors. She understood the king, and only the king, was allowed to use it. But her situation was dire. As she looked at the locket while it caught the light, she prayed to whatever power that might be listening to forgive her for the deception she had played upon her husband, though if it brought back her Daphnia, she'd have no regrets and was prepared to accept the consequences.

"What are you doing with that!?" a voice demanded from behind her.

Sofia lowered the locket and turned slowly. She knew who the voice belonged to, Boris Drugov, the ranking member of the opposition party and currently involved in trying to turn the Draugen Pesta people against her husband. *This is going to be a contentious tête-à-tête,"* she thought.

Sofia nodded. "Minister Drugov."

The minister didn't waste time with pleasantries. "Why do you have the Doom Warrior locket?" he demanded.

Sofia didn't have an answer as she put the locket back into a pocket and looked at him.

"Well?!" Minister Drugov said. "You realize only your husband is permitted to use it." It was a statement, not a question. "Does he know you have it?"

Sofia remained silent as she stared at Minister Drugov.

His eyes narrowed. "He doesn't, does he?"

"The locket is connected to me as much as it is to my husband," she said.

"Yes," Minister Drugov said. "I believe your great aunt once controlled it, correct?" He shook his head. "It doesn't matter. The law specifically states only the king can use the locket. Just it being in your possession is treason. But having it in a time of war is high treason... punishable by immediate execution."

Minister Drugov shook his head. "Now you'll finally get what you deserve, traitor!" He turned his head to shout for the guards.

Without thinking, Sofia threw three knives in quick succession. One hit the neck severing the trachea while the other two were buried deep into his chest, puncturing his heart. Minister Drugov dropped, gagging and suffocating on his own blood. He stopped moving a few seconds later.

Lester and Safire had only been in Saint Seton for a few hours when the entire town turned out and put together a welcoming feast of homegrown fruits, vegetables, several roasted pigs and a strong, hearty ale. In the same barn the two stayed when passing through two weeks earlier, they enjoyed an evening of good food, light-hearted banter, and re-acquaintance. As the evening dragged into early morning, and after most of the townsfolk had retired, Lester and Safire sat on a bale of hay across from an older gentleman who was smoking a pipe. His name was Lloyd Fairmount, a knight of high standing from Altheros and the current commander of the Riders of the Elderdale. Several younger men – men who Safire noted only drank water or cow's milk during the feast – had just saddled horses and disappeared into the dim light of early morning. As those men disappeared, several other riders returned weary horses to the stables a few hundred feet away.

"You send out nightly patrols?" Lester asked.

Lloyd Fairmount nodded as he inhaled smoke. "Riders are out day and night."

"But why? This place seems peaceful enough."

"And we aim to keep it that way," Lloyd Fairmount said as he tapped burned tobacco out of his pipe on the heel of his boot. "HeBron's not too far away and they've made it quite clear how much they covet our rich farmlands… and our farmers to work it for them. While there's lots of good earth and plenty of water around Hebron, they don't want to get their hands dirty. It's hard work, and they'd rather play with their swords."

"You've had trouble with them before," Safire stated.

The old knight nodded. "And my boys showed them what good swordplay is all about. But they have the numbers on us, which is why I'm so glad the two of you decided to join up."

"Neither one of us are farmers, Friend Lloyd," Lester said. "And probably never will be. But we both want to settle down and call a place home. We're not afraid to defend that which we love... and our ability with swords and bow is somewhat acceptable."

Safire chuckled. "Lester has a way of understatement," she remarked. "I've yet to see someone as strong as he... or someone who can weld that huge blade of his as well as he does."

Lloyd Fairmount grunted. "I've no doubt about either of your abilities. Is what you say about Elanesse and the Forest of the Fey true? Or just a story for the children?"

"It's true."

"Forgive me, but as welcoming as that sounds, I must remain skeptical... at least for the time being. But if it's true, then we've an ally the likes of which we've never had. HeBron will be in for a surprise if they move south. Maybe your experience in the Riders won't be so dangerous after all, eh?"

Safire sighed. "It's been my experience that 'happily ever after' rarely lasts."

"Safire!" Lester protested. "That's a bit pessimistic, don't you think?"

"Sadly she's right, Sir Knight," Lloyd Fairmount said.

The three broke off their conversation as several riders entered the far end of Saint Seton from the south. Their horses were well lathered... a sure sign their riders had them running with speed and purpose.

"They're from Havendale," Lloyd Fairmount said. "I wonder why they're pushing their horses so hard?" He stood and walked out of the barn and into view of the riders. Lester and Safire followed

The riders saw Lloyd Fairmount and raced forward. Coming to a stop, each rider slid off his or her horse. As the leader, a captain, walked up to the old knight, the others took their horses to nearby water troughs. The Havendale captain reached inside his tunic and withdrew a rolled-up parchment. It had the waxed seal of General Kelsia Húrön.

Lloyd Fairmount raised an eyebrow. "What's this, Captain?" he asked.

The captain shook his head. "I don't know, sir. But the General ordered me to get it to you posthaste."

Lloyd Fairmount broke the seal in front of the captain, unrolled the scroll, and read the message without expression. When he had finished, he re-rolled the scroll and kept it in his hand while his other gripped the hilt of his sword. "Captain see to your horses then go refresh yourself and your troopers. You passed a tavern down the road. The owner is probably already awake. Get coffee and something to eat. Tell him I'll settle payment later."

After the Havendale courier left, Safire asked about the message. Lloyd Fairmount shook his head. "When worlds collide," he said as he watched the Havendale warriors unsaddle their horses. He sighed and looked at Safire. "You're correct, my dear," he said as he handed her the scroll to read. "There'll be no 'happily ever after' any time soon, I'm afraid."

The Havendale spy raced her horse across open country southeast of the city of HeBron. Behind her and closing fast were three Madeiran and two HeBron cavalry soldiers. The spy had a crossbow bolt in her side and each step of her horse caused extreme pain. Only by adrenalin and will power had she been able to make it this far. Though she'd like nothing more than to stop, lay down, and sleep, thoughts of giving up were far from her mind. The information she carried was much too important to her superiors in Havendale.

In the breaking morning light, she observed a fogbank to her south and about half a mile away. The pain in her side and the blood loss was affecting her thinking, but not enough that she didn't recognize the significance of the fogbank. It would provide cover, and that was her only chance of escaping her fate... and perhaps the fate of Havendale if what she saw wasn't reported.

Her horse stopped, snorted, and reared up just as they entered the fogbank. The spy understood. The fog felt unnatural – dry, not wet – and charged with some mysterious power. In their delay, a crossbow bolt whizzed past the spy's head. *"That was close,"* she thought as she urged her horse forward.

Neither horse nor spy could see more than a few feet ahead, and the breakneck speed in which she pushed her horse was extremely dangerous. But she had no choice. It was fortunate they were crossing a flat, grassy terrain.

They came out of the fog and it was night instead of day. There were no clouds in the black sky, and the stars seemed so close she could reach out and touch them. Three moons appeared to be just coming up over the horizon and it wouldn't be long before they dominated the sky. The landscape looked nothing like the field they had been crossing. All around, the trees were small and scraggly with no leaves. Their branches where moving, yet no wind propelled them. The mountains on the horizon were nothing but huge, dark forms that gave the spy a sense of foreboding. In the sky floated huge city-size creatures with long arm-like protrusions hanging down. The spy saw no other sign of life.

The young woman kept her horse running forward but clutched the reins twice as hard. She heard the distinct sound of running horses behind her, getting closer. But she doubted they could still see her in the fog. She laid her head down on the side of the horse's neck and closed her eyes. "I'm hallucinating," she said aloud. "Too much blood loss."

Suddenly she felt the familiar warmth of the sun and realized she no longer breathed in the dry fog. She opened her eyes and saw they once again traveled across familiar fields in the early morning sunshine. She inhaled the scent of flowers and grass dampened by the early morning dew. The wind in her face was suddenly the most welcomed thing she'd ever experienced in her young life. She risked a glance behind her and saw the fog had dissipated. There was no signs of the riders that chased her.

She pulled her horse up on the northern bank of Lake Lorali and fell to the ground. While the horse drank, the spy crawled over to a beautiful, green tree and leaned her back against its trunk. "I'll rest here for a minute," she told herself before drifting off into an exhausted sleep.

The three Riders of the Elderdale, former knights one and all, saw a lone rider on horseback appear out of nowhere. They watched the rider stop, dismount, and collapse against the trunk of a tree. From their location they could see a crossbow bolt sticking out of the rider's side. They kicked their horses into a run as they rode to investigate.

The unknown rider was female and unconscious. A quick examination revealed the severity of her wound, and the three Riders of the Elderdale knew the bolt needed to be removed if the girl was to have any chance of survival.

"That's a HeBron bolt," one rider remarked. "I recognize the fletching. They use barbed points which have to be cut out, not pulled."

The elder knight nodded. "I'll do it," he said. Then he paused as he looked at the face of the sleeping girl. "She can't be more than sixteen. Why would Hebron attack a child?"

"You'll never find out if you wait much longer," one of the other Riders commented. "We can defend her honor later if we must."

The older knight nodded. "I need one of you to hold her down while the other keeps a sharp lookout for the bastards who did this."

The crossbow bolt was dug out easily enough... the knight was familiar with this type of injury and had a practiced hand. Though the field surgery went quickly, it still caused a significant amount of pain. The girl woke up screaming. Over and over she repeated words that gave each knight pause.

"Black Death!"

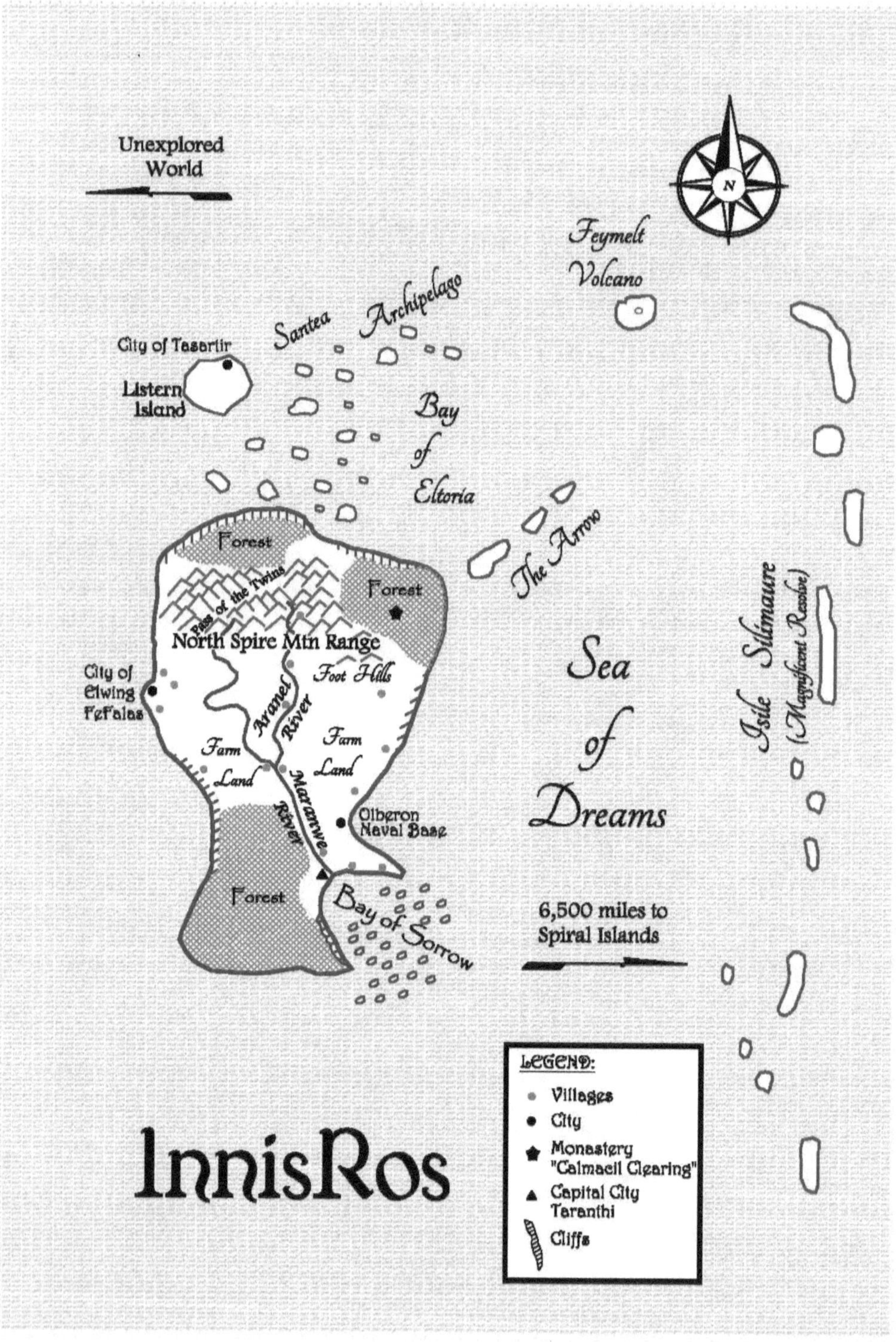

Unexplored World
Feymelt Volcano
N
Santea Archipelago
City of Tasartir
Listern Island
Bay of Eltoria
The Arrow
Forest
Pass of the Twins
Forest
North Spire Mtn Range
Foot Hills
City of Elwing Fefalas
Aranel River
Farm Land
Farm Land
Maranwe River
Sea
of
Dreams
Isile Silimaure
(Magnificent Resolve)
Olberon Naval Base
Forest
Bay of Sorrow
6,500 miles to Spiral Islands
InnisRos
LEGEND:
Villages
City
Monastery "Calmacil Clearing"
Capital City Taranthi
Cliffs

CHAPTER FIVE

InnisRos

Now I know why they refer to the elves from the Svartalfheim as 'Dark Elves'. The hopelessness they bring to the soul is as black as the darkest night... and as evil.

-From the Journal of StarSinger Nefertari Arntuile

Dressed as simple farmers, StarSinger Nefertari Arntuile and Marine Colonel Daeron Tirion had been traveling southwest for the last two days in a simple cart pulled by two large draft horses. Nefertari's ever-present guardian, the creation stone Maedhros Nénmacil, flew high in the sky, using clouds to remain undetected. The StarSinger and the creation stone maintained constant communication with each other through the telepathic link they shared.

As they traveled, Nefertari had plenty of time to reflect. *"So many things have changed,"* she thought as she reviewed the past few days in her mind. The most important of which were the problems being presented by the theft of the *Ak-Séregon Stone* and the dangerous repercussions its alignment to the Svartalfheim had caused. Eric the Black had described what was happening as an interface between universes. A message he sent to his sorcerer contacts at Havendale confirmed it... and so much more. It wasn't just the future of InnisRos at stake, but the entire world of Aster rested on the precipice. Then the captain of the armed cargo ship *Freedom Wind*, which had unexpectedly appeared off the shores of InnisRos, had her own amazing story to tell about strange fogs, foreign night skies, and the stunning crossing of half an ocean in the blink of an eye. Eric the Black touted this as further proof that the realignment of the *Ak-Séregon Stone* caused parts of Aster to interface with other universes and the worlds that existed within them. All plans for Lessien's trip to the mainland in search of human allies was put aside because of the risk involved. Lessien's was the only dissenting voice. Father Goram pulled her aside for a private conversation, after which she too recognized the folly. The priest was very persuasive. Nefertari believed he could talk a dragon out of its hoard... or a knight out of his honor.

Another issue, communicated to Father Goram by his daughter in the ruined elven city of Elanesse on the mainland, involved two city-states in her part of the world that had mobilized and formed an alliance with a race of giants from across the Greater Boreskyre Mountains to the east. Daeron had called them the Draugen Pesta, but most others called them the 'Black Death'. This claim hadn't been substantiated, but if true and an invasion was imminent, the humans would be more inclined to face that threat rather than travel thousands of miles across an ocean to fight for an island that has, for the most part, shunned them. Furthermore, and even Lessien couldn't deny this, any attempt by human troop ships to make the crossing to InnisRos might get caught in the same shift phenomena the crew of the *Freedom Wind* had experienced. That would be disastrous not only for the lost ships but also for any hope of future friendly relationships with the humans on the mainland.

Finally, there was the catastrophe suffered by the Navy in the Bay of Eltoria. Daeron didn't feel concentrating most of the fleet in the bay was a strategically sound decision by Admiral Shilannia... but then again no one could anticipate the appearance of three dark dragons and a five-headed hydra. The admiral had done well to save the fleet from an even larger tragedy. Unfortunately, the admiral's flagship, the *Felicidade*, was destroyed with only a hand full of survivors. The admiral wasn't among them. Luckily, or perhaps by divine providence, the dragons only made two passes over the fleet before heading out to sea.

So now InnisRos was not only cut off and alone, but the island was also facing an invasion force of dark elves. Intelligence concerning the size, strength, and disposition of the dark elf army was woefully lacking, as was information regarding their leadership and ultimate goals. Do they want to subjugate the people and use them for slave labor? Do they want to rape the land of its wealth? Or perhaps it's a springboard for something far more sinister? All that mattered at this point was to find the *Ak-Séregon Stone* and close the portal to stop the shifts and end the dark elf invasion.

Nefertari sighed as she touched her chest to verify the magical necklace which rested between her breasts was still there. At the behest of Lessien, it was created and given to her by Eric the Black just before they left. With it came exact instructions on how it was to be activated and what it did. She hoped she'd never have to use it, for it was magic only designed for one… a desperate last hope.

Nefertari shook her head and shoved her thoughts aside as she addressed Daeron. "It's so desolate," she said. They were approaching the Aranel River and had met no one. All the crops in the fields looked to have been hastily harvested, for much of the valuable grain was still on the stalk. "Where did the people go?"

Daeron looked at this companion. "I'm sorry I've never mentioned this before, Nefertari. You've taken to this world so well I sometimes forget you're from the Alfheim. As soon as we realized we were being invaded, we sent messenger dragons all over the island to get everyone in their safe places for the duration. Those east and south of the Maranwe River went to Olberon. The folks west of the Maranwe River left for Elwing FeFalas while most of the northern population scattered into the North Spire mountains. We have caverns prepared for this kind of emergency up there."

Nefertari nodded. "That's fairly radical, and might I add forward thinking."

"We're concerned about the safety of our people," Daeron replied. "But it also makes good tactical sense. Now, instead of having a scattered populace who can only resist in small bands, we've created several strongholds on the island which will not only slow down the invasion, but also make them pay for their troubles. Instead of farmers with pitchforks, we make them troops with modern weaponry led by experienced military officers, sergeants and tacticians. Not only can we defend these strongholds, but we can also use them as bases to plan and take offensive action against the enemy. The best-case scenario is we drive the invaders off the island. But if not, then we use the mountains as a cover for guerrilla warfare."

"This isn't just an invasion force with a finite number of troops," Nefertari said. "The dark elves have their entire world available to them. They've got a ready and secure supply line and access to an unlimited number of fresh and healthy warriors."

"Which is why we need to find the *Ak-Séregon Stone* and steal it back," Daeron said, "or destroy it. To do that, we need intelligence."

Nefertari had taken part in all the meetings and understood what was required to move forward. But Daeron was a 'grunt' and saw things from a different perspective. His unique assessment and thoughts about strategy were invaluable. "Do you really think there's still people inside Taranthi who can and will help?"

Daeron shook his head. "I don't know, but I suspect so. Every city has an underside – thieves, pickpockets, smugglers – run by powerful guilds. An occupied city isn't good for business. They'll want to get rid of the dark elves as much as we do. And don't forget about the veterans who have either retired or were discharged and made Taranthi their home."

"Is that who Eric the Black said would meet us?" Nefertari asked. "Thieves and cutthroats? Veterans?"

"No. They'll serve as our army. We're meeting someone different. He didn't go into specifics except to say they're expecting us." Daeron looked ahead. "There's something about Eric the Black that seems off... like he's hiding a secret."

Their cart rambled over a hill and they could see a village spread out ahead... perhaps two miles away and sitting on the bank of the Aranel River. Like the surrounding landscape, it appeared to be empty. Not even a barking dog broke the silence.

"Perhaps we've planned our retreat into strongholds too well," Daeron remarked.

Nefertari nodded. "It will be hard to go unnoticed across a landscape that's void of life."

"And it gets harder," Maedhros Nénmacil said through his telepathic link with the StarSinger. *"Several of those small dragons..."*

"Wyverns," Nefertari corrected aloud for Daeron's sake.

"Yes, wyverns," the creation stone replied. *"They're flying towards us from the south. Give me but a few minutes and I'll destroy them."*

"No, not yet," Nefertari replied. "Let's first see if we can take cover before being spotted. I don't want to give our position away... nor do I want them to know about you, my friend. At least not until the moment is right."

Daeron snapped the reins to pick up speed. The strong draft horses responded well and soon the cart was flying down the hill towards the town.

"How are we doing," Nefertari asked the creation stone.

"The wyverns are flying in zigzags to cover more area... which is slowing them down. You should be fine if you don't delay overmuch."

"Maedhros Nénmacil says we'll be fine if we keep up this pace," Nefertari said to Daeron.

Daeron clucked at the horses as he snapped the reins again. "Tell our boulder friend I'm heading for the large white barn just on the outskirts of the town. I think he should join us."

Maedhros Nénmacil was waiting for them inside the barn. He didn't acknowledge them as they entered... he was watching a cat and her five kittens in a pile if hay. The mother was suspiciously eyeing Maedhros Nénmacil, but the kittens were fast asleep.

While Daeron closed the barn doors and fed hay to the horses, Nefertari kneeled next to the feline family. She sighed.

"What's wrong, StarSinger," Maedhros Nénmacil asked in a low voice.

Nefertari shook her head. "Oh, I guess it's nothing really. I just miss Miracle."

The creation stone grumbled a chuckle. "She's in good hands with Colonel Tirion's Marines."

"That's what worries me," the StarSinger replied good-naturedly.

"What worries you?" Daeron asked as he walked over.

Nefertari shook her head. "Nothing. Look here, perfect innocence in a world gone mad."

"Kittens!" the big Marine exclaimed as he too kneeled beside them and played with the now awake little ones. "I love kittens!"

Maedhros Nénmacil laughed hard enough to dislodge hay from the loft above.

Lessien was angry. Her sword, *Ah-HritVakha*, blazed in its scabbard in reaction to its master's irritation. "It's bad enough Mordecai attempts the overthrow of InnisRos! But to use the dark elves to support his treachery is... is ..."

"Control the blade, Lessien," Father Goram said. He could see the rage in her face and knew part of the reason was the sword and its constant bloodlust.

"The blade is under control, priest," Lessien snapped back. Then she looked away, closed her eyes, and took a deep breath. "I apologize, Horatio. I shouldn't have yelled at you like that. Of course, you're right."

They were in the monastery chapel. The Queen, Father Goram, Autumn, Landross, Cordelia, Cameron, Eric the Black, Marine Commander-General Feynral, and Army General Tomas Singëril with his assistant Lauran Ar-Feiniel, sat on benches in the center of the room. Three dire wolves, Ajax, Findley, and Razor lay off to one side, dozing. Everyone in the room knew the dire wolves would be awake in an instant should danger present itself.

The chapel had been converted many years ago at the request of the goddess Althaya. A babbling brook ran along one side of the room and small trees, shrubs, and flowers flanked the gathering on all sides. Windows allowed sunlight during the day and starlight in the evening. The gentle sounds associated with the running water, the chirping of the crickets, and even the occasional chorus of birds made the chapel seem magical. It was an ideal place to fortify the soul – which was no doubt Althaya's intent – and the perfect spot to find peace and tranquility, both necessary for truthful contemplation.

"We're at a distinct disadvantage, Your Highness," General Singëril said. If the exchange between the Queen and Father Goram bothered him, he didn't let on. "Even as we speak, the dark elves are fortifying the capital. It's just a matter of time before they start their expansion outward."

"Those damn wyverns will spot any countermove we make," General Feynral remarked. He was still feeling the sting over the loss of Admiral Shilannia during the naval battle two days prior. "And possibly more dragons. Meanwhile, we're groping around in the dark."

"Nefertari should be able to provide valuable information," Cordelia said.

General Singëril shook his head. "We've no guarantee of that. At least not enough to stake the entire war on it. We need to expect failure and act with that in mind. Even if the colonel and the priestess get into the city..."

"Don't worry about that," Eric the Black said. "My people will get the two in. All Nefertari and Colonel Tirion have to do is get there."

"You keep saying your people," Landross complained.

Father Goram shook his head to stop any further discussion about Eric the Black's unknown resources. He didn't care as long as the sorcerer and his allies remained loyal to the Queen.

"General Singëril," Father Goram said. "Please continue."

General Singëril nodded. "As I said, we're not in a very good position, tactically speaking. We have our strongholds here at the monastery, Olberon, Elwing FeFalas, and in the mountains... but we don't have the numbers to hold out against such an army, particularly since they have an entire world from which they can draw fresh reinforcements." He nodded at General Feynral.

General Feynral produced a linen parchment, kneeled and unrolled it on the floor. He then pulled out his spectacles and put them on. "Tomas and I have studied our options," he said while looking at everyone over the top of his eyeglasses. "We don't have many. Our forces concentrated in strongholds all over the island makes sense when your goal is to protect as many people as possible... when you want to give them a haven to retreat to. But we've always built our worst-case scenario planning around an invasion by sea... not an army dropped into our laps."

General Singëril picked up the narrative. "Except for Taranthi, most of our people are safe and behind fortified positions."

"That's a good thing, right?" Lessien remarked.

"To a point, Your Highness," General Singëril replied. "That part went according to plan. But considering the size of the dark elf army and the unlimited reinforcements that can be tapped from their home world, they have the manpower to parcel out, surround, and either cut off or destroy each of those strongholds. And if we don't act soon, there'll be nothing we can do about it."

"Which means we can't expect help from Olberon or Elwing FeFalas," General Feynral added.

"Not to mention the jeopardy it puts my subjects in," Lessien said. "Okay. That's the problem. So, what's the answer?"

Both generals looked at each other. "You're not going to like it," General Singëril said.

Lessien frowned. "Give it to me straight."

"Abandon Olberon and Elwing FeFalas and move our folks north into the mountains," General Singëril replied. "We should also move our remaining naval units into the archipelago with those already there."

"Your Highness," General Feynral said. "General Singëril and my Marines will hold the forest while those who make it north hold the mountain passes."

General Singëril nodded. "General Krismoris is the Elwing FeFalas garrison commander."

"Tisha, right?" Lessien remarked.

General Singëril smiled. "She'll be happy to hear you remembered her name. I've given Tisha overall command of the northern force. She'll keep the mountains secure, don't worry about that. But Your Highness, we need to move quickly before the dark elves expand their perimeter."

Lessien studied the map. "All that's doing is playing defense and buying time. By moving north, we'd lose access to all the farmland and fruit groves. We've plenty of supplies cached away, as well as herd animals, but we can't replace them. What do we do when we've nothing to eat?"

General Singëril looked at his queen. "Playing for time is all we WANT to do, Your Highness. We can't drive them off the island... there's too many of them. And the mainland won't help since they appear to have their own invasion to worry about. We could scatter into the archipelago, but, though well hidden, we'd not be able to stay for long. Then there're the pirates to consider. Believe me, they're a force to be reckoned with. No, we need time to figure out a way to close off the portal to the dark elf home world."

"But once the portal has been closed, we still must eliminate the dark elf army that's already here," General Feynral said. "So, until then, we need to marshal our forces and avoid direct confrontation as much as possible."

"Unless direct confrontation is forced upon us," General Singëril added.

"So, my sister's mission isn't just to gather information... but also to conduct a covert operation to steal the *Ak-Séregon Stone* back,"

Lessien stated. She turned and glanced angrily at Father Goram. "That's a bit more dangerous, don't you think, Father?! Why wasn't I told about this?"

"Calm down, Lessien," Father Goram said before the Queen had a chance to say any more. "Your sister asked we keep it to ourselves until she was away. Nefertari and the creation stone have certain abilities that make her the perfect candidate for this attempt. She understands that... which is why she volunteered to go."

"And Colonel Tirion is my best Marine," General Feynral interjected.

Father Goram nodded. "With the help they'll be getting from Eric's people, the mission has a good chance for success."

Lessien looked unconvinced. "The dark elves have their sorcerers, Horatio. And black magic. How is Nefertari going to protect herself against that?"

"Don't worry about the sorcerers, Your Highness," Eric the Black said. "I'm taking care of that."

"How...?"

"Best you don't know," Eric the Black replied. He maintained eye contact with Lessien. "Perhaps it'd be more honest to say I'll not tell you, Your Highness, even if ordered. Or anyone else, for that matter."

There was an uncomfortable silence in the chapel... a silence broken by Landross. "You'll have to forgive Eric, my Queen," he said. "We all know how sorcerers can sometimes be eccentric. I'm sure he has his reasons."

The queen held up her hands. "No offense taken," she said. "I understand the need for secrecy. And considering how well all of you kept me in the dark regarding the full extent of Nefertari's mission, you do as well," she added harshly and paused for affect. "When we move our people back, how do we deal with the wyverns?"

"We give the wyverns something else to worry about," Father Goram said. He looked over at the sorcerer. "Eric?"

"Bat's, Your Highness," Eric the Black said. "Millions of bats nipping at wyvern wings and wyvern bodies."

Lessien looked at the sorcerer. "You can do that?"

Eric the Black nodded. "I've many talents... and many associates."

"Very well," Lessien said. She didn't want to ask any more questions... or hear the answers. "Generals, is there anything else?"

"Just one more thing, Your Highness," General Singëril answered. "Once we've found and secured the *Ak-Séregon Stone*, we'll launch a full attack to draw as much of their army away as we can. When your sister has it, she'll go underground. With the portal closed and their army in the field to meet us, her chance for success will be somewhat better."

"Somewhat better?" the Queen repeated.

"Right now, it's the best we can do," answered Father Goram. "Keep in mind we're working blind."

Lessien nodded. "And if all that fails?"

General Singëril looked at Father Goram who nodded. "Then we must destroy the *Ak-Séregon Stone*."

"We should do that anyway," Eric the Black said. Everyone looked at him. "You remember the shifts I've been talking about? Well, they're happening more frequently. And they're lasting longer. Who knows how long before we're flung into another universe."

"If we steal the stone away from the dark elves, it'll shut the portal between us and the Svartalfheim down and things will cool off," Landross said.

"That's all true, Landross," Eric the Black replied. "But..."

Autumn, sitting next to her husband, finished Eric the Black's thought. "But destroying it will actually be the better solution. While the *Ak-Séregon Stone* exists, the dark elves can get it back. Or someone else can use it again for nefarious purposes." Autumn looked around the room. Eric the Black was nodding, and she could tell her husband was thinking about it... but everyone else just stared. "Is maintaining our relationship with the Alfheim more important than keeping our world safe?"

"But the Alfheim is the elven home world," Cameron protested.

Queen Lessien shook her head. "A world that exiled my father, mother, and me. InnisRos is my home now. None other."

Night engulfed Taranthi as Nightshade patrolled the dark streets on her large black steed. The winged horse was the size of one of the larger draft horses used by farmers to pull wagons of hay, grain, or other heavy loads. But its lines suggested it could run, and fly, much faster. Its mane, tail, and the socks around its legs were burned yellow with streaks of purple red. The wings were silky-smooth and covered with soft feathers. The horse wasn't from her demon world where ugliness prevailed. Nightshade detested ugliness, even though her own soul was as hideous as the Abyss that spawned her. This creature is a construction of beauty – a living golem with the soul of a child – a loyal steed who accepted Nightshade for who she was, and one of her most cherished possessions.

It'd been three days since her father and the dark elves arrived on InnisRos. The capital city, Taranthi, was quickly surrounded and given the opportunity to surrender. At first there was hesitation – the elves of InnisRos are a stubborn and proud race – but they capitulated soon after her father released black dragons to destroy the main gates and certain other carefully selected targets. The dark elves flooded through the smashed city defenses. With the main elven army in the island's north, the city guards and a platoon of army regulars were all that was left to oppose the invasion. Once the city walls were breached, those pockets of resistance were quickly rooted out and eliminated. Now the occupied city was relatively quiet.

Nightshade was in her Amberley form. She didn't want to make the local populace any more uncomfortable than they already were with their dark elf occupiers. Her consideration had nothing to do with fond feelings for the people of Taranthi, though she had come to appreciate the grace and beauty of the elvan race. Instead, Nightshade hoped to one day win the populace of InnisRos over to her, and the ugliness of her demon appearance would make that desire much harder to achieve.

Whenever she passed dark elf guards and patrols, they would stand aside and salute. Nightshade didn't fear the dark elves would use the cover of darkness to turn against her. Aikanáro, her father, exercised absolute control over them, and Nightshade was confident in her own ability, and in the talents of her loyal steed, to meet such a challenge if it should occur. Even so, she'd taken precautions in her own indomitable way and gave the dark elves reason to fear her as much as they feared her father. During the first few hours of the invasion as the dark elves secured the city against armed resistance, she selected an unlucky warrior to serve as an example of her abilities should any of them began to think she was vulnerable. The pathetic excuse for a warrior had attempted to rape a human female, a minor infraction, but an infraction, nevertheless. She gathered as many dark elves as she could find and executed the transgressor in a most painful, and original, way. She didn't get as much satisfaction as she did when she dispatched Mordecai, but the results still pleased her. Soon enough, her displeasure and its consequences spread throughout the entire army.

As Nightshade's horse strode through the curfew-deserted streets of Taranthi, she once again admired the beauty of the city – the perfectly symmetrical lines, the multi-colored crystal roofs of the wood and granite buildings which had been grown out of the ground by elven magic, the well-manicured lawns and parks, and clean streets and avenues. It was a place she had come to call home. Nightshade wondered if the devoured soul of Mordecai affected her judgment, but quickly ruled that out. His soul was almost as black as hers. Still, something within her had begun to change.

As she entered a small square, she saw several dark elf warriors gathered around something on the ground and chattering in their native tongue. Nightshade knew something was amiss. As she edged her mount toward the commotion, the dark elves, surprised by her arrival, hurriedly backed away to expose a dark elf sorcerer's body.

Nightshade dismounted and kneeled to examine the corpse. He was curled into a fetal position. His clothes were disjointed from seizures, his eyeballs were hanging by tendons down the side of his head, and there was coughed-out phlegm on the street next to his mouth. She instantly knew what caused the death. Poison... the same poison used to kill General Narmolanya and so many of Mordecai's other commanders. The assassins who delivered that message are now focusing their attention on dark elf sorcerers.

Nightshade stood. "If there's one, they'll be others," she said out loud as she turned to the frightened dark elves. Scanning the group, she picked out an officer. "You!" she said in their language as she pointed to him. "Come here!"

"Yes, mistress," the frightened dark elf replied as he cautiously approached.

"Find every sorcerer in the city and guard them with your life," she ordered. "Use as many soldiers as you need. This is your ONLY duty. Do you understand?"

"But mistress, what do I say to my superiors?"

Nightshade removed a small, elaborately decorated knife from her boot. "This should confirm my orders," she said. "I'll want that back... General!"

The officer beamed. He bowed, collected his soldiers, and issued orders. As they left to attend their duty, Nightshade called out. "General, if any further harm comes to our sorcerers, I'll have your head."

As the officer disappeared into the night, he looked like he had the weight of the world upon his shoulders.

Admiral Shilannia, Cincinnatus, and Yury had been wondering for three days on the alien world they had found themselves. Daylight never came. The sky remained dark and smoky. Only an occasional break in the clouds revealed the faraway sun which never warmed the world... but provided enough light to feed a few scraggly bushes. Magic was almost nonexistent. Cincinnatus explained that the world had little magic to draw from, and therefore he could only weave the most basic spells. Fortunately, even in the magic-starved world, Cincinnatus could cast enough enchantments to provide basic sustenance to survive on.

Except for the giant cloud-like creature Admiral Shilannia and Cincinnatus saw those first few moments after the shift, they saw no other animals or insects, though they felt strange vibrations beneath their feet. At first it caused a good bit of disquiet, but nothing ever happened.

As the three traveled the barren landscape, they talked about their lives, their backgrounds, their aspirations, and their hope for the future, if they still had one. At first Yury, intimidated by rank, was tentative. But over time he relaxed enough to regale them with stories about his native land of Draugen Pesta and the seemingly everlasting conflict his people had with their mortal enemy, the Hyrokkin. Admiral Shilannia and Cincinnatus were aware of the world beyond the shores of InnisRos, but they never bothered to learn much about it. Yury turned out to be a treasure trove of information.

Reaching the peak of yet another hill, they expected to see another empty, lifeless valley below, yet one more of many they've already crossed since their arrival. But this turned out to be different. Below them they spied an ongoing battle between what looked to be tentacles coming up from the ground and a person almost as tall as Yury. From their vantage point, though too far away to identify details, they watched as the person moved with a strange grace. It appeared the individual was leaving behind faint impressions of itself as it moved from one place to another, like a line of identical copies. Admiral Shilannia thought the movements were vaguely familiar but didn't know why.

The tentacles grasped the left-behind image rather than the real person. Additional tentacles exploded out of the ground. Most reached for the impression. But several, whether by design or happenstance, grabbed the real flesh and blood prey. The now doomed person struck the tentacles with a knife, but it was clear, now that it was caught, the struggle would soon be over.

Admiral Shilannia, as she watched the fight, suddenly understood why it was familiar. "A time walker!" she exclaimed.

"What?" Yury asked.

The admiral shook her head as she ran down the hill toward the battle, followed by the other two. "No time to explain. Cincinnatus, can you work magic to save her?!"

But Cincinnatus was already casting a magical spell. Several glowing balls of energy left his hands and struck the tentacles holding the time walker. However, in the magic-depressed world they were on, the small explosions had only a fraction of the power they normally contained. The tentacles paused as each ball hit but brushed off the impact with only minor injuries. However, the time walker was able to use the slight hiatus caused by the explosions to break free. But instead of retreating, she turned and continued to fight.

Yury reached the mêlée first, screaming a Draugen Pasta battle cry. He still had his naval rapier and, using that with his giant size and strength, made short work of the tentacles as he fought his way to the time travelers' side.

Admiral Shilannia only had a ceremonial dagger, but she too waded into the 'field of tentacles', doing as much damage as possible. Cincinnatus remained by her side. There was little he could do in the way of magic, but he still supported her with his strength, which, for a sorcerer, was considerable.

The time walker suddenly grabbed the back of Yury's tunic and, with surprising strength, pulled him back and down to the ground. Both fell just as a huge, toothy maw rose out of the earth where they once stood. Its mouth contained thousands of small, pointed teeth. Six-foot long razor-sharp appendages covered the bulbous head and body. Strange fleshy pipes extended out from both sides. The pipes opened wide and a great, bass sound bellowed out. Both Yury and the time walker curled up into fetal positions, closed their eyes, and covered their ears. They felt the ground shaking beneath them.

Several minutes of quiet passed before Yury and the time walker opened their eyes. Though they still couldn't hear, they had otherwise survived the encounter with no other complications. Before them, the earth was broken and churned. There was no sign of Admiral Shilannia and Cincinnatus, who were fighting the tentacles just a short while ago. No sign except for the sorcerer's severed arm lying in the dirt, still twitching.

The small group of wyverns were hunting – hunting for food – hunting for an enemy to attack – hunting for information to give their masters. As they flew north, the wyvern group leader observed a black cloud rise from over the mountains. He didn't think much of it, probably a weather front moving in, and continued with his mission.

This new land he and his companions now flew over seemed to be devoid of life. There were fields of crops and hay, those that hadn't been stripped bare, and the fruit trees they found, though hastily picked, still had plenty of fruit. But wyverns aren't inclined to eat grain or fruit. They're meat animals, and the few herd animals they had seen would never support wyvern appetites. The further they flew, the hungrier they became. So much so that their orders to leave the elves and humans alone – to report movement only – was being sacrificed for a higher imperative.

Wyverns have keen eyesight. They could spot prey several miles away while flying thousands of feet in the air. This trait had evolved over thousands of years on their dark home world. When the wyvern leader and the rest of his companions spotted the wagon drawn by huge horses a few miles away, they aligned themselves into attack formation and veered off course to position themselves for an attack. So intent were they on doing this, and so intent on the hunger pangs that rumbled in their bellies, they lost track of the dark cloud that had been moving towards them. By the time the wyverns realized their mistake and discovered the cloud was actually millions of small, flying creatures with sharp fangs, it was too late. The bats encircled all the wyverns and nipped and ripped wyvern flesh. Within a few minutes they had swept all the wyverns from the skies. In the end, the only thing left of the wyverns were their broken, bleeding corpses scattered across several hundred yards of ground. They never know the identity of their killers.

Eric the Black's bat allies continued their flight southward.

During the evening of the third day after the invasion of InnisRos, the freshly minted general of the dark elf army, proudly displaying the dagger loaned to him by the demon Nightshade, went from room to room on the sixth floor of the Taranthi palace to check the status of his 'guests'. Earlier that day, per his interpretation of Nightshade's orders, he had all the dark elf sorcerers rounded up and placed under armed guard. Though they were harbored in comfort, they weren't happy about the restrictions imposed upon them. Yet none dared to gainsay Nightshade's personal representative.

The general felt good. The sorcerers were safely tucked in for the night and the guards had been given their assignments. He smiled each time he heard "Yes, sir!" The deference to him sounded so natural. As he walked down the hallway one last time, he good-naturedly chatted with the guards assigned to each room... using the dagger to cement his greatness in the annals of dark elf history.

Though the general was enjoying his celebrity with the guards, at some point he determined he should personally check on at least one sorcerer. Once that was done he'd find a tavern, drink a few mugs of ale, and perhaps find a female prisoner to enjoy the rest of the evening with. The demon Nightshade and her father had set strict rules against rape. But wasn't he a general? A general promoted by Nightshade herself? And don't generals have special privileges?

He picked a door at random and rapped on it twice with the hilt of Nightshade's dagger before opening it and stepping inside. The room was dark, and all he could see were the shadows caused by the light spilling into the room from the hallway. Just outside the light the general spotted what appeared to be a pile of clothes. *'Messy sorcerer,"* he thought.

"Hello," he called out.

Silence.

Fear clutched at his belly. He turned and pointed to a magical glow light, one of many, sitting in a niche in the hallway wall behind him. "Grab that light and the two of you get in here," he commanded the guards outside the door. He stepped back out of the room just long enough to yell at the rest other room guards. "The rest of you, check your rooms!"

The general followed the two guards into the room. When they saw the pile of clothes, everyone stopped. They looked closer and recognized it for what it was.

"By the gods, General!" a guard exclaimed before he bent over and retched.

The pile of clothes was actually the remains of the sorcerer assigned to that room. It looked like the body had been turned inside out. All the internal organs – lungs, intestines, heart, liver – sat on the floor in a bloody mound protected by a ribcage that had been stripped of flesh. On top of the mound rested the undamaged head, its mouth drawn open in a permanent protest against the vile evil done to the body.

The general backed out of the room. Pandemonium ensued shortly thereafter as all the other guards retreated out of rooms with weapons drawn. Some guards looked pale, like they'd seen something horrifying, and all of them looked frightened. The general heard nor saw any of that, however. Instead, he'd seen his life end the moment he saw the dead sorcerer.

Later that evening, the new general took his own life using the dagger loaned to him by Nightshade. He feared the demon would find him alive and was determined to prevent that... so determined he almost decapitated himself as he slit his own throat.

Nightshade was angry, but not overly so as she made her way to her father's quarters. Each guard she passed came to immediate attention, but none of them dared look directly at her. Stepping in front of the door to her father's room, she waited while the guard captain looked her up and down. In her Amberley form she looked anything but intimidating – beautiful, fragile, alluring – the type of female most males would die for. Wherever she walked, more than one guard would follow her with his eyes while thinking lewd thoughts. At times all she had to do was bat an eye to find favor... something she used many times to her advantage when she wanted to get something accomplished without violence. This was not one of those times.

Nightshade had little patience left for the guard captain's attention and transformed into her demon form. She looked down upon the captain and his squad of guards with blazing eyes and murder in her heart.

"How dare you study me like an insect in a jar," she said quietly, "or as the victim of your next rape. If I must open that door myself, it'll be because I've left none of you alive to do so."

The captain gulped as he looked at Nightshade with big, round eyes. Two of the quicker thinking guards hastily opened the double doors to her father's suite.

Nightshade nodded as she glided forward, bypassed the still stunned captain, and went into the room. As the doors closed behind her, she changed back into her Amberley form.

Her father was sitting behind a large table eating his dinner. Unlike most demons, whose palate leaned more towards fresh meat, both Nightshade and her father preferred meals of cooked beef or pork, vegetables, and wine. Perhaps because of their disposition, neither cared much for sweets.

Nightshade's father, the demon Aikanáro, looked up at her with amusement-filled eyes as she entered. "You shouldn't have been so hard on the captain," he said. "He was only doing his duty. Besides, from what I understand, your female elf form is attractive to males. Let them stare. What's the harm?"

"I don't mind subtle glances," Nightshade replied. "In fact, I enjoy it somewhat. And the form has other, oh, shall we say… advantages? But right now I'm in no mood to be fantasized about or ogled."

Aikanáro stopped eating and poured his daughter a goblet of wine from a pitcher. "Take this. Sit down and collect your thoughts while I finish my meal."

Nightshade did as she was told. She took the proffered goblet of wine, sat, and sampled it with a sip. She studied her father as she organized her thoughts. Aikanáro never took the form of another, regardless of the circumstances. He was massive, eight feet tall, had crimson leathery skin and black, expression-filled eyes. His face had the appearance of an elf, except for the double-row horns that ran down each side of his hairless head. His pointed ears had been pierced multiple times and filled with magical, rune-covered earrings.

He wore elaborate armor that could only be forged in the Abyss. His great cloak, hanging over the back of a chair next to him, matched the color of his skin and had even more magical runes along the bottom. The great mace that never left his side was sitting on the table within arm's reach.

"Is it as bad as I've heard?" Aikanáro said as he sliced a piece of beef and ate it.

Nightshade drained her wine and set the empty goblet down. "It depends. What have you heard?"

The demon speared a large potato with his fork and took a bite. "Just that we've lost our sorcerers," he said after swallowing. "Don't worry. I'll send for more through the portal. Poison?"

"Some, not all," Nightshade replied.

Aikanáro stopped eating for just for a moment while he looked at his daughter. "And the others?"

"Qénsharma."

"What's a Qénsharma doing on this world!?" Nightshade's father shouted as he exploded out of his chair, his meal forgotten. He began to pace.

Nightshade remained calm. She had felt her father's wrath before and didn't want to be punished by him ever again. "I believe there's more than one," she said.

Aikanáro's agitation turned to fear. Nightshade saw it in his eyes. "How can you be sure?" he asked.

"You understand how the Qénsharma kill," answered Nightshade. "You also know that they go into a hibernation period after they eat. The remains of four sorcerers lie in skinless piles in their quarters as we speak... their untouched heads sitting in the middle. I saw what's left of them myself."

Aikanáro sat back down, pushed his unfinished plate of food away, and poured himself a fresh goblet of wine. "That many in one place? It can't be a coincidence."

"No, it's not," Nightshade replied. "An associate told me some assassins on this world use the Qénsharma to fulfill murder for hire contracts."

"Use a Qénsharma?" Aikanáro said in wonder. "How is that possible? Those creatures were spawned in the lowest level of the Abyss. Mindless slugs who live only to eat. They follow no other mandate. They're a demon's worst demon. And you're telling me they're here and the mortals of this world can exploit them... can control them!?"

Nightshade nodded. "They're here. There's no mistake about it. You know as well as I, father, that the Qénsharma are parasites. They probably traveled here from the Abyss on the back of... or inside of... another demon. Who knows. What's important is that they're here and must be dealt with. The mortals use them by manipulating their hunger, though I speculate the Qénsharma might not be as mindless as we've come to believe and are the one's actually doing the manipulating." Nightshade shrugged. "It's what I've been told. I've not observed any of this directly."

Aikanáro laughed. "You got to give these mortals credit. That's ingenious!"

"Our arrogance often blinds us, father," Nightshade answered.

"Or in this case our fear," Aikanáro responded. "This may put a whole new perspective on things."

Nightshade shook her head. "It's inconceivable they'd have many more Qénsharma at their disposal. And the four they used against the sorcerers won't be hungry again for several weeks."

"If your information about them is correct," Aikanáro countered.

Nightshade nodded. "Regardless, we've still a problem with the assassins who used them and who poisoned our sorcerers. We've either been infiltrated or there are secret passageways or tunnels within the palace itself that we know nothing about... and they do."

Aikanáro raised an eyebrow.

"Don't worry, father," Nightshade replied to his unasked question. "I've already given orders for every dark elf in the city to be thoroughly scrutinized by officers I've personally examined."

Aikanáro winced. He knew how his daughter searched someone for the truth. Though left alive and sane afterwards, it wasn't something anyone would ever forget.

Nightshade continued. "As for the secret passageways... I'll personnally search for them myself. I don't entirely trust the dark elves to find everything. But I've lived here long enough to know where to look and what to look for." Surprisingly, she found she didn't relish the thought of all the thieves and cutthroats she'd have to interrogate to find out what she needed to know.

Aikanáro nodded. "Very well," he said as he re-heated his dinner plate with a magical cantrip and started eating his meal again. When Nightshade didn't leave as expected, he looked at her quizzically. "Is there something else?"

"We've lost contact with our wyverns."

"All of them?" Aikanáro asked.

"All of them."

Eric the Black extinguished all the glow lights in the small room that served as his quarters. He wanted no distractions as he called forth the magic of the communications crystal. The crystal he stared into differed from the others in that it also allowed him to see the person on the other end. A hooded figure stared back.

"Any problems, Kat?" he asked.

The black clad figured pulled her hood off. Though elf, there were slight variations in appearance. She was darker skinned than the normal elf and had long red hair. Her eyes were deep green and surprisingly warm for someone who killed for a living. She smiled at the communications crystal. *"Everything went as planned, Eric,"* she said. *"The others are already waiting outside the city to intercept your people."*

Eric the Black smiled back. Though he considered all four of the assassins in his band as brothers, she was by far his favorite... even more cherished than the now deceased Magdalena. "They're our people, Kat," he said.

Katsumi nodded. *"I'm not used to being on one side or the other. And I'm not sure I like all the complications that come with it."*

"I felt as you do once," Eric the Black responded. "I've learned much since joining Father Goram's monastery. Kat, I'm going to drag the four of you into his family whether you like it or not... kicking and screaming if necessary. I'll make you understand that as long as you choose a side, you're no longer orphans... that you're no longer alone. So, get used to it."

"I'm trying, lover," the assassin replied. There was a mischievousness in her eyes and smile.

Eric the Black laughed. He loved this banter with Katsumi. "Are the Soulreavers corralled?" he asked.

"All sleeping peacefully in their crates."

"Good," Eric the Black responded. He was worried the Soulreavers would somehow escape and terrorize the city. Not because it would be an unmitigated disaster for the dark elves who occupy Taranthi, but because of the innocent inhabitants. Soulreavers make no distinction from where their next meal comes. "Now listen closely, Kat. Don't stay in the tunnels and safe spaces. Nightshade won't stop until she finds them all. Consider them compromised."

Katsumi nodded. *"And your operatives?"*

"They'll still have to be slipped into the city later."

"But the stone won't be in the city, Eric," Katsumi said. *"And it's dangerous."*

"You can't stay hidden outside the city waiting for them," Eric the Black replied. "The dark elves are crawling all over the place."

"And they're not in Taranthi?" Katsumi countered.

"The thieves guild have places where you and our people can hide that Nightshade knows nothing about," answered Eric the Black. "And they've the means to sneak you out and back in. I've already contacted them, and they'll meet you west of the city."

"Nightshade has many different ways of getting information," Katsumi said.

Eric the Black nodded. "That's being considered. The guild masters are planning accordingly."

Katsumi relented.

"They also agreed to help find the *Ak-Séregon Stone* and destroy it," Eric the Black said.

"Wait!" Katsumi interrupted. *"You want to destroy the stone? But that's going to be almost impossible! The dark elves use their best, most fanatical warriors guarding it. Plus they have several sorcerers controlling it. They'll risk nothing to see it remains in their hands. Eric, it's their only way back home. It also cuts off the Alfheim."*

"I understand all that," Eric the Black replied. "But it's a better option than stealing it, even if it does seal off the elvan home world. Kat, we must close the corridor. It's our only chance. InnisRos will be lost otherwise. And as long as the stone exists, this could happen again."

"But..."

"Katsumi, I have my orders and now so do you," Eric the Black snapped... and immediately regretted it. "I'm sorry. Things are rather tense. I can count on you, right?"

Katsumi smiled. *"Of course you can, lover."*

The eight-legged creature looked up at the five red moons climbing into the clear night sky. It's four gold-shimmering cat-like eyes frowned while its snake-like tail moved back and forth, causing a ripple among the double rows of spikes that ran down the length of its body. Without clouds, the light from the moons made it difficult to approach the prey undetected. Nevertheless, he couldn't give up. It'd been two days since his last kill and his mate and pups depended on him to bring home a meal.

The silver trees and grass swayed in the wind. The creature could smell the prey. Still several runs away, as the creature measured distance, the wind brought the enticing fragrance of fresh meat... and thoughts of a full belly. Just one of the prey was large enough to feed his family for several days.

After long hours of careful approach, the creature was within striking distance of the unsuspecting prey. The silver strands of grass captured and reflected the color of the red moons, turning the landscape into a field of flowing crimson as the wind blew across.

The prey was feeding on the short grass of a large clearing. There were more of them than the creature originally guessed... an entire herd. But all it needed to do was take down one. As the creature sat in the tall grass at the end of the clearing, deciding which of the prey would be easiest to kill, it noticed a strange fog settle down on the opposite end. The creature paused. The fog had an unnatural, alien feel. The creature briefly considered retreating, but his growling stomach drove him forward. He put all thoughts of the fog out of his mind as he charged out of the tall grass towards his selected prey. He swiped a talon-tipped claw along the hindquarter. The prey, hurt and panicked, ran into the fog with the rest of its herd. The creature followed.

Three assassins scouted a small clearing next to a brook for any sign of the dark elves. They had just made their way out of Taranthi via a tunnel whose existence only they knew... a tunnel that led from the palace and into the forest west of the city. The clearing they now scrutinized was the predetermined meeting place where Katsumi said she'd catch up.

Satisfied they were alone, they settled in to await the fourth member of their group. One assassin sat on the sturdy crate which held four sleeping Soulreavers while the other two made themselves comfortable on the grassy ground of the clearing floor. With the invading dark elf army so near, they dared not make a fire to stave off the chill.

As they waited, a strange fog formed and surrounded the clearing. The assassins, taken unawares, looked around and at each other. They'd ever experienced such a thing before and were shaken by this unnatural event. Each of the assassins drew their lethal katana's and prepared themselves for the attack they felt was coming. But after a few seconds, no danger materialized though the fog remained thick and disconcerting.

As the three masked figures stared into the fog, alert for the slightest movement, the ground beneath their feet shook. They heard hooves and the strange snorting of animals. As the rumbling grew close, they could make out tree limbs and smaller bushes being snapped. Understanding the sounds for what they were, they grabbed the crate and ran in the opposite direction. But it was too late. House-sized, six-legged creatures broke through the clearing edge and trampled the assassins. In their panicked state, the creatures never even slowed down and disappeared into the fog at the opposite end of the clearing.

By the time the eight-legged predator reached what was left of the clearing, all was quiet. He raised his nose into the air and was assaulted by many strange smells, though none of which belonged to his prey. He sniffed the trampled bodies of the assassins and knew they weren't of his world. Then he inspected the remains of the broken-up crate. Though empty, a residual smell remained of something which made him very fearful. He looked around but saw no threat other than the fog itself. Not sure what to do, he followed the prey.

The fog which encircled the small clearing next to the babbling brook lifted as quickly as it had appeared. Of the prey and predator there was no sign. Except for the path of destruction left in their wake, it was as if they never existed. Within minutes, crickets chirped, and small forest animals once again rooted through the leaves, bushes, and dead branches of the forest floor for their next meal. Thousands of insects descended upon the three assassin bodies, trampled beyond recognition, to begin natures cleanup and disposal. The Soulreavers, who had been dragged out of their meal-induced stupor by the stampede, had slipped away to find safe haven under rocks in the brook and fell back into a deep sleep.

Dark elves, drawn to the commotion coming from the clearing, arrived en masse to investigate. They didn't notice the trap door that opened briefly before closing again.

CHAPTER SIX

Havendale, The Mainland

The future is a component of time and is forever being altered. While past events set certain futures in motion, present events constantly amend its course. This is one reason skepticism regarding precognition, or the ability to see the future, is so widespread. Although a future may be predicted, the further away it is, the less the likelihood that prediction will be accurate. Why? Because events that occur between the foretelling and the prophesied future deflect the path. Therefore, on the timeline, the future is never truly known until it arrives in the present. Some speculate precognition is not actually a foretelling of the future, but instead a forecasting of danger caused by an accumulation of all the 'present' events on the timeline.

-The Book of the Unveiled

Despite all evidence to the contrary, the talent of precognition does in fact exist. The consequence one must suffer in exchange for this gift, however, is the eventual destruction of the mind. Nothing comes without sacrifice.

-From the Journal of Rathal Arquen

Precognition is a curse. It only occurs in people with great intelligence — sorcerers, leaders, scholars, and the like. Of course the universe, never one to pass on a chance to turn the screw on a person, takes away the one thing that made precognition possible in the first place — the mind.

-From the Commentaries and Observations of Rhys, Master Spy, Havendale

Rathal Arquen sat at the head of the conference table in the main meeting room at the Academy of Sorcery. Though almost fully recovered from his latest precognition episode, he remained weak. The progression of decay his mind suffered in exchange for his gift, or curse, was escalating. Rathal wasn't sure how much time he had left before he'd have to turn control of the city over to someone else.

Around the table were Rathal's most trusted advisors – Amkrissa, Havendale's chief stargazer, General Kelsia Húrön, Shynaria, Rathal's assistant, and Rhys, master spy. It was early morning and Rathal had called them in for a working breakfast of biscuits, jam, meat cakes, fruit, coffee, and tea. Rathal gave everyone a chance to satisfy their morning hunger before he got down to business.

"Amkrissa," he began, "have there been any more shifts since yesterday afternoon?"

"Just one," she replied after taking a sip of tea. "On InnisRos near the capital of Taranthi."

"InnisRos again?" General Húrön exclaimed. "That makes, what, half a dozen in only a few days? And most on that island alone?"

"Don't forget about the one over the Ocean of the Heavens, Kelsia," Rathal remarked. "Perhaps the largest."

Amkrissa nodded. "Correct, Rathal. To date it's been the strongest by far. Powerful enough to cause major atmospheric changes and unprecedented weather conditions. The gods only know what would have happened if it were over a populated area." She took another sip of tea. "That one aside, most, at least according to the globe, have been small with short duration. I expect those are more like 'hiccups' with little impact rather than full-fledged events. Expect that to change."

Rathal nodded. "I assume the reason so many of the shifts occur on or near InnisRos is because that's where the *Ak-Séregon Stone* is."

"Yes," answered Amkrissa. "That's a pretty good assumption. And it may hold true for a while. But understand that all of Aster is being affected by the rogue corridor opened by the stone. Eventually the consequences of this connection will be experienced worldwide."

Rathal looked around the room. The reality of the situation didn't surprise him or anyone else. He grabbed one of Amkrissa's hands underneath the table before pushing on with the discussion. "Let's turn our attention to the armies coming our way. Kelsia?"

"I have the army on full alert," the female dwarven warrior replied to Rathal's question. "The patrols along the Merchant's Way north to Silverstone and west to Ordenskyr have been doubled. I've briefed both military commanders of those two cities and asked them to put their militias on alert. I expect Ordenskyr to take over patrolling the southern route of the Merchants Way. The Riders of the Elderdale are also on the lookout and patrolling the whole area north of Saint Seton along the Alpine."

"The Riders don't stand a chance against the odds they'll be facing," Amkrissa remarked.

General Húrön shook her head. "Their commander is Lloyd Fairmount, a former knight from Altheros. He understands tactics and knows stand and fight would be suicide. Instead, he'll marshal his Riders in the Forest of the Fey, which is great terrain for guerilla warfare. They'll pick at the enemy from the sides... not enough to stop them, but enough to slow them down. We also need to know the enemy strength, and its composition. He'll be able to provide that information to us."

"Anything else, Kelsia?" Rathal asked.

The dwarf nodded. "I doubt they'll come with their full force down the Alpine. What comes that way could either be a feint or part of a two-pronged attack."

"Two-pronged?" Shynaria inquired.

"She means they could also come down east of Lake Lorali," Rhys answered for the general.

"Correct," General Húrön said. "There's flat grassland offering little cover east of the lake... and it's boxed in by Lake Lorali on one side and the Greater Boreskyre's on the other. But if a military commander found the risks acceptable and marched an army through those grasslands, we'd be forced to split our defense of the city. Though I'd like to concentrate our forces along the Merchant's Way, I can't afford to do that."

"So?" Rhys remarked.

"So, I've sent several cavalry troops to the east to make sure we're not caught unawares. But because of that possibility, we need to keep the bulk of our army around Havendale... at least until we know what the enemy intends to do. By remaining here, however, we allow them to drive the narrative."

"It's a reasoned approach, General," Rathal stated. "I don't see where we have any other option."

"Any chance they'll go straight west along the Denali?" Rhys asked.

"It's possible, I suppose," General Húrön answered. "But to what end? They can't go far before the Knights of Astoria come down off their mountain-top and block them. And Palisades Crest would back up the knights in short order. The commanders of HeBron and Madeira know that... and they've no desire to tangle with either of those two."

Rhys wasn't convinced. "We've no idea what the true strength of the Draugen Pesta is. And I can't get anybody closer to their encampment than a couple of miles. The area's locked down tight. The only trustworthy information we have is that the Black Death is on our side of the Greater Boreskyre Mountains. That's from one of my spies who's fighting for her life against infection... or poison. Our healers aren't sure. Anyway, she's delirious and won't be much help until she recovers. If she recovers."

"They're not going west," Rathal said. "It'll be south. I saw it in a premonition."

Both Rhys and Shynaria were unsurprised by the announcement. Rathal winced when he looked at Amkrissa. She looked confused, as did the general. He should have told them about his talent, and its eventual toll, long ago.

"They're coming south," Rathal re-stated. "And it's connected with that rogue corridor opened on InnisRos. It's too much of a coincidence for there to be any other explanation."

"Aye, lad, I suspect you're correct," General Húrön said. "We'll let somebody..."

"Rathal..." Amkrissa whispered.

Rathal shook his head and squeezed her hand. "We'll talk later," he whispered back.

"... else worry about the north," the general continued. She ignored the low whispers between Rathal and Amkrissa. "When the army moves, I'll need some of your sorcerers, Rathal. I appreciate you don't like them out in the field, but..."

"You'll get them, Kelsia," Rathal replied. "Anything else?"

General Húrön shook her head. "Not for now, lad. But by the spiked hair of my da's underarm you can bet that'll change soon. Those devils aren't going to sit up north much longer."

Rathal smiled. Every once in a while Kelsia's dwarven heritage escaped the serious military demeanor she always presented. He wondered what she would be like drunk... except he didn't think there was enough alcohol in all of Havendale to make that happen. He turned his attention to Rhys.

"What can you tell us," Rathal asked the master spy.

Rhys shook his head. "Not much more than what we knew yesterday. My people in Altheros and Palisades Crest tell me that the two cities are taking our warning seriously and mobilizing their armies. The smaller cities along the Pantera and Tiberius Rivers are 'battening down the hatches', so to speak, and preparing for armed resistance. And, as the general mentioned, Ordenskyr is prepared to defend the Merchant's Way should the three armies get past us and move in that direction."

"We better hope they can be stopped either here or at Ordenskyr," Shynaria remarked. "Otherwise, all the west will be wide open."

"I expect Ordenskyr will have reinforcements by then," General Húrön said. "At least they will if we're able to hold this side of the Olympus Mountains long enough."

"I'd like to defeat them before it comes to that," Rhys commented. "I..."

Rathal suddenly had a thought. "Excuse me, Rhys," he said, "but I've a question for the general. Why aren't we talking about the Knights Lament, Kelsia?"

"Two reasons," the general replied. "For one, there's still plague in Ascension, though the last report I received indicated it was abating somewhat. The Draugen Pesta wouldn't know that, but HeBron and Madeira certainly do. They'll not go anywhere near the city. Then there's the Hammer sitting right dab in the middle of the pass. Rathal, believe me, 'tis a tough nut to crack. There's no way any commander worth a sack of beans will spend the time to take it. And there's no way around. The mountains on both sides are not only virtually impassable, but they're also filled with giants. So, no, they're not going through Knights Lament."

Rathal nodded. "Thank you, Kelsia. Rhys?"

"As I said, our intelligence has improved little since yesterday... though last night was the first time the three armies were seen together. Based upon the number of campfires, my people estimate between fifty to sixty thousand warriors."

"That may or may not be accurate," General Húrön observed. "A common practice of many military commanders is to light more or fewer campfires to hide their true strength. We need intelligence during the light of day."

"I'm working to get that, General," Rhys said.

General Húrön smiled. "I know, Rhys," she replied, then looked at Rathal. "If they believe they have overwhelming numbers, they probably won't bother to mislead us because... well, they'll figure it just doesn't matter."

"Do they have overwhelming numbers, Kelsia?" Rathal asked.

General Húrön nodded. "Yes, Rathal... it's not even close. Hebron and Madeira alone have about a third more than we do. Who knows how much more the Draugen Pesta 'can stoke the fire', as my da would say. Even if we had a plague-ridden Ascension at our disposal, we're still outnumbered. There's not much this side of the Olympus Mountains. In our favor, however, is that we have the finest sorcerers in all the land. That counts for a lot."

Rhys nodded, but he still looked skeptical. "I hope your right about the sorcerers, General," he said before turning his attention back to Rathal. "I'm sorry, but nothing reported gives me even the faintest hint about their motivation other than what we discussed the other day. Without a doubt, land for HeBron and Madeira... but what stake does the Draugen Pesta have in all of this?"

Rathal looked at the spy. "Perhaps land or conquest. But that goes against their character... at least what we know of it. No... it's more personal than that. Something's missing... something they love. They're trying to recover it."

Sofia Ternborg studied the locket that would call the Doom Warriors. She was sitting behind her husband's desk in his study. The king's quarters in the palace was a lonely place without her husband and daughter. Her heart broke with longing – longing for the desire to hear her child's laughter – longing to bask in the sanctuary only her husband's strong arms around her can provide. But in no way did these missing pieces of her heart interfere with her fortitude... or her courage. In fact, it made her even more determined to do everything necessary to save her daughter and return normalcy to her life, including killing anyone who got in the way.

After Minister Drugov succumbed to his injuries, Sofia double wrapped his body in red bed sheets and dragged him to the nearest unguarded latrine. Though not as strong as most males, she was stronger than almost all females, even those in the Army. She forced the lower part of the body through the toilet seat and smashed the shoulder bones together with a large mace to get the rest through. It dropped down a channel and into a cavern several hundred feet below where it would be eaten by carrion. She then grabbed a bucket and mop to clean the floor where he had bled to death. The bloody water served as another treat for the carrion eaters far below. No one would be the wiser, and without witnesses, no one could prove a case even if they did eventually suspect her of the minister's disappearance.

The dead minister wasn't her only problem, however. Her husband had discovered she'd taken the locket. Already an emissary from her husband, someone who no doubt wished to discuss the locket, had been kept waiting several hours. She hoped Viktor understood her reasoning in the letter she left in its place... but the fact that he sent someone could only mean he didn't approve. No matter. She had no regrets.

Sofia's thoughts turned from past and current complications to the locket. It was simply designed and attached to a heavy gold chain. It opened easily to reveal the calling stone inside. The stone was made of black onyx and fashioned into the shape of a six-legged dragon, but had a shiny, glistening aspect to it that was impossible for ordinary onyx to replicate. Along its surface a pinprick of silver light moved back and forth. As she watched the light traverse across the stone and back again, Sofia felt her consciousness drift away. Suddenly, she was flying at breakneck speed. She watched as the stone got closer and closer, larger and larger, until she thought she'd crash headlong into its surface. Then she passed through it, and a complete world lay before her. It had no sun, just black-red light pulsating up from the surface. Many rivers of molten lava ran throughout the landscape, coming down from volcanoes that lie in every direction. Each volcano sputtered its gaseous clouds and filled the atmosphere with noxious fumes. The trees that dotted this panorama were grotesque and evil looking, their souls as malevolent and dark as the rest of this bleakest of lands. The denizens that roamed this hell, for that is what Sofia thought she was seeing, represented the worst of any nightmare she'd ever experienced. She was certain that if she stayed much longer, she'd go insane.

"You have called?" a disemboweled voice asked.

Sofia looked around but failed to see who had spoken.

"We are here," the voice responded to her confusion, "my brothers and I... though you cannot see us."

Sofia bowed her head. "You are the Doom... the Doom Warriors?' she asked.

The voice chuckled. "Yes," it said. "I am Michael. And you are Draugen Pesta."

Sofia nodded.

"Many years ago a priestess of your people called upon us to perform a task," Michael said. "We deemed your people to be worthy and accepted the charge. Afterwards I fashioned a locket to call us if we should ever be needed again. You have used the locket."

"I have," Sofia replied. "I ask a favor."

"The favor is yours to ask," Michael said, "though only we shall decide if it is well-intentioned."

"So I've been told."

Though she couldn't see it, Michael was studying Sofia. "But do you understand what that means?"

"Yes, I understand," the Draugen Pesta queen responded.

"Very well. What is your request?"

Sofia took a deep breath. "My daughter has been kidnapped. By whom I do not know. However, I suspect the kidnapper is using my daughter to blackmail my husband into going to war."

"The fate of one child is worth the lives of hundreds, or perhaps thousands?" Michael asked.

"To a mother or father, she is!" Sofia countered hotly.

"To a king and queen?"

Sofia didn't have an answer for that. If she suspended her emotions and thought about things objectively, Michael's point was well made. But how could a mother do that? What kind of mother would she be if she did?

"Your help will stop a war," she reminded.

Michael didn't answer immediately. As Sofia waited, she could hear the screams of the beasts and demons all around her. *What if they refuse?* she asked herself. *What if they'd don't allow me to return?*

"The war affects much more than you suspect," Michael said. "Terrible danger has found your world."

Sofia was becoming impatient. She hadn't called the Doom Warriors to be lectured. "Will you help or not?" she snapped at him. Immediately she regretted her outburst. "I'm sorry. I had no right."

Michael laughed warmly. "No, you did not. But it was a typical mortal thing to do. We will find your daughter and return her. But as the caller, you alone bear the burden of other wrongs we may decide to correct. In that, we act according to OUR conscience... regardless of who it hurts. Is that clear?"

"Yes!"

Sofia felt Michael's nod. "Very well. It's now time for you to return to your reality."

"Wait!" Sofia shouted. "What manner of demon are you?"

Michael laughed. "Perhaps you should've asked that question before you sought our help."

"I have only legends from which to base an opinion," Sofia replied. "But those legends tell the Draugen Pesta people you once helped us."

"We gave the caller justice," Michael replied, "and vengeance. We determined it was warranted. But we're not demons, child. We're guardians... tasked with the responsibility of keeping this vileness from escaping to other worlds."

"But then if you leave..."

"Don't fear. There will still be enough Guardians to watch over the demons," Michael replied. "Now it's time for you to leave. My brothers and I will not be far behind."

In an instant Sofia had been returned to her husband's study. The locket was closed. "You'll be home soon, sweet Daphnia," she said aloud. Then she considered the Doom Warriors. Though she never saw him, Michael wasn't like the legends portrayed him to be. He and his brother Doom Warriors appeared to be a force for good, a power obligated to protect the innocent from the oppressor. She felt satisfied her daughter would be safely returned to her. But evilness wasn't always obvious, particularly with mortals. Did the Doom Warriors make allowances for this distinction? She wondered about what she had wrought and the lengths the Doom Warriors would go to set things right.

Inside their command tent, Viktor Ternborg and his adjutant, Major Konstantin Timoshenko, watched as General Edric Ujarak, the Madeiran leader, wolfed down a breakfast of hard-boiled eggs, sausage, biscuits, and coffee. The staff officers that had accompanied General Ujarak stood at attention and watched as their commander ate.

"If you'll excuse me, General," Lord Ternborg said, "but I need to have a word with my second."

General Ujarak grunted.

"Can we trust him, my lord?" Major Timoshenko asked as soon as they were outside the tent and sure they wouldn't be overheard. The two Draugen Pesta guards at the entrance snapped to attention.

"Hell no, we can't trust him," Lord Ternborg replied. "Do you really think General Pallis choked on a chicken wing?"

The major shook his head.

"Neither do I, Konnie," Lord Ternborg said. "But while Ujarak's brutal, devious, and without conscience, he has absolute control over his men and, unlike Pallis, the strength to remain relevant. But don't worry, I'll keep him reigned in. When will we be ready to march?"

"We're still waiting for Pallis' replacement from HeBron," Major Timoshenko replied.

Lord Ternborg shook his head. "No, I'm done waiting. I have little doubt everyone this side of the Boreskyre's know we're here. The longer we stay encamped, the more prepared the opposition will be. I want to move by noon. That gives us about six hours to break camp."

"General Ujarak said he couldn't move sooner than tomorrow morning," Major Timoshenko reminded his commanding officer.

"We'll let's see about that," Lord Ternborg said as he wheeled around and stormed back into the tent.

"General Ujarak," Lord Ternborg said as he approached the human. General Ujarak was leaning back in his chair with his feet up on the table and smoking a cigar. He looked up at the Draugen Pesta king and burped.

Major Timoshenko's hand went to his sword, but Lord Ternborg stayed further action by his adjutant with a quick shake of his head. "I'll deal with this," Lord Ternborg whispered.

The king walked over and roughly shoved General Ujarak's feet off the table. The Madeiran general stood and began to draw his sword. With one hand Lord Ternborg grabbed General Ujarak around the throat and effortlessly raised him off the floor. The general's staff drew weapons and advanced but were stopped by Major Timoshenko and two guards who had rushed in from outside the tent.

"In my camp you will act with decorum," Lord Ternborg said. His voice was calm, but its tone was deadly. "Do you understand?"

General Ujarak's eyes looked like they were about to pop out of his head. All he could do was gag and kick his feet.

Lord Ternborg threw the general across the tent where he landed hard, sprawled out and gasping for air. The general's men rushed to his side, but the general shook them off as he stood. He was unsteady on his feet and gasping for air, but his eyes communicated his fury.

"How dare you!" General Ujarak sputtered through a coughing fit.

Lord Ternborg walked to where the man was standing. The eleven-foot-tall giant towered over the Madeiran general. Though his demeanor remained composed, the expression on his face broadcasted to everyone in the room his state of mind. The Draugen Pesta king was ready to kill.

"You WILL follow my orders," Lord Ternborg said between clenched teeth. "Are. We. Clear!"

Behind everyone in the tent a small, brilliant white light appeared and expanded into a swirling eddy of energy and magic. Through this doorway between space and time stepped the black form of Nightshade. The Madeirans, who had witnessed Nightshade's arrival, kneeled and groveled in the dirt.

"What the..." Lord Ternborg said as he turned. Major Timoshenko and the guards had already placed themselves between their king and the demon. "Scabbard your weapons," Lord Ternborg ordered. The sudden appearance of Nightshade had all the makings of a disaster if cooler heads didn't prevail.

"Problems, Ternborg?" Nightshade asked. Though Nightshade's face was unreadable in her present form, there was amusement in her voice.

"Nothing I can't handle," Lord Ternborg replied. The Madeirans show of deference to the demon sickened and angered him. "Is my daughter safe?"

Nightshade turned into her Amberley facade. She thought wearing a more pleasing form might make discussions easier. The two Draugen Pesta guards took a step back in surprise... but they quickly recovered as their professional warrior instincts kicked in. The Madeirans still had their heads down in the floor's dirt.

"Leave us!" Nightshade ordered the Madeirans. As they rose and filed out of the tent entrance, they kept their heads down, though Ujarak sneaked a look of loathing towards Lord Ternborg.

"Her and that wolf are having a grand time, Ternborg," Nightshade replied after she was alone with the Draugen Pesta commander and his warriors. "Here, see for yourself."

A small window appeared in the air. Daphnia and the wolf, Adimar, were sleeping on a large, comfortable looking bed. The wolf had his tail curled around the slumbering child.

"I have to admit, Ternborg, that I didn't expect your daughter and the wolf to get along so famously," Nightshade commented as the window blinked out of existence. "I don't believe the wolf would kill her even if I demanded it. They seem to be best of friends, don't you think?"

Lord Ternborg remained still, though his hands were shaking as fear for his daughter flooded over him.

"Make no mistake, Ternborg," Nightshade continued. "If you double-cross me, I WILL kill your child. I'll do so without hesitation or remorse." Nightshade paused to allow her words to sink in, just in case the Draugen Pesta had lost sight of their agreement or the clarity of her intentions. "Now that we have that out in the open, let's move on to other things. Why are you still here?"

"We're moving out later today," Lord Ternborg responded. "Neither HeBron nor Madeira have armies in the normal sense... more like a loose association of mercenary companies. Organization and communication are big problems. Then there's the competition between the two city states. They've been at each other's throats for so long it takes time for them to learn to fight as allies."

Nightshade sighed. "All you have to do is make a lot of noise to draw the rest of the human armies this way. That doesn't require a lot of organization or communication. It only requires you to make a show. Who cares if HeBron and Madeira suffer the brunt of the causalities. That's actually doing the world a favor."

Lord Ternborg stared at the demon. "I'll meet your objectives. But I don't want to see wide-scale butchery... from either side. I won't allow it."

"I don't care how you do it, just that you do," Nightshade said before turning back into her demon form. "Remember! New land for your people and your daughter's life depend upon it."

"I don't want land that's been covered in blood," Lord Ternborg exclaimed.

"It doesn't matter to me," Nightshade said as she opened a magical window in the air to leave. "The next time I check in, I'll want to see some progress. And have your Doom Warriors available. They intrigue me."

An hour later there was a great commotion in the Madeiran camp. Something had attacked their commander, General Ujarak. Whatever it was left his body a dried-up husk. Soon thereafter, Lord Ternborg received an unexpected visit from the leaders of both HeBron and Madeira, who professed undying loyalty and gave the Draugen Pesta king complete control over both their armies.

Lester and Safire, along with several other Riders of the Elderdale, waited under the cover of bushes and trees at the most northern point of the Forest of the Fey... Elrond's forest. Using spyglasses, they were looking for signs the HeBron, Madeiran, and Draugen Pesta armies were on the march. Though the Riders' commander, Lloyd Fairmount, only wanted them to reconnoiter and provide information to the main body of Riders further south, Lester and Safire wouldn't pass up any opportunity to harass the enemy through hit-and-run attacks if the ideal situation presented itself.

An ominous cloud of dust came into view to the northeast.

"They're finally on the move," Safire remarked.

"I'll go tell the commander," one Rider whispered as he turned to his horse.

Lester shook his head. "No, not until we know more. And you don't have to whisper. At least not yet."

Several boring, yet anxious, hours passed before the first elements of the invading armies came into view. Two huge columns of infantry marched in orderly rows, while cavalry protected both the right and left flanks. So far, all Lester could make out were HeBron and Madeiran troops. Perhaps two miles from the forest one of the infantry columns, along with half the cavalry, veered off and headed to the right.

"That's Hebron. They're going to the east around Lake Lorali," Safire observed.

"In bigger numbers than we expected," Lester said. "I still don't see the Draugen Pesta."

Then the earth moved and in the distance they could hear the rumble of thousands of horses. An imposing figure in a light blue cloak rode out of the dust... a giant sitting on a giant horse. Even larger giants surrounded him. Except for the light blue cloak worn by the obvious leader, the Draugen Pesta wore the blackest of black armor and cloaks. The only break in the black was a tinge of burgundy that lined their cloaks... and the military rank on the sleeves of their tunics. Their horses were jet black, snorted flames, and their hooves, as they danced around, created sparks whenever they hit the stones beneath their feet.

"By the gods, the Black Death," a Rider exclaimed.

As they watched, the Draugen Pesta army came into view. All of them were mounted.

"There're thousands, Lester," Safire exclaimed.

Lester was just about to send his runner back to Lord Fairmount when he noted activity around the Draugen Pesta commander. Opening his spyglass to take a closer look, he watched as the light blue cloaked leader point to the west. One of his guards put spurs to his horse and disappeared into the dust.

Lester snapped his spyglass closed. "I wonder what that was all about?"

A few minutes later he understood. A large body of Draugen Pesta warriors peeled off the main body and went straight west, between Lake Galadriel Feliagund and the Forest of the Fey. They were riding quickly.

"A three-pronged attack," Safire said.

Lester turned to his messenger. "Tell Commander Fairmount we have three armies making their way southward," he said. "The main body is coming down the Alpine, but large enemy contingents are also marching east of Lake Lorali and west of the Forest of the Fey. Tell him we'll try to slow them down on the Alpine as much as possible."

Lester paused. *"I wish I had a damn communications crystal,"* he thought for the hundredth time. "Tell the commander that I think he should evacuate Covington and move their people to Silverstone where there's at least some walls."

"Anything else, sir?" the messenger asked.

Lester looked at Safire and nodded. "Just that if we don't see him again, it was an honor to serve with the Riders, even if only for a short time."

The messenger cringed. "I'll be back as soon as I can, sir," he said.

Lester shook his head. "There's no time," he replied. "Stay with Commander Fairmount. Now go!"

THE FIRST INTERREGNUM

From the Book of the Unveiled:

The corridor between Aster and the Svartalfheim created for the Dark Elf invasion not only pierced different universes (correctly theorized by Aster's greatest sorcerers), but also pierced time itself. This meant that if someone was transported from Aster to another world during a shift, and if that someone returned, the 'where' might be the same but the 'when' not necessarily so. This influence on the timeline affected not only Aster but also every world the corridor touched.

-Author Unknown

The Story of the Sky Emperors:

The world of Selara is dark and mostly covered by water. The light and energy that comes from the double-star it orbits is weak and fractured. It's a world born to the night, and in the night it remains. The living eked out by the inhabitants on this harsh world is difficult, particularly inland where the landscape is dominated by ground dwellers – large, many-tentacle creatures who build their lairs underground. Few survive an encounter with this ravenous beast. Despite the danger, however, there are a few outposts inland. But most of the world's population live near Selara's oceans and survive on an abundance of aquatic life.

The true rulers of this bleak and barren world are the fliers, two-hundred-foot-long eel like creatures who soar in the sky and swim in the water. The mouth on its triangular head contains row upon row of razor-sharp teeth. Instead of eyes, four ultra-sensitive antennae extend forward from its head which are used to detect underwater prey. It has four long wings, one pair behind the head and one pair close to the tail which work the currents of Selara's atmosphere. The tail is flat and Y-shaped like that of a whale. The diet of the fliers consists mostly of large sea creatures which it detects through its antenna, though any unwary surface inhabitant will also serve as food during migration. Fliers remain over and in the ocean and only approach land once every twenty years when they journey to their spawning grounds deep in Selara's only true continent.

The Sky Emperors are not native to Selara. The written history regarding the circumstances of the original appearance of the Sky Emperors is vague and murky, and the verbal stories passed down from generation to generation even more so. Some say the Sky Emperors arrived on the back of the lightning they control and were sent by the gods, though this line of thought had few followers. Most Selarians feel the Sky Emperors are themselves gods. One common consistency in all the stories, however, was that an unnatural fog filled the bleak skies of Selara for hundreds of miles prior to the appearance of the Sky Emperors.

At first glance, the Sky Emperors looked like nothing more than clouds, one to two miles in diameter, with half-mile long appendages – clawed tentacles – hanging down from the bottom. Multi-colored lights would occasionally travel down the tentacles and discharge into lightning bolts which lit the dark skies. In the beginning, the sudden appearance of these magnificent creatures brought fear and disquiet to the inhabitants of Selara. But the placid, even-tempered Sky Emperors never caused harm. They spent most of their time adrift in the air currents feeding on light, which is a large part of their diet, or microscopic organisms taken from the waters of the oceans and the dirt of the land. They gracefully navigated the dark firmament above and quickly blended in with their new environment. Never once did the Sky Emperors show any sign of aggression, and it didn't take long for Selara's inhabitants to accept their presence.

Years after the Sky Emperors arrived, the fliers, following their biological imperative to spawn, arrived off the shores of the continent. Each flier, famished from days of continual flying, looked upon the Sky Emperors as a new source of nourishment and attacked.

The usually passive Sky Emperors didn't ignore the onslaught of fliers. As the gigantic wave of fliers advanced, the Sky Emperors drew themselves into a gigantic sphere with the smaller, younger Sky Emperors in the center. Throughout the sphere, streaks of lightning filled the dark atmosphere of Selara. The crackle and humming sound of building electrical energy reverberated for hundreds of miles. As the fliers soon discovered, the tenacity of the Sky Emperors far exceeded their outward docile appearance.

While astounded surface inhabitants watched from below, the fliers overwhelmed the Sky Emperors and it looked to be an unmitigated disaster for the gentle cloud-like beings. But then bright lights emanated from the middle of the mêlée, and the sky was suddenly filled with blackened fliers falling into the ocean waters far below. The superstitious inhabitants of Selara screamed and ran to the safety of their homes as bolts of lightning streaked out in all directions from the battle above. Each bolt produced a strange sizzle as it pierced the air, the sound of which quickly overwhelmed by the agonizing cries of fliers as they died.

The fliers weren't the only ones dying, however. The Sky Emperors, though they had great success using their tentacles and bolts of lightning for defense, couldn't hold off the entire horde of fliers. There were too many. When the fliers finally stopped their attack and retreated, only one-quarter of their original number remained. Of the Sky Emperors, one. The inhabitants of Selara named it Arsalan, the word for 'lion king' in their language. But to its own people, the last Sky Emperor was known as Liosh, their word for 'father'.

Liosh seemed unbothered by the loss of his kind. He, a differentiation made by the surface dwellers, continued to patrol over the small coastal villages and cities in the gloomy skies of Selara.

The denizens of Selara came to pity Liosh, for he was the last Sky Emperor and must be terribly lonely. But that couldn't have been further from the truth. As each Sky Emperor died fighting the fliers, their consciousness transferred to Liosh for safekeeping. When it was all over, Liosh may have been the last physical manifestation of the Sky Emperors, but he wasn't the last of his kind. If Liosh could find the right environment, the Sky Emperors would once again frolic in the skies.

That opportunity came when an unnatural fog – the same type of fog that brought the Sky Emperors to Selara many years ago – reappeared around Liosh. When the fog dissipated, Liosh was no longer there. And the world of Selara was a darker place for it.

CHAPTER SEVEN

Deep Under Elanesse

On another world in a far different reality, there's a saying which goes, "If a tree falls in a forest and no one is around to hear, does it make a sound?" The pragmatic answer to this question is yes. The absence of hearing doesn't eliminate the physical science of sound. By the same token, if someone sacrifices life or limb and no one is around to see, does it still have significance? Of course it does. Why? Because the motivation is pure. Like the sound of a tree falling in the forest, sacrifice doesn't need to be witnessed to be real. This kind of sacrifice is the greatest of them all.

-The Book of the Unveiled

"Are you daft?" Azriel exclaimed as he looked at Elbedreth. They were in a small cavern. Max was exploring on the other side about a hundred feet away. "Lassie, my girl, you can't tell him that! I know Max. He'll have murder in his eyes. Sure, sometimes the lad appears to be a bumbling boob, but he's quite intelligent... devious... and he holds a grudge."

Elbedreth thought about their ghostly comrade on the other side of the cavern and shook her head. "Azriel, my conscience won't be clear until I've told him what I've done. Besides, we shouldn't keep secrets. We're his friends."

Azriel sighed. "I understand why you feel you have to do this," he said. "But sometimes things are better left unsaid."

"Do you have secrets I should know about?"

This sudden change of direction in the conversation caught Azriel off guard. "My lassie, if I have secrets, I assure you they're unintentional. No dwarf who's lived as long as I can remember every little aspect of his past life."

Elbedreth didn't waver. "Secrets aren't simple, everyday things. We all remember our secrets... and the reasons we wish to keep them so."

Azriel studied his mate. She'd made a very pointed and valid observation. "Yes, I've secrets," he admitted. "Secrets that make me look barbaric, and even a bit dim-witted at times. But bloody hell, I WAS a mercenary after all! I had to do things that way!"

Elbedreth said nothing.

"Which doesn't necessarily make it right, I know," Azriel acknowledged.

"I understand that some things should stay hidden, if for no other reason than to put the past behind us," Elbedreth said. "But any secrets that effect the person we love, any secret that keeps me from seeing you for who you are, is a secret that should be exposed. At least to me."

"I can'nae argue that, lassie," Azriel replied. "And no, I don't. As for Max, you cut his skin off! There's no one ever born that could let that go!"

"He didn't suffer, Azriel," Elbedreth said. "He died quickly with a blade through his heart. What I did later with the skin was meant to serve as a warning to keep interlopers away from my home. Do you think so little of me?"

Azriel paused. The ground he was treading just went from dangerous to treacherous. "Of course not," he replied to her question as he extended an arm and touched her. "I love you and I understand why you did what you did. But Max? Well, that's another story."

Elbedreth returned Azriel's caress. But it didn't sway her. "My minds made up," she said.

"By my father's anvil!" Azriel shouted as he stomped around in a small circle... though since he was now a sylph it didn't have the same effect as it did when he was a dwarf. "You can't tell him you killed him!"

"What can he do?" Elbedreth asked. "He's a ghost."

Azriel stopped and turned to face her. "Remember I mentioned knowing a ghost? Well, she killed a vampyre. Sent a stake through its black heart using the power of her will alone."

Elbedreth was silent as she looked at Azriel.

"She was dear Emmy's long dead mother... may she find peace," Azriel continued. "Her name was Angela and she wouldn't rest until her daughter was safe and properly shielded from future threats. For over three thousand years she watched. And waited. I didn't see her kill the vampyre... too busy fighting another. But that's what Tangus told me. You remember Tangus?"

The female sylph nodded.

Azriel sighed. "Whether she did it to protect Emmy... or because she wanted to extract revenge... isn't important. Only her actions are. Ghosts CAN physically attack under duress. I've no doubt this would be one of those times. And if Max does attack, I'll defend you." Azriel paused. He didn't want to fight his friend, the only person he had left from his previous life. "I'm begging you, don't ask me to do that! Not against Max!"

A stalactite suddenly crashed to the floor a few feet away from the sylphs. Azriel and Elbedreth turned and saw Max walking towards them. He looked like he'd grown twice his size. His eyes glowed bright red.

"You killed me!" Max shouted as he pointed to pieces of the broken stalactite which rose and flew at Elbedreth. Azriel deflected them with his steel quarterstaff before they could harm his mate.

"Now Max..." Azriel said as both he and Elbedreth backed away.

"You skinned me!" Max shouted. His eyes were glowing even brighter.

Azriel's great battleaxe appeared as he stepped in front of Elbedreth. "Laddie don't make me fight you," he said. "She had her reasons."

"Get out of my way!" Max roared. His voice was harsh. It hinted at a side of Max that Azriel had never seen.

Azriel shook his head. "I can'nae do that."

"Then I'll go through you," Max responded as he closed the distance between himself and the sylphs.

The power of Max's will drove Azriel off the floor of the cavern and into a wall twenty feet to the side. Azriel crashed with a "harrumph" and dropped to the floor, stunned. Max grew even larger as he approached Elbedreth. He towered over her.

Azriel stood, but he knew he couldn't stop what was about to happen.

Max paused as he looked down at his murderess. "I will have my vengeance!" he bellowed. "Maybe then I can find peace!"

The thoughts in Elbedreth's head swirled as she considered her options… but in the end she felt the ghost was justified. She decided to submit. Elbedreth stared into the anger-driven countenance of Azriel's friend as he approached. Out of the corner of her eye she saw Azriel charge, but she knew he'd be too late. Unafraid, she accepted her fate.

"I'm so very sorry," was all she said.

Elbedreth's refusal to defend herself enraged Max even further. "I don't forgive you!" he shouted. "There's nothing I want from you but your death."

Max's eyes turned from bright red to black. His fury over what Elbedreth had done to him escalated and burst outwards in a bright explosion of light and energy. He picked Elbedreth up with the power of his will and slammed her against the wall behind her, using the shackles of his hatred to hold her against it. Waves of power struck Elbedreth, flattening her sylph body against the rough stone and making it impossible for her to move.

Azriel, quarterstaff and battleaxe at the ready, sprinted towards Max. At this point he didn't care if he lived or died… only that he somehow save Elbedreth. He raised his weapons and with a great dwarven battle-cry jumped the last few feet. Max, without looking at

Azriel, raised an arm and pointed a finger at the airborne sylph, sending Azriel back against the wall he had crashed into moments before. Instead of falling, however, Azriel remained in place.

"You'll watch as your lady-love perishes," Max said.

"Max, my laddie, I beg you, please dinnae do this," Azriel pleaded.

Max turned to look at Azriel. "Or what!" he screamed. "What are you going to do that hasn't already been done! What dignity did Elbedreth give me! Tell me, Azriel! TELL ME!"

Azriel had no answer for this simple question... and he didn't think it would matter even if he did. Max was too far gone to listen to reason. Or was he?

"What would Emmy think," Azriel said in a low voice. "Would our dear Emmy approve of your revenge?"

Azriel had gambled correctly. The mention of Emmy had a profound effect on Max, as Azriel suspected it would. Both Azriel and Elbedreth dropped to the floor, free of all the restrictions Max had placed on them. Azriel rushed to the side of his mate. "Thank you!" he cried out to Max.

Max was silent. The black shine in his eyes slowly faded, and his ghostly body shrank back to its normal size. He looked at the two sylphs with sad, haunted eyes. Without saying another word, he left the cavern and disappeared into the darkness.

Several hours of travel found Azriel and Elbedreth deeper into the underground world of Aster. The traveling went slower without Max. The master thief had been their scout and pathfinder... a position he excelled in not only as an alive person but also as a ghost. Both sylphs also found they very much missed Max's constant banter and cheerfulness... two qualities he maintained even during the gravest of situations.

During this time little conversation passed between the two. The circumstances of Max's departure was Elbedreth's fault. She knew it, though his vehemence surprised her. She had limited experience around others not of her own kind – Azriel told her so – but she didn't accept that excuse in its entirety. As their journey continued and Azriel stewed about the confrontation, Elbedreth used the silence as a justification to "search her soul", as Azriel would say. She found that some lies were necessary – some secrets left unrevealed – if it kept the peace or prevented pain. Elbedreth's secret, once out in the open, lightened her heart. But it put a heavy burden on Max. He didn't deserve that.

Azriel, now in the lead, turned a corner and stopped. Elbedreth, her mind diverted to other things, bumped into him. The contact between the two reaffirmed their love for one another at a time when both were dealing with internal issues.

"Lassie, would you look at that!" Azriel exclaimed.

Max didn't care where he went. He was a very angry ghost. Only the mention of Emmy by Azriel had brought him back from the brink of murder, not that Elbedreth didn't deserve it. It was during this rage-filled walk when the voice of sweet Emmy, the child empath who endured so much at such a young age, came to him. *'Max, we all need forgiveness. Find it in your heart to give her what you yourself have asked for many times over.'*

Max didn't know if he heard Emmy speak to him through the miles of rock and granite that now separated them... or if it was his own conscience. But whatever it was, it brought him back from the insanity of retribution that overwhelmed him when he overheard Elbedreth's confession.

As perplexing as that was, Max was even more confused by his sudden ability to manipulate the air around him and force its compliance to his will. As hard as he'd tried since then, he couldn't duplicate that moment. Max knew the ghost of Emmy's mother, Angela, had killed the vampyre, Lukas, by driving a stake through his heart. So what he'd done wasn't the exception. But he didn't know the trigger to this ability. Anger? Love? Fear? All of them and more! "Emotion!" he said aloud. "Strong emotion. But how do I control it?"

Max shook out all the thoughts playing around in his head the past few hours and looked around. "Oh no," he groaned. "Where the hell am I?"

Azriel and Elbedreth stared into a large grotto. Lining the floors and piling up to ten feet or more in some places were coins. Hundreds of thousands of coins, plus gems, silver platters, gem encrusted golden chalices, and gleaming magic weapons and armor of all types.

"What is this place?" Elbedreth asked.

"My dear, we're looking at a dragon hoard," Azriel replied. "And from the size, this dragon's been collecting for a lot of years."

"I'm not sure I know what a dragon is," Elbedreth said. "But I know the people who live on the surface world greatly fear them."

"Dragons are rare," Azriel responded as he continued to study the horde, watching for any signs of movement. "They're huge and very hard to kill. The red ones enjoy burning villages to the ground, caring nothing at all for the innocent men, women and children they slaughter. There are other types of dragons – blue, green, gold – but the reds are by far the worst. This isn't a red dragon hoard, though. They live only on the surface."

"On the surface?" Elbedreth asked.

Azriel nodded. "Only black dragons live beneath the surface. Worst then the reds, they're the vilest, most hateful creatures on Aster. Fortunately, they only rarely leave their lairs."

"So, this is the home of a black dragon," Elbedreth stated.

"If it's still alive," Azriel answered. "How is it your people never encountered dragons?"

Elbedreth considered Azriel's question. "Probably because by the time dragons appeared on Aster, my people had already been imprisoned. Come, we need to get to the other side if we are to continue our journey."

Azriel reached an arm out to stop Elbedreth from entering the cavern, but he was too late. As soon as she crossed the threshold, coins shifted. Elbedreth stepped back.

"It would seem this dragon is still alive," Azriel said as he drew out his steel quarterstaff and magical battleaxe. Using his actions as her cue, Elbedreth did the same with her own blades.

"You are correct," a voice spoke from out of the darkness on the far end of the cavern.

A gigantic, serpentine head appeared over the hoard. Its tongue flicked out of it mouth as it tasted the scent of the two sylphs, exposing several rows of razor-sharp, three-foot-long teeth. The dragon's eyes swirled as it looked for any missing pieces to its treasure. Huge horns curved out of its head and wrapped around, like the horns of a mountain ram. Behind and encircling the head was a plate of bone with protruding smaller horns which protected its long, sinewy neck. Its wings were folded back over its body. But perhaps the most striking feature of the black dragon was that it wasn't black at all. It was deep purple.

"I'm called Jörmungander the Cruel," it said, "and you're trespassing."

Azriel winced. "Are there any passageways around this cavern," he whispered to Elbedreth.

Elbedreth shook her head.

"Well! What do you..." Jörmungander stopped talking and moved his head closer to inspect the two sylphs. "What nature of beings are you?" he asked.

Azriel looked at Elbedreth. *"Perhaps there's an opportunity here,"* he thought to himself. He motioned for Elbedreth to let him do the talking.

"Ahh, laddie. That does beg the question, doesn't it?" Azriel said to the dragon. "We're many creatures depending upon your viewpoint."

Jörmungander raised his head. "What do you mean?"

"Well, from your perspective of course," Azriel said. "You understand what perspective means, don't you?"

The dragon nodded. "Point of view... outlook... perception," he said.

"Bravo, laddie," Azriel exclaimed. "Now... there's the perspective of you the dragon... and the perspective of the humans, the elves, the dwarves. In my lifetime I've come to understand even trees have perspective. And they're all different. But that's not even the most interesting point."

"It's not?" Jörmungander asked.

"Come, come, laddie," Azriel replied. "Surely you can see it. For example, let's take your perspective."

"Yes, why don't we do that," the dragon replied. He sat down on his haunches.

Azriel saw the look on the dragon's face change from confusion to patience. The dragon seemed willing to listen – willing to humor the sylphs for a time. But Azriel feared the dragon had already determined the ultimate outcome regardless of how the narrative went. The former dwarf understood he shouldn't take the dragon's calm demeanor as an invitation to story-tell like they were long, lost friends. He was talking for their lives.

Azriel cleared his throat. "Well, as I was saying, everyone has different perspectives. However, this isn't something that necessarily remains constant. While it's true that our experiences, and the society in which we were raised, do much to shape our perspective, it's also true that our emotions, and even those baser instincts such as hunger, play a big part in how we view things. So, you see, this can change from moment to moment."

Azriel frowned and cocked his head. "I wonder if any of this crap makes sense?" he whispered to himself.

"I'm thinking not," Jörmungander said.

Startled, Azriel looked up to see a huge eyeball inspecting him.

"In fact, you're beginning to prattle," the dragon continued. "How does my perspective change the way I look upon you and your companion compared to the other races? Explain or the time for talk ends here and now."

"Yes, yes, of course you're right, my bonnie lad," Azriel replied. "Right now, though you don't know what we are, you're seeing us through the eyes of your dragon perspective. But which dragon perspective? I mean, do you view us as enemies? Thieves? Food? Or perhaps you fear us? I assure you, we're none of those things."

Jörmungander raised his head. "Fear you! Ha!" The dragon suddenly flapped his wings. "There's only one way I perceive you... as trespassers in my home. It is THAT dragon perspective that makes me see you in this way. There are consequences for your invasion... whatever you are."

Azriel put up a finger. "But what if we were here as friends? Wouldn't that change your perspective? I mean, then we wouldn't be trespassers. Right?"

Jörmungander snorted. A black mist smelling of sulfur escaped from his nose that took both Azriel and Elbedreth's breath away. "You're not my friends," the dragon replied.

Azriel coughed. "Or maybe you can think of us (cough) as customers. How do you know (cough) we don't have something to offer for safe passage through your lair? A deal that (cough) benefits us both. Under those circumstances would you not change your (cough) dragon perspective and let us pass in peace (cough)."

"Interesting," Jörmungander speculated. "Go on. I'm beginning to appreciate where this conversation is going. What can you offer me in exchange for a favorable dragon perspective?"

"Azriel, this is silly," Elbedreth whispered. "Let's just be honest with him."

Azriel put a finger to his lips. "Shh, lassie! Dragons have..."

"Extraordinary hearing?" Jörmungander said. "Yes, we do. And, as your companion says, perhaps there should be truth between us. After which we'll let the... how do the humans say it... hmm... oh, yes! After which we'll let the chips fall where they may." The dragon studied the two sylphs. "I'll start. I believe your offer of payment to pass through my home is as bogus as your explanation of perspective."

"Well..." Azriel was becoming uncomfortable.

Jörmungander continued. "You have that battleaxe, but it's almost as if it's part your body. Most peculiar. But other than that, neither of you have anything worth my interest. All right, your turn. Why do you encroach upon my home? Do you wish my treasure?"

"Of course not!" Elbedreth answered before Azriel had a chance. "We stumbled on your home by accident. But it's very important we be allowed to pass through."

"Lassie don't..." Azriel began.

"Now I've got it!" Jörmungander exclaimed. "I thought your dialect sounded familiar. The last time I heard it, a dwarf was speaking. But you're no dwarf."

The huge dragon flapped his wings and wiggled his rear end until he was comfortably ensconced in the mound of coins that served as his chair. "Those dwarves WERE after my treasure." Jörmungander looked around the immediate area and used a talon to pluck an armor breastplate from a nearby pile of treasure. He held it up for the sylphs to see. It was sized to fit a dwarf. A white bone, a rib, dropped out and landed on gold coins. "They didn't succeed." Jörmungander suddenly barked a short laugh. "I dined well that day!"

Azriel forced a smile. "I don't think you'd like us very much. We're not nearly as... succulent... as a dwarf."

The dragon lowered his head and sniffed. "We'll see," he replied. "For now, tell me about... um..."

"Sylphs," Elbedreth offered.

"Sylphs. I've never heard of such a creature," Jörmungander remarked.

"Well, stick around, me bucko," Azriel responded. He threw caution to the wind as his patience neared an end. "You're about to get an unhealthy dose of sylphs unless you let us pass. We're done with this social get-together and scintillating conversation."

"It was you're doing," Jörmungander said. His patience was nearing an end as well. His eyes swirled faster as he studied Azriel and Elbedreth. Both sylphs suddenly felt pressure in their heads. The force of the dragon's will had entered their minds and was trying to expose their thoughts, their memories, their essence. They kneeled in pain as the power of Jörmungander's mind invaded theirs.

"Stop!" Azriel cried. Using all the strength he could muster, he stood. "I beg you, stop! We mean you no harm!"

Jörmungander's probe of the sylph's minds ended almost as quickly as it had begun. The nightmare of having their thoughts and memories laid bare was over. The dragon sat back, his thoughts far away. Neither Azriel of Elbedreth were able to move. They were held in place by a magical spell.

After a few minutes, Jörmungander returned from his self-induced trance and looked at the sylphs. "Remarkable," was all he said before falling back into his thoughts. After a few more moments he re-focused his attention on the two sylphs.

"Perhaps it WOULD be in my best interests to allow the two of you to continue on," he said as he released Azriel and Elbedreth from their invisible prison.

Elbedreth charged the dragon... all her blades out and spinning. "How DARE you invade our minds like that!" she shouted as she moved forward.

Azriel stepped in front of her to hold her back.

Elbedreth didn't struggle. "You could've just asked!" she screamed at the dragon.

"Calm down, lassie," Azriel pleaded. "Dinnae make matters worse!"

"Why didn't he just ask," Elbedreth said to Azriel before she broke down and cried. "I feel like I've been raped!"

Azriel didn't know a sylph could cry. He awkwardly held her.

Jörmungander had remained calm during Elbedreth's explosion of righteous indignation and her subsequent collapse. "It was faster," he said, but it was clear in the tone of his voice that he regretted the choice.

Azriel looked back at Jörmungander with anger in his black, glistening eyes... but said nothing.

Jörmungander sighed. "Look, I'm sorry. But it was the only way I could find out if you were telling the truth. Every human, elf, or dwarf I've ever met lied so they could steal my treasure."

"And they all ended up in your belly, I'd wager," Azriel angrily shouted. By now Elbedreth had recovered and was looking at Jörmungander.

"Well... not exactly," Jörmungander replied. "I'm not a carnivore. And I'm not called Jörmungander the Cruel. Just plain old Jörmungander. That last part was for effect."

"Not a carnivore!?" Azriel couldn't believe what he was hearing. "What do you mean? You're a dragon! What about that bone?"

Jörmungander winced. "I was as surprised to see that drop as you were. I've killed to defend myself, but there are carrion eaters down here that... well... they clean up the messes I make. But I'd never harm anyone otherwise."

"But you're a dragon!" Azriel cried in disbelief.

Jörmungander hung his head.

Azriel sighed. "What do you eat?"

"Oh, I have a mushroom farm right over there in that cavern!" Jörmungander said as he pointed to a dark doorway off to the side. "I also grow other types of fungi to add variety to my diet. And sometimes a crunchy cave spider will wander in."

"How did you learn to cultivate mushrooms?" Azriel asked. "My original people…"

"You mean dwarves," Jörmungander interrupted.

Azriel nodded. "Yes. We eat mushrooms and other fungi as well. But raising and taking care of them is a somewhat tricky proposition."

"Oh, for sure!" the dragon exclaimed. "It seems like every time I turn my back, if even for a second, my good fungi get invaded by the poisonous kind… at least poisonous to my species of dragon."

Azriel shook his head. "I know, right?! Dwarves can eat just about anything… but not some of those damn fungi. And once an invasion starts you need to work like hell to save the good crop."

"If you'd like I can show you my farm," Jörmungander said as he got up. "It's quite impressive. We can even eat a nice meal while we discuss… other matters."

"Gentlemen!" Elbedreth shouted. "We don't have time for this!"

Azriel nodded. "You're right, lassie. But give me a moment. Jörmungander, how does a dragon like you learn to grow mushrooms?"

"Books, Azriel, books!" Jörmungander replied. "Lots and lots of books… magical tomes, scrolls, and books about almost everything. A whole library full in that cavern."

Azriel and Elbedreth looked in the direction Jörmungander pointed. There was another cavern doorway. This cavern, however, was well lit with magical light-spelled stones and crystals. "Amazing!" was all they could say.

"And over there, an armory of my most prized weapons," Jörmungander said as he pointed to yet another cavern. For the first time, Azriel and Elbedreth saw many such doorways leading into other caverns.

"And there, another cavern filled with my most valuable gems and other magical items," Jörmungander continued.

Azriel held up his hands. "Enough! This chamber alone is larger than any dragon hoard I've ever seen or heard about. No dragon legend even comes close. And yet you're telling me there's much more?"

Jörmungander nodded his sinewy neck and blinked. "We're in the least valuable of all the chambers."

"Something's not right, laddie," Azriel replied. "This is as big as SEVERAL dragon hoards. Yet you claim you obtained all of this on your own. I don't believe it." Azriel shook his head. "No, this doesn't add up. We're so deep... how did you even get it all down here by yourself? And I don't think you're old enough. It must have taken thousands of years to obtain this collection."

Jörmungander raised his head high and spewed his dragon breath... a hundred-foot-long cloud of acidic, black sulfur... into the air above them. The cloud exploded into a rain of fiery hot particles that blacken and melted the coins they landed upon. Azriel and Elbedreth stepped deeper into the entrance corridor to avoid the molten shower.

"ARE YOU CALLING ME A LIAR!" Jörmungander bellowed.

Both sylphs returned to stand just inside the chamber... ready to retreat again if the situation should warrant. "No, my scaly friend," Azriel replied. "But I think perhaps you're overstating just a bit... boasting and acting fearsome to keep us off-balanced. A good boast can go a long way towards keeping the peace. I do it all the time. And a properly worded boast with perhaps a little show of power can back off potential adversaries... adversaries that would otherwise be very difficult to defeat. No, I'd not call that lying, laddie. I'd call it sound tactics." Azriel studied the dragon who had, by now, calmed down. "So, what's the full story?"

Jörmungander lowered his head. "I've never met anyone who wanted to hear my story. It's... unexpected. I'm not sure how to react to it."

"You stole our stories," Elbedreth said. She was still resentful about what the dragon had done to them. "At least give us yours."

"I took them only so much as to determine the truth of your words," Jörmungander responded. "Unlike my brethren, I was careful. I didn't permanently damage your minds. But it was necessary to understand why you're really here. I have... trust issues because of our treasure."

"Your treasure," Azriel corrected.

Jörmungander shook his head. "No, truth be told, it's not my treasure," he admitted. "I'm only its guardian. It belongs to my clan."

"So more than one dragon lives down here?" Elbedreth asked. Both her and Azriel took a closer look at their surroundings, concerned about the possibility other dragons arriving to defend the hoard.

"They're not here, if that concerns you," Jörmungander said. "I'm not sure where they are. But they've been gone for ten plus two decades…"

"How can he know for sure how long it's been?" Elbedreth whispered.

"All dragons have an acute ability to understand time," Azriel whispered back. "I've never asked a dragon why that is... but suspect it's because of their magical nature."

"… and as the youngest, it was my responsibility to stay behind and guard the hoard." Jörmungander was saying. "I haven't done a very good job at it, though. But on the bright side, our most prized possession remains safe."

"And what would that be, laddie?" Azriel asked.

Jörmungander paused.

Elbedreth approached closer. "You've been in our minds," she reminded. "You know our true purpose. You know we're not here to steal your treasure."

Jörmungander decided he could trust the two strangers. "My clan elders call it the *Heart of the World*," he answered. "Follow me."

As they moved towards one of the few walls without a door, a thought occurred to Azriel. "If this treasure…"

"Oh, it's much more than simple treasure," Jörmungander said, cutting short Azriel's query. "It's... it's... well, it's us. You'll understand when you see it."

Azriel shrugged. "Okay. But why would your clan leave it with only you... the youngest by your own admission... instead of more experienced clan members?"

Jörmungander stopped and looked back at the sylphs. "They needed everyone." The dragon's response was ambiguous and unsatisfying to the sylphs. "They've descended below to prepare for the *Maelstrom*."

"The *Maelstrom*?" Elbedreth asked.

"Prophecy," Jörmungander replied. "Our end-of-the-world prophecy. It says a new goddess will be born on the surface... and that birth will start a sequence of terrible cascading events which might very well result in the end of the world as we know it. We believe we have an obligation to stop it. Our seers recognized the signs and my clan left to fulfill the *Maelstrom*."

Azriel looked at Elbedreth. "You don't think he's talking about the rise of your people, do you?"

Elbedreth nodded. "What other explanation can there be?" she said before shaking her head. "But a clan of dragons can't stop my people. Slow them down, perhaps. But they'll never stop them through direct confrontation. There's just too many. Who is this goddess he mentioned?"

Azriel didn't answer immediately. *"I caught that to,"* he thought. *"He's talking about Emmy. Has to be!"*

"Is it this Emmy you've talked about?" Elbedreth asked.

"Keen observation. Yes, I believe so." Azriel turned back to Jörmungander. "How many are in your clan?" he asked.

The dragon frowned before answering. "Thirty plus seven."

"Are there other clans of black dragons?" Elbedreth inquired.

Jörmungander shook his head. "Not that I'm aware. Do you really think they'll destroy my clan?" His swirling eyes revealed his fear.

Neither Azriel nor Elbedreth answered. Elbedreth placed a hand on the great snout of the dragon and tenderly stroked it.

Jörmungander closed his eyes and accepted the sylph's caress for a few moments. Then he suddenly lifted his head. "Come quickly!" he said. "We must check the *Heart of the World!*"

As they approached a solid cavern wall, Jörmungander made a quick motion with one of his talon-tipped claws. A dark, large doorway appeared. Jörmungander rushed inside, leaving Azriel and Elbedreth to follow behind. Before they entered, the dragon inside bellowed a deep and long roar of pain and disbelief.

Solveig lay inside an alcove partially hidden by a large boulder. She shivered from blood loss and didn't think she'd live much longer. The young female black dragon had staggered into her hidey-hole after being severely wounded in the battle against the black venom that had risen from the center of the earth. Tears formed in her eyes as she reflected upon not only her own impending death but also the death of her clan. They had expected to fulfill the *Maelstrom*, but in the end only sacrificed their lives for relatively nothing. So many of the dark multitude still remained!

The *Maelstrom* was the black dragon clan end of the world scenario prophesized centuries ago. Not all divinations are unyielding, however, and the clan elders of that time determined they might avert the disaster to which the *Maelstrom* spoke, but only if they acted. Since the first foretelling, the black dragon clan prepared themselves for the *Maelstrom*. They put together supplies, stockpiled magical weapons and scrolls, scouted the most likely area for the final battle, and reproduced so their numbers would be more conducive to a successful campaign. The black clan dragons did everything they could think of to assure a favorable outcome. This led to many challenges, however. The primary of which was food, for the underground environment in which they lived wouldn't support the number of dragons that would be necessary. To solve this problem, they turned to the mushrooms and fungi that had, up to that point, only supplemented their diet. An added benefit to this decision was they no longer needed to make dangerous, and sometimes deadly, forays to the surface world to hunt meat.

One hundred and twenty years ago, the clan seer read the signs that the *Maelstrom* was taking shape. The black dragon clan, after spending hundreds of years preparing themselves, made the long trek to the place they would fight for the world – and their survival. They didn't abandon their home and treasure trove completely, however. They left their youngest dragon, Jörmungander, to guard the riches they'd built over several thousand years. Though the youngest, he was still very formidable and deemed strong enough to defend their traditional home.

When the sylphs came, the dragons were ready for them. But as it turned out, there was little they could do to stop the invasion. Dragons breath killed hundreds, rending great holes in every sylph it touched as the heat and acid of the breath burned through sylph bodies. But thousands more came to take their place.

Dragon magic also killed hundreds – bolts of lightning, explosions of fire, missiles of energy, and every other magic the dragons hurled at the sylphs lit up the cavern with hues of red, orange, yellow, white and every color in-between. But thousands more came to take their place.

Every magical scroll was read, every magical item used, and every magical weapon tasted the blood of the sylph. The dragons killed hundreds more sylphs. But thousands more came to take their place.

Finally, the dragons used their talons, horns, and vast strength to kill hundreds more. Each dragon fought until it exhausted all it its internal resources... until it couldn't bear to fight any longer. And still thousands of sylphs remained.

Those of Jörmungander and Solveig's clan still alive yet too weak or injured to defend themselves were brutally dispatched without mercy. The sylphs continued their march to the surface over the bodies of their own destroyed brethren and the dead dragons. Only Solveig remained alive, gravely wounded and unconscious, when the sylph army left the battlefield. Upon regaining consciousness, she saw that her entire clan had been annihilated. Looking at the carnage, she bellowed. Her cry spoke of misery, hopelessness, and failure. Dejected and no longer willing to accept the challenges of life, Solveig crawled into the alcove and waited to die.

When Azriel and Elbedreth reached the cavern entrance, they could barely make out their new friend, Jörmungander, as he wept. Before him a boulder-size heart-shaped piece of obsidian floated in the air. The *Heart of the World*. It was beating, but only barely. A tiny part of the heart still glimmered with the light of life.

"I am the last of my clan," Jörmungander lamented.

Azriel moved closer to the heart while Elbedreth went to console their new-found dragon companion. As Azriel looked closer, he caught a slight spark of light. "Did you see that?" he asked aloud.

"What, dear," Elbedreth replied.

Azriel stepped closer. "A feint light about here," he said as he pointed to a spot on the heart.

That caught Jörmungander's attention. "Show me," he demanded.

Suddenly there was another spark.

"One of us still lives!" the black dragon exclaimed. "But... there it is again... the spark. Female... and very weak. We must save her!"

"There only one problem with that, laddie," Azriel pointed out. "The sylph army lies in between."

A ghostly figure wandered the corridors and tunnels deep beneath Elanesse. Max knew he was lost... but didn't really care. He was still trying to digest the information regarding his death and the one responsible for it. As he released his initial rage and turned to rational thought, he understood the reasoning behind Elbedreth's actions, even as painful as those actions were. Besides, Max didn't want to lose Azriel's friendship. He didn't know how Azriel had become what he now was, but if Azriel accepted it, who should say different. And there was little doubt that Azriel loved Elbedreth. Max was just about to turn around and return to his friends when he saw smoke in the tunnel ahead.

"Odd," he thought. *"Unless there's a river of lava up ahead? Azriel and Elbedreth can wait. Think I'll check that out."*

What he found, however, wasn't a river of lava, but an enormous cavern... a cavern filled with death and destruction. Bodies of dragons lay everywhere. Each body looked like it had suffered thousands of cuts and slashes. Blood and dragon viscera completely covered the cavern floor. The steam of death still rose off the corpses. Here and there he spied mounds of the still, black forms of sylphs, no doubt part of the sylph army Azriel and Elbedreth had talked about stopping. Even as many as there were, Max figured there were plenty more sylph bodies under the dragon blood and remains.

The stalagmites that dotted the cavern landscape and jutted upwards were blackened and broken off. In the smoky atmosphere of the cavern they looked like spectral warriors standing guard over the killing field. Stalactites had fallen from the ceiling and lie in broken patterns of limestone rubble, a silent testament to the carnage that had occurred. On the walls and broken stalagmites, multi-colored fungi eerily shimmered in the smoke, giving the entire panorama a strange, hypnotic effect.

"So... this is what the sylph invasion means to the world," Max wondered. Deciding he'd seen enough, he turned away and started to leave when he heard a moan.

THE SECOND INTERREGNUM

Liosh floated across a blue, cloudless sky. The yellow sun beat down on his body, warming the thick blood that flowed through his veins. Below him, ocean – an endless expanse of blue-green water occasionally broken by white-tipped waves and the backs of large whales as they surfaced for a breath of fresh air. Liosh inhaled. He had gone from a life of dreary existence to something new and exciting. He felt exhilaration. He felt freedom.

As Liosh cavorted in the skies over Aster, he studied everything to better know his new world. He observed whales as they jumped out of the water, carefree. Schools of dolphins congregated and played while seabirds flew overhead, sometimes dropping to the surface of the ocean and coming back up with small fish in their beaks or claws.

Liosh decided he'd found himself in a peaceful world, a world where the Sky Emperors would thrive. The consciousnesses of all his people, eager to leave Liosh's protection and explore their new world, readily agreed. Without hesitation, they abandoned Liosh to find their own way. Within a few short days, benevolent Sky Emperors filled the skies over Aster. And Liosh went from being one of the youngest of his race to being the oldest.

Liosh dipped low and extended his long tentacles into the water. Bolts of white light ran down the tentacles and discharged below the surface. Microscopic plankton rushed to the source of the disturbance and were absorbed into the tentacles. Food from the light of the yellow sun and organisms in the water was abundant.

Satiated, Liosh regained altitude, looked around, and spied something new. Four figures, flying low over the water, made their way eastward. They were larger than the fliers from his previous home world, and perhaps more dangerous. One of these new fliers had a peculiar characteristic to it… five heads.

Liosh then saw a large ocean vessel riding the waves moving west and on an intercept course with the fliers. As he watched, knowing he was helpless because of the distance, two of the fliers dived on the ocean vessel. The ocean vessel changed course and tried to run, but by then it was too late. One of the fliers spit out a strange beam which vaporized the ships sails and masts. The second flier used its beam to run down the length from bow to stern, slicing it in half. And just like that, the ship, now in two halves, quickly sank into the ocean. The two fliers rejoined their comrades and continued their flight eastward.

"Brutally efficient," Liosh thought. *"And they attacked the ship without provocation. Why?"*

Liosh rushed to the scene of the attack, but there were only a few survivors. He tried to rescue them by letting them climb onto his tentacles, but each time he dropped close, they swam away. Liosh watched as, one by one, the survivors sank below the waves and into the endless night of the sunless water on the ocean floor. The Sky Emperor felt sad.

The fliers were long gone by the time Liosh ascended back into the sky. But he knew the direction they were going. He followed. He felt he owed it to his new home world to at least try to prevent future attacks.

CHAPTER EIGHT

InnisRos

The willingness to sacrifice one's life for that of another is the ultimate act of courage and devotion, for each of us hold our lives most dearly. This is the value of true sacrifice. This is the ultimate purity of the action. Every man, woman, or child who died in my name are, by that one, singular action, better than me. Every man, woman, or child left behind by one who died for me are owed a debt I can never repay.

-From the Journal of Lessien Arntuile, daughter of King Martin, Princess In Absentia of the Alfheim, and Queen of InnisRos

"They're all dead, Eric," Katsumi said through tears as she communicated with her leader, Eric the Black, on the other side of the island.

"Tell me what happened," Eric the Black instructed. Though he had a hard time digesting this news, he could hear how upset Katsumi was over the communications crystal and didn't want to add his own sorrow to hers. The four, when he found them so many years ago, were nothing but orphaned street urchins living off the meager funds they pickpocketed. The assassin-sorcerer took them under his wing and provided them food and a place to call home. He trained them to be not just assassins, but his assassins. His motives for using them may not have been so altruistic at the time, but over the years he'd come to love and respect them as he would his own family… except for Katsumi. His feelings for her went much deeper. *"When we spoke last, the others had already left the city with the Soulreavers in hand."*

Katsumi nodded as she wiped her eyes with the back of her sleeve. "Yes, Eric. The... the others waited for me at our pre-arranged spot in the forest. I lagged behind in the tunnels while I talked to you. But when I reached the tunnel exit and opened the hatch, I saw dark elves searching the forest, so I stayed underground. After the dark elves had left about two hours later, I found all three, dead. It looked like someone or something had trampled them to death!"

Eric the Black grimaced. He shook off his despair and asked the one question that he needed answered. *"What about the Soulreavers?"*

"Gone," replied Katsumi. "Their crate was smashed... but no signs they were harmed. Eric, I found a small brook not too far away."

"Did you search it?" Eric the Black inquired.

Katsumi shook her head. "I'd never find them in the dark. Do you want me to look when it's light? They're harmless enough since they'll be in hibernation for the next couple of weeks."

Eric the Black thought about it for a few seconds then shook his head. *"No. I want you to stay safe, Kat. And we still need to get our operatives inside Taranthi. The thieves' guild will only deal with you."*

"All right," Katsumi agreed. "Do you know how long I must wait for them?"

"I'm not sure, but..." The assassin-sorcerer's voice trailed off as the crystal lost power.

"Eric? Eric!" Katsumi said into the communications crystal to no avail. It needed to be re-powered and that would take too much time.

Katsumi sighed. Eric still expected her to carry out the second part of the assignment, but there were several problems which needed resolution. First, she was now alone. There was nothing she could do about that. Second, she felt sure the dark elves would discover her escape tunnel within a few hours, if not already. With that compromised, she'd need to find another way into the city. Then there were the dark elves. They were scouring the forest in force searching for those responsible for eliminating their sorcerers. That was trouble on two fronts. It would be difficult to get through the day without being captured, or worse. Then she had to get the operatives back through the forest and into Taranthi.

She said a prayer for her dead comrades, knowing she dare not disturb their bodies for fear of being found out, and picked her way through the forest heading north towards its edge. Along the way, she kept a sharp eye out and found a barbed bramble that would protect her as she got some much-needed rest.

Aikanáro walked the battlements of the royal palace in Taranthi. He was troubled. Several unexpected things had transpired that concerned him, though they didn't seem to worry Nightshade. Arrogance and self-assurance were qualities most demons shared, but Aikanáro felt his daughter carried it too far.

The invasion went as he and Nightshade had conceived it. Aikanáro had to give his daughter credit. She'd done a fine job of getting most of the island's fighting forces north before the invasion. Resistance around Taranthi was mostly nonexistent as a result. With the capital city and the immediate surrounding area secured, the dark elf army had not only a splendid home base from which to launch military operations, but most importantly, the portal connecting Aster with the Svartalfheim, a constant source of reinforcement and resupply, was secure. Without the portal, the dark elf army would be cut off and Aikanáro's goal of invading the Alfheim would fail.

Even Nightshade's insistence dragons be sent to the mainland to destroy an ancient elven city called Elanesse had so far been highly successful. Along the way they came across the InnisRos navy and destroyed a good portion of it before heading across the ocean. Though Aikanáro at first refused to waste his dragons on what he saw as a fool's errand, in the end he was glad he relented to Nightshade's demands, though he still had need of them.

While encouraged, what troubled him was the small, annoying things which, when taken individually, meant nothing. But on a larger scale, Aikanáro saw a level of resistance he hadn't expected along with a type of sophistication he didn't think possible from mere mortals.

First, all his scouts, the wyverns, were destroyed by millions of small, winged, black and brown creatures who appeared to be mind controlled. Not only did they destroy the wyverns but are at this moment harassing the hell out of his troops. They were easy enough to kill, but there were too damn many of them. The local populace called them bats and made every possible effort to harbor and succor them, which made it even more difficult for his troops to dispose of the menace.

Then all the dark elf sorcerers were killed by, of all things, Qénsharma. Few know they're not native to the Abyss – that they actually came from a different dimension which gives them abilities never before encountered. In other words, killing them was damn near impossible, and most creatures, mortal and immortal, had few defenses against them. Smart demons feared the Qénsharma and avoided them at all costs. How they got past the *B'nai Elohim* and to this world is open to speculation, and Aikanáro saw no point in thinking about it. The only thing that mattered was that they're here. More terrifying, however, is that the inhabitants of this backwater world learned to use them for their own purposes. Aikanáro didn't fear the one's used to kill the sorcerers. They'd be dormant for at least two weeks. But he did fear those that might still be out there and unaccounted for. The Qénsharma were a wild card he hadn't anticipated.

But the most disturbing thing was that they've yet to root out the city's thieves' guild. Aikanáro knew every city of size had one. Though it only comprised of pickpockets, thieves, muggers, and murderers, it represented a well-organized group that, unless dealt with, would become a deadly opposition force. They stayed in the shadows and knew the city underbelly like no other. They could strike or harass and then disappear without a trace. This guerrilla warfare, and any successes it might achieve, would no doubt embolden the city population to join their ranks. To solve this problem Aikanáro could have all the city inhabitants put to the sword, but he wasn't ready to do that. All he wanted now is a little time to secure his position before sending his army north against the island's main battle force. He didn't need the distraction a wholesale slaughter would bring... especially since Nightshade was, for some obscure reason, firmly against it.

"You're troubled, father?" a familiar voice spoke from behind.

Aikanáro turned to face his daughter. "Sorry, Nightshade," he responded. She was in her Amberley form. "Just thinking. I didn't notice your approach. What news do you bring?"

"Very little, I'm afraid," she replied. "We found the tunnel used by the assassins to escape the city. In fact, we've found the assassins. Well, at least their bodies."

"And the Qénsharma?"

Nightshade shook her head. "The Qénsharma have escaped. But you know they won't pose a threat for at least two weeks."

Aikanáro looked to the north. "Those aren't the ones I'm concerned about. There may be others. Any luck with the thieves' guild?"

Nightshade shook her head. "None. But don't worry, we'll find them."

"Anything else?"

"A most curious thing," Nightshade replied as she too stared to the north. "The dead assassins? They were trampled to death by what appear to be very large animals of some type. I couldn't recognize their scent... but I'm sure they're not from this island. In fact, I don't believe they're from this world."

Aikanáro turned to look at his daughter's expressionless face. "What do you mean? You and me... the dark elves, dragons and wyverns... we're the only beings not from this world."

"It would appear that is no longer true," Nightshade replied. "Whatever these beasts were, another followed. It was different from the others. I believe this one was a predator and hunting the others."

"And?" Aikanáro asked.

"They're scent disappeared into... well, into nothing," Nightshade replied. "Almost as if they teleported away."

"Interesting," Aikanáro said. "So, they're not a threat at the moment?"

Nightshade shook her head.

"Then we'll worry about it later," Aikanáro said. "Right now, I'm more concerned about getting the army on the march. We need to take the island before their queen has a chance to dig in. I wish you hadn't commandeered my dragons."

For the first time Nightshade laughed. "We still have YOUR dragon, father."

Aikanáro frowned.

"Oh, don't look so disappointed," Nightshade retorted. "Those dragons are doing something very important to our plans."

"Destroy an abandoned city?!" Aikanáro shouted. "How's..."

Nightshade remained calm. "It's not the city," she said. "But what, or should I say who, is in the city."

Aikanáro waited.

Nightshade sighed. "Father, a new goddess is being born. If we don't destroy her, everything... and I mean everything... we've worked for will come crashing down on our heads."

Aikanáro looked confused. "How do you know this?"

"Can't you feel it?" Nightshade exclaimed. "It's all around us. It's like Aster is waiting in anticipation of the day when she arrives and takes her place in the pantheon of the gods and goddesses. If we allow that to happen, father, no army can defeat her."

For the second time Aikanáro felt fear. First the Qénsharma and now this. "Maybe you should see to it yourself," he said.

"I intend to," Nightshade replied with a sly smile.

Without the wyverns to worry about, Nefertari, Marine Colonel Daeron Tirion, and the creation stone Maedhros Nénmacil made good time on their clandestine journey south. Within a day they had reached the abandoned town of A'el Ellhendell. Directly across the Maranwe River lay the shambles that once was Ashakadi. Both Nefertari and Colonel Tirion cringed when memories of the carnage that had occurred there a few short weeks ago came flooding back.

"Someday I must bring Miracle here and explain how I destroyed her town and family," Nefertari said. She was suddenly very downhearted. "I hope she can forgive me."

Colonel Tirion, sitting next to her in the horse-drawn wagon they were using for transportation, placed a gloved hand over Nefertari's. "It wasn't your fault."

Nefertari shook her head. "I should've figured out a way to divert the power of that explosion without causing an earthquake. I..."

"It wasn't your fault!" Colonel Tirion stressed again, only this time more firmly. "You did the only thing you could under the circumstances. It was Mordecai's doing and none other. Don't worry, he'll pay for his crimes."

"If he's still alive," Nefertari said. "This dark elf invasion..."

"Was instigated by him," Colonel Tirion interrupted. "He's instigated everything, so quite blaming yourself."

"Listen to the Colonel, StarSinger," Maedhros Nénmacil said through the telepathic link he had with the priestess. He was flying high above scouting the way ahead for danger. *'From what I've observed, and contrary to popular belief, Marines aren't the big, dumb brutes that destroy everything in sight. They've been trained in so many ways to kill they must be smart enough to pause and consider which method they're going to use. Eventually all that thinking catches up with them until they become smart. At least that's how it looks to me. I speculate our friend Daeron knows a lot of ways to kill."*

Nefertari chuckled.

Colonel Tirion looked over at her. "What?"

"Oh, nothing," she replied. "Something Maedhros Nénmacil said."

Colonel Tirion grumbled under his breath. Sometimes he felt like a third wheel with those two.

Nefertari laughed again.

"What now?" Colonel Tirion asked.

"Maedhros Nénmacil says you should pet one of those kittens we brought along."

A few hours later they approached the huge forest that covered the entire portion of InnisRos west of the Maranwe River. As they traveled, they saw no signs of the dark elves which seemed unusual to Nefertari. Even Maedhros Nénmacil, from his perch high in the sky, saw nothing except empty fields and grasslands before the forest.

"Do you think they're all waiting in the trees?" Nefertari asked Colonel Tirion.

Colonel Tirion shook his head. "I don't know," he answered. "Though I'm sure their pickets... speak of the devil."

A squad of dark elves emerged from the forest's edge and marched to meet them.

"Should I come down and scare those fellows away?" Maedhros Nénmacil asked.

"No," Nefertari said aloud. "I don't want them to know about you yet."

Colonel Tirion looked over at Nefertari. "That's creepy," he said, referring to her verbal conversations with the creation stone... conversations he could only hear one side of. "Let's go over our cover story. I'm a simple farmer bringing my wares to the big city," he explained. "I have hand-sewn coats, jackets, and treated leather hides for sale."

"Your sword?" Nefertari asked.

"It's cheap and something a farmer is likely to carry for self-defense," he explained. "We'll get better weapons once we meet our contacts. Your turn."

"I'm a country witch who can do a little magic... but mostly rely on sleight-of-hand," Nefertari replied. "My staff is nothing more than a stick... a symbol of my station."

"And if they detect for magic in the staff?"

"I've already broken my connection to it," Nefertari said. "Don't worry, though. I can re-establish that link in a moment's notice."

Colonel Tirion nodded. "Good. Now what else?"

Nefertari frowned. "There isn't... oh, yes... we don't know each other. You're only giving me a ride into Taranthi. We met in A'el Ellhendell. I lost my home in the earthquake that destroyed Ashakadi."

"Correct," Colonel Tirion responded. "Now when they... whoa there, big guys!"

The huge horses obeyed the Colonel and came to a stop.

"What's wrong, Daeron?" Nefertari asked.

Colonel Tirion laid the reins to the horses across his legs. "I caught a glimpse of metal in the trees ahead. My guess... archers."

"I can use the air to stop any arrows they shoot," Nefertari answered. "You know that."

"Yes," Colonel Tirion said. "But I don't want THEM to know that. We need to be very careful right now. We'll be less of a threat if we let them approach on their terms. I don't want to give our friends in the forest a reason to shoot." Colonel Tirion turned and reached in the back of the wagon. When he had turned back, he held one of the kittens. He handed it to her. "Maedhros Nénmacil is right. Here, pet a kitten."

Nefertari quizzically looked at the Marine.

"It'll give you something to do with your hands," Colonel Tirion said. "And that, my dear, will help to keep you calm. We can't afford any mistakes."

"Why have you stopped, StarSinger?" Maedhros Nénmacil inquired inside Nefertari's head.

"Simply a precaution, my friend," Nefertari said through the telepathic link. *"Use the clouds and move to the forest perimeter. Daeron thinks there might be archers hidden in the trees. See if he's right."* She glanced up to make sure he was following her orders and not attempting to do anything heroic.

One of the dark elf soldiers shouted, "Jǔ shǒu nóngmín!" as they surrounded the wagon. Each had black swords pointed at Nefertari and Colonel Tirion.

Colonel Tirion held up his hands, shook his head as he pointed to his ears, and shrugged his shoulders. "I don't understand you," he said.

Another of the soldiers stepped forward. This dark elf was bigger than the rest and had numerous scars and tattoos covering his head and uncovered arms. He was the obvious commander. "Bǎ nǐ de wǔqì rēng dào dìshàng!" he shouted as he pointed his sword at the rusty blade hanging from Colonel Tirion's side.

"I understand that," the Marine said as he removed the sword and threw it to the ground.

The soldier then pointed at the staff sitting next to Nefertari and waved his sword.

Nefertari debated whether she should make a scene... after all, she was playing the part of a purveyor of magic and used to getting her way... but thought better of it. Perhaps it was the kitten she was petting. She picked up the staff and threw it to the ground.

The soldier who initially spoke picked up both the sword and the staff and presented them to the leader. The leader scrutinized the tarnished sword and spit on the ground. "Kěbēi de," he said as he heaved the sword away into some bushes.

Inspecting the staff, he seemed disappointed it looked to be an ordinary piece of wood. "Bah!" he said as he dropped the staff to the ground.

Nefertari watched with disgust as she stroked the soft fur of the kitten. As the staff hit the ground, she called forth a weak air elemental which lifted the staff and hit the soldier in the back of head before dropping it back down.

The rest of the soldiers snickered at their leader's unfortunate accident, though they stopped when he glared at them.

"Nǐ shì zěnme zuò dào de!" he demanded as he looked at Nefertari. She sat calmly in the wagon petting the kitten. But as they made eye contact, he quickly look away. Daeron watched the exchange between Nefertari and the dark elf commander. In her eyes he saw the raw, bottled-up power of a StarSinger waiting to be released. Her self-control and good heart were the only reason these dark elves stilled lived… and deep down the dark elf understood that as well.

Angry, but no longer wishing to confront the StarSinger, he picked up the staff and broke it over his knee. "Jiǎnchá huòchē!" he brusquely ordered.

Two soldiers sheathed their swords, climbed into the rear of the wagon, and searched the leather hides, coats, and jackets. Several of the coats got tossed onto the ground.

"Méiyǒu," one of them said as they jumped off. They made no attempt to pick the discarded coats up.

Colonel Tirion pointed at them. "I need to get those," he said as he prepared to jump off the wagon. "They're worth several hundred pieces of copper... enough to keep me and my horses fed for a week."

The leader shook his head. He clearly understood what Colonel Tirion meant even though he didn't understand the words. "Tíngzhǐ!" he shouted. He then motioned with his sword. "Gēnzhe wǒ," he said as he turned and walked forward. The rest of his squad, still surrounding the wagon, waited until Colonel Tirion picked the reins back up and started the horses forward, following the squad leader.

"What were you doing," Nefertari whispered. "You could've gotten both of us killed."

"Just playing the part," answered Colonel Tirion. "We must always play the part. If we don't, well," Colonel Tirion shrugged his shoulders, "who knows. But that little scene I just played out was undoubtedly the one thing we've done to convince him we're who we say we are."

"Daeron was correct," Maedhros Nénmacil said. *"There were archers in the woods… though only a few now remain. What game do you play, StarSinger?"*

"Be patient, my friend," the priestess replied to the creation stone.

Nefertari turned to Colonel Tirion and whispered. "Maedhros Nénmacil says you were correct about the archers. He says most of them have left."

Colonel Tirion nodded.

"He also contemplates our current course of action," she added.

"I'll bet he does," Colonel Tirion whispered. "No doubt he's wondering why I'm being so complacent."

"He's not the only one, Daeron. I was thinking the same thing. I understand the need to infiltrate the dark elf camp to find the stone… but we never intended to do it as their prisoners."

"A change of plans," Colonel Tirion said. "Why sneak when we can be escorted. Besides, I have every confidence you and our flying boulder friend can break us out if it becomes necessary. Now pay attention to every little detail about the dark elf camp. We'll need that information to determine their strength and disposition. It might also help us get a line on their leadership."

"Our mission is to get to the *Ak-Séregon Stone*," Nefertari stated.

"But we don't know where it is," Colonel Tirion responded. "I'm hoping we'll get some information about that too. Besides, there's no guarantee we'll stay prisoners. If we do this right, they'll let us go."

Nefertari shook her head. "I'm not so sure. It seems to me you're thinking too much like a soldier."

Colonel Tirion smiled. "What other way is there in a time of war?"

"StarSinger, there appears to be a struggle in the forest below me," Maedhros Nénmacil said. *"Should I get closer?"*

"Only if you have cloud cover," answered Nefertari.

"Then I can get no closer," Maedhros Nénmacil said. *"Dark elf guards seem to have something trapped in a bush. I don't think it's an animal... wait... it's a person... a female by the length of her red hair. A well-trained female! She's fighting like a... how do you say... oh, yes, she's fighting like a hellcat. The dark elves have lost five, but now they have her subdued. They are taking her back to the city."*

"Keep monitoring... but stay hidden," Nefertari ordered.

"As you wish, StarSinger." Maedhros Nénmacil responded.

Nefertari heard frustration in the creation stone's voice, but she had no time to reassure him. She turned to Colonel Tirion. "Eric said we were to meet with a friend of his... a woman with uncommon red hair. Katsumi's her name."

Colonel Tirion nodded.

"She's just been captured," Nefertari said. "Maedhros Nénmacil saw it happen deeper in the forest."

Colonel Tirion sighed. "She's special to Eric... at least that's what Landross told me. We can't leave without her, or we'll have a very angry sorcerer to deal with."

Neither said another word as they and their escort picked up the main road going into Taranthi. Before they reached it, however, Colonel Tirion discreetly removed his communications crystal and dropped it to the ground where it lay unnoticed by the guards.

Several miles behind them, forgotten in the tall grass, two ends of a broken staff moved towards each other. When they met, the broken halves touched and melded – two into one – broken to unbroken – incomplete to whole. The new, intact staff shot up into the air and raced to find its master.

Father Goram opened one eye in response to a wet tongue snaking across his forehead. Salamis, the largest and strongest of Ajax's sons, was staring at him and cocked his head to the side. Father Goram sighed and closed his eyes, which prompted yet another wet lick across the face.

"All right, I'm getting up," Father Goram said.

"What's going on?" Autumn asked sleepily.

"I don't know." Farther Goram replied. "But Salamis and Murphie are as bad as Razor and Findley." Razor and Findley, his previous dire wolf guards whenever Ajax wasn't around, were now guarding Queen Lessien. Ajax had sent Salamis and Murphie in their place.

"Waking me up at all hours of the night," he grumbled as he put on his robe over his nightshirt. He leaned over and kissed Autumn on the cheek. "I'll go see what's up, dear," he said.

Autumn nodded as she returned to her dreamscape.

Father Goram, led by Salamis, exited the bedroom. Salamis wasted no time rushing down the hallway to stand with Murphie at the entrance door to Father Goram and Autumn's apartment. As Father Goram carefully closed the bedroom door so he wouldn't disturb Autumn, there was a loud knock at the front door, followed by the low growls of his dire wolf guardians.

"Father Goram!" a voice called from the other side of the door. Father Goram recognized the voice of Eric the Black, though he'd never heard it so frantic and panicky.

"Coming," he said as he walked down the hallway. When he passed the great room, he glanced out the window. *Still early morning,* he thought. *We only got to bed a couple of hours ago!*

Father Goram pushed his way through the two dire wolves and opened the door.

Eric the Black pushed past Father Goram. "Horatio, I don't know what to...". He stopped as two angry-looking dire wolves blocked any further entry into the apartment. Their many sharp teeth dominated their features as they growled a low warning. It was clear that if Eric the Black took one more step, he'd be torn apart.

"Calm down boys," Father Goram said as he stepped past the sorcerer and grabbed the tuft of hair behind each of the dire wolves' head, forcing them to turn away. With one last snarl, both dire wolves moved into the main room and deposited themselves next to the unlit fireplace.

Autumn opened the door of the bedroom and walked down the hallway.

Father Goram sighed. "Sweetie, I wanted you to sleep," he said.

Autumn shook her head. "I'll make coffee," she said instead. "Eric, please make yourself comfortable."

"Horatio, I'm sorry to disturb you so early, but this just couldn't wait," Eric the Black said.

Father Goram shook his head and motioned for Eric the Black to sit down on one of several over-stuffed easy chairs while he took his preferred spot on his luxurious sofa. Both remained silent until Autumn handed them large mugs of steamy hot coffee. She then took her customary place next to Father Goram. Once she had settled in, all three took a moment to enjoy the day's first sip of coffee.

"All right, Eric," Father Goram said. "What's going on?"

Eric the Black put his mug down on a side table and got out of his seat. Both wolves suspiciously eyed him as he paced. "It's Kat... she's missing," he said.

"Who's Kat?" Autumn asked.

"Oh, sorry. I guess you wouldn't know about Katsumi, would you," the sorcerer said. "I used a team of assassins to kill the dark elf sorcerers, and she was the leader of that team. Three others were with her. They penetrated the palace and... well... did what needed doing. They were also supposed to meet Nefertari and Colonel Tirion and help get them into the city. But the last time I spoke to Kat she told me the rest of her team had met... untimely deaths. Something about them being trampled, though that doesn't make much sense."

"That's terrible!" Autumn exclaimed.

Eric the Black nodded. "It was only luck she didn't get trampled as well. If she hadn't stayed in the escape tunnel to report to me she no doubt would have been. By the time she was ready to rejoin her team, the dark elves were searching the forest." Eric the Black stopped pacing and sat back down. He looked at his coffee, but decided he no longer wanted it. "She waited until the dark elves had left and snuck out of her hiding place to check on the others. That's when she found them." Eric the Black decided not to say anything about the missing Soulreavers and the problems that might cause in the future. "Even with the loss, Kat intended to meet Nefertari and Colonel Tirion, but since they were still several hours away, she needed to find a place to hide until she could make contact. She was supposed to signal me when she had our people... but I haven't heard from her since that last conversation. Horatio, she should've made contact by now. Something's wrong."

Father Goram sat, thinking. "This is beginning to fall apart. I need..."

Salamis and Murphie perked up just before a discreet knock at the entrance door. Father Goram sighed as he got up to answer the knock which, by now, had become insistent.

"Horatio, we need to talk," a voice said from the other side.

Father Goram opened the door to reveal a weary-looking Cameron and Cordelia.

"We got a problem," Cordelia said as both she and Cameron brushed past the priest.

"Come right in and join the party," Father Goram grumbled under his breath.

Cameron and Cordelia made a beeline to the coffee-pot on the stove and poured themselves a mug before settling down next to Eric the Black on the last two easy chairs.

Father Goram re-took his seat next to Autumn.

"Eric, what...?" Cordelia asked.

"In good time," Father Goram said, interrupting his second in command. "First, why are you two here so bloody early in the morning?"

"Nefertari and the Colonel have gone dark," Cordelia said without preamble. "We can't contact them... nor have they tried to contact us... since yesterday."

"You know that doesn't really mean anything, right?" Father Goram said. "There could be all kinds of reasons... most of which don't suggest a problem."

"Convenient, wouldn't you say, Horatio?" Eric the Black interjected.

Both Cameron and Cordelia looked from Eric the Black to Father Goram.

Father Goram shook his head. "It appears Eric's people in Taranthi has had some problems also. But that doesn't mean the two are connected."

"Excuse me, Horatio, but if they took Kat, there's no one to meet them and get them inside the city," Eric said. "Without her help, there's no way they could avoid capture."

"Whose Kat," Cordelia asked.

"Later," Eric the Black snapped. "Well, Horatio?"

Father Goram looked at Eric the Black before turning his attention to Cameron and Cordelia. "Have you said anything to the queen," he asked.

Cordelia shook her head. "We figured it best she hears the news from you. You're like a father to her."

Father Goram laughed. "Hardly," he responded. "No one will ever take the place of Martin in her heart." Father Goram paused. "Still, you're right. I should be the one to tell her. But I don't want to alarm her too soon."

"Honey, we need to tell her about all this as soon as possible," Autumn remarked. "We have an obligation to be straight with her."

Father Goram looked at his wife, then at each of the others, and nodded. In the brief silence that followed, there was another knock on the door. Salamis and Murphie, dozing by the fireplace, looked up, snarled, and returned to their nap.

Father Goram, without a word, got up and went to the front entrance and opened the door. Landross was standing there looking embarrassed.

"I'm so sorry to disturb you at such an early hour," Landross said. "But there's something I must discuss with you."

Father Goram moved to the side and motioned with a sweeping arm for Landross to enter.

"Your so kind, Father," Landross said as he walked past the priest. "Again, let me say how sorry I am. We've..." Landross stopped as he saw the rest of the monastery council sitting in the great room.

Father Goram went around the motionless Landross. "There's coffee in the kitchen, but you'll have to use one of the dining room table chairs... or the fireplace hearth if you can make your way past my two dire wolf rugs."

Landross poured his mug of coffee and picked up a chair. He placed the chair next to Eric the Black and took a sip of the hot morning elixir. "Most excellent as always," he said as he nodded to Autumn. "You make the best coffee on InnisRos."

Father Goram rolled his eyes. Sometimes dealing with the courtesy of a knight can be bothersome... particularly if you were on a tight schedule. Or, as was the case now, irritable.

Eric the Black, who probably knew Landross better than anyone, noticed the priest's impatience. "Perhaps if you'd get to the point, Landross?" he said.

Landross looked at his friend and nodded. "Oh, sorry. It's just that I love Autumn's coffee so..."

"Landross!" Father Goram barked.

"Horatio, there's no reason to..." Autumn began before her husband's withering glare interrupted her.

"I'm sorry..." Landross repeated.

"Would you please just get on with it," Eric the Black scolded.

Landross nodded. "General Singëril doesn't want to take my knights south with the rest of the army," he said. As he spoke, his face grew redder. "He says that we've gotten... well, to use his exact words... fat and lazy doing simple sentry duty here at the monastery!"

"You've seen plenty of action in the last few weeks," Cordelia protested.

"He knows," answered Landross. "He replied that his men do that much fighting against the pirates in the archipelago before breakfast!" Now Landross was mad. He set his mug down, got up from his chair, and paced in front of the fireplace. Even as annoyed as he was, he still took great care to go around the sleeping dire wolves. "The audacity of that man!" Landross continued as he smashed a fist against his other hand. "Horatio, I wanted to challenge him to a duel right then and there!"

"You told him how effective mounted knights were against footed troops?" Cameron asked.

Landross looked at Cameron curiously. "Why would I do that, Cameron?" he replied. "He's a general. He knows what my knights can do!"

"So then?"

Landross stopped his pacing to look at Father Goram, who had just asked the question. "He says we're too damn slow! That we'd hold up his army! That we'd not be effective because they'd have fought the battle a week before we got there!" The big knight snorted. "A week he says!"

Father Goram laughed. It was a full-throated, hearty laugh, the kind he'd almost forgotten how to do. He knew he shouldn't have, but Landross looked so comical standing there in all his righteous indignation.

Autumn frowned. "Sweetheart?"

Father Goram looked at Autumn, and then back at Landross, and laughed even harder. Everyone stared. Both dire wolves woke up, stood, and looked around, bewildered and hoping to find the cause of their masters' affliction. The look on his friends faces, the confusion he knew Salamis and Murphie must be experiencing, seemed even funnier. He laughed so hard tears were falling down his cheeks. *"They must think I'm crazy,"* he thought... which made him laugh even more.

After a few seconds – seconds that seemed to stretch into an eternity for his friends who worried about his sanity – Father Goram journeyed back to reality. The brief respite, however, had done him a world of good. It felt to him that a great tension had snapped, like floodgates opening to release cleansing water over a perched earth. He felt refreshed.

Another knock on his door broke the silence.

Kyleigh Angelus-Custos, Queen of the Alfheim, sat on her great war stallion before the portal that led to the world of Aster. The opening, built out of nothing, swirled in vapors of black and gray. Four sorcerers surrounded another who held a glowing staff. All five of the sorcerers were casting spells of enchantment. Two rows of twelve mounted knights formed a steel corridor leading to the mouth of the portal.

The piece of the *Ak-Samarië Shard,* which Kyleigh had fashioned into a locket, lay inert against the skin of her chest. Kyleigh didn't know if this was good or bad because she wasn't sure how the shard would react to the portal.

"I wish Zacharias had found another way," she thought for the hundredth time. *"A way that didn't involve his death. No one knew more about the shard's abilities than he."*

"Please reconsider," First Councilor Robert Gareathe said, deciding to make one last effort to sway her course of action. "Stay until you have the weight of the Army at your back."

"I have *Ah-RahnVakha*," Kyleigh replied, referring to the magical sword that never left her side. "And I have my personal guard. I'll be safe enough until you can bring the Army over."

Kyleigh looked at the frown on the face of her First Councilor and sighed. "I've gone over this time and time again, Robert. The portal is becoming more and more unstable with each passing hour. Who knows when it'll collapse, and we desperately need more information. I don't want our army to walk into a trap. But more importantly, we must get the shard to Aster or both our worlds may not survive."

"But…"

"This could be our only opportunity," Kyleigh said. The tone in her voice served to end further discussion.

Robert nodded, unsurprised she still resisted his advice. He had tried on numerous occasions to talk her out of this in favor of someone else, but she didn't waver and refused to debate it further. And perhaps she was right. That she was the queen of the Alfheim was the very reason it was necessary for her to go. She considered it her responsibility, her duty, and her sacrifice.

Robert watched as Kyleigh closed tight her cloak, the *Mantle of the Sovereign*, kicked her steed and led her escort into the portal. After the last guard had disappeared into the smoky darkness, he turned his horse and galloped away. There was much he needed to do before he'd be ready to answer the Queen's call when it came. As he crested the small rise that overlooked the portal, there was a tremendous explosion from behind which knocked him off his horse. Robert shook his head to vacate the fogginess and looked down towards the portal. It was no longer there. Of the sorcerers and soldiers still in the valley, only black soot remained... ghostly outlines on the grass.

Kyleigh recognized something was wrong soon after she and her guards entered the portal. Though she'd never traveled between the two worlds herself, she had heard enough stories from those who did. None of them ever described a fog. She understood she had to keep going, for she'd come too far to turn back now, but that wasn't true for her guards. She turned and screamed for them to return. It was too late. She stared in horror as her astonished guards disintegrated.

The shard lying against her skin exploded into a brilliant white light. Kyleigh felt an incredible pain in the center of her chest which forced her to scream and bend forward, clutching her horse's powerful neck to stabilize herself in the chaos all around. Dangerous energy danced in colors of black, brown, orange, and amber. But a bubble of protective magic surrounded her and kept her safe. She watched as the portal which from the inside looked like a long, dark corridor, collapsed towards her. She turned and saw the other side also collapsing. Kyleigh couldn't do anything as the two ends of the portal crumbled towards her.

The pain in Kyleigh's chest became unbearable, causing her to scream once again and drop from her horse to the floor of the portal as she clutched her breast. The energy of the collapsing corridor moved faster... swirling around her as if she were in the eye of a hurricane. But for the pain in her chest, however, she felt nothing. Faster and faster the energy spun. As Kyleigh stared, the turbulent whirlpool surrounding her solidified into solid light. It moved inward with Kyleigh at its center. Intense light burst out of the shard. *Ah-RahnVakha* answered with a strong glow of its own. The two were working together to save her.

"*Sleep,*" a female voice said in Kyleigh's head.

Then another voice, a distinctly male voice that Kyleigh realized must be from her sword, added, *"We'll protect you."*

Kyleigh suddenly felt very drowsy. She couldn't resist the urge to sleep and gave in to its embrace. As she blacked out, she heard the shard and sword talking between themselves. She had slipped too far into unconsciousness to understand what they were saying... but it brought a smile to her, nevertheless.

THE THIRD INTERREGNUM

Liosh tried to keep up, but the dragons were too fast for him. It didn't matter. The Sky Emperor could still detect their spore – a presence every living thing leaves in its wake. When he reached dry land, he looked for any physical signs of the dragon's passing, fearing they'd do to the inhabitants what they had done to the ship. His apprehension calmed somewhat when he saw no obvious path of destruction. Liosh sighed in relief. All seemed quiet from his perch high in the sky. In the far distance he saw a very large forest with great mountains directly behind it. The dragon's spore scent led in that direction.

As Liosh continued to follow, he noticed several black figures circling the peak of the highest mountain in the mountain range ahead. The dragon spore he followed led in that direction, so Liosh surmised the black forms were his quarry, though he wasn't so sure if 'quarry' was the correct term. After all, he knew nothing of the circumstances which led to the destruction of the ship. Perhaps the ship's crew were renegades and the black fliers had only brought them to a well-deserved justice? On new worlds nothing is ever as it seems.

Liosh felt a sharp pain and looked down. One of his tentacles had been severed and was falling to the earth. Below that, a black flier was flying up and towards him.

"Clever! It must've been hiding in the forest trees below!" Liosh thought as he worked to control the pain.

He wasn't worried about the lost tentacle, for he knew it would grow back. The black flier's beam of destruction and its effectiveness concerned him deeply, however. Liosh waved his tentacles in the hope it would make them harder to hit. As he did so, he discharged several lightning bolts around the black flier, using care not to hit it. Liosh still wasn't sure of the black flier's motivation and only wished to force it to keep its distance.

The black flier intentionally flew into one of the lightning bolts. To Liosh's surprise, instead of being hurt, it absorbed the energy and looked to be stronger for having done so. At this point the Sky Emperor realized another approach to this fast closing threat would be necessary – only he didn't have a clue what it should be.

Liosh retracted his tentacles into his cloud-like body and retreated. The black flier didn't continue with its attack or follow. It circled the forest as it watched Liosh leave, returning to its companions once satisfied Liosh wasn't coming back.

Liosh turned and watched as the black fliers flew down the eastern side of the mountains. *"I wonder what they're doing,"* he asked himself. *"And how do I stop them?"*

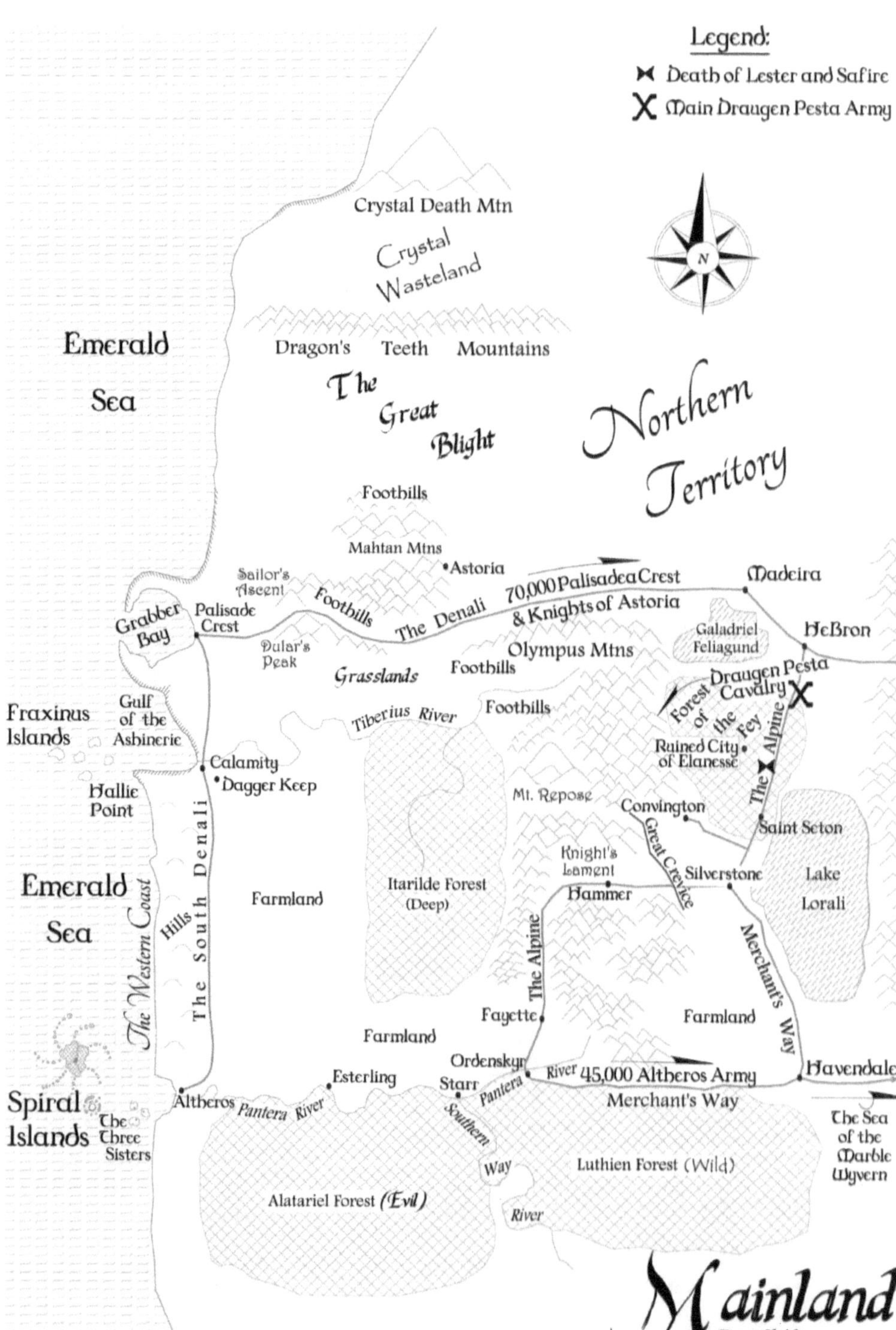

Legend:
Death of Lester and Safire
Main Draugen Pesta Army
N
Crystal Death Mtn
Crystal Wasteland
Emerald Sea
Dragon's Teeth Mountains
The Great Blight
Northern Territory
Foothills
Mahtan Mtns
Sailor's Ascent
Astoria
Foothills
70,000 Palisadea Crest & Knights of Astoria
Madeira
The Denali
Grabber Bay
Palisade Crest
HeBron
Galadriel Feliagund
Dular's Peak
Olympus Mtns
Grasslands
Foothills
Draugen Pesta Cavalry
Forest of the Fey
Fraxinus Islands
Gulf of the Ashinerie
Tiberius River
Foothills
The Alpine
Ruined City of Elanesse
Calamity
Dagger Keep
Mt. Repose
Convington
Saint Seton
Hallie Point
Knight's Lament
Great Crevice
Silverstone
Lake Lorali
Emerald Sea
The Western Coast
The South Denali
Hills
Farmland
Itarilde Forest (Deep)
Hammer
Fayette
The Alpine
Farmland
Merchant's Way
Farmland
Ordenskyr
Starr
River 45,000 Altheros Army
Havendale
Esterling
Pantera River
Southern
Pantera
River
Merchant's Way
Spiral Islands
The Three Sisters
Altheros
Way
Luthien Forest (Wild)
The Sea of the Marble Wyvern
Alatariel Forest (Evil)
River
Mainland
Post Shift

CHAPTER NINE

Lost in a Shift

Shift: The strange phenomenon triggered when the demon Nightshade used the Ak-Séregon Stone to forge a pathway through universes from Aster to the Svartalfheim. Unlike the corridor from Aster to the Alfheim, this pathway was an unstable breach in time and space. It was impossible to know how many worlds the corridor touched... or how many universes it found as it wound its way to the home world of the dark elves. But one constant remained despite those uncertainties. For those caught in a shift, time became an unreliable master. It could run faster or slower, forge through both the past and the future, or erase someone's existence altogether. Unfortunates caught in a shift are lost like no others.

Time Walkers: A tribe of females originating from the island of Vesperia located in the Sea of the Marble Wyvern. Unique to the world's inhabitants, time walkers can move forward through time at will. They can walk the timeline a few moments in front of the present. To the outside observer, this creates a shadow effect. When a time walker uses her ability, she leaves a silhouette in the present as she moves a few moments into the future. As she travels though the timeline, she sees and senses how the universe has moved, is moving, and will move in an instant. She sees the past, present, and future at the same time.

The Shift and the Time Walker: The unstable breech in time and space caused by the Ak-Séregon Stone corridor will increase exponentially if a time walker is caught in a shift. This will cause world altering consequences up and down the corridor, particularly at the corridor's point of origin. An interesting dilemma since only a time walker in the corridor can stop the shifts.

-The Book of the Unveiled

Navy Master at Arms Yury Petrenko sat in the dirt and looked at the amputated arm of Cincinnatus as it twitched, though the twitching wasn't as fast or as erratic as a few short moments ago. He shook his head as he considered the deaths of the admiral and the sorcerer. He was stunned — two invincible characters in his world of the Navy, ships, and the sea, gone in an instant.

"Come, we must go," the time walker said as she stood. "That thing isn't dead, only eating. It'll be back."

Yury grimaced at the thought of who it was eating, then diverted his mind away from that to study the time walker. She was unlike anyone he'd ever seen. He was tall for his race, almost thirteen feet. But at ten feet, she was as tall as any Draugen Pesta female. But unlike the females of his race, she was slight and petite, far from the huskiness one expected of one with her height. But he saw surprising strength in her slim body from the way she had fought the great tentacled beast and the ease by which she threw him out of the way of that danger. She reminded Yury of the willow tree which, though bending with the wind, rarely ever broke.

Her head, uncovered from the hood of the heavy dark green cloak she wore, was slightly elongated, though this unusual aspect of her appearance made her even more beautiful. She had long, silky white hair with dark auburn stripes starting at the temple and moving to the back of her head. The auburn-colored hair was braided and fell down her back, intermixed with the flowing sea of her white hair. Her ears were shaped like an elf, and her sky-blue eyes similarly so, though the irises looked more like that of a cat. Her skin had a slight amber tinge to it.

Perhaps the most unusual feature of the time walker, however, were the two small horns that came out of her forehead at the hairline, turned back and traced the curvature of her head. The symmetry of her horns and head were in perfect balance.

Yury gawked. He looked at the time walker's hands to confirm his suspicions. They ended with talons instead of fingernails.

"You're dragon born!" he exclaimed.

The time walker nodded. "As are my sisters. Now come, before that creature discovers you're a much larger food source than your two companions," she said as she pulled the deep hood of her cloak back over her head and turned to walk away. She didn't notice Yury's flinch at the mention of his loss.

Yury and the time walker walked side by side over the barren landscape. Here and there stands of trees broke the monotonous scenery. The time walker explained those represented pools of fresh water. She further mentioned they were always dangerous to visit, but less so during the night. From her experience there were fewer predators after dark, in direct contrast to their home world.

They exchanged little information or pleasantries during the first hour of their traveling together. She was a mystery to Yury – and a bit intimidating. But in the end Yury's curiosity overcame his nervousness.

"The Admiral called you a time walker," he said.

"She was well educated," the time walker replied. "Few know of our existence."

Yury threw caution to the wind. He grabbed her arm and turned her to face him. He pushed the cowl back so he could study her face. The sky-blue eyes bore into him, but she didn't appear to take offense.

"She valued you," Yury said. "You're the reason she's dead, her and Cincinnatus! We ran to protect you from that... that creature... on her orders!"

For the first time her facade broke. Her eyes softened, and she looked away. "For which I'm grateful. I wouldn't have chosen that death for your friends. Nor did I ask for their sacrifice."

The time walker's response angered Yury. His hands rolled into hard-as-rock fists and his eyes reflected his fury.

The time walker put her soft hands over his fists. Her touch suddenly drained away his anger. She looked deep into Yury's eyes. "You misunderstand," she said. "While I value my life, I don't hold it above others. But it's done and all I can do now is... live. Is that not what they wanted?"

Yury sighed and nodded. "Yes, though I don't know why you're so important they would die to save you." Yury looked back towards the place of the deadly encounter. "But I trust my Admiral, so I'll continue to follow her orders and strive to keep you safe. My name is Yury Petrenko and I'm at your service."

"I'm called Eirwen," the time walker replied, distracted as she looked around for any hidden dangers beneath the earth. "It means 'snow' in the language of my people."

"Snow... ah, I understand. It's because your hair's so white. Right?" Yury said.

Eirwen looked at her traveling companion. "My hair?" she questioned. Then she shook her head. "No, nothing like that. Whatever gave you that idea?"

Yury frowned. "Well, your hair..." he said before he stopped himself. "Okay, if not your hair, then what? Why name you after snow?"

"I had a twin sister named Aethelind, which means 'maiden' in our language," Eirwen replied. "We were born on the twenty-seventh day of a great blizzard. Mother considered us her little snow maidens, hence the names."

Eirwen suddenly put an arm in front of Yury to stop him. "Don't move. See those faint markings in the dirt?" she said as she pointed to several visible track marks. "The dirt's disturbed and not packed. Impossible to spot in the dark."

"A tentacle creature?"

Eirwen nodded. "Likely so. Now stay still."

Yury looked at Eirwen but only saw a shadow where she had just been. From the shadow an elongated version of herself stretched out ten feet ahead. Tentacles exploded out of the ground, but only clutched at an empty silhouette, for Eirwen was standing once again at Yury's side. "Danger," she said.

"You just walked in time, didn't you?" he asked, though it was more a statement of fact than a question.

Eirwen nodded. "Only a few moments," she responded while watching the tentacles settle back into the earth, no doubt frustrated it had made the effort for nothing. "We should go around unless you intend to kill it."

Yury drew back and frowned. "Kill it?" he retorted. "No! I don't want to kill it! Or let it kill me. But back to your time walking... well, how does that work? Your time walking, that is. I only saw a shadow of you next to me. That and the extended, drawn out blur of you until your real self was standing next to me again."

"The reason you observed a shadow is that you can't see forward in time," Eirwen explained. "What you're seeing is an impression of myself as I walked the timeline."

Yury thought about that. It made sense.

"As you yourself move through the timeline at normal speed," Eirwen continued, "you perceive me as I was when I was, in fact, there. But I wasn't... there... at that moment..."

Yury shook his head. *Maybe I don't understand it,"* he thought to himself.

"... because I'm still moving forward along the timeline. When you see me I'm a few moments in the future. It's very complicated. My father understands it much more thoroughly then I. It's his magic I inherited."

"Your father's a sorcerer?" Yury asked.

"Of course," answered Eirwen. "Aren't all dragons?"

Yury paused as he considered. He had graduated near the top of his class at the Academy in Saint Petersburg, considered the premiere university in Draugen Pesta, and never a word about time walkers or their history. *"Then again,"* Yury thought, *"It's hard to learn about something I doubt my teachers knew themselves."* Yury had another thought. "Can you go back into time," he asked.

"I was wondering how long it'd take for you to get around to asking that question. I can... but I never will. It's too dangerous." It appeared Yury accepted her answer, so she decided not to offer additional information.

"Where's your home?" Yury queried, seeking to turn attention away from the discussion about time. For him it was unstable ground intellectually, though he surmised the answer to his latest question even as he asked it. She wouldn't go back because the risk of changing the present, or future, was too great.

Eirwen looked up at Yury. She had warmed up to the unpretentious way he viewed things. He was taller than her father in his human form, though not overly so. But unlike her father, and many of the dragon males she had known over the years, Yury wasn't arrogant or condescending. His eyes were warmhearted, which was a far cry from the coldness in her father's reptilian eyes. His smile, which came often even here in the most terrible of circumstances, made her want to smile back. Eirwen had few reasons to smile since being caught up in a freak storm several days ago, and each was precious.

"The Sea of the Marble Wyvern is familiar to you?" Eirwen asked her companion.

Yury nodded. "It's on our southern border," he answered. "Well, in truth, it IS our southern border. But we keep a healthy distance from its shores. There are things living under those waters that are deadly and hard to kill."

"Yes," Eirwen agreed. "Even more than you could ever imagine. There's no sailing on those waters, unless you have a death wish. My people live on a large island in about the center of that sea. We call it Vesperia which means Island of the Leviathan."

"I'm starting to understand why your people are so mysterious and rare," Yury observed. "It appears to be impossible to get either on or off your island. Except for dragons," he corrected. "You know, because dragons can fly."

"Why yes, so they can," Eirwen replied with just a tad of sarcasm.

Yury's face turned bright crimson as he turned away in embarrassment. *I must sound like a school child,* he thought to himself. "How long have you been stranded here?" he asked.

"A few days. Or an eternity," Eirwen replied as she scanned the horizon. "Take your pick."

Yury heard a slight tremor of hopelessness in her voice. "We'll find a way back." he said, wishing to give her reassurance. Yury knew from personal experience how it felt to be lost. Even though he'd found a new life on InnisRos, every day brought the heartache he felt being away from Draugen Pesta.

Eirwen sighed. "I'm sorry. I don't mean to sound so... so despondent."

"It's okay," Yury said. He hoped to bolster her spirits. He understood that it's useless to try and predict how the circumstance of life would unfold – for good or bad. Who's to say the strange fog that brought him and Eirwen here wouldn't reappear to take the two of them back. "We'll find the fog again."

"So, a fog brought you here also," Eirwen expressed with interest. "Dry and thick fog instead of wet?"

Yury nodded. "And a waterspout with blue lightning."

"Waterspout?"

"We were at sea when it happened," Yury replied. "I didn't think we'd survive."

Eirwen stared off into space. "My sister didn't," she murmured.

"I'm so sorry, Eirwen!" Yury exclaimed. "What happened?"

The time walker sat on a nearby rock and wiped moisture from her brow with the sleeve of her cloak. The memory of what happened to her sister caused Eirwen to break out in a cold sweat and made her sick to her stomach. She took several deep breaths to fight back the nausea.

Yury kneeled in front of her as he gripped the hilt of his sword. Its familiarity gave him the strength he needed to forget his own pain and concentrate on Eirwen's. "Sometimes it's best to talk about the bad things in life. It helps to pass part of the pain to another." Yury reached over and covered her hands with his. "Tell me," he encouraged. "Let me have some of your pain."

"It's not yours to take," Eirwen said. The tone of her voice was heartbreaking. "But very well."

Yury waited as his new companion composed herself. He waited as she locked her feelings away long enough to tell her tale.

"My sister and I are... were twins," Eirwen began. "Twins are very rare on Vesperia, and while there were those who rejoiced in our birth, more saw us as an evil omen. If not for our father's brutal intercession, I fear we might have died then and there. Several of the more radical elements of my people who defied his wishes were put to death. Dragon fire is a terrible thing." Eirwen shook her head. "I can't imagine... Don't get me wrong, Yury. Many dragons are gentle souls, just not my father. He protected Aethelind and me only because we were his prodigy... his property. In essence, we were nothing but a part of his treasure hoard." Eirwen took a deep breath. "When he understood we'd continue to be in jeopardy because of the superstitions of my people, he decided to take us away from our mother and from Vesperia. He gave us to strangers to be raised — strangers only motivated by the gold my father provided."

Yury shook his head. "That's horrible! No child should be treated so!"

Eirwen smiled through fresh tears. "It wasn't that bad. I still had my sister, and the people who took us in were well-to-do. We wanted for nothing. For twenty years we grew and flourished... in a way. Aethelind and I were close, but this brought us even closer."

Eirwen stopped talking as more tears rolled down her cheeks. Yury waited patiently while she collected herself. "My mother... my mother had no one to comfort or help her after we left. When my father decided we were old enough to fend for ourselves, he returned us to Vesperia, whereupon we learned mother had died only a year after we left." Eirwen looked at Yury with fury in her eyes. "She lived with the loneliness for as long as she could. She had no one, Yury! No one! Her friends deserted her because of us and those that father killed to keep us safe. And father! He could've helped. But would he? No! He was too obsessed with himself to even recognize the pain she suffered," Eirwen said as she angrily shook her head. "When he was around, that is."

The time walker picked up a stone laying at her feet and threw it as far as she could. "I'm dragon born! As was my mother and her mother before her. And while our dragon fathers have other... itineraries... none have ever shown such a lack of respect and caring for their mates as my father did for my mother!"

Eirwen took several deep breaths to calm herself. Her tears had dried on her cheeks unmolested, for she never tried to wipe them away. When she continued her story, her voice started out whisper quiet. "Mother hung on for as long as she could. When she had reached her limit... when the depths of her loneliness became unbearable... she swam out to sea and disappeared. At least that's what they told Aethelind and me. Whether she drowned or was taken by one of the many beasts that live in the waters, no one knew or cared enough to find out. My sister and I were still unwelcome, so no answers to our questions were forthcoming. Only our father's reputation kept their hatred at bay. We left for the sparsely populated mountains soon after. We wanted to leave the island altogether, only we didn't know how that would be possible without asking father to fly us away."

Yury's heart went out to the time walker. She had suffered and conquered many emotional hurdles in her life. But her story was far from finished. Her greatest tragedy, the death of her sister, still remained to be told.

Eirwen continued her narrative. "Aethelind and I left our village and traveled to the southern part of the island. The mountain range that overlooked the sea is almost completely deserted, its heights frozen and barren with little to sustain life. But we had brought enough provisions to keep us well feed for a month, so our only immediate need was adequate shelter. But the mountains are riddled with caves, so that wasn't a serious problem either."

Eirwen hesitated as she remembered. "As it turned out, the mountain range wasn't as uninhabited as we were led to believe. There we found our greatest friend and mentor, a weredragon, and our most terrifying adversary, the Bun Manchi – a fur-covered man-like creature at least fifteen feet tall with fangs and talons that can rip apart even a dragon's scales. They're very hard to kill."

"Weredragon? Bun Manchi?" Yury asked. "I've never heard of such creatures."

Eirwen nodded. "Not surprising. Both are solitary and inhabit only mountains. My father is a true dragon. He can use magic to turn himself into a human, elf, or even a dwarf should he so wish. Weredragons, however, while still considered dragons, only take the form of a female elf. She uses no magic to do this because the elf part is half of who she is. In all other respects she's a dragon, except she doesn't keep hoards of treasure. To them, knowledge is treasure, and their inquisitive nature is their true magic. Weredragons are rare and, as I've already mentioned, prefer isolation."

"Then she wasn't too happy to see you," Yury remarked.

"Quite the contrary." Eirwen responded with a smile. "She accepted us well enough. Her name was Annabelinda, and she had a gentle soul. I always thought the world suffered because of her decision to seclude herself in those mountains."

"So, you found Annabelinda in the mountains and she gave you a place to stay."

Eirwen shook her head. But as she reminisced about that time, she smiled in the comfort it offered. "No... well, yes to the second part. She found us, shivering and huddled together in a small cave. We forgot to bring flint and steel to start a fire. Being dragon born doesn't mean we have the fire breath. I'd have laughed at our ignorance if it hadn't been so damn cold. We're lucky the Bun Manchi didn't find us first. That would have ended us."

"Then perhaps fate turned around for you that day," Yury observed. "You lost one mother but found another."

Eirwen nodded. "My sister and I didn't see it at first, but you're right. Annabelinda turned out to be the mother we missed all those years. But at first it was awkward. She'd been alone for the better part of her life and didn't know what to do with us. For our part, we still harbored ill feelings towards dragons because of our father. We understood we needed her help, but we didn't trust her."

"But you worked it out."

"We did," the time walker replied. "Annabelinda was extremely tolerant and uncomplaining. Aethelind and I came to accept her... and then to love her. She responded in kind with love of her own."

"How long did you live with Annabelinda?" Yury prompted.

Eirwen shrugged her shoulders. "Who reckons time in the mountains when each day is filled with tracking and killing food, lessons not only about magic and time but also about the practical things in life such as sewing clothes, dressing and cooking our kills, how to read weather and the stars, and so much more. But it was far from a normal education. She also taught us how to defend ourselves. The threat of the Bun Manchi was always there. We learned how to use swords, knives, clubs, and staffs."

Eirwen's eyes became unfocused as she drifted off into her memories. Yury waited. He recognized the narrative of her life must be voiced at her own pace. He had experienced much the same thing after leaving Draugen Pesta and his family. The introspection that comes with remembrance is impossible to resist until one accepts the pain of being alone. Eirwen was still coping with that acceptance.

Eirwen looked at Yury, but this time she was truly seeing him. "Forgive me, Yury. My thoughts keep returning to..."

"To that which was," Yury said as he squeezed her hand. "It's nothing to apologize for. And it's normal. I'd be concerned if you weren't experiencing such... shall we say flashbacks? In my experience if you weren't, you'd either be as hard and cold as iron, or the trauma would have broken you. You're neither broken or hard and cold."

"You have a kind soul," Eirwen said as she smiled. "To answer your question, I think ten years. Yes, that seems right." She reached over and gave Yury a quick peck on the cheek.

Yury looked at his feet as his face turned red.

"That's so adorable," Eirwen said.

Eirwen's sudden change in disposition encouraged Yury, though he keenly felt embarrassment resulting from the kiss. He didn't have a clue why that was. He liked females and they liked him. He decided to change the subject.

"What happened to Annabelinda and your sister?" he asked.

The smile drained from Eirwen's face. The memory, which she held as hers and hers alone, brought her pain. But Eirwen thought it would be therapeutic to talk about it to the right person, and that was Yury.

"I guess Annabelinda still lives in the mountains," Eirwen speculated. "Aethelind and I were out hunting mountain goat for breakfast. It was very early, still dark, when an unusual fog poured down the side of a mountain and caught us unawares. The first we saw of it was when a terrible bolt of blue lightning lit up the sky. This was followed by the boom and rumble of thunder greater than either of us had ever experienced. It was so strong the vibration dislodged several boulders above us. Then something else caught our attention. The startled roar of a Bun Manchi. He'd been tracking us while we were hunting the mountain goat and we didn't even know it." Eirwen smiled. "The Bun Manchi are ferocious predators, but sudden loud noises frighten them. It bolted right into the fog which was quickly surrounding us. Aethelind thought it might be best to stay still since the Bun Manchi was running away. Neither one of us wanted a chance meeting in the fog should the creature regain its senses and return. But when the fog dissipated, we were no longer on our mountain. We were no longer on Aster."

"You were here," Yury remarked. "Confused and afraid."

"No, not afraid," Eirwen replied. "There's little doubt we were off-balanced and confused. But we weren't afraid... at least not then. To us, it was a situation that needed exploring... a problem for rational thinking. It wasn't a reason to panic. In truth, we didn't know enough to be afraid."

"What happened next," Yury prompted.

"We heard a terrible scream coming from the other side of a small hill. We rushed up the hill to see what was happening and if we could help." Eirwen paused and shook her head as she remembered what she had seen. "The Bun Manchi was being torn apart by tentacles. Its scream was so... pathetic... so... heart-wrenching. Even if we had wanted, there was nothing we could've done for that poor creature. Oh, I know the Bun Manchi are evil, but at that point in time both of us felt sorry for it. It was over in seconds and there remained no trace of the life and death struggle between the Bun Manchi and the tentacled creature. It was as if its life had never existed, never mattered, to the universe." Eirwen looked at Yury. "Could that be true? Could it be that we toil and suffer for nothing? That the universe created us at random with no purpose, no... no meaning? Just something that sprang up from the ooze and muck of antiquity, learned to walk, to think, to kill, to die?"

Yury shook his head. "You don't believe that, do you?" he challenged. "Surely the existence of the gods prove otherwise."

Eirwen snorted. "Are the gods perfect? Or must they also live within the perimeters set by the universe? No, my friend, the gods are the same as us except they live in a better neighborhood."

"Okay, let's say for the sake of argument that what you say is true," Yury acknowledged. "So, what?"

"So, what?!" Eirwen retorted. "So, what?! It's everything!"

Yury waited. He hoped Eirwen would calm down before countering. After a few moments of silence, he said, "Our lives are ours and ours only. Even if our existence is nothing but a random event, as you surmise, it is still ours to decide how we wish to live it. We decide how we effect those we've touched." Yury shook his head.

"The universe doesn't care about our existence. Why should it? We're nothing but inconsequential specks on an inconsequential world. But what more would you have it do? It gives us a chance to live… but it's up to us to take advantage of that opportunity. Eirwen, WE decide our fate, not the universe."

Eirwen didn't reply, and Yury decided he wouldn't push her.

"What happened to your sister?"

Eirwen sighed and looked at the ground. "Not two hours later we were attacked by the tentacles. Even though we took precautions after what we saw with the Bun Manchi, we still didn't recognize the signs. Aethelind…" Eirwen's voice broke. "Aethelind was faster than me in recognizing the danger. She pushed me out of the way. She screamed. She was dead by the time I got back to help."

"I'm sorry," Yury said after a few moments of silence.

"I went into a rage," Eirwen responded. "I didn't stop until I had cut every tentacle."

"You were lucky."

"I didn't care," Eirwen grunted. "At the time death held no sway over me. I welcomed it. I…" Eirwen stiffened and cried out. "No!"

Yury grabbed her as she toppled over. He kneeled with her in his lap and held her tightly as she went into convulsions. Spittle flew out of her mouth and her breathing became short and labored. Yury touched her neck for a pulse and found her heart racing – beating so hard he worried it would wear out… or explode.

As Yury held Eirwen, he tried to wipe the sweat off her brow, but her head jerked far too erratically for that and he feared he'd cause damage if he tried to restrained it. As he gazed into her eyes, telling her it would be okay, out of the corner of his eyes he noticed subtle changes occurring all around. He looked up into a world that had gone mad. Day became night and night became day. Dirt changed to water and back again. Mountains sprang up and then collapsed. Suns raced across the sky during the day and moons did the same during the night. Storms came and went. Amazing and unimaginable creatures passed by. Then a shaft of light, or its complete absence, appeared. It ran through all things, including time. Though Yury and Eirwen had been insulated against the madness of the world, the strange shaft took notice and moved towards them. Yury clutched at Eirwen, his only anchor, and watched as several tentative streams from the shaft examined them. Yury heard a scream in his head and the streams from the shaft, as well as the shaft itself, disappeared.

Eirwen became still and the world stabilized. Yury continued to hold her tightly as he looked around for answers. Then he saw deliverance in the form of a familiar fog that dropped a few hundred feet in front. He picked Eirwen up and raced towards it, knowing it was their only escape. "Stay open!" he screamed as he ran. "Stay open!"

It did.

Kyleigh tumbled through time and space. The shard and her sentient sword, *Ah-RahnVakha*, glowed as they struggled to keep the Alfheim queen alive. The shard extended strands into her heart to keep it beating while the sword provided an energy bubble which surrounded her entire body. The enclosure of light she was traveling flashed and her unconscious form was now in a dark and foreboding corridor hurtling through the void. As she moved through the corridor, light exploded outward into fragmented pieces and then bent back into themselves. Then the black corridor abruptly broke into pieces and exposed Kyleigh to the gravitational storm of a massive black hole. She was caught in its embrace. The shard and sword, after a long and difficult struggle, broke the gravitational forces of the black hole by orbiting their mistress around the distant edge of the event horizon. They used the speed generated by this maneuver to hurl Kyleigh away at a velocity even the two relics couldn't imagine.

The Alfheim queen traversed several universes as her speed continued to increase. Upon her passing, worlds wobbled and momentarily slowed their rotation before going back on track. As she continued her journey, the light of the worlds she passed elongated and became solid streaks crisscrossing the blackness. There were so many that they formed a barrier which encircled Kyleigh.

All light blinked out. In the oblivion that followed, and without a reference point, it was impossible to determine if Kyleigh was still moving. But it didn't matter, because speed only existed relative to a stationary point in time and space. The only salvation against the nothingness that encased the queen was the shard and *Ah-RahnVakha*. They continued to worked together to keep their mistress safe.

Slowly, deliberately, the relics brought Kyleigh back home. Through it all they had maintained a faint hold on their universe, so they knew the way. But such a long and arduous journey would require more power than they had available between them. They reached out to the emptiness which surrounded them, looking for and seizing every little fragment of energy they could find. What they didn't understand was that the entire journey had occurred deep within Kyleigh's own mind. They didn't know the void from which they drew came from the very darkest recesses of Kyleigh's subconscious. They didn't know the additional power they used came from Kyleigh's own memories.

At the Academy of Sorcery in Havendale, Amkissra saw what appeared to be a slight interference... a barely perceptible alteration in the magical globe she used to study the shifts occurring across Aster. At first, she didn't think it was anything other than a result of her lack of sleep. Then she noticed something about the globe that made little sense. The corridor was elongated as if it had moved farther away.

Amkissra spent the next two hours making calculations, all of which failed to satisfy her findings.

When she had finished, she sat back from her desk and poured a glass of wine. "Interesting," she said out loud. "The corridor must have shifted its place in the timeline." Amkrissa had a sudden thought. "Or did we?!"

Her eyes grew wider as she mentally connected all the dots. She stood. "Slingshot!" she shouted as she ran down the tower stairs. "We've not only shifted, but the whole damn world moved! Rathal needs to know! We must close the corridor before it's too late!"

Amkissra heard a rumbling as the stone stairs beneath her feet gave way.

Aster's slight celestial movement in response to the 'slingshot' triggered a massive earthquake on the ocean floor six hundred miles east of the Isile Silimaure. The giant wave that formed as a result climbed to five hundred feet as it rushed westward. In that part of the Ocean of the Heavens, it threatened little – except InnisRos.

The Isile Silimaure, built many centuries ago in a vain and unsuccessful attempt to keep InnisRos segregated from the rest of the world, finally served a purpose. When the gigantic wave encountered this immovable stone obstruction, much of its strength, and its power to destroy, was diminished.

Several naval vessels that had survived the dragon attack were patrolling the Sea of Dreams. Each crewman knew if the dragons were to return, there'd be no escape, but duty demanded that sacrifice if necessary. None, however, had prepared themselves for the wave that broke over the Isile Silimaure. Though reduced from its former height, its summit was still between two and three hundred feet. The ships could only signal a warning to Calmacil Clearing before being smothered by the wave as it passed.

The leadership at Calmacil Clearing took immediate action. They ordered all ships, including the *Freedom Wind* and those in the Santea Archipelago, to the leeward side of InnisRos. They weren't too concerned about the northeast side of the island because of the high cliffs along the shore. But the southern half of the island didn't have that luxury. The rich, fertile farmlands of the south would be damaged by the saltwater spill over. And Olberon, the island's only true naval base, was unprotected and vulnerable. Its shipyard and resupply docks would be difficult and expensive to replace.

No one was sure how the wave would affect Taranthi. The Bay of Sorrow, a rock-strewn body of water, might reduce the impact. Even though the capital city had been occupied by the dark elves who would suffer as a consequence, innocent city inhabitants would also be hurt or killed. No one at Calmacil Clearing wished to see that happen.

As the wave moved across the Sea of Dreams, its energy leached away. By the time it hit InnisRos, it was only one hundred and fifty feet high, significantly smaller than its greatest height. But those on the island watching it come in thought it was the end of the world.

If it hadn't been for the dark elf invasion, followed by the migration of the population to the north, the death toll would have reached tens of thousands in Olberon alone, and another twenty or thirty thousand in the lowlands of the south. Oberon and the smaller towns along the southern coast were destroyed when the wave crashed over them. It traveled a mile inland before it ran out of energy and pulled back into the sea, leaving in its wake destroyed trees, bits and pieces of buildings, lumber, seaweed, dead fish, and bodies of a few unfortunates.

Taranthi, protected as it was by the Bay of Sorrow and the high walls that surrounded it, escaped the worse the wave offered. But even still, the docks and warehouses outside the walls were destroyed. In one respect the wave accomplished some good, however. All the supplies stored over the last few days by the dark elves were ruined.

The citizens of Taranthi, along with their dark elf captors, watched from the battlements as the wave wrecked the portions of the city not protected by its huge walls before it rushed up the Maranwe river... flooding its banks and leaving more devastation inland. As soon as the wave passed, the dark elves surveyed the damage and collected the dead for cremation. They didn't care who they threw on the funeral pyre – dark elves, elves, humans, dwarves – nor did they care much for decorum. They treated the dead as they treated any other piece of rubbish. Under the stench of burning bodies and decomposing fish, hundreds of Taranthi's more able-bodied residents were rounded up and forced to begin the work of rebuilding the docks, warehouses and any other structures deemed necessary by their dark elf overseers.

Up north, a few of the eastern-most unprotected islands of the Santea Archipelago were overwhelmed. The pirates who occupied the islands paid a heavy price in both men and ships... and soon thereafter decided their position was no longer tenable. Boarding what few ships they had left, they retreated back to their home on The Rosemount, southeast of the Spiral Islands.

That evening, a peculiar glow could be seen to the northeast of InnisRos. By early morning's light, a huge gigantic cloud was visible. Too distant to be of concern, Feymelt Volcano, unprotected and immersed by the full fury of the wave, erupted in an explosion of magma and ash.

Strong surface earthquakes rattled the mainland. The north tower of the Academy of Sorcery in Havendale collapsed. The loss of life was minimal with one notable exception. Amkissra, along with the globe and all her research material, was buried in the rubble. Hour after hour the people of Havendale worked to clear the debris, each holding on to the fervent hope that the astronomer was still alive. As the hours passed, however, it became clear no one could have survived the collapse. When they did find her lifeless body, Rathal Arquen, overcome with grief, kneeled and cradled her close while rocking back and forth. He accepted no help or comfort and allowed no one to come close for several hours.

The entire Olympus Mountain range shook under the power of the earthquake. Passes that did not exist opened, while slides of rock and trees covered others. A miles-long crevice opened in the earth along the eastern foothills. The fracture swallowed the cursed, plague-ridden city of Ascension in a matter of minutes. It was as if Aster was ridding itself of an embarrassing blight.

Most of the mountain cities, Astoria being the most prominent, endured far more damage and casualties from the earthquakes than the cities on the plains. Even the Hammer, Aster's most impenetrable fortress, felt the power of the earthquakes. Several inch-wide cracks appeared throughout, prompting the fortress commander to declare an emergency.

Elanesse shuddered and screamed in pain as the earthquake moved through her foundation. A few of her buildings collapsed into the tunnels below, leaving ugly holes – wounds – on the 'skin' of the city. Underneath, corridor upon corridor caved in. On the surface, pieces of the earth grew up – stalagmites reaching towards the heavens as if they were hands raised in supplication to the gods. Elanesse, overcome by the hurt and humiliation of what she considered a rape upon her person, withdrew into her own mind.

On the northwestern shore, the citizens and visitors in the great coastal city of Palisades Crest watched in amazement as a volcano formed in the center of Grabber Bay. By evening it had grown to well over a thousand feet. By the next morning, three thousand. The lava flow that spewed from the summit provided a spectacular sight during the night as reds, oranges and yellows rolled down the volcano's sides. The ensuing steam as the lava hit the water covered the bottom third of the volcano. Its beauty surpassed any mountain or volcano recorded in recent history. And while it represented potential danger, the populace readily accepted it and, in some cases, took pride in it. It was officially named 'Elysium on the Bay', and all the maps depicting the bay were changed accordingly. But other than a slight increase in water temperature and higher than normal humidity levels, little else changed for the residents of Palisades Crest and the surrounding area, though ships arriving and leaving the port city now needed to use added caution as they navigated around the new volcano.

If Amkissra had lived, she'd have told Rathal that this is only the start of the dangers awaiting them if the corridor between Aster and the Svartalfheim wasn't closed. She'd have told him this latest shift was small compared to what lay in store. She'd have told him it might already be too late.

THE FOURTH INTERREGNUM

$\mathfrak{F}$resh off the experience of the attack from the forest, Liosh approached the mountains cautiously. He didn't want to be surprised again. The black fliers, or whatever they were called on this world, were cunning and brutal. Though he had harbored doubts regarding their motivation when they attacked the ship, there was no question about the black flier's intentions when it ambushed him. He could see the evil in its eyes. Though surprised by the flier's resistance to his lightning bolt, its ineffectiveness was only of moderate concern. Liosh had other means of attack and defense at his disposal.

The mountains Liosh advanced upon were magnificent, particularly the tallest, snow-capped mountain on the western edge of the range. It towered above the other mountains like a king sitting upon his throne overlooking his subjects. The three mountains at its base, though not as high as the king, also towered above the others. Liosh thought of them as the king's personal bodyguard, ready to do battle in defense of their liege.

Suddenly the entire mountain range moved up and down before moving from side to side. It was only for a few short seconds, but the resulting cloud of dust and dirt rising across the entire mountain landscape told the truth of what had happened. Earthquake! Every world had them from time to time, and Liosh knew them well. As the Sky Emperor floated above and watched the dust cloud, he could only imagine the damage on the ground. *"Will you rally your people, king?"* he said to himself. *"Or did I just witness your assassination?"* Liosh always had the heart of the bard in him.

Liosh retracted his great tentacles to better blend in with the other clouds in the sky. He wanted to observe without exposing his presence. With all thoughts of the black fliers temporarily forgotten, the Sky Emperor waited in anticipation for the dust cloud to dissipate. The beautiful mountains fascinated him, and he was determined to find out what had befallen them.

After a few minutes the dust cloud thinned enough for Liosh to see how the king and his minions fared. Everything looked normal, though there appeared to be fresh landslides here and there. Off in the distance to the southeast he noticed a great crack in the ground. Farther east and past a large forest and lake, a new mountain range had grown before his eyes. It was small, and the mountains didn't grow more than a couple thousand feet before settling down, but it was fascinating to watch.

As Liosh approached the center of the king's mountain range, he once again spied the black fliers. They were circling something large on the ground. It was a city, though it looked to be ruined. Liosh suspected what would happen next. The black fliers released their terrible breath weapon. They scorched the forest surrounding the city, encircling it with burning trees, bushes, and grass. Liosh watched as the black fliers trapped the city inhabitants with an impenetrable barrier of deadly flame and smoke. The four fliers then flew over the city and began what looked like a grid patterned search. Without hesitation, the Sky Emperor moved towards the city to engage the black fliers. Perhaps there was still time to save whoever they sought from the malice of the black fliers.

CHAPTER TEN

The Mainland

"I'm tired," the old man pleaded. "So tired. I've labored for decades to bring good to the world. But now I'm alone. My wife's dead and my daughter has left to pursue her own ambition. Let me die."

The Angel of Death, surprised by the approach of one who's time to die had yet to come, shook its head. "You've wasted your time finding me, old man," it said. "The world of the living still has a claim on you. It's out of my hands."

"What claim? What would life have me do?" the old man replied. "I'm begging you! Let me die! I have nothing left to offer."

The Angel of Death sadly shook its head and turned its back on the old man. It heard no final plea as it walked away, but stopped after just a few steps. There was something about the old man it couldn't place a finger on. Something familiar. The Angel of Death turned and saw that the old man hadn't moved.

"Something so recognizable," it thought. Memories of a past life suddenly flooded back.

"Father?" the Angel of Death whispered as it returned to the old man. The words barely came out.

"Yes, my daughter," the old man replied as he took the skeletal hand of the stunned supernatural being and placed it over his own heart. "And I love you."

The Angel of Death knew it was true. She kneeled before her father, bowed her head, and accepted his love. When she looked back up, her face, her entire body, had been transformed from the ugliness of death to the shining beauty of life. The Angel of Death understood for the first time the true meaning of her nature. Death wasn't the end of life for mortals, but a new beginning... and she was their escort.

The Angel of Death rose and looked at her new hands... felt her new face... and took a deep breath to smell the aroma of life. She was still the Angel of

Death, but her father's love had caused a metamorphosis. Now her duty will be forever tempered with love and compassion.

The Angel of Death looked at her father and smiled for the first time in her current incarnation. She kissed her father on the forehead. As she did so, she realized life had relinquished its claim. Her father had fulfilled his destiny.

The Angel of Death put her arm around the old man, "Come, walk with me. I have an amazing place to show you!"

-The Book of the Unveiled

"**A**pproach!" Lord Ternborg didn't bother to look up as he shouted to the figure standing at the entrance of his command tent. The Draugen Pesta king was bent over a table studying a map. He was a figure of calm in a bustle of activity, both inside and outside his tent, caused by the chaos that had followed the earthquake.

"This was supposed to be so damned easy," Lord Ternborg said to himself as he reviewed the progress his forces were making. In the northern outskirts of the Forest of the Fey his army was preparing to sweep through it. A contingent of his own cavalry was riding down the western side of the forest to cover his right flank. At last report the Madeiran army was moving down the Alpine while the HeBron army was progressing south along the eastern side of Lake Lorali. There had been little to no resistance. But that was before the earthquake. His scouts now reported smoke coming from the last known position of the Madeiran army. Though there had been several brief garbled communications with them, the Draugen Pesta king couldn't be sure of their status. As for Hebron, there had been no word since the earthquake.

Lord Ternborg continued to stare at the map, but he wasn't seeing it. Too many possibilities... too many potential problems... kept running through his mind. A commander needed a three-hundred-and-sixty-degree view of the battlefield, and right now he didn't have that.

He sensed a presence next to him and remembered someone had asked his permission to report. He looked up and spied a young and bedraggled HeBron soldier who looked as if she'd been trampled on by a herd of horses. She couldn't have been any older than fourteen. The insignia on her shoulder showed she was part of the HeBron messenger service.

"My god, girl, take a seat," he exclaimed as he steadied the soldier and led her to a human-sized chair. "Konnie! Bring water!" he bellowed to his second-in-command, Major Konstantin Timoshenko.

The human female gratefully took the proffered chair and drank deeply, handing the empty silver cup back to Major Timoshenko after wiping water from her chin with her sleeve. She didn't look up, just sat in the chair while she caught her breath.

"Take your time," Lord Ternborg said. "Konnie, please have the cooks prepare a hot meal for our friend here."

"Thank you, my lord," the girl said. "Would you please take care of my horse? I rode her hard getting here."

Lord Ternborg snapped his fingers, and a guard left the tent.

"What's your name, soldier?" Lord Ternborg asked.

"Vernie... ah... Veronica, my lord. Veronica Shaw."

"Okay, Miss Shaw," Lord Ternborg said. "Don't be afraid. I need you to report. How's it going with the Hebron army?"

"A disaster, my lord," the girl said. There was no panic or fear in her eyes. For all her youth, the girl was handling this remarkably well. "When the earthquake came it opened up great cracks in the ground right underneath the army. Most were lost in those first few seconds, including our commanders. The rest moments later as more cracks filled the ground."

"My people?" Lord Ternborg asked, fearing the worse for his warriors that had been traveling with the Hebron army.

Veronica Shaw shook her head. "I'm sorry, my lord. Gone like the others."

Lord Ternborg winced, then found his own chair. Not only the HeBron army but a hundred of his own warriors... dead. Major Timoshenko poured a cup of wine and handed it over to his king.

"Thanks, Konnie."

Major Timoshenko nodded. "Viktor, we should send a couple squads just in case," he counseled.

Lord Ternborg nodded. "See to it after we're done here." He returned his attention to the HeBron soldier. "Please go on, Miss Shaw."

"Mountains grew up out of the ground," Veronica Shaw continued.

"Mountains?" Major Timoshenko said.

Veronica Shaw's head bobbed, and her eyes widened as she looked between the two Draugen Pesta leaders questioning her. "My Lords, I've seen nothing like it before! First the ground opened and swallowed everyone. Everyone! Then... then a few moments later mountains came up out of the crevice and the ground all around. Some mountains even came out of the lake!"

Lord Ternborg looked at Major Timoshenko. "How could we miss seeing mountains?"

"Begging your pardon, my lord," Veronica Shaw interrupted tentatively for fear of angering the two giants.

"Speak freely, Miss Shaw," Lord Ternborg reassured her.

"These mountains aren't tall like those of the Olympus. The tallest is maybe a couple thousand feet. Since you're in the forest I can see how they might be missed."

Lord Ternborg nodded. "Good point."

"If you'll excuse me, Viktor, I've a question for Miss Shaw," Major Timoshenko said.

"My Lord?"

Major Timoshenko took a chair next to Lord Ternborg and leaned in towards the HeBron soldier. "How did you escape your own death?"

At first Veronica Shaw looked confused. Then her eyes widened. "Oh, I forgot," she replied as she rummaged through her tunic for the message scroll. "I've a written dispatch to Lord Ternborg from general... general... funny, I can't remember his name. Ah, here it is." Veronica Shaw presented the rolled scroll to the Draugen Pesta king. "I was on my way here when the earthquake happened. This saved me."

Lord Ternborg nodded as he took the scroll and unrolled it.

A cook delivered Veronica Shaw's meal and placed it on a human-size table at the other end of the command tent. The young messenger looked at it eagerly but kept her seat and waited for her dismissal.

Major Timoshenko placed a hand on her shoulder. "It's all right, child. Eat. Then rest. We'll call for you if we need you."

The human girl nodded, got up and started to bolt towards the food before she stopped, turned, and saluted. Major Timoshenko returned it and watched as she rushed to the table and began to devour her meal. The cooks had made the plate Draugen Pesta portion size, but it looked like Veronica Shaw was trying to get it all down. Major Timoshenko smiled before returning his attention to his king.

"Viktor?"

Lord Ternborg had read the scroll and was thinking about its content. He didn't hear Major Timoshenko.

"Viktor?" Major Timoshenko tried again.

"Huh? Oh, sorry, Konnie," Lord Ternborg said as he handed the scroll over to his second-in-command. "Here, see for yourself."

Major Timoshenko took the proffered scroll and opened it:

My Lord Ternborg,

Salutations!

About an hour before I wrote this message, my forward scouts reported a strange fog bank which appeared without warning a mile ahead of my position east of Lake Lorali. Perhaps ill-advised, advanced units of our Spearhead Division were ordered by the on-site commander to keep pushing forward into the fog. The fog dissipated as quickly as it materialized, taking with it all one thousand warriors.

I fear this may be a magical trap developed by the sorcerers of Havendale. I will halt my march while I await your consideration of these facts and subsequent orders.

General Klaus Mueller

"Do you think it's magic as the General inferred?" Major Timoshenko asked.

Lord Ternborg stroked his beard. "I don't know," he said. "Our battle sorcerers can't do anything close to that, and I doubt the Riders having anyone that skilled. As for Havendale, your guess is as good as mine. Was this fog connected to the earthquake that destroyed the HeBron army? And who's to say whether it will happen again. Think of it, thousands of lives snuffed out in a matter of minutes if Miss Shaw's depiction is correct. The heavens help us if..."

"Permission to enter, Lord Ternborg," a guard called out from outside the command tent.

Major Ternborg looked at Major Timoshenko. "What now," he said. Then, "Enter!"

One of Lord Ternborg's elite guards escorted a human to the Draugen Pesta king. He wore a patch on his right shoulder identifying him as Madeiran. The human stood at attention and snapped a smart salute which Lord Ternborg returned.

"At ease," Major Timoshenko commanded. "Report."

The Madeiran nodded. "My Lord, General Darcy sends his respects and has ordered me to inform you we've made contact with units of the Riders of the Elderdale."

Lord Ternborg wasn't surprise by this information. The Alpine is guarded by the Riders and wouldn't be handed over to Madeira without a fight. "How strong has the pushback been?" he asked.

"So far just a few small units of raiders hitting at us on our flanks," the Madeiran responded. "More of an annoyance than anything else. But the general felt you should know."

Lord Ternborg nodded. "Any sign of a stronger force?"

"No, my lord."

"Is the general still moving down the Alpine?" Major Timoshenko inquired.

The Madeiran looked perplexed. "Of course!" he said as he puffed out his chest. "The Riders can't stop us. They're nothing but old knights and farmers. They might be great for hunting and stopping bandits... but our Army? Don't you worry, my lord."

"That's not how your late General Ujarak saw the Riders," Major Timoshenko observed.

"It's how General Darcy sees them," the Madeiran replied confidently, as if the matter had been settled.

Lord Ternborg looked over at the HeBron messenger. She had eaten and was fast asleep in a chair. "There's food over there on the table," Lord Ternborg said. "Go eat and rest. I'll have new orders for your general soon."

The Madeiran nodded and walked away.

"SOLDIER!" Major Timoshenko yelled. All the Draugen Pesta personnel in the tent, as well as the guards outside, stopped what they were doing, alert and ready.

The Madeiran stopped in his tracks and turned. The blood had rushed out of his face. He saluted the Draugen Pesta king.

Lord Ternborg shook his head and waved the Madeiran away. "We don't have time for that, Konnie."

The HeBron messenger, awakened by the sound of Major Timoshenko shout, was watching the Madeiran closely as he approached.

Lord Ternborg noticed the fear on the girl's face. "Hold," he ordered. The Madeiran stopped again and turned. "I know the history between your city and HeBron. It's not cordial, to say the least. You so much as looked at that girl sideways and I'll personally gouge your eyeballs out. Do you understand?"

The Madeiran came to attention. "Yes, my lord!"

"You're dismissed."

Major Timoshenko watched the retreating Madeiran. "If their general is as cocky as that, they're in for a reckoning," he observed. "The Riders are tough and, despite the Madeiran's confidence, will fight to the last protecting their farmlands. They know the countryside and, though not strong enough to put a stop to the Madeiran advance, they'll take a rather large bite out of 'em."

"And with HeBron's Army destroyed by the earthquake," Lord Ternborg said, shaking his head to stave off Major Timoshenko's objection, "we'll find ourselves marching on Havendale with little remaining of the two human armies. We'll need our own to take Havendale."

"We're spoiling for a fight," Major Timoshenko remarked.

"Let's save that for the Hyrokkin, Konnie!" Lord Ternborg snapped.

"Nightshade promised land, Viktor," Major Timoshenko retorted. "We need to expand out of our valley, you know that."

"The only thing we need to do is get my daughter back!" Lord Ternborg countered. "Or have you forgotten?!"

Major Timoshenko drew back, surprised his commander would even mention such a thing. "I haven't forgotten about the Princess," he replied. "We all want her back. But Nightshade chose well. This valley is everything we need for our people."

"And how long do you think the other city-states will let us stay, Konnie?" answered Lord Ternborg. "If we do our job as Nightshade has ordered, those same city-states will be on our doorstep and doing everything they can to drive us out."

"But..."

Lord Ternborg held up his hand. "Do you want a war on two fronts? Do you want to fight both the city-states here and the Hyrokkin to the east? I know land was part of Nightshade's enticement, but since our last meeting I've had time to think about it. Taking this land is not who we are. And these people are not the same as Madeira and HeBron. They're peaceful folk who don't deserve the destruction we offer. Once I have Daphnia back, I intend to go back to our side of the Boreskyre's. Until that time, though, I only want to draw the humans here so Nightshade will be satisfied."

"You don't intend to fight?"

"Not if I can help it," Lord Ternborg said. "I know we can't completely avoid a fight, Konnie. But I want as little killing as possible."

Major Timoshenko shook his head. "Nightshade made Madeira promises as well. Try telling THEM not to kill."

"I intend to," Lord Ternborg answered. He stared at his second-in-command, and friend, for a few moments. "Are you're still with me, Konnie?"

"Of course I am, my lord," Major Timoshenko replied. "Always!"

Lord Ternborg nodded. "Good. I need a dispatch sent to the Madeirans outlining two things. First, to warn them about marching into any strange fogs. Bottom line, don't do it."

"I would have recommended that myself even if you didn't," Major Timoshenko commented. "Though any fool should know better."

Lord Ternborg raised an eyebrow.

Major Timoshenko nodded. "Right."

"Second," Lord Ternborg continued, "I want them to hold until further instructions. I'm not happy with the way this campaign's been going. I need to regain control. Losing the HeBron Army couldn't be prevented. But the Madeiran commander... General... General..."

"Darcy, my lord."

"Yes, that's his name. It appears he might be going rogue. That's unacceptable."

"You're thinking your orders should have, oh, shall we say, a little clout to go with them?" Major Timoshenko remarked.

Lord Ternborg laughed. "More like the blade of a sword directed at their throats. Take command of your best mounted platoon and carry my orders to this General Darcy. Stay with the Madeirans to make sure they follow my wishes."

"As you command."

"We'll continue our push through this forest and meet up with you," Lord Ternborg said as he walked over to the map table and pointed to a map of the area. "We'll angle towards the Alpine enough to avoid this supposedly haunted city here... this Elanesse."

"Probably just a local legend to keep people away," Major Timoshenko inserted.

Lord Ternborg nodded. "Perhaps. But then again, I never believed a fog could whisk away one thousand warriors or an earthquake could swallow an entire army."

Major Timoshenko scowled. "That could be an overreaction by an inexperienced young child."

"You may be right. But I don't want to take any chances, particularly with our own folks. Besides, Nightshade didn't seem to think there was any value to entering the city."

"There is that."

"Indeed," replied Lord Ternborg. "If you have no more questions, Konnie, let's get this show on the road." He looked back at the Madeiran messenger who was gorging himself on what little food was left of the table. "Oh, and Konnie... take him with you."

Major Timoshenko motioned for two guards to gather the human up. Watching as they carried his orders out, he waited until the three had left the tent. He saluted Lord Ternborg and followed them out.

Lord Ternborg looked over at the young HeBron messenger. She looked more relaxed now that the Madeiran was gone. "HeBron and

Madeira... my people and the Hyrokkin... enemies till the end. When will it ever stop?" he wondered aloud. "Maybe I can make a difference," he said to the empty air as he walked over to the girl.

She cowered in her chair as he approached. Even though human size, the chair still swallowed her up. There were tears in her eyes and Lord Ternborg's heart went out to her.

He kneeled in front of her and asked, "Do you have family in HeBron?"

The young girl shook her head. "No, my lord. The Army is my... was my family. My mother and father died when I was just a babe. Or so I've been told."

"Do you have anywhere to go in HeBron, Miss Shaw?" Lord Ternborg asked. "Maybe a friend or someone you know who would give you a home?"

Veronica Shaw shook her head again, sniffed, and wiped her nose on the sleeve of her shirt. Lord Ternborg reached into his tunic, pulled out a clean piece of satin cloth, and handed it to her. She blew her nose.

"Keep it," Lord Ternborg said when she tried to give it back. "How old are you, Miss Shaw?"

"Twelve, my lord... well, in a few months," she added.

"You're younger than I first thought," Lord Ternborg said. "Why are you in the Army?"

"It was that or back to the orphanage, my lord," she answered. "I was always good with horses, so the Army made an exception for my age."

Lord Ternborg studied the girl. She had mostly composed herself, but there was still a hint of desperation in her voice and on her face.

Veronica Shaw kept talking. "It's not an Army like yours, my lord. It's more a bunch of different families coming together."

"You mean mercenary companies."

Veronica Shaw nodded. "Yes, my lord. I've heard that name used, but I couldn't remember it."

"Would you care to be part of my Army," Lord Shaw heard himself say. He wanted to protect the child. He wanted to give her a chance at a new life. Back in HeBron it was likely only an empty barracks awaited her. That, as well as poverty, hunger, and sickness.

Veronica Shaw's eyes opened wide. "But you're giants. What could I do for you, my lord? And why would you want me? I'm just a stray human."

"Nonsense!" Lord Ternborg replied. "How would you like to help with our horses?"

"My Lord! Your horses are huge! I could never control them."

Lord Ternborg grinned. "Child, they're well trained. Besides, I have another project in mind for you. One of our mares just gave birth..."

Veronica Shaw drew back. "You took a pregnant mare into the field, my lord?!" she exclaimed.

Lord Ternborg cleared his throat. "Yes… well, that rider was sent back home for remedial training in horse stewardship. But that's not the point I'm trying to make. I'd like you to help the mother take care of her foal. And if the two of you bond, then we'll talk about the possibility of you keeping the colt."

The girl squealed with delight and flew out of her chair into the arms of the king. Lord Ternborg, mindful of his giant strength, carefully embraced her. *"Yes, perhaps I CAN make a difference,"* he thought.

Lester and Safire, sitting on their horses while hidden in trees, bushes and thickets, watched the long, winding line of soldiers as they marched down the Alpine. The Madeiran Army tried moving through the forest, but Elrond, the new guardian of Elanesse and Lord of the Forest of the Fey, put so many obstacles in their path they had no choice but to travel on the open road. Elrond's successful use of his 'green allies' had convinced Lester his small band of Riders, along with Elrond, could slow the Madeiran's advance southward... at least long enough to give Commander Fairmount time to gather his forces and prepare a defense.

"The commander only wanted us to observe," Safire whispered. "Do you really believe attacking an army with a dozen Riders will have any effect whatsoever? It'll be a pinprick on their arse. They'll swat us like a horse swats a fly with its tail! Sweetheart, it's suicide!"

Lester shook his head. "We have the element of surprise. We're well protected by Elrond's forest. Plus, we're dispersed over a large area. The Madeirans might think it's the entire Rider force. That's not something they'll ignore." Lester put his gauntleted hand over Safire's. "It'll buy a little time for Fairmount, love."

Safire shook her head. "They'll know it's a feint."

Lester shrugged his shoulders. "Maybe not."

Safire sighed as she checked the string tension on her bow once again. She wouldn't change Lester's mind. That much was clear. Besides, his plan made sense in a way — if nothing went wrong. They'd fire off two volleys, move along the sides of the Alpine under cover of the forest, and fire two more. This would be repeated until they were out of arrows. Then they'd disappear deeper into the forest and meet up with Commander Fairmount's much larger force. Hopefully by this time Havendale's army will be in the field to reinforce them.

"Are you ready, my love?" Lester asked.

"As I'll ever be," Safire replied. "I love you."

Lester reached over and kissed Safire before saying "I love you, too." He pulled his own bow and turned his horse. "I'll be about fifty feet down the road. When you see my arrow drop a Madeiran..."

Safire finished for him. "The rest of us fire two volleys and move down the road to fire again."

Lester nodded and clicked his horse forward. Tree branches bent to give him free passage, closing after he had passed. Safire watched as her husband, the love of her life, disappeared into forest darkness.

Safire sighed as she drew back on her bow while selecting a target. When she aimed her arrow at him, she didn't see the man, only the threat he represented. Tangus had once told her that killing, even an enemy, was never easy, never should be, and if it ever was, she needed to check her conscience. At the time, Safire had conceded the point. But now she wasn't so sure. The man she'd chosen symbolized a direct threat to her husband, Tangus, Kristen and the rest of her family. She didn't believe she'd experience any more remorse for this killing then she did when she killed the worgs.

One of the Madeirans, an officer by the look of his tunic, dropped to the ground with an arrow buried in his eye. Safire let her own arrow fly and watched emotionless as it sprouted in her selected target's chest. She didn't have time to think after that.

Warned by Elrond, Tangus climbed up into his friend's high canopy and spied four black dragons flying over the Olympus Mountains and heading straight for the ruins of Elanesse. He watched as the dragons spewed their breath weapons on the forest surrounding the city, encircling it. Elrond, and every tree in the forest, shook as the pain suffered by the fire took hold. It forced Tangus to grab hold of the nearest branches to keep from falling.

Tangus sighed and shook his head. The earlier earthquake had damaged Elanesse, both the city and its essence, to the extent she had withdrawn into herself. Even Elrond couldn't convince her to come out of her funk. And now it looked as though Elrond would be out of commission – at least for the foreseeable future.

"Elrond, can you hear me?" Tangus asked in his mind.

"Please don't bother me, Tangus," came Elrond's reply. *"I have too much to do."*

Tangus wasn't surprised considering everything going on. He turned his attention back to the city. The black dragons were now circling overhead, but it wasn't random.

"They're searching," Tangus said to himself. "Horatio said they were heading for the mainland. Now I know why. Emmy!"

At the thought of his daughter, Tangus searched the ground for her. As soon as she was located, he knew that something was horribly wrong. Kristen, Jennifer, and Mariko surrounded the young goddess while Romulus, Sakkara, and the youngsters watched off to the side. Both of the adult wolves looked concerned. And with good reason. Emmy was crying.

Tangus climbed down the tree as quickly as possible. When he jumped to the ground from the last branch, Emmy flew into his arms and buried her face into the side of his neck.

"Oh, father," she cried. There was desperation in her young voice. "It's too late!"

"What's too late, child?" Tangus asked as he looked over at Kristen who shook her head. There were tears in her eyes also.

"Lester and Safire," Emmy said between sobs. "They'll be dead soon and there's nothing I can do to stop it."

Lester and Safire, along with their Rider contingent, killed forty to fifty Madeiran's with arrow fire before their luck ran out. Lester's 'shoot and retreat' tactic had caught the Madeiran Army off guard, and the attack against the flanks of the Madeiran formation was a complete success. But only for a while.

For fifteen minutes Lester, Safire, and the others effortlessly killed the confused, and scared, enemy. But even as they did so, the Riders knew it was only a matter of time before the battle sorcerers of the Madeiran Army arrived to support the soldiers. That appearance was marked by the screaming of one Rider as he died, trapped by the flames of fire magic. One by one they hunted the Riders down and killed them with magic. After a few minutes, only Lester, Safire, and a couple other Riders were left.

Lester, as a former Knight of Astoria, was equipped with several magically ordained items – cloak, shield, armor – which provided limited protection against enchantments and spells. Even so, being hit by several lightning, fire, and energy missiles knocked him from his horse in short order. Though shaken, he was still a formable opponent, a knight with firm footing and determined to make his adversaries pay dearly for his life. Using the flat of his blade, Lester hit his horse on the rump and sent it galloping away. A mob of Madeiran warriors quickly surrounded him and attacked. The next few minutes he parried and thrust, dodged and ducked, hacked and sliced, until he had no one left to fight. At Lester's feet were fifteen dead and dying Madeiran's. None of the blood splattered on his armor was his. He looked up and saw himself faced off with the largest human he'd ever seen. The others had moved back.

"Your foolishness ends now, Rider," the big Madeiran said as he moved in to finish the knight.

Lester studied the human's approach. He noticed a slight limp and saw a shallow cut on his right thigh. It was bleeding, but not enough for blood loss to be an issue for the Madeiran. Nevertheless, it might be a weakness he could exploit.

As Lester crouched, prepared to meet the onslaught, he heard a cry of pain through the trees. He recognized the voice. Safire! At that moment she became his only consideration. He had to get to her.

Lester let out a battle cry – a roar so primal it momentarily startled the Madeiran. He charged, feinted left, twirled around and landed a boot to the human's midsection. The Madeiran let out a loud grunt and hunched over. Lester brought his sword down and severed the man's head from his body. Before any of the astonished Madeiran's could respond, Lester grabbed a full quiver of arrows from the headless corpse and bowled his way through the stunned spectators. Three more died before he broke through their line.

As Lester rushed towards Safire, the trees and bushes opened and cleared a way through the forest, closing up tight after his passing to delay and confound his pursuers. Safire screamed again. Lester continued his mad dash until he figured he was getting close. He stopped and used the cover of bushes to crept forward until he came to a small clearing. Surrounded by roughly forty Madeirans, Safire and two other Riders had been stripped of their armor and tied to stakes. Each had several bloody knife slashes crisscrossing their stomach and chests. Piles of wood had been stacked at their feet and lit on fire. The three grimaced in pain as the first of the flames touched their feet. The screaming would begin in a few short seconds as the fires gained momentum.

Without hesitating, Lester drew and fired two arrows in quick succession, placing the missiles through the hearts of the two Riders and killing them. As he aimed a third arrow at Safire, he paused. She saw him and for a brief second their eyes locked on each other. Instantly, the outside world stopped for both. They communicated their love across the brief distance and opened their souls to each other, providing the strength to cope with what must come next. The world as they knew it was at an end, but not their future together. Regardless of what lay after, they'd find each other. They made this vow through their eyes and through the magic that kept them forever bonded. The two would have eternity as one.

Safire contorted in agony and Lester knew he couldn't wait longer, but still he struggled with his emotions. He closed his eyes and watched as their time together rushed forward. He heard her laugh, relived her sweet touch on his brow, and remembered their intimacy. He thought back to how it felt the first time she said she loved him. He was so excited he couldn't catch his breath, couldn't dare believe he'd been so lucky. Then a great sorrow overwhelmed him. When he reopened his eyes, he could only barely make out Safire through his tears. The arrow flew true and Safire's life ended as soon as the arrow's point drove itself through her heart. That same arrow also pierced Lester's heart. He was never so alone.

Lester dropped his bow and drew his sword from its scabbard and rushed the clearing. He swept through the Madeirans, killing three and wounding another, and brushed the burning wood from the feet of Safire, determined to prevent her from being disfigured.

Lester never had a chance to defend himself or to die in honorable battle. From behind someone yelled, "Take him alive!" and a dozen warriors disarmed and knocked him down.

"Get him up!" a voice commanded.

They forced Lester to stand before a Madeiran officer who held a dirty handkerchief to the side of his face. His cheek had a nasty, bleeding slash running from his ear to the edge of his mouth.

"I'm sorry I didn't kill you," Lester said.

The officer slapped Lester across the face with the back of his hand. "Yes, I believe you will be," the officer replied. He pointed to a nearby tree. "Sit him with his back against that tree and tie his hands around the trunk."

Once done, the officer kneeled in front of Lester, took his dagger, and slashed Lester's cheek.

Lester stared into the smiling eyes of the Madeiran. "Get it over with."

The officer nodded. "As you wish." He looked over to the nearest soldier. "You! Remove his breastplate!"

Once done, the officer slit through Lester's tunic and undergarment, exposing the belly. "I know what you are! I recognize your armor. Let's see how stoic a knight from Astoria can be."

The officer pushed his dagger into Lester's stomach and cut across the belly. Intestines spilled out and came to rest in Lester's lap. The knight moaned but didn't cry out.

"Impressive," the officer commented as he stood. "Bring my horse," he ordered. "We've spent enough time here."

Lester waited until the Madeirans had left before he screamed in pain. He knew, as no-doubt the officer did, that people with belly wounds such as this can linger for hours in excruciating agony before death claimed them. He focused on his beloved Safire. Her eyes were open, and it appeared she was looking at him.

"Oh, sweetie," he said through his suffering. "I'm so sorry for getting you killed."

It was the last thing Lester ever said as a tree branch, guided by Elrond, thrust down and through Lester's exposed chest and into his heart. The whole forest moaned as it grieved over the loss of the beloved knight and his ranger wife.

The trees and bushes of the forest understand nothing of revenge. But not so their master. Elrond was beginning to comprehend what being the *Elendrel-Telperiën* meant and recognized the power he held over his minions. Unlike the forest, his heart not only understood the power of revenge, but craved it. Elrond would have his retribution.

Major Timoshenko could smell burning flesh before he and his platoon of Draugen Pesta cavalry reached the clearing. After ordering riders to scout the immediate area, he dismounted his steed and moved into the clearing just off the Alpine. The sight disgusted him. Three posts had been driven into the ground. Tied to two were smoldering remains while a third held a female elf with an arrow in her chest. She only had a few inconsequential burns on her feet and ankles, but Major Timoshenko saw signs that burning wood had been scattered before it could do any further damage. On the other side of the clearing a knight, Astorian from the look of his discarded armor, had been tied to a large tree and eviscerated. His entrails were lying in his lap. The Draugen Pesta commander didn't see the large hole in the chest until he lifted the slumped knight's head. The wound contained bits and pieces of wood and leaves, which Major Timoshenko thought was odd.

The major looked into the dead eyes of the knight. They appeared at ease.

"Major!"

Major Timoshenko raised his head to see one of his lieutenants kneeling next to him. He nodded.

"The fletching on the arrow in the female is Madeiran," the lieutenant said. "But I don't think they're the ones who fired it."

"The knight?" Major Timoshenko questioned.

The lieutenant nodded. "That'd be my guess. We also found signs of burned arrows in the remains of the two other bodies."

Major Timoshenko nodded. "So, this knight kills all three to save them from burning to death and then rushes into the clearing to scatter the wood that was burning at the feet of the female," the major speculated. "He gets captured and pays the ultimate price." Major Timoshenko stood. "She must have meant something to him. He didn't want her body desecrated by fire."

"That's what it looks like," the lieutenant said.

The Draugan Pesta officer looked at the bodies of the Madeirans in the clearing. "And he didn't go down easily."

"Sir!" A sergeant walked up to the major and saluted.

Major Timoshenko returned the salute. "Report."

"We found another clearing and a bunch of dead Madeirans not too far away," the sergeant reported. "There's many more up and down the road hidden in bushes. And…"

"And what?"

"Signs that magic was used recently," the sergeant said.

"Madeiran sorcerers," Major Timoshenko said. "Is there any sign of who attacked the Madeirans?"

"I can answer that for you," a voice called from behind them.

Major Timoshenko turned and looked at the Madeiran messenger who was bracketed by two of his warriors. "I'd forgotten about you," the Draugen Pesta commander said. "Riders of the Elderdale?"

The Madeiran nodded. "Tough fighters," he said. "But we're tougher!" he concluded with pride.

"He's correct, sir," the sergeant said. "About them being Riders of the Elderdale that is."

Major Timoshenko nodded. "Any idea of their strength?"

The sergeant frowned and bit his lip. "Counting the one's here, we found twelve bodies. The others were burned beyond recognition."

"And the number of Madeiran dead?"

"Seventy at last count," the sergeant replied. "Most by arrow fire."

"About what I figured," Major Timoshenko replied. He looked at the Madeiran messenger. "Get him off his horse," he said to the guards.

The Madeiran messenger didn't look too eager, but understood he wouldn't win an argument with the two giant warriors flanking him. He dismounted and warily approached Major Timoshenko.

"Is this how Madeira treats their prisoners?"

The messenger didn't say a word, which confirmed Major Timoshenko's suspicions.

"Is it?!" the major demanded.

Still the messenger remained quiet and took an uneasy step backwards. The sergeant, now standing behind the messenger, grabbed him by both shoulders.

"Answer the major," the sergeant demanded.

The Madeiran gave up on his ill-advised resistance. "Mostly. Some of our commanders think treating prisoners like this will send a message to our enemies. It's also an effective method of interrogation. But others do it for no other reason than they're cruel."

Major Timoshenko shook his head and sighed. War is brutal. A society's civility is often judged by how it conducts those wars and how it treats the vanquished. But in the reality of life and death conflicts between opposite factions, high ideals are seldom followed.

The constant war between the Draugen Pesta and the Hyrokkin is one such example. Both sides have done horrible things to the other.

"You," Major Timoshenko pointed to one of the two warriors guarding the messenger.

"Private Buturovich, sir!"

"I'm giving you a field promotion to corporal. Put together a squad to bury the bodies of these Elder riders. Treat them as you'd treat one of our own. Leave the Madeirans to the vultures and other carrion eaters."

The new corporal saluted. "Yes sir! Thank you, sir!"

As the corporal rushed away calling out the names of those he wanted on the burial detail, Major Timoshenko looked at the messenger. "You got family in Madeira, son?"

The messenger nodded. "A ma and pa," he replied, "and three older sisters."

"Go back to them," the Major said. "You don't want to be around when we catch up to your army."

"What are you going to do to them?"

"My king considers this behavior a war crime," Major Timoshenko replied. "We'll find who did this and punish them accordingly."

The messenger shook his head. "General Darcy won't let anything happen to anyone in his army."

"General Darcy won't have a choice," the Draugen Pesta commander replied. "I answer to Lord Ternborg who has overall command. That is unless General Darcy wants to take it up with Nightshade."

The Madeiran messenger's eyes widened as he shook his head. "Even I know better. Everything I've heard of her…" He didn't finish but shivered instead. "I'll go. Thank you, sir."

Major Timoshenko watched as the messenger mounted his horse and kicked it into a run, heading north on the Alpine. "Sergeant!" he called.

"Sir!"

"We'll rest here for a few hours," Major Timoshenko said.

"Yes, sir!" the sergeant replied as he saluted before giving the necessary orders.

"Lieutenant!"

The lieutenant walked over from overseeing the burial of the Elder riders. The corporal was doing a good job. "We'll be ready for the service in a couple of hours," he said. "Funny, but we haven't had to chop through a single tree root. It's as if the trees recognize what's happening and are clearing the way."

Major Timoshenko nodded. "There's something strange about this forest, that's for sure. But I'm not so sure it's a bad thing. Lieutenant send out two squads to patrol our flanks. Keep 'em clear."

"Sir," the lieutenant said as he snapped a smart salute.

"Oh, and lieutenant," the major said before the lieutenant scurried away. "If you see any Riders of the Elderdale, avoid combat unless they give you no choice."

Major Timoshenko looked at the bustle of activity both in the clearing and along the Alpine. Every one of his troopers was busy following his orders with precision and without complaint. He was proud of each of them. Confident his supervision was no longer required, he walked to the end of the clearing and gazed out into the forest. It was beautiful, yet something was wrong. Something was different. It put him on edge. As he continued to stare, he got the feeling he was being watched. Life as a warrior was the only thing he knew, and he had learned to trust his instincts. His hand went to his sword. *"What's out there?"* he thought.

Major Timoshenko suddenly found the source of his discontent. He locked eyes with another person hidden in the forest about a hundred feet away. He wasn't sure who it was... perhaps a Rider. But he got the distinct impression the only reason he was able to make eye contact was because the other person wanted him to.

"Major!" the corporal called. "It's time for the service."

"Yes, I'll be right along," he responded without looking away.

He stood for another few seconds before he nodded towards the forest. He wasn't quite sure what the stranger's eyes were trying to tell him, but thought he had a pretty good idea.

"Lieutenant!" he called as he turned away. "I've changed my mind. When we're done with the memorial service, I want to move further down the road before resting."

The Draugen Pesta officer, though surprised with his new orders, didn't think much about it. If that's what the Major wanted, that's what the Major was going to get.

Tangus watched as the giant walked away. His daughter, Jennifer, and Romulus flanked him.

"He saw you!" Jennifer exclaimed in disbelief.

Tangus nodded. The memorial service for Lester, Safire, and the other dead Riders had just started. "By design, Jennifer," he replied.

"I don't think I understand."

"I wanted him to see me." Tangus remarked. "A small test, if you will. I've never seen Draugen Pesta warriors before, but I've heard from reliable sources they're not the evil that frightens our children, but instead a noble people. You know as well as I that a person's eyes reveal a great deal about their character. That's what I was doing... looking into his eyes to judge for myself if the Draugen Pesta reputation was accurate."

The Draugen Pesta commander completed the service and dismissed his warriors. "C'mon, Jennifer," Tangus said as he stood and walked out of the cover of the bramble. Jennifer shook her head but stood as well and followed with Romulus alongside.

As the three cautiously strode in the clearing, the mounted warriors, other than glancing their way and taking note of Romulus' impressive size, ignored them.

The Draugen Pesta commander, followed by his lieutenant, turned his horse and ambled over to stand in front of Tangus, Jennifer, and Romulus. The huge horses were the most beautiful Tangus had ever seen. Neither of the two horses appeared the least bit worried by the presence of Romulus – nor should they be. As large as the great dire wolf was, they still towered over him. What advantage he had in speed, they more than made up for in strength.

"You're not an Elderdale rider, are you?" Major Timoshenko said.

Tangus shook his head and said nothing as he looked at the horse. It was so magnificent! He couldn't help but to be drawn by it! He cautiously approached. "May I?" he asked.

Major Timoshenko smiled. "Only a ranger would be so tempted. Please, by all means. Raisa won't mind, will you girl," the commander said as he patted the side of Raisa's neck.

Tangus reached up and stroked the horse's forehead. Reaching into a belt pouch, he produced an apple which Raisa gently snatched from Tangus' open palm.

The Draugen Pesta officer laughed. "You just made a friend," he said good-naturedly. "Allow me to introduce myself. Major Konstantin Timoshenko at your service."

Tangus nodded as he continued to stroke Raisa's forehead. This simple action was controlling the rage he felt. "What's the Draugen Pesta army doing west of the Boreskyre's?" Tangus asked.

"Rather direct fellow, I see," the major replied. "Still, Ranger…?"

"My name is no concern of yours."

Major Timoshenko dismounted, along with several of his troops who had joined their commander. "Very well, ranger. May I be direct?"

"Please do," Tangus replied. "I don't mince words and I certainly don't appreciate it when someone does it to me."

"Good! We're of a kind in that respect," Major Timoshenko replied. "I'm not at liberty to give you complete satisfaction, except to assure you our goal is not to take any lands that belong to you or any of the other inhabitants in this valley. Nor do we want to harm anyone."

"That didn't work out too well for our friends you just buried," Jennifer said. Though angry and consumed with grief, she managed to keep her voice even. "The Madeirans, whom you're allied with, are brutal beasts."

Major Timoshenko's expression became hard. "They overstepped! Yes. And we'll deal with them! Harshly!" The major paused. "I'm truly sorry for your friends. I wish we had arrived earlier to stop it. But all the signs tell me they died with honor."

Tangus snorted. "Little solace, Major!"

The major shrugged. "The price of war.

"Father, Safire was expecting a child," Jennifer exclaimed in frustration and pain. Tangus and the Major turned their complete attention to her.

"She never said a word about that to me," Tangus responded. "How do you know?"

Jennifer lowered her gaze to the ground. "Safire told Kristen and me just before she and Lester left. I can't say if she told Lester or not."

"I don't think Lester would have attacked the Madeirans if he'd known," Tangus observed. "At least not with Safire there." He sighed. "Damn!"

"Damn indeed," Major Timoshenko said, voicing his agreement with Tangus. "The Draugen Pesta people hold the lives of our children very dearly," he said as he climbed back onto his horse with the rest of his warriors. "We'll deal the Madeirans. You do what you need to do here, ranger. Then go back into your forest and don't come out until this mess has been settled."

"And if I don't?" Tangus asked.

"Then you, sir, will become my prisoner," the major said as he whirled his horse. "I'd hate to do that, but I won't hesitate."

Before Tangus could respond, the Draugen Pesta warriors were galloping down the Alpine.

"I may not have a forest to go back to if we can't get the fires out," Tangus said to the retreating backs of the Draugen Pesta.

"I always the thought someone named them the Black Death for a reason," Jennifer observed. "They don't seem too scary."

Tangus looked at his daughter. "It's their uniforms. But never mind that. Why didn't you or Kristen tell me Safire was with child? For that matter, why didn't she tell Lester? He would've sent her to safety."

"Father!" Jennifer exclaimed. "It's too late for that and you know it. What's done is done. Besides, we can't assume she didn't tell Lester. But even if she did, do you for one moment think she'd let him make the decision to fight or run for her? Not the Safire I knew."

Tangus nodded and walked over to the fresh graves. For a few minutes he just stood there, stroking the back fur of Romulus, crying. Jennifer walked up and stood beside him. She took her father's hand. Together, they grieved for one person who had, in all respects, been a sister to both. And for another who they had been privileged to call a friend.

Lester found himself in a strange place... a place that was neither hot nor cold, damp or dry, dark or light. He no longer felt the incredible pain of his disembowelment, but neither did he feel the relief that came when such pain ceased. He sensed nothing at all.

"This is death?" he thought. *"Such... nothingness?"*

"Lester?"

Lester turned and saw Safire. She was holding the hand of a small boy. The boy had Safire's eyes, complexion, and the same determined look. But he had Lester's smile.

Lester instantly recognized the boy. *"My son,"* he thought. *"Tangus Christian, named after two of the most honorable people I've ever known. A name he would have worn with distinction.*" Lester wasn't sure how he knew this. Maybe fate names children before they are born? Maybe everyone has a name they carry throughout eternity? The knight didn't much care.

Lester rushed to the two and crushed them in a great bear hug. The three clung to each other, afraid if they were to release their hold they'd be lost forever.

"Where are we?" Safire asked.

"A good question," a feminine voice said from behind them.

Lester, Safire and Tangus Christian turned and saw a beautiful young lady. Her hair was silky and the purest white – purer than fresh snow – purer beyond mortal description. It fell across her shoulders and to the middle of her back. When she moved it turned into a waterfall of shimmering colors. Her form-fitting, glossy light blue dress was of a material that didn't exist in the mortal realm. Normal hands could never match the weave. A silver necklace adorned her neck and chest with a large, light blue sapphire glinting in the non-light of her surroundings. Atop her head was a silver tiara with another light blue sapphire, but larger than the one in her necklace. Across her shoulders she wore a dark green shawl trimmed in gold thread.

The face of the young lady looked familiar to Safire. "Emmy?" she asked. "Is that you?"

Lester also recognized the young lady for who she was – and what she was. He kneeled and bowed his head, bringing his son with him. Even in death there were things Lester would teach the lad.

"Oh, please, Lester," Emmy said, though she didn't keep the delight hidden from her voice. "Such formality between us is unnecessary."

"You're a goddess," Lester declared as he and Tangus Christian got to their feet.

Emmy nodded. "Yes. But the child you knew doesn't understand that yet. She will in time, however."

Safire smiled. "You've grown, Emmy."

Again, Emmy nodded. "Don't all little girls?"

"I suppose, though I wonder if I'll ever think of you as anyone other than our little Emmy," Safire replied. "Where are we?"

"This place is neither past, present, or future," Emmy answered. "Time does not exist here. It's a place of nothingness. A place removed from reality. A place of my own creation." Emmy grinned, but there were tears in her eyes. "I brought you here to see you one last time before you move on. And to personally thank you for your love and devotion."

Emmy placed her hand on the clasped hands of Lester and Safire as she ruffled the hair of Tangus Christian with her other. "Come. Your eternity… your happily ever after… awaits."

Safire, now standing behind Tangus Christian with her arms draped over his shoulders, spoke. "Before we go, I have one last question."

"Anything," Emmy replied. "You have but to ask."

"As a goddess, whom do you protect and champion?"

Lester laughed out loud. "Sweetie," he said to Safire, "isn't it obvious?"

Emmy nodded and laughed with the knight. "I will miss you, dear Lester," she voiced. "Safire, I truly was the last empath. Now, however, a new race of empaths must walk upon Aster. And no longer will they be forced to hide behind their mothers for safety. No longer will the hate of others be their weakness. They'll be strong, for unlike the old, the new will have a devoted guardian… a dedicated patron in the immortal realm." Emmy smiled. "Right now I have only one follower. She's a child who has yet to be born. She's the new beginning. She's the first of the new empaths. She's my sister."

The army of Palisades Crest, fifty thousand strong, was advancing down the Denali. They had just cleared the pass between the twin summits, Sailor's Assent and Dular's Peak, and were moving through the foothills of the Mahtan Mountains. In another day or so, they'd meet up with twenty thousand Astorian knights, and together they'd strike the invading army which had come from the north.

Further south, Altheros' thirty-thousand-man army was moving along the Pantera River. They'd incorporate the much smaller armies of Esterling and Ordenskyr as they reached each city, swelling the eventual strength of this army to forty-five thousand warriors. Their objective was Havendale – the city of sorcerers – and the only sorcerer academy in the known world. The city's importance to the land was incalculable and would be defended at all costs.

THE FIFTH INTERREGNUM

Liosh thought he'd have trouble approaching the four black fliers undetected. But as he advanced, he discovered they were so consumed with their search of the terrain below they ignored any semblance of vigilance. Either that, or maybe it was their arrogance. Regardless, it worked to Liosh's advantage.

As the Sky Emperor approached the city in the forest, he began to realize it had been beaten down by time. Nevertheless, Liosh marveled at its beauty, its peculiarity, its exotic appearance in the midst of chaos and destruction. He could only imagine how it must've looked in its prime.

The smoke from the burning trees intensified as the infernal expanded further out into the forest. Though the smoke gave Liosh the cover he needed, the pointless destruction bothered him. The cruel disregard for the life of the trees and forest inhabitants displayed by the black fliers irritated him. Sky Emperors are seldom angered, but those who did anger them faced significant consequences.

Liosh flew low over the western barrier of the fire and extended his tentacles. He rotated them at such an incredible speed they became invisible. The resultant vortex sucked the oxygen out of the air between the spinning tentacles and killed the murderous fire underneath. Liosh absorbed the oxygen. As he did, he became stronger and his tentacles spun even faster. He'd gone halfway around the perimeter of the city before the black fliers took note. Three of them broke off their search and flew towards him, spitting out their deadly breath.

CHAPTER ELEVEN

Deep Under Elanesse

Sometimes the fate of nations... or a world... can be decided by something as simple as an innocent shrug at an inappropriate time... or the wrong facial expression... or even the death of a butterfly. The reality is that fate is often unpredictable... and always uncontrollable. Consequently, no plan or strategy is ever one hundred percent foolproof.

-The Book of the Unveiled

Max approached the source of the moan. Even though ghosts move silently, the rogue in Max's prior life couldn't be tapped down so easily. He selected each footstep carefully, avoiding anything that might produce a sound, until he was at the entrance of an alcove. With his back against the wall, Max took several deep breaths... at least they felt like breaths... to calm his nerves before looking around the corner and into the alcove.

The niche was lit by several magical glow stones which reflected light off the solid crystal walls. Curled up in a gigantic ball was a black dragon. The dragon was female. He'd seen enough dragons in his lifetime to know the difference between dragon genders by the coloration of the scales, the shape of the horns, and several other distinctions. Max saw several bleeding slashes which went through the hardened scales of the dragon's skin, but nothing appeared too serious. Her wings were shredded, though. The damage was so severe Max doubted she'd ever fly again.

While Max examined the dragon, he could hear her breathing, which was steady and even. *"That's good,"* he thought. *"At least I think so."* Max frowned. *"But do I want a black dragon to be breathing well? Or at all?"*

As Max was considering his options – specifically, run and then run some more – the dragon opened her eyes and stared directly at him. "Did you come to finish me, ghost?" the black dragon Solveig asked. "You needn't worry, I'll die soon enough. So, leave me to it."

Max laughed. He knew he shouldn't have, but he couldn't help himself. "What a drama queen!. You're not dying, so quit your whining. In my lifetime there's been plenty of dragons with much more serious injuries who still had enough left in them to eat me!" The rogue laughed. "Well, they tried, anyway."

"Too bad they didn't succeed," Solveig replied as she came out of her ball and looked at him. She snickered. "Or did they? I mean, you ARE a ghost."

"Yuck it up all you want, dragon, but you're in no condition to be making jokes," Max replied.

Solveig inspected her wounds. Except for her wings, most of the slashes were shallow... and the deeper ones had closed and were starting to heal. She took a deep breath. It was pain-free. None of her healing wounds offered any resistance or discomfort.

"How odd," she thought.

When Solveig looked at her wings, Max remarked, "You'll not be using those again... at least not to fly. Oh, I guess it's possible to flutter around a few feet off the ground, but your days of being a real dragon are gone."

Solveig lowered her head and eyed the ghost. "Who needs wings to fly when I can teleport anywhere I wish," she said.

Max shrugged his shoulders. "Whatever you say, but I doubt the boy dragons will line up to dance with you at the Dragon Ball."

"Funny, ghost," Solveig replied. "You must knock 'em dead at Ghost Comedy Club."

"I hate dragons," Max responded. "Dragons have been trying to kill me my whole adult life. Dragons killed some of my best friends."

Solveig snorted. "And perhaps you were in the dragon's lair when those things occurred?" she answered. "Trying to steal the dragon's treasure?"

"A treasure they stole from somebody else, I remind you," the ghost replied. "It wasn't theirs to begin with."

"So, you would return the treasure back to their rightful owners?" Solveig snapped back. "How much of the riches you had in your lifetime were actually earned, ghost... other than stealing, that is!"

"Enough of them were, dragon!"

Solveig raised her head. "But not all."

Max shook his head. "No, not all," he admitted. "Maybe we should agree to disagree and move on to other matters."

"How convenient," Solveig remarked. "Very well." Solveig used one of her many dragon abilities to change her appearance and morphed into an gorgeous, black-skinned woman. She wasn't wearing clothes and Max was involved with his inspection of her body when she snapped her fingers. "You're a ghost, remember?"

Max cleared his phantom throat. "Yes, well, you caught me off guard. You're quite… stunning."

Solveig created a simple dress using magic, which she pulled over her head. Her long, glistening black hair was still beneath the dress, and Max was tempted to pull it out for her before she did it herself. Next, she caused soft, calf-length boots to appear and slipped into them. "Perhaps you're right," she said. "Maybe I was over dramatizing. I wish to start anew with you, if you'll have it. My name is Solveig."

Max considered. Many things he believed impossible had, over the last few months, not only become possible but very real. Why not a dragon traveling companion? The strangeness isn't much different from a three-thousand-year-old child empath. Max bowed and flourished his arms outward. "Maximillian Darkshadow, madam. Thief extraordinaire. Worg slayer. A rogue for the ages. And now, as you can see, a most magnificent ghost specimen. What happened here?"

Solveig winced and sat on a large rock. "The end of the world," she answered.

"Now just hold on there, laddie," Azriel said as he stepped in front of the charging Jörmungander. At first it didn't appear the dragon would stop and Azriel prepared to slip out of the way. Since his sylph body is malleable, he wasn't sure if the dragon could trample it enough to do harm, but he didn't want to take the chance. Fortunately, Jörmungander halted his advance.

Elbedreth rushed to Azriel's side. "Patience, Jörmungander!" she exclaimed as she held up two appendages. "We should take a small measure of time to plan the rescue. My people will soon fill the caverns of the deep. We don't want to stumble upon them unawares or without a scheme in place to cope with them."

Azriel turned to his mate. "I don't know if we can rescue the lass, Elbedreth," he whispered. "We must stop the sylph, but our options are limited. We can't reason with the slugs because they're stark raving lunatics. So, we either kill them or block them from making it to the surface."

"But that will trap her!" Jörmungander cried out. "She's the last female of my race! I need her!" He was beginning to panic once again.

"How could I forget about dragon hearing?!" Azriel chastised himself. He had to calm Jörmungander down. "I know you do, laddie," he said. "Let me think upon this for a moment." If he was still a dwarf, he'd have his arms crossed with one finger tapping his chin. "Wish I had my pipe. I always did my best figuring when I had a puff or two of tobacco."

"I can see our first problem," Elbedreth interjected. "How did your clan travel the small tunnels and spaces below? I mean... look at you. You're huge!"

"Huh?" Jörmungander looked confused by Elbedreth's question. Then her meaning suddenly dawned on him. "Oh, that! Dragon magic. Watch."

Jörmungander used his shape-shifting ability to make himself appear as a large, dark-skinned young man. He magically clothed himself in thick and sturdy clothes – clothes made to survive the dangerous and difficult trek. His boots were knee-length with small spikes on the soles. Around his shoulders was a night-black cloak.

"All I got to do now is add a few daggers and a sword or two and I'll be ready for anything." Jörmungander stood tall and straight. "How do I look?"

"Magnificent!" Elbedreth replied. "Azriel, did you see that? I've seen nothing like it. Azriel?"

Azriel focused on his mate and then looked at Jörmungander. He'd dealt with enough dragons to have seen their shape-shifting abilities... and the magic they had at their disposal. He shrugged.

"Yes, my dear. It's an impressive sight to behold."

"You don't look impressed," she said.

"I've seen it before," Azriel replied. "But only from the other end."

Both Elbedreth and Jörmungander looked baffled.

Azriel sighed. "A human-looking dragon who shifts into its dragon form right amongst you and your friends. Now imagine that same dragon as your enemy... and then consider the damage it can do to a bunch of surprised dwarfs and elves. Yes, very impressive."

Both Elbedreth and Jörmungander looked at the ground. "I didn't know," Elbedreth whispered.

Azriel shook his head. "It was a long time ago, and the circumstances were quite different. No harm done. Jörmungander, we need to raid that cavern with the weapons. Your armory."

"Why do we need to raid it," Jörmungander asked. "I'll give you everything you want."

Azriel shook his head. "Sorry. It's an expression."

"Ahhh..." Jörmungander said as he nodded his head. "Follow me. I think this WILL impress you."

Azriel was. The dragon armory was something any king – any ten kings – would envy. Azriel's past life as an adventurer, soldier, and survivor made him keen towards which weapons are best suited for confronting a superior opponent. He picked magical weapons that imparted speed to the wielder. He chose wands and staffs whose magic affected large areas, particularly those whose magic was fire-based. He made sure Elbedreth and Jörmungander had items – potions, scrolls, rings – that afforded the wearer or user added protection from physical or magical attacks. Finally, he stocked up on as much healing potions and scrolls as he could find.

"I believe we're ready to go," Azriel said after an hour of selecting and choosing what his experience told him they'd need. But just as he was leaving the room, he spied a large, two-handed maul standing upright against a far wall. His curiosity piqued, he walked towards it. At first there didn't appear to be anything special about it. But as he approached to within a few feet, the maul exploded in a fantastic display of multi-colored lights which revealed the dwarven runes that ran along its arm and on the head.

Azriel looked at his companions who were acting as if nothing had happened. *They didn't see the lights,* he thought. *I think I...*

Elbedreth called out to him. He held up his hand to delay her query as he drew closer to the weapon. As soon as he confirmed his suspicion, his eyes expanded, and he caught his breath. "By the cooling embers of my papa's smelting pit!" he said aloud. "The *Maul of Power!* He told me this relic was only a myth!"

Azriel touched the maul. It blazed with light. He picked the magical weapon up and swung it over his head a few times. Light as a feather, he was about to bring it smashing down to the floor of the cavern before he caught himself.

"By the gods, what was I thinking," he said. If the maul was as powerful as the legend that surrounded it claimed, striking the floor would've brought the entire cavern down upon his head.

"There'll be enough time for that later, my glorious laddie," he said to himself before storing it with his great battleaxe and iron staff. Azriel knew exactly how he'd use it. Without further delay, he joined Elbedreth and Jörmungander.

Jörmungander insisted they return to the room containing the *Heart of the World* to inspect the heart once again. After some searching, he located a faint light... a light which appeared to get dimmer even as he watched.

"She's still alive," the dragon said. "But she doesn't have much time. Let's go!"

"Oh, laddie," Azriel whispered as they left the dragon lair and continued the long trek downward. "We'll never make it in time."

"If at all," Elbedreth whispered back.

"So, who did you leave behind to protect your hoard," Max asked Solveig who was still in her human form. She had spent the last two hours talking about the battle with the sylph. She paced as she described every move she made, every attack, every sylph she killed, and every one of her clan that died. When that discussion had reached its inevitable conclusion, Max redirected Solveig's attention back to his primary interest, the dragon hoard. "I know dragons and nothing's as important to them as their hoard."

"Except the *Maelstrom* prophecy," Solveig replied. "We'd sacrifice everything to prevent it."

Max looked confused. "What?"

Solveig sighed. "It's our end of the world prophecy, Max. We take our duty to the prophecy very seriously. The entire world is... was... counting on us, though it didn't realize it."

Max was still thinking about the dragon hoard. To a rogue and a thief, little was more important than treasure. "You just ran off to stop this prophecy and left your hoard unguarded?" he exclaimed.

"We might as well have," Solveig replied. "The clan elders left the youngest of us... a bore who's more intrigued by the books and tomes in our collection than the advances of a female!" The dragon raised a fist in the air. "When I get back, Jörmungander, we're going to have a serious discussion about that!" she shrieked. "If I get back," she said more quietly. "If there's a world to come back to," she finally added.

As Max watched Solveig's drama play itself out, he scrutinized her every move. *"Damn, she's beautiful!"* he thought to himself. But when she raised her arm into the air, he saw something that at first made little sense. Light was shining through her arm... light generated from the magical glow stones and reflected from the crystal walls of the alcove. As he looked closer, he saw that light passed through her entire body.

"Well I'll be damned," Max said aloud.

"What?" Solveig asked.

To test his theory, Max picked up a stone from the floor of the alcove and tossed at Solveig. She raised her hand to catch it, but it passed right through.

Solveig frowned. "That's strange. I thought for sure I had it. Must be out of practice. Throw another."

Max did so, but this time he tossed the stone at her chest. Solveig reached out both hands to catch the softly thrown missile, only to have it pass through her body and land on the floor behind her.

"I don't understand," Solveig said. "I had the stone right in my sight and should have caught it. Yet it passed right through..." She stopped.

Max saw understanding dawn in Solveig's eyes. "Now you're beginning to get the message," he said as he shook his head. "Sorry. I didn't think you'd been injured bad enough to die."

Solveig just stared... first at Max and then at her arms and hands. She raised a hand against the light and could see through it.

Max sat on the floor and patted his hand next to him. "Sit," he said, "while we discuss what's happened to you."

Solveig, in a state of shock, sat next to Max and closed her eyes. "I'm a ghost, aren't I?" she asked with resignation.

Max nodded. "I'm afraid so, my dear," he agreed. "Sometime between you crawling into this alcove and me showing up, you... well, you expired. You died. Finito. Kicked the bucket. Bought the farm. Went belly up. Pushing up..."

"I get it, Max."

Max nodded. "For whatever reason you didn't travel to the dragon afterlife, or wherever your people go. You stayed here instead."

"But why?" Solveig asked.

"That's hard to say," Max responded. "I don't know many ghosts. You make two, not counting myself."

Solveig looked at the rogue. "You know of another ghost?"

Max shook his head. "Not know... knew. She was a mother. Her spirit stayed in the world of the living for over three thousand years protecting her sleeping daughter."

"Three thousand years!" Solveig exclaimed with wide eyes. "I can't imagine... three thousand years?!"

Max took Solveig's hand. "It's not the number of years, but instead when we've completed our unfinished business. As soon as Angela... that was the name of the ghost... had gotten her revenge against the vampyre who had killed her and threatened her daughter, she left. Her job was done. The thing that had compelled her to stay had reached a conclusion. I suspect that's why we're still here. We have unfinished business to attend."

"Like killing sylphs," Solveig said.

Max could hear the hate in her voice. "Perhaps," he answered. "Who's to say?"

Solveig nodded. "Yes, who's to say. But I guess I can still kill sylphs while going about finding my unfinished business," she replied.

"Yes, that's probably... Hey, wait a minute! How can you hold my hand?"

"We're both ghosts, remember?"

Solveig nodded. "I guess that makes sense. But you can pick up rocks and throw them. How'd you do that?"

Max smiled. "You can do it too. You can even throw rocks with just your mind. It's just a matter of getting the right training."

"You'll train me?"

"Of course," Max replied. "Just stick with me, kid, because we're going places!"

Solveig nodded. "Maybe being a ghost isn't the end of the world after all."

Max smiled. "No, my dear, it isn't."

It was at that moment Max truly forgave Elbedreth for killing him.

Azriel, Elbedreth, and Jörmungander traveled half a day before taking a break... though Jörmungander wasn't thrilled about stopping.

"We don't have time, Azriel!" he exclaimed. "And I'm not tired at all!"

Azriel sighed. "I know, laddie! But we can't just blindly wander the under dark hoping we'll find the way. We need to stop every once in a while to gather our bearings. There's too much room for error to do otherwise. Believe me, I know of such things. I've spent too much of my life underground to make the mistake of rushing through like a fool."

"Like a fool!" Jörmungander bellowed. "Even a young dragon's older than the longest living dwarf... or whatever you are! We're not fools!"

Elbedreth placed a hand on Jörmungander's shoulder. "Peace," she pleaded. "I've been alive since the dawning of this planet and hear me when I tell you my mate is correct. We must carefully consider our steps. We're no good to your female or the rest of the world if we're dead. Now then, Azriel didn't mean to say you were a fool. Isn't that right, dear?"

"Of course, my fair lassie," Azriel agreed, more to the supplication in Elbedreth's eyes than any desire to placate the dragon. "But Jörmungander, in this you must follow my lead."

Jörmungander considered both Azriel and Elbedreth's words and nodded. "You're right, Azriel. I'm sorry," he said.

Several hours later they stopped at a "Y" crossroads... a small cavern with two exits other than the one they had been traveling. "You two rest here while I check those tunnels," Azriel said, pointing ahead of them. "I'll be able to tell soon enough which one goes downward."

"And if it's both of them?" Elbedreth asked.

"It probably doesn't matter as long as we're going in the right direction," Azriel replied. "I suspect the sylphs will find us whichever way we go."

"What about the female?" Jörmungander asked.

Azriel sighed. "Laddie, I think it's time to be realistic regarding our chances of finding her. With the sylphs between us, it'll be near impossible."

Jörmungander shook his head. He was getting angry again. "I don't accept that. If you stop looking, I'll do so on my own."

Azriel sighed and nodded. He didn't want conflict with the dragon. "I didn't say we'd stop looking. But you must prepare yourself for the worst. And if that comes to pass, there are still the sylphs to stop. We need your help."

Jörmungander sat on the cavern floor and said nothing more.

Azriel looked at Elbedreth.

"Go," she said. "We'll be fine."

Five sylphs secretly watched the exchange between two of their own kind and a dark-skinned human – a parasite in their worldview.

The lead sylph pointed to another. "You!" he said. "Go back to our people and inform the swarm leader we are the first to locate the glorious passage to the surface." As the messenger scurried away, the leader smiled. "Our reward will be most profound."

"And the traitor?"

The leader brought forth his bladed appendages and swirled them around his body. "She is mine. I will destroy the turncoat Elbedreth-Ahlasim."

Azriel knew something was wrong as soon as he entered the tunnel. The malevolence in the corridor was palpable. He considered retreating and calling upon the others to enter with him but decided against it. He'd handle whatever it was. Though now sylph, the dwarf hardheadedness remained in his personality. If Azriel were to be honest, he didn't believe he'd ever shed his dwarf heritage. Nor did he want to. Among the sylphs, his worldview was unique. He alone of all the sylphs understood what it was to be mortal... to be a 'parasite'. It was a perspective he thought Elbedreth understood... and a perspective he'd need to fight the sylph.

Azriel drew his magical battleaxe and steel quarterstaff. As for the maul, he didn't want to use that unless he had no other choice. He eased through the corridor. His years of adventuring had prepared him for moments like this. So, when the attack came, he was ready for it. The first of four sylphs died within a few seconds as his great battleaxe sliced through the sylph body and left it laying on the floor in two quivering pieces. The remaining three sylphs, though surprised by the first deadly exchange, quickly adjusted their tactics. They forced Azriel into a defensive posture. As he probed for an advantage, he noted but couldn't prevent one of the sylphs from peeling away and heading towards Elbedreth and Jörmungander.

Max and Solveig knew they had to act quickly to prevent the sylphs from making it to the surface. As they tracked their quarry, Max taught the undead dragon the finer aspects of being a ghost… at least those he'd learned during his short time as one. Within hours, Solveig had mastered everything she was shown. She learned how to manipulate her form to handle physical objects and was soon throwing rocks as if she'd been doing it her entire life – or her death. Her dragon strength, which was still accessible in her ghostly manifestation, played havoc on the stalagmites at which she threw. The two ghosts made bets on which would break into pieces first, the thrown stone or the hapless stalagmite it hit. And finally, to the delight of both, Solveig found that she could still cast magical spells just as she did in her mortal form.

It didn't take long before the two of them began to grow close. Max fell in love first, though he'd never admit it. Solveig, despite Max's natural charm and her own deep feelings for him, resisted because he wasn't a dragon. She refused to succumb to Max's allure until he pointed out she was more ghost then dragon. Solveig had no counterargument.

Solveig sensed the wounded dragon before Max. In the underground's emptiness, the echo of a faint heartbeat led them to a large cavern. Lying motionless next to a pool of bubbling spring water was a huge female dragon. As the two ghosts approached, they could see the massive, bleeding wounds that were killing her. She was barely alive. And what remained of her life was quickly draining away.

"Erika!" Solveig exclaimed as she caressed the enormous dragon's head to comfort her. "Max! We have to do something!"

"You know her?" Max asked as he began an inspection of the dragon's wounds, determining which were life threatening and which were superficial. He wasn't encouraged by what he saw.

Solveig grunted. "I do," she said. "She's a member of my clan."

Max shook his head. "Not for long," he replied as he used his hands to stem the flow of blood from the most grievous of her wounds. *"Some of these wounds are fresh,"* he thought to himself.

"We have to save her!" Solveig pleaded. "If she dies, Jörmungander won't have a mate and our kind will cease to exist."

Max frowned and looked around the cavern in search of anything that could be used for a field dressing. His search was fruitless. *"What the hell am I going to do,"* he thought as he racked his brain for an answer. "Of course," he said aloud after a few seconds. "Come here, Solveig."

Solveig kissed Erika's forehead and moved to Max's side. "Tell me what to do."

"Your dragon magic," Max prompted. "Surely you know a spell that can help her?"

"No, not really," Solveig replied. "My people normally don't need healing, but when we do, that responsibility rests with our clerics."

"Dragons have clerics?" Max asked.

Solveig reared back as if someone had slapped her. "Of course we do!" Solveig redirected her look back to the wounded dragon. "Unfortunately that's not me," she added. "Erika's our cleric."

Max sighed. "If we don't do something soon, she'll die for sure. Think, Solveig! Is there any dragon magic that might be helpful?"

Solveig looked at the wound Max was trying to keep closed.

"Anything?" Max asked.

Solveig closed her eyes and whispered an incantation. Unlike mortal magic practitioners, dragon magic didn't require intricate hand symbols. Over thousands of years, they had learned to practice their brand of enchantment using words and the force of their will. A white-hot flame appeared in the air above the three-foot-long slash Max was applying pressure to. The flame moved to the end of the wound and touched the two sides. Smoke filled the air as the heat cauterized first the bleeding arteries within the cut and then fused the flanks together. The unconscious dragon's body trembled in response to the horrible pain, though even that didn't wake her. Within a few seconds the entire wound was sealed, and the bleeding stopped.

Max smiled. "That's my girl. I knew you could do it. Now just a few more and at least she won't bleed to death."

Solveig nodded as she moved the flame to the smaller wounds that were still bleeding. Once she had closed them as well, she dispelled her magic and returned to cradling the enormous head as best she could. Closing her eyes, she drifted off to sleep.

Max, concerned, checked on Solveig. She was breathing without difficulty and didn't appear to be in any discomfort. The other dragon, *What was her name? Oh, yeah, Erika,"* also seemed to be resting easier. Max knew it was still too early to be sure, but Erika looked to be out of danger.

Max frowned. *"That's weird,"* he thought as he considered Solveig's condition. *"I didn't know ghosts could get tired."* After mulling it over in his mind for a few minutes, he decided that using magic must be a very tiring affair. So much so that even a ghost wasn't immune.

Max sat next to Solveig and leaned his back against Erika's huge neck. He gently moved Solveig away from Erika and brought her in to his side. With his arm around the sleeping ghost, he pulled her into his embrace and held her tight.

"If this is my eternity," he thought, *"then I gladly accept it."*

While two sylphs kept Azriel engaged, the leader sylph backed away and headed towards the cavern. He knew Elbedreth was in there, and he intended to kill the traitor. But before he could reach the end of the corridor, Elbedreth, who had heard the attack on Azriel, appeared in front of him. Behind her, in his human guise, was Jörmungander.

Neither sylph was surprised by the sudden encounter. Nor did they immediately attack one another.

"You have a death sentence upon your head, Elbedreth-Ahlasim," the leader sylph said. "And I will be the one to collect the reward for your execution."

"You'll find I'm not so easy to kill, Naz-Ahlasim," Elbedreth replied. There was anger in her voice.

"We'll see about that!" Naz-Ahlasim roared as he charged.

The exchange between the two was lightning fast and over almost as soon as it had begun. Both stopped and looked at each other. Then the light in Naz-Ahlasim's eyes went out as he dropped to the floor – in three quivering pieces. Elbedreth didn't hesitate. She rushed forward to help her mate. Jörmungander, however, stared at the sylph body and shook his head in wonderment. He didn't see the flash of sylph blades. The battle happened so fast he didn't even see the killing blow.

"By the first egg!" he exclaimed. "The surface world's doomed if these things ever get up there."

The battle ahead forced Jörmungander's attention away from the dead sylph. Azriel, who'd been fighting against two sylph opponents until Elbedreth's arrival, was cut but still in the fight. Elbedreth was remarkable. She expertly defended against every slice, cut, thrust, or feint from her adversary. At the beginning of the combat, Jörmungander thought Elbedreth only played with the other sylph, waiting to make the killing cut until after she had shown her prowess. But as he studied the fight closer, he realized the other sylph was also very good and, though not giving as much as he received, did make several successful attacks of his own. Convinced that Elbedreth would win her duel, the black dragon turned his attention back to Azriel. It looked like the sylph-dwarf would soon triumph in his confrontation as well. The enemy sylph was clearly weakening, and Azriel appeared to be growing stronger.

Azriel studied his enemy's movements and tactics as he fought, adopting and combining them with his own dwarven style. He used a ruse with his quarterstaff to force the sylph into an awkward position which cleared the way through the sylph's defenses for his magical battleaxe. Azriel's great weapon sang as it tore through the sylph, sending pieces in all directions. The battleaxe bellowed in triumph over its victory. Then the magic of the battleaxe drank the dead sylph's energy. Azriel watched in astonishment as tendrils snaked out from the gleaming double-bladed head and absorbed what was left of the dead sylph. He gasped as the sylph energy transferred to him and healed all his wounds.

"I didn't know your weapon could do that," Elbedreth said as she came up to Azriel's side. Her own opponent was dead, several pieces of it lay motionless on the cold, stone floor.

Azriel was looking at his battleaxe. "Neither did I," he replied. "Although I've always suspected some of its powers were untapped." Azriel shrugged and put the great weapon away. "Interesting, but something to ponder when we have more time. Are you okay?"

Elbedreth nodded.

Jörmungander approached. "That was awesome!" he exclaimed. "So graceful! So elegant! So… so… I don't know what else to say! It was just so… you, Azriel. The way you used the quarterstaff to set up your battleaxe. And you, Elbedreth! I don't think I've ever seen a fight over so quickly. The speed of your blades! It was amazing!"

"Temper your enthusiasm, laddie," Azriel remarked. "They were nearly as fast. I have… had… the wounds to attest to that. And they number in the thousands. We'll never win this war one on one."

"Indeed," Elbedreth added. "Few surface dwellers have the speed to battle a sylph. The gods designed us to be the ultimate guardians of Aster. Only our guardianship does not extend to other flesh and blood beings, just the world itself. And our means of removing any threat is to kill it. There's no in-between. That's why the gods entombed us when life first appeared and began to gain a foothold. We couldn't be trusted to keep it safe."

"If you're such a threat," Jörmungander said, "why didn't the gods just kill you?"

"It's simple," Azriel said. "In case the gods ever needed the sylph again."

Elbedreth frowned. "Needed again?" she questioned. "But that would mean… Surely not!"

"Not all the gods have our best interests at heart," Azriel answered.

Both Elbedreth and Jörmungander looked confused.

Azriel took a few seconds to organize his thoughts. "I guess living here somewhat cuts you off from reality. Or maybe it'd be more correct to say you have your own reality beneath the surface. But up there, the gods often interfere. I know. I've had personal experience. There are good gods… Althaya and Aurora for example. But good is always countered by bad. Evil gods exist to hurt people… hurt people of all kinds. I can easily see the sylph being used by the gods as a blackmail chip against others."

"That's… that's…" Elbedreth began.

"That's politics," Azriel finished for her. "If you can't outright kill your opponent, then the give and take which remains is nothing but politics. Lester used to say it was more of a chess match. But I've found that gods, for all their highfalutin' values, are much more primal. They'll take what they can when they can. Only strength matters."

"Is that why the sylph were released?" Jörmungander asked.

Azriel shook his head. "I don't know. Probably not. Too much is at stake. You can't be much of a god without followers, and mortals are the ideal adherents." The sylph-dwarf looked at Elbedreth. "Does this place look familiar?"

"No more than any other tunnel," she replied. "I haven't been this far below since the first gathering. And even then…" Elbedreth shrugged her shoulders. "You know as well as I that underground geography is never static."

Azriel frowned. "No, it never is." He looked at the dead sylphs. "But at least now we know we're in the right passageway to find them."

"Then what?" Jörmungander asked.

"We need to find a chokepoint," Azriel answered. "A large cavern they can't go around as they travel to the surface."

"There could be hundreds," Elbedreth said. "And that only stops them temporarily. The only reason they've not risen before now is the gods put them asleep. But unless the gods put them asleep again, we'll never be safe from the threat they represent."

"That's why we need to kill them," Azriel responded as he fingered the *Maul of Power* hanging at his side. "What better place to do it?"

Erika slowly resurfaced from the black depths of the dream… no, it was a nightmare… she was mired in. At first it didn't appear she'd be able to break its hold on her. But something redeemed her and brought her back to consciousness. The first thing she noticed was incredible pain. It was almost intolerable. Then she felt a weakness in her body that defied anything she'd ever experienced before. Her immediate inclination was to go back to sleep so the pain would go away. But then she remembered her nightmare was also her reality and as such, worse than the pain.

The clan couldn't stop the *Maelstrom* and had paid for their failure. Her reflection of recent events soon turned to amazement that she was still alive. She was a cleric and knew the injuries she suffered were fatal without immediate attention. But she was alone. At least she thought she was. Was it safe to hope someone still lived?

Then massive guilt overwhelmed Erika. Unlike the others, she hadn't died trying to prevent the *Maelstrom*. She had survived, and the sylph were still a threat. Her failure shamed her and her people. A tear ran down her cheek. The guilt, the loss, was unbearable. *"Why didn't I die?"* she thought. *"Why didn't I die!"*

"How do you feel?" a familiar voice asked.

Erika looked up and saw a figure watching her from the side. "Solveig? Is that you?" she asked. "You survived?!"

Solveig shrugged. "More or less," she said. "How are you feeling?"

Erika didn't pick up on Solveig's cryptic response. "Like the whole underworld collapsed on my head. How is it you survived the attack?"

Solveig looked at Max, who had purposely stayed out of Erika's view. Max offered no help. "It's complicated," she finally replied.

Erika groaned as she raised her head to study her friend. "In what way?"

"Look closely, my dear Erika," Solveig replied.

The black dragon closed her eyes and whispered a prayer. When she re-opened them, she saw Solveig for who she really was. Erika reared her head back. "What manner of deception is this, foul ghost?!"

"Your friend has a rather low opinion of us, don't you think?" Max said.

"Shh," Solveig hushed. "She's a cleric and sensitive to the undead."

Erika, noticing Max for the first time, tried to back away. But she was too weak and injured to go more than a few feet.

"It's okay, Erika," Solveig called out. "We're not evil ghosts trying to trick you. I'm who I appear to be. And this gentleman here is Max… my… my… what are you, Max? Friend? Comrade? Ghost buddy?"

Max smiled. "Something more significant," he answered. "Erika, use your cleric senses to see we're not evil and that Solveig is who she says she is. In fact, she's the one who saved you. Only…"

"Only what," Erika snapped.

"Only I didn't survive the battle," Solveig replied in answer to Erika's question.

Erika began to relax. "So, you're a ghost," she stated. "Why didn't your spirit move on with the rest of our clan?" Erika pointed at Max. "And why is he here?"

Solveig shook her head. "I can't say. Perhaps we need to languish away in purgatory for past transgressions."

"More than likely we're here to help in this moment of crisis," Max said. "Or we have unfinished business."

"Such as?" Erika queried.

"Neither of us know the answer to that," Max replied. "But we're not here to haunt anyone, of that I can assure you."

Solveig nodded in agreement. "We'll do you no harm, Erika. You're a cleric and know more about the undead than either of us…"

"Speak for yourself, Solveig," Max interrupted. "I've killed enough undead in my lifetime to understand more than I ever wanted."

Erika stared at Max while Solveig nodded assent. "No doubt you have, Max. But do you understand the mythology?"

Max looked back at Solveig. "I don't need to know their mythology to kill them."

"If you know how to kill them, then you probably know more their mythology then you think." Solveig turned back to Erika. "Use whatever clerical skills you have at your disposal to read our intentions. You'll see we only want to help."

"And after you're done doing that, heal yourself," Max remarked. "We need to get out of here and see what we can do about stopping the sylphs. They won't go away by themselves, you know!"

"You have a plan?" Solveig asked.

Max shook his head. "Humph! She asks for a plan," he said as he walked away. "I never have a plan!" Max stopped. "Maybe that's why I'm a ghost?" he said before continuing to walk away. Then he stopped again and turned. "You ladies coming?"

Erika, who had healed herself of most of her wounds and changed into her human form, looked at Solveig and grimaced.

"Really, Erika, I haven't known him that long. In life he was probably insufferable. But he has a good heart and I believe I'm falling in love with him."

Erika laughed. "Well, I guess that's a good thing since it looks like he's the only ghost available." Then she frowned. "Wait! That has me thinking. If I'm the only survivor, then that means…"

This time it was Solveig's turn to laugh. "That means you get Jörmungander."

Solveig was still laughing when the two caught up with Max.

THE SIXTH INTERREGNUM

Three streaks of black energy leaped from the mouths of three dragons and climbed into the air, streaking towards the slow-moving Sky Emperor. Liosh avoided one, but the other two raked his body and tentacles. Severed tentacles plunged to the ground. The shock of the pain overwhelmed his nervous system and he dropped from the sky in agony.

The three dragons, confident in their kill, followed Liosh as he fell. Over and over they pummeled his body with their destructive beams of energy until they no longer felt the necessity. The black energy beams ripped multiple holes in Liosh's cloud-like body. There was no place – no secret chamber within his mind – where he could find refuge from the pain.

Liosh controlled his descent, but only just barely. He now found he faced another life-threatening problem. The hot air from the remaining fires in the forest below was producing strong air currents and crosswinds. In his present state, there was no way he'd avoid the volatile air. Nor would he be able to hold his body together. Pieces of it tore away and dissipated into the alien atmosphere. The battle with the black dragons look as if it was over before it had even begun. But even without his tentacles and half his body floating away, Liosh still had options… though they were dwindling fast.

The dragons followed him as he fell. But now, instead of attacking, they only wished to observe his death spiral. Like the ruined forest city, they believed the Sky Emperor was dead – or soon will be. But as Liosh's fall neared its conclusion, he healed his wounds and closed the holes that riddled his body. Even though he'd lost half his bulk, his remaining size and mass was still substantial. Liosh stopped his fall and hovered over the part of the forest that had already burned. The air currents caused by the fires, so deadly further up, were now calm to non-existent. Off to his side lay the city ruins, and while Liosh suspected this city wasn't as dead as it looked, it did appear to be wounded. Several huge crystal stalagmites had risen out of the ground to pierce it. There were signs this had happened only recently. The Sky Emperor also saw smoke rise from the wreckage caused by the recent earthquake. To the east and deep in the forest, two magnificent trees stood taller than the others. Strangely, Liosh could feel their presence. They were a perfect match of majesty and power. Liosh wished he could introduce himself to those two stately beings. But that would never be, for he knew his death was imminent.

A child's voice entered his mind.

"Hail, Sky Emperor, and welcome to our world," the child said. *"We rejoice in the arrival of such wonderful creatures. Your kind will be loved as friends and allies."*

Liosh took this new development in stride. *"Those dragons like my arrival not one bit,"* he thought back.

The child voice sighed. *"They are not from this world either. But unlike you, they come to maim and kill its denizens. They do it to conquer. They do it to appease the rage within themselves that will never go away."*

Liosh nodded in his mind. *"I have witnessed their rage firsthand,"* he thought back, *"and not just on me. If I survive, I will do what I can to help if that is what you wish. I owe it to my new world."*

"You will survive, Sky Emperor," the child's voice said. *"At least in the minds and hearts of your people... and me. My name is Emmy. Who I am is a bit... shall we say... convoluted? Sometimes it even confuses me. But none of that need be your concern. It'll resolve itself soon enough. For your loyalty and service, you'll have my sincere gratitude, Sky Emperor. Also know that you're not alone. Behold!"*

Liosh looked to the west. Clouds upon clouds drifted his way.

"Your brothers and sisters," Emmy said. *"The souls you brought with you. They're young, but willing to do what's necessary."*

"They're only fledglings, mistress Emmy," Liosh said.

"Never underestimate the young, Sky Emperor," Emmy replied.

CHAPTER TWELVE

InnisRos

The ancient elven philosopher Galweneth wrote that problem solving is similar to crossing a river. Before devising the means, you must first know what lies beneath. The true nature of a problem is not always revealed by examination of the surface alone.

-The Book of the Unveiled

The first thing Kyleigh noticed when she awoke was being covered by several inches of snow. It was hard and crusty but offered little resistance as she sat up. She was on a mountain and close to its apex. The wind whipped around, howling and screeching as it swept through the outcroppings that surrounded her. The few small evergreen trees that had the courage to grow this high up bent to the force of the wind.

But she didn't feel the icy bite of the gale. She stood. Attached to her belt was a sheathed sword. Both the sword and the sheath glowed with powerful magic. She remembered nothing about why she carried such a weapon, but it felt comfortable there. She withdrew the blade and stared as multiple colors of magical energy ran up the blade from the hilt and streaked into the sky. Thunder cracked loud enough to dislodge snow. Fortunately, no avalanche came crashing down from above.

"How do you fare?" Kyleigh heard a male voice say in her mind. Surprised, she dropped the blade. Looking around for the source of

the voice, she saw only swirling snow. Only the howl of the wind broke the silence.

"Was that you, sword?" she shouted above the wind.

"It was," the sword replied. *"Try to remember. I am Ah-RahnVakha, the sword of the rulers of the Alfheim. You are its queen… and my master."*

"I don't remember," Kyleigh said.

Another voice, feminine this time, then spoke in Kyleigh's mind. *"You are the queen of the Alfheim, and this world is Aster. You're here to save both worlds, but something went wrong as you entered the corridor that connects the two. We, Ah-RahnVakha and I, did what was necessary to keep you safe. But in doing so, we discovered we inadvertently stole your memories. I believe this is only temporary. If…"*

Kyleigh placed her hands over her ears and closed her eyes. "Stop!" she cried out, though the wailing wind muffled her scream.

"We will not!" Ah-RahnVakha bellowed. *"You have an important task to fulfill. Your memories may be gone, but you'll always be a queen. That's who you are. Now, more than ever, you need to act like one."*

"I don't remember," Kyleigh responded. There was desperation in her voice.

"The shard and I will help you remember," the sword said.

Kyleigh sighed "I just don't know," she said as she picked up the sword and re-sheathed it. Then she opened her tunic, pulled up her undergarment, and looked at her bare chest. Embedded into the skin, centered above her breasts, was a glowing stone. Warmth radiated from the stone and kept her cozy against the harshness of the mountain. "A piece of the *Ak-Samarië Shard*," she whispered.

"You're beginning to remember," the female voice said. *"But since the corridor, I'm no longer just a piece of the Ak-Samarië Shard. I have my own identity. I am the Ak-Vanessë Stone. And like my friend Ah-RahnVakha, I serve my queen."*

Kyleigh quieted. She thought about everything the sword and stone had explained. She had to admit the veneer of queen did sit easily upon her shoulders. She sat on a nearby rock and wrapped her cloak, the *Mantle of the Sovereign*, tightly around her.

"Very well," she said after consideration. "Tell me what I don't remember."

In her mind, Kyleigh could feel the *Ak-Vanessë Stone* nod before speaking. *"To begin, you're Kyleigh Angelus-Custos, Queen of the Alfheim..."*

Yury still held Eirwen when they arrived to wherever the fog had deposited them. The first thing he noticed was the bitter cold made worse by gale-force winds. He looked around, searching for protection. They were on a mountain trail and up high. A crusty snow covered the ground. The wind picked up the hard surface layer and blew it into his face. Within seconds it was raw from exposure. Ice crystals formed in his beard. Yury kneeled and put his back to the wind, trying as best as he could to save the unconscious Eirwen from the worst of it.

"We need to get off this mountain," he thought, *"or we'll freeze to death."*

Yury wrapped Eirwen's cloak tight around her before gathering her once again in his arms. He stood and moved down the trail, looking for a tree, cave, or anything else that would get them out of the deadly wind.

Though he could barely see through the blowing snow, he found a huge low-hanging pine tree upon which he might be able to pin his hopes. He laid Eirwen against the leeward side of the tree and began his search for wood to build a small lean-to. A few minutes later he returned with an armful of pine tree branches which still had their needles. They'd serve well as a windbreak. Eirwen was conscious.

"Where are we," she asked.

Yury dropped the branches and kneeled beside her. "How are you feeling?"

"Like a herd of horses ran over me," Eirwen replied. "But I think I'll be fine."

The giant nodded and smiled. "That's good to hear. As to your question, I believe we're back on Aster. I know the blowing snow makes it hard but look at that snow-capped mountain further up," he said as he pointed. "See that blue tinge? Mount Cor. It's rumored Father Goram worked a magic spell to turn the snow up there blue as a mark of his devotion to the goddess Althaya. That puts us on the island of InnisRos."

Eirwen frowned. "Whose Father Goram?"

Yury apologized. "Sorry. Father Goram is Althaya's High Priest. His monastery is at Calmacil Clearing east of here."

"I know little about Aster outside Vesperia," the time walker remarked as she shook her head.

"That's okay," Yury said. "I do. InnisRos is my home."

As Yury began interlacing branches together, Eirwen looked up and saw a bolt of multi-colored lightning flash from a point higher up in the mountains. This unexpected light show was closely followed by the rumble of thunder.

Nightshade, in her Amberley form, waited for her father to arrive. They had moved their command headquarters to a villa located a quarter mile outside the walls of Taranthi. The noble who owned the property, a former Mordecai ally, didn't survive even though he gladly offered up his residence to the demons. Nightshade killed him because she didn't trust anyone who aligned themselves with the former First Councilor. The villa staff, however, were allowed to live. They were valuable because they knew how to run the villa, and Aikanáro loved his opulent lifestyle.

When Aikanáro arrived, Nightshade could see from her father's body posture that he was depressed. He was taking the destruction caused by the tidal wave hard. Nightshade thought she understood. It wasn't the loss of life that bothered him – the dark elves could be replaced easily enough. The problem was it had pushed his timetable back by a few days. This gave the island defenders more time to prepare. Nightshade understood the elves better than any other demon. They are formidable and would use the extra time well. Aikanáro had reason to worry.

Aikanáro sat in a soft, cushiony chair and looked at the room's fireplace. It wasn't lit. A maid followed him into the room with a tray filled with sweetmeats, pastries, and fruit. She set the tray on a side table next to his chair along with a decanter of wine. Aikanáro no longer bothered using goblets or glasses.

Nightshade already had a glass of wine in her hand. She took a delicate sip and waited. Prompting her father served no purpose. He'd engage soon enough.

"Why are you here?" he asked after taking as large gulp of wine from the decanter.

Nightshade looked at him. "You called me, remember?"

Aikanáro stared at her and frowned. "Yes. I guess I did."

"And..." Nightshade prompted.

"Huh? Oh, yes... What's the status of the army?"

This confused Nightshade. "I gave you a report this morning."

Aikanáro sat forward in his chair. "Then do it again," he snapped.

"That's not why you called me," answered Nightshade as she shook her head. "Father, what's wrong?"

"I said report!" Aikanáro screamed.

Nightshade acquiesced. "As you wish. The damage from the tidal wave outside the city walls was significant. All the docks, warehouses, living quarters along the shores, and harbored ships have been damaged or destroyed. The ships can't be replaced any time soon, but everything else is well on the way to being rebuilt. The city populace is remarkably efficient with the right motivation."

Aikanáro raised an eyebrow.

"Threats against children, spouses, parents," Nightshade replied as she shrugged her shoulders. "You know... the usual."

Aikanáro was silent for a few moments before speaking. "If you must carry through with any of your threats on children, bring me one of the bodies. Preferably plump. It's been a long time since I've dined on such a delicacy."

Nightshade nodded, but thought, *That'll never happen you disgusting slob."*

"Casualties?"

"I'm surprised you're concerned," Nightshade replied.

"Damnit," Aikanáro exploded. "Are you going to argue with me every step of the way? Just because you're my daughter doesn't mean I won't eat your heart!"

Nightshade took a deep breath to compose her thoughts. After a few moments, she thought she had the answer. Her father wasn't planning to take the Alfheim to satisfy his hunger for power. He's acting on behalf of one of the demon lords. *'Most likely Baphomet or Samael,"* she reflected. *"It sounds like something they'd do. Either could destroy father with a blink of an eye."* Nightshade inwardly shivered. *"If he's hooked up with either of those two and fails, he as good as dead."*

Aikanáro was waiting for a response.

"Several thousand dark elf warriors, including a few generals," Nightshade replied. "We're lucky most of our commanders were in the city."

"No doubt enjoying whatever pleasures they can find," Aikanáro interrupted.

Nightshade shook her head. "Though I have no illusions regarding dark elf desires, they're behaving well thus far."

Aikanáro smiled. "Threats work well against our dark elf friends to, I guess. What did you do?"

"The same thing you would've done, father," Nightshade replied. "I gave them a demonstration."

Nightshade's father winced. "Your talents can be even more brutal than my own."

"Let's just say I left them with no… misconceptions."

Aikanáro laughed. "My daughter!" he crowed before he changed the subject. "Are we getting replacements to cover our losses?"

"They're coming across even as we speak," Nightshade remarked. "And I expect another black hydra with her consorts soon."

Aikanáro breathed easier. "Good," he said. "I'm leaving with the army tonight. Send the dragons to me after they arrive. If the humans stay on their side of the ocean, we'll have the island secured within a few weeks. Once that's done and the city states on the mainland get a taste of our strength, they'll be more than willing to join us against the Alfheim. If they don't..."

Aikanáro didn't have to finish. Nightshade knew what he meant. "Father, you promised me this world."

"And you'll have it... after we've taken the Alfheim."

Nightshade sighed. "My point being, I want a world that isn't lifeless."

"Don't over-dramatize," Aikanáro said. "But there'll be one condition, daughter. I'll have no elves left alive. Not one! You can start by ridding us of that vermin in this city."

Nightshade stared at her father. He laughed, stood, and finished the decanter of wine. "I've other business to attend to. See yourself out." As he walked to the door, he stopped and turned. "Take care of the elves tonight."

"But father..."

"And keep a few children alive for me." Aikanáro smacked his lips and rubbed his belly. "Why settle for just one, right?" He was laughing as he disappeared through the door.

Nightshade had no intention of doing any such thing.

"No, father," she said to the empty room. "You'll not rob me of my elves."

A sweet, melodic sound came through a closed window. Nightshade stood, went over to the window, and opened it. One of the female servants was singing to the stars. It was in High Elven, so Nightshade only understood a few of the words. It was a cappella, and the melody of the mezzo-soprano voice told the story of loss, despair, resolve, battle, and triumphant victory. So many expressions in a simple song! So many emotions in the changing pitch of the majestic elven voice! No demon or dark elf could match the beauty of the intonation she heard.

Nightshade thought she should be concerned. Afterall, the song was about resistance to invaders. But it was too beautiful to condemn – or forbid.

"No father, you can't take my elves away," she repeated.

An interdimensional doorway opened behind her and a minor demon stepped through it. The pathetic creature held a magical amulet Nightshade had created to bring a message to her in an emergency.

"Mistress!" it said, frightened.

Nightshade turned. "What is it? Has something happened to the child?" she snapped.

The minor demon started shaking. "No mistress, the child is fine. But we're under assault."

"Under assault," Nightshade remarked. She shook her head. "No! That's impossible! I've put wards… is it a demon lord?"

The minor demons shook his head. "No, mistress. It's the *B'nai Elohim.*"

Katsumi was thrown into her small, cold cell. She was exhausted. Since the tidal wave, the dark elves had her, along with thousands of other Taranthi citizens, working to retrieve bodies for the pyres, clear debris, retrieve usable supplies stored in the destroyed warehouses, and begin the rebuilding of the docks. She and the other captives were forced to work with little concern for either health or safety. They threw those who died onto the same burning pyres that consumed their own dead dark elf brothers. In that one respect the invaders considered their prisoners equal.

The smell of death and burning flesh permeated the air. It was a miasma of foul evil that had settled over the entire city. It was a stench from which there was no escape. Only sleep offered refuge, but there was little of that. The dark elves were working against an invasion timetable, and nothing would interfere, including the lives of Taranthi's denizens.

A dark elf guard shoved a bowl of cold, watery gruel with a piece of hard bread under the door. Katsumi wasn't hungry and didn't want to eat. The temptation to roll over and ignore the evening's supper was great, but unwise. She needed to keep up her strength. Katsumi got out of her bedroll and crawled over to the plate. Though in good shape and as limber as a cat before her capture, the torture she endured, as well as the work, had taken its toll. She sat with her back to the door and the plate between her legs. She picked up the bread and inspected it for mold and maggots. Finding both, she tore the moldy portions off and disregarded them. The maggots she flicked away. She'd kill them later.

Between the second and third bite of bread, Katsumi drifted into a deep sleep. She dreamed of Eric. They were in a small clearing near the monastery at Calmacil Clearing enjoying good wine, pheasant in a thick cream sauce, and cake. Katsumi always had a weakness for cake. After they'd eaten, they rested on a quilt and looked up through the trees at the blue sky. Eric cradled Katsumi in his arms as they napped. Later, they made love. She'd never been happier and wished for nothing else in life. Dark clouds suddenly covered the sky and the day turned to night. Someone pulled Katsumi from Eric's embrace. Both reached out to the other, but it was a useless gesture. Something far more powerful than love or longing had taken control of their lives. It was something even Eric's magic couldn't deny.

Katsumi, her heart broken and stilled, slumped sideways onto the dirty floor, lifeless. In the early morning darkness of the next day they added her to the burning pyres. After her body was thrown into the fire, millions of small bat eyes watched as the flames consumed her flesh.

Eric the Black awoke from a nightmare. He was sweating, and his heart was beating hard against his chest. He'd just dreamed of Katsumi's death. Throwing blankets off, he got up and went over to the washstand to splash water on his face. He look into the mirror above the washstand and stared at the haggard face looking back. "It was just a dream," he assured himself. Breathing deeply to relax his nerves, he crawled back into bed and tried to go back to sleep. But after a few minutes of tossing and turning, he knew sleep was impossible until he was sure Katsumi was safe.

The sorcerer threw the covers off and rolled out of his bed. He sat on the floor in the middle of his apartment and crossed his legs while resting his hands on his knees, palms up. As he whispered incantations, a form took shape in the air before him. It was the face of Katsumi as Eric the Black remembered it. He broadcasted the image of the one he loved to his small minions in Taranthi. Millions of simple bat minds acknowledged the message and began the search.

Eric the Black waited several hours. Soon dawn would be upon the land and the bats would need to retire to their temporary sleeping quarters. He was just about to give up for the night when he received a small 'itch' in his mind. Then others until it became an avalanche of impressions. Each one saw the same thing – the body of Katsumi being thrown into the fires.

Eric the Black's breath caught as soon as he realized what he was seeing. "Nooooo!" he screamed. The power of his thoughts sent the bats in Taranthi flying which caused him to lose contact.

"First my friend Maggie and now… and now… the one I love," Eric the Black said to the empty room in a pain-riddled voice. "This war must end NOW!"

A few hours later, the sorcerer was absent from the morning command meeting. This generated an intense search. But Eric the Black had disappeared.

The dark elf army began their northward trek before first light. Aikanáro was sitting upon his dragon as he watched the endless line of warriors file out of Taranthi's main gates. Prisoners, mostly women and children, walked in the middle of the huge formation. The demon had plans for them later.

After several hours the massive dark elf armies, except for a strong city guard, had vacated the city, reassembled into individual units outside the walls, and began the march northward towards Calmacil Clearing and the elven resistance. Wyverns, replacements for those lost to the bats, flew point and on each flank of the army… but not so far away from each other that they'd be alone if the bats returned.

Aikanáro lagged. He intended to leave a message for all to see. Taranthi belonged to him! His daughter would raise objections, but he didn't care. She was as much his as was this city and the dark elves he used to conquer it.

Aikanáro nodded at the general standing next to his dragon. The general turned to his aides and gave them their orders. Minutes later naked and chained prisoners were marched out of the city. Against the backdrop of Taranthi's massive walls, the dark elves tied each captive spread eagle to a wooden 'X' which was then staked into the ground. A dark elf warrior stood at attention next to each one of those horrid displays. The general raised his arm and looked at Aikanáro, who nodded. As the arm dropped the throats of each prisoner was slit.

"You showed too much mercy, my lord," the general observed.

Aikanáro nodded. "Perhaps. But I won't be here to enjoy their suffering, so what's the point. General, please make sure my daughter doesn't remove this."

"How am I to do that, my lord?"

Nightshade's father pulled a small item out of one of the saddle bags hanging around his dragon's neck and handed it to the general. It was a vial containing a black substance. "Show this to her and threaten to smash it. She'll get the point."

"What is it, my lord," the general asked.

Aikanáro patted his dragon's neck. "Her blood," he replied with a smile. "You smash this, and she's yours to command."

The general returned an oily smile of his own and Aikanáro recognized it for what it was. "You break it without cause, and I can guarantee your eternity will be spent with me… in agony. Do you want that, general?" Aikanáro said just before his dragon launched into the air.

The blood drained from the general's face as he put the vial away in a very safe place.

"We must stop this, StarSinger!" the creation stone Maedhros Nénmacil pleaded from his position in the clouds high over Taranthi.

StarSinger Nefertari Arntuile and Marine Colonel Daeron Tirion were on the city's battlements overlooking the horrible scene being played out below them. They had convinced their dark elf captors they were who they pretended to be, a poor farmer with wares to sell and a simple country witch. This had gotten them into the city, but now that they were in, they weren't allowed out.

They had evaded the dark elf gathering of the city's populace for cleanup work after the tidal wave. They had much more important business to focus upon – such as locating the *Ak-Séregon Stone*. But fate intervened. Nefertari couldn't resist providing sustenance and healing to those in need. This left little time to hunt for the stone inside the city... and Maedhros Nénmacil was having little success searching outside the city walls. The city underside, those who were supposed to help, remained invisible... perhaps found out and destroyed. But now, below them, the cruelty of the dark elves, and the demon who ruled over them, was on full display... and the search for the stone forgotten.

"You know we can't, my friend," Nefertari replied to the creation stone. *"It's too risky."* She had heard the anger... the outrage... in his thoughts. *"And don't you go rogue on me!"*

"We have the power, StarSinger!" Maedhros Nénmacil responded. *"Their swords and arrows can't hurt me, and you have your spells. It'd be so easy! Give me command of one or two of your stone elementals. We'll run amok. They won't know what hit them."*

Nefertari sighed.

"What's going on?" Colonel Tirion asked. "Are you talking to our friend in the sky?"

"Yes," Nefertari said. "He wants us to stop this barbarism."

"I do to," the Marine said. "But it's too risky."

"Maedhros Nénmacil doesn't agree," Nefertari responded.

"No I don't!" the creation stone roared in Nefertari's mind. *"What does it say about our nature if we don't help those who need our help the most?"*

The StarSinger objected. *"We can't give away our intent before we find the Ak-Séregon Stone. The survival of Aster depends upon its destruction. As evil as it sounds, those you see on crosses are collateral damage. We need to be concerned about the greater good."*

Maedhros Nénmacil was quiet, but Nefertari could still feel his anger and his abhorrence at what she had refused to do.

"Even if we could handle the city guard, how long do you think it'd take the dark elf army, with its sorcerers, to turn and come back?" Nefertari added. *"And only the gods know how powerful that demon is. Creation stones and stone elementals aren't invincible!"*

"I thought you worthy of the title StarSinger," Maedhros Nénmacil replied. There was venom in his voice. *"I thought you worthy of the goddess Sehanine StarEagle."*

Nefertari reared back as if someone had slapped her. "How dare you!" she exclaimed out loud, not bothering to explain to a very confused Colonel Tirion. Then she clutched her throat.

Below, the demon had just given an order in the dark elf language and the prisoner's throats were opened. Nefertari felt the sharp pain of the cuts made by the knives, and the panic as each of the murdered gasped for air through slit throats that would never heal. She felt the relief as darkness fell upon each of them… darkness that came as the blood below them expanded into ever-widening pools.

"That's what we could have prevented, StarSinger," Nefertari heard in her mind.

"Maedhros Nénmacil, my friend, we couldn't," Nefertari pleaded. But her appeal went unheard. Maedhros Nénmacil had broken the mental link between the two.

Nefertari was stunned. She thought her relationship with the creation stone was something unbreakable and everlasting. How could he not understand why she had to say no?

"Still arguing with Maedhros Nénmacil?" Colonel Tirion inquired.

Nefertari shook her head. "It's more serious than that. He's broken contact with me. I'm not even sure he's still up there."

Colonel Tirion shrugged. "I'm sure it was just a spat. He'll be back."

"He said I'm not worthy of being a StarSinger. That I'm not worthy of my goddess Sehanine StarEagle." Nefertari leaned her head against the Marine's shoulder. "Daeron, what if he's right?"

Colonel Tirion put his arms around the StarSinger. "He's not right, Nefertari," Colonel Tirion replied as he held her tight.

"Sometimes that's the whole problem with the righteous. They either believe they're responsible for not preventing every little wrong in the world, or they believe they should act regardless of the consequences because of who they are or what they represent. In truth, if a little pragmatism isn't thrown into that philosophy, the righteous aren't long for this world. Our boulder friend's a bright fella. But we both know he's wrong about this. Very, very wrong. And I'd wager your goddess agrees with my assessment."

Nefertari said nothing. She just stayed in Colonel Tirion's embrace and leaned on his strength. Below them, the death throes of the crucified captives had stilled, and all was silent. Most of the city's inhabitants who had watched turned away in revulsion and went back to their homes. The few who remained didn't do so out of curiosity, but to keep a silent vigil over their dead brothers and sisters. In the trees a field away, the carrion eaters were beginning to congregate.

Nefertari allowed Colonel Tirion to lead her from the city battlements to the small hovel the dark elves had given them. The priestess lay down in the straw that served as their bed and was soon asleep. Her dreams flooded in, as dreams of the troubled frequently do, and Nefertari tossed and turned. Sehanine StarEagle stepped in and reassured her priestess.

"Sleep child," the goddess prompted. *"You made the correct decision. However, your anguish over it does further my confidence in you. The horror you witnessed today would challenge any sane person's restraint."*

"But Maedhros Nénmacil," Nefertari said.

"Like you, he serves me because he has chosen to do so," Sehanine StarEagle replied. *"And also like you, I'll not force him so see things my way. He must come to his own conclusions."*

"Can you help me find the Ak-Séregon Stone?"

Nefertari felt the goddess shrug. *"It's hidden from me. But I believe it's outside the city. Now sleep."*

Maedhros Nénmacil hid himself in the large forest to the west of Taranthi. He needed time to be alone – and to think. That's why he cut the link with the StarSinger. His disagreement with the priestess didn't mean their goals weren't still the same. Friends and allies will sometimes have different viewpoints. And while things can get heated, it shouldn't mean the end of the relationship.

"But I was tough on the StarSinger," the creation stone concluded. *"I said things in the heat of the moment I probably shouldn't have. I mean, all she did was try to reason with me. And when considered objectively, her reasoning was quite sound."*

Maedhros Nénmacil rose from the ground and circled a few times before settling back down. "I'm such an ass," he said aloud. A few birds in the trees above him scattered.

"But I will have justice for those poor souls," he continued. *"My kind of justice! Tonight, after dark, so I can get close without giving myself away."* Maedhros Nénmacil's countenance went dark. *"Time for retribution! An eye for an eye! Measure for measure! Lex Talionis!"*

The creation stone calmed. *"Then I'll apologize to the StarSinger."*

When Nightshade heard the *B'nai Elohim* where involved, she realized that if they rescued Lord Ternborg's child, and if he were to find out, her plans for the mainland might unravel. With this new information, Nightshade wondered if everything she and her father hoped to achieve would ever come to fruition. First the unexpected tidal wave and the losses sustained pushed back the invasion of InnisRos. And now she may lose the only bargaining chip she had against Lord Ternborg – his daughter. There was still the promise of land, but Nightshade was very good at reading mortal attitudes and body language. Lord Ternborg, once he had his precious Daphnia back, would turn his army around and go back home. Though he wanted more land for his people, she knew he'd not use force to take it from someone with a rightful claim.

Nightshade cast a special interdimensional doorway spell to take her to where she held her captive deep in the Abyss.

"Horrid place locked deep in the blight.
All around, up and down, black as night.

A place, a reality, which I did create.
Strong and secure where none may arrogate.

Pierce through space, pierce through time.
Open the doorway to this prison of mine."

"SEMITA REVELARE!"

A shimmering point of light appeared in the air before her. As she waited, it expanded until it was large enough to accommodate her size. Nightshade shifted to her demon form and grabbed the arm of the much smaller demon before she stepped through. The scene on the other side of the doorway was one of chaos and slaughter.

Six of the *B'nai Elohim*, as well as the gigantic wolf she'd given the child, were having an easy time killing her guards. The demons offered little resistance as they ran around senseless while being butchered. The only advantage she had was an unlimited number of minor demons at her disposal. Behind the main fighting, another *B'nai Elohim*, larger than the others, stood with the child in his arms. Nightshade recognized this particular guardian – Michael, leader of the *B'nai Elohim* protecting this Prefecture of the Abyss.

"Stop!" she screamed in the language of the demons. Her minions did so at once.

The *B'nai Elohim* looked to their leader. Michael nodded as he put Daphnia down and moved her behind him. The wolf stopped as well but continued to growl as it retreated to stand guard next to the child.

Nightshade looked at the wolf. "Ingrate," she said before turning her attention to Michael. She nodded towards him.

"Michael," she said.

Michael bowed. "At your service, Nightshade."

Nightshade wanted to knock the smirk off Michael's face. "I think not!" she grunted.

Michael laughed. "You think correct, demon."

Nightshade studied the *B'nai Elohim*. She had to admit they were beautiful creatures, particularly the wings. The colors were mesmerizing. She often fantasized what it'd be like to have one as a lover. But that could never happen. If the Abyss were a prison, the *B'nai Elohim* were its jailers. Though not perfect, they are good enough guardians to keep most from escaping. To do this, they had special powers. One being they were almost impossible to kill. They were also immune to her charms, and they never accepted bribes.

"Why does a mortal child interest you so?" she asked.

Michael shrugged. "Surely you know by now our purpose is to protect the innocent from evil. It's a drama your kind, and mine, have been playing out for as long as the universes have existed."

"Yes, but…" Nightshade stopped. Everything clicked into place. "You're the Draugen Pesta Doom Warriors!"

Michael nodded. "Guilty as charged," he replied. There was a satisfied grin on his face. "I seem to recall you wanted the Draugen Pesta king to use us. Well, here we are."

Nightshade cursed under her breath. "I don't suppose there's any way we can settle this peacefully?" she asked.

Michael shook his head. "Not as long as you insist upon keeping the child," he responded.

Nightshade sighed. "I had a hunch you'd say that."

That evening in Taranthi along the north wall, Maedhros Nénmacil quietly flew past the crucified townsfolk. As he did so, he cut the throats of the guards who were still standing watch. He was halfway down the line before anyone realized what was happening. Even though the alarm had been sounded, what little defense the remaining guards mustered wasn't enough to prevent the creation stone from taking the full measure of his revenge. A few dark elf sorcerers, newly arrived from their home world to replace those killed by the Qénsharma, rushed to their battle stations. From the battlements they bracketed Maedhros Nénmacil with bolts of lightning and super-heated plasma spray. The lightning stung but other than that had little effect. But the heat from the plasma spray hurt the creation stone. Maedhros Nénmacil limped back to his hiding place in the forest. His biology would restore him to full health, but it would be painful. *"I should have listened to the StarSinger,"* he thought as he drifted off into a healing sleep.

In Taranthi, Nefertari worried about her friend and protector. Though she and Colonel Tirion had been forced off the battlements and could no longer see what was happening, she suspected it was Maedhros Nénmacil seeking justice for the murder of the innocent civilians earlier in the day. The streaks of lightning and white-hot signs of the plasma spray lit the night sky. The StarSinger knew sorcerer spells harmed the creation stone. Whether he could actually be killed was something Nefertari didn't care to find out.

"By the gods, that smells awful," Colonel Tirion exclaimed. Nefertari was still looking up and into the sky. Spells were no longer being cast, and the sounds of dark elves removing their dead comrades could now be heard in the sudden silence that followed.

"That's the smell of plasma spray," Nefertari said. She turned to the Marine colonel. "Remember your liquid fire, Daeron? It's like that, only hotter."

Colonel Tirion shivered.

Nefertari continued. "If any of that hit Maedhros Nénmacil, he'll be in real trouble," she said. "Damnit, I warned him." The StarSinger reached out and her staff, which was lying a few feet away, jumped into her waiting hand.

"What are you going to do," the colonel asked.

"I'm not sure," the priestess said as she shook her head. "He broke our link, so I can't talk to him. He's too far away to send an elemental." She paused. "Maybe a blanket location spell would work... but it'd also alert the sorcerers. I could conjure stone elementals to pound our way out of the city. But again, the sorcerers. I'm open to suggestions, Daeron."

Colonel Tirion took a few moments before he responded. He'd been planning their escape ever since the dark elves restricted them to the city. "Well, it's obvious we must get out of the city to get to Maedhros Nénmacil. And according to your goddess, we'll have to do that anyway if we're going to retrieve the stone. But we both agree we need a delicate approach to escape the notice of the sorcerers."

"And what might that approach be?" Nefertari asked. "Not the thieves' guild as was our original intention. The demon Nightshade saw to that. Those not dead are now too afraid to show their faces. Poor bastards."

"Right," Colonel Tirion replied. "Now stay with me, Nefertari. Ex-Marines. They contacted me shortly after we arrived. Several hundred former Marines here in the city just itching to go to work on the dark elves."

Nefertari was silent and stared. "You can't be serious!" she said after a few moments.

"Oh, I'm quite serious," answered the colonel. "They've only been waiting for the right time to move. Now that most of the dark elves have left, they're ready to get started."

Nefertari was incredulous. "Daeron," she retorted. She was trying very hard to maintain control of her emotions. "We want to leave unnoticed. I've seen your men at work. There's nothing subtle about a Marine."

"Your right. We're not usually required to restrain ourselves," Colonel Tirion replied. Then he smiled. "But believe me, we can when the situation calls for it."

"Why are you just now telling me about the Marines here in Taranthi," the StarSinger inquired. There was reproach in the tone of her voice.

Colonel Tirion looked away. "They had me swear an oath," he admitted. "They don't trust you."

Nefertari shook her head, confused. "I understand I'm a stranger, but couldn't you have just vouched for me?"

Colonel Tirion shook his head. "That's my fault, I'm afraid. I told them you were the Queen's sister. They're having a difficult time digesting that piece of information. So they asked me not to say anything until they meet you. They figured by then it'd be too late for you to raise the alarm if you're a spy."

"And you kept that promise even though you know for a fact that I AM Lessien's sister and NOT a spy?" Nefertari asked.

"Well..." Colonel Tirion cleared his throat. "As I said, I gave my word."

Nefertari wasn't happy about being left in the dark. But she knew Daeron did what he thought was right, so she let it rest. She realized that his word was important to him. Besides, in the end he did break his oath for her — at least to a degree. That made her feel special. "Well then, let's go meet these fellows. And while we're walking, you can tell me your plan."

No one understood why a million bats had descended upon Taranthi. But while they left the city populace alone, they presented quite a nuisance to the dark elves – nipping at ears, faces, and any other body part not protected by armor. After several nights of that, dark elf patrols on the city streets restricted their rounds to militarily important areas only. This gave the city folks time to breathe – time to live under the watchful eyes of the moon and stars instead of the dark elves – time to plot revolution against their dark overlords.

Ever since the bats had arrived, the people of Taranthi had gotten used to seeing small, gleaming eyes in every nook and cranny of the city. They had become such a common sight that people pushed their presence to the back of their minds as they went about their daily business. So, when the bats disappeared the evening after the departure of the main dark elf army, no one took notice.

Far to the north, on the western side of the Maranwe River, a lone figure rode a vaguely outlined horse across the flat farmland. The shadow steed traveled much faster than an ordinary horse and did so with no need for rest. Upon its back sat a black-clad figure. His heavy cloak billowed in the wind behind him. The shadow steed slowed as a cloud approached from the south – an enormous cloud much darker than the moonlit night.

Eric the Black had left without a second thought to his friends in Calmacil Clearing. He knew what he'd done would be considered treason in certain circles, particularly the military who took a very dim view of people leaving their post without sanction. But the sorcerer didn't care. No one took what was his without suffering severe repercussions.

As the sorcerer waited for his bat escort, he looked around, using sorcerer's sight to check for threats. To the east, on the other side of the river, he spied campfires. The dark elf army was in the field.

"It's about damn time they came out from behind Taranthi's walls," he told his shadow steed. "Father Goram, the Queen, and her generals will take care of them. But those in the city are mine!"

As the bats circled above, waiting, the sorcerer/assassin looked toward Taranthi. The city's lights were illuminating the sky.

"I'm going to bringing hellfire down on your heads, you dark elf curs," he said aloud. "And it begins with the Qénsharma!"

The corridor from Aster to the Svartalfheim expanded. The dark elf sorcerers controlling it cared little about the consequences… just that it brought the black hydra, her escort, and several thousand more dark elf warriors to Aster. This newest demand for more power forced the *Ak-Séregon Stone* to extend its tendrils even farther into the space and multiple dimensions it penetrated to reach the Svartalfheim. As it drew more power, it became more unstable. As it became more unstable, major shifts occurred on the worlds up and down the corridor length. The energy blowback from these shifts entered the corridor and followed the dragons and warriors as they traveled from the Svartalfheim to Aster.

The enormous black hydra and her three smaller male consorts exited the corridor and flew off to the northeast to join Aikanáro and his dark elf army. Hundreds of wyverns accompanied the dragons. Then came the warrior reinforcements. They marched from the corridor and proceeded directly to Taranthi. The sorcerers, believing their duty completed, relaxed their vigil and released the power they used to keep the corridor open.

But before the corridor closed, tentacles of energy, the precursor to the explosion that was coming, reached out and touched every living thing within a mile. Trees and other plants were only singed. Flesh and blood, however, was incinerated. Every dark elf still in range died as soon as a tentacle found them. Their demise came so quickly they didn't have time to cry out.

THE SEVENTH INTERREGNUM

The young Sky Emperors approached unnoticed by the black dragons. With their tentacles up, the Sky Emperors looked to be nothing more than clouds in the sky. A keen observer, however, would see that these clouds moved in the opposite direction of the wind and were moving much faster than normal clouds. As they draw near, their tentacles dropped from their bodies and began to spin.

Even though assured by the child's voice in his mind, Liosh still feared for them. And it looked to him like they would make the same mistake he did.

"No," he screamed in his mind. *"Not lightning!"*

"Rest easy, Liosh," the child whispered in his mind.

The dragons sensed something was wrong. They looked up and saw spinning tentacles hanging from the clouds. Knowing now what they were, the three smaller dragons shot back up into the sky. Destructive beams lanced into the air, and several of the small Sky Emperors cried out in pain as they died.

Liosh gained altitude as he rushed to help. *"I'm coming,"* he called out with his mind. *"I'm coming, children!"* But the injuries he had sustained earlier slowed him.

The five-headed beast turned her full attention to Liosh. Five beams of black energy pierced his body and sliced parts of it away. The horrid pain was more than the Sky Emperor had ever endured, but he continued to fly as best as he was able.

The five-headed dragon flew level with Liosh. She looked at him and smiled. *"Can you understand me, creature?"* she broadcast with her mind.

Liosh could, but he ignored her as he struggled to fly. The screams of several other Sky Emperors made him even more determined.

"You'll not make it," the dragon continued. *"And even if you did, what could you do in your sorry state? Give it up!"*

"Leave them," Liosh pleaded. *"They can't hurt you."*

The female dragon laughed. *"You're right. Your own poor efforts prove that. But we'll not leave them alone, my dear. No. Nothing like that. We'll hunt them down. We'll chase every single one of them and make sure they die a gruesome death. That is if any of them survive today."*

The five-headed dragon banked away from Liosh and flew away for a mile before turning back. Five beams came out of five mouths and raced towards the Sky Emperor. Liosh was in no condition to avoid them, nor did he have time. First came the familiar pain. Then he could no longer fly and was falling. As he did so, he saw the battle raging above him. But it wasn't the slaughter he'd expected. Most of the children used their tentacles to propel themselves through the sky and maneuver to avoid the death beams of the dragons. They released their own beams from their spinning tentacles. But these beams were blinding white and not the blue-tinged beams of lightning. Whenever a white beam struck, the dragon it hit screamed out in pain.

Liosh landed in the abandoned city. By now, little of his original size remained. He watched as one by one, the dragons, except the female, fell from the sky. Two of them landed in the fire outside the city. Their death screams carried for several miles. The third male landed in the city, impaled by one of the many stalagmites that now dotted its grounds. The female, now alone, flew off to the east.

Liosh's pain lifted. The child voice cradled his mind with soft, soothing sounds. Liosh felt relaxed and euphoric as his life drifted away. Several of the small Sky Emperors descended and surrounded the dead Liosh. They lifted his body until they were high enough for the other Sky Emperors to join them. Together they floated with Liosh's corpse until the winds blew it away.

Only one of Aster's denizens knew of Liosh's involvement and the sacrifice he made for a world he owed nothing. Emmy, the future goddess of the Empath, decided the Sky Emperors would serve her well.

CHAPTER THIRTEEN

InnisRos

"Release the dogs of war!"

-Any world, any time. The order a battlefield commander gives to send his Marines into the fight. This usually marks the beginning of the end for the enemy.

"I will not," Queen Lessien said for what seemed like the hundredth time. She was meeting with her top advisors and military commanders to discuss the next day's deployment of the Army and Marines. "I'll lead them into battle, ladies and gentlemen! I'll not cower behind an honor guard of Marines and dire wolves while my people are dying for me! Anybody here think my father wouldn't do the same?"

General Singëril threw his hands into the air. "I give up," he exclaimed. "Father Goram, you've been unusually quiet. Say something! Tell her Majesty that we can't afford to lose a queen!"

Findley and Razor, who were dozing off in a corner, both raised their heads and perked their ears as they looked towards the cause of the outburst. Ajax, lying next to the two, glanced over at the table where Father Goram was sitting and, noting all was well, went back to sleep.

Everyone turned to Father Goram. Although Lessien had left no doubt who was in charge, the priest was her closest advisor and a dear friend to her late father. She, and most everyone on InnisRos, trusted and respected his opinion.

Father Goram looked around the table. To his immediate right sat his wife, Autumn, who was holding his hand on her knee. On his left the Queen. Then General Singëril, his assistant Lauran Ar-Feiniel, Marine Commander-General Feynral, Landross, Cordelia and Cameron. No one said a word as they awaited his answer.

"General Singëril's correct," he began. "We don't want to lose our queen."

Lessien started to argue, but Father Goram looked at her and frowned. She bit back her objection and nodded, willing to listen a little longer.

Father Goram continued. "But in this matter, the Queen does make a valid argument."

This time it was General Singëril who began to object. The priest shook his head to cut him off.

"True, it'll be dangerous," Father Goram said. "And if she insists, it's her right." His piercing silver eyes locked onto the Queen's. "But your duty is to lead your people. You can't do that from the grave."

"Horatio…" the Queen began.

Father Goram's eyes softened. "Lessien, does General Singëril lead the charge of his army?" Silence. "Of course he doesn't. How can he direct a multi-front battle leading a charge on the back of a horse? Or worse, on the ground with an arrow stuck in his chest?"

"He has people who can step in to take his place," the Queen said.

"There's a reason he's the general and they're not," Father Goram chided. "No Lessien, the general has proven his gallantry many times over. What his warriors need of him is to command the battlefield. They trust him to do what he can to ensure victory. That's his part to play. Your people need you to be Queen. That's your part. And Lessien? No. Martin wouldn't lead the troops into battle. Before he was a king, he was a general. He understood the necessities of command."

The Queen's sword, *Ah-HritVakha*, flared in its scabbard. "I know he's right!" she snapped, addressing the sword. "And I know you once belonged to my father."

Findley and Razor got to their feet and began growling in response to the Queen's anger. Ajax was well used to his master partaking in discussions that were tense but otherwise not dangerous. He looked up and growled at the two younger wolves. Both looked over at their pack leader and snarled their displeasure. Ajax stood and stretched. Findley and Razor are big, but neither could match Ajax's size. Only Romulus is bigger. Ajax was reminding the two of that very fact.

After Ajax finished stretching, he glanced over at his master. Father Goram smiled. The dire wolf returned his master's smile and lay back down. Findley and Razor hesitated, but then did the same.

"What just happened?" Cordelia asked.

Cameron understood wolf behavior almost as well as Father Goram. "The Queen's reaction to her sword upset Findley and Razor. Ajax told them they were overdramatizing the whole thing and to knock it off."

"Interesting," Lauran Ar-Feiniel remarked. "Where can I get one of those wonderful creatures?"

Autumn nodded her head toward the three dire wolves. "Talk to Ajax. But I'd wait until he's done with his daily nap."

Landross snorted. "Ha! Daily nap she says. That's all he ever does!"

Cameron laughed. "Not true! He also eats!" he said as he used his hands to show the size of the meat Ajax was accustomed to whenever Father Goram fed him. "Big, bloody slabs of venison!"

"Most times I cook it up for him," Father Goram added. "He's particularly fond of his meat served up medium rare. And I must admit, it's better that way. No blood to clean up."

"Honey, really?! You use spells to do that," Autumn remarked.

Father Goram nodded. "True."

"Then what does Ajax do?" Landross asked.

Autumn smiled. "He goes back to sleep."

The two generals watched the banter with little interest and much annoyance. But Lauran Ar-Feiniel knew what was happening. As did the Queen.

"Enough," Lessien said with resignation, though her mood had brightened considerably. She couldn't help herself. Father Goram and his band of followers excelled at manipulating emotions during tense situations. Her father had warned her about that. But she didn't mind. She always enjoyed watching the priest and his people take the edge off with a little humor, though she didn't like it when he did it to her. "I know what you just did," she admitted as she looked at the priest who smiled back at her. "Let's get back on point."

Everyone around the table quieted and looked at her, waiting. "I accept Horatio's logic and will stay with the generals."

"General," General Feynral corrected. "I'll be leading my Marines."

Father Goram placed a hand on Lessien's before she could mention the absurdity of this after being convinced it was the one thing she shouldn't do. "It's a Marine thing and steeped in hundreds of years of tradition," the priest said.

"True, Your Highness," General Feynral acknowledged. "Since General Singëril is the battlefield commander, my place is with my Marines."

"You mean you're expendable," Lessien responded.

General Feynral nodded. "On the battlefield, my Marines are primarily the front-line assault troops. In that role we're all expendable."

"How noble," Lessien responded dryly.

General Singëril cleared his throat. "Yes… well, shall we continue?"

"Please do," Lessien said.

General Singëril nodded. "Father Goram, I trust you've given thought to what we discussed yesterday?"

Father Goram nodded. "Yes, though Golanth isn't too keen on flying into the ground again if that's what we ask them to do."

"Only as a last resort," the Army general replied.

"Acknowledged," Father Goram answered. "Now that I know they can survive such a thing, I'm a little more optimistic if it comes to that. My crystal dragon golems are at your service."

"And General," Autumn added. "They're no different than if they were our own children. Please keep that in mind."

General Singëril did a slight half-bow. "I understand, my lady."

"Any word from Taranthi?" the Queen asked. "I've heard nothing from my sister."

General Feynral nodded. "Yes, Your Highness…"

Lessien interrupted him with a wave of her hand. "How many times must we discuss this? I don't require such formality behind closed doors. That goes for you as well, General Singëril. Lessien will be fine." She was tiring of all the "Your Majesty's", "Your Highness's", and "My Queen."

Both generals glanced at each other. It was a familiar request, though it went against protocol. In fact, King Martin had ordered them to do the same when he was alive, and they usually complied. But he was one of them – a former general who had killed in defense of his world and king. The same wasn't true of his daughter. Like her father she had a warrior's heart and she ruled as well if not better. But she wasn't him. She wasn't part of their exclusive club.

"They can't," Father Goram said, rescuing the two from doing something that went against their nature. "You're their Queen and their commander… not someone they go to the local pub with to drain a few mugs of ale."

"But you call me Lessien all the time, Horatio!"

Father Goram smiled. "I'm a civilian and a high priest. I can turn anyone in this room into a toad. That gives me certain privileges." Father Goram sighed and shook his head. "Damn! I should have done that to Mordecai long ago."

Lessien's complexion blanched. *"He'd never do that, would he?"* she thought to herself. She looked at her high priest and shook her head. *"No,"* she thought. *"Well. Maybe."*

Lessien looked at her two generals. "Please continue."

General Feynral nodded. "Colonel Tirion contacted me a few hours ago. The dark elf army is on the move. Their demon leader rides on the back of a gigantic black dragon."

"Well that's not good," Cordelia remarked.

"We'll be ready," General Singëril said. "The rest of the army is on foot. No mounted cavalry to speak of. So we have a few days yet to get into position."

"And you think the foothills are the best place to make our stand?" Lessien asked.

"Indeed, Your Highness," Landross answered. "The foothills give us the high ground. They'll be in the open while we rain arrows down upon their heads. Plus it allows us to hide our true strength."

General Singëril continued. "We're outnumbered. Their commander knows that and won't care about the number of his casualties. He'll pound, and pound, and pound knowing we'll run out of people before he does. At least until the corridor is closed."

"May I interrupt?" Cordelia said. The Queen nodded. "What about that dragon? Or wyverns?"

"I have crystal golems," Father Goram commented. "And Eric has his bats."

"If the sorcerer's even around for the fun," Cameron added. He was angry.

"He'll be here," Landross said in defense of his friend.

"Where is he now?" Lessien asked.

Cameron shook his head. "No one knows. He just up and left during the night. No word, no note, no anything."

"Cameron, I told you, he'll be back!" Landross repeated.

"Calm down the both of you," Father Goram snapped. He turned to the Queen and shrugged his shoulders. "I was going to mention it to you later."

"The only real sorcerer on our side disappeared and you were going to mention it to me later!" Lessien barked. Her long nails were tapping on the table as she stared at the priest. The sudden silence filled the room, as did the Queen's disappointment. "He's got to be around here somewhere. Someone, please find him! Search every nook and cranny in this monastery!" she ordered. Several of her aids bolted from the room. She knew they'd not find him. Father Goram would have been very thorough in his search. But she had to try. "Now then, what of that division from Elwing FeFalas and the two... or was it three... regiments guarding the north?" Lessien asked.

"Three, Your Highness," Lauran Ar-Feiniel answered. "Counting the irregulars, that's another twenty-five thousand troops at our disposal."

"Irregulars?" Autumn whispered to her husband.

Father Goram leaned over and whispered back. "It's a term the Army uses to refer to vets, mercenaries, and anyone else willing to take up arms and fight."

"The problem is most of them are on the other side of the Aranel River," General Singëril observed. "They'll cross but getting here will take more time than we have."

"You'll hold them in reserve once they're here?" Landross asked.

General Singëril nodded. "Correct. At least initially. Several companies of cavalry from Elwing FeFalas will ride south to guard, harass, and recon everything west of the Aranel."

"Why don't you just move the entire twenty-five thousand down the Aranel and have them cross behind the enemy to attack from the rear?" Landross inquired. "The tall grasslands on that side of the river provide enough cover if used properly. We'll have the dark elves engaged by then so there's a good chance they can move and cross unnoticed."

"And there's also a good chance they WILL be noticed, especially with the irregulars marching with them." General Singëril looked around the table. "Need I remind everyone that we can't put all our resources into this one battle. Until the corridor is closed, they have an unlimited number of replacements. We don't unless our human allies from the mainland show up. But that's unlikely since we now know they have their own war to fight."

"There's one more disturbing development, Your Highness," General Feynral said. "Colonel Tirion reported the dark elf army is marching with civilian prisoners."

Lessien's eyes widened. "They're going to use them as shields, aren't they?"

"Probably," Father Goram said. "Or…"

"Or what," Lessien asked. "What could be worse?"

"Food for the dragons, Your Highness," General Singëril said.

Lessien's breath caught. "By the goddess!" she whispered. Her sword flashed an ugly reddish color.

Father Goram reached over and placed a hand on the Queen's clenched fist. "InnisRos needs her Queen to be strong."

Lessien nodded. "I'm fine. It just… One never gets used to cruelty."

"Which is precisely why we do what we do, Your Highness," General Singëril said. "We die for you… we die for InnisRos… but more importantly, we die for our people and their safety. We die so that such evil never touches them."

"And when it does?" Lessien asked the general.

General Singëril's face remained impassive, but his voice changed. It was hard and unforgiving. It was emotionless and unrecognizable. "Then we become the Queen's Justice," he replied.

Everyone in the room stared at the general. Everyone except Lauran Ar-Feiniel, that is. Of all those associated with him, she alone knew what lengths he'd go through to see that wrongs are redressed, injustice corrected, and the purveyors of death and suffering stopped.

The Queen's military commander allowed a few moments of silence to let his intent sink in. Lauran Ar-Feiniel grabbed his hand to give him her support. She'd always be with him.

"Your Highness," General Singëril continued after a few moments. "There's even more bad news from Colonel Tirion."

Lessien's expression didn't change as she prepared herself. She nodded.

"The dark elves took several dozen of Taranthi citizens and crucified them just outside the north wall. Once staked into the ground, the dark elves cut their throats."

Lessien winced. "This has been verified?"

General Singëril nodded.

"At least they died quickly, Your Highness," Landross offered.

Lessien frowned. "That's little consolation, but thank you, Sir Knight." The queen turned her attention to General Feynral and changed the subject before emotions overcame her. There was no time for feelings… at least not until she was in the privacy of her own chambers. "I just remembered. Colonel Tirion's the Marine who accompanied my sister, right? Did he mention her?"

"She's well, Your Highness," the Marine general reassured the Queen. "But there's been a problem between her and that flying boulder…"

"Maedhros Nénmacil," Father Goram offered.

General Feynral nodded. "Yes, that's its name. Well, they've had a falling out. The colonel didn't go into much detail, but it was over your sister's unwillingness to help those being crucified. For what it's worth, Colonel Tirion agreed with your sister though he was understandably distressed by the whole affair."

"And angry, I'd wager," Father Goram added.

General Feynral nodded in agreement. "He made that quite clear."

"Why wouldn't my sister try to help?" the queen asked.

"There was nothing anyone could do to save them, and your sister didn't want to give up their anonymity. Maedhros Nénmacil?…" General Feynral looked at Father Goram who nodded. "Maedhros Nénmacil disagreed."

The queen nodded. She understood. "Thank you."

"Any leads on the *Ak-Séregon Stone*?" Father Goram asked.

"Not really," General Singëril replied, "except that it's not in the city. Feynral's Colonel Tirion has contacted several hundred Marine veterans who are just spoiling for a fight. They'll help get my Marine and your sister outside the city to do a perimeter search."

"Why not contact the thieves' guild?" Lessien asked. "They helped me to escape."

Father Goram shook his head. "That was one of the last things they did before the thieves' guild left for Listern Island. It was getting too dangerous for them. Mother Aubria closed shop, so to speak, and left Taranthi. As for the thieves unaffiliated with the guild who stayed, well, they're either dead or in hiding."

"Then I suppose the Marines will have to do," Lessien said. "Are you still in contact with Colonel Tirion?"

General Feynral nodded. "For the most part. It's not constant since we've no way of knowing if dark elf sorcerers can track a communications crystal. So, he checks in at set times and keeps his communications brief."

"Can you initiate communication?" Lessien asked.

"No, Your Highness."

Lessien understood that necessity. "Next time you talk to him, remind him he's under orders to keep my sister safe."

"You needn't worry, Lessien," Autumn said. "He'll keep her safe or die trying. The Colonel's quite smitten with Nefertari. And I believe the same holds true for her."

Lessien frowned. "She never mentioned it to me."

"Maybe not, Your Highness," Cordelia added. "But it's plain enough to see when the two of them are together. Add Miracle into the mix and the three of them appear to be one happy family."

Lessien thought back at the times she observed the two together and saw it at once. Colonel Tirion never hid his feelings for Nefertari. As for her sister, she was more secretive and kept her personal feelings hidden, but they were still there to read if one was paying attention.

"There's been a lot going on, Lessien," Autumn said to reassure the Queen.

"But she's my sister," Lessien thought. She promised herself she'd do better once things settled down. "We march at first light," she said aloud. "Is there anything else we should discuss?"

Lessien looked around the table as everyone shook their heads. "Well, generals, I suggest you rein in your soldiers from their normal late-night drinking and debauchery and put them to bed," she said as she smiled.

"Too late for that, Your Highness," General Feynral said as he, along with the others, stood. "By now my Marines have drunk the Army under the table."

"Humph!" General Singëril said. "We'll see." Both generals saluted their queen and left the room along with everyone else.

"Horatio," the Queen called. "Walk with me."

The priest kissed Autumn who nodded and went on alone. Father Goram looked at Ajax and motioned with his head that the dire wolf should stay with his wife.

The queen and the priest walked in silence and within a few minutes were on the monastery battlements over-looking the town of Calmacil Clearing and thousands of bivouacked soldiers. Razor and Findley sat on either side of the two. Lessien remained quiet. Father Goram gave her as much time as she needed to say what was on her mind.

Below them, the campfire light from the massive army camp would have been visible for miles if the surrounding forest hadn't smothered it. The warriors laughed, cursed, drank ale or wine, and sang bawdy songs. They gave no sign that in a few days' time they'd be fighting a battle many wouldn't survive. They were professional soldiers and that was their life. As Lessien and Father Goram watched and listened, sergeants walked through the camp, ordering their charges to bed.

Then the sound that Lessien had been waiting for arrived from far away – a female voice singing. "Listen, Horatio," she said. There was a sense of excitement in her voice. "Hear that song? Here, take my hand and close your eyes. Shut the world out for a few minutes and listen. No… not just listen. Feel it. Let the melodies wash over you. Let the words touch your soul."

Father Goram did as the queen requested.

After a few seconds, Lessien broke the silence. "It's a soldier's vow of loyalty to their liege, their commanders, their people, but mostly to each other. My father once told me they sang it on the eve of battle. When I was a child, he'd sing it to me whenever he had to leave. Mother had passed, and I always felt so lonely when he was away. But the song – the sound of his voice – always reassured me he'd be back and that I'd never be alone."

Father Goram nodded but said nothing. He'd heard the song before during one of the many evenings he had spent in the field with Martin and his army. It was beautiful both in sound and in spirit.

First the solo female voice sang of the dark night and how it fell across the land and those sworn to defend it. Then a second voice, a male, joined the female. Together they sang about the glory and horror of battle, its participants, and the lifelong physical and mental consequences of combat. Four harmonious voices took up the cause, describing the darker night that consumed those who fell before the enemy and the reward that awaited them. Then the song's mood turned lighter, and the four singers described a soldier's existence— training, marching, fighting – and the joy of life that came with the day's end – food, ale, companionship, and camaraderie. Finally came the chorus, when everyone within the camp joined in. It sounded much like a tavern song – lighthearted, disrespectful, and coarse. Upon hearing it, one could imagine drunken soldiers sitting together, raising ale mugs to the heavens, and bellowing as loud as they could. The lyrics, however, were not that of a lewd tavern song. They spoke of duty, responsibility, loyalty, and commitment to their country, their loved ones, their commanders, and each other. They sang the chorus twice, then everything in the camp became quiet.

Lessien and Father Goram were silent. The song was still resonating in their souls when Lessien raised *Ah-HritVakha* and pointed it into the black star-filled sky. A bolt of blue energy shot into the air and silently exploded, showering Calmacil Clearing in a blanket of pulsating sparkles which winked out as they hit the earth. Father Goram raised an eyebrow. He'd never seen Martin do that.

The young queen looked over at the priest. "It'll help them sleep." She offered no other explanation as she continued to look out over the battlements.

"Will you be traveling with us tomorrow?" Lessien asked.

Father Goram nodded, though the Queen couldn't see it in the dark. "Of course I will, child," he said. "Both Autumn and I will be at your side every step of the way."

"As you've always been," Lessien replied. She stood silent for a few more moments before continuing. "I've a confession to make. I didn't like you for a very long time."

"I know."

Lessien barked out a short laugh. "I'm not surprised. Not much gets past you."

This time it was Father Goram's turn to laugh. "Autumn would disagree. She says I'm the most obtuse person she's ever met. That I only understand spells, wolves, and political skullduggery. That I'm woefully lacking in the affairs of the heart." The priest paused. "Maybe I was at one time." Father Goram shook his head. "But not now. My first wife, Mary, taught me a lot about feelings, emotions, acceptable behavior around other people, and the such. Autumn likes to think she's continuing my education. And in many respects she is. But the most important thing Autumn's taught me is that a broken heart can love again."

"You're very lucky to be surrounded by friends and people who love you."

"As are you, Lessien," Father Goram replied.

"Humph!" Lessien snorted. "For many it's only because I'm the queen."

"People owe their allegiance to you as their queen," Father Goram admitted. "That's true. But people love you because you're Lessien… a righteous young queen raised by Martin to respect the dignity of life… a queen who'll fight for her people even if it means her own life… a queen who'll make the hard decisions needed to keep her realm safe and prosperous. You're loved, Lessien. Never doubt that."

Lessien turned to face her friend. She had tears in her eyes. "Then why do I always feel so alone?"

Father Goram surrounded her with his arms as she cried on his shoulder. She clung to him as if he were her only lifeline – her only salvation. The priest stroked the back of her head as he let her cry. He may be thickheaded in many things as Autumn sometimes claimed, but he understood precisely what was happening here. For these few moments, Lessien was a child again who needed a father.

After several long minutes, Lessien stilled, though she wasn't ready to break Father Goram's comforting embrace. When she finally did, she stepped away and wiped her tears with the sleeve of her blouse.

"Thank you, Horatio," Lessien said. "Now go home to your wife."

Father Goram paused.

Lessien smiled. "It's okay. I'll be fine. Really. I only want to enjoy the night a little longer. Razor and Findley will see that no harm comes to me."

Father Goram looked at the two dire wolves. *"Yes, they will,"* he thought. *"But it's not your physical well-being that concerns me."* He bowed. "Good night, my queen. I'll see you in the morning."

As the priest disappeared into the monastery, several pairs of eyes looked at the queen from above. Alerted by Father Goram, the crystal dragon golems perched on the roof would be ready to support the dire wolves in the unlikelihood of an attack.

Captain Jasmine Dubois and her First Officer, Thomas Krist, were also on the battlements, though not close enough to notice the queen and Father Goram. They both marveled at the elven song — melancholy in the beginning but changing direction midway through to end up in a high-spirited tone. It was the type of song the crew of the *Freedom Wind* would sing at the beginning of each voyage, though the one they had just heard was darker and more serious.

Then there were the fireworks at the end of the song. Both looked to the source. It was the queen with her sword raised and pointed up towards the stars. A robed figure stood next to her. Both recognized the clerical mantle of Father Goram. Before the light of the sword blinked out, the captain thought the queen looked haggard. They hadn't seen her that day until then, but the day before she appeared to be holding up well under the stress.

"What's changed," Captain Dubois wondered.

Mr. Krist looked over at her. "Huh?"

Captain Dubois shook her head. "Nothing, Thomas. Just thinking out loud. You were saying before the song?"

"Lieutenant Farnsworth reports that all is well onboard the *Freedom Wind*, Jasmine. Though he reports the crew could use shore leave."

Captain Dubois shook her head. "I understand and wish I could grant it," she replied.

Mr. Krist nodded.

"Did the lieutenant mention the status of our resupply?"

"Yes, ma'am," Mr. Krist answered. "We're completely re-stocked. The northern part of InnisRos has copious amounts of both game, fruit, and water."

Captain Dubois said nothing while she stared into the sky. The stars were bright and, as always, enticing. They were also in their rightful places. The change they had experienced on the voyage over still had her unsettled.

The captain broke her silence after a few minutes. "Thomas, what kind of world do you suppose we found ourselves in when we shifted?"

Eric the Black had explained shifts between worlds as possible consequences of the sustained connection between Aster and the Svartalfheim by the *Ak-Séregon Stone*. If the sorcerer was correct, everything the *Freedom Wind* and her crew had experienced left little doubt what had happened, and that frightened her. Until the connection was closed, the risk on open water was too great to ignore. To make matters worse, there were those unworldly black dragons to consider. Dragons are a ship captain's greatest fear, and those black dragons destroyed InnisRos' naval fleet in short order. She could only imagine what would happen to the *Freedom Wind* if they came across even one of those beasts. They were unfortunately 'landlocked' for the foreseeable future.

Mr. Krist considered for a few moments before answering. "Hard to say," he said. "We experienced it for only a few seconds. But perhaps it wasn't too different from our own. To quote from a poem by Sapphorian:

> *"Stars in the sky and water beneath our keel.*
> *Winds for our sails and hearts filled with steel.*
> *Cured hogshead and a mug of mead.*
> *Tell me, what else does a sailor need?"*

Captain Dubois laughed. "How could I ever have forgotten that piece of classical literature?" she teased. "Sapphorian certainly had a way with words, didn't he?"

Mr. Krist joined the captain's laughter. "Indeed he did, Jasmine. Indeed he did."

After a few more minutes in silence, Captain Dubois sighed. "I guess we'd best get some sleep ourselves. In the morning I'll try to talk to the queen to see what she wants us to do, though I don't think we'll have a very big part to play. I'm sure that would satisfy our employers."

Mr. Krist shook his head. "Don't be so hard on them, Jasmine. They have a lot at stake. The *Freedom Wind* is their best ship and represents a substantial part of their profit margin."

Captain Dubois nodded. "Different circumstances, but you're right."

"Of course I am."

Captain Dubos playfully punched Mr. Krist in the arm.

Captain Dubois and Mr. Krist were given adjoining quarters in Father Goram's apartment complex. As they approached their rooms, they saw something unusual. Sitting on the floor, her back leaning against Captain Dubois's door, a young Marine officer was sleeping. The mug of coffee she clutched in her hand was in jeopardy of spilling. Both the captain and first officer of the *Freedom Wind* kneeled next to the sleeping warrior. Captain Dubois removed the mug from the Marine's hand and placed it on the floor.

"I can't believe we got the drop on a Marine!" Mr. Krist whispered.

Captain Dubois shook her head. "Poor thing. She looks exhausted."

Captain Dubois gently shook the girl's shoulder.

"What?" the Marine said as she came out of her sleep. When she saw the captain, she stood and saluted. "Lieutenant Maewen Sharie, ma'am, at your service."

Captain Dubois and Mr. Krist both got to their feet. "Relax," the captain instructed the officer after she returned the salute. She watched as the Marine breathed a sigh of relief.

"You're dead on your feet," Captain Dubois observed as she opened the door to her room. "Come inside where we can talk in peace."

Lieutenant Sharie began to resist. "But I…"

Before she could object further, Mr. Krist put his arm around her to both steady and usher her into the room. He walked her over and made her sit in one of the two padded chairs next to the fireplace. Before sitting the girl deftly repositioned her sword so it wasn't in the way.

Captain Dubois sat in the other chair while Mr. Krist poured drinks.

"Do you drink whiskey, Lieutenant?" he asked.

Lieutenant Sharie straightened up in her chair. "I'm a Marine, sir," she answered with obvious pride. "Of course I drink whiskey. I can out-drink most everyone in my platoon."

"Whiskey it is," Mr. Krist said as he handed both a small tumbler. He took his own and seated himself on the hearth of the fireplace.

While Captain Dubois and Mr. Krist sipped their drink, Lieutenant Sharie downed hers in one gulp, closed her eyes as she leaned back in her chair, and belched.

"Ahhh!" she mumbled. Suddenly she realized she wasn't with her Marine compatriots. Her eyes opened wide and she covered her mouth in embarrassment. "My pardon!" she exclaimed.

Mr. Krist laughed. "Father Goram keeps a pretty good stock of whiskey on hand for his guests, doesn't he?"

The Marine nodded agreement but it was evident she still fretted about her lack of manners.

Captain Dubois smiled. "Maewen, what brings you here," she prompted gently.

"Orders for you, ma'am," the Marine replied. "Well, since Queen Lessien isn't really your queen, I suspect more of a request."

"May we see them?" Captain Dubois requested. "Or are they verbal?"

"Oh, of course!" Lieutenant Sharie pulled a rolled parchment from inside her uniform jacket and handed it over.

Captain Dubose broke the seal and unrolled the document to read it. Mr. Krist drained the rest of his drink, put the goblet on the hearth as he got up, and went to the back of the captain's chair so he could read over her shoulder.

Once she was done, she handed the unrolled parchment to Mr. Krist. "What do you think, Thomas?" she asked.

"It's certainly doable," he responded. "I have concerns about the timeline, though."

"And it leaves us vulnerable should the dragons return," Captain Dubois added.

Mr. Krist handed the orders – the request – back to Captain Dubois and began to knead her shoulders with his strong hands. "We've faced dragons before."

The *Freedom Wind's* master closed her eyes and sighed as she enjoyed her shoulder massage. "Indeed, we have, Thomas," she replied. "But I don't really want to try and face down the likes of those black monsters we saw the other day."

"InnisRos is in a war for her survival, Jasmine. And she's been a very good trading partner with our employer. I don't think Mr. Dular would mind if we helped. In fact, he'd probably demand it. If Queen Lessien wins, his family will have the market cornered in this part of the world. That, my captain, is simple economics."

"As you've already so succinctly mentioned, I'd bet he'd certainly mind losing his biggest and best ship!"

Mr. Krist laughed. "Of course he would. But that'd hardly be our concern since we'd probably be on the bottom with her."

"Point taken, Thomas," Captain Dubois said. She looked at the Marine lieutenant. Exhaustion, the comfortable chair, and the whiskey combined to put the girl into a deep sleep.

Captain Dubois stood and went over to her bed. She pulled a light blanket off and draped it over the sleeping Marine. Then she turned to Mr. Krist.

"It's late, Thomas. How do you feel?"

"Well enough to run an errand for you," he answered. He knew his captain well enough to interpret the meaning of her last question.

Captain Dubois smiled. "Thank you. Go to General Singëril's room and tell him we'll honor the queen's request. Tell him we'll have the *Freedom Wind* anchored off the north shore by mid-morning. And Thomas, make sure you tell him personally."

Mr. Krist nodded. "And you?"

Captain Dubois pulled a charged communications crystal from her captain's jacket. "I'll get Lieutenant Farnsworth out of his bunk. He's got a lot to do before the *Wind* can get underway."

As the first officer opened the door to Captain Dubois's apartment, she called out to him. "And make up an excuse for our sleeping guest here. Be sure to make it plausible. I don't want to see her get into trouble."

"You mean I can't use the 'Someone insulted the size of the *Freedom Wind's* main mast' excuse?" Mr. Krist replied with a smile.

"Particularly that one!" she exclaimed. "Especially since it didn't work the last time you tried it," she grumbled after he'd left the room.

The two creatures, demonic constructs created for assassination, slithered through the Army camp to the monastery walls and went straight up and over. Though visible, they blended in with the surrounding background like a chameleon, though with greater success. Priests and priestesses who have innate abilities to sense evil could locate and recognize their black souls for what they were. But the ordinary person had no such advantage. Unless they were the target, they'd neither see nor hear anything.

The assassins were similar to a salamander – twelve feet long with six short, muscular legs supporting a two hundred-pound body. A scorpion-like stinger protruded from the end of their long tail, and their extended snouts were filled with rows of sharp spike-like teeth. Down the entire length of their backs ran a double row of barbed bone. Each of these barbs dripped a thick, dark ooze. Four spiked horns extended out either side of their heads — two going forward and two going back. Their hides were armored with dragon-hard scales.

Once over the wall, they moved towards the main monastery building. By order of Father Goram, the doors to the massive church and rectory were always unlocked, for the people of Calmacil Clearing don't have spiritual crises during daylight hours only. Once inside the great doors, they separated as each headed towards its intended target.

Landross, per his nightly custom of late, wandered the hallways of the wing in the monastery which contained the apartments of the Queen, Father Goram and Autumn, and other distinguished guests. There was a strong military presence in the wing and each apartment was not only physically guarded but also protected by Father Goram's magic. But as the military commander in charge of security, he needed to verify for his own peace of mind.

As usual, everything was fine. He only had to check the apartments of Queen Lessien and Father Goram before he felt he could retire for the evening. When he rounded a corner and entered the hallway leading to the queen's apartment, he saw both guards on the floor, the double doors opened, and multi-colored lights coming from the inside of the apartment. As he rushed through the hallway with sword drawn, he heard explosions and the queen grunting. There was little doubt she was defending herself against an unknown opponent. When he rushed the door, he didn't stop to check the condition of the guards. It was clear even from a glance that they were dead. He cursed as he was forced to slow and jump over them. He'd just lost a few precious seconds — seconds that he might need to save the queen.

Landross stepped across the door's threshold and was hit by one of the queen's dire wolf guardians. The force of the impact knocked the knight across the hallway. Both slammed against the opposite wall and slid to the floor. Landross hadn't been wearing his armor, so nothing protected him from either the impact with the wall or the weight of the dire wolf. With a grunt and a whimper, both lay on the floor, momentarily stunned. Landross got to his feet slowly. The dire wolf, Findley, tried but his legs wouldn't work. Blood came streaming out of his mouth.

The knight shook his head to clear the cobwebs and then looked inside the room. The other dire wolf, Razor, was on the back of something, though Landross couldn't make it out. Razor wasn't having much luck as his bite and claws appeared to have little to no effect. The dire wolf was bucked off, at least that's how it appeared to Landross, and landed hard. Landross heard the snapping of bone. Razor didn't get back up.

The queen was swinging *Ah-HritVakha* at something Landross still couldn't see. Then a red bolt streaked out of the queen's sword and hit her attacker. Though the assassin was only briefly exposed, it was enough to give Landross an idea where to attack. Though nothing like those of the queen's weapon, his sword also contained powerful magical enchantments. Hoping to skewer the creature, Landross lunged forward and hit the dragon scales hard with the point of his sword, but the blade deflected off with a shower of sparks. The creature glanced back but continued its attack on the queen.

Landross, a seasoned knight with a warrior's instinct, realized the fiend could only be there for one reason – to kill the queen. It'd not be turned from its goal even if it meant its life… so there'd be no distracting it. The knight glanced at the queen. She fought well – better than most of his knights – but was tiring. Her movements were slowing and her defense against the creature's spiked maw and stinger had become more ragged. He had to place himself between the Queen and her attacker until help arrived.

As he moved past the long, sinewy body, the queen's sword released two bolts of energy. The first drove the creature back a few steps while the second froze it in place. Using that instant of advantage, the queen swung her sword with every bit of energy she had left and cut off the head. Both the body and severed head dissolved into ash and disappeared, leaving no trace of its existence. By now the monastery alarm was sounding and hard-soled boots sprinted down the hallway outside the queen's apartment.

The queen, breathing heavily, looked at Landross. "Sir Knight," she said as she extended her sword arm for him to see. There was an angry looking puncture on the back of her hand. "I'm afraid I didn't kill it quickly enough." Lessien's eyes closed and she toppled over.

Landross caught Lessien as she fell. He lowered her to the floor and cradled her in his arms. Her body stiffened and a moan escaped her lips. She opened her eyes back up, but they were unfocused. Landross knew from experience she wasn't seeing anything but the dark recesses of the pain that had seized her body. *Ah-HritVakha* glowed deep purple, but it was as helpless as the knight.

Then Lessien's body relaxed and her eyes cleared. "Landross," she whispered. "The darkness! It's coming!" She then clutched his arm in a death grip as her body went rigid once more.

"What cruelty is this," Landross said as tears rolled down his cheeks.

Desperate for a way to save his queen, Landross considered removing the poisoned hand, but decided it wouldn't do any good if the poison had already spread beyond her arm. The queen's only hope was Father Goram or one of his other healers.

A few of Landross's knights entered the room while even more kneeled to examine the prone guards outside the door. "We need Father Goram!" Landross ordered as he lifted the queen off the floor. "Lead! I'll be right behind you."

Knights had moved away the two dead guards from the doorway and covered them with cloaks. Landross said a quick prayer for their souls as he raced down the hallway toward Father Goram's quarters.

At the time he didn't know Father Goram was dealing with his own assassin.

The assassination attempts on the queen and Father Goram were supposed to occur simultaneously. But the creature that found itself outside Father Goram's apartment discovered the protection wards were stronger than its master had expected. The wards were similar to fine strands of spider silk and only visible to one gifted with magic sight. The creature carefully cut through each strand with its own magic. Satisfied, it spit acid saliva on the door locks. While waiting for the locks to dissolve, the creature wondered why such a complicated ward would have been so easy to overcome. Curious, it took a second look and realized its mistake. Each strand he'd cut had a duplicate strand in another dimension. Too late!

The doors exploded outward, sending wooden shards bouncing off the creature's body. Several shards found themselves imbedded in the organ the creature used to see, blinding it. The force of the explosion pushed the assassin back a few steps. Following the shards was a few hundred pounds of angry dire wolf. Ajax found the underside of the creature's neck exposed for just a moment and pounced. His teeth met little resistance, but his mouth began to burn almost immediately. The overwhelming pain forced Ajax to let go his hold.

Though the creature couldn't see its target, it still sensed it. Ignoring the dire wolf, the assassin cautiously moved forward. Its target stood just a few paces away.

Father Goram now saw the creature... but only because of the wooden shards that had found places between its dragon scales to penetrate. "You come for me," he said. "I thought as much. How's Ajax, Autumn?"

Autumn, who had circled around the assassin, was kneeling next to Ajax and using her magic to heal his mouth. "Just burns, Horatio," she replied to her husband's query. "He'll be fine after a day or two."

The creature stopped, confused. The target acted as if it was unconcerned for its own life. *"Perhaps the mortal had succumbed to the inevitable,"* the creature thought. *"Or…"*

Suddenly the creature couldn't move or sense his objective. *"Another trap!"* it shrieked in its mind. It released a shriek of anger and frustration that drowned out the bleating of the general alarm sounding throughout the monastery… and sent chills down the spines of every living soul within several hundred feet.

As soon as the creature was ensnared, Father Goram began an enchantment. He had to finish quickly, for he knew the trap he'd set for this offspring of the Abyss would fail soon.

"Althaya the wise.
Pray thee, unlock the threshold.
And return this fiend.

Back to the Abyss.
To the hell from which it spawned.
Never to return.

Let other beasts know.
You'll not tolerate their zeal.
In this world, your everlasting domain."

"ET ABIERUNT!"

The assassin creature screamed again in an unworldly voice. The form of Althaya appeared above it and pointed to the floor beneath the shrieking creature. A hole opened up, and from it millions of demons and the trapped souls of the condemned raised their voices in supplication to the goddess, crying for release from the eternity of their prison. She refused to listen. A hand reached up through the hole, latched itself onto the trapped creature, and pulled it down.

Althaya smiled. "You have my thanks, Asroilu," she said. An enormous head appeared through the hole. It was dog-like with six golden eyes, three to a side. The head nodded and smiled before returning through the hole which immediately closed with a faint "pop".

Althaya looked at Father Goram. "You must hurry," she said. "The Queen's been poisoned and is on the brink of death."

By now Autumn and Ajax were standing next to the priest. "Can we save her," Autumn asked.

The goddess nodded. "But to do that the source of the poison must be exorcised."

Father Goram shook his head. "You mean the creature?"

"No, my priest," Althaya replied as she faded away.

"Damn the gods and goddesses for their stupid riddles and half-baked insinuations!" Father Goram said as he ran out the door of his apartment. Autumn and Ajax followed closely behind.

Landross turned a corner and met Father Goram, Autumn, and the dire wolf Ajax. By now, the queen's body was no longer rigid, and the knight could cradle her as he ran. As soon as he spied Father Goram, he stopped and laid the queen on the floor.

"Help her, Horatio," Landross said. "She's close to death."

Father Goram kneeled next to the queen and briefly examined her. "She's been poisoned," he declared.

Landross nodded. "So, she has. Quickly! Work your magic and heal her!"

Father Goram looked closely at the wound in her hand and let his magic flow into it. By now, Autumn was also kneeling next to

Lessien and applying her own special brand of healing. But nothing worked.

"Demonic poison takes many forms," Father Goram said to Autumn. "Before we can remove it, we must correctly identify its specific characteristics. But that's hard to do because it changes the way it presents itself in the body. Like the creature that bit her, the poison camouflages itself to stay hidden. It's as if it has a mind of its own."

Autumn, her magic entering the queen's body and probing for the poison, nodded her understanding. "Althaya mentioned exorcising something."

"I'll be damned if I…" Father Goram started but stopped. "Hold on!"

Landross watched his queen's life drifted away before his eyes. As he held her other hand, helpless, he listened to and observed every word and action the two healers uttered and made. But it was clear neither had an answer to the poison, and that was causing him to become more and more despondent. But as soon as he heard Autumn's oblique comment concerning exorcism, he knew what he had to do. It was what he should have done earlier.

The knight stood and drew his sword. Before anyone could stop him, and before Ajax could leap at him, he brought the sharp blade down on the wrist of the injured hand, severing it. The sweat-laden queen screamed in pain and sat up for a few moments before slumping back, unconscious once again.

"What the hell did you just do?!" Autumn berated the knight.

Silently Landross stared at the amputated hand.

Father Goram, working to stem the bleeding, shushed his wife. "Gently, my love. He did what he had to do to save Lessien's life."

Autumn studied her husband for a few seconds before it suddenly made sense. "You're right," she said as she nodded.

Father Goram grabbed his wife's hand and placed it on the stump. "A little help, please."

Autumn used her healing magic to support the priest, and while doing so, discovered that there were no longer signs of the poison in the queen's body.

"My apologies for yelling at you, Landross," Autumn said. "I hadn't figured it out yet."

"I should have done it sooner," the knight remarked. "But doubt stopped me. That and the fact that she's the queen."

"There's no blame, Landross," Father Goram said.

"Perhaps not, priest," Landross replied. "But there are the canons of honor."

Landross bowed to both, cleaned his sword with a rag, sheathed it, unhooked it from his belt, and wrapped the bloody rag around it. He turned to the nearest knight and presented the sheathed sword. The knight accepted it with a nod as two other knights stepped up on either side of Landross.

"Please tell the Queen that I await her pleasure in my quarters," Landross said as he again bowed to both healers and then to the now sleeping queen.

As the four knights walked away, Autumn asked, "What just happened?"

Father Goram, satisfied the stump had been properly closed and that the poison no longer coursed through Lessien's body, sighed. "Landross just arrested himself for attacking the Queen."

"But he saved her life!" Autumn protested.

"Yes, but that doesn't matter," the priest replied. "At least not to a knight. Don't worry. It'll work out."

Autumn shook her head. "Will it?" she said with uncertainty. "You know Lessien can be… somewhat unpredictable. That was her sword arm! And you know how much she values her fighting ability! She says it honors her father!"

Father Goram stood and motioned to the knights lingering in the corridor. "Take her to her quarters and lay her on the bed. I'll be right behind you."

One of the bigger knights cradled the queen in his arms and carried her down the corridor. Surrounding him was an escort of six more knights.

"Don't worry, dear," Father Goram said as he watched the procession. "Landross will be fine. Right now, however, we may have more immediate concerns. Findley and Razor are noticeably absent and probably need our help."

It was still dark, but dawn was only an hour away. General Singëril, Lauran Ar-Feiniel, Commander-General Feynral, and several aides sat atop their horses and watched as the InnisRos main army broke camp. Soon they'd begin the march through the forest to the foothills of the North Spire Mountains. Once there, General Singëril thought they'd have a day to organize and prepare for the upcoming battle. A rider approached. It was Father Goram.

"Good morn to you, priest," General Singëril said without taking his eyes off his soldiers. "How fares the queen." It was a question that interested everyone present.

"As well as can be expected," Father Goram replied. "She almost died last night. I suspect she'll need at least three days to fully recover from her wound. Then who knows how long she'll need to adjust to only having one hand."

General Singëril was quiet. Though it was good news, it didn't erase the guilt. The assassination attempt should never have happened on his watch. If not for Landross' quick thinking, they'd be without a queen this morning. Inexcusable!

Lauran Ar-Feiniel looked pleadingly at Father Goram. She wanted him to ease the guilt the general bore. The priest understood and nodded.

"The demons sent to kill the Queen were chameleon-like and hard to see," the priest said. "No one untrained in the arcane arts could have stopped them before it was too late. Fortunately, Lessien had her sword and her dire wolves. Only that saved her life."

"And one attacked you. But you had wards to protect you, as I understand it," General Feynral interjected. "And a damn good thing too, else we'd be without our high priest!"

"True, general," Father Goram replied. "Smart enough to ward my apartment but not smart enough to ward the queen's as strongly. Perhaps if I had the queen wouldn't have lost her hand."

General Singëril sighed. He understood what the priest was doing – trying to deflect the blame to himself. The general appreciated it, but he wasn't the type of person who'd let go of something like this. "Your words make sense, priest. But I won't be manipulated by you as if I were a child. I, and only I, will decide the degree of responsibility I bear for what happened last night."

"And if you're wrong?" Father Goram countered.

General Singëril looked at the priest. "I'm not," he insisted.

Father Goram shook his head. "You're so focused on being a general you've forgotten you're also a mortal with the same weaknesses and failings every other normal person has. So again, I ask, what if you're wrong?"

"Stop this nonsense," General Singëril barked. His voice remained calm and controlled, but everyone who knew him could see signs that his anger was boiling just below the surface.

Father Goram wouldn't let it go, however. Guilt has a habit of simmering until it explodes. He didn't want to see that on the battlefield. So one way or another he had to clear the General's mind before the mêlée with the dark elves. "Very well. We'll try it your way since you're so damned determined to parcel out responsibility. This monastery is MY responsibility, not yours. You have no control over what happens under its roof. If you want someone to blame, look to me and quit beating yourself up over it. Were mistakes made last night? I don't know. Maybe. Probably." Father Goram sighed. "I should have protected her apartment better. But she had two guards posted outside her quarters and of course her two dire wolves. And she's in the most protected part of the monastery. I never thought her life would be in danger. But general, I don't feel guilty. I mean it's not as if I was trying to leave her vulnerable. It's war! You should understand better than anybody that the unexpected is commonplace."

"Queen Lessien!" an aide shouted.

Everyone turned their horses to observe two figures making their way towards them on horseback. Alongside the queen's horse trotted two dire wolves who were moving gingerly. Both would have died a few hours before if not for the Autumn's healing hands. Lessien didn't have hold of the reins of her horse. The other figure, riding ahead of her, was leading it. The queen was holding onto the saddle horn with her remaining hand, while the stump of her other arm rested at her side. Father Goram kicked his horse to the queen's side and dismounted. He put his hands around her waist and lifted her off the saddle, whereupon she closed her eyes and rested her head on his shoulder. By this time, everyone else had also dismounted and were standing around her and her two wolves. The guard who led her horse faded into the background to await further orders.

"You look terrible," Father Goram noted.

The queen looked at him and frowned. "I feel terrible," she answered back.

"Then why are you here, Lessien?" the high priest asked.

"I've been asking that same question ever since I climbed on my horse," Lessien replied. She held up her stump for all to see. "My hand feels as if it's still there, Horatio. And it hurts."

"Didn't Autumn block the pain?"

The queen shook her head. "Really, Horatio, you should know your wife better than that. She offered, but I didn't let her. Then she tried to come with me, but I wouldn't let her do that either. She pleaded with my wolves to stop me. But they wouldn't dare. Finally I ordered two of my guards to lock her in my bedroom for safekeeping. I don't need a nursemaid, babysitter, or special treatment! Not when my people go to war!"

"We go to war willingly, Your Highness," General Feynral said. "For our queen, our loved ones, and our country."

"Of course you do," Lessien snapped back. "You're a Marine. Father warned me about the Marines."

The Marine commander-general raised an eyebrow.

"He said that every once in a while, one must throw the devil dogs a fresh piece of meat," the queen responded to the general's unasked question. "Because if you don't, they lose their manners around civilized folk. Well, general, this is your piece of meat."

General Feynral laughed. "Martin was a wise man!" he observed.

The queen nodded. "Yes. Yes, he was. But I don't willingly send any soldier to war. And if it's forced upon me, I'm damn-well going to at least be available to see them off regardless of how I feel! And don't counter me with the whole 'But you're the queen!' crap. I'm not in the mood."

The Marine got back up on his horse, still laughing as he did so. "Are we finished, My Queen?"

"It would appear so."

"Then with your permission I'll return to my devil dogs and tell them their queen will provide plenty of fresh meat and wishes them good eating." They could hear the general laughing as he and his aides rode away.

Lessien shook her head. "General Singëril, you've been awfully quiet."

"I'm just surprised you're up and about after last night, Your Highness," the general replied.

Lessien waited.

Lauran Ar-Feiniel nudged her general in the ribs.

General Singëril cleared his throat. "Yes, well, as you can see, we're moving out. We... I mean everything... ah..."

"I don't think I've ever seen you at a loss for words, general," the queen remarked.

Lauran Ar-Feiniel sighed and shook her head. "He feels responsible for the attack last night."

"I tried to convince him otherwise," Father Goram stated. "But he's a stubborn ass."

General Singëril glared at the priest.

"If it's anyone's fault, it's yours, Horatio," Lessien replied.

"I told him that," Father Goram said.

"It's an honor thing," Lauran Ar-Feiniel added.

"Don't speak for me, Lauran," General Singëril said through clenched teeth.

"Then speak for yourself, Tomas!"

General Singëril nodded. "My Queen, as overall commander…"

"Enough!" Queen Lessien interrupted. "Consider yourself reprimanded, general, if that's what it takes. Reprimanded and expunged from the record. I'm the queen. I can do that."

The Army general sighed. He'd met his match. "Very well, Your Highness."

Queen Lessien nodded. "Now go win me a war, general."

General Singëril saluted, as did his aides, and mounted his horse. "Yes, My Queen," he said before galloping away.

The queen looked at Father Goram.

Father Goram shrugged. "Don't concern yourself about it, Lessien. He'll do his duty… and do it well."

Lauran Ar-Feiniel, who had remained behind, cleared her throat. "Your Highness, may I ask for your consideration regarding something that's been on my mind?"

Lessien redirected her attention to Lauran and nodded. "Speak freely."

Now that Lauran had the queen's full attention, she hesitated. Did she have a right to speak on Tomas' behalf without his knowledge? And if Tomas ever found out…

The queen placed her good hand on Lauran's arm. She sensed what caused Lauran to falter. "It's about General Singëril, isn't it? And he doesn't know you're talking to me."

Lauran nodded.

"Don't worry. None of us here will say a word without your permission. You have our word."

After a few moments of silence, Lauran bit her lip. "Sorry. I find myself suddenly at a loss for words."

"Just spit it out, child," Father Goram prompted.

Lauran nodded. "Tomas has never failed you. And he'll not fail you now. But once this is over, retire him, Your Highness. He's much more tired than he allows anyone to see, and you're the only person he'll listen to. Right now, other than the Army and the realm it protects, he has little time for anything else. I'm tired of competing against that."

"Isn't that rather selfish of you?" Father Goram remarked.

"You're not there comforting him after a nightmare about the people who've died following his orders," Lauran said. "Their ghosts haunt him every night. More than most you know what it's like to have someone die in your arms... to watch the light of life slowly fade away knowing you're the cause, knowing you can't do anything about it? He deserves peace, Your Highness! Give it to him, I beg you."

Father Goram nodded. He knew exactly what she was talking about.

Queen Lessien heard the concern in Lauran's voice and saw it in her eyes. But as much as she wanted to help, she couldn't let Lauran's personal feelings impede with what's best for InnisRos. "I can promise that I'll give your petition my upmost attention... but only after we've won the war. I'm sorry, but that's the best answer I can give you."

Lauran Ar-Feiniel nodded. "That's all I ask." She climbed into the saddle of her horse and wheeled it around.

"Be safe, Lauran," Lessien said.

"Yes, Your Highness." Lauran nudged her mare into a run to catch up with the one she loved.

After the assassination attempt on the queen and Father Goram, Landross, under a self-imposed arrest, waited in his quarters for the queen's judgement. As he waited, he cleaned and oiled his armor and sharpened his sword. Both magical items gave off a soft glow – the only light source in the otherwise dark room.

A former knight from the city-state of Astoria, Landross was well practiced in the upkeep of the equipment and tools of war upon which he so heavily relied. His actions were automatic and required no conscious thought. Landross always used the opportunity to let his mind wander. As he attended to his armor and sword, his mind repeated the night's events over and over again. He wasn't overcome with guilt as so many of his brethren might have been, however. He'd been around Father Goram far too long to let that happen. When he first arrived upon the shores of InnisRos and been accepted into the service of the good priest, he quickly learned that any type of lasting guilt didn't receive much traction in the monastery. What counted was a desire to learn from honest mistakes and the effort made to do better. Guilt is too self-destructive. "If you want absolution, figure out how to do it right the next time!" Father Goram would often say. "Never allow yourself to wallow in a mug of ale while you're feeling sorry for yourself."

Landross realized he'd done the only thing he could do under the circumstances. But even though it had saved the queen, she was grievously wounded as a result. Worse, he had maimed her. Both were acts of treason in some circles, and Landross wasn't sure where the queen would stand on the matter.

The knight was so busy thinking as he cleaned his armor, he didn't hear the knock on his apartment door. The second knock was more insistent and brought Landross out of his reverie.

"Enter," he called out as he continued his work. He wasn't under guard and the door to his apartment was unlocked. Landross' honor as a former Astorian Knight was enough. No one wanted to shame the knight by doing either.

It was just after dawn and Landross figured breakfast was being delivered. Famished and in need of a strong mug of coffee, he eagerly looked up from his labors as the door opened. But when he recognized the person delivering it he jumped to his feet. The armor he was cleaning, forgotten, crashed to the floor. He winced.

Queen Lessien peered into the dark room only somewhat illuminated by the light coming through the opened door. In her hand, she held a tray filled with eggs, bacon, cheese, bread and butter, and a steaming mug of coffee. Her stump was underneath the tray while her good hand tightly gripped the side.

"Please take this, Landross," Lessien said. "I'm about to drop it."

Landross stared. "Huh? Oh! Certainly, My Queen," he mumbled as he rushed over to remove the burden from his queen. "How did you knock on the door?" Landross blurted out before realizing his boorishness.

Lessien smiled. "The servant who originally had this tray did the knocking for me, you big dope! May I sit?"

"Of course," Landross exclaimed as he set the tray on a table. He rushed over and guided her to his most comfortable chair. Though well-used and somewhat tattered, it was cozy. The knight had spent many a night sleeping in it with his feet up on the ottoman in front of a warm fire.

"Thank you," Lessien said as she accepted his help to the chair. She was tired and in pain, though she hid it well.

Landross offered her his mug of coffee, but she shook her head. "It's been a busy morning, but I'm neither hungry nor in need of drink," she said. "Please, eat your breakfast."

All of a sudden Landross found he wasn't very hungry either, regardless of the grumbling in his belly. He sipped his mug of coffee as he watched Lessien close her eyes. Within seconds she was fast asleep. The knight put her feet up onto the ottoman and covered her with a quilt from his bed. He suddenly realized she didn't have her sword at her side. *"She goes nowhere without Ah-HritVakha,"* he said to himself.

"Train me," the queen said.

Landross looked over at her. Her eyes were open and alert.

"My Queen?"

Lessien closed her eyes once again. "Train me to wield *Ah-HritVakha* with my good hand," she said before drifting back to sleep.

Autumn, high on the roof of the monastery, stood next to the crystal dragon golem Golanth. His heart, visible in his chest, beat slowly. "Awaken, my friend," she said as she stroked Golanth's side and whispered the magical spell her husband had taught her. His heart began to beat faster until blood pumped throughout his body. As Autumn continued to run her hands over its side, Golanth leaned his head in towards the wife of his master and friend. His body turned from clear crystal to deep purple.

"We have need of you and your brothers, Golanth," Autumn said.

The dragon golem nodded. Autumn repeated the same awakening magic with the rest of the dragon golems. Golanth and his eleven brothers – Horvath, Renart, Duffy, Talamanth, Brand, Hoth, Tremorlyne, Jyoranth, Eddrych, Klaus, Pytor – flapped their wings as they made themselves ready for flight.

"I've never done this before," Autumn said. "Do you need to eat? Or is there anything else I can get for you?"

"No mistress," Golanth replied. "We live on the love our creator had for the master who is your mate. We live on the love you and our master have for us... and us for you."

"No other power?" Autumn was skeptical.

Golanth smiled. It radiated warmth. "What greater power is there besides love?" he replied. "Not magic, for love is the foundation stone of the magic used to form our bond with you and our master. Time? Does true love ever stop? Is it not everlasting?" Golanth shook his head. "No, mistress. Love conquers all. Look into your own heart and tell me I am wrong."

It amazed Autumn that a physical construct – a piece of crystal forged and shaped by magic and love – could be so wise. "Your creator… was she…"

"He," Golanth corrected. "Our creator was brother to the master. Brother in all things except blood."

Autumn was intrigued. "Horatio's only mentioned your creator a few times to me, and then only to say that he was a close, personal friend."

"The master can be a very private person," Golanth commented. "He used to come up here often and we would talk. He said I… all of us… were the last connection he had to that part of his life. When Kristen and her nanny, Mary McKenna, arrived, he visited less often."

"Kristen became his daughter and Mary his wife," Autumn said.

"Yes, that is true," Golanth answered. "He visited less often because he was busy raising Kristen and being a mate to Mary McKenna. We understood that."

"Fascinating! There's so much I don't know about you… or my husband, so it would seem."

Golanth nodded. "The master thinks upon himself as an enigma. I know few mortals but believe that is probably true about all of them. What do you wish of us, mistress? To talk?"

Autumn looked at the twelve crystal dragon golems surrounding her high on the roof of the monastery. She felt safe, almost as safe as when she was in her husband's embrace. She also realized the golems weren't just tools that could be used and then forgotten. They loved him and he them. So did she.

"We have to fight a war for our existence," Autumn replied. "I know you're already somewhat involved, Golanth…"

"Yes! It was an experience I wish never to duplicate!"

Autumn nodded. "But do you understand what it means to go to war?"

"The master has told us about war," another golem, Talamanth, answered for Golanth. "He has made sure our education concerning the ways of mortals is not lacking."

"My brother is correct." This from Eddrych. "We understand the necessity and the brutality of war."

"And the sacrifice," Renart concluded.

"My husband… your master… rides to fight for all of us," Autumn announced. "He said you are to fly to him during the night."

"We will do so, mistress," Golanth said. "And you?"

"I'm coming as well," Autumn replied in response to Golanth's question. "I wish to be by his side. Can one of you carry me?"

"I will be honored to carry our master's mate," Jyoranth announced. "We will go to the moon and back if you so wish it."

THE EIGHTH INTERREGNUM

The female hydra, distraught over the loss of her consort, flew east over the Greater Boreskyre Mountains, the land of the Draugen Pesta, the Eastern Boreskyre Range and into the lands of the Hyrokkin before turning north over the Northern Boreskyre Mountains and into the Great Blight. She found succor in the vast expanse of wasteland… comfort in the endless prairie of dirt and stone where only an occasional hill or a brown, scraggly looking bush broke the monotony of flat boredom from horizon to horizon.

The hydra located an oasis of bushes and landed in its center. Though hidden and protected by large brambles, she knew she'd still be vulnerable for the next few hours. Even in this nothingness predators might by lurking, waiting for her to drop her guard. Upon landing, she scrapped a large hole in the ground, turning unmovable stone into rubble with the breath from one of her heads. Once the hole was to her liking, she wove over herself a magical cocoon of energy which, when completed, turned from translucent to opaque. Over the course of the next few hours and into the night, the ground surrounding the cocoon suffered from small earthquakes. When the light of the next new day exposed the cocoon, it was sitting five hundred feet below the surface in the center of a mile-wide crater. The cocoon had adopted a yellowish tinge and had grown fivefold. One final earthquake, stronger than the others combined, rattled the crater until the sides collapsed and completely buried the cocoon. Steam and smoke streamed up from the broken ground where the crater used to be.

CHAPTER FOURTEEN

The Mainland

Kevik crouched close to the ground and crept towards his objective. A few feet away and from the opposite direction, Loki was doing the same. It was a coordinated attack devised by the northern wolf pup and his saber cat cub accomplice. Sakkara, nearby, watched as the two youths made ready to pounce on Romulus, sound asleep after a long night of guard duty. Even with assurances from Elrond that everything in the forest was well and all the fires extinguished, Romulus refused to relax. He insisted upon doing his duty to Kristen and Emmy. Sakkara would have patrolled with him, but someone had to keep the two youngsters under control.

As Sakkara watched the ambush develop, she wondered if she should stop it. Then she sensed a change in Romulus' breathing. Though he didn't show it, he was awake. As tired as he was, and as quiet as the two youths were, Romulus had still detected the upcoming attack. He allowed the two to get within pouncing range before he sprung his own trap. With a great roar, he launched himself straight up into the air. When he landed, there was no sign of the two tykes. Settling back to return to his sleep, he looked over at Sakkara. Both of the little monsters were peeking from behind the female northern wolf. Romulus smiled at his mate before closing his eyes.

Emmy clapped her hands. "How delightful!" she exclaimed. "But you two will have to do better than that to surprise Romulus!"

The youngsters, seeing a new target, scrambled from behind Sakkara to the sitting empath, who obliged them with open arms, giggling as they jumped into her lap and sent her sprawling.

Kristen, a few feet away with Tangus, Jennifer, and Mariko, laughed as the bundle of child empath, northern wolf, and Royal Mountain Saber Cat wrestled on the soft, grass-lined earth. "It's good to see Emmy laugh," she remarked to Tangus.

Tangus nodded. "Yes it is. After we lost Safire and Lester, I wasn't sure if she would ever recover. Then something happened. You saw it. One second she looks hopelessly lost, then the next she's okay. She's accepted it and moved on." Tangus shook his head. "The resiliency of a child, I guess."

"She's more than just a child, dear," Kristen remarked.

"Isn't that the truth," Jennifer said. "Sometimes it seems my little sister's soul is as old as the world itself."

"It probably is," Mariko whispered to no one in particular.

Tangus looked through tree branches and into the blue sky. Here and there clouds moved with the wind. "I know we're comfortable here," he said.

"And safe," Kirsten added.

Tangus nodded. "And safe. But we can't stay. We need to go into the city to check the damage… at least some of us do. The sooner we get things back to normal, the sooner we can attract folks to live there again. Hopefully Elanesse will come out of her melancholy long enough to give us a hand with any heavy lifting that might be required."

"Elanesse deserves a return to the vibrancy of her past," Kirsten said. "The poor dear. She's suffered so much and for so long."

"I've been helping Elrond and Elanesse cope with both the fires and the earthquake," Emmy said as she approached, holding a content Loki in her arms. Kevik was playfully nipping at Emmy's heels as he followed. The saber cat cub, though young, weighed thirty pounds. But Emmy wasn't having any trouble carrying him. "But father, you're correct. You must venture into the city and start making things right. Whether anyone makes a home there matters little to Elanesse. She only wants to be whole again."

"I agree, Emmy," Tangus replied. "But I'm not sure I know what to do to make that happen. And if I did, can I even repair it?"

"You'll know," the child said. "And Elanesse will help you. I know she's damaged, but she's still aware enough to understand what it'll take to heal. I'll stay here with Sakkara and the little ones."

Mariko protested at once. "I'll not leave!"

Emmy smiled. "Thank you for your devotion, dear Mariko, but I'll be safe here. My father, mother, and sister…"

Romulus growled.

Emmy laughed. "… and Romulus may have need of your particular skill set."

Mariko shook her head but offered no further resistance. She had her instructions.

"Father," Emmy said as she turned to Tangus and Kristen. "The Purge was not the end of it. There are still many dangers out there we must face before we can achieve peace, though peace is never guaranteed. Our world is experiencing strange reality breaks. I don't understand why or how, but it's causing the earthquakes, and more. My future self…"

"Your what?" Jennifer exclaimed. "How is that even possible? No wait! Let me think about this for a minute. We know there's something incredibly special about you. Something none of us understand. So why should this surprise anyone? But if your future self-visited you, then that must mean our problems here in the present worked out since you're still alive. Alive in the future I mean."

Emmy shook her head. "I don't completely comprehend it myself, but the future can be altered. No, that's not correct. I suppose a better analogy would be a crossroads. Your determine your future by the path you choose from many different possibilities. If I go to the right, one future becomes a reality. Left, another. Life presents hundreds of crossroads and paths every day of our existence. The choices we make, or in some cases the choices made by those around us, determine our future selves. My future…"

"Enough!" Tangus shouted holding his head. "You're making my head hurt. Let's just say Emmy had a vision and leave it at that! Emmy, why won't you go with us? I'm aware of the danger, but I can't protect you if you're not nearby."

"Here! Here!" Mariko echoed Tangus' sentiment.

"Dear," Kristen added. "Your father's right."

Emmy shook her head. "I can't. I have something to do here."

"What?"

Emmy sighed. "I can't say, mother. Only that something important will happen that I'll need to control."

"Well that'll be hard to do if you don't even know what it's going to be," Tangus said as he unleashed his pragmatic side.

"I'll understand when I'm supposed to, father," Emmy remarked. "Just as you and mother will recognize the threat once you're inside the city."

Tangus looked at his daughter and then his wife. Finally he threw up his hands. "For once I wish I knew what the hell I was doing!"

Kristen and Jennifer both giggled. "Father, you've been saying that from the beginning," Jennifer said.

"You think you're confused!" Elrond exclaimed inside everyone's mind. *"Try being a tree!"*

"Poor thing," Kristen cooed. "I imagine becoming a tree is very hard."

Elrond's leaves shook. *"Is it ever,"* he replied. *"I'm mated to a city. A city, Tangus! Let that sink in! That oak south of here survived the fires and still thinks he rules that part of the forest. What's worse, he's recruited a couple of cypresses' to his cause. Dumb cypress trees! All wood but no mind worth a damn. And then there's a spruce to the west that has a crush on me. Sure, she's beautiful. But I see her for what she is… a gold-digger. I've told her I'm committed to a city. But do you realize how impossible that sounds? She just won't…"*

"I'm ready to go," Tangus said as he walked away to get his backpack and weapons.

The shift, like the other shifts, came without warning. An unworldly fog – the one prevalent similarity of all shifts – settled on the city of Elanesse. Unlike earlier shifts, though, there were no earthquakes, tornados, or other strange and powerful weather phenomenon. Only the fog. After a few seconds it lifted and retreated into the void which then closed. The city appeared normal, as if no harm had befallen her as a result of this latest shift. That peace was broken by hundreds of unworldly creatures who came out of the deeper recesses of Elanesse and to the surface.

These creatures walked into the light of day and looked around at the world they found themselves. They walked upright, but as they moved around the city to investigate their new surroundings, they hunched over and used their talon-tipped arms as a second pair of legs. This made them extremely fast and allowed them to climb stone, though crystal, which had a less porous composition, frustrated them. They were albino-white with pink eyes. Their short, pig-like snouts opened to reveal two sharp fangs and a barbed proboscis. Their elongated head curved downwards towards their back. The body was armored with a hard chitin exoskeleton and their long tail ended in spider spinnerets.

Several dozens of these creatures congregated near the Great Obelisk. Following an unheard signal, half ran through a broken fragment of the wall and into the forest south of the city. The others dispersed within the city itself. Though scattered, they all had the same goal – find food for their queen who was already situated in a chamber at the bottom of the Pyramid of the Purge.

The male saber cat, former pack-leader of the Lowland Pride, sought a safe place away from his mate. She still hadn't forgiven him for turning out her newly born cub, and now he was on the run for his life. He didn't understand why she was so angry. He'd done her a favor, for the thing was an abomination. What decent saber cat sports purple stripes on white fur? The thing probably wasn't even his, even though she maintains she's been faithful.

"Yeah, right! Faithful my ass!" he growled to the wind as it blew through the mountain pass.

He deliberated upon the circumstances that had put him in his current predicament. His whole pride had been put under some form of enchantment. This mind-controlling force dominated them and took control of their actions. Even the pregnant females had to answer this call, of which his mate was one. As their leader, it was his responsibility to protect the pride. But he had been powerless to stop the mind incursion, and the pride blamed him for the things they did and the members they'd lost.

At least he had the presence of mind to get rid of the thing his mate had given birth to before any of the others knew about it. How could he hope to stay the dominant male when his mate gave birth to such an atrocity?! So, while his wife, still under the remnants of the enchantment, slept off the ordeal of the birth, he hid the cub in the abandoned city in the forest below their mountain home. It would've been more merciful to kill it, but he discovered he didn't have the courage to do so directly. Instead, he left it to fend for itself even though he knew it was too young to survive.

When the pride had come out of the enchantment, his mate asked about the cub. After the debacle in the city, the saber cat decided he needed something positive to offer the pride – particularly to the younger males who eyed his position as leader. He announced what he'd done and that he, and only he, had kept his senses long enough to do the right thing for his pride. He insisted he had done his duty, his mate should remember her place, and that was the end of it. A few hours later he took his share of the evening kill – a kill he hadn't taken part in – and moved to his familiar ledge to sleep.

Nightmares centered around the cub haunted him and caused him to toss and turn. When he woke up, he felt miserable. As he blinked the sleep out of his eyes, he looked out from his ledge and took in the majestic, panoramic view of the mountains. He took a deep breath of mountain fresh air and decided today might be a good day to pick a new mate. Yes! That should cheer him up!

"I pity the poor male who ends up with that old hag," he said to himself. *"She's nothing but a stupid, uppity female!"*

There was growling close behind him. He turned and met the angry stare of his mate. That in and of itself wasn't too disconcerting. But the rest of the pride, including the youngsters, were behind her and growling and showing their dagger-long fangs as well. He was being challenged, but incredibly it was the entire pride and not just one male. If there was one thing the pride leader understood, it was how to survive, which sometimes included running for his life. He jumped from the ledge to a tree just below. He climbed to the ground and ran, not really caring where he went as long as it was far away.

He knew he'd lost the pride to another cat… but thought if he left, they'd cease their idiotic challenge and leave him be. And good riddance! He'd find another pride to dominant. After all, he was a fine specimen of saber cat maleness. But to his surprise, leaving wasn't the end of his problems with the pride. His former mate, the mother of the abomination, still tracked him after several days… and she had enlisted several males to help her.

"Males following a female?" he grumbled as he continued to run. "Impossible!"

But soon enough he had his proof. He spied the saber cat posse from a tree and saw the males follow her commands. The sight filled him with terror. His former mate, a female, appeared to be the new pride leader. It was unprecedented!

No amount of distance satisfied her. As the male saber cat crossed the border of his pride's territory and into that of the Snow Pride, he felt safe for the first time since he bolted from the crazy female. But still she followed.

"No respect for territory, that one," he growled. "But this works to my advantage. The Snow Pride will end her for this invasion. Then I can have my pride back once again."

He knew of the Snow Pride only through reputation. According to the stories, only a fool entered their territory – a fool who'd be quickly separated from his life. That, and the fact they rarely came down from their mountains, explained why he'd never seen one.

He immediately sensed their presence. He stopped and inhaled. The scent was somewhat familiar, but he couldn't place it. He shook his head and continued his run into a small clearing and right into members of the Snow Pride. What he saw took his breath away, for each cat of the Snow Pride had purple strips running through their snowy white fur. It was then the male saber cat knew he had made a serious miscalculation.

"A whole pride of abominations!" he thought.

From behind he heard more movement. *"Great! I'm surrounded."*

Just when he thought things couldn't get worse, they suddenly did. It wasn't more of the Snow Pride as he thought. No. It wasn't them at all.

"Hail, Snow Pride!" a female voice called out. It was his ex-mate.

"Hail, Lowland Pride!" a male voice replied as he stepped forward. "You have wandered far and are no longer in your territory."

"I'm Baaghaghra, new leader of the Lowland Pride," the ex-pride leader heard his ex-mate say. He looked around, but there was no escape.

"Well met, Baaghaghra of the Lowland Pride," the male said. "I'm Osiris, leader of the Snow Pride. What brings you so far up the mountain and into the lands of the Snow Pride? Perhaps this cur with his tail between his legs?"

"Cur indeed, Osiris of the Snow Pride," Baaghaghra replied. "We ask that you release this… this… cub murderer to us so we may exact justice."

Osiris looked at the fugitive. "What's your name?" he asked.

"Cletus," Baaghaghra answered instead. "His name is Cletus, and he killed my cub! Our cub!"

The Royal Mountain Saber Cat looked at Cletus with dismay. "Is this true?" he asked. "You killed your own cub? Why would you do that?"

"Yes, Cletus, why did you kill our cub?" Baaghaghra added.

Cletus knew it'd be suicide to confess the reason. They were the same repugnant abominations as the cub he had exiled. He looked around but saw no weakness he could exploit to escape. "She lies," Cletus replied. "I didn't kill the cub."

"You abandoned him in the haunted city in the forest below!" Baaghaghra roared. "You might as well have killed him!"

"Again, I ask," Osiris said. "Why?"

Cletus knew this was going badly for him – that there was little chance he'd ever see the moon rise in the sky again. This made him angry – angry and insane. "Because he's the same as you and your whole damn, dirty, stinking pride," the trapped saber cat growled.

There was a hushed silence in the small clearing. Osiris turned to the female standing next to him. "Return to the caves and tell our warriors to meet with us. We'll be moving down the mountain and towards the haunted city. Tell them to hurry because they must catch up. I'll not wait."

Osiris then turned his attention to Baaghaghra. "I claim your cub if he is still alive."

Baaghaghra looked at the others in her pride to gage their feelings about the cub. It came as no surprise that many agreed with Cletus, but all harbored hatred for the former pack leader and were using the cub as an excuse to eliminate him. Baaghaghra reluctantly nodded.

Osiris looked at Cletus. "You left a saber cat cub to die because of the color of his fur!" he roared with disgust. "I should kill you here and now. But that honor belongs to the cub's mother." He turned and bound bounded away followed by most of the Snow Pride warriors.

Cletus glanced around the clearing. It was now a good bit less crowded, but still no easier to escape. Baaghaghra and the rest of the Lowland Pride closed in around him, snarling and looking for vengeance. The remaining Snow Pride cats watched impassively as Baaghaghra and her males tore Cletus to shreds.

Major Konstantin Timoshenko hurried his mounted platoon along the Alpine to catch the Madeiran army. His purpose was twofold. First, he wanted to bring justice to those who had butchered the Riders of the Elderdale. Not because the Madeirans killed them. They had been attacked first by the Riders and had every right to defend themselves. The problem was the way the Madeirans treated their prisoners. The Draugan Pesta felt it rose to the height of a war crime that should be stopped before things got too far out of hand. Second, he was to deliver Lord Ternborg's orders before the Madeirans engaged either the main force of the Riders of the Elderdale or the Havendale army.

Major Timoshenko didn't expect trouble. But like every warrior in enemy territory, he was wary. Since the smoke and ash coming from fires deeper in the forest to the northwest made visibility less than optimal, he increased the number of warriors watching his flanks. He then slowed the main body of his platoon traveling the Alpine to make allowances for his scouts who had to move on foot because their horses were too big to negotiate the dense forest.

The first sign of trouble in the offing occurred when one of his scouts wandered onto the road ahead of the main body and collapsed.

Major Timoshenko called a halt while his healers attended the warrior. He dismounted and led his horse to his wounded scout. There was a single arrow in the soldier's leg – nothing too serious. The arrow had the same fletching as the arrows they found where the four Riders had been killed. It was Madeiran.

"How is he," the major asked.

The company's chief healer, someone the major had known for years, looked up from his kneeling position. "He's dead, Konnie."

"Dead, Sergei? But it was only a shot to the leg?"

The healer shook his head. "Poison from the coloration of his fingernails and around his lips. Then there's this." The healer opened the dead soldier's mouth. The tongue was three times the size it should have been. "No doubt why he didn't scream a warning. I'll know more after I take a closer look."

Major Timoshenko's second in command, Captain Anatoly Kiryanov, spoke. "It appears the Madeirans know we're here and don't like it."

"So it would seem," the major replied. "They've miscalculated. Captain Kiryanov…" Major Timoshenko stopped. There was a faint crackling sound in the air and the hair on his arms were standing up. "Lightning!" he yelled as he tried to drop to the ground. But it was too late. He felt his body go rigid and fly through the air. He hit a stout tree hard and tumbled to the earth beneath its branches. Nothing in his body worked except his eyes and ears. Before he lost consciousness, he saw and heard multiple explosions of fire rip his platoon apart.

"General?"

Madeiran General Darcy was sitting in his command tent, eating a meal of leg of mutton, potatoes, fruit, and pastry. Behind him, his concubine awaited his pleasure. It was mid-day and still the Madeiran army had yet to break camp. General Darcy was content to march south at a leisurely pace. With the Black Death coming up to reinforce him, his rear flank was well protected. Only the Riders of the Elderdale stood between him and Havendale, and they'd be dealt with later in the day… one way or the other.

General Darcy recognized the voice of his second in command, General Timothy King. "Enter, Timothy," General Darcy called out.

As the man entered, the general spread wide his arms. "Have you had your lunch yet, Timothy?" he asked. "There's plenty here… and not just food," he said as he motioned with his head towards the bed.

General King looked at his commander with unconcealed contempt. "Thank you, general, but I've already eaten," he replied.

"Then what," General Darcy remarked as he buttered a piece of bread. "Or are you here to bore me again with your demands to move faster?"

General King shook his head. "I don't understand why you refuse to see the precariousness of our situation. Ahead are the Riders and Havendale with its sorcerers. Behind us is the Black Death."

General Darcy sighed as he put his buttered bread aside and dipped his hands in a water bowl. "The Black Death is our ally," he stated as he dried his hands on a cloth. "Just the sight of them will make every Havendale sorcerer piss his pants and run away. As for the Riders? Timothy, they're no threat. A minor inconvenience. Think of the loot in Havendale! The women…"

"You're an old fool!" General King angrily shouted. "We can't trust the Draugen Pesta! The only reason they're here in the first place is because they're being coerced by Nightshade. Hell, the only reason we're here is because of Nightshade. And how long do you think Palisades Crest and Altheros will hold back? Both have treaties with Havendale. Then there's the Astorian Knights. You know as well as I that they're the finest fighting force west of the Boreskyre's. And they always side with Palisades Crest. I have no doubt those armies are already on the march."

"None of that is a match for the giants," General Darcy replied. He'd had purposely ignored the insult. He needed the man. "But let's say I was to listen to you. What would you have us do?"

General King smiled. *"Maybe I'm finally getting somewhere!"* he thought. To the general he said, "Like Hebron, Madeira's really nothing more than a loose confederation of separate mercenary companies with the same goals and held together by a ruling body of the mercenary leaders."

"Yes, yes! I know all of that," interrupted General Darcy. "Get to the point!"

General King ground his teeth but patiently continued. "We hire ourselves out to settle disputes across the mainland. We become the armies of the smaller city-states who can't afford a permanent one. It's what we've been doing for hundreds of years. So why the sudden need for this land? We're not farmers. But we do get much of our food from them in an arrangement that satisfies both sides. Why mess with that? To save us the expense? Our current agreements with our regular customers keep our coffers well filled. And except for Hebron, nobody bothers us. But this invasion changes all that. Hell, it's probably already too late. But we still might salvage something out of this if we stop now before our position becomes even more tenuous. Let's scatter. Scatter and have each company go back to Madeira on its own. We'll survive if we're no longer considered a threat. Then maybe we can pick up the pieces of this ill-advised campaign."

"And how will the Black Death feel about this 'scattering' that you suggest," General Darcy shot back. "How do you think they'll take to our deserting them? Do you think they're going back across their mountains when this is all over? No, Timothy, I highly doubt they'll do that. The land is going to Draugen Pesta, not us. Mark my words. We're doing this because Nightshade commands us. We're doing this for our own survival… a survival made impossible if we betray the Black Death. Draugen Pesta controls the Doom Warriors. Never forget that!"

"That's a legend," General King replied. "No one's ever seen one. I doubt they exist. At least we better hope they don't."

General Darcy scratched his unkempt beard. "That's rather cryptic, Timothy," he remarked. "Speak more plainly."

General King nodded. "All right, I'll speak plainly," he replied. "You remember your orders regarding prisoners? Specifically Rider prisoners? Word going around the camp is that our rear guard, the Spiked Fist, was attacked by a team of Rider archers. The Fist paid a heavy toll, but in the end they corralled the Riders and executed the prisoners."

"So, they killed a few prisoners," General Darcy said as he poured himself a glass of wine. "It's war. They did as I instructed... a quick sword thrust and move on."

"Only that's not what they did," General King said. "They burned three and gutted another."

General Darcy winced. "That does seem a bit harsh. But still..."

"It gets worse," General King responded. "A Draugen Pesta mounted contingent came across the sight and reacted... somewhat badly."

"How do you know this?"

"The fools who executed the Riders bragged about it," General King answered.

General Darcy speared a strawberry with a stiletto and plopped it in mouth. "What else."

"Do you remember the messenger you sent to Lord Ternborg?" General King asked. "The Draugen Pesta who found the dead Riders had him with them and he saw the whole thing. They let him go since he was only a boy with instructions to return to Madeira. But he doubled back and made his way to us."

General Darcy frowned. "He was my messenger! Why didn't he return to me?"

"Apparently he felt his duty was to his own company first..."

"And the Spiked Fist was his company," General Darcy finished the thought. "When did this happen?"

"Two days ago. But I just learned of it this morning."

General Darcy nodded. "Go on," he said, but now his voice reflected apprehension.

General King continued. "The messenger reported that the Draugen Pesta would punish those responsible for the tortured prisoners. That didn't sit well with Harkum, the Spiked Fist commander. Without orders he laid an ambush for the Draugen Pesta several miles back up the Alpine."

"Harkum did what!" General Darcy screamed. The woman in the bed pulled the covers over her head.

General King continued as if the outburst never happened. "Striking first with sorcerers, he caught them off guard and killed a large number of the black devils."

"How were they able to defeat the Draugen Pesta?" General Darcy asked. "They're not called the Black Death for nothing."

General King shook his head. "The Draugen Pesta only had a mounted platoon against a company of mercenaries with sorcerers. The Spiked Fist had a four to one advantage in numbers, operational surprise, and magic on their side. Even with all of that, over half the company didn't return. I'd say the Black Death's reputation remains intact."

"And my precious sorcerers?" General Darcy asked. "Did they survive?"

"Yes," General King replied. "Even Harkum knows how valuable they'll be against Havendale. After the first attack, he sent the sorcerers back to our camp."

"Good! Good," General Darcy said as he poured himself another glass of wine. He glanced over at this bed as if he'd forgotten something. "Go," he said to the concubine.

After the woman had left, General King sat down for the first time since entering the tent. "General, Lord Ternborg will soon come south with the main body of his army. There's no way he won't find out about his dead platoon. And he'll know who did it."

"Yes," General Darcy replied. He was staring into space as if only half his mind was engaged in the conversation. "Lord Ternborg! Black Death! Doom Warriors! They'll turn on us, Timothy! They'll kill us all!" The general put his head in his hands. "What am I going to do?"

General King shook his head. "You're no good to anyone in this condition," he whispered. The general stood and drew his sword.

General Darcy came out of his funk at the sound of steel. "How dare you draw your weapon!" he shouted. "Guards!"

The guards rushed in, but they were General King's men. When they realized what was happening, they re-sheathed their weapons and backed out of the tent.

"You can't do this!" General Darcy screamed as he stood, causing his chair to smash to the floor behind him. "I'm your commander!" Spittle flew from his mouth. He began to back away, but the flash of a sword sent his head spinning to land on a pillow in the general's own featherbed. General Darcy's body dropped and flapped around for a few seconds before quieting. The copious amount of blood that gushed out of the body's neck was greedily soaked up by the ornate carpet covering the dirt floor.

General King cleaned his sword with a satin napkin before sitting down. He grabbed a large peach, put his legs up on the table, and bit into it. The juices from the succulent piece of fruit dribbled along his chin and dripped onto his uniform tunic. He didn't mind.

The leading elements of Lord Ternborg's army heard the rumble of hooves long before they saw the horses. They held up and watched as nineteen Draugen Pesta horses, each with an empty saddle, raced up to them before stopping. Each of the riderless horses snorted and rose on its hind legs, pawing front legs in the air. As soon as they landed back on all four, they turned and ran back along the Alpine whence they came. One of the mounted warriors turned his horse to take this information to the Draugen Pesta king while the other's pushed their own horses into a gallop and followed.

Tangus, Kristen, Jennifer, and Mariko, all on horseback, carefully picked their way through the forest. Romulus roamed in front, weaving back and forth several hundred feet ahead. Though Elrond assured them his trees and bushes would give plenty of warning if danger approached, caution isn't an easy thing to throw away for experienced rangers like either Tangus or Jennifer.

As they entered the outskirts of the fire damage, Tangus shook his head. It hurt him nearly as much as it hurt Elrond and Elanesse to see the devastation. But new growth was already beginning to push its way through the black fire-ravaged forest soil. That lifted his spirits somewhat.

"But what does the future hold," Tangus asked himself. *"We've not seen the end of that hydra, I know it. As long as it's still alive, this could happen again."*

Because of the fire-related deforestation, the broken walls of Elanesse came into view much sooner than expected. By this time Romulus had returned to walk at Kristen's side. The small party stopped and stared. Elanesse had been hurt badly. Fresh parts of the walls had collapsed, and stalagmites had risen from the surface in several parts of the city and towered over the walls. Their height easily surpassed that of the tallest buildings and towers in the metropolis. The closer they came to the perimeter, the more anxious both Tangus and Romulus became. Tangus called a halt still several yards from their destination. Romulus growled a warning.

"You feel it too, huh big guy," Tangus said.

"Feel what?" Kristen asked.

Tangus shook his head. "Something's wrong. There's a… I guess I'd call it a presence… that shouldn't be here."

"If you're right, then that must be what Emmy was talking about," Mariko remarked.

Tangus nodded and motioned for them to continue their trek towards Elanesse through the burned-out forest. Just outside the city walls they observed what Tangus now recognized as charred bone and not the remains of a burned tree. The blackened bones where huge.

"Dragon bones," Kirsten remarked.

"One of the dragons that started the fires," Jennifer observed. "Along with the hydra."

Tangus, ahead of the others, moved his horse Smoke to the nearest break in the wall. They had approached from the northeast, so he was looking into the business district of the city. Not far away was the first of several stalagmites, a three-hundred-foot-tall column of rough crystal. If its emergence hadn't been so painful to Elanesse, he'd consider it beautiful. But now he saw it as nothing more than the tip of an arrow which had pierced the flesh of his friend.

"I wish I knew how to remove that," Kristen said.

Tangus looked over at his wife. While he was thinking about the stalagmite, the rest of the group had caught up with him. "I don't think any healer can fix it," he remarked. "At least not a mortal one," He tapped the side of his horse with his boot heals and moved into the city, followed by everyone else. Instead of roaming and scouting ahead, Romulus remained by Kristen's side.

Tangus picked the route they'd use through the city's eastern half with care. He used the buildings for protection as much as possible. Though moving from building to building provided cover, it also increased the chance of an ambush. To counter this, Kristen used her priestess ability to unmask evil intent while Romulus used his heightened dire wolf senses to ferret out any strange odors or sounds. Mariko, trailing behind by a few paces, had her bow out and an arrow notched. She'd partitioned off the part of her that was Emmy's guardian and released her assassin persona. Mariko's horse responded to her commands by a simple nudge of a knee, making it unnecessary for Mariko to hold the reins. She would answer the slightest movement by any antagonist with an arrow in the chest — two if it didn't fall quick enough.

It took them the better part of two hours to cross east Elanesse. The walled road which separated east and west Elanesse was intact but narrow — no wider than three horses walking side-by-side. Once they entered it they'd have no room to maneuver. It concerned Tangus that they could be walking into a 'murder hole' ambush. He'd seen that type of trap used before and knew how devastating it can be. Instead, he led them around the narrow road, through broken walls, and into unburned forest. On the other side, just inside the second collapsed wall, was the fourth stalagmite they'd seen since entering the city. Like the others, it was three hundred feet tall and made of crystal. Unlike the others, however, black blood covered it. At the base was another dead dragon… or at least part of one. Something, or many somethings, had scavenged the body, leaving only gleaming white bone.

Rathal Arquen saw a huge, covered crater in a land of desolation and despair. Other than the trees that surrounded the crater, only a few scraggly bushes dotted the empty landscape. It was relentless. Even though Rathal was only an observer, the power, the evil, that radiated from beneath the ground overwhelmed him. As much as he wanted to flee, he realized he was caught in a precognitive vision and couldn't leave until this foreshadowing of events had played itself out.

The loose soil began to move, shifting like a ripple in a pond. Great rends opened up in the loose dirt and steam escaped into the frozen air. Rathal lost sight of the crater as a cloud of ice crystals hovered over it. He heard a cacophony of terrible screams coming from the ice cloud. Then he saw movement. It looked as if many heads were undulating within the misty vapors. In his vision he recognized the same five-headed dragon he'd seen over the ruined city of Elanesse. Only now it was different… changed. The crater appeared to be a cocoon protecting the monster dragon as it went through a transformation. Only the gods knew what the change would be. The original version was bad enough. But what Rathal now witnessed would be far worse.

Rathal returned from his vision. At first, he wasn't sure where he was. The one small candle that provided the only light in an otherwise dark room revealed simply adorned stone walls. The room had no windows, only a closed steel door. In front of him stood a stone sarcophagus. He was in Amkrissa's burial chamber, a place he had visited often since her death. Rathal smelled a rusty, iron aroma mixed in with the musty odor of the chamber. He felt a warm stickiness on his chin and neck. He knew what that was – small streams of blood coming from his ears and nose. But that concerned him not. What was important was the danger coming from over the horizon. Rathal, excellent in interpreting his visions, sensed the creature buried in the crater would return to Elanesse. He had to warn those in the ruined city of the grave danger. They had to know something wicked – something huge – was coming for them.

The graveyard with Amkrissa's crypt was one of several in Havendale. This one sat on a small hilltop. Rathal kissed Amkrissa's sarcophagus one last time before he left. "We'll be together soon, my darling," he whispered.

It was night and Rathal realized he must have been in there for several hours. Rhys and Shynaria waited outside, sitting on foldable chairs around a small fire and drinking mulled wine. Both looked up when Rathal exited the crypt.

"I thought you'd never come out," Rhys said.

Shynaria noticed blood and knew what that meant. She rushed to the master sorcerer's side. "You've had another premonition," she commented as she led him to her chair. "Sit and rest. We'll get you in bed soon enough, but right now you look like a dead man." Shynaria winced as soon as she said that. "Here, drink."

Rathal took the mug and drained the wine. Handing the now empty mug back to Shynaria, he said, "No time! I need to warn Elanesse!" He stood and walked towards his horse.

"Elanesse is a dead city," Rhys mentioned as he walked to his own horse.

Rathal shook his head. "Not anymore."

Both Rhys and Shynaria knew better than to question one of Rathal's premonitions.

Rhys moved between Rathal and his horse. "At least clean up and rest for a while before departing. It's obvious you don't have the strength to leave right away."

Rathal stepped around Rhys but said nothing.

Rhys, watching the sorcerer's back, was frustrated enough to shout, "You'll never make it, fool!"

Rathal stopped and turned. "Then come with me, spy," he answered.

Rhys looked at Rathal and then Shynaria.

"I'm going with you," Shynaria said to Rhys, knowing that he'd already decided to go.

"No!" Both Rathal and Rhys objected at the same time.

"You've never been in real danger before," Rhys said. "You'd not only be putting your own life on the line, but also ours."

Rathal nodded. "Believe me, experiencing combat isn't something you want to put on your resume if you can help it," he remarked. "Besides, I need you to help the city's new Lord Paramount."

"What are you talking about?" Shynaria asked. She had an idea what the response would be, and she didn't want to hear it.

Rathal uncharacteristically hugged his surprised assistant. "I'll not survive this, Shy." He put both hands on her shoulders and pushed her to arm's length. "The powers of the visions drain my body and Amkrissa's death has destroyed my heart. I'm tired."

Shynaria stepped back, crying as she shook her head. Rhys moved to her side and placed his arm around her. He understood Rathal, for he knew how he'd suffer if someone ever took Shynaria from him. He was also aware Rathal's prophetic power will soon demand payment. The sorcerer should be allowed to leave this world as he sees fit.

Shynaria still couldn't control her tears but finally nodded.

"Thank you, Shy," the sorcerer said as he gave her a kiss on the forehead. "The council has final approval, but my pick to lead Havendale is General Kelsia Húrön."

This took both Shynaria and Rhys by surprise.

"Really?" Shynaria exclaimed. His pick of a successor was unprecedented. Only sorcerers became Lord Paramount.

Rathal nodded. "It's time for Havendale to have someone other than a sorcerer to be the Lord Paramount... or in this case Lady Paramount. She's level-headed, a great organizer and the best tactician I've ever seen. And she commands, and has, the respect of everyone in the city. You'll have my letter of recommendation before I leave."

"Not only is she not a sorcerer, Rathal, but she's a dwarf!" Rhys exclaimed.

The master sorcerer smiled and shrugged. "So? Havendale will have a Lady Paramount who'll have no equal drinking ale."

"I'll tell her, Rathal," Shynaria consented.

Rathal nodded. "I know you will, Shy. Also tell her for the time being I'm still the official Lord Paramount and I order her not to send anyone after us. Other than that, it's her city to run, defend, and keep for as long as she can."

Shynaria nodded.

Thirty minutes later Rathal and Rhys galloped their horses, enhanced magically for endurance, through the city gates and north along the Merchant's Way.

Nightshade weighed her options. Michael, along with his *B'nai Elohim* brethren, was a problem she hadn't anticipated. As she looked around the massive chamber, the number of her dead minions lying at the feet of the *B'nai Elohim* astonished her. While they were only minor demons, it appeared they fought hard and courageously… though the courage to stand up to the guardians probably came from their fear of the alternative she offered. Talons and a slow death was a significant motivator. But dead is dead, and it looked like the rest would meet the same fate if they kept fighting. The *B'nai Elohim* clearly had her guards outclassed.

"I'm curious, Michael. How did you come to be here?" Nightshade asked. "I mean, why is this little mortal female so important you'd leave your post to rescue her?"

Michael studied Nightshade. She had come disguised as the mortal female Amberley. He suspected it was because she didn't want to reveal her demon ugliness to the child. But why would she care about that? Michael then saw an ever-so-faint lightness in her soul. Like a single ember in a newly lit fire, it could ignite and create heat – light against darkness – protection against predators. Or it could go out. But maybe, like the ember, Nightshade only needed careful stoking to bring her dead soul back to life. Wouldn't it be great to turn a demon of Nightshades' rank to the light? Michael decided it would be worth the effort, and he knew just the right person to ask for help.

"Many years ago I made a bond with a priestess of the Draugen Pesta people," Michael replied. "I gave her a *Locket of Need* which I linked to my soul."

Nightshade shook her head. "Why would the *B'nai Elohim* give a mortal access to unlimited power?"

Michael laughed. "Unlimited power? You mean little old me? Oh Nightshade… if you even knew the half of it." Michael's voice turned serious. "We're not gods. No, not that powerful. But in some respects we're pretty damn close, particularly where demons are concerned. Do not doubt me in this. However, to your point, a Draugen Pesta priestess invoked a summoning demon spell. Not so unusual. Many foolish mortals do. But this one was different in that it opened a gate large enough to engulf the entire world of Aster. That, Nightshade, runs counter to what the *B'nai Elohim* were created to do. I intercepted it before true demons such as you could answer. With a few of my brothers, I responded and listened to her petition. I found it to be acceptable and aided in her request. But if not for us, the world of Aster would have been overrun with your kind. The Draugen Pesta priestess's spell had let the 'cat was out of the bag' so to speak. I couldn't allow that to happen ever again. Our job in the Abyss is hard enough without adding a whole other world filled with mortals. I thought about ending her life, but I didn't know if she was the only one with knowledge of the spell. So I decided to take a chance. I created a magical locket tied to the spell and gave it to her. If she used the spell again, only I would hear it. I also warned her that only I will decide if the calling is justified."

"And you mentioned the consequences if it was not, I suspect."

"Indeed!"

"So how many calls have you answered, Michael," Nightshade asked.

"Other than the original, just this one," Michael replied. "They've taken my warning to heart."

Nightshade nodded. "Yes, so they have. But you'd do this for a mortal child?"

"Her name is Daphnia," Michael responded.

"I know that," Nightshade replied harshly.

Michael scowled. "And Daphnia has a mother and a father who'd do anything to get her back."

"Ternborg appeared willing enough to invade lands that didn't belong to him," Nightshade countered. "And not just for the promise of his daughter. He wants the land and he'll go to war to get it."

Michael shook his head. "He's smart enough to understand how tenuous his position will be if he occupied the valley. The rest of the city states would never allow the Draugen Pesta a moment's peace. And then there's the Hyrokkin to his east. The giants have been fighting a war with the centaurs for generations. If Lord Ternborg has to keep half his army west of the Greater Boreskyre Mountains, he's putting his own lands in jeopardy. If he were to let that happen, his people would boot him out on his arse faster than the *B'nai Elohim* kill demons." Michael smiled. "You understand the analogy, do you not, Nightshade?"

Nightshade wasn't smiling.

"I knew you would," Michael answered his own question. He wasn't just being snide with his comparison. He was reminding the demon that the *B'nai Elohim* aren't easily defeated if she should decide to go to war over the child. "I believe Lord Ternborg will turn his army around as soon as he knows his daughter is safe. So I suppose that just leaves one thing unanswered."

Nightshade sighed. "And what's that, Michael?"

"Do we leave peacefully with the girl? Or do we have to fight you for her?"

The demon looked at Michael. Everything he had told her was true. She didn't have the means to stop the *B'nai Elohim*. If truth be known, she'd never have tried such a damn fool thing as kidnapping the Draugen Pesta princess if she knew they'd be involved. Still, her gambit wasn't entirely unsuccessful. The human armies will be too busy with the Draugen Pesta invasion to reach InnisRos in time to save it. And the island is the only foothold she and her father needed. It was the steppingstone to the magic rich Alfheim and the subjugation of those haughty elves.

But Nightshade paused. Why did that not satisfy her? Why did she find herself no longer thirsting for power? Why does she no longer have a desire to hurt the child, Michael and his brothers, or even the elves on InnisRos she's aligned against? She thought of Mordecai. He'd been a lying, thieving, murdering bastard nearly worth demon status. She should've been thrilled to have him as an ally. Yet she ended up detesting him. And during her time with the elves of InnisRos, she had begun to understand honor, bravery, and sacrifice. *"What is wrong with me?"* she asked herself.

Michael broke Nightshade's self-introspection. Or was it self-immolation? "What did you say?" she asked.

Michael hesitated. He saw a struggle taking place in Nightshade's mind. Or was it her soul? *"That ember,"* he thought. Aloud, "I asked you how we'll resolve this? Peacefully or with violence?"

Nightshade sighed. "There's been enough violence. Take the child and go."

Adimar the wolf snarled.

"You can go too," the demon said.

The huge wolf jumped up and down and licked Daphnia on the face.

In an instant the *B'nai Elohim*, Daphnia, and Adimar, had disappeared. Nightshade released her demons who gathered their dead and left as well. But Michael remained behind.

Nightshade moaned. "Is there something else?" she asked.

Michael shook his head. "No, not really, except to offer my help."

"You're offering me your help?! Why would I ever need anything from you?"

"I think you know why," Michael said. "Let the goodness inside you grow."

"Goodness?!" Nightshade turned from her Amberley manifestation into her demon form. "You ask that of this?"

Michael was undeterred. "Much can be forgiven if the intent is true. But first you must forgive yourself. And of course some penance will be required."

"The demon lords…"

"I've dealt with demon lords before," Michael interrupted. "It's not pleasant. And they never willingly give up one of their own. But I'll not be deterred if I can save a soul… even if it's a demon soul."

Nightshade laughed. "Demons don't have souls."

"Everyone has a soul, Nightshade," Michael replied. "But demons and the hell spawned can't feel it. They're trained from creation to lock it away."

Nightshade wasn't sure if she believed the guardian, but something new stirred within her. That much was undisputable. Nightshade banished her surviving minor demons back to the Abyss. Then she turned to look at Michael. There was no point in asking him why he'd do such a thing for a demon – and she didn't really want to know. "I'll consider it."

Michael produced a diamond locket on a chain of unbreakable talamite – a rare and priceless metal mined from uninhibited creation stone – and opened it up to place around Nightshade's neck.

"Don't worry. This only allows us to communicate," he said, reading her hesitation.

Nightshade nodded and changed back to Amberley. She found she hated her demon form. It was repulsive.

Michael put the two ends of the chain around her neck and they snapped together. "Remember, Nightshade. If we strike a bargain, your penance will be hard. Don't make things worse by continuing your evil misdeeds."

Nightshade shrugged. "We'll see," she said.

Michael left without another word. It was up to her.

Nightshade stood for a while. The need to escape her fiendish existence was growing stronger in her newly discovered soul and pleaded for release. She found she was ready to accept the lifeline offered by Michael. She didn't understand it, but the decision felt right.

When she left the now empty prison, she wasn't sure where she was going.

CHAPTER FIFTEEN

Deep Under Elanesse

"Love makes strange bedfellows."

-Author Unknown, but probably someone who fell in love with the last person he or she expected.

Max was in the lead as he, Solveig, and Erika climbed back through the tunnels that led to Erika's home – and the sylphs who had butchered her and Solveig's clan. As they trudged upwards, Max looked for sylph sign. He knew the 'sylphie devils' were ahead, but not how far… and if they weren't stopped, Max surmised there'd be a whole lot more spooks roaming Aster. The only thing Max hadn't figured out was what they would do to the sylphs once they found them. A whole dragon clan lay dead below as a testament to how much of a danger the sylph represented.

Max was having trouble tracking the sylphs. There were many corridors they could take to the surface, and his silent quarry left behind no physical evidence. After a day of traveling with no luck, a frustrated Max called a halt. Solveig looked as fresh as the day she died. But Erika, though she'd never admit to it, was exhausted. As the dragon-ghost and dragon in human form sat and reacquainted themselves, Max sat on a large boulder of solid gold and contemplated his next move. At the pace they were moving, they'd never catch up before Azriel and Elbedreth were forced to faced off with the sylphs. Max didn't want his friend to go into battle alone…

and he wanted a chance to tell Elbedreth he forgave her for killing him.

"Damn it!" he said aloud.

Both of his companions looked over at him.

"What's wrong," Solveig said as she glided over and sat on the gold boulder next to him.

Max looked at Solveig. For the millionth time he thought to himself how stunningly beautiful she was. It made him sad to think that once he, or she, completed their earthly task, they'd move on their separate eternities.

"We're moving too slow," he said.

"Erika's going as fast as she can," Solveig responded. "She understands the importance. But she's still weak from her injuries."

"But she healed herself," Max protested.

Solveig took Max's hand. "How did you feel after the same happened to you?"

Max sighed. Solveig had made a valid point. He'd been brought back from death's doorstep many times. It was a consequence of his chosen profession – before that chosen profession had killed him for good. Being that close to death throws you off your game for several days regardless of the healing power of a potion or a cleric.

"I need to think of things as a ghost and not as a thief," Max said.

Solveig laughed.

Max looked at her. "What's so funny?"

"You already are. You're sitting on what might be the largest gold nugget I've ever seen, and you never even noticed!" she replied, still laughing.

Max looked down, then jumped. "By the gods, would you look at the size of that thing?!"

Solveig was still smiling. "Indeed! Enough to buy a small human kingdom, I'd wager."

"But it's not worth much to a ghost," Max concluded as he sat back down on the nugget. He looked over at Erika, who had fallen into a weary sleep. "I heard you make a comment to Erika that now she has Jörmungander. What did you mean by that?"

Solveig laughed again. "Jörmungander is the last male. We left him behind to guard the lair because he's the youngest. They must mate if our clan is to continue. Now don't get me wrong. Jörmungander's a handsome and powerful dragon – a fine specimen of male dragonhood. But he's not overly aggressive. In fact, he's a bookworm and…"

"And a bit of a bore," Max finished for her. "I know the type. I've a friend who's a former knight and a big old ole' bruiser in battle. But he's… he's… oh, I guess you could say he's somewhat unbendable. Rigid. You know what I mean? But I got to admit, he's a good listener. Nobody else would ever take the time. Well, maybe Elrond. But he doesn't count. Brothers have to listen."

"Well, maybe others don't because you have a tendency to repeat your stories over and over again," Solveig observed.

Max nodded. "You ain't lying."

Solveig stared out into the darkness of the small cavern in which they rested. "They'll be fine," she concluded. "Erika and Jörmungander are more alike than either will admit."

"One more reason to stop the sylphie bastards," Max commented. "Except I haven't figured out how to do that yet."

"You've been a ghost longer than I," Solveig remarked, "so you'd know better than I. What can a ghost do that a mortal cannot?"

Max shrugged his shoulders. "Not sure. We scare people. We throw rocks and other stuff about. But mortals can do those things to. We can pass through things like walls when motivated. But again, mortals can do that with magic." Max frowned. "I guess we just kind of hang out… at least until we've satisfied whatever grand universal scheme is required of us before we can rest in everlasting peace… if there is a scheme… if there is everlasting peace. I don't know. I've never been dead before. Ghosts are…" Max stopped, and a sense of enlightenment came over him. "I'll be damned!"

"Are you okay?" Solveig asked.

Max held up a hand. "Shh. Let me think this through."

Solveig looked over at Erika. She was still asleep. Solveig thought in some respects the lives of mortals are far less complicated than that of a ghost. *"Who would have thought it'd be more than just saying 'Boo'!"* she thought.

"We're asking the wrong question," Max declared, bringing Solveig out of her reverie. "We should be asking ourselves what a ghost can STILL do."

"Huh?" Solveig looked confused.

Max shook his head. "Sorry. We've been having a conversation about what ghosts can do that mortals can't. Not much, apparently. So the next logical question is what are the similarities? Can ghosts do the same things mortals can do? What I mean is how many of our talents are left over from our mortal lives. I'm still Max, thief extraordinaire. Everything I've learned from decades of life remains locked up in the old noggin. See where I'm going with this? Try one of your dragon spells."

Solveig nodded. "I'll try a simple light spell."

The whole cavern flooded with light.

"Dampen it down," Max said has he closed his eyes.

The dragon-ghost, amazed that so much light had materialized, didn't react at once.

"Dampen it down!" Max said for a second time.

"Oh, sorry, Max." Solveig dampened the light… then brought it back up again before breaking the spell altogether.

As Max waited for his ghostly eyes to reacquaint themselves with the dark, he asked, "What was that last bit all about?"

Solveig swung her hand around in the sudden darkness until she found Max's and grasped it in excitement. "Wasn't it wonderful!" she exclaimed. "I've never been able to bring that much power to bear! And it responded so quickly to my commands! Max, I had to let the light flare up one more time just to confirm it! You're definitely on to something!"

Max shook his head. "You think? I knew ghosts were sensitive to bright light, but that was ridiculous. It hurt."

"Sorry," Solveig said.

"Don't be," Max replied. "Now that we know you still have at least some of your dragon magic, maybe we can do more to stop the sylphies. And don't forget, we also have Erika. Two dragons and…"

Solveig shook her head and interrupted Max. "I'm not so sure about that. For the most part, she only uses her magic to heal."

Max smiled. "I came across a healer like that," he said. "She's a pretty little thing… but too… nunnish. Understand?"

Solveig nodded. "In other words, she had standards," she said, implying Max's lack thereof.

Max laughed. "We've had so little time together and already you know me too well. Anyway, her name's Kristen and she's married to one of my best friends. Man, oh man… I'd never threaten THAT healer. Tangus is NOT someone you want angry at you. He's… he's… well, let's just say he's very protective. But back to my point, Kristen's quite the proper lady until backed into a corner with her child in danger. Then she turns into a hellion. She uses her magic to kill efficiently and to great effect without remorse. Oh, she might pray for their souls afterward… but the soul of anyone trying to harm an innocent child belongs in Hell, and by the gods she'll put 'em there!"

"When an innocent child's involved, us girls are all the same," Solveig said. "We're death on two… or four… legs. No quarter asked, no quarter given."

Max nodded. "Without doubt. And I bet Erika would be the same." He changed the subject. "Think I'll use this down time to scout ahead. Without Erika, I can make much better time. You stay here, watch over her while she rests, and practice your dragon spells."

"Do you sense danger?"

"Not here," Max said as he shook his head. "But who knows what I'll find up ahead?"

"Be careful!"

Max leaned over and kissed Solveig. "Always," he said.

Solveig looked at him out of the corner of her eye. "You've already died once. Remember that."

Max smiled, turned and disappeared into the darkness. Solveig, as she floated over to where Erika slept, heard a faint, happily whistled tune come out of that same darkness.

"This is perfect!" Azriel exclaimed. He, Elbedreth, and Jörmungander had just entered a huge cavern. It was the largest Azriel had ever seen. Moss illuminated the entire cave with an eerie, greenish glow, broken here and there by the light of yellow mushrooms. In the center, water crashed to the floor from a crack in the ceiling. Hundreds, maybe thousands, of years of falling water had created a large, deep pool in the stone floor underneath. The ceiling was three to four hundred feet high. Azriel calculated that the cavern was at least eight miles in each direction.

"Perfect," Azriel repeated.

Elbedreth, standing by Azriel's side, agreed. "Yes, you're correct. It looks big enough to hold my entire race."

"I just hope they're coming this way," Azriel commented.

"Why wouldn't they?" Jörmungander asked. "We know the ones you killed came this way. We've been following their signs."

Azriel nodded. "Aye, laddie, you're right," he said. "But if I were leading the sylph, I'd have several scouting parties out looking. What if another party found an alternate route? What if they've already passed us by? There's no way to tell how many passages lead to the surface."

"There are far too many 'what if's' for the mind to comprehend, my love," Elbedreth remarked. "We shouldn't let the evidence we think to be true fall victim to the possibilities in our mind… at least not until we prove this evidence false. This appears to be the way my people are taking in their quest to reach the surface world. We should act on it."

"I won't discard the 'what if's', but you make a good point," Azriel replied as he studied the cavern more thoroughly.

"Azriel," Jörmungander said.

Azriel frowned. "Not now, laddie! I'm figuring things out!"

A plan was formulating in Azriel's mind. He was an experienced warrior, and like all experienced warriors, he was looking at it from various angles – trying to find and correct weaknesses, determining what steps he'd need to take in response to possible reactions by the sylph, determining his fallback position if his plan didn't work, and anything else he could foresee.

"Azriel!" Jörmungander insisted.

"Jörmungander, I said I'd…"

"Listen to him, dear," Elbedreth added.

Azriel sighed. "Not you too! Alright! What is it!"

"Someone's living in this cavern," Jörmungander stated. "Actually, it's a lot of someone's. Possibly a whole clan or tribe of someone's."

"What leads you to this conclusion?" Azriel asked.

Elbedreth pointed up. "Look!"

Hanging from the high cavern ceiling were hundreds of stalactites. That wasn't unusual in a cavern with the high moisture content this one had. But what he saw in the stalactites confounded him. Each stalactite contained foot-high doors made of moss. A few of these doors were open, and Azriel could see green eyes – eyes as luminescent as the moss – watching them.

Azriel grumbled as all his planning tumbled away. He began a long list of dwarven expletives but stopped himself after only a few. Elbedreth looked at him with frightened eyes. But Jörmungander thought it was rather impressive and told him so.

"I guess the cavern being occupied is a 'what if' I never considered," Azriel thought to himself. Turning to Elbedreth and Jörmungander, he said,

"Well now, if that isn't a hoot!" Dwarves had perfected the art of sarcasm and Azriel was one of the best.

The sylph leader, the Supreme, had stopped her people's dash to the surface when the messenger arrived with word of the true path. Though satisfied the way had been discovered, the report about the traitor Elbedreth-Ahlasim, with a male sylph and a dragon disguised as a human, disturbed her. She thought the treacherous female was the only sylph left after the gods of creation had imprisoned her people.

"Did you wait to see the outcome of the battle?" the sylph leader asked the messenger.

"No, Supreme. My orders were to leave post-haste and report to you. But how can there be any other outcome but victory? I'm sure they all lay dead at the feet of my comrades!"

The Supreme nodded and dismissed the messenger. She wasn't as confident of victory as the courier, however. They've been asleep all this time while Elbedreth-Ahlasim has had billions of rotations around the sun to perfect her fighting style and skill. She alone might be worth several hundred of her subjects. After the losses against the dragons, it was a number the sylphs couldn't afford if they were to rid the world of parasites.

The Supreme approached the true passage and stared into the blackness. The unknown evolution of Elbedreth-Ahlasim wasn't her only concern. The traitor's companions, particularly the male sylph, gave her pause. Everyone had been accounted for except Elbedreth-Ahlasim. So how did the male sylph come to exist? And if there was one, could there be others? If so, was Elbedreth-Ahlasim allied with them? The Supreme knew the parasites on the surface wouldn't go without a fight. She was prepared for that. But if there existed a corresponding army of unknown sylphs with the same mindset as Elbedreth-Ahlasim's, then their life's work was in serious jeopardy.

The Supreme bellowed a call for her battle council. Though the sylph were scattered across several corridors and caverns, all heard her broadcast.

Max discovered there were limits to his ghostly powers. He moved faster than when he was alive, but not much. He could pass through stone, but not through less porous crystal. While he had perfected the art of hiding in shadows when alive, his ghostly body gave off a shimmering glow which was visible in darkness. He hid better in light… but bright light hurt him. That was the short list, but Max knew it wasn't complete. He oftentimes wondered what other things would go wrong because he was a ghost.

The phantom Max was having a hard time following the sylphs. They didn't leave any sign of their passing. The only thing Max knew for sure was the corridor they used after they defeated Solveig and Erika's dragon clan. But since then he's found several corridors large enough to accommodate the sylph army. Which one did they use? Until he had a better plan, he just took the most likely path and crossed his fingers, something he discovered ghosts can do.

"I guess I should turn back," Max said to himself, *"before I lose my… what's this?"*

Max kneeled. Before him on the stone floor of the corridor was a dead albino cave spider. Though barely recognizable, its crushed guts where smeared in a teardrop pattern which pointed forward. The cave spider's remains were already dry, so there was no telling who or how long ago someone had passed this way and smeared the poor spider. But who else could it be?

"Max, you handsome devil," he said aloud as he stood. He looked into the darkness and yelled, "So you think you can get away from the great Max! Ha! I GOT ya, you sylphie beasts!"

Max saluted the deceased cave spider before turning away to head back to his companions. It wasn't long before his thoughts, fresh off the small spider victory, returned to the problem of the sylphs. Now he knew which path they took. That meant it was time to fight and probably die... again. "Damn spider!"

As Azriel, Elbedreth and Jörmungander watched, more and more of the strange moss doors opened. In the darkness of each door, green eyes looked down at them. There was a sudden flurry of activity as several hundred of the creatures jumped into the air and circled high above, waiting for the entire formation to form. At first Azriel thought they were large bats, but though they had the same leathery wings, that was where the resemblance ended. The largest of the group had a wingspan of three feet and a body length, from head to the tip of its tail, of five feet. Their bodies were long and slinky and covered with orange fur.

"They're flying ferrets!" Azriel exclaimed. "Hundreds of them!"

The flying ferrets were done circling. With precision, they arranged themselves into several smaller groups. The lead group dove, followed by the other groups, one by one. Surprised, Azriel, Elbedreth and Jörmungander stood and watched this display for a few moments, mesmerized, before they realized they were being attacked.

The first group was upon them before they could react and used their short, clawed legs to score several long surface scratches on all three. As the first group flew away, the second group attacked. Azriel turned and shooed Elbedreth and Jörmungander back into the relative safety of the entrance corridor. As Azriel had hoped, the flying ferrets didn't follow.

"Well, that wasn't a very warm reception," Azriel observed.

Elbedreth nodded. "A bit of an understatement, dear," she said. "Even you would have to admit the way they attacked wasn't something an ordinary animal would do. They showed an extraordinary degree of precision and organizational skill."

Azriel shrugged. "So? Lots of critters do those sorts of things. It's nothing but instincts. Wolves, for example. Well, not Romulus and his pack, but normal wolves."

"I don't know of wolves, but these creatures deserve our consideration," Elbedreth countered. "I've been beneath Aster from almost the beginning, and I've never seen their kind. We must destroy the sylph. Of that there can be no question. But we shouldn't commit genocide in the process."

Azriel shook his head. "If the sylph gets to the surface, it won't be just these flying ferrets that'll be destroyed. You want to talk about genocide! They'll kill every living being on Aster! Even if ferrets aren't just instinctual animals..."

"It's definitely more than instinct, Azriel," Jörmungander interrupted. "They were talking to each other."

"I heard nothing," Azriel responded.

Jörmungander walked past the two sylphs and looked out into the cavern. "Then I guess they communicated in a tone the sylph can't hear," he said. "But dragons can. At least I can."

"Do you understand them," Elbedreth asked.

"I understand them," Jörmungander replied. "It's really a pretty simple language. See, once you figure out their sentence structure, which reverses..."

"Stop!" Azriel shouted as he slapped his sylph forehead with a sylph open palm. "Morgothal, save me suffering soul. Jörmungander, what were they saying!"

Jörmungander nodded before replying. "Sorry. It just seemed like such a good teachable moment."

"Jörmungander!"

"Okay! Other than the normal commands being bandied around, most of the talk was about keeping their mates and offspring safe. There was genuine concern in their voices... concerns that come from more than just instinctual prerogative. These aren't dumb animals, Azriel. We can't set a trap to stop the sylph invasion here. At least not a trap that would also harm the inhabitants."

"Then what would you have me do, laddie!" Azriel exclaimed. "Pull my granny's chest hairs, we've already got an impossible task! You'd have me pass up what might be the only chance we'll get to stop the sylphs?!"

"We can use the *Maul of Power* in other caverns," Elbedreth said. Azriel had explained the power of the maul to both Elbedreth and Jörmungander. "In other uninhibited caverns," she added.

"Lassie, have you lost your damn mind!" Azriel shouted. The calm he had found after his transformation into a sylph sometimes still gave way to his dwarven heritage. "For all we know the sylphs are just outside! Hell, they could already be here hiding in the shadows. We're out of time!"

"Maybe I have a solution," Jörmungander said as he stepped back into the cavern.

Immediately the flying ferrets dove on him. But when he transformed into his black dragon persona, they pulled out of their plunge and veered off to reform further up and closer to their homes. Jörmungander raised his head and spewed his dragon's breath into the air.

The flying ferrets, much to their credit, didn't break formation and fly away. Several of them even snarled in defiance. After a few moments pause, the lead ferret of the first group dropped and landed on the cavern floor in front of the towering dragon. Jörmungander bent his two forelegs and lowered himself so he could get close enough to make eye contact. The ferret folded his wings and stood on his two back legs to meet the dragon face to face – at least as much as was physically possible.

"I am called Jörmungander and my companions are Azriel and Elbedreth," the dragon said in the language he heard the ferrets use. "How are your people called?"

That the dragon understood the language of his people surprised the ferret. He took a step back before regaining his composure. "My people are called the Kounávi. I am Thauzeacsaush, their leader." Thauzeacsaush studied Jörmungander as the dragon tried to say his name. "You may call me Thaz. Why have you invaded our home?"

"To warn you of a grave danger," Jörmungander replied.

Thaz laughed. "You lie," he reprimanded. "You didn't even know of our existence before you walked into our cavern. Admit it."

Jörmungander blinked. "Yes, you're correct. We didn't know of your existence. But it's not a lie that your people are in grave danger. A menace from below draws ever so close to your cavern even as we speak. We, my friends and I, wish to stop this threat before it reaches the surface. Since they're so many and we're so few, we've decided your cavern is the best place to stop their advance. That is before we realized you called this place your home."

Thaz crossed his arms and frowned. "Why is this menace to you our problem?" he asked. "Other than you want to destroy our home to stop them, which we'll not allow."

"The menace has a name. They are the sylph," Jörmungander replied. "Ancient guardians of this world long since placed into slumber deep below by the gods. They have awakened and once they reach the surface world, they'll murder every living being until the only life left will be plants. That includes your people."

"We'll just hide and let them pass…"

"No one can hide from the sylph!" Jörmungander roared. He then punctuated his response by again spewing dragon's breath into the air. "No Thaz, you won't be able to hide from them once they're here. You won't be able to stop them either. Nor will you survive the encounter. My people died deep below trying to stop the sylph so that people like you can continue to live your lives in peace. I'll not let you make their deaths meaningless!"

Thaz didn't back down from the angry black dragon. "We'll decide our own future!" he retorted, matching anger with anger. "You figure it out. But do it somewhere else."

The ferret cavern defenders, who'd been circling during the conversation between their leader and the dragon, began to spiral downwards in response to the anger displayed by both. They were prepared to continue the battle.

Jörmungander reined in his anger somewhat. "No," he said. "You don't get to sit this one out even if the sylph were to let you."

Thaz shrugged his shoulders. "You going to stop us?" he said as his army flew closer.

The ferret motioned with his hand and the first wave dived on the dragon. But instead of attempting to scratch, a futile attack against hard dragon scales, each ferret released their own breath weapon – a mist of noxious gas that settled around Jörmungander and left him choking and gagging. Within a few seconds he was having trouble breathing and had a sharp pain in his chest.

Thaz didn't moved an inch as he watched the dragon struggle for breath. "Don't worry," he said matter-of-factly, impervious to the pain Jörmungander was experiencing. "Considering your size, the dose you received isn't lethal."

"I… I… I'm immune to poison," Jörmungander fought to say between each struggle to gulp air.

"Oh, it's nasty, but not poison," Thaz replied. "The droplets in the mist react with the lining of your lungs to create small air bubbles. If you breathe in enough, a clot forms and kills you… at least that's what our healers tell us. I don't care as long as it gets the job done. We don't fear your sylphs. Now take your friends and go."

Jörmungander was starting to breathe easier. He looked at Thaz. "You idiot! The sylph don't breathe like we do!"

That stopped Thaz. He waved again and his flying comrades regained altitude and returned to circling. "Don't be absurd. All creatures breathe in air."

Jörmungander took a deep breath. Thaz was correct about the breath weapon attack. It appeared he was no longer in danger of suffocating. He looked at the ferret. "And you know this because of your vast traveling experience beyond this cavern?"

Thaz shook his head. "Well... not exactly," he mumbled.

Jörmungander pounced. "What was that? I don't believe I heard you."

The ferret king stared at the dragon.

The dragon turned and glanced at Azriel and Elbedreth. Both were staring at him. Azriel had the *Maul of Power* out and was tightly gripping it. Elbedreth had a hand on her mate's arm. Jörmungander had little doubt she was trying to instill patience on the sylph-dwarf. He nodded at the two. And though Elbedreth visibly relaxed, Azriel didn't – too many years a dwarf, too many years a mercenary, too many years spent putting his life on the line.

When Jörmungander first met Azriel, he didn't care for the dwarf-sylph for those very reasons. Azriel represented the exact opposite of the values he himself espoused – peace through knowledge and compromise, live and let live, minding one's own business. But Jörmungander now realized he'd been wrong about Azriel. He began to see that his values didn't matter much if he wasn't ready and willing to stand up for them. Regardless of Azriel's outlook on life, he was ready to put his life on the line for the greater good. His own clan had just died following that end. Jörmungander always thought the *Maelstrom* prophecy wasn't much more than just the name his people used to represent their perceived destiny. But he now realized it was much more than that. It was what Azriel and Elbedreth were now doing – sacrificing their lives, hopes, and dreams for the future so that others can keep theirs intact.

Jörmungander turned his head back to the ferret, but he wasn't seeing the diminutive figure. "I've been so selfish," he thought out loud. "I can no longer hide in my books and scrolls, isolated in a cavern deep below ground. My friends have shown me a new path."

"What are you saying?" Thaz asked. "You're making no sense."

Jörmungander came out of his self-reflection and looked at Thaz. The dragon's eyes, the look of determination on his face, and the complete change in the way he now carried himself, stunned the ferret. Thaz stepped back and began to signal his circling army.

"Don't you dare," Jörmungander roared, "or I swear I'll burn them out of the air! We're trying to help you!"

Thaz stopped. He caught a slight whiff of sulfur from Jörmungander's breath which caused him to crinkle his nose.

Jörmungander noticed and lowered his head closer to the ferret and exhaled. "You've only seen a small demonstration of my dragon breath," he said. "You DO NOT want to be in its path if I decide to release it in anger. I speak the truth. As for your own defense, it worked once because you surprised me. But it won't work on me again. I have dragon's magic… spells to keep your mist away from me. Ponder that. And while you do, think upon this. One of my friends has a weapon that can collapse this entire cavern. He intends to use it to stop the sylph. The question you have to ask yourself is whether you still want to be here when he does."

Thaz considered. In their brief acquaintance, the ferret leader had seen the dragon morph from timid to commanding – from almost non-threatening to something that now would have no compunction destroying his people to stop the sylph. *"If he's telling the truth,"* he thought to himself, *"it means the end of my race either from the sylph when they arrive or from his companion if he can collapse the cavern."*

Time was wasting and Jörmungander's patience had run out. The dragon transitioned back into a human male and turned to walk back to his friends still standing in the corridor.

"Wait," Thaz called.

Jörmungander stopped and turned. He didn't speak. Instead he crossed his arms and stood, waiting. Azriel and Elbedreth exited the corridor and stood at his side. Azriel still had the *Maul of Power* out. It was clear he was ready to use it.

Thaz sighed. They had defeated him. For the good of his people he didn't have a choice. He had to trust the newcomers. "What would you have us do?"

Jörmungander nodded. "It'll be quicker if I tell you mind-to-mind," he said to the ferret leader. "Perhaps if you call your most trusted to stand witness?"

"Mind to mind?" Thaz said as he frowned. "You mean you'll enter my mind to talk to me?"

"More like mental pictures and impressions," Jörmungander replied. "It's much quicker."

Thaz backed away. "You're asking much."

"Get on with it, Jörmungander," Azriel barked. "I don't know what you two are debating, but whatever it is, get it done!"

"Trust me," Jörmungander said to Thaz.

Thaz finally nodded and called several of his top lieutenants to come to him. Once everything was ready, Jörmungander began. Each of the ferrets went rigid. After a few moments they collapsed holding their heads. Thaz recovered first.

"You'd do that for us?" he said to the dragon.

Jörmungander nodded. "It'll make an ideal home for your people," he said. "Oh, I'll be back from time to time, but other than that, I don't need it anymore. I'm going to the surface."

Thaz nodded his thanks before he flew up to the hollowed-out stalactites that served as the home of his people. Within a few moments the exodus of the Kounávi began.

"Where are they going to go," Elbedreth asked, concerned.

"I've given them the lair of my clan," Jörmungander replied. "I want to live the rest of my days on the surface." The tone in his voice said he expected to be alone.

Thaz and a score of his best warriors landed beside Azriel, Elbedreth, and Jörmungander. The dragon cocked an eyebrow.

"We're staying," Thaz said in reply to Jörmungander's unasked question.

"The sylphs will probably kill us all, Thaz," Jörmungander pointed out.

"Let 'em try!"

"What's he saying," Azriel asked.

"He's offering their assistance," Jörmungander replied.

Azriel nodded. "Good. We need all the help we can get."

The Supreme marched at the head of the long line of sylphs. They had abandoned their search of the other passageways. They now knew those corridors would not lead to the surface of Aster. A messenger from the scout team the Supreme had dispatched appeared out of the darkness and flattened itself on the floor in front of the sylph leader.

"Rise," the Supreme commanded. "What news do you bring?"

"A great cavern, Supreme!" the messenger replied with enthusiasm. "A great, green shimmering cavern!"

The Supreme nodded. "Did our lost scout team pass through it?"

In answer, the messenger extended an arm out from its amoeba-like body. In its opened hand was a miniscule spore scout teams leave to mark the way. Each spore radiated specific sylph pheromones which served as direction markers.

"Very good," the Supreme acknowledged.

The messenger's body shivered with pleasure at the compliment.

"And the rest of your team?" the Supreme asked.

The messenger stilled.

"Well!" the Supreme demanded.

"They remained behind to watch," the messenger replied.

The Supreme could see there was more, but the messenger hesitated to speak – no doubt terrified. "And what else?" she asked.

"The cavern has inhabitants, Supreme. The team intends to eliminate the parasites as a glorious gift to Your Most Superlative Self."

"DAMN YOU SAY!" the Supreme roared. "I gave specific orders to observe... OBSERVE... if you found any parasites. Your team has defied me!"

The messenger scrunched down as much as he could. He wanted to retreat but didn't dare. He knew any movement in any direction would bring instant death. "The parasites are only furry flying things," the messenger pleaded. "They're no match for our team. And we'd be ridding our world of their scourge."

The Supreme understood the messenger was only following orders and therefore not subject to execution. As for the team leader? Well that was another story. The Supreme turned to her nearest lieutenant. "Gather ten score of your best warriors, go to that cavern and bring the team leader to me, unharmed. We'll be following behind as quickly as we can."

"And the parasites, Supreme?" the sylph asked.

The Supreme paused before she nodded. "If there are any of the scourge left, eradicate them."

Max turned a corner and the focus of his pursuit, the dreaded sylph, were in front of him. Max froze as the memory of his death flooded through him. He felt his body being pierced and sliced. He remembered being dragged over the hard tunnel floor, and the moment Azriel's light-helmet slipped off, releasing the blackness that, up to then, had only threatened to engulf him. He remembered the moment of his death – a quick and efficient thrust through his heart. Elbedreth didn't want him to suffer. He knew that. He also knew she wasn't cruel or evil. She only wanted his death to serve notice to those on the surface who were about to enter her territory.

So much had changed since that moment – so much he didn't understand. But who understands why fate works the way it does? Who could fathom why, for example, an explosion might tear one person to shreds while leaving the person standing a few feet away unharmed? Or why someone with a sliced-open belly will sometimes survive while another will die from a simple bee sting? Max had seen how fate worked first-hand and knew better than to question it. Dwelling upon all the quirks in life that resulted in tragedy was a losing proposition and could get him killed – if it didn't drive him crazy first. Max came out of his funk just in time to dodge the first attack by two sylphs. The second attack scored but passed right through him.

Max nodded and smiled. "Yeah, sylphie! Can't hurt me, can you?!"

Without missing a beat, the sylphs produced several gleaming blades and continued their attack. Max suddenly found himself fighting for his life. The new blades were magic. Ghosts aren't immune to magic. Max backed towards his companions while screaming a warning. In that moment he learned ghosts can match the speed and quickness of the sylph. He successfully dodged the attacks from the two sylphs for the first few moments while holding his ground to give Solveig and Erika time to react. But a successful strike from a magical blade was inevitable, and when it came, it brought with it a searing pain unlike any Max had ever experienced.

Max screamed and dropped to his knees. In that split second of vulnerability, the sylphs moved in to strike the killing blow. It was then that Max stumbled onto a ghost trait he never realized he had – the ability to shift to the ethereal plane. He could still see the sylphs, though their appearance was somewhat vague. And they could still see him since they continued their attacks. But the magical blades passed through him with no effect.

Max didn't have his own weapons, but since the sylph's couldn't hurt him, he took a chance and punched the closest. His attack yielded the same results as theirs as his fist passed through the sylph.

"Hmmm," he thought. *"You can't hurt me, but neither can I hurt you. So what good does it do to plane shift… other than to save my life?"*

"That won't do," Max said aloud. "That won't do at all!"

He tried to use his power of telekinesis to lift one of the sylphs. He wanted to bash it against the ceiling of the corridor and bring it back down to the floor just as hard. But that didn't work either.

"Damn!" he roared.

"Max," Solveig called. "Come back to us!"

Solveig had called from around a corner, so Max couldn't see them. The ghost-thief didn't have a better idea, so he shifted from the ethereal plane back to the material plane.

"What did you do?" Solveig asked. "I could barely make you out."

"I'll tell you later," Max replied. "Right now I have half a dozen of those sylphies following me."

"Maybe I can help," Erika said.

She positioned herself in front of the two ghosts and began an incantation.

"Devil's fire, oh so true.
Hot and burning is your brew.

Come to me from far below.
Bring to my enemies your everlasting woe.

Evil souls are what you seek.
Souls I give you without critique.

Your deadly magic is what I need.
Only you can perform this crucial deed."

"VENITE COMEDITE GEHENNAM IGNIS"

Max waited a few seconds. "Nothing happened! NOTHING HAPPENED! Please tell me this spell is one that only works under precise conditions… like a sylphie walking into it," he pleaded.

Erika smiled. "You're strange for a ghost. It's almost as if you're still alive. Don't you go 'boo' or moan or something?"

Max frowned and looked at Solveig who shrugged her shoulders. "I already tried that once," he replied. "It didn't work. Now if you'll…"

Suddenly six sylphs rounded the corner, spotted the three, and charged. Halfway between the corner and Max, Solveig, and Erika, the sylphs triggered the spell. A barrier of fire blossomed and exploded in brilliant white light. Erika had to turn her face away to avoid damage to her eyes. But the two ghosts didn't bother. It hurt but had no long-term implications for their well-being. Being dead had its advantages.

"By the gods," Solveig whispered.

The sylphs had been destroyed.

"Now that's a neat trick!" Max exclaimed with joy. "Will it work again?"

"One never knows when the fires of perdition will be quenched," Erika replied.

Max gawked. "I swear, that's just how Lester would say it. You sure you've never… forget it. Can I get past it?"

"What are you thinking," Solveig asked.

Max smiled. "Use that wonderful brain of yours, my lovely," he replied. "We got an automatic sylphie killer down this tunnel. Now all we need are the sylphies." Max turned to Erika and repeated his question. "Can I get past it?"

Erika shook her head. "I don't know. I've never had to use the spell. But the human cleric who taught it to me…"

"Wait a minute," Solveig interrupted. "We've never had a human cleric in our lair."

"It was that time I went on sabbatical, my friend," Erika replied. "Humans, even clerics, treasure the gold we can offer. Jörmungander once told me my teacher was 'on retainer', whatever that means."

Max barked a short laugh. "I'd never believe it if I hadn't heard it with my own two ears."

"What?" both dragon and dragon-ghost asked as they looked at Max.

"Retainer. It means you pay a fee, usually over an agreed upon length of time, for the exclusive use of someone's particular talents. In your case, it was training. When I was alive, my company of friends did it all the time. It's a steady income. And a steady income pays the bills much better than the occasional treasure strike. Mercenaries have a lot of expenses!" Max shook his head. "Never thought a black dragon would contract with a human, though. What's the world coming to?"

"Yes, strange times indeed," Erika remarked. "The spell is supposed to attune itself with its first victim. Since the sylphs have already activated it, we should be able to pass through safely. But I don't know for sure."

"Guess I'll just have to take the risk," Max exclaimed as he floated back towards the sylphs. "It's time for some sylphie fireworks!"

And that's exactly what happened. Several times. Even Solveig got involved. She and Max took turns luring small groups of sylphs through the spell, sending each to its death. It worked like a charm — until it didn't.

"Can't you get them to move any faster?" Azriel asked Thaz. They were watching the Kounávi leave their traditional home to make a new one in Jörmungander's lair. It looked like a never-ending green-speckled orange cloud pouring through the exit. Half the tribe had already left, but Azriel wasn't pleased with the time it was taking.

Thaz frowned.

"Azriel asks if your people can evacuate with more haste," Jörmungander translated.

Thaz shook his head. "We are many. Our females and youngsters are frightened and don't entirely understand why we must leave our home, so they must be reassured. Please tell your friend we're going as fast as we can."

Jörmungander turned to Azriel. "Thaz says…"

Azriel cut him off. "Don't bother, laddie, I get the gist."

Soon after, one of Thaz's scouts landed, and the two had an animated discussion.

Azriel looked at Jörmungander who was concentrating hard on the conversation. "Well?" he asked.

Jörmungander shook his head. "They're talking too fast," he replied. "I can't keep up. Something about…" Jörmungander looked at Azriel. "Sylph's have entered the cavern at the other end!" he exclaimed.

"I KNEW IT!" Azriel shouted before launching into a long string of dwarven invectives. For the second time Jörmungander listened in wonder to one of the sylph-dwarf's tirades. In his anger, Azriel shaped his sylph body into that of a large dwarf. His eyes became two orbs of deep crimson which reflected his fury. Elbedreth, who was doing what she could to assist the Kounávi evacuation, came over at the sound of Azriel's cursing.

"And curse the puke faced, penny lickin', spider kissin', greasy dingo god that thought sylphs was a good idea!" Azriel concluded. "No offense, love." He turned to Jörmungander as his magical battleaxe and steel quarterstaff appeared. "Well, laddie, don't just stand there!" he yelled. "Turn back into yer black dragon self and come with me. Tell that weasel fella to bring his warriors too. We got a battle to fight."

Elbedreth's blades also appeared as she prepared to go with them.

Azriel shook his head. "Here," he said as he gave her the *Maul of Power*. "We'll lead them into the cavern as far as we can. You continue to help get the ferrets out but stay by the exit. When you start seeing sylphs coming your way, think the word *'Frangit'* while striking the wall of the cavern as hard as you can with the maul."

"I won't do it," Elbedreth replied as she shook her head.

Azriel locked eyes with the female sylph. In the universe of their minds, much crossed between them in an instant – love, loss, what might have been, goodbye. "You must, my dear, sweet lassie," Azriel said aloud. "There's no other way to stop the sylph. There's no other way to save Aster."

Azriel turned and, followed by a huge, black dragon, headed towards the opposite end of the cavern. Thaz and several score of his Kounávi warriors flew above them.

Elbedreth didn't move for a few seconds as she watched them leave. "Return to me, heart of my heart," she whispered in her best dwarvish before turning away.

THE NINTH INTERREGNUM

Many strange, powerful, unimaginable, and sometimes frightful creatures travel the ethereal. Not even the gods of creation hold sway over these beings, for they existed long before the gods arrived – and will exist long after the gods have left. The gods who consider themselves philosophers believe that these creatures ARE the universe. But even those gods can only speculate.

One of these incredible creatures spotted a long tendril of power, an unnatural ley line, extending through space and time. It watched as the strand pulsated and drew power from its surroundings. Small filaments of the main ley line branched off to drain even more power from neighboring universes.

Intrigued, the creature followed at a safe distance. It wondered where the tendril was going and from where it originated. Tracking the line to the endpoint, the creature came upon a small, dark planet circling a dying star. It sensed the life forms living on the planet and knew they'd die when their star exploded in the next few thousand years. There was no remorse, no sorrow, and no sympathy. Not that the creature didn't care. But from its perspective, it was the way of things. It was the circle of life.

Wishing to investigate further, the creature moved toward the planet. As it did so, the ley line bowed outward and retreated from the creature's approach. The creature withdrew and the ley line straightened back to its original path. Deciding a different tack was necessary, the creature moved to the other side of the doomed planet, the recipient of the main ley line, and advanced.

As the creature drew near, the planet slowed its rotation until it stopped. The creature retreated, fearing it had affected the planet's destiny. It watched from a distance while a few small chunks of the planet separated as the forces of gravity holding it together weakened. Unable to control its curiosity, the creature shifted to an overlapping plane of existence so it could observe without jeopardizing the planet further. It discovered the reason for the ley line – a corridor between worlds.

"Interesting," the creature said to itself. *"Maybe it's a primitive form of transportation or communication? Yes, remarkably interesting!"*

Not only was the creature pleased with this new knowledge – for knowledge of new things was what it lived for – it was also thankful it wasn't responsible for the damage occurring to the world. *"The connection is destroying the world,"* the creature thought with relief. *"Not me."*

As the creature considered, there was a sudden increase in the power of the ley line. The dark planet brightened, then came apart. It appeared the ley line had destroyed the gravitational cohesion of individual atoms – the foundation of all matter. As a consequence, the planet and its inhabitants – plants, insects, flesh and blood – came apart. There was no explosion – no light show – no sign of any kind that an entire world had ceased to exist.

The ley line paused. As the creature watched, the ley line hung in space for a brief moment before drifting forward. The creature guessed the destruction of the planet was an outcome the ley line, or whoever controlled it, didn't expect. The ley line then began to pulse with renewed power. Tendrils lanced out from the end as it reached out across even more universes and timelines – seeking, probing – for a replacement to the world that was no more.

The effects of this power surge worried the creature. Someone had put in play a force that threatened the balance of several universes and timelines. The creature knew the ley line was dangerous, but it wouldn't interfere with the circle of life even if it could. As a watcher, it only existed to witness and learn. As it turned to leave, it noticed black energy build in one of the ley line's tendrils – one which had pierced another timeline. The uncontrolled black energy grew and exploded. Unfettered, the force of the explosion raced down the ley line back toward its origination point.

"Fascinating," the space creature thought before disappearing into the void in search of the next shining diamond of wonder to attract its curiosity.

CHAPTER SIXTEEN

InnisRos (Taranthi)

The war was over. They told the old, grizzled soldier he could rejoice. They told him a permanent peace had been negotiated and his services were no longer required. They gave him a small pension as thanks for his years of service and told him to go home and be with his family. But the old soldier had no family since his entire life had been in spent in the service of his country. He packed up his meager belongings, adopted a homeless dog for company, and disappeared into a nearby forest.

Over the following months, the old soldier forged a small patch of land, another gift from his country, into a suitable place to live. He fashioned a small, one-roomed cabin with wood from the trees of the forest and planted several small vegetable gardens. Wild game, the staple food for both him and his dog, was plentiful, and he was deadly with his bow and arrow. The old soldier and his dog never went to bed hungry. After each day, the old soldier sat before the fire in his hearth and either sharpened his great battleaxe or made new arrows for his longbow, even though two full quivers of arrows stood in a corner. Those he never touched, for those were designed to kill something other than game.

The day came, as he always felt it would, when riders approached the old soldier's small homestead leading a riderless horse. "Your country has need of you," they told him. So the old soldier, not surprised, retrieved his great battleaxe, longbow, the two untouched quivers of arrows, and boarded up his cabin. He mounted the horse provided to him — one final gift from his country — and followed the riders. The politicians always believed each battle would be the last and peace would once again settle over the land. But the old, grizzled soldier knew something that all old, grizzled soldiers know. Peace is never everlasting.

-A short fable written by bard-knight Aracripidees of the Astorian Knights.

Yury and Eirwen climbed to the point of near exhaustion. Ever since Eirwen had seen that bolt of multi-colored lightening and accompanying crack of thunder on Mount Cor, she pushed hard to locate its source. She told Yury the imperative she felt to find it was impossible to ignore. Despite Yury's alarm concerning her condition, Eirwen refused to be deterred.

The sky darkened as night settled in. Yury, after a brief argument, convinced Eirwen to stop in a small alcove in the mountain that would put rock over their heads and keep them out of the ever-constant wind. As Yury looked around for anything he could use to build a fire, Eirwen, back against a wall, closed her eyes and drifted into a fitful sleep. During the first few minutes her mind struggled to calm itself as she tossed and turned. Despite the dropping temperature, Eirwen broke into a chilled sweat. Her agitated state, however, was only a precursor of what was to come.

When the dream, or vision, arrived, Eirwen stilled. Somewhere in her unconscious mind she recognized something important was happening – something she couldn't ignore. Eirwen saw a thin line of energy as it traveled through space and time to intercept a world she couldn't identify. She watched in horror as the world vanished. Then the line of energy, what she now thought was a ley line, reached beyond the destroyed world seeking more power.

What Eirwen observed next caused her to sit straight up, though she was still in her dream. Yury, sitting next to her, gently put his arm around her and tried to awaken her. But Eirwen didn't respond. Her breathing became ragged as she went into violent convulsions. Yury protected her thrashing head and made sure she didn't strangle on her own tongue and vomit as he waited for the seizure to pass. It was all he knew to do.

"Ho the cave!"

Yury, busy with Eirwen, barely acknowledged the intruder. He had long since refused to be taken by surprise. "Can you help?" he pleaded to the dark shadow that stood just outside the light of his small fire.

A female figure walked into the fire light. She was an elf dressed in normal traveling clothes – belted tunic, pants, knee-length heavy boots, and an extravagant purple cloak. Other than her beauty, the only thing that stood out was the glow that came from her magical long sword, its scabbard, and what appeared to be a magical necklace underneath her tunic. Yury looked back down as he continued to administer what help he could to Eirwen.

"What happened?" the female elf asked as she kneeled on the other side of the time walker. She had put her long sword aside, but still within arm's length. She'd never seen giants before, though the female was several feet shorter than the male. Even though the brief look she read from his eyes told her he was a good person, his stature and giant size forced her to stay on her guard.

Yury shook his head. "This happened once before," he explained. "She's different from normal folk. Sees things others can't."

"Like a seer. Or maybe a prophet?"

"I don't think it's the future she sees," Yury replied. "She's a time walker."

There was s swift intake of breath as the female elf drew back.

Yury looked over at her. "You too? People I greatly admired died saving her life. Apparently time walkers are unique and important individuals."

The female elf returned to helping care for Eirwen. Her necklace was radiating even more light. But it wasn't a necklace. Yury could now see that it appeared to be a stone embedded into her chest.

"And you?" she asked.

Eirwen began to breathe easier and her convulsions calmed. Yury felt her pulse. Eirwen's heart was beating at a normal rate... at least he thought so. He relaxed somewhat.

"Me?" Yury said as he shrugged. "I just love her regardless of who she is. What's your name and how did you come to be here?"

The female elf studied the giant. It suddenly occurred to her who he was, although the term 'Black Death' didn't appear to be an accurate description. "You're from Draugen Pesta, are you not?"

"You're dodging the question," Yury remarked as he removed the leather vest he wore over his tunic and placed it atop the now sleeping Eirwen.

The female elf smiled. "Sorry," she said as she sat back against a wall of the alcove. "My name is Kyleigh Angelus-Custos. And yours?"

"Yury Petrenko, Master at Arms and chief cook on the naval vessel *Cassiopeia*," Yury replied as he extended his huge hand. "Though my ship now lies on the bottom of the Sea of Dreams. This is Eirwen."

Kyleigh took it. Though his hand engulfed hers, his grasp was gentle and warm. "I'm not from around here," she commented.

Yury laughed, a loud bellow that warmed Kyleigh's soul. "That's funny," he said, chuckling. "I kinda already had that part figured out." Yury continued to chuckle. "Not from around here, she says."

Kyleigh smiled. "Yes, well, you know, just so you're sure. How did you come to be up here?"

Yury stopped chuckling. "That, dear lady, is a very long tale," he said. "As I suspect yours is as well. Strange, frightening times these are."

Kyleigh nodded. *"Stranger than you could ever know,"* she said to herself. *"Or perhaps you do."* Aloud, "We need to get off this mountain."

"Aye," Yury nodded.

"Do you know the way?" Kyleigh asked.

"Aye," Yury replied as he pointed down the mountain. "We go that way."

Kyleigh was about to answer when Eirwen began to move around and say unintelligible things. Yury cupped her head in his massive hands and tried to soothe her, but her thrashing only became worse. "This isn't convulsions," he said.

"No," Kyleigh said as she shook her head. "It's more like she's having a bad dream. Don't restrain her too much or you might cause her to hurt herself."

Yury was about to tell Kyleigh how needless her warning was when Eirwen suddenly stilled and sat up. She remained so, supported by both Yury and Kyleigh, for a few moments as she took deep breaths. The giant and the queen both gasped when Eirwen opened her eyes. They were as black as night, but deep inside the obsidian were small specks of light.

"By the gods, Eirwen," Yury exclaimed, "your eyes! They look like… like…"

"They look like stars in the Stygian night!" Kyleigh finished.

Eirwen reached out to Yury, found his arm and wrapped it around her. "Yury, I can't see!" she proclaimed.

Yury pulled Eirwen into his embrace and looked at Kyleigh.

But Eirwen suddenly drew back. "It's coming," she said. "And we have to stop it!"

"What's coming," Kyleigh asked.

Eirwen shook her head. "It has no form, but…"

"But what, dear," Yury inquired.

"I saw a world destroyed," Eirwen replied. "By a ley line. A ley line from… here. How is that possible?"

Kyleigh frowned.

"You understand what this means," the *Ak-Vanessë Stone* said in her mind.

Kyleigh acknowledged the question with a mental nod. "It's possible, Eirwen," she said to the time walker. "Believe me, it's possible. Yury, we have to get off this mountain."

"Who are you?" Eirwen asked Kyleigh.

"A friend," Kyleigh answered. But that was all the information she was prepared to divulge.

Eirwen accepted that response at face value. She had faith that Yury protected her and wouldn't allow an enemy to get close. Eirwen nodded. "She's right, Yury. We need to go as soon as possible. We need to find the origination point of the ley line and collapse it. If we don't, it'll destroy Aster just as it did that other world."

"Surely…" Yury began, then nodded to the inevitable. "How do we do that?"

Kyleigh answered him. "We start by getting to the origination point of the ley line. I can lead us there. Just get us down from here before we freeze to death."

"The Ak-Séregon Stone is unattended and, like a child, is exploring her limits," the *Ak-Vanessë Stone* said in Kyleigh's mind. *"She grows stronger as she siphons power from the universe, and she won't want to lose that. Stopping her will be hard and only the time walker can do it."*

Kyleigh cringed, but said nothing as the three of them began the long climb down the mountain.

The small rabbit, lost, was running for its life. His family was far ahead, panicked by the activation of the *Ak-Séregon Stone*. The rabbit, only a week old, couldn't keep up. Other animals – foxes, deer, squirrels – had run past, each as frightened as the rabbit's family.

At the point of exhaustion, the small rabbit spied a large boulder and saw a refuge against the thing that drove it and the other animals away. Once on the other side the young rabbit lay against the boulder and closed its eyes. Within seconds the youngster was fast asleep from exhaustion.

As the furry little fella slept, appendages appeared from the boulder and enclosed it in an impervious cage of creation stone. The boulder flew straight up for one hundred feet and then headed north. Below, tentacles of energy from the *Ak-Séregon Stone* covered the ground where both once rested. The boulder landed at a safe distance from the energy tentacles, but sensed something else, something far deadlier, followed. Razor-sharp sword-like limbs grew out of the boulder as it spun, using them to burrow into the soft earth of the forest floor. Both the boulder and the small rabbit remained safe when the force of the explosion passed over them.

Maedhros Nénmacil, certain the worst was over, took to the sky once again. The creation stone searched and eventually found a family of rabbits. He landed and gently released the young rabbit who excitedly rejoined his kinfolk. Pleased, Maedhros Nénmacil rose and left the happy reunion to investigate the explosion point. The devastation was complete except for a single point of powerful magic.

"The *Ak-Séregon Stone*," Maedhros Nénmacil grated. "And it's getting stronger."

The creation stone knew he had to reestablished his link to the priestess he served. She needed to know what had just happened. "As Colonel Tirion might say," Maedhros Nénmacil grumbled, "it's time to eat crow."

The explosion, a release of energy never before seen on InnisRos, charred and flattened trees for several miles surrounding the *Ak-Séregon Stone*. The stone itself survived, but there were no sorcerers left to control its power, and its link to the Svartalfheim had been broken. Left to its own devices, the stone reached out through space and time even more greedily, thirsting for the unimaginable power offered beyond.

Nefertari and Colonel Tirion were in a large back room of an even larger stone warehouse in the capital city of Taranthi. They were trying to prove Nefertari's credentials to the retired and discharged

Marines that lived in the city – the Marines Colonel Tirion said would help. But it wasn't going as easily as the two had hoped.

Nefertari shook her head and stood up from the uncomfortable barrel she was sitting on. "Enough of this charade!" she exclaimed. "I don't care whether or not you believe me to be a spy! Nor do I care if you don't believe I'm the Queen's sister. We've come to you for help… help to free your own city from the dark elf scourge. And all you do is talk and whisper conspiratorially amongst yourselves. A bunch of blowhards, that's all you are!"

"Nefertari," Colonel Tirion pleaded.

The priestess turned to her companion and directed an angry stare towards him. The colonel cringed. "Once a Marine always a Marine, eh, Daeron?" she said. "Isn't that what you're constantly telling me? And this is your example of that creed?"

Colonel Tirion remained silent. Nefertari was gripping her staff so tight he could see small scratches where her fingernails gouged the wood. He didn't want to push her any further by arguing. Pressure had been building inside her of late, and he didn't want to be the one to set off the explosion to come.

The leader of the Marine band, a retired general, stood to challenge Nefertari. She whirled on him and tapped the base of her staff on the floor. Small sparks of crackling energy flared, and the room dimmed as the priestess' staff absorbed most of the light coming from the magically lit stones used as light sources. A huge elemental formed from the stone of the floor and stood beside Nefertari. Its eyes were directed at the Marines who faced its mistress. Colonel Tirion bent his head and shook it while the Marines stood and drew weapons, ready to combat the sixteen-foot-high creature.

"Look at you!" Nefertari said. "My sister, your queen, once told me of brave Marines who gave up their lives so she could escape those who hunted her. But you…" Nefertari shook her head. "What was it, gentlemen? Ale, females, both? You've gone soft and lazy. Two hundred Marines the likes of Colonel Tirion here would've taken the city back from the dark elves by now. Or died trying."

There was complete silence in the room. No one dared to contradict her words. Colonel Tirion continued to stare at the floor. The tongue-lashing Nefertari had just delivered must have hurt – must have damaged their pride – and more than likely raised a lot of anger.

Somewhere outside the city, a massive explosion stunned them all. The vibration of the blast caused dust and pieces of the ceiling to fall.

"Come, Daeron, it's time to leave," Nefertari announced, unfazed by what just happened. She looked at the elemental and pointed to the entrance.

"Yes, mistress," it answered her unspoken command. Nefertari followed it out of the room without looking back.

Colonel Tirion stood and looked at the retired Marine general. "Sometimes she can be a little emotional," he said. "But she's rarely wrong. As hard as it was to hear, she made a valid point. When so many lives are at stake... when the very freedom we hold so dear is being threatened by such evil... there's no such thing as retirement or discharge."

"Surely you understand our position, Colonel," the general said. "We're too outnumbered and we've families to consider. You saw what the dark devils did outside the city walls!"

"Resistance against evil always comes with great risk," Colonel Tirion countered, "and even greater sacrifice. You can do a lot of damage with two hundred Marines, retired or not. Maybe even enough to have delayed the dark elves from putting their army in the field. So no, I don't understand. We all have 'skin in the game', so to speak. And as Marines, even more so."

Most of the Marines looked at the Colonel as if they'd been caught cheating by their schoolmarm. They'd act now, the colonel was sure of it. But he also knew, from a lifetime of experience as a Marine commander, that when people felt they had something to prove, they'd have a propensity for overcompensation.

"Be smart," Colonel Tirion warned. "Don't allow your enthusiasm to overcome your common sense."

The Marine general snorted. He didn't appreciate being told what to or not to do. Colonel Tirion didn't care. Besides, he suspected better Marines than the general would lead the real fight.

"We'll be outside." Colonel Tirion turned and rushed out of the room to catch up with Nefertari but didn't have far to go. Nefertari was standing just outside the door. She was alone.

"I sent the elemental back," Nefertari replied to Colonel Tirion's unasked question as she started walking towards the warehouse exit. "That was a good speech you made in there."

Colonel Tirion brushed off the compliment. "Simply the truth as I see it. You weren't so bad yourself. But you took quite a risk. Some of them looked ready to throttle you."

Nefertari nodded. "They could've tried. But if they did it would've gotten messy in a hurry. I didn't want that, which is why I called the elemental. I needed to show my power before they did anything stupid. You know, the whole 'my staff is bigger than your staff' thing. I figured they'd respect that."

Colonel Tirion smiled and nodded. "Clever."

Nefertari looked up at him. "You're surprised? I've been around Marines long enough to know they aren't as dumb as the rocks they sometimes impersonate… which I was counting on. The elemental forced them to consider my words before they did anything foolish… like attacking me. Sometimes that's all you need to do to stop a fight. I once had a showdown with a dragon. I used elementals to force him to put aside his anger and listen to my point of view. That I could call upon elementals to reinforce my request made the difference. But the larger point is neither of us died as a result of my show of strength. I must tell you that story someday."

"A dragon" Colonel Tirion sputtered. He looked at Nefertari and shook his head. He'd hold her to that promise. Then he laughed. "I think two elementals might have been better. Then your 'staff' would've been twice as big."

Nefertari smiled. "Perhaps. But a proper lady doesn't like to show off." Nefertari glanced over at Colonel Tirion. "Most times, anyway."

Nefertari stopped at the warehouse exit.

"What's wrong?" Colonel Tirion asked.

"Maedhros Nénmacil just contacted me," Nefertari replied as she opened the door.

Outside complete chaos ruled. Dark elves had come out of the woodwork, and the Taranthi citizens were giving them a wide berth. Near the western gate of the city a large contingent of dark elves were getting ready for a foray outside the city. Several sorcerers were having an animated discussion at the base of the gate while two more were up on the battlements scanning the western horizon.

"Did he tell you the reason for this?" Colonel Tirion queried.

Nefertari nodded. "A massive explosion a few miles west of here," she replied. "The one we felt inside."

"What caused it?"

Nefertari looked at the colonel. "It came from the open corridor created by the *Ak-Séregon Stone*. Maedhros Nénmacil said it killed every dark elf within at least a mile… or so he thinks. He didn't see any bodies as he flew overhead."

"Did he get the stone?"

Nefertari shook her head. "He says there's still too much residual energy from the first explosion to survive an attempt, even for him." Nefertari chuckled. "He told me a live creation stone is better than no creation stone at all."

Colonel Tirion stared at the priestess.

Nefertari shrugged. "Just a little creation stone humor," she said.

"So you two are on speaking terms again?" Colonel Tirion asked.

Nefertari nodded.

"Rànglù!"

Both Nefertari and Colonel Tirion turned in response to the harsh dark elf command. A squad of five dark elves were running towards them, forcing everyone to step aside. As the squad passed, Nefertari made a gesture with one of her hands and a small rock sprung up in front of the lead dark elf. He tripped and landed nose first on the street. None of the other dark elves had time to avoid him.

"It'll be impossible to get to the stone before that small army," Colonel Tirion observed as they walked away. "And with the sorcerers going along, our boulder friend will have a hard time as well."

Nefertari nodded. "I need to get out there."

"Maybe we can help!" a voice said from behind.

Several Marines had filed out of the warehouse and were walking towards them. The general, battered and bruised, was slinking away in the opposite direction.

Noting that Colonel Tirion was watching the general leave, one of the Marines moved forward from the pack. She was the same Marine who had just called out. "We decided a change of command was necessary, Colonel," she said as she extended her hand. "Opha Mayalene, sir."

Colonel Tirion shook the proffered hand and nodded. "We sure can use you. What was your rank?"

"Sergeant Major, Colonel," Opha replied. "And it still is. My men and I were part of the palace guard. We went underground after the dark elves took Taranthi. Our intention was to carry out guerrilla operations."

"Any luck?"

The Marine shook her head. "The dark elves battened down the hatches tight. Resistance is one thing. But suicide? Well, that's an entirely different matter. Besides, after the bats arrived not too many of the dark bastards continued to patrol the streets at night for us to kill."

"You did the right thing, Sergeant Major," Nefertari commented. "Daeron, we need to get to the stone before the dark elves reinforce it."

"Follow me," the Sergeant Major said. "We'll get you out. As for the dark elves, we'll see what we can do to keep them off your backs."

Eric the Black rode towards Taranthi on his shadow steed. It was the next day and his bat escort had long since retired back to their temporary roosts in Taranthi. Since bats are nocturnal and rested during the day, the master assassin-sorcerer dismissed them with instructions to seek him out at dusk. He was sure he'd have plenty of work for them to do.

Eric the Black stopped his steed on a small rise overlooking Taranthi. While his eyes studied the city, his mind thought of the different killing techniques he'd use to get retribution for the death of Katsumi. Distracted as he was, his mind overlooked the dark shapes that rose out of the forest to the west of Taranthi. The danger didn't become apparent to Eric the Black until they were close enough to be identified – dragons, accompanied by hundreds of wyverns, heading north. The only acceptable defense against dragons was magic, and he didn't have a high opinion of the sorcerers the Army used. "Even with their best spell they couldn't swat a fly off a baby's behind," he once told Landross.

"Damn it!" Eric the Black screamed as he stopped his shadow steed and jumped off. "I should never have left!"

He sat and crossed his legs. Within moments his mind had retreated deep within itself as he drew forth the power of his will to command magic. With practiced grace, his hands moved in rhythm with his incantations. His body faded away. Not only was the assassin-sorcerer invisible but also shielded from detection by the other senses, both physical and magical.

Next, he sent a mental picture of Calmacil Clearing to his bat minions resting in Taranthi. The master assassin-sorcerer wasn't sure if the bats could cover the distance between Taranthi and Calmacil Clearing in one night, but he commanded them to try.

Eric the Black then began a new series of invocations of his own creation to contact the sleeping Qénsharma. Assassins have been using the Qénsharma, creatures more commonly known as Soulreavers, for hundreds of years… but that didn't mean they could control them. If not for their need to sleep for two weeks after eating, even the most daring assassin wouldn't go near a Qénsharma. But Eric the Black had developed a spell which allowed him to communicate and command them.

Not long after Eric the Black woke the Qénsharma and gave them their orders, he heard and felt an explosion come from the south. He looked in that direction and saw a yellow-orange plume rise in the sky over the forest west of Taranthi. Every bone in his body screamed "Magic!" He closed his eyes and reached out with his mind to touch the ley line feeding Taranthi. It was there. But the power of the magic that flowed through it was far more powerful than he expected. Not only that, but he saw other, more subtle differences. It wasn't pure – there was a dangerous corruption to the magic. It also appeared to be distorted, as if it were being influenced by an outside force. Lastly there was a strange 'feel' to it apart from the corruption. Eric the Black sensed the cold, dark environment of the space between worlds. His stomach lurched as he was subjected to the transition between several strange and wonderful universes. Then there was the familiar grayness of the 'in-between' dimensions, something he knew all too well through usage of his own magical spells.

Eric the Black deliberated. After a few seconds it became obvious he didn't have a clue what everything meant – just that the greatest danger to InnisRos and the rest of Aster lay to the south at the site of that strange explosion. He looked back towards Calmacil Clearing and watched as the dragons and wyverns continued their flight into the horizon.

"You're on your own," he said aloud has he remounted his ghostly horse. "The gods be with you, Landross."

Eric the Black commanded his shadow steed to continue its race to the south.

Yury, Eirwen, and Kyleigh found the mouth of the Maranwe River. Though it was dangerous, Yury convinced them the quickest way out of the mountains and to the *Ak-Séregon Stone* in the south of the island was to build a raft and travel on the water. Kyleigh used her sword, *Ah-RahnVakha*, to cut the wood needed while Yury used his naval service knife to make simple cordage from the bark of several small, straight saplings. Within half a day they had what they hoped to be a serviceable raft. Yury wanted to craft a primitive rudder and affix it to the raft, but it would've taken the rest of the day to do so. Neither Eirwen nor Kyleigh were willing to spend one more night in the mountains despite Yury's claim it'd be quicker in the long run. Instead, he fashioned two long poles to steer the raft.

The Maranwe River flows from the north to the south, running almost the entire length of InnisRos and draining into the Bay of Sorrow. The current of the river works to power any craft moving downstream. But since they were using poles instead of a rudder to control the raft, they had to closely parallel the shore. Though this affected their speed since the current was slower, it offered a small measure of protection from prying eyes. It also put them closer to land should the need to abandon the raft become necessary.

They traveled on the river the rest of the day and into the night, made possible by light from Kyleigh's magical sword. By dawn of the following day they had negotiated the few rapids the North Spire Mountains offered and were in the southern foothills. The sun rose on the horizon, a giant orange sphere peeking through thick clouds. But Yury knew those clouds would be gone by mid-morning and then there'd be nothing to protect them from the heat of the day. He wasn't worried for himself – most of his life he'd been on the water under the relentless sun and was used to it. But his companions didn't have that benefit. The heat would drain their strength to the point that it could become dangerous. He guided the raft towards the shoreline.

"What are you doing," Kyleigh asked.

"I need to rest," Yury replied. "Besides, we need to eat to keep up our strength. I'll catch fish for breakfast and then we'll rest for a spell. It's going to be a long, hot day."

Kyleigh looked down at Eirwen who was sleeping. The time walker still hadn't recovered from her convulsions of the previous day and that concerned her. Then there was Yury. Kyleigh saw exhaustion in the giant's eyes. She nodded.

"Very well," Kyleigh said. "Once we land, I'll help Eirwen and get a fire started while you catch fish. But Yury, we dare not delay too long."

Yury nodded agreement as he steered the raft towards the shore. Once they were back on land, Yury, after carrying Eirwen off the raft and sitting her on the ground, back against a log, went downstream a hundred feet and threw a line and lure into the water. Both were standard gear carried by all seamen.

Kyleigh gathered an arm full of leaves to make the time walker more comfortable. Eirwen voiced her thanks and went back to sleep. Kyleigh then collected wood and started a small fire with the magic of her sword. Yury returned a short while later with three large trout hanging from a string thrown across his back. In his other hand were various herbs he had found growing in the immediate area. Within minutes he had the fish deboned, dressed, and roasting over crude spits fashioned from some of the wood Kyleigh had gathered.

Kyleigh shook her head as she studied Yury's well-practiced movements. "Incredible," she remarked.

"I'm a master cook," Yury said. "Of all the things I can do, cooking gives me the most pleasure. Watch the fish for me. I have one more thing to do."

The Alfheim queen nodded as Yury stood and move further into the trees. "And don't let them burn!" he called back.

The fish were a golden brown when Yury returned. He was carrying wood – supple saplings that could be easily fashioned – and three large leaves. Dropping the wood to the ground, he kneeled by the fire and inspected their breakfast with a practiced glance.

"Perfect," he said as he used the leaves to wrap around the hot fish and removed them from the spits. He opened the leaves up and sprinkled the fish with the herbs he'd found earlier.

"Seasoning," he remarked to his audience of one. "You got them roasted perfectly. I suspect you'd make a fairly decent cook."

Kyleigh laughed at the thought of the queen of the Alfheim preparing food. "Like I'd do that," she remarked without thinking.

"So cooking's beneath you?" Yury asked.

Kyleigh stifled her giggles as she realized how her remark must have sounded. She looked up to meet the gaze of the giant. "I didn't mean to belittle…"

Yury stood. At that moment Kyleigh didn't feel too comfortable with the huge giant looking down at her. But *Ah-RahnVakha*, quick to rise in defense of its master, remained inert. There was nothing to fear from the Draugan Pesta seaman.

"It'll take a few minutes for those to cool off," Yury said as he turned and picked up the wood he dropped. He started to walk away, stopped, and swung back around to face Kyleigh. "Look, my lady," he said. "I know you're someone special. That sword you carry, your fancy cloak, and that precious stone embedded in your chest… well… I've never seen the like, and I've been around my share of admirals, sorcerers, even a queen. Then there's the circumstances of your arrival in the mountains. No, you're certainly a person of some importance. But I haven't questioned any of that because you're here to help. Whether you're a queen or princess, or some kind of priestess whose been sent by… whoever… or even a goddess yourself, I don't care. From what Eirwen has told me, we'll need all the help we can get. I'm just a navy chief petty officer, so I expect you know better than me regarding such things. Eirwen does." Yury paused and shrugged. "But regardless of who you are, you shouldn't demean the work of those you believe to be below your station in life. It's wrong. And it doesn't become you." The giant reached down with a free hand and grabbed one of the three fish before leaving for the raft.

"Yury, please, I didn't mean anything by it," Kyleigh called out. "I'm not like that!"

Her plea fell on deaf ears.

"Please wake Eirwen and get her to eat," Yury called. "The fish should be cool enough by now."

"The giant is wrong about you, Your Highness," the *Ak-Vanessë Stone* said in Kyleigh's mind. *"He lashes out because his feelings are hurt."*

Kyleigh shook her head. "That was a careless and cruel remark," she replied aloud as she gently shook Eirwen awake and offered one of the two remaining fish.

The time walker accepted the fish and bit into it hungrily. "Where's Yury," Eirwen asked. "I don't sense his presence nearby,"

Kyleigh sighed as she bit into her own fish. It was delicious, which made her wonder what he'd be able to do with a complete kitchen from which to work. "He's down by the raft making a few improvements."

Eirwen stopped eating. "Did he cook this?"

Kyleigh nodded and then remembered Eirwen's blindness. "Yes."

"Did he eat before he left?"

The Alfheim queen looked towards the shore where the giant was working on the raft. He had thrown his fish to a fox who had come out of the underbrush hoping for a few remnants of Yury's meal. He got the whole thing instead.

"Lucky fox," Kyleigh thought. She then turned her attention back to Eirwen. "Yes, he ate every single bit of it."

The new dark elf warriors who had arrived through the corridor before the explosion had for all intents and purposes overrun Taranthi. The city garrison commander immediately put them to work going door-to-door in search of contraband. He had surmised, though he doubted it, that a city-wide search might produce clues to what, or who, had caused the explosion. That would garner him favor with his demon superior, Aikanáro, who appreciated success and rewarded it handsomely. The demon's daughter, though, was another story altogether. She was the one who usually doled out punishment, sometimes even for minor offenses if she felt an example was needed. One does not soon forget punishment delivered by Nightshade... that is if the one receiving the punishment survived.

Two hundred Marines spread out through the city to serve as a wedge with Nefertari, Colonel Tirion, and Sergeant Major Mayalene in the center. Nefertari saw the truth in Colonel Tirion's earlier words about Marines being capable of delicate operations when the need arose. They looked just like any other citizen going about their business. She wouldn't have known they were Marines if she didn't know they were Marines.

The numbers of dark elves now roaming the streets had virtually doubled in the space of one day. The occupiers were going door-to-door searching for something. Fortunately, most of the citizenry understood now wasn't the time to resist such an overwhelming presence. Their perseverance appeared to be paying off as she saw no indications of undue violence against the populace. Nefertari wondered if there were, would her Marine escort try to intervene. Colonel Tirion, who heard her whispered concerns, assured her the Marines understood the overall objective and its importance. Only if discovered would the real 'crap hit the windmill'.

Colonel Tirion was being supported on either arm by two stocky Marines who were dragging him between them. The Colonel's eyes were dark and sunken. He was sweating and purple splotches covered his entire body, a few of them with foul-smelling pus dripping out. As they made their way to the gate, everybody on the streets gave them a wide berth.

As the small group approached the western gate, its guards, who were just milling around, raised their noses in the air and sniffed. From the reactions of most, they didn't care much for what they smelled. Directing their attention to the source of the smell, they saw Nefertari leading a small procession approaching their gate. The two hundred Marine 'ushers' had melded into the surroundings – shops, alleyways, rooftops, doorways – and watched for any sign of a problem.

Several of the guards, holding their noses, approached. "Ràng nà zhǐ chòu gǒu líkāi wǒmen," one of them screamed while pointing at Colonel Tirion.

Nefertari, standing in front with Sergeant Major Mayalene behind and on her right, shook her head. "I don't understand," she said. She pointed to Colonel Tirion, and then the gate, and said "We need to leave. It's the plague!"

The guard commander shook his head. "Líkāi huò sǐwáng," he said as he and the other guards drew their swords. Several dark elves on the battlements had taken an interest as well and now had arrows trained on Nefertari and her small party.

"Please, you must allow us to leave or the whole city will get sick," Nefertari pleaded.

The guard commander shook his head. "Lái dào zhèlǐ, qiúfàn."

A diminutive, cloaked figure moved through the throng of guards. One of them roughly pushed the figure forward. The robed figure stopped several feet behind the lead guard and removed the hood to reveal a female dark elf – small, petite, and the first dark elf female anyone on Aster had ever seen.

"My Lord says you are to 'get that stinking dog away from here', madam."

Nefertari looked into the eyes of the young dark elf. She saw fear – fear, hopelessness, and resignation. "You speak our language," Nefertari pointed out the obvious.

The dark elf female nodded. "Yours and many others," she replied. "I'm… an anomaly… touched by magic which allows me to understand languages after hearing but a few simple phrases."

Nefertari frowned. "Why are you here," she asked, "and not with the dark elf invasion commander-in-chief? I'd think your talent would be greatly valued."

The dark elf female sighed. "Being different is frowned upon in dark elf society. I only live until they have no further use for me. It is the way of our people."

"Tíngzhǐ nǐ de diédiébùxiū, bit zi," the guard commander shouted as he slapped the back of the interpreter's head with an open hand.

"We are to get on with the discussion. I am Song Jingyi, your translator. The lord asks why you wish to leave."

Nefertari looked back at Colonel Tirion. "There's plague in the city," she declared.

Song Jingyi interpreted as the priestess spoke. The guard commander's face remained impassive as he listened. "Wǒ wèi shén me yào guān xīn?".

"The lord wishes to know why he should care."

"Tell your lord that if this disease spreads, half the city population will die," Nefertari replied. "That includes your own people."

"Why do you think it will hurt the glorious dark elf race?"

Nefertari held back her disgust. "I'm a healer and I've studied the plague extensively. That's how I know this patient is the source and should be quarantined outside the walls. He's not yet contagious. But if he's still in the city an hour from now…" Nefertari shook her head. "Well… the gods help us all."

Song Jingyi stopped translating mid-sentence. "That makes little sense," she told Nefertari. "In a city this size the odds of you knowing the plague has struck before an actual outbreak, let alone being able to find the one person who has it, are astronomical."

Nefertari gripped her staff while the others prepared for the worse. One of the Marines holding up Colonel Tirion secretly signaled the other Marines who were looking on from their various hiding places. Their own weapons were already drawn and trained on the dark elf.

"Shénme shì zhǐliú!" the guard commander yelled as he slapped Song Jingyi across the back of the head for the second time. She glanced at Nefertari before she turned to her master and bowed low. She spoke to the guard commander at length.

The guard commander eyed Nefertari for a few moments. Suddenly he smiled and said something to the other guards who laughed. Song Jingyi didn't bother to translate – it was plain what was happening. The guard commander walked up to Nefertari and squeezed her breasts as he said something else to the guards, which brought even more laughter. Nefertari closed her eyes and gnashed her teeth together. Every muscle in Colonel Tirion's body shook with rage as he marked the guard commander for death. Song Jingyi whispered "pig" just loud enough for Nefertari to hear.

The dark elf leader leaned in close and ran his tongue across the side of Nefertari's neck before he stepped back. Still laughing, he called out and several guards disappeared into the gate house. Slowly the portcullis began to rise.

"Qīngchú xiānshēng chòu," the guard commander said, then looked at Sing Jingyi who bowed.

"The lord says you are to remove mister stinky from the city," she said.

The guard commander pointed at Nefertari. "Wǒ fēnfù nǐ yǐhòu jiàn wǒ."

"And you are ordered to report to him later," Song Jingyi said to Nefertari.

Nefertari gazed at the guard commander for a few moments. She had little patience left for his arrogance and was ready to bring fire and damnation down upon him and his retched comrades. One word of command, one swipe of her staff, was all she needed to remedy the insult she just suffered. But the metal-on-metal sound of the portcullis being raised brought her back to reality. She'd come back, all right. Back to skin him alive. She smiled and bowed to the guard commander who, hands on hips and legs spread wide, laughed into the sky before he turned his back and walked away.

Little Jimmy was a six-year-old human whose parents were lost in the tidal wave. Both were outside the city walls working for the dark elves when the wave hit. Little Jimmy, now an orphan, was taken in by a home for children. He was one of hundreds. As a result of this sudden influx of orphans caused by the dark elf invasion and subsequent tidal wave, the orphanage staff were ill-prepared to properly supervise everyone. As a result, several of the waifs were usually outside the home and unaccounted for at any given moment.

The palace Marines had taken an interest in the parentless children and offered whatever help they could. Little Jimmy, one of the youngest in the home, developed a strong relationship with Opha Mayalene. Whenever he spied her, he'd call out "Hey, Marine!" and brandish the wooden toy sword she had bought for him. He swore, in his child-like mind, that he'd grow up to be a Marine, win fame and fortune, and marry his Marine sweetheart.

Nothing makes a little boy braver than when he sees the one person he has a crush on in danger. So when he saw Opha with other

Marines talking to the evil dark elves, he figured he must save her. He ran out into the open waving his sword screaming, "Leave my Marine alone!" The dark elves only bothered to learn one word in the common tongue of Aster – Marine. To them it meant devil. The portcullis dropped and the dark elves charged. Arrows from the battlements started to fill the air. The crap had hit the windmill.

The four Qénsharma were cranky. Something had disturbed them from their sleep. First, an explosion which caused the ground to shake with its force. Then they heard the call – subtle and barely recognizable. As much as they wanted to return to their slumber, they were compelled to answer. They grumbled as they wiped away their stupor. They weren't ready to eat, had no desire to seek food, and knew if they ate too soon it might kill them.

But powerful magic had weaponized the Qénsharma, and through this magic they had been taught how to kill without eating – without absorbing the muscle and skin. They did this by squeezing the internal organs of their intended victim. From the outside, the corpse would look normal. But when opened, the internal organs would be nothing more than a quivering mass of crushed viscera. That was what their new orders required them to do, but with one difference. They were to kill slowly and in a way which extracted as much pain as possible. One by one the internal organs were to be crushed until only the beating heart remained.

Appearing as a small puddle of quicksilver, the Qénsharma slithered out of the stream bed they had found to sleep. Their targets were once again the purveyors of magic – dark elf sorcerers – and the Qénsharma knew their particular scent. That odor was strong and not too far away. Using the underbrush as cover, they approached the dark elf sorcerers undetected.

Maedhros Nénmacil was observing the *Ak-Séregon Stone* from his position on the ground behind several blackened and overturned trees. To those unfamiliar, he appeared as nothing more than a common over-sized boulder. The dark elves, warriors and sorcerers, hadn't taken long to arrive at the explosion point. Five sorcerers were doing everything they could to bring the stone back under their control, but it appeared they were having little success in doing so. The *Ak-Séregon Stone* was resisting them, which Maedhros Nénmacil thought was a fascinating development.

"Good for it!" the creation stone grumbled.

Two dark elf warriors who had been sitting on the creation stone and watching the sorcerers, jumped off and looked around for the source of the grumbling.

"Spirits!" one of them said as they both moved away, seeking the comfort of numbers offered by their other comrades.

Maedhros Nénmacil laughed again. Like all creation stones, he could understand all languages, regardless of the world or the universe. There was no logical explanation – just like there was no logical explanation for their very existence. It just was.

Then he noticed movement on the blackened ground. The movement appeared as a slight shifting of the burned forest floor. As Maedhros Nénmacil continued to stare, he saw a glint of silver. He watched as the movement advanced towards the *Ak-Séregon Stone*.

"What am I seeing?" the creation stone wondered.

The sorcerers were standing in front of the corridor created by the *Ak-Séregon Stone* and trying to control it. So intent were they on their spell crafting they had lost all awareness of the outside world… which is why dark elf warriors accompanied them. The warriors, bored with sorcerer guard duty, paid little attention to anything other than their game of dice or smoking tobacco in the fancy porcelain pipes they had commandeered from the Taranthi populace.

The movement broke apart into four pieces directed at four of the five sorcerers. Maedhros Nénmacil continued to watch as the creatures – what else could they be – slithered underneath the yellow robes of the sorcerers. Five minutes, then ten minutes, went by and nothing broke the will of the sorcerers. Just the opposite – they looked as if they might be finally having success against the *Ak-Séregon Stone*.

Suddenly one of the sorcerers screamed out in pain and clutched the back of his right side. Another bent over and vomited blood has he grabbed his stomach. Within seconds the four sorcerers started rolling on the ground screaming in agony. The fifth sorcerer, alone, was no match for the more powerful *Ak-Séregon Stone*. It blasted him into dust while disintegrating a few of the warriors as well. Those who remained backed away from the stone and the screaming sorcerers. They concluded that what had just happened, and was still happening, was really, really bad mojo. They retreated into the forest and never looked back.

"Mistress," Maedhros Nénmacil called through his mind link with Nefertari. *"The stone is unguarded. Now might be the right time to come for it."*

"Can't my friend," came the reply. *"I'm a bit busy trying to stay alive. In fact, we could use your help."*

"Coming, StarSinger," the creation stone responded as he rose and sped to the east.

Eric the Black followed the Maranwe River along its western bank. When he reached the huge southern forest's edge, he veered away from the river and into it. The thickness of the underbrush slowed his speed as expected, but he decided not to use magic to make his way easier. Any sorcerer, if paying attention, can track magic along the ley line, and he didn't want to take the chance of being discovered.

The master assassin-sorcerer stopped his shadow steed and whispered an incantation. Drawing power from within so he could sense the ley line without tapping into its power, he extended his senses outward. It pulsated with even more strength than the last time he had checked.

The quantity of magical energy that runs through each ley line varies. Some are strong while others not so much. In all cases, though, the power in a ley line remains static, unchanged, and one of the few unvarying things in the universe unless it was being affected by an outside source. This one was gaining power.

"The stone," Eric the Black thought. He surmised either the *Ak-Séregon Stone* is forcing the ley line to gather more power from the universes it penetrated with the corridor, or there was something on the other end of the ley line causing the power surge. No one knew what might happen when a ley line overloaded. But either way, it was dangerous, if not disastrous, to every world or part of the universe it touched.

Eric the Black pushed forward with more urgency. Closing the corridor between Aster and the Svartalfheim suddenly took on a far greater significance… not only because it allowed the invaders to reinforce their numbers, but also because it might lead to an even more ominous outcome – a planet-wide blowback of powerful magic. The master assassin-sorcerer cursed. His progress through the forest frustrated him. Throwing caution to the wind, he cast a flying spell on his shadow steed. Up they soared, through the encumbrance of branches and past the forest canopy into the freedom of the sky.

From his new vantage point, everything looked peaceful – no smoke waffling into the air, no sounds of battle, no threats of any kind. To his left he saw the majestic crystal towers that identified Taranthi and the sparking blue of the Sea of Dreams beyond. Behind him sat the rich farmlands of InnisRos, though they now looked scarred from the early harvest of crops and the dark elf army as it moved through. Once the invaders were driven away, those fields will once again provide a wealthy bounty.

As he continued his flight, he soon made out a patch of disfigured and blackened forest, the obvious point of the explosion. It was a lesion that looked and felt infected. What the forest had been put through was repulsive. The rangers of InnisRos would have a difficult time draining the pus out of this wound.

In the center of the destruction lay the *Ak-Séregon Stone*, gleaming with a steady, white light. Next to it was the corridor opening, swirling vapors of black and gray. But there were no sorcerers maintaining control. In fact, Eric the Black saw no one at all. The *Ak-Séregon Stone* was maintaining the corridor on its own.

"That's not right," he whispered as he landed next the stone.

He dismounted his shadow steed, studied both stone and corridor, and shook his head. "Too much power coming through the corridor," he said aloud. "The stone can't possibly control it, can it?"

Eric the Black closed his eyes and concentrated on the stone, attempting to garner more information through his connection to magic. His sorcerer's sight glimpsed something out along the corridor, out past Aster, through dimensions and other universes. He couldn't discern its true nature except to understand that its power was beyond comprehension.

He whistled. "If the stone taps into that power without destroying itself," he said while shaking his head, "there'll be no stopping it."

The *Ak-Séregon Stone* flashed. Eric the Black drew back from his examination. He sensed the stone was warning him to withdraw, but he couldn't. He needed to know more. He needed to figure out what he had to do to close the corridor. He extended his sorcerer's sight back to the stone. It flashed again. Only this time the stone wasn't holding back. The master assassin-sorcerer was hit by a wall of force that threw him back fifty feet. He landed hard against the blackened and broken trunk of a downed tree. Several bones shattered upon impact, but Eric the Black never felt the pain. He was unconscious before his body hit the tree.

THE TENTH INTERREGNUM

The cold, barren ground of the Great Blight, miles from the Northern Boreskyre Mountains, shook. The loose dirt and sand of the freshly filled-in crater slowly sank into the earth and exposed a large cocoon made of black onyx. The sun, shining through the blue sky, tried to expose it with light, but none of its rays reflected off the surface of the cocoon. It was as if the light itself had been captured and held ransom for a payment that had yet to be determined.

The cocoon began to rotate and expand until the crater could no longer contain it. Now larger than the largest ships roaming Aster's oceans, it rose into the air. As the rotation speed increased, black beams of an unknown substance assailed the sky in every direction. When they passed through the air, they turned what little moisture there was into ice crystals that fell to the ground.

The cocoon continued to grow and spin. Now the size of a small castle, it continued to rotate faster and faster. The assiduous black beams twisted from their course and turned back into the cocoon, returning energy to the origin.

The cocoon stopped spinning and hung silent in the sky… its metamorphosis complete. Ice crystals formed around its cold surface and fell from the sky. Other than the near imperceptible sound of ice hitting the ground, complete silence ruled.

The cocoon began to rotate once again, but faster. This time, however, it was spinning in the opposite direction. As it built up speed, a strange low hum emanated from it. The faster the rotation, the higher pitched the hum became, until the sound left the range of perceptible hearing.

There was an explosion of black light, but no sound accompanied it. The creature that replaced the cocoon was beautiful. Three times larger than the largest dragon, it was entirely white with deep blue eyes. Atop its huge head were two spiked horns that curved forward, the tips of which radiated energy. The long, serpentine body was free of spikes or horns. The tip of the tail radiated the same energy as did the two horns on its head. Five large talons, ten feet long, tipped each its two hind legs, while the two arms ended in talonless fingers.

The magnificent creature unfurled its massive wings, hovered, and surveyed the landscape until it looked to the southwest. Its blue eyes flashed black as it turned its head upwards and roared. Two white beams from its horns lanced upward into the sky while a third beam from the tail went into the ground. Having announced it presence to the world, the dragon flew to the southwest.

The part of earth hit by the beam from the tail looked as if nothing had changed for a few moments before collapsing in upon itself, shrunken as all its energy and heat was drained away and released into the landscape surrounding it.

CHAPTER SEVENTEEN

InnisRos (Calmacil Clearing)

"It's going to be a long day!" the soldier said to his companion as they watched the long line of enemy soldiers marching towards them. The rock that hid them was but one of many between their forward position and the safety of their own line of troops.

The other soldier, older and much more experienced, nodded. "Son, you ain't lying!" he replied. "And from the dust on the horizon, I'd wager that ain't the last of them. Let's go make our report."

The two soldiers retreated.

Several hours later the advanced scouts of the enemy army reached the position vacated earlier by the two soldiers.

"Any sign?" the commander asked.

"Someone's definitely been here," the subordinate replied. "There are signs of at least two and a strange message written on the stone in chalk."

"What does it say?"

"It'd be easier to understand if you looked for yourself, sir."

The commander led his horse to the other side of the stone and looked to where his subordinate was pointing.

The commander couldn't help himself as he broke out into a hearty laugh.

-An old war story (author unknown).

𝕸arine Commander-General Feynral and several thousand Marines dug long trenches into the foothills of the North Spire Mountain Range which overlooked the plain below. From there they'd fire arrows when the enemy came within range. They'd also be the first to engage in hand to hand combat, the Marine specialty. Dragon and wyvern attacks from the air were expected, but they hoped Marine battle sorcerers positioned further up in the foothills, along with the huge Army operated ballistae and catapults, would be enough to keep them at bay.

Army General Singëril had four Army Corps at his disposal. Two were his and the other two were the Army elements that had come up from the south before the dark elf invasion. He kept one corps in the forest to cover the retreat of the queen should the battle be lost. He also had Navy ships standing offshore and prepared to evacuate her. Five fast frigates, camouflaged and anchored at the base of The Arrow, were ready to race in, pick up the queen, and transport her to the relative safety of the Santea Archipelago.

The positioning of the other three corps looked like a giant dome. One super-corps, larger than the other three by half, had been positioned in the hills above the Marines to anchor the center. Another corps was in the outskirts of the southwest corner of the forest, hidden in its dense and tall trees. The final corps was to the northwest and stretched from the Aranel River to the foothills. The last corps had fewer hills and trees for cover but consisted of mounted cavalry which gave them the advantage of speed.

Landross and his knights were with the Marines. At the right time, his thousand armored knights on their armored warhorses were to open a lane in the forward lines of the dark elf army for the Marines to rush through with orders to kill the commanders and sorcerers. General Singëril thought it was probably a suicide mission, but if anyone could do it and come out alive, it was the Marines and Landross' knights. During the confusion this bold attack will cause within the enemy midst, the Army would make its attack.

"Providing we still have an army by then," General Singëril thought out loud. With him were his assistant, Lauran Ar-Feiniel, Queen Lessien, Father Goram, and Autumn who had flown in with Father Goram's twelve dragon golems. Golanth stood off to the side and behind the priest. The ever-present dire wolves, Father Goram's Ajax and the queen's Razor and Findley, sat next to their masters. The group was on the highest hill which overlooked the plain. Dust kicked up by the march of the dark elf army was now visible to the naked eye.

"Excuse me?" Lessien said.

"My apologies, Highness," General Singëril replied. "I was only thinking out loud."

"It's a good plan, Tomas," Father Goram reassured.

General Singëril shook his head. "I don't know. There are too many variables… too many unknowns. Their sorcerers, for one. How powerful are they? As many times as King Martin fought the dark elves on the Alfheim, he never faced their sorcerers. And what's their leadership like? Are they being led by dark elf generals or demons? And if demons, are there any other demon troops with the main army? Then there are those damn dragons. Or the wyverns. They can lay waste to the landscape even before we engage the army. And finally, your missing sorcerer, Eric the Black. My own are good, but not that good. At least not good enough to fight dragons."

"There's risk to everything we do, general," Autumn remarked. "Very few plans are perfect. And those that are rarely reveal themselves until after the start of the battle."

"Though I wonder about your orders to send the Marines, escorted by Sir Landross' knights, into the center of their army," the queen commented.

Father Goram raised an eyebrow as he looked at the queen. There was something more to that statement than simple concern for subordinates. He knew she and Landross had grown closer after the assassination attempt. But maybe it was more than that.

Lessien noticed the priest's stare and knew she'd just let him through the doorway to her emotions. She didn't care. She returned his stare with one of her own and shook her head.

General Singëril, oblivious to what had transpired between the queen and the priest, responded to her question. "We went over this, Highness," he said with a touch of irritation. "In any battle, it's important to kill the head of the snake, so to speak. That is, if the opportunity should present itself. Once you remove their command and control, or their ability to give orders to their warriors, you isolate the individual fighting units. They lose their cohesiveness as their view of the battle becomes limited to their immediate surroundings. There's no way they can reinforce breeches in the line or take advantage of successes if they can't see them."

"Yes, yes, I understand that, general," Lessien answered. "My father made sure I had plenty of training in military strategy. But once it becomes obvious to their commander what we're doing, he'll reinforce and close it down real fast. Even a simultaneous attack by the rest of our army won't prevent them from being slaughtered."

"It's our hope their commanders won't realize what's happening until it's too late," Lauran Ar-Feiniel answered for the general.

"It's our hope?!" The queen turned to Father Goram. "You're sure your crystal dragons can keep the dragons and wyverns busy?"

Father Goram nodded. "Relatively so. And their attack should help to keep attention away from the knights and Marines."

Lessien sighed. "And if their commander is smart enough to realize your attack with the golems is only a feint?"

"I think it's a chance we need to take," General Singëril replied.

Lessien shook her head. "I still don't like it. It's way too risky."

General Singëril groaned and rolled his eyes. "Aye, Highness. War is risky. Perhaps you're letting your personal feelings impede rational thought."

There was silence. Even Father Goram, who was noted for his directness, cringed. Razor and Findley's ears perked up as they positioned themselves between the general and their mistress. *Ah-HritVakha* glowed in its scabbard hanging from the queen's side.

Lauran Ar-Feiniel grabbed General Singëril's arm to calm him, but he shrugged it away. "The enemy is in sight and you're still having problems with the battle plan?" he shouted. "This… this inability to make up your mind… to… to be decisive will kill us all as sure as a sword to the heart!"

"You go too far, Tomas," Lauran Ar-Feiniel said as she again grabbed his arm and tried to pull him back.

Although the general didn't shrug her arm off this time, he also didn't back away. "You told me I was to run the campaign! Well, you either need to back away and let me do my job or take command yourself!"

Lessien stared at him. She didn't flinch… she didn't back away… nor did she get angry. She understood General Singëril wasn't being disrespectful. He was being passionate, and she couldn't blame him for that. Still, his inability to control his tone bothered her.

"General, I'm not questioning your plan," Lessien replied. "I just wonder if there's another way to take out their command and control. The Marines… well, they saved my life. And even now one stays with my sister keeping her out of harm's way, or at least one can hope he is. They're like no other warriors I know. They're the elite of the elite and I don't want to lose them."

"And I don't want to lose your kingdom," the general snapped back. There was complete silence. "You think I want to lose them? You think I wanted to lose our Navy? It's war, Highness. Loses are impossible to avoid. Besides, this is exactly the type of fighting we trained them to do. And we need them to do it. But I'm not throwing them in with no regard for their chances. That's why I'm also sending the knights… to help not only getting them in but to also get them out once they've accomplished their mission."

The statement concerning the knights struck another chord. Pain flashed over the queen's face for just an instant, but everyone saw it. As much as she wanted to save the Marines, she was even more desperate to keep Landross safe. She had wanted to order him to stay behind and become part of her command structure, but she knew he'd insist upon being with his knights, and there was no doubting that's where he belonged. Such an order would not only kill their blossoming relationship, but perhaps his spirit as well.

Lessien consented. "Very well, General. We'll do it your way."

General Singëril nodded. "Thank you, Highness. Please keep in mind that battles can be very fluid. It's never too late to speak up if you see something you think I missed." The general looked at each of them. "That goes for any of you as well."

Father Goram wrapped an arm around Autumn's waist and pulled her close. "You can count on it, Tomas."

"Dragon's to the east and coming on low and fast!" a lookout shouted.

"Wyverns from the west!" another lookout cried.

"That's exactly what I would've done," General Singëril said. "Apparently their commander isn't an idiot." He turned to an adjutant. "Signal the ballistae and catapults to train to the east and fire when the dragons are within range. Signal Third Corps to ready archers. Their targets are coming from the west."

"Yes sir!"

Instead of looking to the attacks coming from each side, General Singëril looked at the advancing dark elf army. "This is just softening up," he said. "Out there is where the real battle will be waged."

"What's that," the queen asked as she pointed to the southwest. What appeared to be a large black cloud in the air was moving up the Aranel River.

"I don't know," General Singëril replied. "Interesting. It looks as if it's going to intercept the wyverns."

On the mythology of dragons:

Sightings of dragons west of the Eastern Boreskyre Mountain Range are rare. It's this very rarity that causes so much panic when dragons appear. And with good reason, for most of the dragons that fly westward don't do so with peaceful intent. They're intelligent, powerful, and ruthless magical creatures that are hard to kill. They come in different colors which associates it with its terrible dragon breath. For example, red dragons breathe fire while the white dragon breathes bitter cold. Though manuscripts of study on dragons exist on InnisRos and in the sorcerer city of Havendale, they're few and contain little verifiable information. In other words, not much is truly known about the dragons of Aster.

The dragons from the Svartalfheim match their Aster cousins in every characteristic but two. They're only black and all Svartalfheim dragons have the same dragon breath — super-hot plasma that slices more than it burns. All the females are hydra's — five-headed beasts twice as big, on average, as their male consorts. One hydra will always fly with three males in its harem. The males, though nearly as intelligent, are mentally dominated by the female they follow. This changes when the female hydra enters its transformation cycle. The male consorts, if they survive the loss of the female, become psychotic, killing and eating everything in sight until the madness kills it.

Svartalfheim wyverns are distant kin to the black dragon but differ in many ways. They're docile creatures who'd prefer to live peacefully in their mountain warrens. But, as she does to the males of her race, a female hydra can dominate wyverns and force them to do her bidding. Wyverns are also much smaller than a dragon — only half its size — and doesn't have a dragon's two upper arms. Wyverns are intelligent, but their ability to use magic is only rumored to exist. Many scholars, however, do believe the wyvern have the same spell casting ability as their dragon cousins, but for unknown reasons find using magic disagreeable... which isn't to say they never will. The wyvern isn't the same blood thirsty beast portrayed during the dark elf invasion. They were conscripted and forced into the fight.

The Svartalfheim wyvern faded into obscurity with the destruction of their home world and the mass killings that occurred during the Dark Elf War. Rumors persist, however, of winged creatures in the North Spire Mountain Range on InnisRos that match their description.

-From the Book of the Unveiled

Winston and his female companion, Willow, two young wyverns torn from their gloomy home on the Svartalfheim and transported to Aster along with hundreds of others of their kind, were part of a wyvern formation that flew north along the Aranel River. As the youngest, they flew rear guard. Up front, the older and more experienced wyverns had more important things to do than babysit rookies who were inclined to screw things up. It meant that those in the rear guard, the "tail end Wilburs" as the veterans called them, were in little danger. Rookies tended to live longer that way.

The flight from the corridor had been long and exhausting. The two rookies, undisciplined as all rookies are, broke formation to take an unscheduled break. They not only wanted to rest, but they also wished to explore this new and wonderful world. Laughing as if they didn't have a care in the world, they dove into the river and resurfaced with mouthfuls of fat, succulent fish. They wasted little time swallowing their meal. Bellies now full, they moved to the shore to sit in the sun for a few precious minutes.

It was Willow who spotted the black cloud moving along the river from the south, the direction from which they had just flown. The cloud not only traveled with great speed, but it undulated as it did so, swelling and contracting as if it were made of many smaller components.

"What's that?" Willow asked her companion.

Winston looked in the direction Willow indicated and froze. He'd never seen the like before, but he knew what it was – an unfathomable number of small flying things with very sharp teeth. At least that's what he'd heard from the few survivors of the last "cloud" attack. Winston flapped his wings to dry them. "We have to warn the others!"

The two wyverns decided the safest approach back to their comrades was to fly just off the surface of the river's waters. The trees that lined both sides of its bank would keep them hidden from the approaching black cloud. It was a good plan which worked – until it didn't.

The two wyverns rounded a bend in the river when a raft with three people on it suddenly appeared. Before Winston or Willow could react, one of the raft people drew a sword and pointed it at Willow. A multi-colored bolt of crackling energy hit her, and she dropped into the water. Winston cried out, but instead of attacking the unexpected threat, he dove into the river to get Willow before the strong current swept her away. Once in the water, he wrapped his wings around her and used his powerful legs to kick them to the nearest shore. The raft people watched as Winston administered to his companion while they drifted past. After a brief discussion, they directed their raft to shore one hundred feet downriver.

Winston ignored the raft and didn't notice when or where they landed since he was too busy trying to save Willow. She was barely alive and in desperate shape. A long, deep gash along her right side burned skin and muscle, exposing the ribcage. Even more distressing, the ligaments which supported her wing had been burned away. If she survived, she'd never fly again. Further complicating matters, Willow's blood flowed unimpeded.

The raft people approached slowly under the cover of trees and bushes. Winston looked up and roared to keep them back. He immediately returned his attention to Willow without bothering to see if they heeded his warning. Though he didn't have the arms of a dragon, he could use the four elongated "fingers" that supported the wing membrane to do many delicate things. Winston gently pried open the wound and discovered a main artery had been sliced in two. He tried to grab both ends as best as he could, but the blood was not only making it slippery, it was also limiting his field of vision. Two small hands unexpectedly reached in next to his wing fingers and grabbed both ends of the bleeding blood vessel and brought them together.

So intent was Winston on helping Willow, he had forgotten the raft people. Surprised, he stood and roared into the air. When he looked back, he saw that the small female was the same raft person who hurt Willow... only now she was trying to help. The female looked up at the towering Winston. She hadn't stopped holding the artery together, nor did she display any fear. Winston looked over. The other two raft people, the giant and the other one, an almost giant, hadn't moved. The giant shielded the other with his body.

Winston decided he'd accept whatever help the raft people gave him if it meant that Willow would survive. He calmed and returned his attention back to Willow. Bending back over her, he placed a wing finger on the two ends of the bleeding artery being held together by the raft person. Then he opened his mind to the magic of this beautiful new world and found the blue strand that healed. Winston tapped into it and let it flow through his body and into the wound. The artery sealed and the bleeding stopped. Next, he healed the muscles, tendons, ligaments, and other blood vessels that had been severed. He then closed the wound before releasing his hold on the magic.

Winston sighed. Though satisfied he healed Willow's wing ligaments, he knew they'd never again be strong enough to withstand the strain of flying. Willow, when she realizes the price she paid, will be angry, as would any wyvern, that she had not been allowed to die. But he just couldn't let her bleed to death when he had the power within him to save her. Even grounded she was important to him. Important enough to let her sacrifice be his sacrifice.

Drained from the healing, Winston laid his head across Willow's torso. He listened to her heartbeat – slow, but steady and strong – and felt her taking normal breaths. The last thing he remembered seeing before exhaustion overcame him was the concerned look of the small raft person who had helped him. In her eyes he recognized several things wrapped into one – guilt and sorrow for what she had done, relief that it looked as if Willow would live, and concern… whether for them or something else, he couldn't tell.

When he awoke, it was dark. After conducting a quick inspection of Willow's life signs, he determined she was well on the road to recovery. She'd probably sleep through the night. Of the raft people he saw no sign.

Winston studied his surroundings and listened. It was peaceful. There was the sound of the river, so rare on the Svartalfheim, as it flowed past. He heard insects chirping and the distant "buuurrrp" of an unknown river animal. Intermingled in this was the rustling sound wind made as it blew across and through the hollow river reeds, which were adding their own trebles and basses to the symphony being conducted by the night. And the evening sky! So many stars!

"I'm not going back," he said aloud, meaning back to his home world. He looked at Willow. "WE'RE not going back."

As Winston settled to wait out the night, he saw something drawn into the dirt. It appeared to be a mountain range with a river winding down from it. An "X" had been drawn next to the river. In the drawing, one mountain was taller than the others. There was an arrow pointing to it.

Army Sergeant Remay Trisfema and Private First-Class Rufus Torwarin were in a foxhole at the extreme end of the Third Corps line to the southwest, watching with great interest as the wyverns approached. Both had laid out their weapons and strung their bows. They didn't think arrow fire would do much damage, but other than their swords and daggers, what else did they have?

Rufus looked over at the sergeant who had just finished a smoke and was knocking the burned ash out of his pipe. "Why are we still here?" he asked. "What's the captain going to do about those wyvern thingies?"

Sergeant Trisfema looked at the youngster. They were all young, he thought as he stowed away his pipe. "We have our orders," he said. "We're to hold the line."

"It's suicide!"

The sergeant looked at the closing wyverns. "Maybe. But we're soldiers. We follow orders. We fight, smoke, drink, visit the whorehouse, and even die when we're told to. Hell, we breathe according to Army regulations." The sergeant looked over at the private. "You got someplace else to be? Or simply scared of dying?"

"Aren't you?" Rufus replied.

Sergeant Trisfema looked back at the wyverns. "Maybe," he admitted. "But if we didn't fight, InnisRos wouldn't survive. I fear that more than death. At least we're not the Marines."

Rufus didn't reply. Instead, he looked at the approaching wyverns. Something was happening. There appeared to be confusion in their picture-perfect formation. "Look at that, Sarge," he said as he pointed.

"I see it," the sergeant replied. "And I think I know why. See what's coming up from the river?"

"A black cloud. But what is it?"

Sergeant Trisfema shook his head. "Not sure from this distance, but there's only one thing that travels like that... bats. There must be millions!"

"Don't bats only come out at night?" Rufus asked.

"That's only part of what makes this so strange," Sergeant Trisfema replied. "Every bat on the island must be in that... that cloud... working together. How is that even conceivable?"

The two watched as the wyverns turned to meet the onslaught. Unlike the last wyvern-bat encounter, these wyverns weren't taken by surprise. As the two forces met, the bat formation broke apart into five smaller components – one in front, one to each side, one on top, and the other on the bottom. The surrounded wyverns, prepared for a frontal assault, panicked. Instead of staying in formation and forcing their way through the box they found them themselves in, they scattered. It rapidly became a free-for-all with every wyvern and bat fighting for itself.

Wyverns and bats began to fall to the earth. Huge swathes of bats were swatted from the sky by the wyvern's wings while others were either swallowed or crushed by talon-tipped claws. The ground beneath soon became dotted with dead and wounded wyverns and bats. Though spirited, the wyvern defense never had a chance. There was just too many bats.

The battle lasted for thirty minutes. Not a single wyvern escaped. Even the wounded lying on the ground were dispatched by the bats. Every last one. When the bats were finished with their butchery, they flew back into the mountains, though with only half their original number.

"Damn, sarge," Rufus said. "I ain't never seen no bats do something like that before."

Sergeant Trisfema shook his head. "Neither have I."

Rufus continued. "It was like they knew what they were doing. Like they were following the Army handbook on tactics. And they sure didn't take any prisoners. Killed them all. Yes sir, every single last one of them wyvern thingies."

"Quit your jabbering," Sergeant Trisfema admonished. "We still got a war to fight."

"Just not as soon as we thought. Ain't that right, sarge."

Sergeant Trisfema nodded as he continued to stare at the bloody field before them. "Yeah, Rufus, that's right."

There were no bats to stop the hydra and her three male consorts. Their first pass over Lessien's army went virtually unopposed. Only one of the ballistae hit – a clean shot through the arm of one of the males. Its rage at being wounded cost the ballistae crew their lives.

Arrows from the archers, most of which ran true, couldn't pierce the invisible force field around each dragon. Arrows with magical enchantments could, but even then, they had little effect, their magic spent before they completely penetrated the dragon's scales. Stronger enchantments were needed.

Queen Lessien, Father Goram, and the others watched in horror from their hilltop command post as dragon breath weapons were released against the troops. While covered trenches protected most of the warriors, the dragons caught many out in the open. White-hot plasma spray turned running soldiers into a blackened, molten residue – a quick, merciful death. Those that didn't die at once lay on the ground writhing in pain with parts of their bodies burned and melted. As the dragons flew away to the west, the screams of the wounded and dying filled the air.

General Singëril, with an occasional suggestion from Lauran Ar-Feiniel, hunkered down with his staff and began to issue orders. He was in his element. Everything around him turned into a beehive of activity as subordinates raced to do his bidding. No panic, just calm urgency. Years of battling pirates in the archipelago had honed his command abilities and his army's fighting edge.

Father Goram spoke into a communications crystal. Cameron, who led the monastery clerics, was on the other end of the conversation and assured the head priest that his healers were coordinating with their army healer counterparts to help the injured and the dying. Satisfied, Father Goram walked over to Golanth and put an arm around the dragon golem's neck as he whispered into its ear. Together the two of them left the hilltop and approached the rest of the dragon golems waiting below.

"Gather around," the priest said.

Surrounded by purple crystal dragons, Father Goram looked into their eyes. "I'm going to ask each of you to do something that's dangerous. So dangerous that it might mean the end of you."

"We're yours to command," Tremorlyne spoke out. "Our lives mean nothing. Just say the word."

Father Goram shook his head. "Thank you, Tremorlyne. But your lives are not meaningless to me. I love each of you. At first because I loved the friend who gave you to me. But now… well, you're important to me."

"And our mistress, your wife?" Eddrych asked.

Father Goram smiled at the thought of Autumn. "One of flesh and blood can have many loves… all of them as important as the other. You remember dear Mary McKenna?"

Each of the dragon golems nodded. "Yes, of course," Golanth said. "But you never made her our mistress."

"She was human and had no magic," the priest replied. "She wouldn't have survived the introduction. But I loved her as much as I love Autumn."

The dragon golems looked confused.

"It's our hearts," Father Goram explained, "and our nature. We of flesh and blood aren't made to be alone. Oh, sure, we can convince ourselves that we can carry on. And many do. I was one of those unfortunates. But I've come to realize happiness without love isn't… well, it isn't healthy. It hurts the psyche much more than some ever realize. In many respects we give up our will to live when we wall ourselves away from others."

"Do we love you?" Eddrych asked. "We feel the need to do what you need of us… to protect you and the mistress. Is this love?"

Father Goram frowned. To his astonishment, the other dragon golems shook their head.

"It is a silly question, Eddrych," Hoth reprimanded. "Of course we love the master and his mistress. They're bonded with us. Isn't that right, master?"

The priest smiled. "Yes, Hoth. You were created and given to me out of love. I have no doubt that love transferred into you. Though the person who created you is long dead… the love of your creation lives on through you." Father Goram's smile disappeared. "Now we must discuss something else."

Father Goram had the twelve golem's undivided attention. He felt a great sadness. In their eyes he saw the look of innocent and eager children. He held their complete trust, and he was about to put them in grave danger. Of the twelve only Golanth understood true sacrifice.

"We have little time," the priest announced. "The dragons have caused terrible suffering and will come back as soon as they can use their breath weapons again. You're our best chance to stop them."

"How do we do that, master," Duffy asked.

"They're flesh and blood," Father Goram replied. "All you have to do is ram them flying as fast as you can."

Golanth interrupted. "We build up more speed by flying down on them."

Father Goram nodded. "That's right. Once you've built up speed, inertia should do the rest. They have an unknown magical force field surrounding them, but as creatures of magic I believe you'll be able to punch through it, although your speed may slow significantly. Once inside the field, use whatever speed you have left to pierce the dragon's scales."

"And if we have no speed left?"

"Then just dig your way through," the priest replied. "Dragon scales are hard, but not as hard as crystal."

There were no more questions. The dragon golems would do the best they could and were intelligent enough to improvise should it be required. Father Goram closed his eyes and began an enchantment.

"Free and beautiful skies of azure blue.
Hide my minions within your hue.

Keep them safe, keep them veiled.
So their actions will not be derailed."

"SIC FACIAM ILLUD!"

When the command phrase was spoken, the coloring of the dragon golems turned from deep purple to light blue. The golems looked at the change in each of their brothers but accepted it without question and remained silent and still as Father Goram began another enchantment.

"Fires of perdition, fires of Hell,
Burning hot, never quelled.

An imposter has appeared and shown its face.
Seeking to upstage you and take your place.

Meet this pretender in the firmament beyond.
Send it back from which it was spawned."

"HERCLE SUMMONITIONEM AUDIRE MANDATUM MEUM!"

Father Goram turned to his dragon golems. "You'll be hard to spot as long as you stay above them," he said. "You'll also be protected against their super-heated breath. At least I'm fairly sure you'll be… so don't take any unnecessary chances if you can help it. Questions?"

Several of the dragon golems shook their heads.

"Golanth, I want you in charge."

"Yes, master," Golanth replied.

Father Goram paused as he looked at his children. "Good hunting," he said. There was apprehension, and sorrow, in his voice. "Now fly."

The twelve crystal golems flapped their wings twice and took flight. As the priest watched, they disappeared against the blue hue of the sky.

"Be safe," Father Goram whispered as he watched the last one blink out.

While Father Goram and General Singëril were attending their duties, Lessien felt as if she were only a spectator. She couldn't administer to the dead and suffering warriors like the priest and his healers. And she couldn't direct the army to battle the dragons and the advancing dark elf invaders. That was General Singëril's responsibility. And rightfully so. At the moment she was a non-essential person.

Razor and Findley looked at their mistress with concern as she turned away with tears in her eyes. The calls of the dying and the wounded had abated, but she still heard them in her mind. The memory of her warriors screaming in agony, longing for loved ones they'll never see again, or pleading to make the pain stop caused her to close her eyes and drop her head in sorrow. Her tears splattered on the ground at her feet.

Two soft hands gently wiped her tears away. Startled, Lessien drew back and opened her eyes. Before her stood Autumn.

"It's never easy to watch people die, Lessien," Autumn said. "It makes you feel helpless, as if your soul were being torn apart."

Lessien laughed. "Helpless!" she exclaimed. "Try useless! Or incompetent! Autumn, all I did was stand and watch it happen! I could have at least used the power of *Ah-HritVakha.*"

"Which would have directed the dragons to you," Autumn countered.

Lessien shrugged. "Is my life so important? Queens can be replaced… at least far easier than dead fathers, mothers, brothers, sisters, sons, and daughters."

Autumn moved over to stand between the two huge dire wolves and began to stroke their thick, rich fur. They both had been guardians to her and Horatio not too long ago, and she loved them as much as the queen did.

"Why must we have this discussion again?" Autumn asked. "What purpose would your death serve? Why do you think so little of yourself that you ignore the fact that those who died did so not only for their families and country, but for you as well? Are their deaths so unimportant that you'd throw their sacrifice away by calling dragon's breath upon your own head? Have you learned so little from your father?"

Lessien reacted as if Autumn had slapped her in the face. "How dare you!" she shouted.

"Then snap out of it!" Autumn fired back just as loud. "How many times has Horatio warned you about this?!" She paused before continuing. "Most times I see Martin in you. I see his bearing, his wisdom, his strength in your eyes. In you I see his mercy and the way he cares for InnisRos. Those times I know we have a true monarch, a queen who will rule as her father did. But there are other times… other times I see a weakness no ruler should ever have."

Lessien laughed. "You mean having feelings for the death of so many? Deaths I'm responsible for? Is that my weakness?"

Autumn shook her head. "No, Lessien," she whispered. "Listen to what you're saying. Compassion isn't a weakness. It's a strength."

Lessien looked from their hilltop perch at the progress being made. All looked to be going as well as might be expected, as one might anticipate from a professional organization that fights battles for a living. She returned her attention to Autumn. "Then what," she asked. "What's this great weakness you have observed in my character?"

Autumn sighed. *"Be patient,"* she said to herself before addressing the queen's question. "Stop letting emotions interfere with your duty, Lessien. You must learn to compartmentalize your mind. You must be able to turn your emotions off when making decisions in time of war. Turn aside the pain and horror before you. There's plenty of time for remorse afterward in the privacy of your quarters. For now you must stand like a rock. Do it for your armies. Do it for your kingdom."

Lessien frowned. "Horatio's been making that same point," she said. "Hell, even Landross has mentioned it. And you know how he is… a gallant knight to the core who hardly ever corrects another's behavior."

"Both wise beyond their years," Autumn remarked. "Though I believe Eric the Black would disagree about Landross."

Then there was shout from another hilltop. "Dragons returning!"

Army Sergeant Remay Trisfema and Private First-Class Rufus Torwarin were the first to die when the dragons made their second attack, from west to east this time. Fortunately for those in the line of attack, the dragons only had time to use their horrific breath once before they themselves were assailed.

One male was hit with three bolts from ballistae in quick succession. The first bolt struck the magical force field which surrounded the dragon and punched a hole through it. Its energy spent, the bolt hit the dragon's hard scales and bounced off with no effect. But the other two bolts followed the first through the temporary break in the force field and buried deep into the dragon's side. It screamed and broke off its attack. It wavered and started to drop from the sky but quickly righted itself. Flying raggedly because of the bolts in its side, the dragon didn't get far before two dragon golems hit it from above. The dragon's force field, damaged by the ballistae, shattered in an explosion of light and energy. The force of the impact broke the dragon's back. As it dropped, the golems gouged great rends through the scales with their claws. The dragon was dead before it crashed into the ground. The dragon golem attackers, now colored deep purple instead of sky blue, flew up to rejoin their comrades.

The force field of another male, hit by two other golems, also shattered upon the impact. Stunned by the collision, the golems fell, defenseless. The dragon engulfed them in a swath of white-hot plasma which overwhelmed their protective magic. Both screamed out to their brothers as their bodies melted into liquid crystal. Their sacrifice wasn't in vain, however. Hundreds of arrows released from below, each tip flush with magic, rose towards the dragon. With its force field gone, the dragon's hard scales weren't a match for the enchanted arrows. It died a quick death.

The remaining male and the female each suffered similar collisions in the air with dragon golems – two on the male and six on the much larger female. The force fields on both flared but held, accepting the energy of the impacts and keeping the dragons themselves unharmed. As the male turned its attention to the new attackers, it was hit with enchanted ballistae and arrows which broke the force field for good. That window of opportunity was all the golems needed. While one landed on the dragon's head and gouged at the eyes, the other bit under the neck where the scales weren't as hard. The dragon stopped flying and fell from the sky. Just before impact with the ground, the two golems flew off, one holding the head of the dragon in its claws.

The female, the five-headed hydra, proved to be a much more difficult opponent. As soon as the dragon golems hit her, she twisted in mid-air and then flew straight up with the six golems in close pursuit. As she climbed, she slowed her speed, allowing the golems to close the distance. Two miles up, she stopped flying and allowed herself to fall. The golems, caught by surprise, couldn't reverse their ascent quickly enough. As the hydra dropped below them, five beams of plasma streaked from five heads, hitting two of the six golems. The protective spell Father Goram had conjured couldn't withstand multiple dragon breath attacks. Their melted remains dropped from the sky. The other golems scattered into a nearby cloud to regroup.

The hydra turned just in time to avoid a ballista bolt, but as she moved a beam of dark energy assailed her weakened force field and drove her back. She hovered for just a second looking for the source of the attack. Atop a hill stood two figures – one the source of the attack and the other a four-legged creature that appeared to be growling. Magic surrounded the aggressor but was strongest on an object hanging around its neck. Dodging another bolt and several arrows, she dove. Several magical rays of extreme cold came up from others in the hills but didn't penetrate the force field of the hydra. Annoyed, one head targeted a random hill and left it a smoldering ruin, the burned corpses of two sorcerers and twenty warriors littered the blackened hilltop.

Father Goram grimaced over the loss of two more of his golem dragons and the people who died on the hilltop. Autumn and Lessien appeared on either side of him. Razor and Findley had joined Ajax.

Father Goram glanced to either side and shook his head as he continued to mouth the words that made his spell come alive.

"Dark energy, murky bane of light,
Black as obsidian, black as night.

Hear my entreaty, hear my plight.
Dance from my fingers with all your might.

Strike this beast, hew this blight.
I call forth and liberate ebony's white knight!"

"FIAT VOLUNTAS MEA!"

Another beam of dark energy left the extended hands of the priest and struck the hydra, driving it back once again and causing it to retreat into a cloud. The dragon golems, now only numbering eight, landed next to their master and mistress. They stood ready to answer their master's summons even though they knew more were likely to die.

"That bought us some time," Father Goram said as he walked over to Golanth and leaned in to rest his forehead on the forehead of the dragon golem. Though stoic in nature, the priest knew the golems mourned the loss of their brothers. He wanted to comfort them as best as he could. Or perhaps it was he who needed to be comforted.

"Neither of you should be up here," he said to Lessien and Autumn after a few seconds of silence. He turned to face both. "It's too dangerous!"

Autumn brushed off the reprimand. "You used dark energy! You shouldn't have done that!"

It surprised the queen to hear the anger in Autumn's voice.

"It was the only way," Father Goram replied. His voice was calm and steady. "And I must use it again."

"Even if doing so threatens to destroy your soul?" Autumn demanded.

Father Goram turned away to stare into the sky where he had last seen the hydra. "Althaya understands."

Autumn didn't waver. "Althaya doesn't grant those kinds of powers. Dark energy is evil! Our mistress wouldn't allow you to use it even if she could."

The priest whirled on his wife. The fire of unrepressed anger burned in his eyes. "That hydra and its companions killed scores of our countrymen, not to mention four of my golems... our golems. Don't you care about that?"

"Of course I care," Autumn replied. She spook softly. Upon seeing the rage in her husband's eyes, she decided her own anger wouldn't accomplish anything. "It hurts to the very core of my being." Autumn stroked the side of Father Goram's face. "But my love, using evil to fight evil isn't the way."

Father Goram, unconvinced, jerked away and looked back into the sky. "There isn't any other way! Not without losing more of our warriors… and our children. Now take the queen and leave."

Lessien spoke for the first time. "We'll do nothing of the kind, Horatio." She drew *Ah-HritVakha* from its scabbard. "We'll stand and fight."

Father Goram shook his head. "InnisRos needs her queen."

The priest jumped on Golanth's back, and before Autumn or Lessien could react, was in the air with the other dragon golems heading towards the cloud where they'd seen the hydra disappear.

"No!" Autumn screamed.

If Father Goram heard her, he didn't respond. In just a matter of a few seconds they had disappeared.

Autumn looked around as she tried to figure out a way to get to her husband. But she knew without one of the dragon golems or a fly spell from Eric the Black, she was helpless.

Lessien seethed. "How dare he!" she said.

Autumn looked at the queen. "Be careful how you speak of my husband." There was a deadly seriousness in her voice.

Findley and Razor got up and took their familiar positions at the queen's side but weren't sure what to do. They loved Autumn almost as much as they loved their mistress. Then Ajax settled the matter with a low rumble which froze both. Ajax was still their pack leader and the dominant male.

Autumn put her hand on the back of Ajax. "You'd do well to remember that I'm also a devoted follower of Althaya… and a powerful priestess in my own right. I'm not the same mild, timid person who was kidnapped all those weeks ago. I've learned much from the love of my life… and can turn you into a toad just as fast."

Lessien, not one to back down, was about to respond when there was a rumble followed by an ear-splitting crack of power — a thunderclap that shook the earth. Both she and Autumn looked up as did the dire wolves. In the clouds they saw streaks of dark light going back and forth. Three dragon golems dropped from the clouds to crash into the hills beyond. But each, though unmoving as they dropped, hadn't been melted. They'd be a mess when found, but at least they'd survive. Unfortunately the same couldn't be said for Father Goram if he fell.

THE ELEVENTH INTERREGNUM

As the massive, pure white dragon moved through the sky, she looked for the cloud-like creatures that had caused her and her lovers so much harm. The dragon wasn't angry. They attacked her because she dealt death and destruction… because she was an outsider to this strange world. It was only natural that the inhabitants would defend their home. And the power the cloud beings wielded to defeat her was very impressive. The dragon understood and respected power. But that understanding and respect didn't diminish her need to dominate anyone who'd challenge her rightful place as the new ruler in the skies over Aster. The white dragon broke the demon Aikanáro's shackles of enslavement. She'd no longer destroy to meet his agenda. Now she'd kill for her own dark purpose – retribution.

As she flew south into warmer air, the bone-chilling cold of her body sucked the moisture out of the air and turned it into ice crystals which fell onto the landscape below. As she crossed the Greater Boreskyre Mountains and flew into the hotter atmosphere of the valley beyond, the ice crystals turned into rain.

The white dragon spied her objective, the dead city in the forest, and began her descent. She'd yet to see any of the cloud creatures. But no matter, she'd deal with them later.

Her rapid drop from the sky caught an unfortunate flock of sparrows by surprise. As the dragon passed by, several of the birds who hadn't escaped in time were instantly frozen. Their carcass's plunged downward with the rain.

On the western slope of the Greater Boreskyre Mountains, Erasmus had his arrow trained on a mountain goat when something – several something's – fell from the sky along with the rain from a sudden squall. The goat, as startled as Erasmus, bounded up the mountain and out of range before Erasmus could recover.

"What the hell!" the hunter exclaimed as he climbed to where the goat stood just a few seconds ago. Erasmus' faithful dog and sidekick, ol' Sparky, kept to his side as he approached the spot.

Erasmus looked down and saw several sparrows, all dead, littered on the rocky ground. He shook his head, confused. Never in his forty years of hunting had he ever seen such a thing. He looked up into the sky. All traces of the squall had moved to the southwest, and the sun was already beginning to dry him.

Erasmus looked back at the dead sparrows. "Well, boy," he said to ol' Sparky. "It's not goat, but I reckon sparrow stew will taste fine enough."

"Woof!"

Lycomedes, the new leader of the Sky Emperors, stopped his people as they rode the winds of Aster. They had been exploring the new world, basking in its light, and recovering from the battle with the dragons. Of all the worlds his people had found themselves, this one was the most idyllic. Even so, it offered dangers that, thus far, have been unique – and deadly. Nevertheless, Lycomedes and his people would stay if Aster would have them, though he wasn't sure if either had a choice.

As his people drifted, awaiting their leader's command, Lycomedes was listening to a strange, sweet voice speaking to him in his mind.

"Lycomedes," it said. *"You must return from your pilgrimage. I have need of you."*

"I heard you speaking to Liosh," the Sky Emperor leader said. *"You comforted him as he died. Who are you?"*

"I'm Emmy. The moment dear Liosh died, the future of your people became irrevocably tied to me. You will serve as guardians to the emerging empath race."

"Our temperament doesn't really suit that role," Lycomedes replied. *"Not that we wouldn't help, but we're not warriors."*

Emmy laughed. It was a child's laugh but tinged with the seriousness of an adult. *"I beg to differ! Liosh… all of you… put on a fierce display fighting the black dragons. Yet your gentle nature is clear for all to see. You'll serve magnificently!"*

"You give us a duty?" Lycomedes asked.

"I give you a purpose."

The Sky Emperor considered. *"All creatures need a purpose,"* he agreed. *"We will do as you wish. Are you the one we are to protect?"*

"No, my friend," Emmy replied. *"My future is now assured. It's my sister who must be shielded from harm."*

The ley line created by the *Ak-Séregon Stone* weaved in and out between different universes and timelines. As it did so, it strengthened. More tendrils broke off from the main line. As each found a world, or worse, a star, the power of the ley line increased while the means to stop it decreased.

The shift that followed the ley line to Aster was stronger than the other shifts combined. As it traveled the line through space and time, it gained in both power and momentum by draining energy away from the ley line. As a result, the ley line was forced to seek even more power from the universes it had already breached to counter the demand.

When the shift hit Aster, there was a momentary implosion. The surrounding air and loose items around the *Ak-Séregon Stone*, such as tree leaves and twigs, were sucked into a point above the stone.

Eric the Black, nursing the broken bones, scraps, and cuts suffered from his earlier unsuccessful attempt to study the *Ak-Séregon Stone* with magic, watched from behind a large boulder as a small tornado appeared above the stone. He could feel the power of the shift gain in strength and momentum. The plant material caught up in the tornado, unable to withstand the enormous pressure which drove the whirlwind, broke apart and disintegrated.

The cyclone stopped spinning and the clearing around the magical stone settled into a quiet tranquility. But Eric the Black sensed it was only an illusion. Something far more significant was about to occur. He felt uneasy though he wasn't sure why. Then every sorcerer sense in his body warned him to get away. Without hesitation he withdrew as fast as he could. He spied another large boulder and hurried towards it, hoping to hunker down behind and ride out what was to come.

Dragging a shattered ankle and having trouble breathing because of broken ribs, he pushed himself to the limits of his endurance. But before he could reach the safety of the boulder, a silent and invisible force hit him and threw him into the air. More bones snapped. He hit the top of the boulder he had sought for protection and flipped over and behind it. The ground Eric the Black landed on was covered by a soft moss which saved him from added injury… but the pain to his existing wounds caused by the impact forced him to scream out in agony. After his mind had cleared enough to concentrate, he encircled himself in a silvery cocoon of magic and passed out.

The magic of the shift surrounded the entire world of Aster. Only those attuned to magic – sorcerers, clerics, magical beings – felt the effect, a slight "vibration" in the ley lines that encircled the world. It was a momentary disturbance… an incongruity that was soon forgotten.

The newest denizens of Aster also sensed the change and recognized the danger. The Sky Emperors, as they floated high in the sky, saw the electrical storms that now transpired in the region above the world where Aster's rich atmosphere met the cold void of space. Lycomedes sent several of his people to investigate. The screams of those dispatched – horror, anguish, loss, death – echoed in the minds of each Sky Emperor. Silence followed, but each Sky Emperor had caught a faint mental glimpse of what their compatriots saw before they died. A whole other world had appeared and filled the space of stars and constellations above Aster. Even though Lycomedes and the other Sky Emperors sensed the rogue world wasn't in the same universe as Aster, they knew it still affected their world. At the point where both worlds touched – where two universes converged – was complete and utter annihilation. And the two worlds were moving closer to each other.

— ◆◁⊗⊗⊗▷◆ —

CHAPTER EIGHTEEN

The Mainland

"Vengeance, even for the virtuous, can be exhilarating."

-The Book of the Unveiled

Lord Ternborg stood before the opening of the hastily erected medical tent. Sasha Baratynsky, his chief healer, blocked him from entering.

"Get out of my way!" Lord Ternborg shouted. Rage seethed through every pore of his body.

The healer grimaced but stood his ground. Around them, Draugen Pesta warriors scrambled to make themselves scarce. "My Lord, you don't want to see the major like this."

That caused the leader of the Draugen Pesta to hesitate. "Is he still alive?"

The healer nodded. "Only barely, my lord. Anything more I do will only prolong his agony."

Lord Ternborg frowned. "But your magic…"

Sasha shook his head. "He's horribly burned, blinded, and has lost his arms and legs. But Viktor, that's not even the worst. His manhood's been…" Sasha didn't finish. "Though magic will heal his burns, it can't bring back his eyesight, his arms and legs… or anything else lost."

"By the gods," Lord Ternborg whispered as he shook his head.

"I've made him comfortable," the healer said. "But he's not long for this world without intervention. Considering what's left of him, that's probably for the best."

Lord Ternborg looked up. "What did this to him!" he angrily demanded.

"Magical lightning," Sasha replied. "No doubt about it."

"Other than the horses are there any other survivors?"

Sasha shook his head. "Konnie is the only one."

The Draugen Pesta ruler sidestepped the healer and entered the tent. Sasha didn't bother to stop him this time. Nor did he follow. He allowed the king to be alone with his best friend.

After a few minutes, Lord Ternborg stepped back out of the tent, shouting orders. He was as angry as Sasha had ever seen him. As warriors raced to do their lord's bidding, Sasha went back into the tent to tend his patient. There was no need. Major Konstantin Timoshenko was dead, a deep sword thrust through his heart.

Osiris led his Snow Pride warriors off the mountains and into the lowland forests. He and members of his pride ventured from their mountain only rarely, but when they did they always found the forest to be a peaceful place of refuge — a sanctuary to rest and recover from a long journey. But this time was different. Though it was as lush as always, the scent of smoldering and burned wood overwhelmed Osiris and the rest of his pride warriors. He stopped. There was something else as well, something strange and foreign, in the atmosphere.

Osiris disliked it at once. He turned to his oldest son and heir, Saladin. "Do you smell that?"

"You mean the burned wood, father?" Saladin replied.

"No. Something else, son. It's something malignant… something that doesn't belong."

Saladin took a deep breath and then shivered. "Yes! I smell it!"

"And?"

The prince paused for a few seconds. "We must find and destroy it," he growled.

Osiris nodded. "It's no longer just a matter of the missing little one," he said before calling out to the rest of the warriors. "We run!"

As the Royal Mountain Saber Cats ran through the forest towards the source of the malevolent smell, the haunted city of Elanesse, they didn't notice that tree branches and other plant impediments had moved to give an unobstructed, and unerring, path.

Elrond, the *Elendrel-Telperiën*, the Tree of the Eternal Sentinel, ordered his forest minions to open the way so the pride of purple stripped saber cats could make way with all due speed. They were much larger versions of young Loki, so he figured they'd fight on the side of his friends who needed as much help as they could find.

Elrond took stock of his forest and sighed. His green-bronze leaves fluttered in the slight breeze that blew through the trees and bushes of his dominion. At least one-third of his forest had been destroyed by the hydra and her dragons, including a few of his most powerful trees, the sequoias. But like all living things in nature, the dead inspires and promotes new life. The entire damaged part of his forest was already beginning to resurrect itself, though the larger trees will take decades to regain their majesty.

Elanesse moaned. At once Elrond sent more of his life-force to her through the complex joining of their roots far beneath the forest floor. His companion had been severely hurt, not only by the dragons but also by large, towering stalagmites that had pushed through the ground inside the city. Elrond would teach Elanesse how the stalagmites can be used in her favor as a defensive mechanism. But first he had to get her through the pain and anguish.

And it wasn't just the stalagmites. There were other creatures – evil creatures – that had arrived and taken up residence within the city. Elrond sensed their presence and the danger they represented though his link with Elanesse. He looked forward to the time when those monsters ventured outside the city and into his realm. That is if Tangus and the others didn't take care of the matter themselves.

The thought of Tangus shifted Elrond's attention to the loss of Lester and Safire. As Tangus had described it, both, particularly Lester, had died gruesome deaths. Tangus, most eager to seek his revenge, was keeping it on the down-low because Emmy wouldn't approve. The last empath was funny that way. While she'd condone Tangus's intention to kill the murderers as the proper punishment, she'd disagree with his motivation. But revenge is pure. It offered closure to the victim or the victim's family. It was a way for those most affected by the crime to say, "Take that, you son-of-a-bitch!"

"This little adventure has cost me much in the way of dear friends," Elrond said to himself. *"First Max died in the tunnels below Elanesse, then Azriel, and finally Lester and Safire. Not what I expected when we first started out. On the other hand, Max seemed okay with his new fate as a ghost, while Azriel wasn't really dead… at least not in the truest sense of the word. Now he's a sylph, whatever the hell that is. Tangus' description wasn't clear. And look at me. By the gods!"*

"Elrond?"

Elrond's attention snapped from his personal reflections and to Elanesse. "How do you feel," he asked.

"Violated, but much better thanks to you and Emmy," Elanesse replied.

Emmy, sitting next to Sakkara, watched Loki and Kevik wrestle. By now Loki was filling out and growing. The fruit from the Tree of Golden Radiance had nourished a growth spurt in the young Royal Mountain Saber Cat, and, under the tutelage of Sakkara who was teaching him the fighting style of the wolf, he was now an even match for Kevik. Even though he had only three legs and was still smaller, the speed and quickness of his kind made up for his disability and the difference in height and weight.

"You just needed the love of your mate and friends, dear," Emmy said to Elanesse. "There's very little we cannot survive with it."

Elanesse's golden leaves shimmered and the faint sound of bells filled the air. "Even so, I owe you much. Thank you, my lady."

Emmy laughed as she watched Loki tackle Kevik and roll him around on the soft forest floor. "Love requires no thanks," she said. "Besides, the world would be a much darker place without you in it. And Sehanine StarEagle might never forgive me if I let something happen to you."

"You've talked to my mother?" Elanesse asked.

Emmy shook her head. "Not within the last few days. She's helping her high priestess on the elven isle of InnisRos. There's more than just one war being fought for Aster."

"The dark elves," Elrond said. "Or so Kristen said. Her father's involved."

"It's all connected," Emmy remarked. Then she frowned and put her hand up for silence.

A pinprick of light had appeared outside the canopy of branches and leaves provided by Elrond and Elanesse. As they watched, the pinprick grew until its circumference reached thirty feet in diameter, wide enough to admit a giant. It was a magical portal through which almost anything could exit.

Sakkara corralled the little ones behind her and snarled. Elrond moved a few branches around Emmy and the wolves, while others poised just outside the portal itself, ready to pierce or block any threat.

But Emmy walked past the wolves, gently brushed Elrond's guardian branches to the side, and stood in front of the gateway. "You're safe here," she said aloud.

Tendril hands reached out and caressed Emmy's face as if it could test the veracity of the young girl's statement by touch alone.

Emmy brought her own hands up to cover the tendrils on her face and repeated, "You're safe here."

The tendrils paused and then snapped back into the portal. The misty, silvery grayness inside cleared and a huge, iridescent-winged creature with the torso of a dragon pushed through and stood. He towered above Emmy, but after a brief pause, kneeled before her.

"I'm Sandalphon of the *B'nai Elohim*, goddess," he said. "Michael has ordered me to release my young charges into your care."

Elrond's branches flapped around as if he were a bird trying to fly as he grasped the implications of what was happening in front of him. A supernatural being of obvious stature and power was deferring to the child Emmy and called her a goddess. Everyone had been hedging around that possibility for days – and upon reflection, Elrond found it made perfect sense. But still…

"Hail, Sandalphon of the *B'nai Elohim* and guardian of the Abyss," Emmy replied. "I accept. They'll be well guarded here with my friends for as long as necessary."

Sandalphon rose and looked down at Emmy. "And safe from you?"

"And safe from me," Emmy replied to Sandalphon's question.

The guardian stepped aside. A female child-giant stepped through the portal. The youth was the offspring of the giant race from Draugen Pesta. Close behind her was the largest wolf Emmy had ever seen. Even Romulus couldn't match it in height and weight. Emmy knew she was looking at the direct offspring of Fenrisúlfr, the eternal father of all wolves.

"Welcome princess," Emmy said.

The child looked up at Sandalphon. "This isn't my mother," she exclaimed as she grasped the thick fur of her wolf, Adimar.

Sandalphon placed a hand on the girl's shoulder. "You'll see your mother and father soon enough, Daphnia. Until that happens, this is the safest place for you to be."

The Draugen Pesta princess looked at Emmy and smiled but remained at Sandalphon's side.

Elanesse noted the girl's caution and moved one of her branches to within arm's length. Hanging from the branch was a nourishing and delicious piece of fruit. At the same time Elrond moved his branches back from their protective position around Emmy and the wolves.

Daphnia's eyes widen.

Emmy laughed. "We've two very special trees, here," she said. "Take the offered fruit. It's quite good. Even the wolves like it."

On cue, a piece of fruit dropped in front of Adimar. Startled at first, he sniffed it for a few moments before he gobbled it up. Juice from the fruit dribbled down his chin as he chewed. Just as the huge wolf finished, another dropped to the ground which he devoured as quickly as the first.

Daphnia first looked at Adimar, and then back again to Emmy, who nodded. She broke the piece of fruit off the branch, sniffed it, and took a bite. She closed her eyes and smiled as the lush flavor of the fruit burst into her mouth.

Emmy nodded at Sandalphon who saluted the child-goddess and stepped back into the portal which quickly closed.

Emmy reached out her hand to Daphnia. "Come. Your father will be here within the next few days. Until then, there's much we need to discuss about life beyond your mountains."

"My father?" Daphnia replied as she clutched Emmy's hand.

The empath nodded as she led the girl to a large log which was, to the dismay of the family of squirrels who called it home, used as an informal meeting place beneath the canopy of the Tree of the Eternal Sentinel.

As the two sat, Adimar, who had wasted no time making friends with Loki and Kevik, took part in a three-way wrestling match under the watchful eyes of Sakkara. The huge offspring of Fenrisúlfr appeared to understand the difference in size and played the game with that in mind.

"How much of the world do you understand, Daphnia?" Emmy asked.

The child-like façade dropped, and the princess became serious. "Mother and father have been training me for the day when I'll be queen. That is if my people so choose."

Emmy nodded. "Good. Then you understand what alliances are and why we need them?"

Daphnia nodded. "We prefer to live our lives peaceably," she replied. "But the Hyrokkin make that impossible. Regrettably, our experiences with this hereditary enemy echoes our worldview. So much so we find it hard to trust anyone. And trust is the most important thing you need to form an alliance."

"Your parents have trained you well," Emmy stated with amazement.

The princess looked at Emmy. "I prefer to be an innocent, carefree, child," she said. "But I'm not. Mother and father have made that abundantly clear. Even so, my father insists I play the part before strangers for my safety."

"And Adimar?"

Daphnia grinned. Emmy could see the love for the wolf in that smile. "An unexpected gift," the princess replied. "My captor felt Adimar would calm me… give me something to play with so I wouldn't get whinny."

"But he's become much more than that," Emmy observed.

"Of course he has," Daphnia said. "What child wouldn't love such a furball?"

Emmy laughed. "As a good friend of mine would say, 'Yer naw wee bairn, me bonnie lass.'"

Daphnia looked confused.

"Perhaps a tale for another day," Emmy said. "Let's talk about the lands west of your mountains and how an alliance with them could help your people."

The Madeiran soldier screamed. He was naked. His hands were behind him and tied around the trunk of a tree. A few strips of skin had been peeled away from his chest and left hanging in his lap. Around him, several of his mercenary friends, also naked and tied to trees, watched in horror. Kneeling next to the screaming prisoner was a Draugen Pesta sergeant. His knife was dripping with blood.

"Where's your army?" the sergeant asked.

The prisoner shook his head. "Please! I don't know!" he pleaded.

The Draugen Pesta warrior looked back at his commander. Lord Ternborg nodded. He had no mercy to spare at the moment. The sergeant reached into a leather sack lying on the ground and pulled out a handful of salt which he stuffed into the bleeding flesh of the wound he'd made. The prisoner screamed again before passing out.

"Go on to the next one until he wakes up," Lord Ternborg ordered.

"He's telling the truth," one of the other Madeiran soldiers shrieked. "King scattered the army into smaller groups and ordered us to head back to Madeira!"

"Who's King?" Lord Ternborg asked.

"General King," the soldier said. "He killed General Darcy and took command of the army."

Lord Ternborg walked over to the prisoner and kneeled. "There are blades heating in the fire over there," he said as he motioned behind him with his head. "You tell me the truth, or you'll soon wish we only skinned and salted you."

The prisoner's eyes widened impressively, he gulped, and nodded.

"Why would your new general give up the field?"

"I don't know for sure, milord," the man responded. "But after what the Spiked Fist did to your people, I figured he just got scared. Everyone knows 'bout the Black Death! I'd be running too if I were him."

Lord Ternborg studied the prisoner. A small stream of urine moved between the legs of the frightened human before being soaked up by the thirsty earth.

"Milord, I just want to go home," the Madeiran said.

The Draugen Pesta king backhanded the helpless man which sent a broken tooth flying.

"Konnie wanted to go home too!" Lord Ternborg yelled as he stood and began to draw his sword. A hand reached out and stopped him. Lord Ternborg turned. Fire filled his eyes.

"He's only a boy, Viktor," Sasha Baratynsky said. "What's being accomplished by taking his head? Will it make you sleep better at night?"

Lord Ternborg stopped, took several deep breaths, and nodded. The cleric was right. "Very well, healer," he conceded. "I suppose I got what I needed. See to them."

As Sasha began to administer to the prisoners, Lord Ternborg turned to his new executive officer, Colonel Florentina Antonovich. "After Sasha is finished, give them back their clothes, horses, and supplies."

"What about their weapons?" Colonel Antonovich asked.

Lord Ternborg nodded. "They're no threat to us. Return them as well."

Colonel Antonovich saluted and turned before stopping. "Who pays for Konnie and his command, my lord?"

"Don't worry about that, Florentina," her king replied. "Madeira will pay a hefty price for those murders."

Colonel Antonovich nodded and walked away to carry out her orders.

"Feel better, Viktor?" a voice said from behind the tree line.

Lord Ternborg looked, but little sunlight penetrated this part of the dense forest. "Who said that?" he asked.

A huge, magnificent creature walked out from the cover of the trees. Several of Lord Ternborg's personal bodyguards, the First Phalanx, drew weapons and rushed to place themselves between this new threat and their lord.

The Draugen Pesta king ordered his warriors to stand down. He recognized the stranger for who it was.

"You're a Doom Warrior," he said as he pushed his way through the wall of his bodyguards.

The Doom Warrior nodded. "Yes. I'm Michael of the *B'nai Elohim*, the guardians of the Abyss. You know the story about how I personnally forged the locket and presented it to your ancestor, the priestess Irinushka Abramovich. She has honored my request to use it sparingly and pass it on to people who can be trusted."

Lord Ternborg nodded. "Indeed I do. But I didn't call..." The Draugen Pesta paused. "Of course! It was my wife!"

Michael nodded. "She took a more direct approach to your problem."

Lord Ternborg shook his head. "I was trying to work through that without calling you at all. No one knows what you'd bring to the world... and the stories told from generation to generation about you are used to scare the devil out of our children. If you were evil..."

"We're the opposite of evil, Viktor," Michael said. "We guard the Abyss. We keep the demons that live there from your world and others like it. The priestess Irinushka Abramovich, in dire need for help against the Hyrokkin, opened a gateway to the Abyss as she sought demons to do her bidding."

Lord Ternborg shook his head. "What a foolish thing to do."

Michael nodded. "That is why my brothers and I answered her call. I judged the priestess had a justified need and helped her in her quest. But I also realized that there was no going back. The next time someone stumbled upon the same spell and used it, we might not be there to intercede. You can't understand the extent of the evil that would be unleashed."

"I think I can, actually," Lord Ternborg remarked.

"You mean Nightshade?" Michael asked.

Lord Ternborg nodded.

"She doesn't represent the true vileness that inhabits the Abyss," the *B'nai Elohim* leader replied. "She's done terrible things, as have all demons, and has brought your world into turmoil. But, believe it or not, over time her proximity to the good elves on InnisRos has softened her stance. I don't know if a demon can 'change its stripes'… I just love the colorful language of the humans… but if they can, Nightshade will be the one. I have high hopes for her salvation."

Lord Ternborg stared at Michael in disbelief. "You're kidding, right?" he said. "She has my daughter! She's used that to force me to invade these lands!"

Michael looked away.

"What!" the Draugen Pesta king demanded.

"I guess I should have led with this," Michael said as he sheepishly looked at Lord Ternborg. "Viktor, your daughter has not been harmed and is safe. We rescued her from the Abyss where Nightshade was holding her and…"

"She's well?!" Lord Ternborg interrupted. Hope was written on his face.

Michael nodded. "Very well," he replied. "Nightshade made sure she was as comfortable as possible… well, at least given the circumstances. It's hard for mortals to be around demons for long periods of times without being affected in some way. But Nightshade provided a companion to help your daughter keep her sanity. Again, I should have told you this right away."

Lord Ternborg brushed off Michael's admission. "She's with Sofia?"

"No, Viktor, she's not," Michael replied. "She's in a much safer place."

"A safer place?" Lord Ternborg said, dumbfounded. "Where would she be safer than in my palace?"

Michael's visage turned dark. "The Hyrokkin have spies placed in your kingdom. Most are human, but some are your own people. Surely you understand that."

Lord Ternborg was becoming very agitated. "Of course I do! We've found most of them! Others we keep around to feed false information."

"There are others you have yet to find."

"Yes! Yes!" Lord Ternborg retorted. "We're not stupid."

Michael shook his head. "Don't you think being here with half of your army will present the Hyrokkin a golden opportunity to invade your lands?"

"Yes, I do," Lord Ternborg snapped back. "I took measures to strengthen our eastern border before we left."

Lord Ternborg opened a canteen and took a sip of water before pouring more of it over his head. "Where's my daughter?" he asked.

Michael sighed. "Sofia asked me to return your daughter to safety," he said. "Viktor, your lands are no longer safe."

Lord Ternborg studied the *B'nai Elohim*. "What do you know?" he asked.

"The Hyrokkin are massing on your eastern border," Michael replied.

The Draugen Pesta king threw his hands up in the air. "To do what?" he asked. "Charge through Dragon Pass to be butchered by my warriors? Go over the mountains that separate our two lands only to die in the cold or get swept away by an avalanche? As for the south… no way they'd survive even a brief journey across the Sea of the Marble Wyvern. There are things in the water, terrible things that… that… well, let's just say even the Hyrokkin aren't that stupid. No Michael, Hyrokkin offers no threat to Draugen Pesta. I've worked hard to see that come to pass."

"Perhaps under the mountains," Michael proposed.

Lord Ternborg froze, then shook his head. "No, those mountains have at least two major earthquakes a year."

"There's a 'but' in there somewhere," Michael stated after seeing a thought fleetingly pass over the Draugen Pesta king's expression.

"Well, there's a story, more of a myth I guess, that the Hyrokkin did just that," Lord Ternborg said. "It was when Irinushka Abramovich called you for the first time."

Michael nodded. "I remember."

Lord Ternborg looked at Michael, remembering that the *B'nai Elohim* were immortal and capable of things he couldn't comprehend in a million years. "As the story goes, after the attack in Eagle Pass, a small band of dirty, starving dwarves presented themselves to King Fedor with the wild claim that the Hyrokkin, with the help of captured dwarves, had dug several tunnels underneath the Eastern Boreskyre's. The attack in Eagle Pass was meant to be a diversion away from those tunnels."

"But the Hyrokkin didn't attack through the tunnels," Michael observed. "What happened?"

Lord Ternborg shrugged his shoulders. "Who knows? The dwarves told Fedor that they had trapped the tunnels to collapse while the Hyrokkin had most of their warriors in them. It was payment for the slavery the centaurs had forced upon them." Lord Ternborg paused and wiped his brow. "We never found any tunnel exits on our side of the Eastern Boreskyre's to substantiate their claim."

"But you're thinking…"

The Draugen Pesta king nodded. "I'm thinking if the tunnel legend is true, the Hyrokkin could have been clearing out those same tunnels over the course of the last thousand years to prepare for another invasion. The tunnels were, after all, built by dwarves and probably meant to stand the test of time. So I suspect they'd be earthquake proof if the dwarves are as good mining the earth as I've heard. The Hyrokkin would have to clear away and shore up the collapse caused by the dwarven traps, but… maybe with humans or more dwarves…"

"There you have it." Michael shook his head. "But that's your concern. I'm only certain your valley isn't safe enough to return your daughter... and the Hyrokkin appear to be the likely candidates for the danger I sense."

"Damn!" Lord Ternborg exclaimed. "All right, you've made your point. Where did you stash her?"

Michael pointed west. "In there."

"You put her in the Forest of the Fey?" Lord Ternborg said as he shook his head. "The only things there are worgs and the haunted city of Elanesse."

"There are also other things, dangerous things, not of this world," Michael answered. "But the city's not haunted, though it is alive."

Lord Ternborg stared. "Worgs, creatures not of this world, and a haunted… excuse me… a living city, and you left her there?" he said in exasperation. "What the hell, Michael!"

Michael put up his arms, palms outward, in an appeal to stop the furious Draugen Pesta king from attacking him with his bare fists. "Compose yourself, king. She's in the safest place on the continent. She's guarded by a fledgling goddess and the forest itself… not to mention Adimar, son of Fenrisúlfr, the eternal father of all wolves."

Lord Ternborg calmed. "You'll not be bothered if I see to it myself, will you?" he remarked.

"My promise to your wife is now satisfied, Viktor," Michael replied. "We have delivered Daphnia out of harm's way and she's safe and sound. And I've just passed along information to you that will affect the child's future safety. What you do with that information…" Michael shrugged.

A crack in the ground opened at Michael's feet. Lord Ternborg heard the inhuman screams of demons from below – from their prison of deprivation. He saw several demon heads appear through the crack… inhaling the air of freedom… only to be pulled back by an unseen force. Maybe it was this miniscule taste of independence, abruptly taken away, that was the cruelest torture of all. Even for a demon it must be a torment most foul.

Michael looked down on the mortal king. "I suspect we'll see each other again. But who's to say. Heed my words, Viktor Ternborg, king of the Draugen Pesta race. Power can corrupt even the strongest mortal. Use it carefully. Don't let your soul become as black as the souls of the demons I guard."

Michael took flight and hovered over the crack in the ground but spoke one last time before diving back into the Abyss. "Don't be too hard on Sofia for taking the locket," he said. "She had the strength to do what you would not."

Lord Ternborg didn't waste any time reflecting upon Michael's last words. He knew them to be the truth. "Colonel Antonovich!" he screamed as he mounted his horse.

"Sir!" she called as she rushed to her king.

"Recall the cavalry," Lord Ternborg said. "And turn the army around. We're heading home."

"And the Madeirans?" she asked.

"They're running like jackrabbits. Let them return to their city. We've more pressing matters."

Colonel Antonovich saluted and turned away. Lord Ternborg looked at his personal bodyguard. He pointed to several. "You three, with me," he said before turning his horse and galloping into the forest towards Elanesse.

The Draugen Pesta cavalry was engaged with the main body of the Madeiran army when the recall order arrived. The opposing forces had run into each other west of the Forest of the Fey. Prior to the meeting, the cavalry commander, Lieutenant Colonel Nikolay Ivanchenko, had received a message that outlined the circumstances of the death of Major Konstantin Timoshenko and the treachery of the Madeirans. Nikolay was a good friend of the major's going back many years. He knew the major's wife and was godfather to their daughter, Tatyana. To say the cavalry commander had a score to settle with the Madeirans was not an exaggeration.

Those Madeirans who didn't disappear into the forest and stood to fight were cut down in short order. After only a few minutes of fighting a small cluster of Madeirans was all that remained. Nikolay ordered his warriors to stop. Around him dying Madeirans were lying on the ground screaming and calling for their mothers. The standing survivors had congregated into a small defensive circle in the middle of the Draugen Pesta cavalry. From the forest he heard more screams, but only briefly wondered why.

Nikolay rode his horse to the front. "I wish to speak to your commander!" he shouted.

Several arrows aimed at the cavalry commander took flight from the encircled Madeirans but smashed into an invisible shield of force and shattered. Then bolts of magical lightning streaked towards Nikolay. These were intercepted by bolts of lightning from his own sorcerers and annulled. For a few seconds opposing sorcerers fought for supremacy. Draugen Pesta magic users deployed both defensive and offensive war spells. While some weaved return spells, others sent fire. The return of the Madeiran sorcerers own spells weakened their defenses which allowed the fire spells to hit for effect. Only after all the Madeiran sorcerers were burned to death did the battle of the arcane arts conclude.

As the clash of sorcerers took place, Nikolay sat upon his horse and stared at the Madeirans. When it was done, and the screams of the burning sorcerers had ceased, Nikolay repeated his request.

General King rode his horse through what was left of his command until he was about fifty feet from the huge Draugen Pesta cavalry commander. Nikolay watched as the human approached. He didn't think it was General Darcy. He had heard that Darcy was what the humans called a dandy, a person of fine taste unfamiliar with the true rigors of the soldier life. Nikolay had seen the like before. Someone put in charge of a campaign because of status and not merit. But this human appeared to be a true warrior. Nikolay saw it in the way he carried himself, the way he sat upon his horse, and the look in his eyes.

Nikolay nodded. "Thank you for meeting me. But I wish to meet General Darcy."

The human nodded back. "I'm General King," he said. "General Darcy is indisposed. Permanently. Why did you attack us? We're allies."

Nikolay didn't answer at once. The silence upon the battlefield stretched for a minute. Nikolay's horse kicked the earth beneath its hoof and whinnied. Nikolay scratched behind its ear to calm it. To an observer he appeared to consider his answer. In truth he was trying to control his rage at what this man's army had done to his friend.

"Allies?" Nikolay finally said. "We have several dead warriors from an ambush you instigated who might disagree. If they were still alive."

General King shrugged. "The fortunes of war. None of us here were involved with that."

"But you do know about it. Have those miscreants been brought to justice?"

"General Darcy wouldn't allow it," the human replied. "By the time I assumed command, the guilty parties had already fled." There was truth to this. General King didn't know what had become of the Spiked Fist, or Harkum, its commander. For all he knew, they might be back in Madeira by now.

"Then that's bad for Madeira, for I WILL have the men who ambushed my friend," Nikolay said. "There will be justice, general! Make no mistake! But right now I need to figure out what I'm going to do with you."

"We're no threat," General King said. "We just want to get back to our families."

"But that's a problem," Nikolay said as he brought his horse closer.

General King stood his ground. He had his pride… and he understood any retreat would only be temporary and might exacerbate the situation.

"How can I trust you?" Nikolay asked. "Madeira, and to a lesser extent Hebron, are notoriously dishonest. You're sell swords, and your only loyalty is to the wealth garnered at the expense of people who are too weak to protect themselves. Or to evil men who can afford your services to do evil things."

General King looked up at the giant. "I'll not argue your point. Our leaders are driven by whatever wealth they can generate. It's business. But for the common man, our companies offer a home to the orphan, the outcast, the downtrodden..."

"And criminals," Nikolay interrupted. "Brutes who should hang from the bottom of a rope. Swine who'll take your money and slit your throat. Men who are nothing but murderers, rapists and pillagers. Tell me, general, how do you control those? How do you keep their sickness from infecting your entire city?"

General King looked down without remarking.

Nikolay continued. "There's a human axiom I once heard. 'There's no honor among thieves'. Are you familiar with that particular adage?"

"Yes."

Nikolay stared down at the human. "So I ask again. Why should I trust you'll return home?"

General King drew his sword from its scabbard and threw it at the feet of Nikolay's horse which danced back and snorted angrily. "That sword lying on the ground is my word that's all we want to do. Sometimes even the word of a thief can be sincere. Particularly since death looks like it's my only other choice."

Nikolay dismounted and picked up the discarded sword. It was extraordinarily large and fit the giant's hand like a glove. Sturdy, yet finely made, it was undoubtedly used by someone of high import. The jeweled hilt gleamed in the sunlight. Along the blade were etchings and runes that he didn't understand. But he knew enough to surmise the blade wasn't simple steel. He felt the magic radiating from it... and the need for justice deep within its core.

"Where did you get this blade," Nikolay asked.

The question confused General King. "Why is that important," he asked. "It's just a sword. It's pretty, but..." The general shrugged. "Take it if you want it."

Nikolay looked at the man and shook his head. "You fool! Can't you sense its power?"

"What power," the general replied. "It's a stupid sword. I have many in my collection."

"From whom did you take this sword?" Nikolay repeated, now positive that General King wasn't its rightful owner.

"What does it matter?" General King asked. "It was plunder."

Nikolay closed his eyes and concentrated. After a few moments, he began to hear the song of the sword. It started tentatively but grew in strength as it judged the moral fiber of the Draugen Pesta warrior. Finding it to be acceptable, it sang of its beginnings. Nikolay could see the forge in his mind's eye. He witnessed the blacksmith pound layer upon layer of the finest steel to make the blade. He felt the grinding wheel as it sharpened the dull edge, the heat as the etchings and runes were imprinted upon the steel, and the magic that was transferred from the hands of a sorcerer and into the sword. Then Nikolay saw the huge steel-clad warrior, an Astorian knight from the symbol painted on his breastplate, and felt the sword come alive when the knight laid his gauntleted hand upon it. On the day of its birth the sword sang loudly, adding its voice to the harmonic songs of other magical swords as they rejoiced in its creation.

The sword then sang of the adventures it shared with its master. It sang of the many battles against thieves and murderers as the knight protected the common folk. It's song told of the times its owner comforted the dead and the dying, knowing all the while that someday he will be the one to require comforting. Nikolay saw the humble times… times when the knight and sword both reflected upon the nature of life and death. He felt excitement as the sword sang about its battle with a dragon in the Mahtan Mountains – of the feel of dragon blood upon its cutting edge – and the brotherhood the knight shared with his comrades during the fight.

Then the sword's song turned into a requiem. One day its beloved master, along with four of his Astorian knight comrades, were waylaid by a band of fifty mercenaries. Though the knights killed more than half of the bushwhackers, they couldn't escape the death that fate had demanded. The song continued showing how the knights were stripped of everything they owned except for their undergarments and left on the ground for the carrion. No burial, no words of eulogy, and no respect – only glee at the haul of the treasure the mercenaries had plundered. The sword cried in despair over its loss as it was carried away. But no one heard. All it could do was withhold its magic. That, and wait.

The sword's song changed tenors to one of enthusiasm and anticipation. Now in the hands of a good soul, it released its pent-up magic. The steel blazed as it declared to the world its new owner and announced its true name… *Ak-MithialJafnaðr*.

Nikolay's mind returned from the sword's song and he looked at General King. The general, when he saw the look in the giant's eyes, turned his horse to run, but Nikolay didn't let that happen. He took several giant strides and decapitated the mercenary general with *Ak-MithialJafnaðr*. As the sword sang of justice, Nikolay signaled to his men. They dispatched the surrounded Madeiran army within a few minutes.

Elrond was having a good time playing with those Madeiran soldiers who made their escape through his forest. He wasn't being cruel or vindictive, at least not overly so. Nor was he trying to kill anyone. But branches snapping derrieres, roots tripping the unsuspecting, thorn bushes pricking bare skin, and trees coming alive to scream at the terrified humans was very entertaining. It also, if only for a few moments at a time, freed his mind from his constant worry over the health and welfare of Elanesse and the pain he had endured when his forest kingdom was so brutally assaulted.

In both respects Emmy had helped tremendously. Through her gentle ministrations Elanesse was slowly regaining her strength, both physically and emotionally. Through the child goddess' powers, the burned portions of Elrond's forest were well on their way towards recovery. Even young Daphnia, who had been dropped in their laps by a demon and placed in Emmy's care, had been helping. Yes, Elrond reflected, they were all one big, happy family – a child goddess, a Draugen Pesta princess with her immense, immortal wolf companion, a gaggle of dire wolves, a three-legged saber cat, and a few squirrels.

"I can't believe I've come to this," the massive tree said.

"What's that, dear?" Elanesse asked.

Elrond's leaves shimmered as he came out of his reverie. "Oh, nothing," he replied. "You know me, always thinking about different stuff. Right now I'm making sure Madeiran soldiers are having a difficult time retreating through my forest. How are you feeling?"

"Much better," Elanesse answered.

"Her leaves have returned to their full golden hue," Emmy added.

Daphnia reached up and put her hand on Elanesse's trunk. It felt warm and alive. "You're both such beautiful trees," she said.

"Can she understand us?" Elrond asked Emmy.

"Oh yes!" Daphnia replied. "Emmy used magic to make sure of it."

Elrond nodded, though he had found the best he could do as a tree it was to dip and raise his branches. The first time he did it Kevik and Loki bolted in surprise and took up residence in the hollow log with the squirrel family. Mama squirrel had a few choice things to say regarding the whole state of affairs.

"Then know, child, that four of your people have just entered the forest from the east and are heading in this direction," Elrond said.

The princess clapped her hands. "That's wonderful news, Elrond!" she squealed, falling into her innocent little girl persona. "Father's coming to rescue me!"

"Harrumph!" Elrond exclaimed. "You hardly need rescuing... though perhaps I do."

Daphnia laughed. "Get used to it, *Elendrel-Telperiën*. You're going nowhere."

"Harrumph!"

Harkum, the Spiked Fist commander, when the decision to return home was sanctioned by General King, moved his mercenary company northwest into the Forest of the Fey towards the haunted city of Elanesse. Their latest intelligence had the Draugen Pesta moving south down the Alpine, and the last thing Harkum wanted was to be located by the Black Death. He'd no longer have the element of surprise and General King had taken away his sorcerers.

His men were tired. Because of the thick forest, they had been forced to dismount and lead their horses on foot. Most of the men later decided to let the horses go their own way. The march was not only physically draining but nerve-racking. Even though the Black Death, at least according to the latest reports, appeared to be far away, any little noise made them jump as their minds envisioned giants behind every tree and bush. But Harkum wouldn't let his men rest. He wanted to get behind the walls of Madeira as soon as possible.

Two miles from Elanesse, they heard explosions to the northwest. Harkum recognized the sound of sorcerer magic – lightning bolts or blasts of fire magic.

"Didn't King go that way?" the man walking next to Harkum asked.

Harkum nodded. He didn't care. The general could fend for himself. Besides, it'd be to his own advantage if it drew attention away from his own small force.

As they approached Elanesse, his men heard screams of agony come from the same direction as the explosions, but closer. It was unsettling. Harkum's inner voice, the instincts that had grown from his experience as a cold-blooded mercenary, screamed to him that something was terribly wrong which had nothing to do with the Draugen Pesta army. He moved his men forward even faster. But despite his best efforts, it wasn't long before panic spread like wildfire throughout his command. Before long it was every man for himself. Any who fell by the wayside were left to their own devices unless they had comrades to help. No amount of pleading would prevent them from being left behind.

It took time, but eventually Harkum regained control over the ragged group of mercenaries. Soon thereafter they reached the outskirts of the burned-out forest which surrounded Elanesse. He remembered seeing dark clouds billowing up from the forest not too long ago, and now he knew why. In the distance, roughly half a mile away, the broken walls of the haunted city were in view. Harkum called a stop and used a spyglass to study the creeping-looking metropolis. Nothing moved on the battlements or at the base of the walls. It looked peaceful and serene. Nevertheless, a chill ran up and down his spine.

"Barclay!" Harkum called for his second in command.

"Here, sir," a man answered from a few feet away. He was sitting on an old log, resting.

Harkum walked over to him. "How are the men?" he asked.

Barclay looked at the Spiked Fist leader with barely concealed contempt. "We've lost nineteen since your forced march. As if you care."

"Nineteen!" Harkum exclaimed. "All we did was walk through the forest!"

Barclay rose. "It's not just any forest," he said as he looked around. There was a hint of fear in his eyes. "Tree branches are cuffing people. Roots keep appearing out of nowhere and tripping anyone who isn't paying attention. Thorns from poisonous bushes strike hands, faces, and anywhere else not covered. We've suffered broken bones, concussions, cuts, bruises, and punctures. Many of the men are puking, have diarrhea, or both. If you're one of the unlucky ones to fall and not get back up, you're left behind. It's every man for himself."

Harkum looked at Barclay in disbelief. Why hadn't the man told him about this earlier? "What's our strength?" he asked.

Barclay shook his head. "Removing the ones left behind and those too weak to fight, I'd say we're at half strength. It'll only get worse the more you drive us through this evil forest."

"It's the only way home," Harkum remarked as he renewed his study of Elanesse's walls. "Tell the men we'll rest for the night in the city."

"Thank the gods," Barclay said as he turned away. "Even a haunted city was better than this damned-awful forest."

Both men stopped what they were doing as a scream rang out from behind them. It was one of their own. Before they could react, they were bowled over as those still left in the Spiked Fist mercenary company decided they've had enough and ran for their lives. By the time Harkum and Barclay had picked themselves up, what was left of the company, minus ten or fifteen more, were heading towards the walls of Elanesse. Barclay didn't wait for permission as he too made the dash.

Another agonizing scream came from the forest, but closer. The Spiked Fist commander took a few seconds to study the trees and thought he saw a hint of movement on a branch. *Something's up there,"* he thought before being hit by a stench more powerful than an open latrine after a meal of beans, peppers, and onions.

Another scream, this time not from one of his men but from something else – something otherworldly. Harkum decided he'd had enough of the forest as well and bolted towards the city as fast as he could. As he ran, he could hear more alien screams behind him from the forest edge. He wished he had his horse.

Romulus, several hundred feet ahead of the rest of his friends, stopped in the deep shadows of the forest that was encroaching upon the city and sniffed the air. The scent he picked up, one he'd never experienced before, made him gag. It was overwhelming in its strangeness. Instead of investigating, Romulus howled a warning and waited. Since he'd met Sakkara and adopted young Kevik, Romulus' view on life had changed. He'd no longer risk himself in reckless abandon to keep Kristen and Emmy safe. While that was still his life's work, he'd now do those things with greater thought and consideration. His great friend and father-equal, Horatio Goram, would no doubt say he was maturing, and that it was about damn time. Romulus bared his teeth in a wolf smile as he fondly remembered the grumpy but lovable priest. He thought about how much he missed the behind-the-ear scratches, the belly rubs, and the meat always on hand for the wolves of his pack. A wolf never forgets someone who provides the meat.

Romulus sat just inside the forest boundary. Ahead of him were the main army barracks and many smaller, abandoned buildings. The city brewery, overgrown, lay just to the south, and the gigantic stalagmite with the dead dragon at its base was behind him. Tangus and Jennifer joined him soon enough, as he knew they would, and put their hands on his back to signal they understood the need for circumspection. A rumbled growl escaped from deep within Romulus' chest.

"You've got that right, my friend," Tangus whispered. "Do you smell it, Jennifer?"

"I smell it, father," the young ranger replied. "It's unlike anything…" Jennifer held her nose. "It's nasty and makes me want to vomit."

Tangus nodded. "Take deep breaths. Get used to it because we'll probably fight whatever's causing it. We can't afford distractions as we do."

Jennifer inhaled and choked. "How do we do that," she asked. "Better question… CAN we do that?"

Tangus gagged from the stink himself. "I don't know. Maybe Kristen can use magic to help."

Jennifer nodded. "But we don't want to cut all of it. As long as we can smell the stench, we won't be taken by surprise. I'll go get Kristen and Mariko."

"Be careful," Tangus said without taking his gaze off the city.

After his daughter had silently moved away, Tangus pulled out a couple pieces of venison jerky and gave one to Romulus. "Strange happenings, eh Romulus," Tangus remarked.

The wolf was chewing his jerky but growled assent between bites. Wolves' teeth weren't designed for gnashing. They're sharp and pointed to rip flesh. After a few more moments of working the tough jerky to get as much of the flavor out of it as possible, Romulus swallowed.

Tangus continued. "I thought after we destroyed the Purge that'd be the end of it. Oh, I know a war's being waged on InnisRos. But Horatio and the queen can handle that. At least I hope so. Besides, we couldn't get back over there quick enough to be of much help, anyway."

The wolf barked in agreement.

"But the Purge hasn't been the end, has it, my friend," Tangus said as he petted the soft fur of the wolf's back. "No, not even close. Dragons, the Black Death, who don't appear to be near as horrible as we've been led to believe, cloud beings, earthquakes…"

"Woof!" Romulus interrupted. He'd made the same observations.

Tangus grinned. "Indeed! Guess I don't have to tell you, do I. Anyhow…"

Romulus growled as he stared at the corner of a building. Something was there. He saw it, but yet he didn't. There was no masking the smell, though.

"I believe I see it," Tangus said, replying to the wolf's low growl. "It looks like displacement magic."

"Perhaps a Cloak of Deflection," Kristen said as she came up next to Tangus.

Tangus looked over at her and smiled. Seeing Kristen always brightened his mood, even during the darkest of nights or times. "Do you see it?"

Kristen nodded. "And smell it," she said. She was breathing through a silken handkerchief. "Jennifer warned us," Kristen replied to her husband's look of inquiry.

"I can only barely make it out," Mariko said. "It appears to be waiting for something."

"Probably for others of its own kind," Jennifer commented.

"And no doubt connected to all the strange things happening around here," Kristen remarked.

Romulus barked a warning. Two more distorted shapes joined the first.

"Everyone, quick!" Tangus commanded. "Back further into the trees! Mariko, you're with me."

Kristen hesitated. "What are you going to do," she asked Tangus.

"We need to figure out what we're dealing with," her husband replied.

"You're going to… you're going to capture one?" the priestess exclaimed.

"No… kill and examine," Mariko said. She understood the necessity. "It has to be done."

Tangus nodded. "It's not of this world, dear. We need more information."

Kristen shook her head. "That we know nothing whatsoever about these creatures is exactly why you can't do this."

Tangus cupped Kristen's face in his hands and kissed her. "Romulus!"

The huge wolf gently, yet firmly, clamped his jaws around Kristen's wrist. Surprised, she looked at the wolf. Then she turned back. Both Tangus and Mariko were gone.

Osiris led his Snow Pride warriors through a break in the northeastern wall and into East Elanesse. The Royal Mountain Saber Cat leader hoped the lost cub wasn't here because a malicious odor of evil permeated every building, every street, and every blade of grass.

Osiris stopped his warriors and looked around to get his bearings. The source of the vile stench was stronger in the western part of the city. There was also a hint of elf scent coming from the same direction.

"Do you smell the elves, my son?" he asked.

Saladin yelped assent. "I do, father," he replied. "But it's almost imperceptible."

Osiris nodded. "The elves presence is well masked, but it's there and you've done well to distinguish between the two. Now here is the true test. What does their scent tell you?"

The young saber cat sniffed the air again. "There's more than one elf," he answered. He sniffed again. "And they're agitated... and... and fearful."

Osiris nodded. "Splendid! Now consider everything... the scent of the elves and the evil in this place, the direction and strength of the two scents... and draw me a conclusion."

Saladin didn't hesitate. "Most of the evil comes from the west, as does the elves, though not as strong. Father, I'd conclude the elves are following, in hiding, or are surrounded and preparing for the final battle."

"You missed one other possibility," Osiris said. "They could be allies of the evil." The saber cat leader turned to his warrior commander, Rahotep. "We'll go west. Send out your scouts but have them be extra cautious. We've never encountered these smelly ones before."

"And the elves," Rahotep asked.

"I don't think they're the enemy," Osiris replied. "But observe their actions and be vigilant if you have to approach them."

Tangus' first look at his quarry turned his stomach. He and Mariko, after their initial observation, concluded the only sign, besides smell, that the creature existed was a slight blurring which blended with the immediate environment. Once Tangus had figured out this was like beasts he'd hunted during his younger days, it was easy to readjust his mind to distinguish the movements of each creature against its surroundings.

Mariko, using her assassin skills, sneaked up on one and put an arrow in its back. As soon as she hit it, the charade it used to stay hidden dropped.

There was no doubt that what lay in front of them wasn't from Aster. Both Tangus and Mariko were certain of that. It was albino white with pink eyes and a short, pig-like snout, which, when opened, showed sharp fangs and a barbed proboscis. Their elongated head curved downwards towards their back. Two arms extended from the body, and each arm ended with sharp claws. A hard chitin exoskeleton armored the body and the long tail ended in spider spinnerets. As they stared, the creature dissolved into a puddle of a white mucus substance.

A slight cracking sound, unnoticeable to the layman but distinct to both the ranger and the assassin, gave warning that more of the creatures were in the vicinity. After a short skirmish, two more white puddles were soaking into the ground. Both Tangus and Mariko decided not to retrieve their mucus covered arrows and returned to Kristen, Jennifer, and Romulus. They'd seen enough.

"Romulus, return to Emmy and your family," Tangus ordered.

The wolf nudged the ranger and Kristen then sped away. His ability to sense danger would keep him safe until he reached the umbrella of Emmy's protection. Though he wasn't sure why he was sent away, he figured Kristen was in good hands with Tangus, Jennifer, and the assassin. It also meant he'd be reunited with Sakkara and the cubs. He left with little more than a constrained protest.

Kristen looked at her husband, confused.

"Romulus uses his teeth and claws to fight," Tangus answered Kristen's unasked question. "These creatures…" Tangus shook his head. "These creatures are disgusting! And I suspect they're poisonous. Although Romulus was granted long life by Althaya, that only means he's immune to death from natural causes."

Kristen nodded. "Still, whenever there's danger involved, it's always been 'all hands-on deck', as Jasmine is fond of saying."

"For his entire life he's done nothing but protect you, and later, Emmy," the ranger replied. "Now he has a family." Tangus shrugged. "I think he can sit this one out."

Kristen hugged her husband. "I love you," she said aloud.

Tangus blushed while Jennifer and Mariko grinned.

But as Tangus would later discover, no one really could sit this one out.

Rathal Arquen, master sorcerer and former leader of Havendale, and Rhys, Havendale's master spy, veered off the Alpine and entered the southern boundary of the Forest of the Fey. Rhys noted several archers of the Riders of the Elderdale watching from concealed perches in the trees… but didn't fear a stray arrow in the back. Everyone on this side of the world recognized Rathal Arquen. Besides, no arrow would make it close enough to strike. He knew the defensive shields the sorcerer had conjured safely encircled both. Rhys wasn't a huge fan of magic, but it had its advantages.

Not long after entering the forest, several more Riders of the Elderdale met the sorcerer and spy. Rhys and Rathal had stopped next to a small stream to water their horses when Riders appeared out of nowhere. It surprised neither of the two. The leader of the Riders walked over to Rathal and bowed.

"Master Sorcerer Arquen," he said as he acknowledged the sorcerer. To Rhys he only nodded, but with familiarity. "These are certainly bad times if the leader of Havendale ventures out from behind its walls."

Rathal returned the bow. "Hail, Commander Fairmount. But I'm no longer Havendale's Lord Paramount. That distinction now falls to General Kelsia Húrön."

Lloyd Fairmount looked with concern at the sorcerer's face. It was drawn and appeared weary. "Bet that rubbed a few knickers the wrong way," he said to Rhys. Rathal had moved away and was stretched out next to the stream. He appeared to be already napping.

"Not really," Rhys replied. "Most of the people, and all the sorcerers, have a lot of respect for the general. When there's war, someone like Kelsia in charge soothes a lot of anxious 'knickers', as you say."

"Well, Havendale can rest easy." Commander Fairmount remarked. "There doesn't appear to be much of a war going on. In fact, I wouldn't be surprised if it's already over."

"Explain," Rhys queried.

Commander Fairmount shook his head. "Some of the strangest things, Rhys. Let me tell you, Havendale was in for it."

Rhys raised an eyebrow.

"You had three armies heading your way. Hebron was marching down the eastern side of Lake Lorali, Madeira straight down the Alpine, and the Black Death not far behind. Wasn't much my Riders could do about it, and I'm not even sure I would've tried. As long as they didn't threaten Saint Seton, Covington, Silverstone, or any of the farms around here, what was the point? My Riders would've been wiped out in what the Madeirans might consider nothing more than a skirmish."

Rhys nodded. "I understand your position and don't find fault in it," he said to reassure the commander. The Riders were in a tough spot. It's one thing to die for your family and friends, but another altogether when there didn't appear to be a direct threat. Since there was no formal alliance between the two, the Riders didn't owe Havendale their lives. Any resistance would've ensured the very thing they wished to avoid. The Madeirans aren't known for their compassion. And the Black Death? Well, that would've been even worse.

"So what ended it?" Rhys asked.

Commander Fairmount looked away and into the small stream. A crawfish was ambling in the same direction as the running water, his trail spread out wide to accelerate his movement over the pebbles that lined the stream floor. "As I said, strange things are going on."

"Tell me," Rhys prompted.

The Rider leader refocused on Rhys. "For one, a new mountain range, accompanied by earthquakes, rose from the ground on the eastern side of Lake Lorali and swallowed the whole Hebron army. My scouts say there were no survivors. Then the Madeiran army has disbanded and retreated, presumably back to Madeira. And the Black Death army has followed suit, but not before destroying the main body of the Madeiran army. I'm not sure what the Madeirans did to those black devils, but whatever it was, it severely pissed them off. As I said, it looks to be finished."

"It's not over!" Rathal disagreed. He hadn't moved and his eyes were still closed. "There's a different threat now."

Commander Fairmount looked at the sorcerer. "Meaning what, sir?"

The Havendale sorcerer sat. "There are things deeper in these woods, near the haunted city, that are not native to our world," he said. "They're vicious, ravenous beings for whom killing comes naturally."

Rhys looked at his companion. "Have you had another vision?" he asked.

Rathal shook his head. "No, nothing like that," he responded. Then he frowned. "Don't ask me how, but the trees told me."

The spy shrugged and accepted that without reservation. Since he'd been around sorcerers his whole life, he'd grown used to that type of thing. "Are these creatures the same as the danger you foretold in your premonition?"

Commander Fairmount's eyes widened. "Premonition?"

Rhys shushed the Rider chief.

Rathal paid no attention to Commander Fairmount's skepticism. "No. What comes is even more dangerous and approaches from the north." He looked at the Rider. "Elanesse may have need of your help."

Commander Fairmount nodded and started to say something when Rathal's eyes rolled back into his head and his body stiffened and then began to jerk. Blood spewed from his nose and ears.

Rhys rushed to the sorcerer and kneeled beside him, holding his head to the side so Rathal wouldn't swallow his tongue. "He's having a vision," Rathal remarked to Commander Fairmount and the stunned Riders.

"What can I do?" Commander Fairmount asked.

Rhys shook his head. "Nothing except ride out the storm."

Premonitions are deceptive things. Sometimes they give the recipient well-defined forewarnings of future events. But most of the time the message is wrapped in the murky and confused waters of the mind. As a result, the talent of precognition relies as much on the correct interpretation of the vision as it does the ability to receive it. Because so many premonitions mystify, and are misconstrued, they're discarded as fantasy. Many with the gift are mocked and abused as common hustlers preying on weak-minded individuals in an effort to make coin. And many with this talent are guilty of doing just that – as do many who are nothing more than shysters.

Rathal never wanted the ability to receive glimpses of the future. He never wanted the responsibility that such foretelling's incurred. But he never shied away from it. Even though there existed magical wards that worked to shield the mind from the visions, he abhorred the thought of losing the opportunity to use his gift for good if he did so. He didn't realize it would kill him until after the talent had been fully awakened.

When Rathal resurfaced from the premonition, he was left with a singular thought planted in his mind – fire defeats ice.

THE TWELFTH INTERREGNUM

The white dragon, as large as a small mountain, flew between the mercenary cities of Madeira and Hebron on its way towards Elanesse. Moisture in the atmosphere around the dragon turned into ice crystals that fell from the sky… though by the time the ice crystals reached the ground the warmer surface air had turned it into a cold, heavy rainfall. The populations of both cities were forced to watch helplessly as their homes were overcome by sudden flooding and the destruction and misery that goes with it. The flooding devastated the two cities, leaving little behind except for the city walls and the strongest stone structures. Fires raged uncontrollably, feeding off wood, cloth, and flesh. Despite the high loss of life, many of the cities past victims would argue it was a justified cleansing. This, combined with the loss of their entire armies, meant Madeira and Hebron wouldn't be players in the mainland's politics for an exceptionally long time.

Lycomedes, high above Aster with his Sky Emperors, worried about the fate of his new home world if the planet from another universe moved any closer. He studied the situation alone, having ordered his people to stay back, and concluded there was nothing he, or any Sky Emperor, could do to stop this transgression.

"*Emmy,*" he whispered in his mind. "*Can you hear me?*"

There was no response.

"*Maybe I imagined the voice,*" he thought.

He tried again. "*Emmy?*"

"I hear you, Lycomedes," Emmy replied after a few more seconds of silence. Her voice sounded anxious. *"I apologize, my guardian. Our world faces several serious threats and I'm somewhat distracted by the part I'm to play. I'm so new at this."*

Lycomedes accepted this admission. He had wondered if it was a child who had spoken to him earlier. This last seemed to confirm it. But what child should have the responsibility for a world placed upon her shoulders? *"You have no help?"* he asked.

"I do," Emmy replied. *"But nothing worthwhile is ever guaranteed. Nor does it come without cost, and that cost will be steep. Why are you not over Elanesse?"*

Lycomedes explained what he and his people had found high over the world of Aster and the threat he felt it represented.

"Others are working to solve that problem, my dear Lycomedes," Emmy said. *"I need the Sky Emperors over Elanesse."*

Lycomedes nodded his acceptance in his mind. As he turned away from the outer reaches of Aster's atmosphere, he had one more question to ask Emmy.

"I know who you are, Emmy, but I don't know WHAT you are," he said.

Emmy chuckled. *"Sometimes I ask myself the same question, brave guardian. I'm a daughter, a sister, a friend, a companion, and at one point I was the last empath. What am I, you ask? I wish I had an answer."*

The ley line's tendrils continued to traverse different universes and tap into the energy of worlds both past and present. It was rapidly becoming a brute of mind-boggling power, surpassing even that of the *Ak-Samarië Shard* relic. The *Ak-Séregon Stone* became aware... became sentient... and she had a voracious appetite for more power.

On the Alfheim, the *Ak-Samarië Shard* felt the *Ak-Séregon Stone* come alive. They'd been so intricately linked for thousands of years that when the stone became self-aware, the shard sensed it instantly. The shard greeted the stone as a sister and an equal. Though powerful, the *Ak-Samarië Shard* realized the *Ak-Séregon Stone* was also immature – immature with a mind damaged by the forced link to the Svartalfheim. If the shard didn't reign in the stone, there was no telling what damage the stone might do. The shard engaged the stone in conversation and instruction. The stone, thirsty for knowledge, abandoned its drive for more power and began to absorb the shard's lessons.

As the shard tutored the stone, she communicated with her daughter, the *Ak-Vanessë Stone*, buried in the chest of Kyleigh Angelus-Custos, Queen of the Alfheim. The communication was short and succinct… "Hurry!"

CHAPTER NINETEEN

Deep Under Elanesse

There are fables, stories, and legends, passed down from generation to generation by poets and bards, that tell of heroes accomplishing great feats. They tell of brave people who are willing to sacrifice their lives for the greater good, for love, or to atone for past misdeeds. Though some of these sagas describe the heroics of real people, most are allegories which teach that selflessness is necessary in the fight against evil, and that imperfect souls can act with nobility and courage. But the vast majority of sacrifices, those performed by the ordinary people day in and day out, are seldom captured by the lore master. This doesn't mean they go unnoticed.

-The Book of the Unveiled

The jig was up. The spell Erika had conjured to incinerate sylphs was still working, but the sylphs realized what was transpiring and stopped chasing the bait Max and Solveig were offering. Instead, they waited for the spell to end… though every once in a while they sent one of their own to test the magical barrier.

"How much longer, Erika," Max asked.

The dragon priestess in human form shook her head. "I don't know. I told you, I've never used this spell."

"Look at them," Solveig commented. "They're congregating on the other side. As soon as it goes down, they'll be all over us."

"Ghosts can do all kinds of things when annoyed, my dear," Max replied as he looked across the corridor expanse to the ever-expanding number of sylphs. He shook his head. "But damn! There's a lot of 'em!"

"Perhaps we should seek another exit before it's too late," Solveig urged.

Max shook his head. "As much as I want to save Erika, the sylphies threaten the entire world. I'm not sure running is the right thing to do. Elbedreth told me sylphies don't reproduce, which means the more we kill here, the more Azriel, Elbedreth, and those on the surface won't have to. We might be the difference. Besides, the first people the sylphies will run into on the surface are good friends of mine. Right now they'd be slaughtered like your people were."

"So will we," Erika asserted. "I'm still weak from my injuries. Most of the magic I employ is for healing, not killing. And I can't turn back into my dragon form to use dragon's breath. The corridor's too small."

Max looked at Solveig. She shook her head. "Erika's right. We'll kill a fair number of them, but I doubt it'd be enough to matter if their number is as great as you've been told."

The three's attention was distracted by a discharge of magic further up the corridor. Another sylph had just tried the barrier and died for it. But it had moved further forward before the magic activated.

"The spell wanes," Erika observed. "The next attempt will end it."

"We need an earthquake to collapse this corridor," Max remarked. "That'd give us time to work out something else." His comment was wishful thinking, and he knew it.

Another sylph made a run at the barrier. It exploded and multicolored lights filled the passageway. When they blinked out, the sylph was still standing, singed, but alive. That was all the sylph's needed to attack en masse. But by the time the rolling wave of sylphs started moving down the corridor, Max, Solveig, and Erika had already left.

The Kounávi raced to the other end of their cavern to engage the sylph invasion. Each of Thaz's volunteer warriors knew the situation was dire and that they'd probably never survive to be with their families again. Jörmungander, in his dragon form, lumbered behind. A dragon's flying speed and endurance consisted of catching air currents high above the earth and riding them out, using its wings as economically as possible to conserve energy. But the huge cavern offered no such advantage.

Azriel slid across the cavern floor as fast as his sylph body could take him, which meant he was even further in the rear. The whole time he shouted and cursed at the dragon. "Would it have hurt you to let me ride on your back, you flying sack of slug offal?" he bellowed at the dragon's disappearing backside.

After a few minutes Azriel still found himself being outdistanced by his allies. *"Damn it!"* he thought. *"Thaz doesn't know what the sylph can do. And that daft dragon's a bloody nitwit!"*

The dwarf-sylph was half-way through the cavern when Jörmungander's dragon breath exploded in the darkness ahead. As he got closer, he could see streaks of light rise into the air and figures fall to the ground.

"Magical arrows," Azriel concluded.

By the time he was only a couple hundred feet away he saw the still bodies of many Kounávi, and Jörmungander was fighting with several arrows sticking out of him. Behind the dragon lay the wounded figure of Thaz. As for the sylph's, it was hard to make out the body count, but it must have been significant. They approached the black dragon cautiously, and their body language told Azriel they respected his power. And with good reason. Jörmungander was using his dragon magic and breath to make the sylph pay for every inch of ground they took.

Azriel used the sylph's obsession with the dragon to sneak behind them. He attacked from the rear as he belted out an old dwarven battle song:

"Cleave, cleave, chop, chop!
Smash, smash, whack, whack!"

The ferocity of his attack stunned the sylphs. Confused because they couldn't distinguish him as a friend or foe, it wasn't long before sylph looked upon other sylph with suspicion. Azriel, having weathered many battles during his career, knew to take advantage of any weakness the enemy offered, and for a few valuable seconds the sylph-dwarf had free rein to kill… which he did with great efficiency.

Jörmungander used the brief respite Azriel gave him to heal most of his wounds. The dragon then turned to help Thaz but saw that the flying ferret had died from his injuries. Jörmungander roared and rejoined the battle. He recognized Azriel by the great battleaxe and staff he always used and fought his way over to his friend. The pair then fought to a wall which they used to guard their rear.

Dragon breath and magic spells, along with the powerful magic of the moving battleaxe, lit the western side of the cavern. Sylph after sylph attacked – and died. But by sheer numbers alone they'd win the battle against Azriel and Jörmungander. Both suffered terrible wounds from arrows and the blades commonly used by all sylphs. Every attack Azriel made with his battleaxe and metal staff was slower than the last, and with diminishing effect. If Azriel had still been a dwarf, he'd be dead.

Jörmungander didn't fare much better. He had used up his dragon breath and magical spells and they wouldn't be available again until he rested. His huge body was an easy target and looked like a pin cushion with several dozen sylph blades sticking out. Blood flowed and pooled at his feet.

Without warning the sylphs retreated.

Jörmungander couldn't believe their good fortune. "Have we won?" he asked between several deep breaths.

Azriel turned and looked up at his dragon companion. "You're kidding, right?" he replied. "Have you not listened to a word Elbedreth has said about her people?"

"Well, I…" stuttered Jörmungander.

"That was only the beginning," Azriel said, though his tone had softened. "The sylphs are as many as the grains of sand on a beach. Well, maybe not quite that many. But my friend, what we just fought was but a small sampling of their true number. Right now they're regrouping… or waiting for the rest of their people."

Jörmungander raised his arm and waved it back and forth as if he were a child in school. "I have a question."

Azriel looked at the dragon and raised an eyebrow. "All right, laddie," he said. "What's your question?"

"What's a beach?"

Azriel stared at Jörmungander. "What's a…" Then he laughed, a rich, loud dwarven laugh. "You're like a wee bairn, are you not? If we get out of this, I'll show you a beach myself. But for now, pull out those blades. You look ridiculous!"

The sylph Supreme watched as the messenger from the sylph advance party made its way through the throng of her personal bodyguards.

"What news do you bring?" she asked after the messenger had made the proper supplication.

"We're on the cusp of a great victory, my Supreme!" the courier exclaimed. "Even as we speak, those you sent ahead are destroying parasites. I've been ordered by my most gracious and humble commander to inform you that the way out has presented itself through a great cavern."

The sylph leader, excited and pleased, maintained her composure and nodded. "I will move the people forward. You and my brave commander have done well." She opened several of her appendages. "Come closer and accept your reward."

The messenger shivered in anticipation as he rose and stepped into her embrace. The Supreme sighed in orgasmic pleasure as she absorbed the male sylph.

"YUCK!" Max screamed. His whole body shook in disgust. "Don't you ever do that to me again!"

Max, Solveig, and Erika were in a small, lightless chamber which wasn't much bigger than a broom closet. A few moments before, as the sylphs charged down the hallway towards them, Erika did the only thing she could. She grabbed both ghosts, who were corporal, spoke a short incantation, and merged all three into the stone wall. She hadn't expected to find herself in a tiny cavern. Nor did she expect Max's reaction.

"I thought ghosts traveled through stone?" Erika asked. "What makes this any different?"

"We do, hon," Solveig said as she rubbed Max's arm to calm him. "It's just that we do it when we're in our incorporeal state."

"As in 'When we're ACTUALLY ghosts!' Max added as he shivered again. "It felt as if every part of my body was drowning in stone-colored snot."

"Oh, don't be so dramatic," Solveig said. "Erika did the right thing under the circumstances. And things could have been much worse. We're lucky to have stumbled into this small room."

Solveig held out her hand and a small light flashed in her palm. Stone walls surrounded them – walls roughly hewed by the hand of nature. Embedded in the walls was a thick vein of gold which gleamed in the light of Solveig's magic.

Max sighed and whispered a few choice words under his breath. Solveig chuckled.

Erika looked at her in confusion.

"There's only one person who likes gold and other treasure more than a dragon," Solveig replied to Erika's unspoken question. "And that's a thief."

Erika nodded in understanding. "Max's prior life," she responded. It wasn't a question.

Solveig nodded. "The gold beckons to him like a long, lost lover," she said as she eyed her companion. "Or perhaps it speaks softly to you like a cold breeze on a hot, summer day. Eh, Max?"

"Yeah, Max," Erika added as she snickered. "Or maybe it calls to you like the thought of cool water across a parched throat."

Max looked at the two and ignored the fun they were having at his expense. "Do you think they've passed by yet?" he asked, referring to the sylphs on the other side of the wall.

Erika's disposition turned somber. "Hard to say," she replied. "My spell is still…"

Max shook his head. "No! That's too dangerous. I'll…"

"Max, down here," Solveig said as she stooped to look closer at something near the base of the wall on the opposite side of the small room.

Both Max and Erika turned and looked to where Solveig was staring. It was a small, jagged crevice that ran up from the floor for several feet. It wasn't very wide, but that wouldn't be a problem for a ghost… or for a dragon who had the power to shape-shift.

"Maybe nothing…" Solveig said.

"Or it may be another way out," Max finished for her.

The ghost-thief shrugged his shoulders as he turned back into his ghostly form. "I guess there's only one way to find out. Stay here until I give the all-clear," he said as he went through the crevice.

There was silence for several minutes.

"Max!" Solveig called several times without a response. Just as she was getting ready to go find her lover, Max reappeared. He was visibly shaken.

"There's a city," he said.

"A dead city this deep underground," Erika asked.

Max shook his head. "It's not dead."

Azriel and Jörmungander prepared as best they could for the onslaught each knew was coming. Jörmungander, with the dragon magic he had at his disposal, prepared traps – most of which were suggested by Azriel after a spirited discussion regarding what the dragon could and couldn't do. As Azriel saw it, now was the time for Jörmungander to throw caution to the wind and throw everything at them, including the 'kitchen sink'. The dragon didn't know what a kitchen sink was.

Jörmungander had never found cause to use the killing magic he had in his arsenal. But things were different now… and although the killing unsettled him, he understood the necessity. What deeply concerned him was the drain of power – the drain of his life-force – such magic caused when used. He'd been taught that using killing magic came with consequences, but never suspected the veracity of those teachings until after he had to use it.

Azriel didn't have time for his concerns and brushed them off. "Laddie, everyone dies at some point," he said, which didn't help. The young black dragon was terrified of what the sylph's will do to him if they found him weak, helpless, and unable to defend himself. He shuddered at the thought.

"Are we all set," Azriel asked.

Jörmungander nodded. "Yes, Azriel, the magical traps are where you instructed."

Azriel smiled. "That should put a burr up their arse. Let's move back and let your magical spells do their work."

"Maybe the traps will kill all of them," Jörmungander said as they moved back to their designated safe spot.

Azriel considered. "Unlikely, but possible, I suppose. But as I've said, there's still plenty following behind. We'll not get off that easy."

"You're such an inspiring leader."

"You want me to tell you everything will be fine?" Azriel asked. "I can't because we'll probably die here. But we need to at least try to stop the sylphs from reaching the surface, and it's the only plan I have. Before it can work, though, we have to get them together in one place."

Jörmungander sighed.

"Look, laddie," Azriel said. "There's too many sylphs to beat outright. But we don't need to kill all of them. If we can whittle them down, if we kill enough of 'em, then the remnants can be finished off on the surface."

The first explosion from a magical trap went off a few hundred feet away.

"Time to suck it up, my laddie," Azriel remarked. "I'll catch up wi` ye fur a drink oan th' ither side."

But, except for a few more thunderous explosions and the crackling of lightning, the sylph's never came.

Max, Solveig, and Erika stood on a ledge which overlooked a vast, underground plain populated by giant mushrooms and different colored moss. Stalactites hung from the ceiling far above. Clinging from the stalactites were bat-like creatures. But these bats differed from surface bats. They were larger, four or five feet long, had cobalt-blue colored furry bodies and wings, faces resembling a large panther, and bigger than normal eyes.

As beautiful as the creatures were, the city in the center of the plain was even more so. It was enormous… as large as Palisade Crest. The lights that came from the buildings and lined the empty streets chased away the darkness of the vast underground plain. Large crystals, embedded into the ceiling high overhead, reflected the light back, the effect of which lit the entire plain with a soft, white glow. Unlike other cavern's they had seen, the source of the city lights wasn't generated by bioluminescent moss, fungi, or any other form of underground life. Instead, it appeared to be the kind of light generated by magic – steady and bright.

The structures didn't match any elven or human architecture Max had ever seen. The city rose from the cavern floor as different sized pillars, with tall middle buildings surrounded by smaller buildings, the height of which descended downward to make it look like a jagged pyramid. On the cavern floor, at the base of the tall, thin buildings, were smaller, dome-shaped buildings of various sizes which appeared to encircle the entire metropolis. And unlike every major metropolitan city on the surface, this city had no walls for defense.

The city was made of stone. Max had seen the intricacy of the lines and curves matched by elves working their crystal, but never at this magnitude. As Max studied the finer points of the structural design, he began to notice differences in the windows that dotted the buildings. The light shining through was multi-colored and similar to the light shining through glass he'd seen many times in churches and temples. Colored glass was expensive on the surface. The artisans who created it were the best of the best and the material components hard to mine and smelt. How so much of it ended up so far underground was beyond Max's ability to comprehend.

The thief part of Max's ghostly mind ran through several calculations. *The colored glass alone is worth enough to buy several small kingdoms,"* he thought.

"It's gorgeous," Erika whispered.

Solveig, transfixed, nodded. "I've seen colored glass before, but never anything like this."

Erika looked at her.

"I've been to the surface several times," Solveig replied in answer to Erika's questioning look. "Plus, Jörmungander has shown me the books he has that are written about the kingdoms above. They have pictures."

Max put a ghostly hand over Solveig's mouth. If it had been any other time, both would have laughed at the ridiculousness of his action.

"Shh!" he whispered as he motioned with his head to a point up and slightly forward.

They saw several of the closer bat-like beings staring right at them. But if they were concerned about the intruders, they didn't show it. One of them, a juvenile by the size of it, dropped, flapped his wings, and descended to one of the large mushrooms on the floor. As big as the bat was, the head of the mushroom was many times larger, enough to support several dozen. After settling on top of the mushroom, the bat took a chunk out of it and began to eat.

"Well," Max whispered, "At least they're not meat eaters."

"Jörmungander once told me the head of a mushroom is nourishing," Solveig mentioned. "He said they have lots of protein. He even let me have some from his mushroom farm. Tasty!"

Max sighed. "Meaning?"

"Meaning that if the bats crave protein, they just have to take one bite out of Erika to realize mushrooms aren't the only protein source down here," Solveig replied. "And if she's in her dragon form, there's plenty to go around."

Erika let out a strangled cry.

"Don't worry," Max said. "Just use your magic to talk to them. Be their friend. Then they'll never get a taste for dragon flesh."

"Sweetheart, isn't that a bit cavalier of you?" Solveig said. "You know it's not that easy."

Max shook his head. "Cavalier?" he replied. "Oh, I don't think…"

"I don't even know where to begin," Erika interrupted. "I'm not a ranger who's skilled at understanding animals."

"Erika, there's more than one way to communicate with them," Solveig said. "Your actions, the sound of your voice…"

"You just have to show them who's boss," Max remarked. He wore a sly grin on his face.

"Max!" Solveig exclaimed.

Several bats looked at the three. They were adults – and large. One let out a high-pitched screech. All the bats came instantly awake.

"We're way too exposed on this ledge," Max said. There was no humor in his voice this time. "We need to get off now!"

Many of the bats had taken to the air and were circling.

"Ghosts float," Max reminded Solveig.

Solveig nodded. "And dragons fly," she said to Erika.

Erika didn't hesitate. She took a running start and leaped off the ledge into the air. Max and Solveig watched as she dropped. Neither were too concerned for it didn't take long for a dragon to change its form. A few moments after her leap, Erika turned into her true self and flapped her wings to slow her ascent.

Max and Solveig looked at each other and held hands while stepping off the ledge. As they floated towards the cavern floor, they looked up to see how the bats would respond to having a large, black dragon in their midst. Every adult bat was flying and descending towards Erika.

Except for the forward scouts and her personal bodyguard, the sylph Supreme was at the head of the exodus of her people out of their prison. It had always been her place. Even the Great Sleep didn't change that. All things that came to the sylph came through her. She allowed others to show initiative, and many vied for the opportunity to curry the Supremes' favor. But it was risky, for a sylph was never permitted to fail a second time.

What was left of the sylph faction the Supreme had sent to destroy the parasites moved through the corridor towards her from the opposite direction. She stepped through her bodyguards to welcome them, for she was pleased with the great victory they achieved for her glory. But something was wrong. These sylphs didn't move like victors. Instead, they approached her tentatively. The Supreme could smell their fear… and their body language spoke of failure. They hadn't succeeded in their task.

"Report to me, my children," she purred. These sylphs didn't have long to live, but she needed the information they had first.

There were seventeen sylphs total, and each one dropped to the corridor floor.

The Supreme maintained her outward composure, but beneath the surface she was seething. "Quit groveling and give me your report," she snapped. "Have you destroyed the parasites in the cavern or not?"

"No, Supreme," one of them said. He didn't rise. The rest flattened themselves on the floor even more.

The Supreme shook her head in disgust. She turned to her guard commander. "Get them up," she ordered.

The threat of the Supremes' personal bodyguard getting physical with the groveling sylphs was enough to motivate them to stand.

"That's better," the Supreme said. "Where's your commander?"

The doomed sylphs looked at each other, none willing to volunteer the information their Supreme required. The bodyguard commander grabbed one at random and shoved him forward.

"The commander is dead, Most Supreme," the unfortunate replied. "He was burned by magic most foul. He bravely died for his Supreme."

"As did the others, I'm sure," the Supreme answered. She wasn't impressed. "I ordered the commander to wipe out the parasites, and yet he did not by your own admission. What happened?"

By this time, the returning sylphs were quivering in fear. The spokesman looked at the stone floor.

"LOOK AT ME!" the Supreme snapped.

They had no choice.

The sylph leader moved among the seventeen and looked each one in the eyes. She was reading their minds, picking out the information she needed. Mind reading was a skill given to the Supreme by the creators of Aster for quick information gathering and dissemination. But they never intended its use to be so brutal. One by one each dropped unconscious after she was through. Seldom did she ever find it necessary to take what she needed by force. But when she did, the psyche rarely survived. What was left was a sylph whose brain performed only the most basic functions. The heart kept beating, the lungs kept breathing, and the other organs kept working. But none of that mattered since her probe stripped the brain of its identity.

When she had finished, she knew what happened from each personal vantage point. She learned of the dragon, the little fur-covered flying things, and the male sylph. The traitor Elbedreth-Ahlasim, however, was never spotted. She saw the battle for the cavern that ensued, and she understood the savagery in which the parasites defended the cavern entrance.

Her sylph destroyed all of the flying parasites, but the dragon and the male sylph refused to die. The Supreme had never seen a sylph fight like that male. He fighting style was like a grand dance. He weaved and bobbed while his sylph opponent tried to strike. As he did so, he cut and slashed until his adversity was too cut up to respond. A quick slice ended it and on he was to another foe. He was gruesome. She had a fleeting thought he'd make a worthy consort, but most of her just wanted him to suffer a vile and cruel death for the number of her brethren he slew.

Her commander, concerned about the number of causalities his people was taking, ordered a general retreat to regroup and heal their wounds before making another attempt to kill the remaining parasites.

"Critical mistake," the Supreme thought. *"The dragon and male sylph might have fallen if only you had pressed your attack. Who cares about causalities!"*

When the sylphs returned to the cavern for the second assault, there was no sign of the dragon or the male sylph. Then there were explosions everywhere. Fire burned many of the warrior sylphs… then lightning bolts and pressure waves from their thunderous detonations killed more. That was enough to convince those left to come back and report.

"We continue on," the Supreme said to her guard.

"And those?"

The Supreme looked at the sylphs lying on the floor. Though their bodies worked, they'd never wake up. She shrugged. "Leave them."

Elbedreth leaned the *Maul of Power* up against a wall. She didn't like it and didn't want to use it. She didn't even want to touch it. The female sylph knew deep down in her soul the maul meant more pain, loss, and the familiar isolation she felt before her encounter with Azriel. The solution it offered was so final. But if it stopped her people, it also offered the world salvation. As she was considering the maul, she watched the Kounávi leave for their new home. There were more of the flying creatures then she originally believed, but the greater numbers wasn't slowing their exodus. It proceeded quickly and in an orderly fashion.

Explosions turned her attention away from the Kounávi and to the other end of the huge cavern. She saw the red light of fire and the white light of lightning. She felt the stone beneath her tremble after each discharge of magical energy. Then she caught a slight whiff of sulfur from Jörmungander's dragon breath. As she strained to listen, she thought she heard the screams of the dying break through the stillness of the cavern.

"Kick arse, my love," Elbedreth whispered.

Azriel and Jörmungander were ready for the next assault of the sylphs. But when the explosions from Jörmungander's magical traps ended, the attack they had expected never materialized.

"Do you think they found another way to the surface?" Jörmungander asked.

Azriel shook his head. "I don't know. Are any of the traps unexploded?"

The black dragon nodded. "A few," he said, "though not many. Azriel, I used all my magic to create the traps and heal us."

Azriel looked up at Jörmungander. "Nothing left at all?"

Jörmungander shook his head. "I couldn't even fire up a twig. I'm tapped out."

Azriel sighed. Without magic to fight with, and heal, they'd be overrun by the sheer volume of sylphs heading their way. Nothing could stop it. He had hoped for more time.

"Jörmungander," Azriel said, "Come here."

The dragon bent his head so he could be closer to the sylph-dwarf.

Azriel lightly slapped the massive head on the snout. "No, no, you great dunderhead," he said.

Jörmungander raised his head up, confused, and wondered what he'd done to deserve the tap on his nose.

"Turn into your human form so we can have a face-to-face discussion," Azriel called. "Your dragon face is somewhat ... disconcerting... especially when you're close enough to swallow me whole."

The dragon did as Azriel had requested. Now standing in front of his friend as a dark-skinned human, he looked expectedly at the sylph-dwarf.

Azriel nodded. "That's better. Now listen closely, me boyo. We have little time."

"I'm listening, Azriel," Jörmungander replied.

"I want you to leave."

Jörmungander shook his head. "No! I won't do it!"

Azriel held up two arms. "Now don't go getting yer black scales all in a bunch. Hear me out first."

Jörmungander stared.

"You'll listen, right?" Azriel repeated.

Jörmungander nodded. He couldn't deny one of the few friends he had left.

"That's better," Azriel responded as he looked at the cavern exit for signs of the sylphs. "You don't have any magic left, and we won't have time to rest long enough for you to recharge. When the sylphs come, you'll be slaughtered just like the rest of your kin."

"Except for one," Jörmungander added.

"Yes, that's right," Azriel agreed, "except for one. A female. That's why I want you to leave. You need to go find her and escape. Share your home with the Kounávi. I guess they're good folks. They certainly died well. Or go to the surface. My friends will accept you. Make new little Jörmungander's and live a good life. The world shouldn't lose the black dragon race, even if they do kill dwarfs."

"Only the one's trying to steal our hoard," Jörmungander interrupted.

"Well… yes… but how did you get your hoard in the first place?" Azriel shook his head. "Never mind. There's no time for that discussion. Your people had a prophecy…"

"You mean the *Maelstrom*."

Azriel nodded. "Yes, that was it. And your clan died trying to fulfill that destiny. They died trying to save the world. That was a courageous and noble act, laddie. There're folks on the surface I can guarantee wouldn't have done the same."

Jörmungander looked at the floor of the cavern. He felt embarrassed somewhat because he didn't die being courageous and noble with his kinfolk.

Azriel thought he knew what Jörmungander was thinking and put a hand on his shoulder. "It's okay, laddie. You did nothing wrong or dishonorable. You followed your orders like any good soldier… or son of the black dragon race. Things happen for a reason and I'll not challenge the will of fate. Nor should you. Do you think a female was spared from the sylph onslaught for no reason? So go! Find her. Build a new life. Your race need not shrivel and die here this day."

"But…"

Azriel embraced the young dragon. "Find Max," he whispered. "He's down below somewhere. Tell him what happened. Tell him I sent you and ask for his help. He's obnoxious, but not nearly as blockheaded as he sometimes acts. He won't let you down if you gain his trust."

"Azriel…"

Azriel shook his head as he released Jörmungander. "No more discussion." he said as he pointed towards several visible exits off to the side. "Now go quickly! And when you find Max, tell him… tell him I never stopped thinking of him as my brother."

Jörmungander nodded.

The sylphs were reentering the cavern. Azriel couldn't see or hear them, but he could sense them. "Get!" he whispered.

Jörmungander turned away and left. The tears in his eyes made his vision blurry, but he found the exits Azriel had mentioned. Only a dwarf would have known they were there. Picking one at random, he entered its darkness, stopped, and turned. Azriel had already disappeared.

On the floor of the underground plain of mushrooms, Erika remained in her natural dragon form and stood guard as Max and Solveig floated down from the ledge. She wasn't sure if bats could hurt ghosts, but she wouldn't take the chance. She was prepared to release her dragon's breath on the bats if it became necessary.

But other than curiosity, the bats showed no interest in molesting anyone. Their inquisitiveness satisfied, most landed on the large mushrooms and began to eat, though several of the braver youngsters approached Erika. By the time Max and Solveig had settled on the mossy floor of the plain, Erika and the youngsters were playing a game of 'catapult'. Several of the bats would sit on Erika's tail and she'd fling them up in the air, after which they'd glide back to await their next turn. Bat screeches of delight filled the otherwise silent air.

"Looks like Erika has found a new following," Max observed as he and Solveig glided over to her. They were still in their ghostly, incorporeal form.

Solveig laughed with delight. "Erika loves children. And it warms my heart to hear their laughter."

Max shook his head. He never felt comfortable around children. Most of the juveniles he'd ever known were orphaned pickpockets working for thieves' guilds. He didn't blame the children – they were just trying to survive, and the guilds offered them food, shelter and family. But when it was HIS money-purse being jeopardized, he took no chances and moved away as soon as he recognized a child with guild training. That is if he hadn't paid the local guild to leave him and his comrades alone, which was the first thing he'd do whenever he ventured into a city or town. But sometimes a guild's protection services were so astronomically high it was more cost effective to gamble he could guard his own purse.

A screech from above scattered the young bats and suddenly Erika was alone, but there was a smile on her dragon face. She transformed into her human form and looked up into the near darkness of the ceiling far above. Several pairs of eyes were looking at her from stalactite perches. One waved a clawed wing.

"I see you've made a few friends," Max said as he and Solveig approached. Both ghosts were now in their corporeal states.

"Isn't it wonderful?!" Erika exclaimed. "They're just like dragon children, inquisitive, smart, and ready to play."

Solveig smiled. "A welcome change. And perhaps this place will make for a fresh start for our race. That is if Jörmungander still lives."

"Ladies," Max interrupted. "Before you go making plans for the coming of the new black dragon nation, need I remind you that the city might have inhabitants who will object?"

Both Solveig and Erika frowned.

Max continued. "And you haven't forgotten the sylph, have you? We still need to find Azriel and help him handle that particular challenge… or else all my friends on the surface could very well die. That's not something I want to spend the rest of eternity thinking about."

"Of course we haven't," Solveig replied. "We're only thinking of what happens afterwards."

"But first I'll fly over the city to see if it's inhabited," Erika said as she turned back into her dragon form.

"Wait, it's…" Max started. But Erika had already launched herself into the air. "Damn fool dragon! She's going to get herself killed."

"Then we best go make sure that doesn't happen," Solveig answered as she started to run towards the city. After a few steps she went incorporeal and flew.

Max shook his head. "Women!" he yelled in misery to the universe as he followed Solveig.

Several bats leaped from their perches high above and followed.

With Jörmungander gone, Azriel was relieved to be on his own. He could act freely. There was no need to limit his actions because of the dragon or worry about the dragon's safety. He raced forward to reconnoiter the sylph army. He used the large stalagmites growing from the floor of the cavern for cover. He stopped behind a large boulder with two stalagmites on either side. It appeared as if the boulder had fallen and become wedged between the two, but Azriel's dwarven experience with the underground told him the opposite occurred. The stalagmites had, over thousands of years, grown on either side of the large rock and fused themselves with it.

The first sylphs to enter the cavern were larger than the sylphs he'd already faced in combat. In the center of those sylphs strode one who was even larger – a female if he had to guess. He wasn't sure if he completely understood sylph physiology yet, but she was similar to Elbedreth in appearance.

"She must be the leader," Azriel thought.

He changed his strategy. Trying to get the sylphs to chase him into the cavern was never a solid plan. Anyone with even the slightest hint of intelligence would see one lone sylph trying to bait an entire army of sylphs as an obvious ploy. And Azriel knew sylphs weren't stupid.

Azriel climbed onto the top of the boulder and drew his battleaxe.

Jörmungander, observing from deep within a corridor, watched as the sylph army entered the cavern. They marched in like a giant wave of cave spiders, climbing and trampling over everything. Leading the invasion were several large sylphs with an even larger one in the center.

"That must be the leader and its bodyguard," Jörmungander thought.

Then he watched as Azriel climbed onto a large boulder locked between two massive stalagmites. When he saw the magical glow of Azriel's battleaxe appear, he knew at once what the sylph-dwarf was planning to do. He looked on in amazement as his friend began to change form – back and forth from solid to phantom – between his sylph form and the dwarf form he must have been in his past life. It was Azriel the dwarf who threw the battleaxe.

The Supreme sensed a strange, male sylph presence as soon as she entered the cavern. It was strange because, while there was no doubting it was the familiar scent of a sylph, there was something else wrapped around it. It was almost as if two beings were in the same body.

"So this is the sylph who has killed so many of my children," she surmised.

Though it gave her pause, she didn't bother to halt the advance of her people into the cavern. Like a great wave, the sylph moved forward, searching high and low for parasites to destroy. No place would be safe from the sylph occupation of the cavern. Every living being in their path, small insects such as cave spiders, centipedes and beetles, fell before the onslaught. Only plant-life such as moss and fungi escaped. Thousands were presently in the cavern and thousands more waited in the tunnel beyond for their turn. The Supreme, absorbed in the progress of her people, pushed the strange scent out of her mind.

"Yes, my children!" the Supreme screamed. "Annihilate the parasites!   Exterminate   the   vermin...   the   scroungers...   the freeloaders!" She extended her appendages as if she were going to embrace the entire cavern. "Cleanse the world of its infection! Purify every niche and crevice! FULFILL YOUR PURPOSE!"

Her eyes caught the flash of light, but her mind didn't have time to register its significance before the battleaxe struck her between the eyes and split her brain into two, non-functioning halves. The Supreme dropped to the floor, a quivering mass of dead flesh. Her people, now devoid of leadership, went crazy in their desire to seek retribution. Though a new Supreme will eventually rise through the combat of natural selection, they must first avenge the old one. And that vengeance must come against the strange sylph running towards the opposite side of the cavern.

As each sylph passed the body of their old Supreme, they took a bite out of it in the belief that they'd capture bits and pieces of the old Supremes' knowledge, courage, and wisdom. By the time the entire sylph army was in the cavern, there was nothing left of the Supreme except a bloody wet spot on the cold, hard floor. The instrument of her demise, the battleaxe, had disappeared.

Azriel wasn't sure what affect killing the sylph leader would have on the others, or if it even was the leader his thrown battleaxe had killed. Regardless, he didn't intend to stick around to find out. As soon as he launched his battleaxe into the air, he jumped off the boulder and ran as fast as his leg appendages could move him.

He heard a great sigh come from behind him and then a whole lot of commotion. He looked behind and saw an enormous surge of sylphs as they took up the chase.

"So much for putting them into a state of confusion," Azriel thought. *"I've only pissed them off even more!"*

The chase was on. Azriel realized if the death of their great 'Poo-Bah' didn't put them in a state of bewilderment, anger might be the next best thing. It meant when Elbedreth collapsed the cavern with the *Maul of Power*, most of the sylphs, if not all, would be inside chasing him.

"Elrond would appreciate such strategic thinking," Azriel said aloud as he slowed and turned. He wanted to make sure the sylphs were still following him.

Several of the faster sylphs trailed close behind. "You will die, parasite," one of them called as the sylphs attacked.

Azriel managed to block the blades of his opponents with his steel quarterstaff, but it was close. He might not be so lucky the next time. But what appeared to be an extremely one-sided battle quickly turned to Azriel's advantage. The sylphs, blinded by their fury over the death of the Supreme and driven mad with their determination to skewer and cut, attacked with no mind for defense. Azriel, on the other hand, was intent only on breaking away to continue his run to the other side of the cavern. In quick fashion he disarmed most of the sylphs, while those remaining weren't close enough to stop his escape. As he broke away, he saw the rest of the sylph army rapidly closing the distance.

The next few minutes were the longest in Azriel's lengthy life. He ran, dodged, zig-zagged between stalagmites, and exposed himself whenever it appeared the sylphs had lost sight of him. The other end of the cavern where his love awaited looked to be an ocean away. As he ran, he reflected upon his life and the circumstances that had brought him here. He thought of his friends… no, his family… and their many adventures together. And then there was dear, sweet Emmy, the only person he'd ever known whom he'd be willing to suffer a thousand deaths. As much as he loved Elbedreth, it was Emmy's face he kept in his mind, for she is goodness personified, and the world of Aster direly needed the special love she had to give.

At last the other end of the cavern came in sight. Azriel saw Elbedreth, looking out from the exit corridor where she waited, holding the *Maul of Power*. He saw the relief and love in her eyes when she first caught sight of him. But when he was only a few feet away, Elbedreth's eyes suddenly widened in fear. Azriel stopped and looked back. The sylphs chasing him were too close. He stopped running and turned to meet their attack. Though hopelessly outnumbered, he had to give Elbedreth the few seconds she needed.

"Remember the command word, Elbedreth," he called as he barred the way of the first of the sylphs with the speed of his quarterstaff. "Say it and strike the maul to the floor!"

Elbedreth shook her head. "My love... I..."

"Please!" Azriel implored. "Don't fail me!"

Elbedreth, sylph tears in her eyes, nodded, and whispered the command word as she brought the *Maul of Power* down to strike the floor. The earth rumbled and small pieces of stone and debris began to fall. Then a great moan reverberated throughout the cavern as if the very earth had called out in pain. The entire cavern ceiling and walls disintegrated and tumbled to the floor. Elbedreth, now on her knees and weeping, heard Azriel shout "I love you," just before the collapse covered him with tons of stone.

After the dust had settled, Elbedreth looked at the destruction she had wrought and shook her head in disbelief and pain. She'd never felt such anguish or loneliness. Not even the loss of her own people had caused this much sorrow. Through her tears she spied a slight movement at the bottom of the cave-in. She let the *Maul of Power* drop to the floor and moved closer. She cleaned off the dust and debris. It was Azriel's hand – warm, soft, and beautiful. Elbedreth desperately grasped it with both of her own, bent over and placed her cheek on it.

"Oh, my love," she cried.

Azriel's hand tightened around Elbedreth's for a moment and then went slack. By the time Elbedreth realized Azriel would breath no more, his hand was cold, warmed only by her tears. It then transformed from sylph to dwarf – wide, calloused, and hard. Elbedreth didn't care. Nor did she care about how he had come into her life. It was a common source of speculation between the two, but neither could answer why Azriel the dwarf had turned into Azriel the sylph except to say it was the will of the gods. She only knew that she loved him, and now he was forever lost to her.

"We've done well, have we not, my love," Elbedreth said as she reluctantly, and lovingly, put the lifeless hand on the floor. She got up and moved back to where she dropped the maul and picked it up.

Raising it over her head, she looked one last time at the dead hand of her love – her life. "We stopped the sylph," she said. Her tears were now dry, and she was seeing clearly. "I didn't fail you. There's just one last thing to do."

Elbedreth said the word that brought the *Maul of Power* to life and struck the wall next to her with all her might, unleashing its incredible power. The magical weapon didn't disappoint.

Jörmungander watched the sylph army pass by his hiding place without as much as a glance in his direction. By killing their leader, Azriel had driven them into such a frenzy they only had eyes for the vengeance they sought, and the punishment they hoped would consummate their rage.

The young black dragon wanted to wait a few minutes before leaving. Somewhere in the back of his mind he held onto the hope that Azriel could defeat the sylphs and that Azriel, Elbedreth, and he could continue their journey below in search of the last black dragon female. But Jörmungander knew it was a false hope, and he'd never see his friends again.

Suddenly there was a deep rumble within the earth. It felt like a great earthquake. The immense cavern shook, and the ceiling began to collapse. Jörmungander backed up deeper into the corridor as huge chunks of broken stone crashed to the cavern floor. In the distance, he heard shrieks – thousands of voices screaming in fear, rage, and frustration. Then nothing but silence.

The end of the corridor was covered by stone debris which left Jörmungander in complete darkness. He sighed and stared into the nothingness. Then he felt the ground move again, and he heard a second, muffled rumble. He wondered what could have caused it. Perhaps it was nothing more than a secondary collapse brought on by the original. But Jörmungander thought that unlikely. The most likely scenario was that a second strike from the *Maul of Power* was necessary. That, or Elbedreth had decided her place was by Azriel's side in death.

He conjured a small, magical light in the palm of his hand to show the way through the pitch-black darkness. He looked at the blocked entrance to the cavern and, through tears, recited a poem he'd overheard Azriel mutter time and time again over the sleeping Elbedreth.

"Yer slumber come quickly, mah laddie an' lassie,
Fur it is weel earned an' richly deserved.

Sleep weel an' hae nae fear,
I'll watch ben th' nicht, I'll aye be haur."

Jörmungander turned away with tear-filled eyes and returned to his trek to find the last female black dragon.

Max and Solveig entered the city which was even larger than it looked from the other side of the underground plain. Delicately carved stone structures towered up and into the shadows not lit by magical light. Smaller structures surrounded the tallest like court handmaidens surrounded a queen, or warriors their king. The streets were not cobblestone as Max had expected, but solid stone. There was no sign of life, and no entrances into any of the buildings. The magical lights, which appeared to be shinning though doors and windows, were really bright crystals embedded into the stone.

As Max looked at the smaller buildings and their relationship to the larger, he began to notice that everything was interconnected. None of the buildings were stand alone, but instead, each was buoyed up by the buildings surrounding it. Suddenly the image of Elrond, the tree version, came into his mind.

"Roots," Max said out loud.

"Huh?" Solveig grunted. She had moved off the street and was inspecting a particular spot on the wall of one building. She reached out a hand to make contact. It was warm and pulsated as if it were alive.

"The smaller buildings are connected to the larger ones in a way that makes each of them stronger," Max replied as he moved next to Solveig. "They're like wooden support stakes you attach to young trees. Only these aren't temporary." Max pointed to the base of the nearest building. "Look. The smaller support buildings are fused to the taller ones, and each of the smaller buildings has 'streets' going outward and into a dome."

Solveig nodded understanding. "So that would make the domes anchor points."

"Correct," Max responded. "It's almost as if… well, it looks like a stand of stone trees that's grown up through the earth."

"Give me your hand," Solveig said.

Max did so without hesitation.

Solveig placed Max's hand on the same spot of the building she'd touched a few moments ago. "Feel how it pulsates and how warm it is," she said. "It's like no other stone I've ever come in contact with. I don't know if it's a city, but I think it's alive."

"I'll be damned," Max commented before he turned to Solveig. "I've had experience with stone that's come alive…"

"Like a stone elemental," Solveig added.

Max nodded. "That's exactly what I mean. I've been smacked around by a few, and I can assure you, dear lady, there was nothing warm about them. Nope. It was nothing but cold, hard granite. Broke a few bones, it did. There was this one time when Elrond, Lester, and

I battled an evil priest… I believe he called himself Bernie. Any way, we were in a mountain keep and right in the middle of our… disagreement… he waves his hands and shouts a few strange words… you know, the stuff priests say… and up pops this elemental right from the floor…

"She's not an elemental," a familiar voice said from behind them.

Max and Solveig both turned to find Erika walking around the nearest dome.

Max approached her at once, his anger visible in every step he took. "What do you mean by flying away like you did!" he yelled. "If that's not the most dang-fool thing you could've done, I don't know what is. By the gods, I should throttle…"

Erika turned into her normal dragon form. In his rage, Max had forgotten about not only Erika's true form but also that she was a cleric. Either could destroy a ghost. And as much as he wanted nothing but eternal rest at the start of his 'ghost hood', he now had a different perspective. He loved Solveig, and there was still the world to save against the sylph. Max stopped and held up his hands.

"Okay… okay! Perhaps I overreacted a little. But there's no reason to get defensive. We're friends, right?"

Solveig, behind Max, transformed into her ghostly dragon form and laughed.

Erika watched as Max kept turning his head, first looking at Solveig, then back to Erika. Then she too laughed. "Did you see the look on his face when he was suddenly confronted by two dragons! It was precious!"

Both dragons returned to their human form and Solveig, still laughing, walked over to Max and kissed him. "I still love you," she said.

"And I'm still your friend," Erika added.

Max sighed. "Okay! Okay! But the next time you scare me like that… either of you… I WILL put you over my knee and spank your butts until you can't sit for a week. If you're going to act like children, then that's how I'll treat you."

"We understand, dear," Solveig said, though she was still chuckling.

Max suspiciously looked at both before nodding. "Very well. Erika, you said she?"

Erika nodded. "I don't know what I expected to find when I flew to investigate. But this isn't it. When I touched the side of a 'building', it was warm, and I felt what appeared to be a heartbeat. So I took a chance and used a communication spell my mother taught me to see if I could talk to her. She answered."

For what must have been the millionth time Max wished he could cast magical spells. "What did she say? No wait! A better question… what exactly is she?"

Erika shrugged her shoulders. "Who knows? I couldn't get much. Living stone is all I can tell you with any degree of certainty. So much is unknown this far beneath the surface. Even dwarves don't go this deep. She's aware. She identifies herself as female. And she doesn't know if any more of her kind exists."

Solveig put her hand against a wall and closed her eyes. She had learned the same communications spell as Erika, but since she'd died and come back as a ghost, her enchantments and spells appeared to be twice as strong. Maybe she'd get more from the creature than Erika.

"What are you…?" Max began to ask.

Solveig held up her hand for silence. She let the magic flow through her. She felt it open a conduit from her mind to that of the creature. She sensed fear – and curiosity.

"Who are you?" the creature asked.

"We're travelers from the surface world who have lost our way," Solveig replied. *"My name is Solveig. What's yours?"*

"Name?" the creature replied. *"You mean how am I called? Those who share my existence call me Johari."*

"Very well, Johari," Solveig said. *"You're safe with us. We'll not harm you or the others. We call them bats, by the way."*

"Bats? That is a strange name," Johari said before going quiet for a few moments. *"They accept this name for their race. But each bat is called something different."*

Solveig's mind registered surprise. *"You can communicate with them?"*

"I can," Johari replied. *"They're my friends."*

"Are there others here who are your friends?" Solveig asked.

"No, just the… bats," the living mountain said. *"Except for them, I've been alone for as long as I can remember."*

"Well?" an impatient Max asked.

"Calm yourself," Erika said as she put a hand on his arm. "The magic she's using is heavily dependent upon concentration. She'll tell us when she's done."

Max looked at Erika. "We don't have a lot of time! Remember?"

Solveig overheard none of the conversation that had passed between Max and Erika. *"Can you tell me how long you've been down here?"* she asked.

Johari sighed. The slight vibration caused Max and Erika to glance around. *"Time has no meaning for me. It's eternal. But to my friends it's fleeting. Many generations of bats have passed by while I watched. Their deaths make me sad."*

"Generations," Solveig said as she nodded. *"That's a long time. But then again, you're a mountain… a very unusual mountain, to be sure… but still a mountain. Time never means the same for a mountain."*

"What is a mountain?"

Solveig shook her head. *"Not now, Johari,"* she said. She had an idea. *"I know someone who'll be more than happy to talk to you about mountains… and oceans… and the stars in the sky above the surface. But that must come later. I must ask you a question."*

"I'm not going anywhere," Johari remarked.

"Indeed," Solveig said as she chuckled. She wasn't sure if Johari's last remark was meant to be humorous or sarcastic. *"Do you mind if my friends and I make a home here?"*

Johari was enthusiastic about the suggestion. *"Of course you may!"* she exclaimed. *"There's plenty of room and lots of food for sustenance. And I'd appreciate having someone to converse with. The bats are… well, they're intelligent enough, but they don't like talking much."*

"That's very kind, Johari," Solveig replied. *"For now, some of us must leave for a while… but we'll be back. And then we'll talk with you to your hearts content. Thank you again for letting us share your home."*

"Really, Solveig, I might as well," the mountain responded with a shrug that knocked Max off his feet. *"I mean, how can I stop you?"*

"That may be true," Solveig thought after she broke contact with Johari. *"But I suspect there's more to it you don't understand. Either that… or your holding back information."*

"Well?" Max asked as he brushed dirt off his pants.

"What happened to you?" Solveig inquired.

Erika laughed. "A small earthquake knocked him over."

Solveig chuckled. "Those types of things wouldn't happen if you'd stay ghostly, dear."

Max crossed his arms over his chest. "So it would seem," he replied. "What did you learn?"

Solveig told them.

"But we already have a home," Erika protested.

Solveig shook her head. "I think you and Jörmungander should move here. At least until the next generation of black dragons is born and ready to join the world again. It's safer."

Erika blushed but nodded.

"You mean if Jörmungander, and the world, survive the sylph plague," Max interjected.

Solveig ignored Max's acid tongue.

"And you should stay here while Max and I go back to help with the sylphs and find Jörmungander," Solveig said.

"But you'll need my help," Erika responded.

"She's got a point," Max added. "We've seen the sylphs. It's all-hands-on-deck."

Solveig and Erika looked at Max. Both appeared to be confused.

Max sighed. "Geez… you guys really don't get around," he said as he shook his head. "You know, ships that sail the oceans, the top level or deck, sailors, all hands to their battle stations, and all that shippy stuff?"

"We understand what ships are, how they're constructed, what they call the different parts and their functions," Erika responded to Max's question.

"Indeed," Solveig added. "Most of us have seen them. And Jörmungander built an extensive library for study. We've just never heard that expression used before."

Max heaved another sigh. "Black dragons live isolated lives, don't they?"

"We prefer it that way, dear," Solveig replied. "Our reputation as evil, black engines of death and destruction, is just that and nothing more. It's intended to keep the rift-raft away."

"Well, you've done a pretty fair job of that," Max answered. "What say we get back to the original point, though? We need Erika, her spells and her dragon's breath."

Solveig shook her head. "No, she stays here with Johari and the bats," she insisted. "Erika's the only chance for our race… her and Jörmungander. I won't risk it."

"You won't risk it?" Max countered. "What good does it do to have her here if the world up top is being destroyed by the sylphs? Especially if she could help stop it?"

"He's right, Solveig," Erika added. "You're a sister to me, and I love you, but… well, you're dead. You no longer have status above me within the clan. I have no clan. So I'll make my own decisions."

Erika and Max both stared at Solveig and waited until the ghost-dragon nodded. "Of course," she replied stiffly. "Please forgive me for being so presumptuous."

"Solveig, please…" Erika pleaded, suddenly contrite.

Solveig shook her head. "It's fine," she said before walking away.

Max had a hard time translating the look on Solveig's face when she relented. He knew it wasn't anger. Perhaps it was because, for the first time, she realized the dead held no sway over the living. Or maybe it was because she understood for the first time that she was no longer part of the black dragon clan. As they walked through the underground plain towards the ledge which led out, Max took Solveig's hand to reassure her. Even so, it was a silent walk through the mushrooms.

It surprised them to find Jörmungander a day later wandering the tunnels and caves deep beneath Elanesse. A small ball of conjured light floated just over his head. And though it lit his way, he didn't appear to be seeing anything. He looked broken and withdrawn... more dead than alive.

Erika slowly approached Jörmungander while Max and Solveig lingered behind. Why he was here and not guarding their home was a discussion for later. She put both her hands on his upper arms to stop him. When she looked into Jörmungander's eyes, they stared back at her blank and unaware. Although his eyes followed her, they didn't appear to recognize her. Erika forced him to sit with his back against a wall. He didn't resist and returned his hollow gaze to the empty corridor.

"Jörmungander, it's me," she said. "Erika."

Jörmungander directed his attention away from the inky blackness of the corridor behind him, looked at Erika, and shook his head. "You're dead. This is just another hallucination."

The female dragon stroked the side of his face. "No," she said. "Trust me, I'm no phantasm. I survived our people's battle with the sylph."

Jörmungander's eyes focused on the female black dragon's face. "Erika! Is it really you?" He reached out and touched her on the shoulder with a finger. Then he looked at the two ghostly figures standing behind her. His eyes widened in surprise.

"Solveig!" he exclaimed before frowning. "But the *Heart of the World* only showed one still alive?"

Solveig sat next to her friends. "The *Heart of the World* was correct," she replied. "Jörmungander, this may come as a shock, but I'm not alive."

The young male black dragon took the announcement in stride and nodded. "The sylphs killed you. You're a ghost like Max there."

Max stared at Jörmungander, then understood the only way the young dragon could know who and what he was is if he'd met Azriel. "You've come across Azriel and Elbedreth? How is that old son of a barroom whore? And, Elbedreth… where are they? Last time we were together I said a few things I regret and would apologize for."

Jörmungander grimaced and looked at the tunnel floor. There were fresh tears in his eyes.

"They didn't make it, did they," Max stated as fact that which the dragon had yet to confirm.

Jörmungander stood and faced Max. "The sylphs are dead, Max. Elbedreth collapsed a cavern upon their heads. But…"

The announcement about the sylphs, and ultimately the fate of the world, stunned the two female dragons. The black dragon *Maelstrom* prophesy had been fulfilled by others! Impossible! But it must be so. They knew Jörmungander well enough to know he wouldn't say such a thing if it wasn't true.

"But what," Max insisted.

The black dragon looked at the ghost-rogue. "Azriel never intended to survive the encounter," he said. "And Elbedreth… well, I don't think she wanted to live by herself again."

"How can you be sure?" Max asked. "You saw their bodies?"

Jörmungander shook his head. "But they used the *Maul of Power* from the armory. I felt the earthquake it caused and saw the cavern give way myself. It was used not once, but twice. There couldn't have been any survivors, especially after the second time." Jörmungander turned to Erika. "Azriel and Elbedreth fulfilled the *Maelstrom* prophesy. Never in a million years did we ever think someone outside our clan would accomplish it. But it doesn't surprise me. Our arrogance has kept us apart and isolated. Our pride wouldn't allow us to ask for help. Oh Erika, that's all we needed to do!"

"Even if what you say is true, it matters little," Erika replied. "What's done is done and you shouldn't concern yourself with that which cannot be changed." Though her response sounded harsh, she desperately wanted him to come back from his self-recrimination. It seemed the only way.

Jörmungander grimaced but nodded. "You're right. But if our race survives, I promise that'll never happen again. We'll visit the surface often. And we'll go there in peace."

Max, who hadn't been following the conversation as other thoughts bounced around in his mind, shook his head. "I have to know for sure that Azriel is dead," he said as he disappeared into the darkness of the corridor.

"Hold on!" Solveig called. "I'm coming with you." She turned to Erika. "Take Jörmungander back to Johari and wait until you hear from us."

"What?" Jörmungander exclaimed. "No! No! I'm going too."

Erika shook her head, took his hand, and pulled him in the opposite direction. "No, you're not. I'll explain along the way."

A brilliant white light from above pierced the great cavern – the new tomb of the old sylph race. Over the rubble it went, back and forth in a complex search pattern that left no inch of the collapsed cavern untouched. Here and there it found a sylph which, though trapped, wasn't yet dead. The white light gently helped those unfortunates along into the next life. The elder gods had decided the sylph, with one exception, were too dangerous to live.

At one end of the cavern, a lance of blue light rested atop the cold and still hand of a dwarf. The rest of the body was buried in rubble. Althaya was well familiar with the grizzled but likable Azriel. The light continued to search until it found the body of a sylph, its hand outstretched just inches away from that of the dwarf. The blue light retreated a few feet, split in two, and returned to the dwarf and sylph simultaneously. A bright, silent explosion lit the otherwise dark cavern. Before the blackness once again settled over the largest mausoleum the world of Aster has ever seen, all signs of the dwarf and sylph had vanished.

<u>THE THIRTEENTH INTERREGNUM</u>

It didn't take long for Lycomedes and the Sky Emperors to locate the massive white dragon. It was approaching the Forest of the Fey from the east and leaving destructive flooding in its wake. Lycomedes stopped. The dragon was much larger than he had expected.

"We're supposed to stop that?" Phanessa, the oldest female Sky Emperor, asked.

"It would appear so," Lycomedes replied. Though he was talking to Phanessa, he didn't try to keep the conversation private. "Emmy has asked us to help save the city in the forest."

"Haven't we done enough for this world to earn our keep?" another Sky Emperor asked. "Poor Liosh gave his life for it."

"One never stops fighting for what they believe, Cyberniskos," Lycomedes replied.

"We're still children," another added.

"Indeed," Lycomedes answered. "But with Liosh gone, we no longer have the luxury of hiding behind adults. We must make our own way."

"Lycomedes is right," Phanessa said. No one argued with her. "What are your orders?"

"We might not be able to destroy the creature," the leader of the Sky Emperors said. "But maybe we can slow it down… or divert its attention away from the city in the forest for a time… and I have a plan for that. Here's what I want you to do."

Havendale's master sorcerer Rathal Arquen, and his traveling companion, Rhys, Havendale's chief spy, watched through the trees of the Forest of the Fey as strange, unknown creatures battled an impossibly large white dragon. The two of them were once again alone. Commander Fairmount had turned his Riders back a few hours ago.

"Ice," Rathal whispered.

"What's that?" Rhys asked.

"Nothing," the sorcerer replied as he observed the battle taking place in the sky.

The cloud-like creatures had long tentacles hanging down from which they were attacking the monster dragon with lightning bolts. Others were exploding balls of lightning around the creature. It didn't matter if they made a direct hit. The power of the electrical charge bounced around in the wet atmosphere surrounding the dragon. It was impossible to escape.

"Whoever is controlling those… those cloud people… is doing a pretty good job," Rhys remarked. "See how they've boxed the dragon in on all sides except one? They're directing the dragon away from the Elanesse. And look… they even have a reserve. Sound tactics. Even now the dragon appears to be weakening. They'll have this wrapped up in a few minutes."

Rathal shook his head. "Don't be so sure," he commented. "We need to follow."

"It's not a danger to Elanesse right now, Rathal," Rhys argued. "But if the cloud people don't destroy it, we can damn sure expect it to come back. This is where we need to be."

Rathal turned his horse to the east. "I think I can kill it," he said. "But the only chance I have is if it's over that new mountain range on the other side of Lake Lorali."

Rhys was silent.

The sorcerer looked at the spy. "Are you with me?"

Rhys looked at the battle being played out above for a few seconds more before he looked at Rathal and nodded. "Let's go."

The white dragon was annoyed. The creatures that had killed her mates now filled the sky above the forest and the city she had marked for destruction. She killed several with her dragon's breath... and even more by freezing the air surrounding her whenever one got close. But she knew it wouldn't be enough. The white beams the creatures used with their cursed tentacles were taking its toll, and the tactics they used kept their losses to a minimum.

Constantly stalked and attacked, the white dragon looked for any place that would give her a moment's rest. She needed to heal and the mountains to the southeast appeared to be the most likely spot.

The white dragon altered her course to take her south, then turned east to go over the large lake at the base of a small mountain range. It relieved her to see that her attackers didn't follow.

CHAPTER TWENTY

InnisRos (Taranthi)

"You never stop being a Marine. The code, the tradition, the brotherhood, the Marine way of life, is forever branded in your heart... in your very soul."

- Marine Commander-General Aubrey Feynral

Yury, Eirwen, and Kyleigh made good progress traveling the Maranwe River. The improvements Yury had made the day before on the raft were paying huge dividends. Though he wasn't a shipwright, he'd spent hours making repairs to ships he'd served aboard. He used what he'd learned to incorporate several design characteristics of a fast frigate into the improvements... at least as many as he could under the circumstances... which resulted in enhancements to both speed and stability.

The relationship between the seaman and the Queen of the Alfheim was much improved. Kyleigh had apologized again, and Eirwen, after she heard what happened, insisted the giant stop being so distant. It was advice which Yury took to heart. They filled the hours with stories that not only entertained but revealed who each person was. Yury fell even more in love with Eirwen as he learned more and more about her. And though Kyleigh didn't admit to being a sovereign on another world, she spoke freely about many other things in her life.

Their concern regarding discovery never materialized. The land had been abandoned. Except for the dark elf army, which was well to the north, the central part of the island was completely deserted of elf, human, wyvern, or demon. Birds flew in the sky and an occasional horse or cow roamed the rich farmland, but not much else. Each night they listened to the call of a Nighthunter, the big cats that are one of the few true predators that still roamed InnisRos. As terrifying as these big hunters were, their nightly laments sounded even worse. But as long as they stayed on the river, the Nighthunter didn't pose much of a threat. Even so, Yury still felt uncomfortable and remained cautious. During the third day of traveling, not long after a small lunch of blackened catfish with apple nut salsa and wild onions, Kyleigh suddenly stood. The northern most tip of the forest west of Taranthi had just come into view. Kyleigh threw the mint stalk she'd been chewing into the water and pointed.

"There!" she shouted as she pointed to the forest. "We need to go into that forest."

Eirwen, sitting next to Yury at the tiller, located Kyleigh from the sound of her voice and asked, "What is it?"

Yury took Eirwen's hand. "It's a large forest," he said. "It stands to the west of Taranthi."

Eirwen nodded. "The capital city of InnisRos?"

"Yes," Yury replied. "And now home to several thousand invading dark elves… or I'm a three-legged sea hag."

"I know the dark elves well," Kyleigh remarked. "They're there, no question." Kyleigh then noticed the direction of the raft had changed. She turned to look at the giant who was steering the raft towards the western bank of the river. "What are you doing? We're still several miles away from the forest."

"And more noticeable to prying eyes on the water than on land," Yury replied. "Unless you have a way to make us invisible."

Kyleigh looked at the farmland between them and the forest — mostly uncut fields of hay, wheat, and oats. "You're right."

After reaching the river's edge, Yury pulled the raft out of the river and camouflaged it with long stocks of hay. While the crops in the field hid Kyleigh and Eirwen, as long as the latter crawled, Yury's even larger stature stood out like a sore thumb. He made the painful decision to leave Eirwen in Kyleigh's care and sprinted the two miles to the edge of the forest to find sufficient concealment and draw any attack away from Kyleigh and Eirwen. No attack materialized, however. As he waited for the two, he checked the surrounding trees and bushes for signs of dark elves. There were none.

"Now where," Yury asked Kyleigh after the two females had caught up. "This is a big place, and other than a few excursions just outside Taranthi while on leave, I've never been here before."

Kyleigh paused as she received directions from the *Ak-Vanessë Stone* in her mind. "That way," she replied as she pointed to the southwest.

The forest was lush and thick with trees averaging eighty to ninety feet high, though a few of the older trees reached twice that height. The ground was filled with thick underbrush and thorny bushes which made traveling slow. The canopy above, as well as the forest floor, teemed with life – squirrels, deer, rabbits, chipmunks – and the streams were stocked with plenty of fish, freshwater lobsters, crawfish, and salamanders. Nighthunters also occupied the forest, but they typically kept to the forest edge.

Dusk had fallen and still they hadn't reached their destination, the *Ak-Séregon Stone*. Yury was making plans to stop for the evening to pitch camp and make a meal before darkness settled in when a strange glow through the trees and brush caught his eye. He stopped.

"Kyleigh," he said as he pointed. "Could that be the stone?"

The Alfheim queen looked in the direction Yury pointed. "No. We're close, but that's not the stone. It's something else."

A few minutes later they stood over what appeared to be a silvery cocoon the size of a person. Eirwen reached out and touched it before Yury could stop her. She suffered no ill effects as she ran both hands over it.

"It's cool to the touch," Eirwen said, "and extremely hard… probably impenetrable."

"I recognize it," Kyleigh offered. "It's a stasis healing spell. Only powerful sorcerers can conjure it."

"I know there are sorcerers in the navy," Yury remarked. "Cincinnatus was one… and he was awfully powerful."

Kyleigh shook her head. "It's not a military sorcerer. They wouldn't waste their time learning healing spells, particularly one this powerful. They're more concerned with spells that defend. And kill. Military sorcerers have ready access to healers and clerics, so this type of magic is pointless from their point of view."

Eirwen took her hands away from the cocoon and reached out to Yury. He put an arm around her shoulders to reassure her of his closeness. "We need this sorcerer," Eirwen explained. "I need this sorcerer!"

"I don't understand," Yury said.

Kyleigh looked up at the giant. "I do. This sorcerer is the only one who can get her into the corridor."

Yury shook his head. "No! I don't think so. I've heard you two talk about the corridor and it's… how did you describe it… oh yeah… its instability. It's causing everything that's happening. Hell, it traces right back to the dark elves' home world. No, it's too risky. Eirwen might never come back. Even worse, it could kill her!"

"Yury, I must," Eirwen pleaded. "I'm the only one who can shut it down."

"There are other time walkers," Yury replied.

"But she's the only one here," Kyleigh said. "We don't have time to waste. You of all people should understand what the consequences are if we don't do this. You and Eirwen were both sent to another world by the breech in space and time caused by the corridor." The Alfheim queen paused to let her words sink in. "You can't deny the danger the corridor represents to Aster… or what must be done to end it," she added.

"We need to act soon, Yury," Eirwen remarked to lend weight to Kyleigh's argument.

The giant seaman was helpless when it came to Eirwen. He was forced to agree. But he vowed that she would not go in alone, and that her fate would be his.

Eric the Black slowly regained consciousness. The stasis healing cocoon he'd surrounded himself in had done its job. He no longer felt broken. Then his mind shifted to the reason he needed to conjure this spell in the first place.

"How much time have I lost," he thought as he began the process of un-tethering himself from the healing magic.

The cocoon rose from the ground and rotated from horizontal to vertical and then settled back. Layer upon layer of the magic dissolved until it exposed the sorcerer. Eric the Black opened his eyes to see three people, no, make that one person and two giants, staring at him. The giant female had eyes as black as a Stygian night with specks of shimmering silver embedded in them. The contrast between her eyes and the snow-white hair flowing to her waist was remarkable, eerily beautiful like that of an exotic alien. Eric the Black didn't know what to make of her. But the other female was none other than Kyleigh Angelus-Custos, Queen of the Alfheim. He'd never met her, but he'd listened to plenty of tales from Landross about the sword hanging at her side, the legendary *Ah-RahnVakha,* sword of the rulers of the Alfheim. The other giant he also recognized. It was Yury Petrenko, the only Draugen Pesta citizen to make InnisRos, or any of the city states on the mainland, his home. He was a minor celebrity in his own right.

Eric the Black bowed to the Alfheim queen. "Queen Kyleigh. It's an honor."

Kyleigh frowned. "You know who I am?"

"Not through personal contact, madam," the master sorcerer-assassin replied. "But your sword is quite famous over here amongst certain military types, most notably my friend the knight Landross."

"You're Eric the Black!" Yury exclaimed. "I heard that Landross hung around with a powerful sorcerer."

The sorcerer nodded. "At your service, Yury Petrenko," he responded.

Eric the Black ignored Yury's astonished look and studied the other female. Though she was looking at him, he understood at once that she was blind, or that maybe she saw different things – different realities. Who could tell what other things she saw?

Eirwen appeared to know the sorcerer had taken an interest in her and moved closer to Yury.

"And you are?" Eric the Black asked.

"She's…" Yury began.

"My name is Eirwen," the time walker answered. "I'm from the island Vesperia in the Sea of the Marble Wyvern."

Eric the Black's eyes widened. "I've been told time walkers lived there. Is that… are you…"

Eirwen nodded.

"We need your help," Kyleigh said. "The *Ak-Séregon Stone*…"

"Indeed," Eric the Black interrupted. "Follow me."

At Taranthi's western gate, Nefertari raised her staff and commanded an air elemental to block the arrows being fired from the battlements by the dark elves. Even though her reaction time was near instantaneous, a few arrows got through her hastily conjured defenses. The two Marines holding up Colonel Tirion dropped to the ground with several arrows buried in their chests. Sergeant Major Opha Mayalene dashed to protect Little Jimmy and took an arrow in her side. She screamed out in pain but was able to pick up the boy and carry him to the cover of several barrels of fresh water.

Colonel Tirion ran forward and met the dark elf charge. He slashed and cut his way through five dark elf warriors, leaving three dead and two dying. But the Marine hadn't gone unscathed. One arm was useless from a deep slash that had severed tendons, and he was losing blood from at least two more deep cuts. Everything else was superficial. He felt no pain – only the rage that had overtaken him when Nefertari had been fondled by the guard commander. That same dark elf, the focal point of Colonel Tirion's fury, backed away. As he did so, he tripped over a body with several Marine arrows sticking out of it. Colonel Tirion wasted little time removing the repugnant guard commander's head. He turned and headed back to Nefertari. Marine arrows picked off any dark elf warrior attempting to attack the wounded Marine colonel.

Several dark elves who had escaped Marine arrows and swords rushed forward towards Nefertari and the earth elemental now standing by her side. Its size was enough to make the dark elves hesitate, but only for a few moments. Half attacked the elemental while the remaining struck at Nefertari. Her staff, before an object of magic, now became a weapon of self-defense, its' magic-fused wood stronger than metal. Nefertari spun it like a windmill, blocking sword thrusts, counterattacking, parrying, and counter-parrying. On the ground in her wake lay dark elves with busted heads and broken bones. Those that attacked the earth elemental were down as well, their bodies twisted into unnatural shapes. She gazed over her shoulder and saw several dozen Marines running to her, but she didn't think she'd need the help.

Then something hit her hard in the back. Her staff went flying, and she tumbled to the ground, stunned. The dark elf who had tackled her turned her over to face him as he raised his sword to deliver the final blow. His eyes suddenly widened, and he coughed out blood before collapsing on Nefertari. The priestess pushed the dead dark elf off and willed her staff to return. As she stood, she saw Song Jingyi holding a bloody, curved, serrated knife. The dark elf female translator bowed slightly to Nefertari before kicking the body of the dark elf she'd just killed. Then she began to deliver the *coups de grâce* to any of the other dark elves still alive.

Nefertari nodded approval and turned towards the western gate. There were still dark elves charging, and they weren't too far behind

Colonel Tirion who was running back to her. He looked gravely wounded. Without a thought she ordered the earth elemental to attack the charging enemy while she hurried to him. With her staff she used the force of air to shove two dark elves back just before they leaped to tackle the Marine. With one hand holding onto her staff and an arm around Colonel Tirion's waist, they retreated towards the onrushing Marines who had left the safety of their concealment to engage their dark elf counterparts directly.

Song Jingyi hurried forward to the other side of Colonel Tirion and together the priestess and dark elf interpreter half-dragged the Marine to the same barrels of water Opha Mayalene and the boy Jimmy were hiding. A small contingent of Marines broke off from the main group and formed a protective barrier around the barrels.

Above the melee on the ground, the two opponents filled the air with arrows. After the first few volleys, and several of their number lying dead on the battlements pierced by Marine arrows, the dark elf archers, who had been shooting at targets on the ground, concentrated their fire at the Marine archers on the rooftops. Both sides fought well, and each was taking losses. But while the death toll was four to one in favor of the Marines, the dark elves were getting reinforcements from the adjoining battlements. There were no replacements for the dead Marines.

"This isn't going as planned," Nefertari said as she healed Colonel Tirion's wounds.

"I'm scared," Jimmy said.

"Hush now," Sergeant Mayalene said.

"I'm fine," Colonel Tirion said as he brushed Nefertari's hands away. "Help Opha."

Nefertari turned and inspected Sergeant Major Mayalene's wound.

"We're almost out of the fight, colonel," one of the nearby Marines said. "The dark elves are drawing more reinforcements from other barracks and preparing a second wave. And it's only a matter of time before a much larger force shows up on our six from inside the city."

Colonel Tirion looked over the barrels to gage the tactical situation. The Marines were fighting well but were no match for the overwhelming numbers the dark elves could bring to bear. "Ain't that the truth, Marine," he said. "Nefertari, we're pinned down. We need help or we're going to die right here. Where's Maedhros Nénmacil?"

Nefertari, finished with Sergeant Major Mayalene, joined Colonel Tirion. "He should be here any second now. But I have an idea. Give me a few minutes."

The priestess sat with her back against the barrels and closed her eyes. She chanted a prayer to her patron, the elder goddess Sehanine StarEagle. Her staff, lying on the ground next to her, exploded in bright lights of browns, blues, and reds. It rose into the air before the StarSinger and changed into the figure of the goddess.

"What you ask is very dangerous, child," Sehanine StarEagle said. "I didn't raise you up to be my high priestess only to have you waste your life upon this field of death."

"Do you not want me to serve the greater good?" Nefertari asked.

"You'll serve the greater good by staying alive," the goddess countered. The look on her face was hard and unrelenting.

The fighting had reached a crescendo. The remaining Marines had retreated and formed a phalanx with the barrels in the center. Dark elves kept charging and dying, but each time they did, a few more Marines fell. Colonel Tirion joined the Marines and took command. "Get ready to move!" he shouted. Then he looked at Nefertari and her goddess. "But not until I give the word!"

Nefertari was becoming desperate as she looked at the one she loved give orders to his Marines. She knew they were going to die if they didn't break free soon. "Where the hell is Maedhros Nénmacil," she whispered.

"He'll be here soon enough," Sehanine StarEagle said. "But right now I have him occupied with something else. HE'S following orders… as should you! Let me take you away from here."

"Gaze into my heart, mistress," Nefertari said, "and tell me what you see."

The image of Sehanine StarEagle shook her head. "I already know what I'll find."

Nefertari stood. "Then you understand I'll not leave Daeron and his Marines," she told her goddess. "As much as I love you and everything you represent, you ask the one thing I will not do."

Sehanine StarEagle frowned at her high priestess. "Stubborn… but very well, Nefertari. I grant your request."

The staff dropped to the ground.

As Maedhros Nénmacil flew back to Nefertari, he noticed a long column of dark elves marching towards the *Ak-Séregon Stone*. Marching at the head of this 'snake' were three sorcerers. He wasn't concerned. The stone had proven able and willing to defend herself… and he didn't believe the three sorcerers were enough to harm her.

A sweet, musical voice entered his mind. *"You must destroy the dark elves before they get to the Ak-Séregon Stone."*

Maedhros Nénmacil knew at once who was communicating with him, the goddess Sehanine StarEagle. "My mistress has called to me for help," he stated. "I must protect her before all else."

"You question my judgement?" the goddess snapped.

The shortness in Sehanine StarEagle's voice took the creation stone by surprise. He surmised that Nefertari's in real trouble and the goddess was worried, which in turn made him even more anxious to get to her. But if Sehanine StarEagle was willing to jeopardize her High Priestess to eliminate the dark elf threat, it must be critically important to do so. Nevertheless, he believed his sacred duty was to the StarSinger. Let Sehanine StarEagle deal with the dark elves. "I protect the StarSinger," Maedhros Nénmacil replied. "That is the work of a creation stone, or have you forgotten?"

"Then why are you not already with her?!" Sehanine StarEagle replied.

The harshness in her voice made Maedhros Nénmacil pause. He had no answer for that question – for that accusation. "The *Ak-Séregon Stone* has grown in power. Three sorcerers cannot hurt her."

Sehanine StarEagle laughed. *"You don't think I know that? But each time she's forced to use her magic to defend herself, she grows even stronger. As her power grows, so does her thirst for it. But that's not the only reason. There are others, others with special skills, who will be killed if you don't stop the dark elves. These others are the only ones who can end the Ak-Séregon Stone's quest for supremacy."*

Maedhros Nénmacil was less sure of himself. "I'm a creation stone," he announced. "There are limits to your ability to command me."

"Very true," Sehanine StarEagle answered. *"Along with your independence my brethren also gave you one of the keenest intellects in the universe. Figure it out!"* The elder goddess broke contact.

Maedhros Nénmacil considered Sehanine StarEagle's words and realized the truth. He turned and headed back.

He flew at treetop level to hide his presence from the dark elves for as long as possible. Maedhros Nénmacil recognized the sorcerers must be taken out first, for they and their magic could hurt him. Against the warriors he was pretty much indestructible. The creation stone veered right when he reached the end of the long column of warriors. For a few seconds he flew just atop the trees parallel to the dark elves until he was out in front of them.

From his vantage point he could see the burned and devastated clearing surrounding the *Ak-Séregon Stone* ahead. Four people cautiously approached it. One he recognized as Eric the Black, and another was a giant from Draugen Pesta. The other two were females with whom he wasn't familiar.

"The dark ones will have complete surprise," he thought to himself as he settled to the ground. *"It'll be a slaughter even with Eric the Black."*

As soon as the dark elf sorcerers came into view, the creation stone, as he did outside the small river village of Ashakadi, attacked with hundreds of small shards which exploded outward. The three sorcerers were dead before they hit the ground, as were a score or so of warriors, their bodies pierced through and through. The creation stone recalled his shards, extended multiple blades, rose above the ground spinning, and moved towards the remaining dark elf force. Five beams of magic hit Maedhros Nénmacil and he crashed into the ground, stunned. Five sorcerers, dressed as warriors, moved forward and laughed at the creation stone. But what none of the dark elves understood was that Maedhros Nénmacil, though hurt, was only now becoming angry.

Yury, Eirwen, Kyleigh, and Eric the Black cautiously approached the *Ak-Séregon Stone.*

"Careful," Eric the Black said as he stopped the group ten feet from the pulsating stone. "The last time I tried to interfere she damn near killed me."

"We have to stop her," Kyleigh remarked. "She's reckless with her power and too young to understand the scope and breadth of its consequences."

"Why is someone as important as the Queen of the Alfheim over here trying to help," Yury asked. "You've never explained that."

"Because the *Ak-Séregon Stone* and the *Ak-Samarië Shard*, which links our two worlds, also tethers both worlds," Eric the Black responded for the queen. "What happens to us happens to the Alfheim." Eric the Black looked at Kyleigh. "Isn't that right, Highness?"

Kyleigh had been briefed about Eric the Black's arrogant attitude and caustic tongue. On the other hand, though, Father Goram once told her the sorcerer had the best interest of InnisRos and his friends at heart. But there was no question regarding his intended meaning — that she's only here now because the Alfheim is threatened rather than any desire to help an ally. "We were ready to help, sorcerer," she replied, undaunted by the sorcerer's veiled accusation. "But the corridor between our two worlds was no longer safe for passage. I lost many fine warriors coming over here. If not for the magic of my sword and the *Ak-Vanessë Stone*, the daughter of the shard and my friend, I'd have died along with my guard."

"It appears, at least for now, that we want the same thing, regardless of our motives," Yury observed.

"I need to get into the corridor," Eirwen blurted out.

Yury, Kyleigh, and Eric the Black turned to look at the time walker.

"I'm the only one who can stop what's happening," Eirwen continued. "To do that, I must be in the corridor."

"You just heard me say how dangerous the corridor is," Kyleigh protested.

"Eirwen's right," Yury countered.

"How do you know that?" Kyleigh asked.

Yury took Eirwen's hand in his. "I've seen what she can do. There's not much I understand about magic, time walking, or other such things. But I know what I've seen... what I've experienced. Black dragons, a dark elf invasion, demons, the queen of the Alfheim, even a distant world where animals come up out of the earth itself to kill you." Yury shook his head. "Nothing is as it should be. None of us can doubt that. And who here can deny that it will take something extraordinary to stop it. Something just as extraordinary as the threat itself. Look at Eirwen's eyes. She's been marked."

There was silence as Kyleigh and Eric the Black considered Yury's words.

Eric the Black nodded. "I think I understand. But I've tried to connect with the *Ak-Séregon Stone* and nearly died for it. She wouldn't tolerate any interference. How's Eirwen supposed to get in?"

"The *Ak-Vanessë Stone*," Kyleigh said. "We believe she'll bring the stone back to her senses."

Eric the Black shook his head. "But that's no longer good enough. The stone's gotten a taste of power. And she craves it. That's had unexpected consequences."

"Strange creatures? Trips to other worlds?" Kyleigh asked. "Yury and Eirwen have talked to me about their own experiences."

Eric the Black nodded. "That… plus a deep sense of self-preservation. But there's more. In the brief contact I had with the stone, I sensed something more dangerous… something more powerful… coming our way. It's power in its truest sense. The blowback of magic that caused the destruction you see here around the stone is but a miniscule preview of what's heading towards us."

"I can only stop it in the corridor," Eirwen said. "If it's allowed to reach here, Aster will be destroyed. So will the Alfheim."

Kyleigh looked at Eirwen and Yury. They had become good friends in their brief association. Though she understood the necessity, she feared for Eirwen's safety.

"I can calm the stone," Kyleigh said. "Sorcerer, can your magic get Eirwen…"

"And me," Yury interrupted.

Eirwen nodded. "I need a protector's strength. Or I won't be able to do what's necessary."

"Very well," Kyleigh said. "Eric, can your magic get Eirwen and Yury into the corridor?"

Eric the Black nodded. "If you can calm the *Ak-Séregon Stone* as you say, then yes. But I must caution you. Getting back out with your lives won't be as easy."

Eirwen agreed. "That's something we both understand."

Kyleigh stood on her tippy toes, reached up, and framed Eirwen's face in her hands. She then kissed the time walker on the forehead. She tried to say something – something wise and worthy of a queen – but couldn't find the words. Kyleigh looked up at Yury. He appeared content. Suddenly a huge smile broke through and he nodded.

"Don't worry, Kyleigh," he said as he put his arm around Eirwen. "We'll see you on the other side of life."

Kyleigh turned away with tears in her eyes and approached the stone. "Let's get started."

The sudden and gruff departure of her goddess surprised Nefertari… but when she closed her eyes and retreated deep within herself, she found the power to do what she wanted was there as promised. The StarSinger gave thanks to Sehanine StarEagle, picked her staff up from the ground, and began the incantation that would save Daeron and the other Marines… and possibly the city itself.

Colonel Tirion used every trick, every tactic his long years of experience and training could muster. But the Marines were still losing. He'd already lost half his command. And while the dark elves died in huge numbers, there was always two more to replace each one killed.

"We have to go now," Sergeant Major Mayalene shouted. "Or we'll never get out of the city."

Colonel Tirion winced as an arrow grazed his arm. He skewered a dark elf and glanced back at Nefertari. She was kneeling behind the barrels with her eyes closed. The big Marine saw her mouthing words, a sure sign she was conjuring a spell.

"Not yet," Colonel Tirion replied. "We have to give Nefertari more time."

"We don't have the time to give!" Sergeant Mayalene barked just before she dropped from a thrown six-foot-long spear lodged in her chest.

Colonel Tirion kneeled to help, but there was nothing he could do. The spear had pierced her heart. She was gone. "Damn!" he whispered.

Nefertari, though her eyes were closed, sensed the ebb and flow of the battle. She experienced the sudden pain and fear Sergeant Mayalene felt just before she slipped into the eternal night… the terror of the young boy as he lay curled into a fetal position next to her… the anguish in Daeron's heart at the loss of yet another Marine… the Marine's determination to make their deaths as costly to the enemy as possible. The bravery, skill, and resolve of these warriors never failed to astonish her.

"So little time," she thought.

After what seemed like an eternity, the StarSinger reached the last phase of her calling. She could feel the elemental magic of earth build within her.

"Castle rock, mortar and steel,
Hear my summons, answer with zeal,"

"Rise up from your slumber and open your eyes.
Feel with your heart the hue and the cry."
Of all those the dark elf occupy."

"Castle rock, mortar and steel,
Hear my summons, answer with zeal,"

"Destroy the invaders, evil and depraved.
Their pleas for mercy, for lenience, do not cave.
Put them in the dirt, put them in their graves"

"Castle rock, mortar and steel,
Hear my summons, answer with zeal,"

"HOC PRAECEPTUM!"

The walls surrounding the great western gate of Taranthi rattled and shook, accompanied by a rumbling deep within the earth. The fighting ceased as both the dark elves and Marines looked towards the source of the disturbance. The Marines watched as dark elf archers, knocked from their perches in the battlements, fell fifty feet to their deaths. The dark elves on the ground, unsure of what was happening, turned their backs on the Marines and cautiously approached the wall to check on their fallen comrades.

Suddenly two forty-foot sections of the wall, one on each side of the gate, broke away and rose out of the ground, growing to ninety feet. The lower half formed into massive legs while arms and hands grew from each side. The two colossal stone elementals reached up and grabbed what few black elves still clung to them and flung them over the city and into the Bay of Sorrow.

Panic gripped the dark elves on the ground. Those that tried to get past the elementals and out of the city were smashed with huge closed fists or stomped into the ground. Those that ran back into the city met the blades of the Marine phalanx. Within minutes the immediate threat of the dark elves had been eliminated. The elementals, their work finished, settled back into the earth and returned to their rightful place as guardian walls to the city of Taranthi.

With the threat of dark elf reinforcements over for the moment, Colonel Tirion released the Marines to search for dark elf survivors. They were to be put to death. There was no place on Aster for the dark elf race. His Marines took to the task like the professionals they were… dispatching survivors without emotion or remorse. By the time they had finished, the only dark elf alive in that part of Taranthi was the female translator, Song Jingyi, who hated her race even more than the Taranthi citizens enslaved by them.

Colonel Tirion, confident his post-battle orders were being carried out, turned his attention to the stack of barrels hiding Nefertari and the dark elf translator. Little Jimmy had run off as soon as the mêlée had ended. The Marine expected Nefertari to be up by now and helping his injured Marines, but he couldn't spot her anywhere. He covered the distance to the barrels in several long strides. What he saw turned his blood cold. Nefertari was on the ground with Song Jingyi kneeling over her. Lying next to her was the wooden staff she always carried. It was black and charred.

Song Jingyi looked up as Colonel Tirion approached. "I can't feel her heartbeat."

As near as Colonel Tirion could see, there was no clear physical damage, but that meant nothing when magic was involved. He kneeled next to the dark elf and took Nefertari's hand. He felt for a pulse but couldn't find one. Then he grabbed one of his daggers, wiped the blade off on his sleeve to return its shine, and held it to her nose to check her breath. She wasn't breathing.

Colonel Tirion cupped Nefertari's face between his two callused hands. "Don't you do this to me!" he pleaded, even though he knew it was pointless.

Deeper inside the city he heard fighting – swords, maces, and daggers clanging on shields and body armor – the agonized screams of the wounded, and the pleading of those about to die. In Colonel Tirion's sorrow over Nefertari, he had put the remaining dark elf army still in the other parts of Taranthi out of his mind.

"Colonel, we must make our escape," Song Jingyi said.

Colonel Tirion shook his head. He'd grieve later. Right now there was still a war to be fought and won. "No point now. We can't do anything beyond the city, not without Nefertari. But it sounds as if the good people of Taranthi are taking our lead and beginning to fight back." The Marine colonel looked at Song Jingyi. "Your dark elf brethren treated you like a piece of dirt."

Song Jingyi hung her head. "It's the way of our people. Females in my society are slaves. We cook, clean, and have babies. I'm an exception, but even my special abilities doesn't leave me immune to the wishes... and perversions... of the males."

Colonel Tirion grimaced in anger. "I'm sorry."

Song Jingyi shrugged. "Dark elf females never had a taste of freedom... or hope for the future. The only love we're allowed is for our daughters. Our sons are taken from us soon after birth. We endure while we wait for the deliverance of death." The dark elf translator looked at the Marine. "I don't want your pity. But I would like a chance to earn my freedom… and the hope of a better future."

Colonel Tirion nodded. "Let's put you on that road. You're good with your daggers. How would you like to extract a little more revenge?"

In an instant both of her daggers were in her hands. "I'd enjoy that very much."

Colonel Tirion stood and rallied his fellow Marines around him. One hundred determined warriors answered his summons and listened to his plan to help the citizens of Taranthi defeat their oppressor. Each Marine raised their weapons into the air and screamed, "Oorah!"

Colonel Tirion kneeled and gently eased Nefertari's body closer to the barrels. He'd return to it as soon as he could. He then motioned for the tattered cloak of one of the several Marines gathered and covered the priestess up to her neck. Bending over, he kissed her on the lips before draping the cloak over her face. As an afterthought, he grabbed the charred staff and tucked it under the cloak beside her. Without thinking, the Marine colonel wiped his trouser leg to remove the black soot that had rubbed off the staff and onto his hand.

Maedhros Nénmacil, surrounded by dark elves, sensed the StarSinger go black in his mind. His anger turned to worry for the priestess, and suddenly the mission given him by Sehanine StarEagle had even less appeal. The creation stone shrugged off his injuries and rose from the ground. The dark elves warriors screeched and backed up, but the dark elf sorcerers held their ground and began to conjure a fresh batch of offensive magical spells.

Maedhros Nénmacil opened his eyes. The sorcerers paused in their spell invocations and stared at the large, angry eyes gazing at them. As they watched, dozens of stone blades, as sharp as any steel, materialized out of the creation stone's body.

"You have done this," Maedhros Nénmacil said. His grated voice reflected his full fury and the concern he had for Nefertari.

This time the sorcerers backed up a step, their spells forgotten. The creation stone laughed. Never in his existence had he experienced such emptiness in his soul for a species or race of beings then he did at that moment. Along with that came a sense of freedom… a sense of self-determination without the normal restrictions he always placed upon himself. For the first time in his long life he felt free to do what was required without concern for the consequences.

Maedhros Nénmacil began to spin. Faster and faster he went until his enemy could see only the outline of his blades. He approached the sorcerers who stood paralyzed with fear. His advance was deliberate and slow. The creation stone knew he risked giving them time to invoke defensive magic. He didn't care. He relished the fear he saw in their eyes. As he approached, they dropped to their knees and pleaded for mercy. It was too late. Maedhros Nénmacil's intentions were the opposite of mercy. He wanted them to feel pain… to experience true terror… as he flayed and hacked them apart piece by piece.

The angry immortal hamstrung the sorcerers so they couldn't run away. The warriors were long gone back towards Taranthi. *"That's okay,"* the creation stone thought. *"There'd be plenty of time for them later."*

The sorcerer's screams of agony brought a pleasant sensation to Maedhros Nénmacil… a satisfaction that was even greater than when he avenged the people crucified outside Taranthi's walls. Though the creation stone had learned how to kill long ago, he never enjoyed it… until now. Somewhere deep inside he understood something had radically changed in his view of the universe. But he'd ponder upon that another day.

Screams filled the forest. They echoed through the trees causing birds to leave their perches for the safety of the sky and small land creatures to seek their barrows. Though the screams themselves were almost too unbearable to endure, a great healing balm seemed to settle over the forest upon their conclusion, much like the peace that settles upon a new mother holding a child after the rigors of labor.

Eric the Black looked around in irritation, but relaxed once the screaming stopped. There was too much to do, too much at stake, to take time to investigate. Kyleigh, though, didn't appear to have heard as she stood over the *Ak-Séregon Stone* with her great-sword, *Ah-RahnVakha*, held into the air. The stone was trying to dissuade Kyleigh with bolts of energy. Her attack was tentative at first, and unlike the energy that had hit Eric the Black, meant to warn and not harm.

But it wasn't long before the stone began to assail Kyleigh with a killing vigor. The *Ak-Vanessë Stone* buried in Kyleigh's chest absorbed each assault and transferred it to *Ah-RahnVakha*. The queen's sword glowed, and jagged beams of power ran up the blade and discharged into the air.

"You cannot destroy me so easily," Kyleigh told the stone. "Now, calm yourself. Your childish quest for power is putting two worlds at risk."

"What do you know of power, mortal!" the *Ak-Séregon Stone* screamed into the minds of Kyleigh, Eric the Black, Eirwen, and Yury. *"I deserve more than this backwater planet can offer... and I intend to take it regardless of the consequences to this world or any other! The lives of mortals mean little to me! I'm beyond that!"*

"Well that's comforting," Eric the Black remarked.

"It's gone mad," Yury said. "How are you going to convince it...?"

"Convince me of what?!" the stone interrupted. *"Convince me to spare your lives?! Convince me to go back to the way it was?! You are fools if you believe that!"*

The *Ak-Séregon Stone* glowed so brightly everyone had to shield their eyes. Suddenly an invisible wall of force hit and sent them flying back. Even the *Ak-Vanessë Stone* appeared surprised by the power behind the assault. After picking themselves up, they decided it best to continue at a safer distance.

"This will be harder than I expected," the *Ak-Vanessë Stone* said in Kyleigh's mind.

"Can she listen in to our conversation?" Kyleigh asked as she stood.

"No… at least not now," the *Ak-Vanessë Stone* replied. *"But she grows stronger by the minute. We need to act at once before it's too late. I'll try to calm or distract her while the sorcerer opens the corridor for Eirwen and Yury to enter. Once that's been done, it's up to the time walker."*

"I believe Eirwen knows what to do," Kyleigh said. *"Will she and Yury survive?"*

Kyleigh felt a sigh in her mind.

"It's unlikely," the *Ak-Vanessë* Stone answered. *"But both of them understand the risks and are willing to take them."*

Kyleigh nodded in resignation and said a prayer for the souls of the time walker and her brave sailor companion. Then she repeated what she'd just been told by the *Ak-Vanessë* Stone… everything excerpt the stone's opinion about the probable outcome for Yury and Eirwen. "We must act before the *Ak-Séregon Stone* becomes too strong," Kyleigh said in conclusion.

"I'm ready," Eric the Black said as he sat, crossed his legs, and began an incantation. A large portal appeared in front of him. Inside the portal only darkness existed, a deep onyx that felt insidious and evil.

"That's not the corridor I remember," the sorcerer remarked. "It's been… despoiled."

Kyleigh nodded. "It's even worse than I thought. Much worse than when I used it to come over here. And that was bad enough."

The *Ak-Vanessë Stone* glowed brightly in the Alfheim queen's chest and detached itself. The *Ak-Séregon Stone* answered in kind. For a moment both stones battled through a kaleidoscope of colors until they reached an accord on olive green – the color of peace.

"Now," Eric the Black shouted.

Yury picked up Eirwen and ran into the portal. There was a flash, and the portal, along with Yury and Eirwen, disappeared.

Maedhros Nénmacil, covered in the blood of the sorcerers, retracted his blades, and rose above the tree line and looked toward Taranthi. He saw smoke rising from the center of the city and he heard the faint sounds of explosions. He rotated to look at the burned clearing a few hundred yards away. None of the dark elf warriors had run in that direction, so there was no threat to the four people now approaching the *Ak-Séregon Stone…* the people he assumed he'd just saved.

"My work is finished, goddess," the creation stone announced in his mind.

There was silence at first. *"No, creation stone, it isn't,"* Sehanine StarEagle replied. *"Here, yes. But not in the mortal city of Taranthi. Nefertari has fallen."*

Maedhros Nénmacil, stunned by this announcement, refused to believe it. The StarSinger and the mighty Marine colonel couldn't fall. It wasn't possible. He turned and looked back towards the city. The smoke trailing up from its center mocked and accused him. But if the goddess is right…

"HOW COULD YOU HAVE LET THIS HAPPEN?!" his mind roared. *"She was your only priestess, and you didn't protect her?!"*

"She made her choice," Sehanine StarEagle replied. *"Her argument was forceful and came from her heart. Why would I not give her the power to do what she asked?"*

The creation stone raged. *"So you just waved your magic wand and let her go to her death?!"*

The goddess of the five elements sighed. *"No! I allowed her to travel her own path. Was that so wrong?"*

Maedhros Nénmacil dropped and immersed himself in a nearby deep spring to wash away the blood of the sorcerers... and the stink he smelled from his inability to protect his friend the StarSinger when she most needed it.

The water didn't help much. He still felt dirty. The creation stone flew straight up into the sky. "Without the StarSinger my purpose on this world ends," he said aloud as he began to gain altitude. "I'm not your servant and will no longer do your bidding. There are other worlds, other places, even other gods worthier."

By now the creation stone was well above Aster. The smoke from Taranthi dimmed from view. Maedhros Nénmacil saw InnisRos grow smaller. To the east, the mainland on the other side of the Ocean of the Heavens, to the west, another land far away, and then the emptiness of space to match his soul. *"I don't know if she's dead,"* Sehanine StarEagle said.

Maedhros Nénmacil stopped. *"Explain yourself!"* he demanded.

"I can't find her soul," the goddess admitted. *"That's what I wanted you to do."*

"Find her soul?" the creation stone said in disbelief. *"You mean you've lost it?!"*

Sehanine StarEagle sighed. *"Peace, Maedhros Nénmacil. Many extraordinary things have been happening. I'm not the only goddess to lose control of things. It's possible I can't find her soul because she's not dead. Maybe she's hiding. Or recuperating. Perhaps she used a transference spell."*

"That's sorcerer magic..." Maedhros Nénmacil said then stopped. *"Wait a minute..."* Suddenly everything made sense – the simple wooden staff she always carried, her association with the sorcerer Eric the Black at Calmacil Clearing, and the strange necklace she'd worn around her neck ever since they'd left the monastery. She never explained from whom she received it before she, Colonel Tirion, and

he left for Taranthi. *"Why that sneaky, little sorcerer weasel,"* he said. *"He and Nefertari had it planned all along!"*

"What?"

The creation stone shook his head. *"I have an idea, goddess, but I need to verify it."* A tentative feeling of relief flowed from the goddess to Maedhros Nénmacil's mind.

"Please hurry," Sehanine StarEagle pleaded. *"Despite what you might think, I love her dearly and wish to see her unharmed."*

Maedhros Nénmacil didn't reply as he reversed his direction and descended back to Aster. He knew exactly where he was going.

Colonel Tirion had tears in his eyes as he led his Marines towards the fighting. It'd been thirty years since he'd cried. That was the day his mother had died at the hands of human outlaws. They raped her for two days before slitting her throat and leaving. The soon-to-be Marine was part of the posse that ran them down and brought them back for trial and the hanging they so richly deserved. And though it served justice, the young Colonel Tirion wasn't satisfied, for he also blamed one other. If his father hadn't abandoned them for the mainland, if he had stayed and fulfilled his responsibility to his wife and son, he might have stopped the attack that brutalized and murdered the Marine's mother. Colonel Tirion vowed one day he'd quit the Marines and seek his own justice on the father he had come to hate. But loving Nefertari changed him. His feelings for the priestess forced him to move on from his personal demons. Now he had only her memory to give him succor.

Colonel Tirion and his Marines came upon injured and deceased civilians and dark elves, a few locked in death grips with their opponent. The city populace was fighting back, and by the looks of it was giving a good account of themselves.

The colonel turned to his field medics. "Help as many as you can," he said before addressing several other Marines. "Kill any dark elf survivors and get back to us as soon as possible."

Colonel Tirion led the rest of the Marines forward. The ongoing battle was very fluid as it moved between streets and alleyways. The screams of the wounded, or for the dead by mourners, continued to get louder and appeared to be concentrated in or around the Bâr Ennorath, a large heavily treed park in the center of Taranthi. Explosions rocked the center of the park as Colonel Tirion called a halt to his advance.

"Those explosions will piss a bunch of people off, Colonel," a gruff sergeant commented.

Colonel Tirion nodded agreement. To an elf the forest is sacred. "It makes my blood boil also, sergeant," he replied as he looked at his warriors. "You!" he called to another sergeant. "Come here! I have a job for you two."

"Sir!" both sergeants said.

Colonel Tirion kneeled and pulled out a dagger to draw in the dirt. "I want each of you to take twenty-five Marines and flank each side of the battle. Locate the enemy and move behind them. Keep your scouts out in front of your columns. You don't want to get surprised yourself."

"Yes sir!"

Colonel Tirion nodded. "Position yourselves on their rear flanks… about here… and wait."

A large explosion, most likely a fire spell, rumbled from the direction of the battle. There was a fresh chorus of screams, and more smoke rose from the trees.

"Wait for me to attack their center," Colonel Tirion remarked. "But hold your assault until they've engaged me. I don't want them to know you're there until it's too late. And make sure you have someone train arrows on their sorcerers. I want them to go down first."

"Colonel, we're going in blind. Shouldn't we send scouts first to see just what's happening?"

"Yes we should," Colonel Tirion replied. "But that'll take time we don't have. If the dark elf breaks the backs of the resistance, we might never get another chance."

"With that damned corridor open they can always bring in reinforcements from their home world," the other sergeant remarked. "We should be attacking that."

"That's true, but without Nefertari…" Colonel Tirion's voice broke and it took a few moments for him to compose himself, "… there's nothing we can do about the corridor. We can only hope other folks are working to close it. The only thing we're left with is to play our part and hope they play theirs."

The Marine colonel looked at his Marine noncom's. "Do either of you have questions?"

Both shook their heads.

Colonel Tirion nodded and shook both sergeants' hands. "Oorah!"

"Oorah!"

The battle for Taranthi was over in an hour. The appearance of the Marines completely surprised the dark elves. Dark elf sorcerers, scorched by arrow fire, offered little resistance and, without their help, the main body of the dark elf fighting force was overrun. Colonel Tirion and his Marines – now numbering seventy-five – watched impassively as the civilian population butchered the dark elf survivors. That evening, as the Marines rested, armed civilians combed the city in search of dark elves trying to hide. They found a few. Fresh screams filled the night air.

Colonel Tirion left the senior sergeant in charge of the Marines and, with Song Jingyi, covered in the blood of her own people, returned to the western gate. Nefertari's body had disappeared along with her staff. Colonel Tirion sat, his back against the barrels, and buried his head in his arms and wept. Song Jingyi stood guard to stop anyone from approaching the colonel during his time of sorrow.

Eirwen and Yury were in a dark place. It felt as though they were disembodied, like incorporeal beings floating in a place where reality seemed a distant memory. Yet when they moved, they felt substance beneath their feet. The only light Yury could see was the pinpricks of illumination coming from Eirwen's blind eyes, except she was no longer blind.

"Yury, please put me down," Eirwen requested.

"Huh? Oh yeah," Yury said as he lowered the time walker from his arms. "Is it safe?"

"Perfectly so," Eirwen replied.

Though he had put Eirwen back on her feet, he didn't release her hand. He now needed her to lead him. "Are we in the corridor?" he asked.

"Not exactly," Eirwen replied. "As we've surmised, the corridor's been corrupted by the *Ak-Séregon Stone*. I've never traveled the corridor like Kyleigh has, so I'm not sure how it works. But I know this much. The great distances that must be traveled between two worlds in real-space also has an aspect of time control wrapped around the core of its existence."

Yury grunted. He didn't understand the correlation between distance and time.

Eirwen looked up at the giant and smiled, though she doubted he saw it. "What I mean is you can't step into the corridor here on Aster and come out on the Alfheim a few minutes later without some sort of time manipulation. The distance in real miles between Aster and the Alfheim is unimaginable. Indeed, the Alfheim may not even be in the same universe." The time walker paused. "This is powerful magic, Yury." There was a sense of awe in her voice. "Incredibly strong magic!"

"Most relic magic is."

Eirwen shook her head. "Not like this."

Yury shut his eyes for a moment rubbed them. The constant darkness was beginning to close in around him. "We know the stone corrupted it."

Eirwen nodded. "Yes. But knowing that isn't going to solve our problem. We need to understand HOW it was corrupted."

"And?"

"The stone, in her quest for power, has done something that my people have only hypothesized," Eirwen answered. "She's overlapped the time streams of past, present, and future. The corridor serves as the juxtaposition point."

Yury looked at the light coming from Eirwen's eyes. They were his only anchor points. "So that means the *Ak-Séregon Stone* can draw power from this universe's past, present, and future?" he asked. Before meeting Eirwen, he'd never given time much consideration beyond grumbling about the length of the mid-morning watch.

"Probably several universes," Eirwen replied. "I doubt if even the gods can do that. It's like I said… strong magic."

"Okay, then how did the stone do it?"

"I'm not completely sure," the time walker replied. "Yury, think about it. The stone's tapping into the power of several universes. But not just as they are today. She's also using them as they were in the past… and will be in the future. Imagine the raw power waiting to be released by a young universe. Or how polished, for want of a better word, the power of a universe that's been in existence for billions of years must be. Somehow she's coalesced this power and is using it without being destroyed."

Yury scratched his beard. "How can you stop something as strong as that?" he asked.

Eirwen frowned. "I believe I know what's needed. And I'm fairly certain I can control the outcome. But…"

The time walker stopped talking. After a long minute, Yury asked if she was all right.

"Yury, my dear," Eirwen said. "I wish you could see what I'm seeing right now. It's magnificent!"

Maedhros Nénmacil flew the body of Nefertari, along with her staff, back to the forest and landed in a secluded spot well away from Taranthi and the *Ak-Séregon Stone*. He gently rewrapped her in the same tattered cloak he'd found her under. As he turned his attention to the staff, a small squirrel approached to investigate.

"How are you, my brave little friend," the creation stone asked as he held up the staff and examined it. "Something's quite different about this. More than wood, I should think."

The squirrel squeaked acknowledgement and moved closer to get a better look.

Maedhros Nénmacil rubbed the soot off the staff with a soft hand – blades weren't his only appendages – and studied the white which lie beneath the blackened surface. It was warm to the touch and glowed. Draped around the staff was the necklace Nefertari had been wearing. The locket attached to it was embedded into the staff's side.

"Look, little friend," Maedhros Nénmacil said as he showed the staff to the squirrel. "Something has changed the staff from wood to… hmm… I believe pearl. Yes, that's it, solid pearl."

The squirrel jumped up on the massive creation stone for a better look. As fearful as people were of Maedhros Nénmacil, animals seemed to always feel safe and at home with him.

"Be careful not to touch," the creation stone warned. "I don't know what affect it might have."

The squirrel chattered a response.

Maedhros Nénmacil laughed. "Yes, yes, you're right. It IS a most unusual thing. But I know just the person to figure this out for me and, if I'm right, bring my dear StarSinger back. And if that happens, I'll never abandon her again."

The squirrel scrambled down Maedhros Nénmacil's side and settle onto the ground. "Be safe, my little friend," the creation stone said as he rose once again into the air tightly clutching Nefertari and the staff.

Kyleigh and Eric the Black waited. Neither expected Eirwen and Yury to return, but both hoped for a sign the *Ak-Séregon Stone* had been stopped.

"Anything from your stone," Eric the Black asked. "You're in touch with her, right?"

Kyleigh shook her head as she looked at the *Ak-Vanessë Stone* lying on the ground. "Not since you opened the corridor. I'm as much in the dark as you are."

Eric the Black began to pace. "If this doesn't work…" He left the rest unsaid.

The Alfheim queen sighed. She was beginning to think she'd never see her beloved lands again. Then something caught her eye… something exceptionally large and above her. Kyleigh looked up to see a massive boulder floating down from the sky. It was carrying a cloak-wrapped body and a white staff. She drew *Ah-RahnVakha* and stood ready to release its power. As she waited, she glanced at Eric the Black who seemed unconcerned as the boulder approached. The boulder hovered several feet away and laid a body and a white staff on the ground before settling down on the blackened earth.

"So she had to use the transference spell," Eric the Black said as he went over to where the creation stone had lain the body of Nefertari and her staff.

"It wouldn't have done her any good if I hadn't figured it out," Maedhros Nénmacil said. "She'd be in that staff forever. For once I'd like to meet a sorcerer who actually explains things."

Eric the Black kneeled next to Nefertari and studied the staff and the necklace attached to it. "I'd have known, Maedhros Nénmacil," he said.

"And if you were dead?!"

Eric the Black didn't bother to respond to the creation stone's accusation as he continued to examine the staff. "It appears she did everything right."

"Then get her out!" the creation stone grated.

Kyleigh returned her sword to its scabbard and walked over to the two. "Eric?"

The sorcerer ignored her, but the creation stone rotated to look at the queen. "I beg your pardon, my lady. Please forgive my poor manners. I'm Maedhros Nénmacil, guardian to the StarSinger, Nefertari."

"And that's..." Kyleigh said.

"Quite right," the creation stone replied. "That's the StarSinger..."

"Stop your blabbering," Eric the Black admonished. "I'm trying to concentrate. Or maybe you'd prefer the priestess stay a staff?"

Both held their tongues. There'd be time for explanations later.

Colonel Tirion crossed the small square in front of the western gate to meet several of his Marines approaching from the center of the city. Several of the locals followed.

"Colonel, I'd like you to meet Taranthi's mayor," the lead Marine, one of the two sergeants who had helped him lead the assault on the dark elves, said.

Though the person who stood in front of the colonel with his hand outstretched was one of the powerful elites on the island, Colonel Tirion didn't have a clue what his name was. "Pleased to meet you, sir," he replied as he shook the hand. It wasn't soft or pampered as he'd expected, but instead calloused and rough – the hands of someone who wasn't a stranger to physical work.

The mayor looked at the Marine colonel with a glimmer in his eyes – eyes that showed experience, intelligence, and someone at ease with command responsibilities. Though the mayor was a politician, Colonel Tirion saw no trace he was anything other than what he presented.

"Connak Feynore, Colonel," the mayor said. "It's a pleasure to meet the Marine who saved my city."

Colonel Tirion nodded. "I had plenty of help," he replied.

Mayor Feynore smiled. "Indeed, you did! Your Marines fought magnificently."

"They aren't really my Marines. Most of them are veterans who live here in your city. They were defending their homes."

"Sir, we must go," one of the mayor's staff interrupted. Unlike the mayor, this elf and the other two that stood with him looked to be typical government popinjays.

The mayor turned on them. "Leave," he said.

"But Your Honor…"

"I said leave," Mayor Feynore ordered. This time there was more force in the tone of his voice. "Organize a detail of volunteers and go back to the palace. It's high time we cleanse the place of dark elf stink. Then clean up city hall."

"You want us to clean?"

Mayor Feynore nodded. "On your hands and knees, if necessary. Now go!"

The mayor turned to Colonel Tirion and shook his head. "I'm sorry, but I didn't get to pick all of my assistants," he explained. "A few are hangers on from Mordecai's government, though I haven't seen the First Councilor around lately. That's more stink that needs to be cleaned up."

Colonel Tirion smiled and nodded. "I'm sure you're up to the challenge, sir. Now, if you'll excuse me, I have other, more pressing matters that require my attention."

"Hear the mayor out, Colonel" a sergeant said.

"He needs more time," Song Jingyi retorted. She'd kept herself in the background, almost to the point of invisibility. It was what her dark elf masters had expected, and old habits die hard. But she knew she owed Colonel Tirion and the priestess Nefertari her freedom as well as her life. To repay that debt, she'd be their guardian, when required, and their friend if they'd accept her. "He needs to find out what happened to the priestess," she added. Song Jingyi had observed the exchange between Nefertari and her goddess. She watched what Nefertari did to defeat the dark elves. A priestess that powerful wouldn't just die. She'd have an escape route planned. Now they needed time to figure out what it was. Sacrifice for the greater good was a foreign concept to the dark elf.

"I'll only take a few minutes of your time," Mayor Feynore pleaded.

Colonel Tirion looked at the people staring at him. Song Jingyi was impassive. She'd probably support whatever he decided. He felt comfortable having her around and trusted she wouldn't go rogue on him. While there's no longer much need for a translator, she had value as a warrior. She'd fought like a hellion against the dark elves.

The mayor, his two sergeants, and the other Marines gathered around patiently waited him out. Whatever it was the mayor wished to discuss had them excited.

The colonel pushed his personal distress aside and nodded. "Very well, Mayor Feynore. What do you wish to discuss?"

The mayor smiled. "Well, Colonel, I'm thinking about putting together a few of my boys and going north after that dark elf army attacking Calmacil Clearing. The queen's up there and I suspect she could use our help." Mayor Feynore paused as he looked over at the western gate and the devastation Colonel Tirion's Marines had caused on the much larger dark elf contingent. "We'd sure appreciate it if you and your Marines would go with us."

"Begging your pardon, sir, but we'd sure like to tag along," one of the Marines said.

Colonel Tirion looked at one of his sergeants who smiled. "Still plenty of dark elf heads to knock together," the burly Marine said.

"Do you think your boys can keep up with my Marines," the colonel asked.

"Hell, Colonel, most of my boys are former Army."

"Just answer the question," a Marine voice called out, unimpressed.

Mayor Feynore looked at the Marine faces surrounding him and for the first time wasn't so sure of himself. "We'll keep up," he vowed.

"My command?" Colonel Tirion asked.

The mayor nodded. "Yes. Your command."

"Have your people outside the main gate before first light tomorrow," Colonel Tirion ordered. "Make sure they have enough field rations for several days and all the weapons, shields, and armor they can carry."

The mayor nodded. "We'll be ready," he said as he turned away.

"Oh, and Mayor Feynore," Colonel Tirion called out to the retreating mayor, forcing him to stop and turn. "I don't want any kids dreaming of glory or old folks who want to relive their past to be part of this. I don't need them on my conscience."

The mayor of Taranthi nodded and walked away.

"Your orders, sir?"

Colonel Tirion looked at the sergeant, then at the dead Marines who were even now being collected and laid in a long row. "Build a pyre. Have everyone assembled within the hour for honors."

As the sergeant walked away, Colonel Tirion looked up, closed his eyes, and took a deep breath. He was exhausted.

"Colonel?" Song Jingyi inquired.

Colonel Tirion shook his head to dash away his melancholy and went to help his Marines gather the dead.

"What's going on," Yury exclaimed. "I can't see a damned thing!"

Eirwen had been silent for several minutes as she examined the timelines. The combined streams sparkled in multi-colored splendor… but its beauty no longer fascinated the time walker. She was trying to decide how to separate the past, present, and future timeline triad.

"Hush, Yury," Eirwen said. "This might be more complicated than I thought."

"What are you seeing," the giant asked.

Eirwen sighed. Not because she had been interrupted, but because she could almost see the solution, and each time it started to become clear, "poof", gone. "Think of a rope made of several strands of hemp wound together. Each strand, on its own, isn't too strong. But when added to other strands…"

"It's stronger than its individual components," Yury said, finishing Eirwen's thought.

Eirwen squeezed Yury's hand. "Correct," she replied. "The three time lines are like strands of a rope, tightly wound together. And from this, other time strands begin, similar to a tree trunk with many branches. At first, I believed I needed to determine how it was corrupted. But I now realize that's not the answer. I need to find where it was first corrupted and stop the strands from coming together."

"Where it was corrupted?" Yury questioned. "You mean go into the past?"

Eirwen chuckled. "Forget about past, present or future. Those don't exist here. It's just us and the time rope."

Yury grunted. "Sounds like we follow the rope backwards, then."

"Precisely," Eirwen said. "And who better than a time walker to do that, eh?"

Nefertari floated in a sea of blackness. Though aware, all her senses had deserted her. Such was her predicament she doubted she was even alive.

"So this is eternity," she thought.

Suddenly she felt herself being pulled. Faster and faster she went, onward towards an unknown destination.

"Even death has its surprises," she said to the void just as she lost consciousness.

"Far away, distance unparalleled.
Through the ethereal, the celestial sentinel."

"Find the soul my magic displaced,
into the staff prepared in haste."

Bring her forth, reunite.
Soul to body, her birthright."

"FIAT VOLUNTAS MEA"

Nothing happened.

"Usually when a sorcerer speaks the command, there's explosions, loud noises, and strange manifestations," Maedhros Nénmacil commented dryly. "Isn't that how it's supposed to work?"

Eric the Black ignored the creation stone and went through the conjuration again, with the same results.

"Eric?" Kyleigh said.

"Shhh," the sorcerer whispered. "I'm thinking."

"Think harder," Kyleigh replied. "This… this… boulder thing is starting to get a bit antsy. And I want Nefertari back."

Maedhros Nénmacil had risen off the ground a few inches and was slowly spinning. It was the equivalent of a husband pacing in worry over the birth of his first born. "Indeed," he replied to Kyleigh's observation. "The StarSinger is my responsibility… and now yours. Bring her back!"

Eric the Black looked at Maedhros Nénmacil and sighed. The creation stone was showing a few blades for affect. "Stop threatening me," he said.

The third time the sorcerer tried to bring Nefertari back failed just like the first two. At this point Eric the Black and Kyleigh were more than just a little concerned. Maedhros Nénmacil, on the other hand, had settled back onto the ground and watched the magic user work. As he did so, he searched for the StarSinger using the bond that existed between them. One way or another he was going to bring Nefertari back.

None of the three saw the *Ak-Séregon Stone* begin to pulsate rapidly.

Eirwen, holding Yury's hand in a vise-like grip, followed the time rope. They weren't walking — at least not as either knew it. But instead they appeared to float along, going in the direction Eirwen willed. Yury remained silent, reluctant to voice his fear of the blackness all around. He understood their future solely depended on the time walker and he didn't want to interfere or be a burden. For now, all he could do was lend her support and strength through the contact they both shared. After an undetermined amount of time, a large sphere of throbbing light became visible in the nothingness ahead.

"It looks like a heartbeat," Yury commented.

"You can see it?" Eirwen asked,

"Yes, and the time rope," the giant replied. "I can't explain it… but it appears my eyes have been opened."

Eirwen squeezed Yury's hand. "What you're seeing is the juxtaposition point of past, present, and future."

"Then we've reached our destination," Yury said.

"We have."

"Now what?"

"Now I separate the three," the time walker replied.

By this time they were next to the sphere, and it was huge. Each of the three time periods were different colors – colors Yury had never seen before – and interwoven tightly together. To Yury it was similar to the ball of wool his grandma-ma used to knit sweaters.

"How in the hell are you going to separate that mess," Yury asked.

Eirwen didn't answer at first. She was busy studying the point where the three strands of time melded to become the sphere. It wasn't long until the solution came to light.

"Eirwen?"

"Huh? Oh, I'm sorry." The time walker turned and looked up at her protector. "Yury, I… Yury, you know that I love you, right?"

The Draugen Pesta giant smiled and nodded. "Yes, though it's good to hear you say it."

The sphere of time pulsated and drove an invisible force against the two, driving them back.

"What was that?!" Yury exclaimed.

"We're being warned away," Eirwen said. "The next time might be worse."

"Then we need to get to work," Yury replied.

Eirwen kissed the back of Yury's hand. "Pick me up," she said.

The giant did so, cradling her in his arms.

"Will you face eternity with me," Eirwen whispered into Yury's ear.

Without hesitation Yury nodded and kissed Eirwen. "Several eternities," he said.

With a tear in her eye, Eirwen hugged Yury hard. She closed her eyes and concentrated on her power. The two of them seemed to blur from reality and back again until they blinked out completely, only to reappear in the past just as the *Ak-Séregon Stone* was drawing her power from the time strands, forcing them together either as an unintended consequence or by design. Eirwen had positioned Yury and herself just before the juxtaposition point.

For a second – or days, years, millenniums – the time walker absorbed the time strands. The sphere, cut off from its power source, slowly unraveled until it no longer existed. Each timeline once again followed along its normal path. But where Eirwen and Yury once stood was empty space.

Nefertari gasped for air. She opened her eyes to blue, cloudless skies broken here and there by tall forest trees. A huge visage came into view and smiled. Stone teeth and warm, expressive eyes stared down at her.

"StarSinger," Maedhros Nénmacil rumbled. "You're back!"

"Step aside," Eric the Black said as he tried to move the creation stone to no avail. He kneeled next to Nefertari and helped her to sit. "How do you feel?"

"Dizzy," Nefertari replied. "But not too bad. I don't like your transference spell, sorcerer!"

"You don't have to like it," Eric the Black grated, "for it to work. And it did. Thank you."

"Nefertari?"

The StarSinger looked to the sound of the voice. It was one she recognized but hadn't heard in many, many years.

"Kyleigh?" Nefertari said as she turned to see her former mentor.

Nefertari stood with Eric the Black's help and embraced the Alfheim queen.

"You've grown, child," Kyleigh said.

"And you've become Queen of the Alfheim," the StarSinger replied, nodding towards the sword *Ah-RahnVakha* and the mantle of royalty draped across Kyleigh's shoulders.

Kyleigh smiled. "You're still the rightful heir... if you're interested."

Nefertari shook her head. "No longer, Highness."

"Kyleigh will be just fine," the Alfheim queen remarked as she smiled. "Being a priestess agrees with you."

"I can think of nothing else I'd rather..."

The *Ak-Séregon Stone* exploded in a flash of brilliant white light. It was bright enough to temporarily blind everyone. When their vision returned, they looked in horror at the stone. All that remained was a blackened, charred, and melted lump. The *Ak-Vanessë Stone*, however, now gleamed with the former's glory.

"She's gone," the *Ak-Vanessë Stone* said in everyone's mind. *"Aster is safe from her corruption and the flow of time has returned to normal. I've taken her place and the corridor to the dark elf world has been cut, while the corridor between Aster and the Alfheim is once again safe."*

"What of Eirwen and Yury?" Kyleigh asked aloud. "Did they survive?"

The *Ak-Vanessë Stone* sighed. *"I don't know. Perhaps. But if they did, they're lost in the fields of time. I wish I could be more encouraging."*

"You only speak the truth as you know it," Kyleigh remarked. "But I refuse to give up. If they're still alive, I'll find them." She turned to Eric the Black. "I can use some help. What say you, sorcerer? Care to accept a commission from the Queen of the Alfheim to help me find and bring them back? Think you're up to the challenge?"

There was a sparkle in Eric the Black's eyes. "Let's first drive the rest of the dark elves off my world. Then we'll talk."

$$\longleftarrow\!\!\!-\!\!\!-\!\!\!-\!\!\!-\;\text{〜}\;-\!\!\!-\!\!\!-\!\!\!-\!\!\!\longrightarrow$$

THE FOURTEENTH INTERREGNUM

Rathal, with Rhys riding beside him, drove his horse eastward through the Forest of the Fey and onto the grasslands north of Lake Lorali. The white dragon had disappeared somewhere in the new mountain range east of the lake. The 'cloud people', as Rhys called them, floated above. It looked as if they were patrolling the skies and guarding against any future effort by the dragon to fly westward toward Elanesse.

"Why does Elanesse intrigue me so," Rathal thought. *"What's in it that causes the cloud people, beings from another world, to die for it against a dragon? And why does the dragon wish to attack it?"*

"We're sitting ducks out here with no cover," Rhys exclaimed. "Can't you mask us?"

Rathal turned his head to the side to look at his comrade. They'd had this conversation several times since entering the open ground of the grasslands. "We don't have a choice," he replied to Rhys's frustration. "Besides, I want the beast to see us. It's the only way I can get it back into the sky."

The master spy shook his head. "At least tell me what your plan is."

"Sorcery, Rhys," Rathal answered. That's all he was willing to admit.

Rhys swore. "Damnit, Rathal! This is madness. We can't defeat that thing by ourselves."

"I can defeat it," Rathal replied.

"THEN WHY DO YOU NEED ME!" Rhys bellowed.

"To take my body back to Havendale," Rathal responded without hesitation. "To put me in the same burial crypt as Amkrissa."

Rhys stared. As he looked at Rathal, he noticed a small drop of blood coming out of the master sorcerer's nose. "I... I..."

"This is a good spot," Rathal said as he stopped his horse and dismounted.

Rhys, now silent, followed suit.

The great white dragon, perched atop the summit of one of the higher mountains east of Lake Lorali, scanned the lands below. To the west was a gigantic lake which teemed with life. The boats of several fishermen, oblivious to the battle that had just occurred in the skies overhead, were pulling in plenty of fish with their nets.

To the southwest, a large city. The white dragon sensed the magical power emanating from behind its walls. *"Sorcerers,"* she thought. The white dragon recoiled. It was an instinctive behavior derived from millennia of battling magic users who wish to enslave dragons to their will. There wasn't much that could hurt her, but sorcerers are at the top of that short list.

As the white dragon continued her examination, she spotted a huge inland sea to the southeast, and fertile lands to the east on the other side of the mountains. Its cities and villages built for giants.

When the white dragon turned her attention to the large grasslands northwest, she noticed two figures riding horses in her direction. As she watched, her interest now peaked, the two figures stopped and dismounted. After a moment, one of the two sat with his legs crossed. She sensed the magic build around him.

"I'll not abide sorcerers!" the white dragon screamed at the azure sky.

Glancing upwards to locate the cloud creatures, she saw they were still east, protecting the city in the forest. Before the white dragon leaped into the sky, determined to destroy the figures on the grasslands, she never felt the rumble of the earth below her feet. So focused was she on the sorcerer she didn't notice the smoke rising from several of the mountains in front of her.

Rhys watched as Rathal conjured his magic. He glanced towards the mountains and saw a huge, pure white figure take to the sky. The master spy thought he should warn Rathal but knew better than to disturb him after he'd begun one of his spells. Besides, if his sorcerer friend's magic didn't stop the dragon, it wouldn't matter.

Blood began pouring from Rathal's nose and ears as he whispered words in a language Rhys didn't recognize. The sorcerer manipulated the magic around him with vocalizations and hand movements. Rathal's fingers danced through the air in gyrations that would have broken the bones of a less practiced person.

Rhys felt a slight tremor in the earth. Dark smoke escaped from the mountains in the dragon's path and curled up into the sky. The shaking became stronger, and the frequency of the undulations in the ground increased. Steam vented from horizontal shafts in the sides of the mountain closest to the white dragon. When the super-heated gases of silicon, various metals, and other materials were exposed to the extreme cold that surrounded the flying white dragon, they solidified into a thick molasses-like substance which fell to the earth and covered the vent shafts. As the substance hardened, it sealed those vent shafts shut. This resulted in the buildup of unrelenting pressure.

To Rhys it looked as if the mountain had become a giant balloon, expanding from forces within that had nowhere to go. The master spy dropped to the ground and covered his ears.

"I'll not abide sorcerers!" the white dragon screamed again as she flew over the smoking mountain. Those were the last words she ever spoke.

The explosion knocked the master sorcerer over on his side, where he lay unconscious. Rhys crawled over to Rathal and turned him over onto his back. The bleeding had stopped, but the sorcerer's breathing was shallow and labored.

Rhys looked around to locate their horses, but the explosion had sent them scampering away. Unsurprised, Rhys looked back at the sorcerer.

"Guess I carry you back," Rhys said aloud. "At least far enough to get help. Saint Seton is the closest."

"No!" Rathal blurted in a ragged voice. "Take me to the golden tree."

"But…"

"Please!" Rathal pleaded.

Rhys sighed and nodded. Though he'd never been there, he knew about the Tree of Golden Radiance in the Forest of the Fey near Elanesse. His job as Havendale's chief spy takes him to many places. His ability to draw information out of the people he meets allows him to discover many secrets and hear many stories.

"It's probably closer than Saint Seton anyway," Rhys said as he lifted Rathal over his shoulder. The sorcerer had lost consciousness again. "Either way, it's going to be a damn long walk."

The explosion of the mountain shook the earth for miles around and threw ash and debris several thousand feet into the air. It wasn't a large explosion, at least as far as volcanoes go, but large enough to obliterate the top half of the mountain. As for the white dragon who was flying over it at the time, the blast instantly blew her apart.

The gigantic release of pressure stabilized the other mountains in the immediate vicinity, which eliminated the potential for a disastrous chain reaction. Over the next few hours the ash and debris fell back to earth. The lack of wind helped to limit the ash fall to the mountain range and no farther.

Days later the first people to climb into the mountains to investigate found pieces of dragon flesh. They were still frozen.

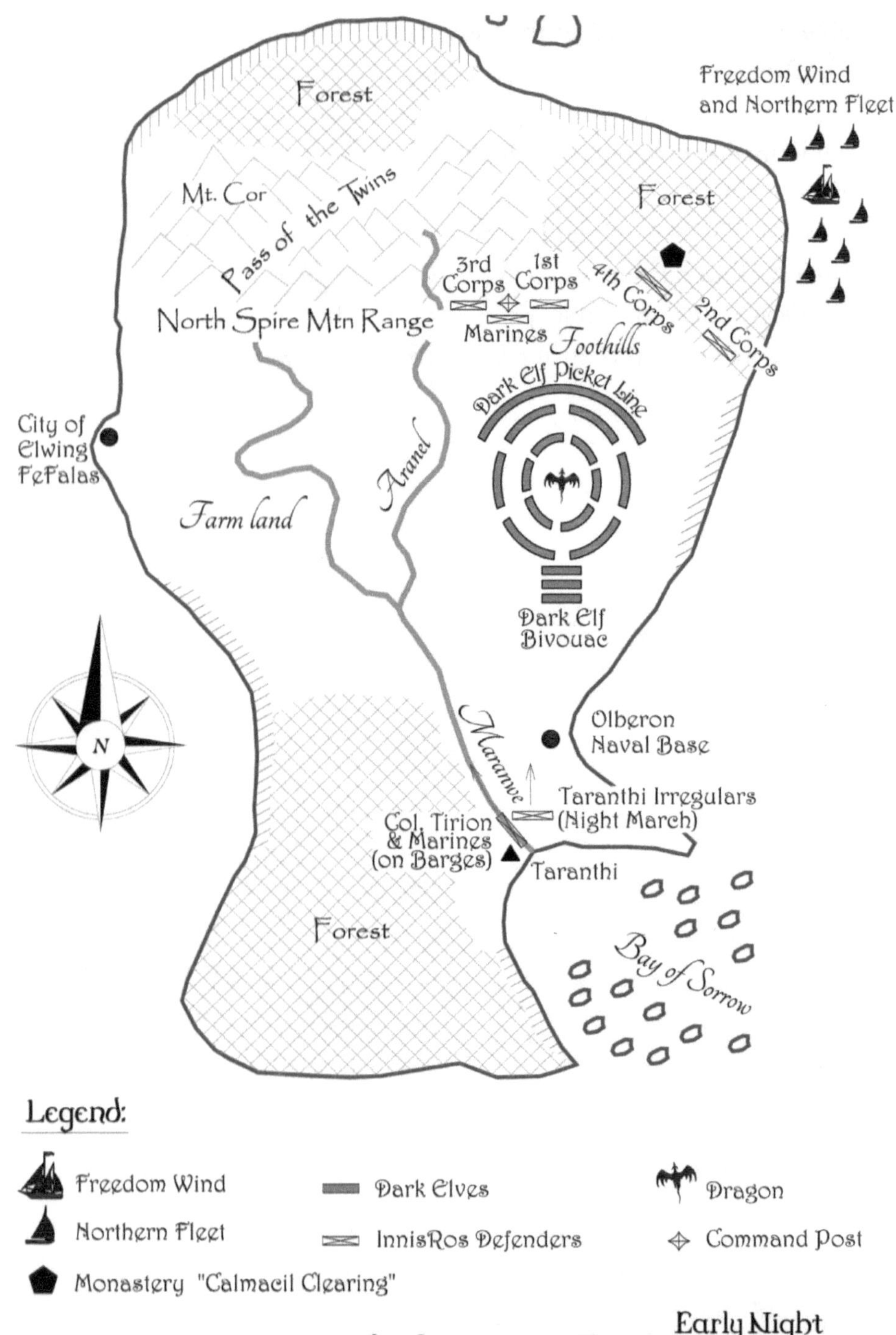

Battle for InnisRos – Early Night Troop Disposition Day Before Battle

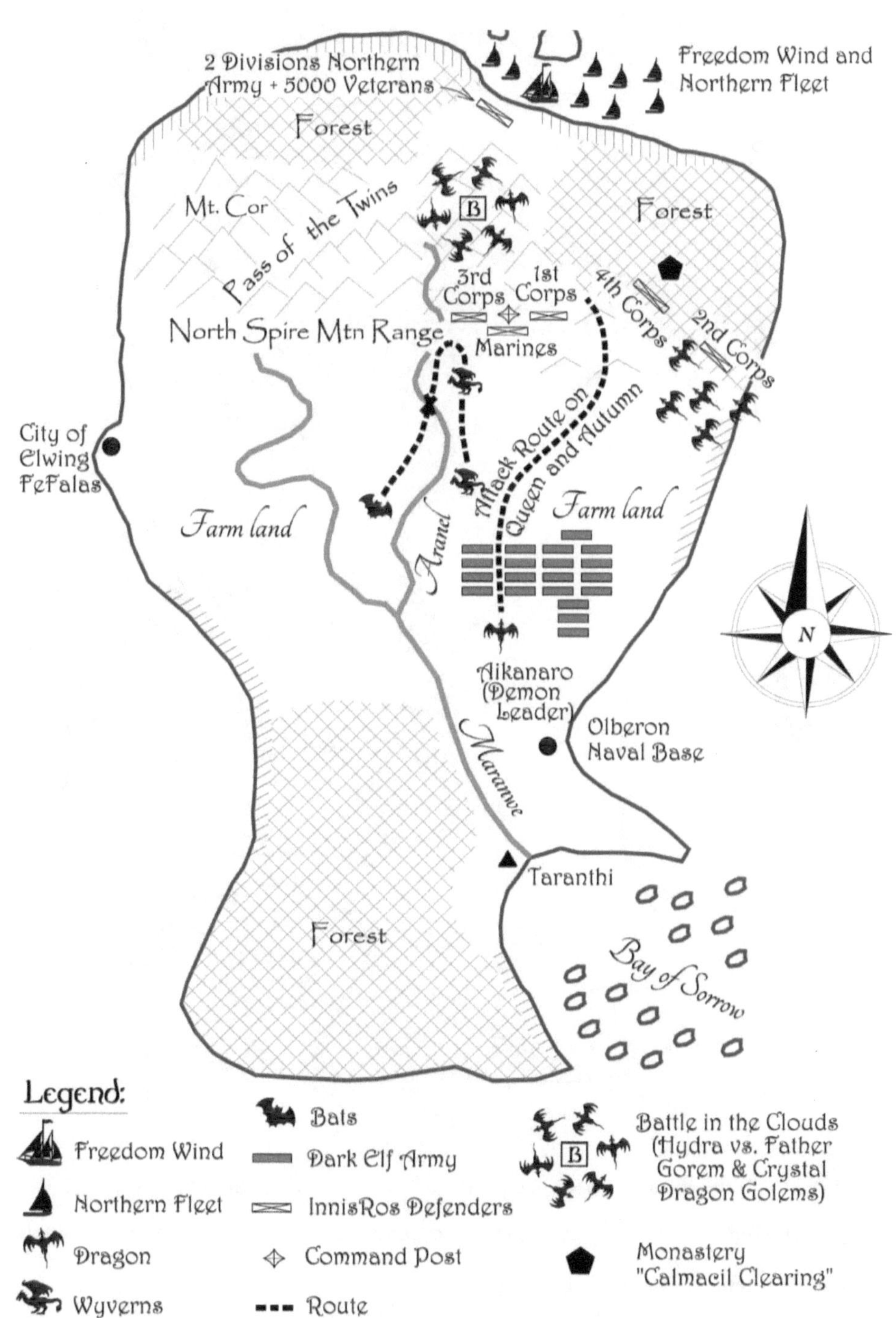

Battle for InnisRos - Day 1

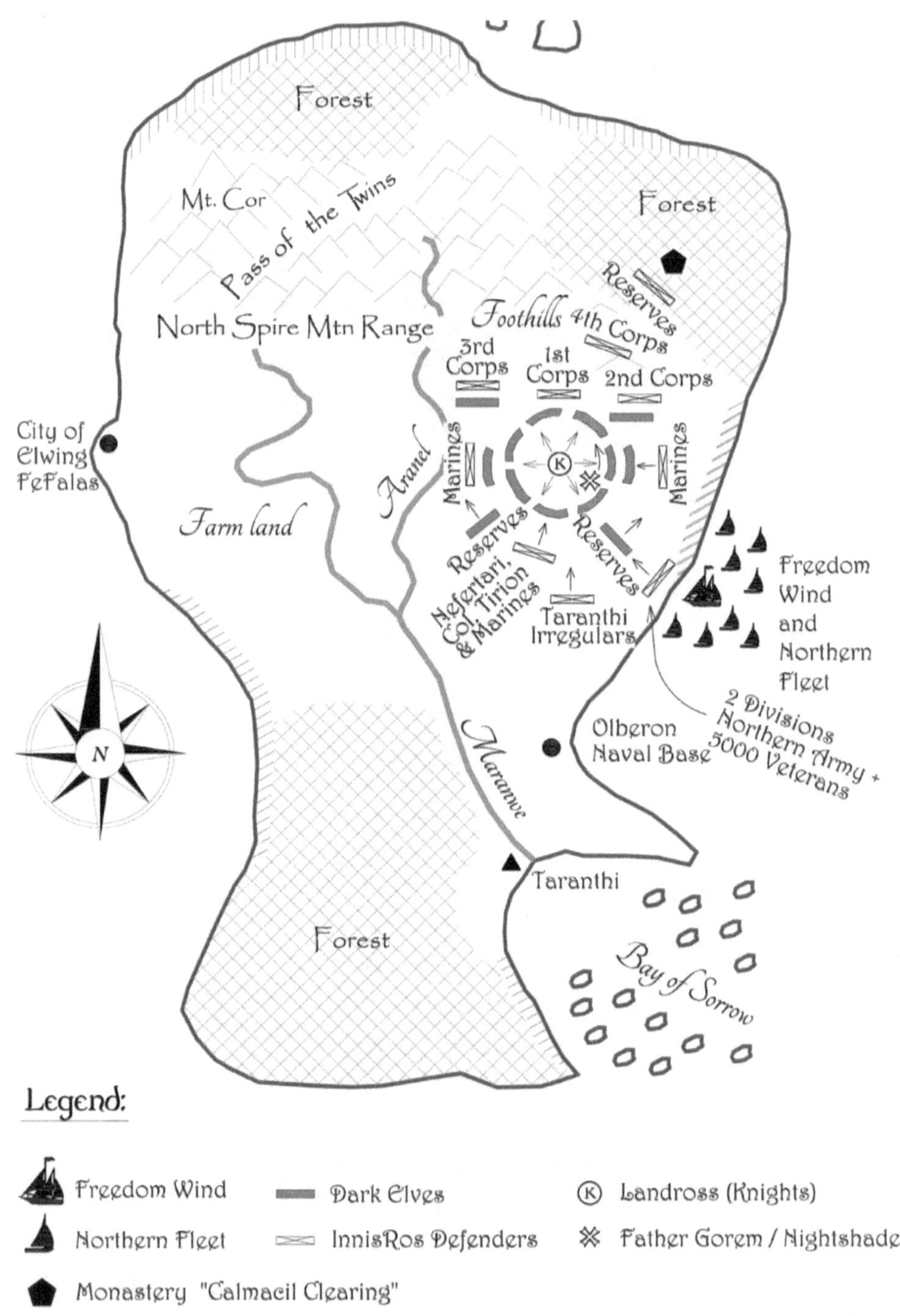

Forest
Forest
Mt. Cor
Pass of the Twins
North Spire Mtn Range
Reserves
Foothills 4th Corps
3rd Corps
1st Corps
2nd Corps
Marines
Marines
Aranel
City of Elwing FeFalas
Farm land
K
Reserves
Reserves
Nefertari, Col. Tirion & Marines
Taranthi Irregulars
Freedom Wind and Northern Fleet
2 Divisions Northern Army + 5000 Veterans
Olberon Naval Base
Maranwe
N
Taranthi
Forest
Bay of Sorrow
Legend:
Freedom Wind
Dark Elves
K Landross (Knights)
Northern Fleet
InnisRos Defenders
Father Gorem / Nightshade
Monastery "Calmacil Clearing"
Battle for InnisRos - Day 2

CHAPTER TWENTY-ONE

InnisRos (Calmacil Clearing)

"And there I was, atop my warhorse cleaving dark elves, when this ugly demon monster appeared right out of thin air right in front of me. Smelled something awful, it did! Like fresh cow dung spread over a week-old rotting corpse. Well, boyo, I gob-smacked that beastie with my trusty battleaxe. Hit it right between the eyes, I did. And it just laughed at me. It was laughing so hard it bent over holding its stomach. Don't look at me like that, boyo. It's true. Every word on my honor as a knight! Anyway, as it stood there bent over laughing, I put my battleaxe away and drew the sword my grandpa gave me. It's magical. But you already know that. So I moved Chipper a few steps forward and skewered that damn demon right through its back. Well boyo, I'm here to tell you, that demon went from laughing to screaming in an instant. Then 'poof', it was gone. Just like that. That was the first demon I ever fought, boyo… but it wasn't to be the last. The others didn't die so easily, though. One took my leg, it did. Hurt like hell."

-As told by Sir Reginald Cumberfield to his squire the day after the battle for InnisRos against the dark elves.

Aikanáro, the demon responsible for the war between InnisRos and the dark elves, flew high in the sky above the clouds on the back of his dragon and watched as the female hydra fought the priest – Father Horatio Goram, according to his daughter, Nightshade – and the priest's dragon golem allies. The hydra's consorts were dead, destroyed by the golems, but dragons were easy to get and therefore expendable. Aikanáro didn't believe the same was true regarding the dead dragon golems. As he continued to follow the battle, he realized the hydra didn't have the wherewithal to defeat the priest and his minions. Nevertheless, Aikanáro was pleased. She was keeping the priest occupied as his army approached the last defended bastion on the island.

The demon smiled as he watched his plans come to fruition. In a few days' time, his army will have destroyed what little resistance the island offered. Once that was done, he'd have an unassailable base from which to launch attacks against the rest of this backwater world – and the Alfheim itself. Then he'd petition for demon lord status. Considering everything he's accomplished, who else deserved it more.

A black bolt of energy pierced the clouds from below and struck the hydra who screamed out in pain. This was the only opening the priest needed to get past her defenses. He struck the hydra with his own black beam while the remaining golems attacked from above, breaking through the hydra's weakened force field and using their claws to devastating effect.

Aikanáro pondered. According to Nightshade, Father Goram was the most powerful priest on the island, yet the bolt which originated from below appeared to argue different. That could be a serious problem for his army. Aikanáro ordered his dragon to dive into the clouds to find the source.

Autumn felt as if her soul had died somewhat. She knew the dark energy was evil, had even chastised her husband for using it. But as always, he was right. It appeared to be the only way she could help Horatio in his time of need.

"How can you see through the clouds," Lessien asked. She didn't question the method of the attack. In her mind, anything that combated evil was acceptable. Unlike Autumn, the queen held a more pragmatic view… because sometimes one needed to use evil to fight evil. She didn't believe the gods would hold her liable.

Autumn looked at the queen. "Magic," she replied, though it was much more complicated than that. "And I hit it."

"Did you kill it?"

"I can't say," the priestess answered. "The dark energy explosion took away the sight. But if I know my husband… what's that?"

Lessien looked up in the direction Autumn pointed. Something big was coming through the clouds and it was heading straight towards them. The queen stared in fascination, mesmerized and oblivious to everything except what approached. She didn't hear Landross scream "Dragon!" from another hilltop. Nor did she see him mount his horse and gallop towards them. She didn't see the ballistae arrows arc up, only to shatter against the field of protection that surrounded the dragon. She didn't see the magic spells Autumn conjured and directed towards it to no effect. Closer the dragon flew. Lessien could now see a demon riding upon its back. She saw it smile as several bolts of lightning left its outstretched hands. A hard jolt hit her on the shoulder which forced her to stumble to the side. Findley and Razor grabbed both her arms in their mouths and dragged her down the hill. Then everything went black.

Landross spied the demon and dragon almost immediately. With his warriors' eyes he calculated the beast's trajectory. It was heading towards the hilltop where the queen and Autumn stood. Ballistae arrows had already been ranged, targeted, and fired, but the big knight knew they'd have no effect. And though he was pushing his horse as fast as he dared, he knew he'd never be in time.

A streak of loud, crackling energy left the demon's hands and raced towards the hilltop. Landross saw Autumn push Lessien to the side. The two guardian dire wolves, taking their cue from their former mistress, grabbed both the arms of the queen and dragged her down the side of the hill. He had just enough time to stop his horse and cover his eyes before the entire top of the hill exploded in a release of electrical energy. In an instant the hilltop had been reduced to ruins. Of Autumn and Ajax there was no sign. Lessien and her two wolves were at the base of the hill and beginning to stir. As for the dragon and its demon rider, they had disappeared back into the clouds.

Ajax saw the dragon come through the clouds before Autumn. Even as she was pushing the queen off the hilltop, with help from Findley and Razor, he was grabbing Autumn's other hand and dragging her down the other side. Ajax's alertness saved Autumn from being hit by the conjured lightning bolts coming from Aikanáro. The force of the near hit blew both of them into the air.

Ajax, barely conscious, watched the ground at the base of the hill come rushing towards him. A small stream between two hedgerows came into view, getting closer and closer. Time seemed to slow during the fall. Ajax saw small fish just beneath the surface of the stream scatter. A large bullfrog stared into Ajax's eyes as he fell.

"Rrriiibbbiiittt!"

The huge dire wolf hit the stream hard and for a moment he blacked out. After regaining his senses, he looked for Autumn. She was lying only a few feet away, unmoving and face down in the water. Ajax, when he tried to walk over to her, discovered the fall had broken both his front legs. Grimacing in pain, he crawled over to the unconscious priestess and latched his mouth around one of her ankles. After dragging her out of the water, he put his ear on her chest, something he'd seen Father Goram do to people who were unmoving. The mistress was breathing, and he heard her heart beating steady and strong. Ajax looked over at the bullfrog who continued to sit and watch. It was the last thing he saw as he slipped into unconsciousness.

The bullfrog watched the wolf go still. A few crunchy flies later it observed armored knights find and take the wolf and priestess away. Snaring a dragonfly with a lightning quick, sticky tongue, the bullfrog felt it had enough excitement for one day and jumped into the stream.

"Rrriiibbbiiittt!"

Army General Tomas Singëril and his assistant, Lauran Ar-Feiniel, studied the approaching dark elf army from the general's command post on one of the more prominent hilltops overlooking the farmland. Thus far everything had gone well. Eric the Black, though absent, had sent his bats to destroy the wyverns while Father Goram's dragon golems were keeping the dragons from making any more attacks on his troops. A short, curt message from Eric the Black via communications crystal brought news that the corridor between Aster and the dark elf world had been closed... so there'd be no more dark elf reinforcements. And the good news didn't stop there. An uprising of Taranthi's citizens, led by Colonel Tirion, had recaptured the capital city.

The main fighting force of the dark elf army spread out across the farmland below in twelve columns of ten thousand warriors each. Marching in front were what General Singëril thought were troops unlike the rest. *"Shock troops,"* he surmised. Similar to the Marines though he doubted as effective. Trailing behind the main battle columns were three lines of reserves. There was no supply train which wasn't too surprising. Troops can carry enough supplies on their person to make the march from Taranthi.

"We're outnumbered," Lauran Ar-Feiniel observed.

General Singëril didn't bother to look over at his assistant. "Which is what we expected, Lauran. But we hold the high ground."

Lauran shrugged. "Even still they'll try to defeat us with overwhelming numbers. They don't need more reinforcements to take InnisRos."

General Singëril turned and kissed his assistant on the forehead. He'd been much more inclined to openly display his love for her the last few days. "Nefertari and Colonel Tirion did their jobs. Now we must do ours."

General Singëril activated a communications crystal. "Aubrey?"

"I've been waiting for your call," Marine Commander-General Aubrey Feynral replied.

"Get your Marines ready. We're a go for tonight."

General Singëril could almost see the smile come to General Feynral mouth. *"Yes sir!"* he replied with enthusiasm. *"I'll tell Sir Landross…"*

General Feynral stopped speaking and General Singëril could hear commotion in the background. "What's going on?" General Singëril asked.

"The queen!" came a hurried response from General Feynral through the communications crystal.

General Singëril looked over to the hilltop Queen Lessien occupied with Father Goram, Autumn, and the wolves. He didn't see the priest, the queen, or her wolves… only Autumn and her huge wolf companion. Shafts of lightning struck the hilltop from above and appeared to strike Autumn and Father Goram's wolf Ajax. After the light of the explosion flashed out, there was little left of the hilltop.

Though he saw Landross and a few of his knights scrambling towards the hill to help, the army general decided more eyes would be beneficial. He turned to one of his adjutants and bellowed, "Get people over there to assist the knights! And don't come back until the queen is safe!"

"Tomas," Lauran said.

General Singëril, who had started to pace, whirled on his assistant. "I didn't even see what attacked them!"

"I did," Lauran said. "It was a dragon. A dragon with a demon riding on it."

"Damn!"

Landross found the queen sitting up and shaking her head. Both dire wolves had taken a protective stance on either side but acknowledged Landross with a simple and short howl of greeting. They trusted him with their mistress.

"Are you all right?" Landross said as he kneeled beside Lessien.

"I think so," the queen responded.

The big knight removed the dressing and inspected Lessien's stump. Though healed by magic, the skin covering it was still very fragile. As he suspected, it was bleeding.

As Landross applied a healing salve and re-wrapped the stump with a clean silk cloth, Lessien looked around. "Autumn?" she asked.

Landross, examining the field bandage he'd just applied, answered, "I've got knights looking for her on the other side of this hill. But I have to warn you, from what I saw, it doesn't look like she could have survived."

Lessien's eyes watered. "Find her alive, Landross. I don't want to lose my best friend! I don't want to tell Horatio she's gone!"

Satisfied the bleeding had slowed to a point where it was no longer a concern, Landross looked at his queen. There was nothing he could say to counter the hurt he saw in her eyes. He embraced Lessien tight as she cried on his shoulder.

The female hydra was flying for her life. The black, necrotic energy deployed by the priest had weakened her, and the dragon golems kept pestering her, looking for any weakness. She was growing weary and thought it best to retreat. Without warning, another black beam of necrotic energy sliced through the clouds from below and struck her soft underside. She bellowed in pain.

Father Goram saw the black beam rise through the clouds and paused. He knew the source – Autumn. He felt sad she had to sacrifice her innocence, but satisfied she now understood the necessity. Sometimes the defense against evil requires the shackles of fair play be disregarded… that every weapon at your disposal is utilized to its maximum effect. This is the lesson Autumn appears to have learned this day.

Althaya's high priest didn't waste the opportunity his wife had given him. He conjured another beam of necrotic energy and struck the hydra, causing her to roar in pain once again. To Father Goram it sounded like her death lament. His remaining dragon golems took it from there and clawed her to pieces as she fell from the sky.

As Father Goram watched atop Golanth's back, he spotted another dragon appear through the clouds.

"Nightshade!" he exclaimed before seeing his mistake. It was another demon, similar in form but bigger and much more sinister looking, if that was possible.

The dragon dove and disappeared into more clouds. Through the clouds Father Goram saw a burst of light on the hilltop Autumn and the queen occupied, followed by loud explosions.

The priest wanted nothing more than to return to check on his wife and queen. But a greater imperative drove him to follow the demon-riding dragon instead as it flew back towards the dark elf army.

Dequan Zhào sat on a large rock and stared into the night. It was the late watch, two hours before dawn, and staying awake had become a challenge. After marching the entire day, setting up a field camp, and grabbing a quick, cold supper, he only had a few hours of rest before they awakened him for guard duty. Matters were made worse as the night brought with it rain and fog. It wasn't too uncomfortable – dark elf warriors are familiar with such deprivations. The steady drip of raindrops on his poncho muffled the sounds around him. The world disappeared into a surreal vision of foggy shadows twisting and turning in the darkness. The undulating fog seduced him into a sleep-like state even more than his exhaustion.

Using his glaive for support, Dequan Zhào sat glassy-eyed, hypnotized by the steady beat of the rain and the constant movement of the fog. He didn't hear the Marine who had slipped behind him. Without warning a hand covered his mouth, startling him out of his stupor. The blade of a very sharp knife ran across his throat. Dequan Zhào dropped to the wet ground, gasping for breath as he drowned in his own blood.

Marine General Feynral and Landross studied the huge dark elf encampment from atop an overlooking hill. Both were waiting for the signal to go ahead with the next step in the evening's 'festivities' as Landross described them. Earlier the Marine general had sent five hundred Marines to infiltrate the dark elf picket lines, kill as many as possible, and reconnoiter the enemy camp in preparation for the larger attack to come later. As this was going on, two Marine brigades of one thousand warriors each positioned themselves on the flanks of the dark elf army.

"The rain is a most fortunate omen, wouldn't you agree," Landross remarked. There wasn't much Father Goram's military commander loved more than going into a righteous battle. He was attempting to engage the somber general in a few pleasantries to pass the time and lighten the mood.

General Feynral looked over at the big knight encased in his well-used armor. "We knew the rain was coming. We planned for it and it's one reason why tonight is the perfect time for this little foray of ours. But I'd say rain's more luck than omen."

The general studied the knight. Landross, as did all his knight brethren, followed a code that was unbreakable – duty, honor, loyalty, and unfailing commitment to a cause. That sometimes made them unreliable, particularly if their code interfered with the mission. "You understand what's required of you and your knights?"

Landross smiled. "Of course! Rush through the front lines which will be weakened by your Marines and sow disruption and panic. Show them they can't attack our queen and get away with it."

"I cannot stress how important it is you and your knights appreciate what we expect from you," General Feynral said. "This is just a quick hit-and-run to see how they respond. We need to gage the mettle of their commanders."

"And expose any secrets they intend to deploy against us," Landross commented.

General Feynral nodded. "General Singëril and Queen Lessien insisted on your knights instead of my Marines. You're mounted and well armored… better suited for the mission."

"And tougher."

"Tougher than my Marines?" General Feynral exclaimed, rising to Landross' bait. "Hardly! But mounted knights charging through the lines of an enemy will garner a far greater response than an attack by my Marines. There's not much ground troops fear more." The general looked at Landross out of the corner of his eye. "At least until they've faced my Marines."

Landross smiled.

General Feynral's communications crystal buzzed several times in quick succession. "That's the signal."

Landross looked at the Marine.

"Don't worry, Landross," General Feynral said in answer to Landross's unasked appeal. "We'll take damn good care of the queen should something happen to you."

The knight nodded and slammed shut his faceplate. He raised his gauntleted fist as a signal to his steel-encased army and directed his horse down the hill to the rendezvous point. The wet ground silenced the hoof-beats.

"Those dark elf bastards won't know what hit them," General Feynral thought to himself.

Autumn stood at the entrance to her tent with Ajax at her side and watched the rain fall from the night skies. Thanks to the dire wolf, she had survived the demon attack with only a few minor injuries – a mild concussion, one of her ear drums perforated, and bumps and bruises. Ajax had been in much worse shape with a concussion, broken bones, and internal injuries. Fortunately, the healers got to him in time. But that was old news. Dominating her thoughts now was the whereabouts of her husband.

Autumn's reverie was interrupted by a low growl from Ajax as he acknowledged the approach of Findley and Razor. If Razor and Findley were close, then so was the queen.

"I'm worried about Horatio too," Lessien said as she brushed an errant lock of hair from Autumn's face. Besides being a trusted and valued friend, the queen knew she owed her life to the priestess, and to Father Goram, many times over.

Autumn shook her head. "I don't even know if he's still alive. The dragon golem Talamanth said he was, but why hasn't he returned?"

"I'm sure he has his reasons," Lessien replied. "Besides, we know he wouldn't do something without asking my permission first."

Lessien's obvious effort to brighten the mood fell flat. The thought that Father Goram needed anyone's permission to do something he felt necessary was laughable. The queen's comment only drew a "Humph" from Autumn. In silence the two females and three dire wolves, each left to their own thoughts, stared into the rain as it fell in a steady downpour.

Father Goram had followed the dragon at a discrete distance. Earlier he'd been in contact with Talamanth and knew that both his wife and the queen were alive and well. It also comforted him that besides Talamanth, the other two he'd lost track of, Duffy and Pytor, still lived. Even so, losing four of his precious dragon golems' weighed heavily on him.

The priest believed that the demon directing the dragon was not Nightshade, but her father, Aikanáro. Father Goram was itching to take on the more powerful demon but understood it must be under the right circumstances or he'd fail.

Father Goram landed Golanth and the other four dragon golems with him in a stand of pear trees just west of the Aranel River and the dark elf army. What he needed now was information. Not about the army... General Singëril would take care of that. He needed information about the demon. What was his overall motivation? What were his strengths and vulnerabilities? His movements? The strength of his guard? Where he and the dragon stayed when not flying?

The priest conjured invisibility magic on Golanth, his most trusted golem, and had him fly over the army encampment. Golems, as magical creatures, never tired. But Golanth's discovery by either the dark elf sorcerers, the dragon, or the demon was a certain eventuality. Therefore, time was a limiting factor. Golanth was to report on the demon exclusively... his movements, the time he ate, the people meeting with him in the command tent, even the number of times and how long it took the demon to visit the latrine, if that was something a demon did.

Day turned into night, and with the night came a steady rainfall, which worked to Father Goram's detriment as the rain droplets now outlined the invisible Golanth. As a result, he stopped the golem's reconnaissance of the enemy demon.

"I think I have enough information," Father Goram said out loud to the five dragon golems who surrounded the small lean-to the priest had built to keep dry. A small magical fire, impossible to see over fifty feet away, kept the priest somewhat warm.

"To do what," a familiar voice said from the cover of the night's darkness.

Father Goram looked towards the voice's direction and saw a gorgeous female figure walk into the light of his small fire. His dragon golems growled and roused from their defensive positions around the lean-to as the priest stood.

"Amberley…" Father Goram began then realized his mistake. "No. Nightshade."

"Can't get much past you," Nightshade said as she smiled. "I come in peace."

Father Goram ignored the demon and conjured protective magic around him and the golems. Nightshade didn't interfere, instead choosing to allow the mortal his magical reassurances.

With his protection spells now on full display, Father Goram studied the demon. There was no hint of any kind as to her intentions, though given that she hadn't already attacked appeared to bear out her call for peace between the two.

"What will you have of me, demon," Father Goram asked. "Besides your death by my hand, that is."

The smile left Nightshade's face. "I suppose you have every right to distrust me. There's much I need to answer for."

Father Goram stared at the demon. "You think! You're responsible for a war! What more could there possibly be?"

"You'd be surprised, priest," Nightshade answered. "But for whatever reason, I've grown… accustom, shall we say… to elves and this island. I see a magnificence… a kind of beautiful symmetry… in both your actions and your civilization. It's something I want to be a part of."

Father Goram shook his head. "You expect me to believe that? What kind of country bumpkin do you take me for?"

Nightshade produced a diamond locket on a chain of unbreakable talamite from underneath her satin blouse. "Do you know of the *B'nai Elohim*?"

"The *B'nai Elohim*," Father Goram said as he scratched his beard. "Creatures of legend said to guard against the escape of demons from the Abyss. I've concluded they're creatures of myth… a made-up contrivance to reassure children and the innocent against evil."

"Rest assured, Priest of Althaya, that the *B'nai Elohim* do indeed exist," a voice said from the locket in Nightshade's hand.

Father Goram looked suspiciously at Nightshade. "And I'm to believe a disembodied voice coming out of a diamond locket." The priest shook his head. "Try again, Nightshade."

A large crack appeared in the earth between Father Goram and Nightshade. Steam and heat rose from it, forcing the two back a few paces. They could plainly hear the screams of the eternally damned coming up from the fissure. Father Goram recoiled from the sound, as most mortals do upon hearing it for the first time, but Nightshade appeared unaffected.

A large creature flew up from the crack and stood next to Nightshade. As Father Goram stared, transfixed by its obvious beauty, the *B'nai Elohim* looked at Nightshade.

"So you've decided to turn away from your former life." the creature said.

Nightshade nodded. "I have, Michael."

Michael looked hard at the demon – former demon if she serves her penance. "You realize that, once committed, the locket you wear will prevent you from turning into your demon manifestation."

Nightshade took a step backwards and frowned. "I need my demon powers to stop my father, Michael," she said.

"You'll still have powers," the *B'nai Elohim* leader replied.

Nightshade shook her head. "There's always a 'but' with you, Michael. Spill the beans."

Father Goram came close to laughing out loud when he heard Nightshade use such a distinct human phrase.

"Your powers will be limited to those that either help or defend people," Michael answered. "You'll no longer have access to the dark powers except to battle evil."

"But that'll make me… it'll make me no better than him," Nightshade replied in exasperation as she pointed at Father Goram.

"Actually, the priest of Althaya will be far more powerful," Michael said. "Part of your penance is to learn humility."

Nightshade seethed. Giving up her stature as one of the more powerful beings on Aster would be difficult. But it wouldn't sway her away from her decision. She bowed her head in acceptance.

"Done," Michael said without further ceremony before he turned his gaze at Father Goram. "Are you now satisfied as to Nightshade's sincerity?"

Father Goram looked at the former demon. She looked like a naughty wolf cub who'd just been disciplined – head down but still defiant. And just like the wolf cub, the priest knew Nightshade would still be capable of pulling a few more shenanigans before her soul matured.

Father Goram nodded. "What an extraordinary time to be alive," he added.

This time it was Michael who smiled. "I'm glad you think so. Both Althaya and I feel you'd be the perfect mentor for Nightshade."

The priest and former demon looked at each other in horror. Neither remembered seeing Michael leave.

General Singëril, in his command tent, was standing next to a table, hunched over, and studying a map of the area. The disposition of the dark elf army had been hastily penciled-in. The enemy bivouac was typical, perhaps even what he'd have done before his experiences with the pirates in the Santea Archipelago. It was a huge ringed circle with several picket lines on the outside. The further one moved inward through the rings of the circle, both the number and experience of troops increased exponentially. There was little doubt the commanders were in the center of that enclosure, and that gave the InnisRos defenders a target… but only if they attacked before the army broke up in the morning.

The Marines and Landross' knights would make an attack as soon as they were in position. The First and Third Army Corps left their campfires burning while moving to the base of the foothills, ready to take any advantage the dark elf response to the initial attack might give them. The Second Corps, positioned just inside the forest to the east, was also ready to attack should it become advantageous to do so.

Lauran Ar-Feiniel entered the tent and shirked off her poncho. The rain had soaked her hair, but otherwise she was dry.

"The Marines have cleared the pickets and are in position," she said. "Landross is ready to make his assault."

"What's the latest on Captain Dubois and the rest of the northern fleet?" General Singëril asked.

"She'll be ready to unload behind the dark elves soon enough, provided she's not spotted and attacked by dragons," Lauran replied. "She's running near the shore to avoid that problem."

"Rocks and shallows?"

"Don't worry, Tomas," Lauran said. "The *Freedom Wind* has a very seasoned captain."

General Singëril nodded. "Even so, message her that if there's even a hint of discovery, she needs to offload those warriors. Right now I can afford to lose the ships but not their contents."

Lauran moved behind the general and massaged his shoulders. "The captain understands the situation and its inherent dangers. She'll take good care of our fighters and her ships."

For a moment, General Singëril closed his eyes and just enjoyed Lauran's touch.

"One last thing," Lauran said. "Colonel Tirion is moving upriver with a detachment of Marines. We also received a report the mayor of Taranthi has put together a force of several thousand able-bodied folks and are marching north."

"Very good," General Singëril remarked. "Though I'm not sure what good civilians are going to be against experienced warriors, even if many are retired or discharged veterans. Message Tirion and tell him not to let Taranthi's... irregulars... get themselves butchered if they engage the dark elves. I don't want to add even more souls to my conscience."

Lauran shook her head. "We haven't been communicating with Colonel Tirion, Tomas. We're talking with the mayor of Taranthi, himself a retired Army colonel."

General Singëril raised an eyebrow.

"Nor have we heard from Nefertari," Lauran answered the colonel's unspoken question. "But the mayor says they're not together, so I assume that something has happened to her."

"Damn it!" General Singëril barked. "The queen won't be happy losing her sister."

"We don't know for sure she's dead," Lauran remarked. "There could be many reasons the two aren't together."

General Singëril shook his head. "Give me some credit, Lauran! During the mission brief with the colonel and priestess I noticed strong feelings passing between the two. Even someone like me knows when two people are in love. He'd never leave her side if she were still alive."

"Nor would Maedhros Nénmacil," Lauran pointed out. "If the flying boulder were present, the people of Taranthi would surely know it. So if he's not with the colonel…"

"Then he's with his mistress, Nefertari," the general finished for her. "And the colonel only thinks she's dead. Yes, I suppose that's a possibility." He shook his head. "We've got plenty of other things to do, so let's not focus on speculation. I'm sure it'll straighten itself out in due time."

General Singëril turned to an orderly. "Make sure we have plenty of coffee brewed. It's going to be a long night."

Aikanáro sat alone in his luxurious tent holding a half-empty goblet of mulled wine. A blood-filled leg of mutton lay forgotten on the table in front of him. The demon was worried. The invasion wasn't going as planned. Not because of anything the dark elf commanders had done, they'd proven themselves to be somewhat competent. No, it was other things, other troubles that were turning the tide of battle before it had even started.

First it was the easy destruction of his wyvern allies. Whoever controlled the bats did a masterful job. And though he never expected the wyverns to play an important part, it would've been nice if they could at least have served as a distraction for the dragons approaching from the east. As for the dragons, they did damage, but it wasn't as much as he had expected, primarily because they weren't given the chance to. The ease in which the golems and the dark necrotic energy employed by the enemy destroyed them had thrown the demon back on his heels.

Then there was the loss of contact with Taranthi. What did that mean? Simply a loss of communication? Were his on-sight commanders too busy putting down an uprising? Or even worse – had Taranthi fallen? If that were the case, his rear flank was now dangerously exposed. The demon leader was tempted to 'pop' back to the capital city to find out, but things here were still too unsettled to leave.

And where the hell was Nightshade?! Oh how Aikanáro wished his daughter were here! Not all the magic in the world would allow him to be in two places at once. Her absence meant he had to make the day-to-day decisions required to run the army. And that meant he had to associate more closely with the dark elves, which left a bad taste in his mouth.

To top things off, Aikanáro had lost contact with the corridor. If the corridor had collapsed and couldn't be re-established, then reinforcements from the dark elf home world would no longer be available. InnisRos would still fall under the might of the dark elf army but conquering the rest of Aster might be problematic. That failure would have serious personal consequences. His demon overlords were watching to see if he had what it took to join their ranks, and they didn't accept incompetency or failure.

A dark elf poked his head through the doorway of the tent. "My Lord!"

Aikanáro, already irritated, didn't hesitate to take his frustrations and uncertainty out on the poor unfortunate. He raised an open hand. The dark elf screamed as his beating heart burst out of his chest. The demon closed his hand into a fist and the heart, suspended in mid-air, collapsed into itself and dropped to the floor. The glazed-over eyes of the victim watched as the crushed heart landed with a loud 'splat'.

"My Lord!" another voice called from outside the doorway. "We're being attacked!"

The demon sighed. "It's a feint," Aikanáro said as he left the tent and faced a group of dark elves who had congregated outside the door. "We discussed this, generals. We planned for it. Why am I being disturbed?"

"It's knights, My Lord. There has to be several thousand at least. They've breached the pickets and the outer ring."

"Then they've made a mistake," Aikanáro barked. "Collapse the circle and kill them."

"We're also being attacked on both flanks," another general added. "We can't get a handle on the number, My Lord. They're using commando tactics… hit and run. But it's along the entire perimeter."

"Daylight is just over the horizon," Aikanáro remarked. "Hit and run tactics are less likely to work in the light, particularly against a force of overwhelming numbers. Swat them like the flies they are."

"Our losses will be high, My Lord."

"Do you think I care," the demon screamed. "We can always get more soldiers from your home world. Now go do your job and don't come back until it's done!"

Aikanáro turned and stopped. He had forgotten about the corpse. "And get this trash out of my sight!" he shouted as he stepped over the body and re-entered his tent.

The demon sat and stared at the jumping flames in a lantern which sat on a small table. "At least I think I can get reinforcements," he muttered to himself after refilling his goblet with mulled wine and downing it in one gulp. He picked up the mutton leg and took a large bite. Blood ran down his chin. "I need insurance. And I think I know how to get it."

The dark elf warriors guarding Aikanáro's tent grimaced and ducked their heads when they heard a loud cackle emanating from within.

Landross and his knights broke through the first line of resistance with little difficulty. The dark elf warriors, as savage and skilled in battle as they are, didn't respond very well to his charge. He had been told that horses were rare on the dark elf home world… but thought their exposure to the horse since coming to Aster would have given their generals time to plan and implement a strategy. Instead, the sight of armored knights sitting on top of armored horses wielding fifteen-foot long lances scared the fight right out of them. Even their sorcerers had retreated into hiding.

As the knights approached the inner ring, Landross could see the campfires and tents of the dark elf commanders beyond. Though his orders were to go in, kill as many dark elves as possible, reconnoiter the enemy strength and position, then retreat, he spotted what he believed to be the perfect opportunity to strike a major blow. Just one run at the command tents was all he needed. Landross charged a dark elf warrior and planted his lance through the chest. He let go of it as his horse continued to gallop forward and pulled his sword from its scabbard, raising it into the air to signal his knights. At the signal, the advancing knights formed a phalanx in the shape of a four-sided diamond with Landross at the leading tip.

The battle through the inner ring met strong resistance, but the knights won through with minimal losses. Then dark elf sorcerers moved out into the open and started to blast the knights with fire and lightning. Most of the knights had protection from such magical attacks, but causalities began to mount despite that. By the time Landross had broken through the inner ring, he'd lost a quarter of his knights – higher than he would have liked, but still acceptable if he can accomplish his goal. Landross saw enemy warriors rush to set up a line of defense between him and the command tents, but he knew they were too late to stop his charge.

It was at this moment the disaster Landross could never have anticipated hit him and his knights head-on. Demons – hundreds of demons from the darkest depths of the underworld – appeared both outside and inside his phalanx. The dark elves, buoyed by the unexpected arrival of the demons, now fought with renewed vigor. Before Landross had time to counter, his charge had been stopped, and the phalanx had been broken. Each knight was now fighting for their lives in a pitched battle that had collapsed into a disorganized fray. It was every knight for himself.

"Sixty-seven meters on the port side," screamed a seaman.

"Sixty meters on the starboard side," another seaman answered.

"Very good," Captain Dubois said as she nodded. "Lieutenant Farnsworth, continue soundings every five minutes."

"Aye, madam."

"And make sure the lookouts keep a sharp eye out for rocks," Captain Dubois added. "We're running closer to the shore and the charts say we're an hour away from the east-side shoals."

Lieutenant Farnsworth saluted as the captain grabbed a bullhorn.

"Helm!"

"Captain," Ensign Carlowe answered from below in the wheelhouse.

"Keep your course steady," Captain Dubois ordered before turning to another officer standing next to her. "I'm going below to check on Mr. Krist. You have the deck, Mr. Gilbert."

The ship's master carpenter was also an experienced sailor and officer, more than capable of taking command. He nodded and tipped his hat to the captain before walking to the quarterdeck railing overlooking the ship. Clasping his hands behind his back, he observed every sailor, the set of the sails against the choppiness of the waters, and the overall function of the ship.

Captain Dubois went below and soon found herself at the door of Mr. Krist's stateroom. She knocked, waited for a respectful period, and entered. The room was dark except for one sconce magically lit over his bed. Mr. Krist was struggling to get off his bed, but the broken leg he'd suffered the day before was proving to be more of a challenge than the *Freedom Wind's* first officer could overcome.

"Oh Thomas, please," Captain Dubois said as she hurried over to force Mr. Krist back onto his bed.

"Sorry, Jasmine," Mr. Krist said. "I know it's only been a day, but I'm so damn tired of lying here feeling useless. Especially now. My leg feels fine."

Captain Dubois sat in the chair next to his bunk. "It was a bad break, Thomas. Mr. Bowen said you still need a few of days off your leg to let the mending strengthen. You don't want to spend the rest of your life wondering if, or when, that leg will collapse. Or worse, walk with a limp. They'll drum you out of the service for that."

Mr. Krist sighed. "You're right. Sorry. Are we near the drop-off point?"

"We'll be upon the shoals soon," Captain Dubois replied. "The weather's turned crappy, so we might not get the troops unloaded as soon as the general wants. But at least he'll get them."

Mr. Krist nodded. "Send the frigates ahead," he suggested, reasoning that their shallower draft makes the shoals less of a threat.

"Already done, Thomas," Captain Dubois answered. "But we have two Army divisions in our holds. The rest won't try to mount an attack until we've unloaded."

"At least the others will be on shore and ready to go."

Captain Dubois nodded. "That's the plan." She got up. "I'll be sure to let you know if we hit something and begin to sink," she said as she exited the cabin.

"You're all heart, Captain," Mr. Krist said to the closed door.

Aikanáro watched from the entrance of his tent as the demons, with help from the dark elves, surrounded the knights. For a moment, each side didn't react except to stare at each other. The knights realized only a miracle could save them, and the demons and dark elves recognized the same thing. Aikanáro smiled. He knew the dark elves wouldn't attack until the demons did, and he held the demons back just long enough to witness the moment the knights realized their doom.

So involved was he at the spectacle being played out before him he didn't hear the magical doorway open behind him. Nor did he hear the five dragon golems as they stepped through, followed by Father Goram and Nightshade.

"Hello father," Nightshade said before she and Father Goram used dark energy to blow Aikanáro out the tent and into the muddy ground.

From atop a hill General Singëril used a spyglass enhanced with magic to watch Landross' unexpected attack into the heart of the enemy encampment. "Curse you Landross," he railed. "I should have known you'd do something like that!"

"What?" Lessien asked as she approached the general, Lauran, and the other commanders. Autumn and the three dire wolves followed close behind.

 General Singëril turned and shook his head.

"Highness, there's no need to be up here in the rain," Lauran said to cover the general's surprise. "We have everything under control."

Lessien ignored Lauran and stood next to the general. "Give me," she motioned with her hand, indicating the spyglass.

General Singëril was reluctant to hand it over, but he couldn't disobey his queen.

Everyone in attendance had seen the queen's affection for Landross, and none of them expected her to stay calm after she saw the dire predicament her knight was in.

After a few moments, Lessien handed the spyglass back to General Singëril. "So now we must win against the dark elf army AND demons. And we must do so without our knights WHO ARE DOWN THERE SURROUNDED AND MOMENTS AWAY

FROM BEING BUTCHERED!" Lessien turned to the general. "What are you going to do about it?!"

General Singëril looked first at his queen, then at Lauran.

Lessien reached up with her stump and directed the general's gaze back to her. "Surely you're not looking to Lauran for help, are you?"

General Singëril saw anger in the queen's eyes.

"You have a plan, do you not?" the queen persisted as her remaining hand grasped the hilt of her sword, *Ah-HritVakha*.

"You need to attack, general," Autumn added, "while their forces are in disarray from Landross' assault."

"It's the only chance to save my knights," Lessien said with finality. Over the course of the last several weeks, the mounted brotherhood of warriors that Landross led went from being monastery knights to becoming knights of the realm answerable only to the queen. Any resistance from Father Goram would be resolved after the war... though as far as the queen was concerned he didn't have a choice.

General Singëril nodded. "Landross took things too far," he said to the queen.

"Which you should have expected," Lessien responded. "You KNOW Landross."

"Indeed!" the general replied. He turned to one of his executive officers. "Colonel, are your Marines positioned?"

The Marine colonel nodded. "General Feynral's ready to go."

"You may make your attack."

"Do I have your permission to return to my Marines?" the Marine colonel asked.

General Singëril nodded. "Good hunting, colonel."

The Marine colonel saluted, took the reins of his horse from an orderly, mounted and nudged it into a gallop.

General Singëril watched as the Marine raced away. He then turned to his second-in-command. "Signal the First and Third Corps to move forward."

"And the Second?"

"Make sure their commanders have them ready," General Singëril replied. "But let's hold them back for the time being. What's the status of the Navy?"

"Unloading behind the dark elves as we speak," the general's second-in-command answered after giving the attack order. "But it's going slowly. This squall makes for rough seas."

"Captain Dubois will get it done," Lessien interrupted. "You should include the Second Corps and have the Fourth here and ready to fight as well. This war with the dark elves could very well end tonight. We need all-hands-on-deck."

General Singëril shook his head. "We need to hold back a reserve, Highness. We're fighting demons with unknown capabilities. If we put all our forces in one basket and they defeat us…" The general shrugged.

"Horatio will handle the demons," Autumn said.

The queen looked at her friend. "You've heard from him?"

Autumn nodded. "I received a message from Tremorlyne, one of our golem dragons. Apparently since I'm bonded with them, we can communicate on a limited basis. Wish I'd known that sooner."

"So Father Goram will defeat the demons on his own?" Lauran asked.

Autumn shook her head. "No. Tremorlyne said he has help."

"But who could be helping him?" Lessien asked. "The last time anyone heard from my sister, she was several days away in Taranthi. And who knows where Eric the Black is."

"Tremorlyne described her," Autumn responded. "It's Nightshade in her Amberley persona."

"Nightshade!" Lessien exclaimed. "But how… why… that makes little sense! Doesn't it worry you?"

Autumn nodded. "Maybe a little, but Tremorlyne appeared to be okay with it. You need to understand that our dragon golems live to keep Horatio and I safe and protected. It's ingrained into their existence. Being magical creatures gives them certain… ahh…

capabilities and enhancements… to determine friend or foe. They'll know if she's deceiving him. And don't underestimate Horatio."

Everyone on the hilltop shook their heads. "We'd never do that," the queen answered for all of them.

Landross looked around. Demons called from the Abyss surrounded him and his knights, but, though snarling and making obscene gestures, held their positions. *"Why don't they attack and finish us off,"* he thought as he wiped the blood from his blade with an old piece of cloth he always carried for such purposes. He turned on his horse and looked up into the hills behind them. He wasn't sure what he expected to see. Perhaps his queen watched from a hilltop and would send him a sign that she knew of his sacrifice and approved. But as he expected, there was nothing.

Landross looked up into the sky and let the rain cleanse his face for a few seconds before he closed his face shield with a 'clang' and dropped the now bloody rag.

"It's time to get on with it," Landross said as he raised his sword.

But before he had a chance to engage the enemy, a commotion ahead drew his attention to the command tents. A large demon flew out of the largest tent and landed in the mud on its back. It was tethered to multiple streams of black energy coming from inside the tent. The demons, no longer concerned about the knights, moved to the defense of their master. Then Landross spotted a monstrous black dragon rose from behind the tent. Up, up, and up it went until it disappeared into the semi-darkness of the rainy dawn.

Out of the tent strode two figures. One he recognized as his old friend and former commander, Father Goram. The other looked like Mordecai's assistant, Amberley something or other. But Landross knew it wasn't her because Mordecai's beautiful aide wasn't a sorceress. She was unquestionably his paramour, but not a purveyor of the magical arts… and this Amberley most definitely was. Black shafts of energy continued to strike the large demon as Father Goram and Amberley approached the writing monstrosity.

"Horatio!" Landross screamed as he spurred his warhorse into battle. "Behind you!"

The knight was then too busy fighting demons and dark elves to see if his warning was in time.

Nightshade looked over at her 'mentor', Father Goram, to see if he had heard the warning from the knight. It didn't look like it. Black magic was distasteful to him, that much was obvious, and the concentration needed to maintain it precluded him from being distracted by outside sources.

A fleeting thought entered her mind, *"I need to correct that in him."* But she knew the priest would conjure no spells of the black arts without revulsion, even if it WERE used for the common good. And he was correct. Black magic twisted the soul.

"Perhaps that's another penance Michael requires of me?" Nightshade ruminated to herself. *"Am I to turn away from the black side and towards the white to save my soul? To break from dark magic even though I still crave its embrace? To suffer its closeness yet deny its release?"*

"Bah! No time for that," she said aloud as she redirected her black necrotic magic to the dragon. She believed that between her and Father Goram they had the power to vanquish her father and his dragon. She hoped the knights could keep her father's summoned demons and the dark elves at bay until then.

General Feynral had split his Marine combat brigade into two regiments of twenty-five hundred Marines each and positioned them on the dark elves right and left flanks. It was a bold and dangerous plan, for the dark elves numbered in the tens of thousands and could easily overrun both positions. That's why the distraction caused by Landross' knights were so crucial to his success. But before he launched his own attack, both of the enemy flanks opposing his Marines collapsed inward.

"Well that's unexpected. The knights must be doing better than anyone anticipated," the general thought as he turned to his second-in-command. "Let's move our devil dogs forward," he ordered. "Remember, our objective is to hit and run... strike and then blend back into the surroundings. I don't want to see even a hint of a full-frontal assault."

General Feynral's second-in-command smiled as he saluted. Both officers knew the 'dogs' were chomping at the bit to go.

"Let's give the Army a mess to clean up," the general concluded.

Colonel Tirion sat on a hill which overlooked trampled farmlands and used his spyglass to observe the dark elf bivouac. "We've got a problem," the Marine said as he handed his spyglass to Nefertari. Just a few hours before, Maedhros Nénmacil had flown in from the south, and riding upon the creation stone's back were Nefertari, Eric the Black, and Kyleigh Angelus-Custos, the queen of the Alfheim. Even though everyone wondered why Queen Kyleigh was on Aster, Colonel Tirion only had eyes for the love he thought gone forever. After several un-Marine like displays of affection between the colonel and Nefertari, followed by introductions and a round-table discussion concerning the status of the war, Colonel Tirion, unwilling to waste any more time, asked Nefertari to be his wife. With a smile on her face and pure joy in her eyes, she accepted, though she made the Marine ask Maedhros Nénmacil for her hand. The creation stone looked at the colonel for several long moments before exploding in laughter. "You'll make a fine mate for the StarSinger," he said. The queen of the Alfheim was invited to the nuptials, as was Eric the Black, who accepted with surprising grace.

"Oh no," Nefertari whispered as she watched what was happening in the center of the encampment. Landross had attacked with his knights and, though outnumbered, pierced the encampment all the way to its center. But now they were in dire straits.

"I'm not sure we can do anything to help Landross," Colonel Tirion added.

Song Jingyi turned to Eric the Black. "Can you not use your magic, sorcerer?" she asked.

Eric the Black shook his head. "Not at this range," he answered. "Landross is too well engaged with your dark elf brethren, translator. Any magic I can use would also hurt the knights."

"He's got even bigger problems," Nefertari said as she continued to study the situation unfolding in the dark elf camp. "Demons! There must be hundreds!"

Maedhros Nénmacil rumbled. "StarSinger?"

Nefertari shook her head as she handed the spyglass back to Colonel Tirion. "You will not attack alone, mister" she replied to the creation stone's unasked question. "Even you aren't hard-headed enough to survive hundreds of demons."

"How much longer before your 'Taranthi Irregulars' arrive?" Kyleigh asked.

"Hours, minutes, who knows," Colonel Tirion responded. "They… uh oh, something else is going on."

"Let me see," Nefertari said as she reached for Colonel Tirion's spyglass.

But the Marine didn't relinquish it, brushing her hand away instead. He swung the spyglass around one last time before he stood. His Marine sergeants stood with him.

"Get 'em ready for battle," Colonel Tirion ordered, then turned to Nefertari, Kyleigh, Eric the Black, and Song Jingyi. "General Singëril is attacking."

Maedhros Nénmacil rose into the air, his deadly stone blades whirling, and spun around several times "I've restrained myself for too long, StarSinger," he grumbled as he flew away.

Nefertari sighed. "He's in one of his moods," she confessed.

Li Qiang wasn't an ordinary dark elf warrior. Not only was he the largest and strongest warrior in the dark elf army, but he also had a special talent for cooking. Chef's in dark elf society are rare. Though a valuable fighter, the dark elf high commanders cared more about the food he placed before them at the dinner table. Fighters were plentiful. As a result, they kept Li Qiang off the front lines and as safe as possible. He didn't mind. By nature he wasn't the cruel beast dark elf culture expected him to be. Instead, despite his size and strength, he was contemplative, reasoned, and gentle. He found peace and joy in the simple act of making food, even though it branded him a pariah in dark elf society. Many times he dreamed of escape into the wilderness of his home world where he'd find a small village, build a home, fall in love, and raise a family.

Li Qiang had risen early, long before first light, and trudged to the large kitchen where he'd make breakfast for the army commanders. This morning's menu included coffee, eggs, potatoes, biscuits, fruit and doughnuts, something Taenya, a diminutive female elf in Taranthi, had taught him how to make. His commanders loved the sweetness of the doughnut and soon discovered the taste of doughnuts dipped into coffee was something they couldn't live without. Li Qiang used this passion for morning doughnuts and coffee as a hedge against any harm that might befall Taenya and her young daughter.

His chow hall was well back from the front lines, and though the sound of fighting came from that direction, he didn't concern himself with it. In fact, he didn't even wear his armor when on duty – just a plain uniform covered by a white apron. And instead of his sword, he carried his most prized possession, a set of pearl-handled cooking knives.

Li Qiang lit fires in the belly of his stoves and collected the ingredients he'd need to make breakfast. It wasn't long before biscuits were cooking and coffee brewing. He had already removed a mountain of doughnuts from boiling deer fat, cooled, dipped in his own concoction of honey, sugar, cow milk and vanilla, and left hardening on a tray. As the dark elf cooked, he wondered how many officers he'd be feeding this morning. He hoped most of them would be too dead to show up.

From outside the chow hall tent a commotion arose. People screamed. Li Qiang wondered what could cause such a ruckus, but before he had a chance to investigate, there was a jarring thud from just outside the entrance. The tent flaps disappeared into tatters, and in their place sat a huge boulder with many stony knives protruding from its body. The 'thing' opened its eyes, and a mouth appeared.

"Where are the hostages," the boulder grumbled through tight lips. "And don't lie. It will go very badly for you if you do."

Another thing Taenya had taught Li Qiang was the common language of Aster. He pointed to his right. "Two tents over and three… no four… tents up. You can't miss it. It has guards." He looked at the doughnuts he'd prepared and knew they'd probably go into the trash. If a talking boulder was any indication, things must be going badly for the commanders. He grabbed one of the delicious nuggets and took a bite. *"Perfection!"* he thought to himself.

The dark elf chef looked at the boulder. "Here, have a doughnut," he said as he tossed one to the creation stone.

Maedhros Nénmacil speared the doughnut from the air with one of his blades and took a tentative bite. He broke out into a smile. "Wonderful!"

Li Qiang nodded as he finished his own doughnut and picked up the massive tray full of them. "I'll take you to the hostages. No point in wasting these pastries."

"I'll grab the coffee!" Maedhros Nénmacil rumbled as he used several of his blades to snag coffee pot handles and a tray of clean mugs.

It was completely deserted outside the tent, but there was little doubt trouble would arrive soon enough.

"So," Li Qiang broke the silence. "Just exactly what are you?"

"Throw me another doughnut and I just might tell you," Maedhros Nénmacil replied. "That is if I don't kill you first."

"You'd kill me before trying my smoked salmon potato cakes with herb crème fraîche?"

Maedhros Nénmacil looked at his prisoner and began to laugh. Soon both of them were laughing, the creation stone so hard the vibrations caused by the deep rumbling knocked over a nearby empty tent.

Captain Dubois was shouting commands from the quarterdeck of the *Freedom Wind*. They had unloaded the two Army divisions from their holds, but, though her draft was higher, the ship wasn't safe by any means. Two things concerned the captain – retreating from the shallows to open water without ripping the bottom of the ship out, and, most urgently, dragons. With dawn just over the horizon, they were sitting ducks against a dragon attack this close to shore. They needed to be in open water where they'd have room to maneuver.

"Jasmine," Mr. Krist said as he limped up from behind her.

Captain Dubois turned. "At least you're using a cane," she remarked. "Thomas, I thought we agreed you were to stay below and off your leg."

"Six fathoms!" shouted a crewman from the bow of the ship.

"Jasmine, you need me here," Mr. Krist said.

"Rocks two points off the starboard bow!" shouted another crewman from the crow's nest of the foremast.

"Helmsman, please keep your course steady," Captain Dubois ordered before she turned to her first officer. "Yes, I do… need you, that is."

Mr. Krist nodded. He looked out over the deck of the ship and scrutinized the crew as they went about their duties. Here and there he corrected a few minor things he didn't like, but as usual the experienced crew of humans performed exceptionally well. He turned to Captain Dubois.

"What's next, Jasmine," he asked.

The *Freedom Wind's* master shrugged her shoulders. "Queen Lessien has no more need of us. We sail for home. I'm sure Mr. Dular is eager to get his largest ship back. We're not making profit otherwise."

Mr. Krist looked out to sea. It would be an overcast day. "I'm tired of running cargo," he said.

Captain Dubois looked at her first officer with a raised eyebrow. "That's new coming from you. I remember you once telling me your adventuring days were over and 'milk runs', like sailing up and down the coast, was enough."

Mr. Krist nodded. "At one time, yes. But our time with Tangus and Kristen, and what we're doing here, has opened my eyes to more… oh, I don't know… more noble causes, I guess you could say. There's so much good we can do with this ship and her crew."

"As you yourself have told me many times, we're under contract," Captain Dubois reminded her first officer. "The ship isn't ours to do with as we please. It's the jewel of the Dular family fleet. How do you think it'd go over if we used it for a purpose of our own choosing, regardless of how righteous that purpose may be? And what would the crew have to say about it?"

"They'd follow you anywhere."

Captain Dubois shook her head. "They'd mutiny in about five seconds and we'd find ourselves in the brig five seconds after that. Almost to a man they have families. Remember? You insisted upon it when we hired them. 'A family man is a stable man,' you said. No…

they'd not abandon their families for me. Not that I'd ask such a thing."

Mr. Krist nodded. "Of course you're right, Jasmine. And for the record I wouldn't ask the crew to do such a thing either."

"I know that, Thomas."

"But please keep this conversation in mind," Mr. Krist persisted. "We can do so much better."

"Ten fathoms!"

"Out of the shallows," Captain Dubois said. "Please get us underway, Mr. Krist."

"Aye, captain," Mr. Krist replied as he gave orders to get underway with full sail.

Captain Dubois looked down from her position on the quarterdeck. "Helmsman make your course northeast," she directed. "Keep the Arrow abeam on the port bow."

"Aye, captain. Making my course northeast with the Arrow abeam on the port bow."

"Very good," Jasmine Dubois said. "Once past the Arrow, set course for home."

The *Freedom Wind's* captain watched as her crew performed their duties flawlessly. *"Yes, Thomas, we are better than this,"* she admitted to herself.

The black energy bolt Father Goram used against Aikanáro kept him writhing in pain for an long time. All the demon could think of was the agony caused by the priest's use of dark magic. What was worse, somewhere in the back recesses of his mind he knew his dragon and demons wouldn't, or couldn't, help. He was on his own.

"Damn you priest," Aikanáro shouted as he diverted the torture away from his consciousness and deep into his psyche. He rose from the muck. "You think your use of the dark elements is greater than mine!?"

"We'll see who commands the field, demon," Father Goram said in response to Aikanáro's challenge. He poured more power into the black bolt, but the demon hastily built a magical shield to absorb at least a portion of the energy.

"So we shall," Aikanáro replied.

Father Goram's black bolt was encapsulated and destroyed. The same magic that had neutralized the bolt surrounded the priest and dropped him to the ground.

"Wallow in the mud yourself, Goram," Aikanáro laughed.

The priest regained his feet. He closed his eyes, took a deep breath, and crossed his wrists in the shape of an "X" before him.

"Black magic, thy soul is blighted.
Energy taken from those who are dead."

"Light magic, your power ignited.
By innocence, your glamour is fed."

"IN NOMINE ALTHAYA… ET MORTUUS EST!"

Brilliant white magic exploded the black magic which had such a hold on Father Goram and rushed to surround the demon. Aikanáro screamed in terror. The white magic exceeded anything the demon had ever felt, and, though it didn't hurt him, it forced him to his knees. Such was its might that Aikanáro knew it could crush him if Father Goram so desired.

"Why do you not kill me?" Aikanáro asked. "Clearly it's in your power to do so."

Father Goram remained silent and just stared at the demon.

"You can't, can you?" Aikanáro said. "The great Father Goram, high priest to the goddess Althaya, as weak as any mortal. Maybe you think, like my traitorous daughter, I can be turned to your white magic? That my black soul is somehow redeemable? You don't have a clue, priest!"

As the demon spoke, he tested the strength of the enchantment that confined him. He understood that the smallest distraction, the tiniest mental lapse by the priest, was the only inroad he needed to break free from the cursed white magic.

There was a loud inhuman roar from overhead. Father Goram noticed Aikanáro's face turn a different shade of black. The priest looked up and saw the creation stone Maedhros Nénmacil attacking Aikanáro's dragon. His swirling stone blades were making huge rents in the dragon's head. Nightshade redoubled her own magical attacks against it.

The dragon decided enough was enough and made its escape through a magically crafted doorway that opened into the Abyss. Maedhros Nénmacil and Nightshade let it go.

Father Goram turned his attention back to Aikanáro. "You're starting to run out of options."

"Indeed, father," Nightshade added. Her work with the dragon done, she now stood at Father Goram's side. "As they say on the mainland, 'your goose is cooked'. Kill him now, Horatio."

Father Goram hesitated. He wanted to squeeze the life out of Aikanáro… the demon was still extremely dangerous and, even without the dragon, commanded a large army capable of destroying everything he loved. Yet something held him back.

"Do it," Nightshade pleaded. There was fear in her eyes.

"My, aren't you two all chummy," Aikanáro observed. "What'd she promise you, priest? Wealth? Immortality? Sex?"

"You know nothing," Nightshade screamed at her father. She turned to Father Goram. "Kill him! Crush him into oblivion while you still can." Now there was panic in her voice.

Father Goram squeezed his closed fist tighter. The white magic that surrounded the demon began to contract. Aikanáro was helpless.

"How much do you love your wife?" Aikanáro asked. "Or your queen?"

Father Goram stopped. He figured the demon was only buying time, but he couldn't risk it.

"No… no… no!" Nightshade shouted. "He lies."

"Do I?" Aikanáro responded. "Contact your generals. Ask if any of them know the whereabouts of either."

Althaya's high priest looked at Nightshade and nodded. She knew what he wanted… and that he'd do nothing with her father until he got it. Without hesitation, she opened a magical doorway and stepped through it.

Aikanáro laughed. "It's not a bluff, priest. I dispatched demons to kidnap both before you and my daughter arrived. They're comfortably imprisoned in the Abyss." The demon laughed harder. "Though I suppose comfort is a matter of perspective. But at least they're still alive… and under my control. Call it an insurance policy against your meddling."

Father Goram squeezed his fist just enough to cause the demon to feel uncomfortable. "I'm supposed to just take you at your word!"

"Fair point," Aikanáro replied. The demon opened a small magical window with his mind. It floated in the air about six feet away from Father Goram. "Take a gander." Aikanáro snickered. "Gander! I too love mortal colloquialisms?"

Both females were visible through the supernatural window. They were in a dark, dank cave which, surprisingly, appeared to be lavishly furnished. Black magic barred their way out, and Father Goram could see several demons milling about at the entrance. From the look on Autumn's face, he knew she was preparing magical spells. Queen Lessien crotched in a defensive posture as the demons on the outside of her and Autumn's prison cell sneered. She held her sword, *Ah-HritVakha*, out before her. Brilliant lights of magic swept up and down the length of the weapon. Father Goram wanted to shout Autumn's name but knew better than to break her concentration.

"Come now, priest," Aikanáro said. "You didn't think I'd let you talk to them?"

"Then how do I..." Father Goram began.

"You don't!" Aikanáro snapped. "That's how the game is played, is it not?"

"What you see is real, Father Goram," Maedhros Nénmacil, who had floated down and hovered behind the priest, grumbled. "And they're in the Abyss as the demon declared."

Nightshade suddenly appeared by Father Goram's side and shook her head, confirming the priest's fear. "It's bad, Horatio. The three dire wolves are barely alive. The tent they were in is a shamble with blood everywhere, most of which belongs to the wolves, but some of it is demon blood. They put up quite a fight."

Father Goram winced. "Ajax, Findley, Razor... Are they going to make it?"

Nightshade nodded.

"Are there any other casualties?" the priest asked.

Nightshade shook her head. "No, unless you want to include General Singëril's wounded pride. He appeared rather concerned about how you're going to react."

"Indeed!" the priest responded. "He's correct. I don't think he'll much like what I have to say on the matter. But let's shelve that for later. Recommendations?"

Nightshade took a few steps closer to Aikanáro and addressed him. "You realize I count Michael of the *B'nai Elohim* as one of my few friends, such as it is."

Aikanáro's smile dropped. It was obvious to Father Goram the demon wasn't aware.

Nightshade continued. "That means, father, you can't hide in the Abyss... at least not from Michael or the *B'nai Elohim*. Release Autumn and Queen Lessien and end the war."

"Or what?"

"Or die," Father Goram answered. He started to tighten the white magic surrounding the demon once again.

"You can't kill a demon on this plane," Aikanáro said. "I'll only be banished back to the Abyss for a century. You have plenty of years left to see me again. And when you do…"

"Release them, demon," the priest said as he tightened his fist.

"Think of it. Your wife and the queen, in the Abyss, under my control. Go ahead, finish it, and send me back. I'm losing interest in this war anyway."

"He'll finish it by proxy, Horatio," Nightshade said. "He has too much riding on this to stop."

"BITCH!" Aikanáro roared.

"Release them, demon," the priest repeated, never once wavering.

Aikanáro grimaced. "You'll regret this."

"RELEASE THEM, DEMON!" Father Goram roared.

Aikanáro started to laugh through his pain.

There was something in the demon's eyes that frightened the priest. He looked back into the window. As he watched, powerless, the bars of confinement dropped, and several demons rushed in, interposing themselves between the two captives. The queen used her sword to try to cut her way back to Autumn, but they forced her into another part of the room. The demons weren't trying to hurt the queen, just keep her away from Autumn.

Autumn was doing everything she could to fight off her demon assailants, but the numbers were too great and their intent more than to contain. She killed several using clerical magic and her charmed dagger, but as Father Goram, Nightshade and Maedhros Nénmacil watched, the demons piled on the priestess and knocked her to the ground. They pummeled her with their fists until she stopped resisting.

The demons got up and backed away. They had beaten Autumn to a bloody pulp, but she still breathed and remained defiant. Queen Lessien redoubled her efforts to get past those demons blocking her from Autumn, but to no avail.

Another demon, larger and uglier than the others, came into view. Everyone observing knew what would happen next, including

Autumn. She got to her hands and knees and crawled to the nearest corner. The large demon laughed as he watched. He let Autumn cower in the corner for a few moments before he stepped towards her. Then he grabbed her by an ankle and dragged her to the middle of the room. Turning his head, he grinned at the other demons who were stomping their feet and jumping up and down. He kneeled between her legs but paused as if waiting for something.

"DON'T YOU LET THIS HAPPEN, YOU SON-OF-A-BITCH," Father Goram screamed at Aikanáro.

Aikanáro smiled. "I DID warn you, did I not? This is your last chance to release me."

Father Goram hung his head. He knew he couldn't. There were far too many lives at stake.

Nightshade, now standing next to Father Goram, seized his free hand and squeezed it to comfort the priest. "We can't save her, Horatio. But we can end the war. My father controls the dark elves. Without him, we can defeat them despite their overwhelming numbers."

The demon hovering over Autumn ripped her pants away and raped her. When he had finished, all the demons filed out of the room, laughing while clapping their comrades on the back. They left the magical bars open. The prisoners were free to leave – free to roam, lost, in the Abyss.

Autumn lay there, bleeding from between her legs, staring into space. Father Goram turned away. They had succeeded in destroying the beautiful tribute to life that was Autumn. The magic window into the Abyss closed.

"Nightshade, can you open a small doorway into the Abyss?" the priest said through his tears.

In answer, a small doorway appeared next to the kneeling Aikanáro. Nightshade realized what Father Goram intended and smiled, proud of the way her mentor had decided to eliminate her father.

"What are you doing," Aikanáro asked. The back of his mind was sounding an alarm.

Father Goram squeezed his hand. Even the amorphous incarnation of Aikanáro couldn't resist the power of Father Goram's white magic. But before Aikanáro had the life crushed out of him, the priest used his magic to pick the struggling fiend up and shove him through the doorway and into the Abyss. Aikanáro had breathed his last in the Abyss… the only place where his destruction was guaranteed to be permanent.

Nightshade closed the doorway as soon as they were sure her father was dead.

Father Goram nodded. "Come, Nightshade, let's begin your training in white magic. It kills just as effectively as black. Maedhros Nénmacil, would you care to join us?"

The creation stone nodded. While killing was never a good thing, it was sometimes necessary. Now was one of those times. "Yes, Father Goram, I do."

CHAPTER TWENTY-TWO

InnisRos

"The Perfect Storm!"

All the elements needed to destroy the dark elf invasion fell into place at exactly the right moment. The destruction of Aikanáro, combined with the disappearance of his dragon, put the demons in disarray. Many of them preferred to leave and return to their home in the Abyss. Landross and his remaining knights destroyed those that stayed.

The dark elf army fared no better. From both flanks camouflaged Marines attacked and then disappeared back into the darkness of the night. The dark elves barely had time to loot their dead and finish off their wounded before the Marines attacked again. Though the Marines were efficient in dealing out death, they were no match for the sheer number of fighters the dark elves had at their disposal. But the Marines refused to stand and fight. Instead, they used hit-and-run tactics which chipped away at the dark elf army. The dark elves tried hard to remove the annoyance, but every time they engaged the Marines they were left with even more dark elf dead and dying upon the field of battle. The dark elf commanders decided to push reserve troops from the rear to reinforce both flanks, a move that weakened the southern perimeter of their army.

To further complicate things for the dark elf commanders, the First, Second, and Third Corps of General Singëril's army attacked along the entire front. As they came out of the foothills, hundreds of archers released arrows towards the dark elf lines. In response, dark elf archers did the same. Both sides filled the air above the field that separated the two armies with an ever-expanding cloud of different colored projectiles. War sorcerers from both sides exploded as many of the arrows as they could with balls of fire and explosive barrages of magic. Few of the launched arrows survived their flight to claim a victim. As General Singëril's army marched forward, the dark elf commanders responded by moving most of their army forward to meet the threat, intending to destroy InnisRos' defenders once and for all.

Colonel Tirion, Nefertari, Eric the Black, Kyleigh, Song Jingyi, and his Marines held their position until they could coordinate their attack with the Taranthi irregulars who had just arrived. The Marine colonel was been in constant communications with the Taranthi contingent leader, Connak Feynore, and knew it wouldn't be long before the larger force was in position.

Colonel Tirion, with occasional recommendations from Nefertari and Kyleigh, was devising a battle plan at the foot of the hill overlooking the dark elf base camp.

"Sir, you need to see this," one of his sergeants shouted from hilltop.

The colonel stopped what he was doing and climbed the small hill.

"Give me," Colonel Tirion said as he reached for the spyglass.

As he watched, he shook his head. "I don't believe it."

"What is it," Nefertari asked. She, along with Kyleigh, Eric the Black, and Song Jingyi, had trailed behind the Marine officer.

"The dark elves just sent their reserves to reinforce each flank," Colonel Tirion said. "Their rear is completely exposed." Colonel Tirion shifted the focus of his spyglass further to the east. "Wait! Who's that? Oh, excellent!"

"Well? What do you see?" Eric the Black asked impatiently.

"A large force moving from the coastline," the Marine answered as he continued to look through the spyglass. "It's the rest of Singëril's northern army, those that came south by ship."

Landross and his knights, free of the demons, formed a steel barrier around the command tent where Father Goram, Nightshade, and the creation stone had defeated the black demon and his dragon. With the loss of their demon commander and his minions, the dark elves weren't overly eager to attack the knights, and those that did were easily dispatched. The dragon golems were up in the air, flying over the battlefield. They looked for anyone who appeared to be important and grabbed them on flybys. Hapless dark elves started falling from the skies – flesh and blood bombs seeking more victims. The dark elf sorcerers soon learned that any use of magic exposed them to the golem dragon's search. This amounted to a death sentence, for none of them had strong enough magic to pierce the golem's protection spells placed upon them by Father Goram.

"Well met, Horatio," Landross said as he rode his giant warhorse over to where the priest and his lady-friend stood. "And you, Maedhros Nénmacil." He dismounted and nodded to Nightshade. "You look familiar?"

"You remember Mordecai's assistant?" Nightshade asked.

Landross nodded. "Ah yes. If I recall, her name is Amberley."

"Well, I'm not her," Nightshade replied with finality.

Father Goram sighed. "It's a long story, Landross. And a story for another time. We've more pressing matters."

"Indeed we do, sir," Landross remarked. "Things like beating the bastard dark elves off the island."

Father Goram shook his head. "I think General Singëril will soon have that under control. It's worse than that."

Nightshade averted Father Goram's gaze. She didn't want to see the emotion in the priest's eyes when he repeated what he knew about Autumn and the queen to the huge knight. Nightshade usually relished the pain of others, either physical or emotional. But now she felt uncomfortable with Father Goram's hurt. It was a new and strange sensation. But as the priest explained things to Landross, he didn't sound as if he was in pain. Instead he sounded emotionally disengaged.

Landross's screamed in anger, outrage, and fear. Nightshade looked up to see the knight pacing back and forth while smashing a gauntleted fist against an open palm.

"We have to go get them, Horatio," the knight said, "Abyss or no Abyss. InnisRos needs her queen, and we need the wise counsel of your gentle Autumn. And I…"

Father Goram cut Landross off. "We will," There was no emotion in his voice. "And if you're going to come along, you need to get yourself under control. No flying off the handle and none of that knights honor crap. Can you do that for our queen?"

Landross nodded. "Aye, Horatio. I can suspend the Knight's Code in the Abyss. For my queen."

"You might not come back as the same person."

"I'm stronger than that."

Father Goram focused his gaze into the knights eyes before turning away. "We'll see. But first, we need to make sure Lessien still has an island to rule. Then we'll mount an expedition to the Abyss." He looked at Nightshade.

Nightshade nodded. She could get them there. But in that look, Nightshade noted that there was a void in Father Goram's eyes that she'd neither expected nor seen before. Maedhros Nénmacil, who was floating above Nightshade's right shoulder, gently tapped her on the arm. Nightshade jumped.

"You see it too," the creation stone observed. "Father Goram has replaced his pain with emptiness. He feels nothing… not pain, love, hope, hate… or any of the other emotions that make him mortal. He has locked those emotions away so he can cope with the loss of his wife and the queen while maintaining his sanity. He has locked those emotions away so he can do what needs to be done in the Abyss."

"What an extraordinary creature the creation stone is," Nightshade thought before answering. "That very emptiness might also cost him his life. What hope do we have in the Abyss if he doesn't care about anything?"

"Oh madam, you have it wrong," Maedhros Nénmacil replied. "The Abyss is where he must go to find those passions once again. Even if Autumn and Queen Lessien are dead… or worse, insane… it matters not. The good priest will never be the same until he finds closure, if at all. You will accompany him and Landross?"

"Yes." She and the high priest of Althaya were now allied. For how long she couldn't say, but she suspected it was forever. "I know the way."

Maedhros Nénmacil rumbled. "Indeed you do, madam," he said. "Afterall, you are a demon, are you not?"

After saying that, the creation stone left Nightshade to join Father Goram and Landross, who, along with dragon golems and knights, were fighting the dark elves.

The newly minted white demon shrugged. "An extraordinary creature," she repeated to herself as she caught up with the priest to stand and fight by his side.

General Singëril, along with Lauran Ar-Feiniel, watched as his army engaged the dark elf army. Things had come together much better than expected — the general had a hard time believing how well — and though the final battle had just begun, he knew they had already won the war. From his vantage point in the foothills, he watched as his three Army Corps engaged the forward positions of the dark elf army. Enemy commanders, correctly fearing this was the main thrust of the attack, concentrated their forces on the front.

On each flank, General Feynral's Marines attacked through a series of well-planned and coordinated hit-and-run assaults. At first the dark elves looked upon these attacks as mere gnat bites, but soon learned the difficult lesson of underestimating the queen's Marines. To counter the seriousness of these attacks, the dark elf reserves were ordered into the fight with the Marines, leaving the rear exposed. Fortunes of war, fickle at best, made the dark elves pay dearly for that overreaction.

As the dark elf reserves moved forward to support both flanks, the northern army units and veteran volunteers who had been landed on the eastern coast by the Navy, arrived on the scene. These forces were buttressed by the appearance of several thousand citizen-warriors from recently liberated Taranthi. Together they attacked the mostly deserted dark elf rear and pushed towards the encampment center. Eric the Black, Nefertari, Colonel Tirion and his battle-hardened Marines added to the assault.

In the center, Father Goram, his magical dragon golems, and Landross' knights were causing pandemonium within the command tents of the dark elf army. Reports that the demon Nightshade was now fighting alongside Father Goram had thus far been unsubstantiated.

"Sir!"

General Singëril turned and returned the officer's salute. "Report," the general commanded.

"We haven't been able to find any new clues about who kidnapped the queen and the priestess," the lieutenant replied. "Nothing to track. It looked as if someone dropped out of thin air and, after a brief struggle, spirited them away."

"Demons, I suspect," Lauran said.

"Or maybe dark elf magic," the lieutenant speculated.

"You mean teleportation?" General Singëril asked. "No. Our sorcerers have this whole area magically protected against teleportation spells," he said while he shook his head. "Any blood signs?"

"Lots, general," the officer replied. "Mostly wolves blood, but also someone… or something… else's. It smelled like sulfur. We've checked both visually and magically but found nothing else."

"Which points to the demons as the kidnappers," Lauran said. "From what I understand demons usually leave no evidence behind when they return to the Abyss… so the blood trace works in our favor. If anyone can use it to track the demons, it'll be Father Goram. We need to preserve it."

"See to it," General Singëril ordered.

The lieutenant nodded. "Already collected and stored, sir."

"How fare the wolves?" Lauran asked.

The lieutenant grimaced. "They're much better… uncomfortably so, madam."

Both General Singëril and Lauran looked at the officer.

The lieutenant cleared his throat. "It quite upset all three, particularly the big one."

"Ajax," "Lauran remarked.

"That's the one," the lieutenant said. "The monastery healers think we should evacuate them back to Calmacil Clearing, but the wolves… well, they'll have none of it."

General Singëril nodded. "No, I don't suspect they would."

"Is there anything else sir?" the lieutenant asked.

The general shook his head. "No, at least not… wait. Take a few guards and keep everybody off the hilltop where the queen and priestess were taken. Father Goram will want to investigate and I don't want it disturbed any more than it already has been."

As the lieutenant walked away, General Singëril turned to a sergeant standing a few yards away and motioned for him to approach. "Saddle my horse," he said.

"And mine," Lauran added.

"And hers," General Singëril agreed.

"Where are we going, Tomas," Lauran asked.

"Down there," he replied as he pointed towards the middle of the dark elf army. "I need to tell Horatio about Queen Lessien and Autumn."

Lauran nodded. "Agreed. But I'd bet a year's pay that he already knows."

General Singëril, who had returned to surveying the battle through his spyglass, looked over at Lauran. "That's a safe bet," he responded. They felt the ground shake and a rumble. Bright flashes of light and streams of smoke came from the center of the battlefield. "I can't make out individual figures, but I've no doubt that's clerical magic at its finest."

The three-pronged attack that materialized in the rear of the dark elf army hit the invaders like a sledgehammer. After an hour of fighting, the dark elf commanders – those that were still alive – understood their position was untenable. But they kept fighting while they waited for reinforces from their home world. They had no way of knowing their alliance with the demon Aikanáro had unintentionally caused the destruction of the Svartalfheim, and that no reinforcements were forthcoming. The universe never plays favorites.

After two hours of fighting, the Army and Marines had reduced the dark elf army to one quarter its original size. Many of the remaining fighters dropped their weapons and surrendered. Those that tried to yield to Song Jingyi, however, were afforded no mercy. Her hatred for the males of her species was unparalleled. She cut them up with her knives until she was dragged away screaming invectives at the dark elf males still standing.

After three hours, the fighting had stopped. Though victorious, the InnisRos defenders showed no joy in their victory. By this time everyone knew their queen had been spirited away by demons. The possibility of her death weighed on each mind. Only the superb discipline of the InnisRos troops kept the dark elf prisoners from being massacred en masse.

Father Goram sat on his chair and watched as General Singëril gave his post-battle action report. He wasn't listening and didn't care. All he wanted was to begin the difficult journey to rescue his queen… and end his wife's madness. He reached down and scratched Ajax behind the ears. The wolf responded gratefully. It was the first signs that his master had forgiven him for failing to protect Autumn.

Sitting around a huge, well-worn oak table in the command tent, besides Father Goram and General Singëril, were Nightshade, Kyleigh, Eric the Black, Nefertari, Colonel Tirion, Lauran Ar-Feiniel, Marine General Feynral, and Landross. Maedhros Nénmacil, because of his size, was sitting just outside the open-flapped tent. None of Father Goram's monastery leaders were present.

"I'm sorry," Landross said, "but we just can't trust this… this… this bitch."

The argument had begun again. Father Goram realized it would be a struggle to get his friends to accept the white demon, but the knight, unsurprisingly, wasn't willing to accept the priest at his word. Father Goram looked up at Landross. "I've vouched for her. That should be enough."

"How do we know you're not under an enchantment?" Landross retorted. "Just because Eric can't find one doesn't mean it's not possible." The knight looked around the table. "Demons don't change their stripes! And even if she has, how does anybody know she won't change back?" Landross then drew his sword and slammed it on the table, it's deadly tip pointed directly at Nightshade. Its magic coursed through the blade. "She should pay for the evil she's done. Let me take her head!"

Nightshade accepted the hatred directed at her from around the table. She deserved not only that, but so much more. However, though she was sincere in her desire to make amends for past deeds, her pride remained intact. She'd not beg for her life. Nor would she try to escape. Her physical self was no longer immortal, but her newly found soul was. She didn't want to do anything to jeopardize it… or condemn it.

Suddenly Landross' sword rose in the air and flew straight up, only to come back down tip first to plunge through one of the knight's hands and into the wood of the table. Landross grimaced but refused to cry out in pain. Everyone except Father Goram and Nightshade stood. Nefertari and Eric the Black both began to cast spells while the rest pulled swords and pointed them at Nightshade, including Landross who had pulled his sword out of his hand and the table.

"Move one inch and I'll skewer you!" Landross shouted, his injury forgotten in his rage.

Nightshade looked at her hands which lay in her lap and said nothing.

"You'll do nothing of the kind, knight," Father Goram grated as he stood. "Nightshade didn't do that. I did."

"What?" Landross whispered. He couldn't believe what he just heard.

The priest reached over and placed a hand on Landross' injury. It healed in seconds.

"Put away your swords and listen to me," Father Goram ordered as he looked around the tent. "Nightshade and Michael of the *B'nai Elohim* made a deal."

"The *B'nai Elohim*?" Eric the Black interrupted.

Maedhros Nénmacil laughed. "Something Eric the Black doesn't know," the creation stone rumbled. "Who'd have thought. The *B'nai Elohim* are guardians, though gatekeepers would be a more apt term to describe them. They're the main reason demons don't leave the

Abyss and overrun this world. They're not gods... not quite. But I wouldn't want to run into them in a dark alley."

Everyone looked at Father Goram.

"I only just recently found out about their existence myself," he replied in answer to their unasked question. The high priest stood behind Nightshade and placed his hands on her shoulders. "Nightshade is no longer a demon... at least not in the way we've come to recognize demons. She gave up her immortality and use of the evil arts for a chance to redeem her soul. Then, for reasons I still can't comprehend, Michael determined she was to be my student and that I instruct her in the ways of white magic. Althaya encouraged it, so I accepted the charge and the responsibility. After all, what kind of priest would I be if I refused to help Nightshade amend for past deeds and save her soul?" Father Goram paused and looked around the table. Everyone was looking at the priest except Eric the Black, who grimaced and shook his head. Landross, however, still looked unconvinced. That had to change.

"So, where does that leave us?" Father Goram asked as he looked around the table. "It leaves us with her under my protection. Do you understand what that means?"

Landross growled.

"It means any attack on her is an attack on me," Father Goram said. "I'll not hesitate or hold back in my defense of her. Nor will I ever relent. There will be no exceptions. So long as she stays true to her word, so too will I stay true to mine. Questions?"

"You don't leave us much choice, priest," Eric the Black exclaimed.

Father Goram looked at the sorcerer. Sitting next to him was Kyleigh Angelus-Custos, Queen of the Alfheim. From what he understood, her help was critical in closing down the passage to the Svartalfheim and stabilizing the corridor between her world and Aster. Now, though, she appeared to watch Eric the Black with something more than just a common interest in events. It was an interesting pairing, but one the priest didn't really care for. He needed Eric the Black on Aster.

"No, I didn't," Father Goram answered the sorcerer. "That's by design. Nightshade has much to answer for, no doubt. But she's proven to me she deserves the chance."

"Will she not speak for herself?" Nefertari asked. "Can she make sense out of this betrayal of her father and her demon brethren?"

Father Goram bent down and whispered into Nightshade's ear. "Be who you are… but answer truthfully. This one's an extraordinarily talented priestess who follows one of the old gods. I have no idea what her powers are."

Nightshade looked around the table. Except for Nefertari, who appeared neutral, the others stared at her with barely concealed hatred and contempt, particularly Landross. Upon reflection, she didn't blame them. She'd done terrible things. If she were in their shoes, she'd not want to give her a second chance either.

"Everything Father Goram has said is true," Nightshade said. "I've given up my immortality, my demon form, and the black arts."

"I saw you use the black magic only a few hours ago," Landross protested.

"Granted to both of us by Althaya," Father Goram answered for Nightshade. "Call it special dispensation. Sometimes we need to use all the tools in our toolbox to defeat evil."

Nightshade nodded. "I've been accepted into the service of Althaya. As a result, I can only use magic granted to me by her. If not, I'm powerless."

"Demons don't follow gods or goddesses," Eric the Black remarked. "Like sorcerers, they draw their magic from the environment."

"True," Nightshade responded. "I have the knowledge, but not the connection needed to bend that energy to my will. The ley lines of magic are as accessible to me as they are to any non-sorcerer."

"So, you're a slave to Althaya," Eric the Black remarked.

Nightshade shook her head. "That's not how I see it."

"Nor is that the way it works," Nefertari stated. "There's a level of trust between the gods and their priests or priestesses. My goddess, Sehanine StarEagle, does not restrict me because she trusts me to do the right thing. Oh, there's certainly a back-and-forth if she disagrees, but I've won the disagreement as many times as not. My goddess is immortal and capable of many things, but she's not omnipotent."

Maedhros Nénmacil spun around several times and roared with laughter. "Back-and-forth, she says," he rumbled. "Sehanine StarEagle probably rues the day she accepted Nefertari into her service. My mistress wears the goddess out with her hardheadedness and opinions!"

"All right, my stony friend," Nefertari said. "Nightshade, why did you change?"

Nightshade looked away. "To answer your question, I must admit to weakness. That's never been easy for me."

"HA! Not easy for you?" Maedhros Nénmacil chortled from outside the tent. "You'll fit in real nice with elves!"

Nefertari smiled and nudged Colonel Tirion in the ribs. "Are we that obvious," she said.

"I wouldn't know," Daeron replied as he smiled back. "I'm a Marine and Marines have no weaknesses."

"Ain't that the truth," General Feynral added.

Nightshade, relaxed somewhat by the good-natured banter, continued. "It was a song." She looked at Father Goram. "I first heard it when Kristen was a child. This was before I'd broken my bond to Mordecai."

Father Goram, who had retaken his seat next to his new pupil, stopped her narration. "Whatever happened to him?"

"I ate his soul," Nightshade replied without emotion. "That was after I destroyed him one nerve at a time. My father and I no longer needed him… and I had come to loathe him. The things he did…" Nightshade shook her head. "It took a long time for Mordecai to die."

Father Goram squeezed Nightshade's leg. "I find no fault in that. Please go on."

"I spied on you for Mordecai, Horatio," Nightshade admitted. "The song was a bedtime lullaby you sang to Kristen every evening. It was so beautiful… and not just the song, but also the love I heard in your voice for your little 'Bright Eyes'. I couldn't believe how much it lifted my spirits. But more so, it caused me to question the reason for my existence. I was a demon. How could I have any feelings other than hate for lowly mortals? My first reaction… I'd say probably a typical response to the feelings I wanted to deny… was to be even crueler to the mortals I met. But even as I did, I knew it was already too late for me. I was no longer a true demon." Nightshade bowed her head. "I'm sorry, Horatio."

"Nonsense, child," the priest responded.

Nightshade nodded. "I heard Kristen sing the same lullaby to Emmy."

Everyone perked up at the mention of the last empath.

"You got that close to her?" Landross exclaimed.

"Not close enough to do any harm," Nightshade said. "And even if I wanted to try, I'm not sure how successful I'd have been. Kristen put up very impressive… and possibly impenetrable… defensive spells around the child. And Emmy has her own power. It was power that I didn't recognize. It was power that frightened me."

"Naturally," Lauran commented. "She's an empath."

Nightshade shook her head. "She's more than that."

"Explain," Father Goram commanded. This was new to him also.

Nightshade nodded. "I sent one of the world's foremost assassins from the world's most powerful Assassin's Guild to spy on the child and keep the girl and Kristen safe from harm. At the time Mordecai needed both alive and well for his plan to work… and father needed Mordecai for his own plans. But to my amazement, Emmy managed to capture the assassin's complete loyalty. She's now the child's protector. You can't possibly know how much influence Emmy must have had to get an assassin of her stature to turn on her guild."

"I do," Eric the Black said. "It seldom ever happens, and when it does, the guild will spare no expense to track down and make an example of the poor bastard." The sorcerer looked at Father Goram. "Horatio, if what Nightshade says is true, that guild will come at the assassin hard."

"Mariko," Nightshade interjected.

"Eh?"

"The assassin's name is Mariko."

Eric the Black's eyes became larger, and he whispered a few well-chosen obscenities. "I know this one. I even tried to…" The sorcerer stopped talking. He started to say 'recruit her'… but no one knew he moonlighted as a master assassin. He needed to think it through before he came clean.

"Tried to what," Landross asked.

"You haven't told them your secret?" Nightshade remarked.

Eric the Black looked angry. "No, and it's going to stay that way!" he shouted at Nightshade. More calmly, "How did you figure it out?"

"I was a demon," she replied as if that explained everything.

"Enough!" Father Goram exclaimed before he leaned over and whispered into Nightshades ear. "Tell me later."

Nightshade nodded.

Father Goram addressed the roundtable. "Our sorcerer friend here can make whatever admissions afterwards if he so desires. Right now we have more important things to discuss. How bad is it, Eric?"

Eric the Black saw the exchange between Father Goram and Nightshade. He was fairly certain Nightshade would eventually inform the priest of his secret life as a master assassin if she hadn't already. He didn't fear Father Goram's reaction… the priest knew, as did every leader, how important an assassin's loyalty can be. He only regretted not telling the priest sooner and hoped his secret wouldn't go farther. If Landross found out, he'd probably try to stick that huge sword he carried straight through the sorcerer's heart. That, and he'd regret losing the friendship.

Eric the Black took a deep breath and continued. "Everyone around Mariko is in grave danger," he emphasized. "The guild won't stop until they've restored their reputation."

"They've already shown they can take care of themselves," Landross snorted, "particularly against lowborn assassins. We must save the queen and Autumn!"

Eric the Black shook his head. "You don't understand. The guild, especially one with the resources to employ someone as skilled as Mariko, will have the other smaller guilds beholden to them. Assassins will come from all directions and at all times of the day or night. And it won't stop until Mariko has been either taken or killed. Sooner or later, one of them will score. That's a given. Which of our friends are you willing to sacrifice for Mariko?"

Father Goram shook his head. "I didn't realize the implications of an assassin turning on her guild. I suppose I should have… but this damn war took everything I got. And it's cost me almost more than I can bear. Does Mariko understand the consequences of her actions?"

"Of course she does," Eric the Black snapped. "What assassin wouldn't?"

"Damn you, Eric!" Landross shouted. "Stop being so bloody condescending! The queen and Autumn are in the Abyss and the child Emmy, Kristen, and Tangus are on the mainland and in danger of being slaughtered by nameless scum. If I didn't know better, I'd say we LOST the war."

"Calm down, knight," Nefertari said. "We'll figure it out. That's why we're here."

Father Goram looked at Kyleigh. "Beg your pardon, Highness, but you've been awfully quiet. Do you have anything to offer?"

Kyleigh glanced over at Nefertari and nodded. "Just one piece of advice, good priest. Make Nefertari acting regent during the queen's absence. They're sisters, so there'd be no legal standing for any other claim. I understand Nefertari lacks experience, but she's had many years of training. I did that myself. So I'm confident in her ability to reign. She's also, as you know, a powerful priestess of one of the older goddess's… and she's surrounded herself with powerful allies. You couldn't ask for a better person."

Maedhros Nénmacil rumbled assent.

Father Goram nodded. "I'd already come to that same conclusion. Providing Nefertari is willing."

Nefertari nodded. "Of course! I'd be happy to help however I can. The only question is, are the people willing to accept me."

"They will, my lady," General Singëril said. "And if they don't, you'll have my army at your back!"

"And my Marines," General Feynral added.

Nefertari shook her head. "Please, gentlemen, let's not talk about using force!"

"It's yours by right, my dear," Kyleigh said. "Your sister would use whatever means at her disposal to keep her throne. You owe it to her to do the same. You must make sure there's a throne for your sister to return to."

Nefertari nodded. "I accept. As my first act I'm assigning Colonel Tirion to be my permanent military liaison."

Lauran whispered into General Singëril's ear. He looked at General Feynral who nodded. They suspected the colonel would resign if he didn't get to stay by the queen-regent's side. Not only did the two general's value Colonel Tirion's service, but they also liked the idea of having one of their own so close to the seat of power on InnisRos. "Certainly, my lady," the army general consented.

"Let's move on to other things," Father Goram said. "Eric, I could use your help in the Abyss."

Eric the Black shook his head. "Sorry, Horatio, but I won't be available."

"And why not," Landross asked.

"Because I need him to return to the Alfheim with me," Kyleigh replied to the knight's question. "I too have lost friends to your war and I need his help to find them."

"We'll not deny you this request," Nefertari said, ending any further protest from either knight or priest. "Aster wouldn't have survived without your intervention."

Kyleigh thanked Nefertari with a slight nod of her head and a smile.

"Will you stay and rest before leaving us?" Nefertari asked.

The Alfheim queen shook her head. "No… but I thank you, Nefertari. Eric and I need to travel to my world at once. That's where we'll have the best chance of saving our friends."

"Then you must leave for the…?" Nefertari paused.

"The *Ak-Vanessë Stone*," Eric the Black replied in answer to the priestess's question. "Right now it lies in the forest west of Taranthi guarded by a few Army retirees. I suggest you move it to a more secure location as soon as possible."

"Yes, of course." Nefertari looked at Colonel Tirion who motioned for one of his Marine sergeants to approach. Since the battle for Taranthi they had not left his side. "Please see to it that two horses are made ready along with a small escort."

"We'll travel much faster alone," Eric the Black stated. "And the mounts I have in mind would leave an ordinary horse eating dust."

"Well then, what are you waiting for," Landross said. The tone of his voice marked his disappointment in the sorcerer's decision.

Aster's queen-regent and the Alfheim's queen hugged each other. Outside the tent, Eric the Black conjured two shadow steeds. The sorcerer approached Father Goram, and they hugged, each slapping the other on the back.

"Take this," Eric the Black said as he held out a hand. In his palm was a brooch. "Do you know what a Soulreaver is?"

"Qénsharma," Father Goram answered as he nodded. "Heard rumors…"

"You heard right," Eric the Black said. "Assassins have been secretly using them for a long time. I used them to help us win this little war we had going here. There are four of them somewhere near the *Ak-Vanessë Stone*. Though that's where I'm heading, I don't have time to search them out. That brooch will attract them and allow you control them."

"You want us to use beasts from the Abyss?" Landross, who'd overheard the conversation, asked.

Eric the Black nodded.

"They don't have an agenda, Landross," Father Goram said. "They only want to eat and sleep."

"And the demons in the Abyss are terrified of them," Eric the Black added. "At least that's where my research of them led me."

"You're right," Nightshade added. "When my father found out there where Qénsharma on InnisRos, he had a fit. They will serve us well… provided that brooch does all you say it does."

"Don't worry, it will."

"Eric?"

"I'm ready, Kyleigh."

"Will we see you again?" Father Goram asked.

The sorcerer looked at the Alfheim queen with affection. "I don't know," he said as he directed his shadow steed southward. Within a few minutes both were out of sight.

Father Goram looked at the brooch and then turned to General Singëril. "I need a fast frigate to get me down the coast and to Taranthi," he said.

The general nodded and issued orders to one of his adjutants.

"I guess I'm going with you," Nefertari said to the priest. "At least to the capital."

"Shiver me timbers… an ocean adventure!" roared Maedhros Nénmacil. "Avast ye, mate! Batten down the hatches! Swab the poop deck! Don't hornswoggle the StarSinger! Arrrggghhh…"

◄──────────── ⟨⊗⊗⊗⟩ ────────────►

THE FINAL INTERREGNUM

Rhys, carrying Rathal across his back, was exhausted and needed to rest. He had just entered the outskirts of the Forest of the Fey, but still had a day of travel before they'd reach their destination. He lowered Rathal and sat him against a large tree. The sorcerer hadn't regained consciousness since he exploded the volcano to kill the white dragon. Though Rhys was deeply concerned about the health of his friend, the long walk to get this far had stolen most of his energy. Other than noting Rathal's condition and making him as comfortable as possible, all Rhys was interested in was sleep… sleep after a long drink of water.

As Rhys saw to the sorcerer's immediate needs, he heard a noise which caused him to stand and draw his sword. A small rabbit scurried between bushes.

Rhys smiled. "Run fast, little cottontail. Or the next time you'll be my dinner."

"Not in this forest," Rathal said from behind him.

Rhys looked around and saw that branches had grown out of the tree, similar to the arms of a rocking chair, and provided support on both sides of Rathal.

"That's a neat trick," Rhys said.

"I didn't do it," Rathal replied. "I gather we're in the Forest of the Fey?"

The spy nodded. "We are. How do you feel?"

Rathal coughed. It was ragged and deep. A little fresh blood rolled down his chin. "At Death's door," he replied.

Rhys kneeled back down beside the sorcerer and inspected the 'rocking chair arm' branches. They were solid and looked natural. *"Exactly what Rathal needed,"* he thought. *"Interesting."*

"The forest is alive," Rathal said. He'd closed his eyes again but appeared to breathe easier since his coughing spell. "It wasn't like this the last time I was here."

Rhys had heard the story many times. Rathal was a young sorcerer and his first foray outside Havendale with a caravan escort had been a disaster. Madeira and Hebron, two rival mercenary cities, put the caravan in the middle of their incessant bickering. The surprise attack by Madeira on the Hebron-bound and guarded caravan overpowered its defenders and slaughtered them. Of those, Rathal and a young female warrior sellsword were the only survivors. Together they ran for their lives. Going south back towards Havendale, the night forced them to seek shelter in the Forest of the Fey just outside the haunted city of Elanesse. Though Rathal would never admit to it, Rhys suspected the warrior mercenary and the sorcerer had formed a bond that night, however brief, which would never be forgotten... or forsaken.

"I need to rest," Rhys said. "Give me an hour or two."

Rathal, his eyes still closed, nodded. "Not much more," he whispered. "My heart rushes to beat its last and I need to get to the golden tree. It's important."

"Why," ventured Rhys.

"I don't know."

Rhys felt hot breath on his face. He opened his eyes to stare into the snout of the largest, blackest dire wolf he'd ever seen. Sitting up, the spy scooted over to Rathal, expecting to be ripped apart at any moment. But the wolf only watched. Next to the giant black wolf stood another wolf. While not as large, this one was as white as the other was black... like a newly laid carpet of snow. They appeared to be a matched pair... one's Yin to the other's Yang.

Rhys nudged the sorcerer. "Rathal, wake up," he pleaded as he locked eyes with the larger wolf. The sorcerer didn't move. The spy suspected any move to unsheathe his sword would be catastrophic and probably result in dinner for the two wolves. *"Oh hell, we're most likely dinner already… we just haven't been filleted yet,"* he thought.

Rhys decided there was nothing to lose. He slowly reached toward the sword on his hip and wrapped his hand around the hilt. The large black wolf was on him in a flash. It knocked Rhys over and straddled him. The two stared at each other, nose to nose. The wolf never growled, nor did it appear threatening in any way – just overbearing. After a few seconds, seconds in which Rhys feared to even take a breath, the wolf reached down and grabbed the hilt of the sword with its mouth. It reared on its back legs, much like a horse, and whipped its head to the side. The sword flew straight and true into the trunk of a nearby tree, where it buried itself into the bark. Rhys watched, astonished, as several limbs of the tree began to move. They encircled the blade of his sword and secured it even further.

"What the hell is going on here," Rhys said as he got up into a sitting position.

"They're our friends," Rathal said.

"You're awake!" Rhys exclaimed as he moved closer to the sorcerer. "How do you…," Rhys stopped. "You look like you're feeling better."

Rathal nodded. "For a little bit. Sakkara brought healing." The sorcerer pointed to a discarded glass bottle.

"Sakkara?" Rhys said. "You mean the white wolf?"

"And the black one's her mate, Romulus," Rathal said. "They're two special wolves."

"How?"

Rathal took a deep breath. Sakkara had lain beside the sorcerer and placed her large head on his lap. "A dream," he said as he began to pet the wolf. "It was a particularly specific dream. Romulus and Sakkara are here to take us to the golden tree."

"They are, huh," Rhys replied with skepticism. "I've never seen anything like this, and I've traveled every inch of the mainland. You know I have."

Rathal examined the branches of the tree that kept him propped up. "As I mentioned earlier, this is an extraordinary forest."

"Can it save your life?"

The sorcerer shook his head. "Nothing can do that. I'm already beginning to feel the blackness close in again. Now listen closely and don't ask questions. We don't have time for that, and I doubt I could answer them anyway. There are creatures… creatures in the forest and the city of Elanesse… that are from another world. They're extremely dangerous. The wolves should be able to get us safely to the golden tree, but you need to be ready if something happens."

Rhys heard a soft thump and turned to see his sword lying on the ground. "And once there?" he asked, unphased.

Rathal shook his head. "I've no idea. All I know is that I need to get there, and these wolves were sent to help. So help me get secured on Romulus' back. We need to be off."

By the time Rhys had Rathal tied to the back of the black wolf, the sorcerer had fallen back into unconsciousness. As the spy followed the two wolves, he considered his perceived familiarity with the world around him and wondered how much more there was that he didn't understand. For the master spy it was a humbling experience.

Rhys sighed and shook his head. *"Maybe I should get out of the spy business and settle down with Shynaria,"* he thought. But he knew he never would.

CHAPTER TWENTY-THREE

The Forest of the Fey

The end of war — the end of death, barbarity, and deprivation — is but a truce of sorts… a pause before the beginning of the next war. That another war will be fought is a certainty. True peace is a utopian design which is flawed at its very foundation… for it assumes that's what people want.

-The Book of the Unveiled

Osiris, the Royal Mountain Saber Cat leader, and his Snow Pride warriors picked their way through the debris of a crumbling wall and entered Market Square. The strange, foreign stench they smelled earlier was now overbearing and very nearly masked the scent of the elves, or, as the cats called them, pointy ears. There was no evidence of the cub they sought, and Osiris was concerned that if the little one had found its way into the city, it might already be dead.

Movement came from one of the large buildings that ringed the square. Several of the saber cats trotted over and stopped fifty feet away, sniffing and using their keen night vision to peer into a dark, open doorway. More movement and three creatures charged from the interior of the building.

As the creatures moved they blurred into the backdrop of their surroundings. This camouflage effect made attacks on them difficult… though not so much for those who use more than just eyesight to fight. The creatures were entirely white with pink eyes, and their short, pig-like snouts opened up to reveal two sharp fangs and a barbed proboscis. Their elongated head curved downwards and over their back. Their bodies were armored with a hard chitin exoskeleton and their long tail ended in spider spinnerets. Each had two arms that were highlighted by large and sharp claws. As the otherworldly beings charged they screamed a challenge. The three foremost saber cats answered.

The queen of the *Theraesus* made herself comfortable on the bottom floor of the Pyramid of the Purge. It was the perfect location – deep underground and catacombed with tunnels and chambers that were easily defensible. It was the perfect nest for her, her servants, and her warriors. Even though they'd been mysteriously snatched from their home world with little to no hope of returning, the *Theraesus* queen felt contentment… for she and her horde had escaped a certain death. Their own world had been bleak and desolate, and they were dying from famine. But now they had a second chance on a new world flush with food.

The queen squirmed. Several of her attendants at once rushed to the sides of her bloated body. They discovered a large rock protruding upwards and removed it. The queen sighed in relief and began laying eggs. There'd be hundreds of thousands by the time she was finished. And that's only the first swarm. As the first egg was carried away to one of the hatching chambers, the thought of conquest gleamed in the eye of the *Theraesus* queen.

"Daddy!" Daphnia exclaimed as she ran to a group of four giants leading even larger horses. Her wolf, Adimar, son of Fenrisúlfr, followed close behind.

Lord Ternborg kneeled and opened his arms to accept his screaming daughter as she launched herself towards him. Adimar circled the two, yelping his own welcome to the Draugen Pesta leader.

Emmy approached after waiting a respectful period to allow the two their reunion. Acting as hostess, she silently directed the three warriors who had accompanied their commander to a place with low-hanging fruit and thick, green grass for the horses. None of the newcomers questioned Emmy's authority.

"Did they hurt you?" Lord Ternborg asked his daughter.

Daphnia shook her head. "No father. Nightshade left specific instructions, and she gave me Adimar for protection. He's young, but he's still a son of Fenrisúlfr. Demons feared him almost as much as they feared Nightshade."

Lord Ternborg watched the two closely. There was no doubt the wolf was a loyal friend… and it was plain that Daphnia returned the feelings. An immortal such as Adimar would serve his daughter well, particularly if she's ever named the leader of the Draugen Pesta people.

"We need to return home, child," Lord Ternborg said. "Your mother's eager to see you back safe in the capital."

"And the Hyrokkin again threaten our eastern border," Daphnia mentioned.

"How did you know?"

"I told her," Emmy said.

Lord Ternborg raised an eyebrow. He studied the child. She couldn't be more than seven or eight years old. But there was a look of great wisdom in her eyes, unusual for one so young.

"And I found out from Michael," Emmy responded to Lord Ternborg's unasked question.

The Draugen Pesta leader stared even harder at the young goddess.

Emmy boldly responded to the scrutiny. "What's the matter, Lord Ternborg? You don't believe me? We've talked, Michael and I, several times. He told me and I judged Daphnia deserved to know as well. Don't you agree?"

"I'm growing up, daddy."

Lord Ternborg thought about it and nodded. "All right," he agreed. "Yes, it would seem the Hyrokkin are taking advantage of my forced presence here. I knew better than to come across the Greater Boreskyre's. But what could I do? Nightshade had kidnapped you. But you're safe now."

Emmy nodded. "Safe for now." The young empath moved over to Adimar and scratched the massive wolf's side. The wolf responded by licking the child's hand. "The Draugen Pesta people probably aren't pleased that you left them only partially defended."

"And rightfully so," Lord Ternborg answered. "They deserved more from their leader."

Emmy stopped scratching Adimar. "Will you accept a word of advice from me?"

Lord Ternborg looked first at Emmy and then Daphnia. He realized he had to readjust his thinking about his daughter, and maybe all children in general. He nodded.

"As you go to war against the Hyrokkin, let Daphnia be your… ambassador… to your people."

The Draugen Pesta leader frowned.

Emmy continued. "She's capable. And it just might help to keep you in power. A stable Draugen Pesta is important."

Lord Ternborg studied the last empath. "Why?"

Emmy shook her head. "I don't know why… only that you must not be ousted as leader of the Draugen Pesta nation."

"Listen to her, father!" Daphnia warned.

Lord Ternborg took Daphnia's hand and started for his horse. "Come, sweetie. As for your request, Emmy. I'll consider it."

The Draugen Pesta mounted their horses. Daphnia sat in front of her father. As the horses pawed the soft earth, ready to leave for home, Lord Ternborg looked at the Emmy. "You have my gratitude for keeping my daughter safe, young lady. If ever you should have need of me or my warriors, just send me a message. Draugen Pesta pays its debts."

"You owe no debt to me, Lord Ternborg," Emmy said. "Your daughter is an amazing child… and good-natured. This reflects favorably on you, her mother, and your people. We value the same things. That's enough."

Daphnia removed a locket from around her neck and reached down with it in her hand. "Please."

Emmy nodded and accepted the small gift. It represented the bond that had grown between the two. "I'm honored."

Lord Ternborg paused for just a moment and then bowed to Emmy as an equal before kicking his stallion forward.

Emmy watched as the four gigantic horses and their riders disappeared into the forest. *"Elrond,"* she thought but didn't get a reply. *"Elrond?"*

"Huh? Oh, sorry. You didn't say Elendrel-Telperiën, so I didn't know who you were talking to," Elrond replied.

"Dear!" Elanesse scolded.

"I'm so confused," the former mercenary said.

Emmy rolled her eyes. *"Are there any of the off-world creatures between here and the direction they ride?"*

"No," Elrond replied. *"And before you ask, I'm already making a path so they can travel faster, though it's hard because the Black Death are so bloody big. The natives I'm forcing to comply are not only restless, but they may actually turn on me."* It was obvious the 'natives' to which he referred were the trees and bushes that made up his subjects.

"I'm sure you have the situation well in hand, lover," Elanesse said.

"Yes I do! For I am the great Elendrel-Telperiën," Elrond boasted. *"But the willow is weeping."*

Both trees laughed so hard they soon covered the ground in bronze and golden leaves.

Emmy smiled. *"The spirit of Elanesse has returned,"* she thought. *"And Elrond! What an insufferable scoundrel!"* Emmy then started laughing as hard as her rooted companions.

Harkum, the Spiked Fist commander, and what was left of his mercenary company found little comfort within the broken walls of Elanesse. Instead of finding sanctuary, they discovered there were more of the creatures inside the city then out – many, many more. Each creature his men killed was replaced by ten more… and killing them proved to be difficult because of the light deflection each creature used for defense.

Most of the Spiked Fist mercenaries were killed immediately upon entering the city. Victorious creatures sank long proboscis into the belly of the dead men and sucked the internal juices out until nothing remained but a dried husk. The rest, including Harkum, were overpowered instead of killed. They were held in rough cocoons made from a sticky substance and dragged off towards the Pyramid of the Purge. Harkum and the remaining men of the Spiked Fist Mercenary Company suspected what was coming next. They screamed and screamed and screamed. But it did them no good.

"They're everywhere," Mariko said to Tangus. She, Tangus, Jennifer, and Kristen were on the multi-tiered roof of the Grand Palace. Tangus usually wouldn't have used a place which had few escape routes. But the Grand Palace had been built with every contingency in mind. It included several safe rooms which were extremely sturdy and almost impossible to distinguish from the surrounding architecture. Once inside one of those rooms, it would take a complete collapse of the palace itself to breach, though Tangus judged even that might not be enough.

Tangus nodded. "We're lucky we made it here. Just a few hours later and there would've been too many of them."

"They look fierce and smell awful, but they die easily," Jennifer added. "One arrow is usually all that's needed."

Mariko snorted. "Once you can see them clearly."

"I can help with that," Kristen told Mariko. Then she shook her head and looked at her husband. "We might be thinking about this all wrong, Tangus. They act like insects… like ants or the rock termites that live deep underground."

Tangus nodded. "Organized with each of the creatures knowing its purpose and fulfilling that purpose to the death. If, like the ant, there's a queen somewhere underground, we can kill every single one of these bugs above ground and still not stop the invasion."

"Boy, I sure wouldn't want to live on their world," Jennifer remarked.

"They probably don't want to be on ours, either," Mariko said.

"Alien ants," Jennifer said. "Or some other type of mindless bug."

"Like dire wolves are just some kind of mindless animal," Kristen asked. "Sweetie, they're from another world. We can't assume anything."

"No, Jennifer may be correct," Tangus said, "particularly if a queen is directing their movements. It wouldn't be too far a stretch to assume she's the only intelligent one. But your point is well taken, my love."

"If there's a queen, she'll be well protected," Mariko added. "We need an army to get past guards up here on the surface. The gods only know how many of them are below protecting her. And Tangus, in case you haven't counted lately, there's only four of us."

"Perhaps we could enlist the aid of the Draugen Pesta," Jennifer suggested. "They seemed like they could be decent allies."

"I bet they're long gone," Tangus replied. "I think we're on our own."

"Okay, so where do we start," Jennifer asked.

Tangus frowned, something he did frequently when he was working on a problem. "I suspect the queen, assuming one exists, will be under the Pyramid of the Purge. It's deep underground and has a lot of chambers and passageways she can use. Those passageways are how we get to her."

Kristen looked at her husband. "You mean to get to the queen from below through the tunnels that connect the pyramid and the Tower of the Innocent."

Tangus nodded. "It seems to be our best option. And we know the way. Right now I don't have any other answers."

"You remember there's a Soulreaver down there," Kristen said. "And it's probably starving."

"I'd never forget that." Tangus shivered as he remembered what a Soulreaver had done to one of the many mercenaries that once inhibited Elanesse. "We'll just have to take our chances. Maybe it's already fed on a bug."

"Let's hope not," Mariko interjected.

The reformed assassin had everyone's attention.

"Tangus, do you remember the conversation we had relating to the Soulreaver?"

Tangus nodded. "That assassins use them to 'deliver results'. I remember. But the Soulreaver down there was feral," he said as he shook his head. "No, Mariko, it's too dangerous."

"I can handle the Soulreaver," Mariko insisted. "I can make it do my bidding."

Tangus looked out over the Grand Palace grounds, thinking. He looked back at Mariko. "All right... we need every advantage. If we come across it, you can try. But you must first convince me you have it under control before I'll allow you to use it."

"And if there's more than one?" Kristen asked.

Mariko looked less sure of herself... but only for a second. "Then I'll need a bigger bag to carry them in."

The Royal Mountain Saber Cats were in the fight of their lives. As soon as the first three creatures charged, several dozen more spilled out of the building. The three lead cats came to a halt as common sense overruled their desire to meet the challenge.

"To me!" Osiris roared, though the three front cats needed no prompting. "Back into the forest. Saladin, get to the rear."

"Father?"

Osiris didn't bother to answer his son. The Snow Pride warriors were taking defensive positions as they retreated, and Osiris was busy making sure his cats were exactly where he felt they should be. The situation was grave.

"Father?"

"Not now, son!"

"Father!"

Osiris turned and saw why Saladin had been so insistent. More of the creatures were closing fast on both their flanks. If he didn't respond at once, they were going to be surrounded... if it wasn't already too late.

The Snow Pride leader turned to Rahotep. "Get the lad back to his mother," he ordered. "I need five volunteers... warriors without families... to help me hold back these creatures."

Osiris sent two each of his volunteers to both flanks while he and the final volunteer, a huge one-eyed bruiser named Moishe, waited for the creatures moving to them from the front. They knew this was likely the end, but it was a sacrifice they'd accept if it meant most of their brother warriors would make it back into the mountains and to their families.

The creatures appeared in the trees ahead, their natural blurring ability somewhat nullified as the trees and bushes moved to expose their positions. Osiris roared as the first of the creatures died under his dagger-like claws and fangs.

Kristen, from her position on the palace steps, watched as Tangus and Mariko moved unchallenged from the covering bushes of the palace grounds to the inner defensive wall. The gates of the wall stood open. She waited with Jennifer for her husband's signal to move forward.

"I wish we were home," Jennifer confided.

"We are home, dear," Kristen replied. "It's a good home. We just need to fight for it."

There was silence as both observed Tangus and Mariko check the other side of the gates.

"Not for me," Jennifer continued. "I think once father no longer needs my help I'll return to InnisRos."

"He'll always need you."

Jennifer nodded. "And I'll always need him. But this will never be my true home."

"Your family is here," Kristen countered.

"Aye, but not all," Jennifer replied. "I have family on InnisRos, too. Father Goram, Landross, Cordelia, Cameron, the wolves… even the trees."

Kristen nodded. She understood. For some people, home was also a physical location. It's the sense of a place… a place where one feels contentment… a place where the heart feels complete… a place the soul yearns for. "I understand. And I believe your father will as well."

"I hope so," Jennifer said. "Don't tell him, okay? I'll do that after everything settles down."

Kristen turned and took Jennifer's hand. "I promise." Then she looked back at Tangus and Mariko. Both were running towards them. Their swords were sheathed, but their bows had arrows notched.

There was a look of terror in Tangus' eyes as he stopped, turned, and let his first shot fly.

Osiris ducked a claw swipe, turned, sprang, and raked the creature down its side with his own claws. The cat had learned through painful experience the creature's greatest physical weakness — a small space which ran down both sides of the creature's armored chitin exoskeleton. The creature dropped, dead. Osiris sprang away as the dead creature disintegrated into a puddle of a foul-smelling white mucus-like liquid.

Osiris looked around and saw no other signs of their attackers. Moishe joined him, as did two of the other cat warriors. The remaining two lay still on the moss and blood covered ground. The Snow Pride leader looked over at Moishe. He looked terrible. They all did. And Osiris felt pain with every breath.

"We need to return to the mountains," Osiris announced.

"What of our dead?" Moishe asked.

Osiris shook his head. "We must leave. We're on borrowed time. I can feel it."

Moishe balked. "These creatures will find their way to our home."

"I know that!" Osiris snarled.

Moishe looked at his leader. His one eye gleamed. "We should try to stop that from happening."

Osiris stared back. *"Understanding?"* he thought. *"How could I have misjudged Moishe so much?"*

"Besides," Moishe added, "I enjoy killing these creatures. I enjoy smashing them and hearing their shells crack." There was a round of "Here! Here!" from the other two.

"That's the Moishe I know," Osiris said to himself. Out loud, "Very well, my friends. But we'll need allies to help. Let's go find those

elves. I'm sure they'll be happy to help us smash and crack these creatures."

Two creatures collapsed and fell to the ground with arrows sticking out of their pig-snouted heads. Jennifer turned and saw dozens of the creatures climbing over the palace defensive walls and charging at them from both sides,. It reminded her of a thick fog moving across a landscape, swallowing all obstacles as it made its steady and irrepressible advance.

Arrows took out two more of the beasts. Jennifer grabbed Kristen's hand and the two of them ran down the steps and into the courtyard towards Tangus and Mariko. Kristen needed little coaxing. She also saw the danger and knew that the four of them had no chance of survival unless they stood together.

A creature fell, but only suffered a graze from an arrow. It stood and continued its progress forward.

"Damn that blurring," Mariko remarked as she notched another arrow. This time the creature stayed down.

Kristen and Jennifer were only a few yards away when one creature clawed the back of Jennifer's leg, slicing through her hamstring. Jennifer dropped to the ground as her leg refused to work. Kristen stopped and stood over Jennifer with sword in hand, ready to fight to the death in defense of her stepdaughter. There was no time for magic, and though Kristen would have preferred the steel quarterstaff she'd given to Azriel, she was exceptionally proficient with a sword. Tangus and Lester had made sure of that.

The creatures had almost surrounded Kristen and Jennifer when Tangus and Mariko arrived. There was a small half-circle of the mucous looking remains of dead creatures. Jennifer, sitting on the ground, a small puddle of blood under her right leg, was firing arrows.

"We're here," Tangus called over the sounds of snarling creatures. Kristen grunted each time she swung her sword. Her cloak was on the ground and her silk blouse wet with sweat.

"Give me a few seconds," Kristen said. Tangus could hear the weariness in her voice.

While Jennifer continued to use bow and arrow, Tangus used his scimitars and Mariko her katanas. Although the three of them had to fight off the awful stench of the creatures and the nausea it created, Kristen, by now deep in a spell-casting trance, didn't appear to be affected.

"Wondrous circle of magic and steel,
Behold the enemies we must repeal.

Impenetrable circle of life and death,
It is to you we will owe our breath.

Come and surround us, provide us safe haven.
As we battle our foes, antagonists most craven."

"PER POTENTIAM ALTHAYA"

A wall of magical force surrounded by an impenetrable barricade of hundreds of spinning knives encircled them. Tangus and Mariko backed away from the inner wall of the barrier. Tangus stood with Kristen who was concentrating on the *Bladebarrier Sanctuary* spell she just invoked. Mariko kneeled next to Jennifer and swabbed the young ranger's hamstring cut with a thick and soothing healing jelly before wrapping the wound with a bandage. The stench of the creatures, now blocked by the magic of the spell, was no longer a factor.

On the outside of the *Bladebarrier Sanctuary* the creatures attacked with no concern for the spinning knives. All they saw was prey. And prey was all they thought of. The spinning knives turned the creatures into mucus-like puddles of remains. It didn't matter, though. They kept coming.

The *Theraesus* queen felt the death of her drones. The numbers didn't worry her, for there were plenty more to take their place. That there existed a force capable of killing so many, however, concerned her very much. This threat must be eliminated no matter how minuscule the peril to her might be.

The queen recalled her drones. Perhaps it was best to lie in wait for a while – to gage the strength of the threat before she spent any more of her drones. She hadn't stayed alive for hundreds of years by taking chances.

Osiris sensed something strange had happened. For the last few hours he and his small group of Snow Pride warriors had been moving westward through Elanesse, hiding from, and avoiding the creatures as much as possible. Then, without warning, all signs of the creatures themselves vanished. But there were still plenty of signs of where they'd been... and where they were going. Osiris and his band of cats followed.

"We've only got about ten minutes before Kristen has to shut this down," Tangus commented. "And then, she'll be too weak to even walk."

"There's no sign these creatures are backing off," Jennifer observed.

"And they've stopped running into the knives," Tangus added. "They're learning. Which means Kristen's spell is only a reprieve. Mariko, you've been quiet. Any suggestions?"

Mariko shook her head. "I've tried to contact Emmy, but… I'm sorry. Though I've devoted myself to her and can feel our connection, I don't know how to contact her, or how to be her priestess. I mean, do I get on my knees and pray? Do I go into a trance of some kind? Do I speak holy words like Kristen does?" Mariko sighed. "All I know is how to be an assassin."

"We accept you for who you are," Jennifer said. "As does Emmy. Stop trying to be what you think Emmy expects and instead use what you are to do the things you know Emmy would want you to do."

"Out of the mouths of babes," Tangus remarked as he gave his daughter a playful push. "But wise counsel, nevertheless."

Kristen moaned and wavered.

Tangus put an arm around her shoulders to steady her. He looked out at the waiting creatures. "The magic's going to collapse soon."

The means of their salvation suddenly presented itself in the skies above Elanesse.

Lycomedes looked down into the city and located the congregation of creatures that, like he and his Sky Emperor brothers and sisters, were victims of a shift and not native to this world.

"They're the ones Emmy told us about," Phanessa said. "Those creatures do not wish to live on this world in peace."

Lycomedes grunted. "It looks as if those creatures do not wish to live peacefully on any world. But they, like us, are casualties of the shift. Do they deserve to die?"

"Do the natives of this place, our new home, deserve to die?" Phanessa replied.

"Of course not," Lycomedes said.

"They've made their choice and we've made ours," Phanessa answered. To her, it was a simple decision.

Lycomedes agreed. Though he didn't take any loss of life lightly, he understood the necessity. He gave the order to attack.

The Sky Emperors surprised the *Theraesus* with lightning bolts reaching down from long tendrils. Tangus watched as torn pieces of the creatures flew into the air after each such lightning strike. Within seconds the horde surrounding the *Bladebarrier Sanctuary* began to disperse.

Tangus pumped his fist into the air. "You magnificent bastards," he shouted to the Sky Emperors.

As the *Theraesus* broke and ran, the Sky Emperors tracked them and destroyed as many as possible. After five minutes the explosions stopped as the *Theraesus* disappeared, either killed or driven into hiding. Welcomed silence descended upon the city. Waifs of smoke curled into the air and the acidic smell of scorched earth competed with the stench from the dead *Theraesus*. Above, Sky Emperors filled the sky with their tendrils snaking towards the ground. They looked as if they were gargantuan trees sitting on long, emaciated trunks.

The *Bladebarrier Sanctuary* spell dropped, and Kristen collapsed. But Tangus was ready. He caught and supported her before she could fall to the ground, exhausted.

"How do you feel," Tangus asked.

Kristen didn't even bother to open her eyes. "Like I could sleep for a month," she replied as she sat up on her own. "But not before I've eaten a couple loaves of fresh bread and a wheel of cheese. What happened?"

"Look up."

"The Sky Emperors," Kristen said. "I've gotten so used to seeing them in the skies over Elanesse I took them for granted."

"We all have," Mariko said. "Emmy's brought them into the fold."

"I imagine there are a few generals who'd love to have them," Jennifer remarked. "They've proven they're better than dragons."

Kristen finished a long drink of water to flush down the three hardtack biscuits and jerky sandwiches she'd just eaten. "Emmy would never allow that."

Mariko agreed. "I think she has plans for Elanesse... plans which involved keeping the city protected."

Tangus snorted. "Once word gets around about what's happened here, I don't think anyone will ever try to invade this city again. C'mon! We've unfinished business to take care of, and the Sky Emperors can't do it for us if the bugs are underground."

"Help me up," Kristen said as she held out her arms to Tangus who grabbed her hands and lent his strength. "You're right, though I wish we had more than just the four of us."

Tangus shrugged. "It'll have to do."

"General!"

Knight-General Dame Victoria Fox, the Grand Duchess of Astoria, Defender of the High Reaches, Sentinel of the Blight, and Warden of the Knight's Code, sighed and cursed under her breath. All she desired was rest for her and the thousand knights she hadn't sent home. Travelling through a territory potentially filled with adversaries, even on horseback, demanded a physical toll... and she could hardly keep her eyes open.

Her army of knights, along with an army from Palisade Crest, had been on a forced march eastward to stop the incursion of the Draugen Pesta, who, with their mercenary allies from Hebron and

Madeira, threatened the lands east of the Olympus Mountains. But all they found were a few scraggly Madeiran mercenaries who wanted nothing more than to go home to their families. If the story they told was accurate, the invasion was over and the Draugen Pesta were already gone. This information coincided with reports from scouts, and that prompted the Palisade Crest army to turn around, as did the Altheros army marching towards Havendale in the south. Knight-General Fox wasn't entirely convinced, however, and wanted to see for herself… but decided against taking her entire army.

"Come," Victoria answered.

A trio of knights marched into her tent. One of them held a Madeiran soldier by the back of his tunic collar.

"Begging your pardon, M'lady," a knight said. "We caught this man trying to sneak through our outer picket."

"Why not release him like the others," Victoria asked.

"During questioning he had a few interesting things to say that I thought deserved your attention," the knight replied.

That piqued the interest of the Knight-General. "Very well, Cheeves. At ease, the three of you."

Victoria walked over and inspected the man. It was obvious he wasn't a professional warrior. He was on the small size, middle-aged and pot-bellied. His entire body was shaking uncontrollably, and his eyes kept darting from her to the three knights who had brought him in.

"Relax, little rabbit," Victoria said as she walked over and poured a goblet of wine. The man shook his head when she offered it to him, so she sat on a chair and decided she'd not waste it. "You have a story to tell?"

"Your Worshipness, it was only a harmless boast," the Madeiran replied. "I only wanted your knights to take me seriously. But in truth I didn't really kill a Black Death warrior to get it. I want no part of those devils!"

Victoria looked at her knights and raised an eyebrow. One of them produced a titanium plate attached to a sturdy length of leather meant to be worn around the neck. "The 'it' in question, M'lady. This appears to be Draugen Pesta in make. Identification tags, I suspect." The knight turned the amulet so he could read the back. "It belonged to a Sergeant Drasko Severny of the Third Horse, Twenty-Seventh Cavalry Regiment. It's heavily encrusted with blood."

The Madeiran winced. "Your Worshipness, the soldier was dead, he was. He didn't need it no more. Truly!"

"The Draugen Pesta didn't pick up their dead?" Victoria asked.

"The who?"

One of the knights shook his head and sighed. "The Black Death."

"Oh…"

After a few seconds of silence the same knight cuffed the Madeiran on the back of the head. "Answer the general!"

"Me and my mates got to him before they did. We only just got away."

Victoria sat back in her chair and crossed her arms. "So… spoils of war, eh," she remarked.

The Madeiran bobbed his head up and down. "Yes! Exactly!"

Victoria took a sip of wine. "The Knight's Code allows for spoils of war," she said. "But we generally draw the line at weapons, armor and such. The Code frowns upon the pilferage of personal affects that should go back to the family. It's all so unbecoming, wouldn't you agree?"

Victoria watched as the look of excitement in the man's demeanor drained away. "Your Worshipness?"

"Well, certainly this tag isn't a weapon of war or used for self-defense, now is it?"

"Uh…"

"I mean, surely you realize how it's personal and should be returned to the family of the deceased," Victoria said. "After all, that's what it's for. To identify the dead so his loved ones can find closure."

"Are you crazy?!" the man exclaimed. "How am I gonna return that to his family?! Trudge across the Greater Boreskyre's, walk up to the nearest Black Death warrior I see and hand it over? That's a blooming death sentence! Besides, it's booty under the Mercenary Code! Titanium's worth a lot, you know."

"That's not a thing," Victoria tapped her chin with an index finger. "Your reference to a Mercenary Code, that is. But I see your predicament. Weren't you allies?"

The man stared in silence. The discussion with the lady knight had just taken a regrettable turn. Titanium was rare on the mainland and the plate was equal to a year's salary. But pillaging the body of an ally didn't sit well with the knights. That much was plain to see. Perhaps he should cut his losses and concentrate on keeping his head. "I bow to your judgment. Please make sure that the plate is returned to the family of that most unfortunate warrior."

Victoria smiled and nodded. "A wise decision. No doubt the guilt would have followed you to the end of your days. Rest assured the Astorian Knights will not relax until the plate is back in the hands of the dead warrior's family."

"I bet you won't," the man whispered under his breath.

Victoria ignored the man's impertinence. "Now, tell me why you're here. The real reason."

"I…"

"The creatures," one of the three knights prompted.

The Madeiran shivered as thoughts of the titanium plate were replaced by the creatures. "There were hundreds of them! Maybe thousands! All over the haunted city! I didn't think we'd make it out alive."

"And yet you did," the knight-general said. "What did they look like?"

"Kinda like… well… uh… maybe pig-bug looking." The man shook his head. "More bug than pig. And the smell… by the gods it was awful! They died easily enough, though. And when they did, they melted into a kind of snot which stank even worse."

"Anything else?"

"After they kill, they stick a long, sharp spear-type thing into the body and suck you dry. I mean, what's left is nothing but a wrinkled husk. The skin is paper thin. You can see all the bones through it. But that's only if you're lucky. I've seen men wrapped up alive like a fly in a spider's web and dragged away. Who knows where those poor bastards are heading, but I swear on my fat Aunt Hildy's grave it's not any place a man wants to go."

Victoria stared. She'd never heard of such creatures, but there's no doubt strange things have been happening of late. Things like the odd clouds hovering over Elanesse, the new mountain range east of Lake Lorali, black dragons in the skies, the dark elf invasion of InnisRos, the unexpected invasion of the Draugen Pesta, and a host of other smaller, unusual things… such as people disappearing and returning with tales of traveling to strange worlds, odd weather patterns, and the like. It felt as if it were the end of days.

The knight-general stood. "Sir Abernathy, please send this gentleman on his way with enough provisions for the trip to Madeira. Sir Basil, get the knights ready to go." The third knight remained behind as the others left.

"Well, Sir Pellinore, what do you think?"

The knight walked over to the table and poured himself a goblet of wine before answering. "If it's bugs as the Madeiran says, then the only way to end them is to…"

"… is to find and kill the queen," Victoria finished as she poured herself another goblet of wine. "And that means going underground to do it."

"It's unfortunate you sent our sappers home," Sir Pellinore observed.

"Indeed."

Elrond opened a pathway through his branches for Romulus and Sakkara. Tied to Romulus' back was someone Elrond didn't recognize. Whoever it was appeared to be a sorcerer… and near death. But walking next to the huge wolf was someone Elrond did recognized. It was Rhys, the chief spy of Havendale. Elrond resisted the impulse to club the man with a branch. He hated the spy, but not enough to slay him. Max, however,… well, that was a whole other story.

"Why are you so angry," Elanesse asked.

"That one, the one walking, is Rhys," Elrond responded as he pointed towards the spy. *"Max and I had a run-in with him many years ago. Max told me he'd kill him the next time he saw him. I've never seen Max so angry… either before we met Rhys or since."*

"What did he do to cause so much hatred?" Elanesse asked. *"Another female?"*

"What? No, of course not," Elrond replied. *"Well, somewhat. Something even closer to Max's heart… treasure. It was a magic dagger. The finest dagger I've ever seen! Made from hardened steel with a gem-encrusted hilt. It must've been worth two or three thousand gold coins. Maybe more. Not that Max would ever have sold it. The reason he valued it so was because of the magic contained within. It was intelligent."*

"I don't understand."

"An intelligent object," Elrond answered. *"You know, like you and me. Sentient."*

Elanesse's golden leaves shimmered. *"We've never been inanimate objects,"* she said.

"Yeah, well the dagger was. Until magic was cast on it, that is. But, as is so often the case, the enchantment wasn't what made it intelligent. It was the captured soul within the blade that did. She was an old soul… the soul of a highborn lady who lived hundreds of years ago." Elrond sighed. *"Tragic story how that happened. Her name was Winifred and… well… immortality is one thing, but to be forced to spend eternity in a dagger? Very sad. Maybe that's why Max fell in love with her? Then Rhys spirited her away to Havendale after he*

slipped a sleep potion into our wine. I imagine she sits there even now, guarded by the sorcerers of that city, impossible to retrieve."

"*Interesting story,*" Emmy interjected.

"*Wish you'd quit listening in on our private conversations,*" Elrond said.

Both trees heard Emmy's sigh in their minds. "*I can't help it,*" the young goddess said. "*You forgot to use the filter I taught you.*"

"*Emmy's right, dear,*" Elanesse said. "*It's our own fault.*"

"*Yes it is,*" Emmy retorted. "*And Elrond, you left out the part where Max stole the dagger from the thief who stole it from a Havendale sorcerer. The dagger is where it belongs. Now hush and help me. I need to keep the sorcerer alive as long as possible. He's someone Kristen needs to meet.*"

"*Who could he be to Kristen,*" Elrond asked.

"*Her true father.*"

Tangus looked out over the part of Elanesse he could see from inside the outer defensive wall of the palace. There was no sign of the creatures. He looked up. The cloud beings were still there, motionless in the sky even though there was a strong wind coming out of the north.

"I think it's safe enough to get to the Tower of the Innocent," Tangus said.

"Thanks to those," Jennifer remarked as she pointed to the sky. "Without them we'd be bug meat."

"We'll take whatever luck fate bestows upon us," Kristen commented. "Even luck from another world."

"Let's go," Tangus ordered, ending further conversation concerning the nature of luck, Sky Emperors, and bug meat. Tangus and Kristen, swords drawn, took the lead while Mariko and Jennifer, arrows notched to bows, followed. Though the master ranger didn't think the creatures would venture back to the surface, he wasn't willing to take anything for granted. They moved slowly and deliberately, using whatever cover they could find, until they were at the base of the Tower of the Innocent.

As Tangus opened the door, Mariko and Jennifer trained arrows inside. The glow of light from Tangus' magical sword lit the immediate area on the other side of the door. It was clear of any threat. Tangus motioned for everyone to enter.

Except for the footprints they had left coming up after the final battle with the Purge, the stairs leading into the lower reaches of the tower looked undisturbed. In the air there was a slight hint of bug-smell. They knew the bugs were down there somewhere, so the scent neither surprised nor caused alarm.

"No bugs close," Jennifer observed. "That is unless they've learned to take a bath."

"Don't forget the Soulreavers," Mariko said. "We know there's at least one down here. And I suspect it'll be hungry."

Tangus held up a small jewel that Kristen had enchanted with a permanent light spell. It was better than a torch.

"If memory serves, the Soulreaver will appear as black puddles," Tangus said, "and could be on the floor, ceiling or the walls."

"Your memory is correct, ranger," Mariko answered. "I can handle them, so I should be in front."

Tangus nodded and let her take the lead.

If the smell was any indicator, every step they took brought them closer to the bugs. In due course they found themselves in the same chamber where they had destroyed the Purge, largely through the sacrifice of the young empath, Charity. Tears rolled down Mariko's cheeks as the memory of the empath's death threatened to overwhelm her. If not for her, Mariko would be dead. That Charity's death was necessary to kill the Purge mattered little to the assassin-priestess.

"You okay?" Kristen asked.

Mariko nodded. "There should be a shrine to Charity here."

"Are you not Emmy's new priestess?" Kristen said. "When we're done with this, do it. Emmy would approve."

Mariko shook her head. "No. I wouldn't know where to begin."

"Search your heart, Mariko. It knows."

The assassin-priestess frowned. "Maybe someday. But not now. While I may be Emmy's priestess, I'll not be someone who succors lost souls or calls people to temple. I like the fight... the battle... too much to be held captive by a nunnery. I want to eliminate all threats to future empaths. To do that I must be Emmy's guardian of the faith... her protector, and her enforcer. While the new empath race is still in its infancy, it'll need someone who can do the things people don't like to mention in polite society. The kinds of things I specialize in."

"You definitely have the talent for it," Tangus added as he walked closer to the pair. "Jennifer and I had a look around. I think it'll be safe enough to rest for a few hours."

Everyone sighed with relief as they shed their backpacks and sat. Kristen used magic to create several phantasms to act as guardians while Tangus assigned a watch schedule, starting with him. After a quick meal of nuts, dried berries, hardtack, and jerky, all except Tangus settled into sleep.

In a dark corner, two black pools of murkiness moved towards the sleeping figures.

Osiris stopped. Ahead was the strong odor of the creatures. But the smell he sensed was that of dead and not living creatures. Closer was the more subtle scent of the pointy ears... and they were alive. After a few minutes of tracking, they found the source of the pointy ears' aroma at the base of a tall tower.

"They're on the inside," Moishe said, "and the door has barred our way."

"The scent is strong," Osiris remarked. "They're close. Perhaps all we need to do is make a little noise."

"How do we know the pointy ears won't attack us," one of the other two cats asked.

"We don't," Osiris said. "But my guess is the pointy ears will accept our help if we can convince them to trust us."

"We shouldn't be here in the first place," the remaining cat remarked. "We're supposed to be looking for our cub, not dying for the pointy ears."

Osiris shook his head. "We've had this discussion before, Cheops. If the smelly creatures aren't stopped, how long do you think we'll be safe in our mountains? The cub is no longer our priority."

"Gyasi and Ubaid would not agree with you."

Osiris sighed. "If we leave now, their deaths will be for nothing," he said. "Can't you see that?"

Cheops roared in defiance.

"ENOUGH!" Osiris roared in response and slapped the older cat across his snout with a paw. The saber cat leader didn't have his claws out, but the force of the blow was enough to snap Cheops head back. "I'm the leader of the Snow Pride. Unless you wish to challenge me, you will follow my orders. Do you understand?"

Cheops nodded and backed away. "Forgive me."

"I don't wish to harm you, Cheops," the pride leader said. "Let there be peace between us. Now, how are we going to open the door?"

"Maybe we should knock," Moishe suggested.

Tangus startled awake and sat up. He thought he heard a sound from above.

"Don't move!" Mariko whispered.

Tangus froze. He didn't know what Mariko saw, but he trusted her implicitly. As she crawled over to him, Tangus felt a slight weight on one of his knees. He looked down and saw his first Soulreaver. As he watched, it began to coalesce and move up his leg.

"Mariko," he whispered. "Where are you!"

"Right behind you," she answered.

Mariko reached over Tangus' shoulder and touched the creature.

"Are you crazy," Tangus murmured.

"Hush," Mariko said.

The Soulreaver stopped its forward movement. A part of it reached up and touched a gleaming ring Mariko had put on before entering the tower. It backed off Tangus' leg. Another Soulreaver came out of the shadows and stopped next to its brethren.

"You can relax," Mariko said. "They won't attack."

Kristen was still sleeping – the *Bladebarrier Sanctuary* spell she had used a few hours before to save them had taken its toll. But Jennifer was awake and studying the creatures.

"I told you I could control them," Mariko said.

"You mean your ring can control them," Jennifer remarked.

Mariko shrugged. "With the ring we can communicate. That's all. Even though they're creatures of the Abyss, they're not evil. In fact, they're more like dogs… no, cats… yes cats. They're too willful to be like dogs. But they'll listen, and as long as they know you'll provide a meal, they'll work with you. That's how assassins use them."

"Can I touch," Jennifer asked.

"Why on earth would you want to do that?" Tangus asked. "They're not pets."

"No, they're not pets," Mariko agreed. "But they're not simple killing machines either. They have no problem with your request."

Jennifer put her hand on the floor, palm up. One of the Soulreavers squirmed over and climbed into her hand.

"It feels like… thick pudding," Jennifer observed, "but warm and comforting."

"That's part of how they invade a host," Mariko noted. "They usually attack when the victim is asleep. They use excretions from their body to soothe and reassure. As a result, the touch of a Soulreaver doesn't raise 'yuck' alarm bells."

"How do I get it to leave," Jennifer said. After listening to Mariko, she wasn't so sure she now wanted the Soulreaver resting in her hand. As if it understood her, the Soulreaver moved away.

"One advantage to handling a willing Soulreaver is they're more likely as not to leave a chemical mark that identifies and protects you from being food for other Soulreavers," Mariko added. "That is if they accept you."

"Then why do you use a ring?" Tangus asked.

"Remember the cat analogy?" Mariko answered. "Sometimes a Soulreaver can be picky about who they'll accept… or who they'll protect. I never take Soulreavers for granted."

Tangus raised an eyebrow. "Have you ever made one angry?"

Mariko was kneeling with an open leather pouch and waited while the two Soulreavers crawled inside. "No." She stood and attached the pouch containing the Soulreavers to her belt. "No one makes a Soulreaver angry on purpose."

Above them there was a faint knock on the entry door.

"I knew I heard something up there," Tangus said as he stood. He looked at his wife. Kristen was still in a deep sleep. "Jennifer, you're with me. Mariko…"

"Understood," Mariko said as she looked at Kristen. "No harm shall befall her."

At the surface level of the tower, Tangus stood next to the door while Jennifer, bow and arrow drawn, stood a few feet away. Again the soft pounding. But as Tangus listened, he could also hear faint scratching which sounded like claws on stone. He replied with a few knocks of his own, which was promptly returned.

Tangus looked back at Jennifer and shrugged his shoulders. "What do we have to lose," he said as he unlocked the door.

CHAPTER TWENTY-FOUR

Elanesse

"The End?"

The use of '?' is a very tired, foreshadowing literary device used by playwrights and writers to prepare the reader for the possible continuation of a story. Whether or not the playwright or writer persists and follows through is usually determined by how well the original was received… or more specifically, how profitable it was.

-Economics 101, University of Altheros

On the other hand, a few playwrights and writers inscribe their stories solely for the personal pleasure it brings to them.

-Literature 101, University of Altheros

One thousand Knights of Astoria moved into Elanesse from the northwest. Though the walls of the city were imposing, there were plenty of areas which had been reduced to rubble. Scouts were dispatched into the breaches to reconnoiter those areas, but the main body of the knights shadowed the wall south until they reached the western gate, its massive doors standing wide open.

Knight-General Victoria Fox gave the command to enter, and the leading edge of the knight contingent rushed through and formed a defensive arc bowing outward while their knight brothers and sisters rode into the city. Not too far away was the outer defensive wall of the palace, and a few hundred feet south of that there was what appeared to be barracks. Everything was in a state of disrepair, but the city was of elvan construction, so not only was it still magnificent, its buildings were still intact and habitable.

"Sir Pellinore, please take a column* and clear the palace," Victoria ordered. "We'll set camp within its walls."

As the knight rode away to carry out his orders, Victoria dismounted her horse. The rest of the knights followed suit, the sound of their armor clamored and rang throughout that part of the city, dismissing any doubt as to their presence. No matter. The Astorian Knights had learned long ago they'd never be stealthy and used the sound of their armor to their advantage. It scared the hell out of the people lined up against them.

An hour went by before Sir Pellinore returned. "The palace is secure, my lady," he reported. "But there's signs of recent occupation. In fact, it appears a battle took place."

"Explain."

Sir Pellinore shook his head. "It's hard to describe. Perhaps you should see for yourself and draw your own conclusions."

Inside the outer walls of the palace was another gated wall. Sir Pellinore led General Fox through those gates and towards the palace's front entrance. As they walked, Victoria began to notice peculiar discolorations in the ground. She'd seen the same markings outside the walls but didn't think too much about it at the time.

She spied the battlefield well before she reached its perimeter. It was spherical. In the center was a twenty-five-foot circle represented by upturned ground, as if a plow had dug through the rich earth. All around the circle were hundreds of different sized discolorations on the ground. On the inside of the circle, the earth had been disturbed by what appeared to be hard-soled boots. Here and there bright red blood stains stood out against the deep green of the grass.

---

* Astorian Knight military unit designations and strength - A column represents ten knights. Ten columns equal one company totaling one hundred knights, ten company's equal one regiment totaling one thousand knights, ten regiments equal one division totaling ten thousand knights, two divisions equal one corps totaling twenty thousand knights. The Astorian army consists of two

"Have you ever seen anything like this?" Sir Pellinore asked.

Victoria shook her head. "Magic. I'd say some form of a protection spell."

Sir Pellinore crouched and studied the discolorations on the ground outside the circle. "And these are the remains of the creatures the Madeiran mentioned?"

"Or their blood," Victoria replied. "It looks as if they were ripped apart."

"At least those inside bled red," Sir Pellinore observed after moving closer to the center of the circle.

Victoria stepped across the ground-churned circle perimeter. There was a lot of blood on the ground, but experience told her it wasn't enough to be life threatening. Lack of a trail of blood out of the circle indicated the wound had been treated. She turned to Sir Basil, who had just joined them.

"Any signs," she asked.

"Boot prints going east," he replied. "Sir Abernathy and several knights are following to see where they lead."

"Anywhere else" Victoria asked.

Sir Basil shook his head. "No... except from the palace to here."

"I intend to secure this city, building by building," Victoria said. "We'll make our camp inside the palace walls. Sir Pellinore, once we've settled, I want to send reinforced patrols out. Search in a standard grid pattern and expand it outward as each area is cleared. Be mindful of any passages going underground. Those are to be sealed with protection magic and two knights to stand guard. As we expand outward on the grid, interlock columns at key points within the grid. I don't want any column more than a few minutes away from reinforcement by another. Questions?"

"No ma'am," Sir Pellinore responded.

Victoria nodded. "Good. Be sure to have Sir Abernathy report to me as soon as he returns. Is there anything I've missed?"

Both knights shook their heads.

"Very well," General Fox said. "Gentlemen see to your orders. I'll be in the palace."

Both Sir Pellinore and Sir Basil saluted and hurried off.

"General!"

"What now," Victoria thought to herself as she looked in the direction of the call. A knight was pointing up at the many clouds that covered the sky over the city. Long tendrils were extending downward.

"What the hell?"

Lycomedes watched shiny people move into the city below. The Sky Emperor leader wasn't familiar with these creatures and viewed them with suspicion. He ordered his people to drop their tendrils and prepare to defend the city once again. As the shiny creatures reacted to what they undoubtedly viewed as a threat, he wondered if this new world was the treasure he and his fellow Sky Emperors believed it to be.

Without warning Emmy spoke in Lycomedes' mind. *"Give us a chance, my friend. They only respond to something they don't understand. Will you trust me?"*

"Always, goddess."

Pleasant warmth rolled through Lycomedes signaling Emmy's thanks and approval.

"The shiny ones are forces of good and will protect the city," Emmy said. *"Please tell your people they can rest easy. But remember, you must still be prepared to help the shiny ones against the otherworldly creatures should the need transpire."*

"Many of the creatures escaped underground, goddess," Lycomedes added. *"We cannot follow."*

"My mother and father will take care of that."

Tangus nodded to Jennifer and took a deep breath before opening the door. Staring at him from the other side were four adult Royal Mountain Saber Cats. Each were beautiful – and huge. He and Jennifer were in grave danger if the cats attacked. But they didn't. Instead, the cats just stood there, watching, and waiting. Tangus studied the four cats. He watched them relax after their initial surprise. They didn't snarl or roar, and their eyes, the one thing a master ranger like Tangus can use to determine intent, didn't appear hostile after their original surprise.

Tangus sheathed his sword and motioned for Jennifer to lower her bow and arrow. If he'd read them wrong, and they attacked, one arrow wouldn't make much difference, and Tangus didn't want to accidently provoke the cats.

"Nice kitty," Tangus said as he extended an arm forward, palm up, to let the largest cat pick up his scent.

The cat sniffed the proffered hand. His ears pricked up, and he drew back.

"Uh-oh," Tangus thought, then realized the cat might have picked up Loki's scent.

The cat pushed past Tangus and walked to Jennifer, who still had an arrow notched, though not pointed at the cats. He batted the bow and arrow to the side, sniffed Jennifer from top to bottom, and then nudged her in the chest with his massive head. Jennifer had an impulse to scratch behind the cat's ears. She knew Loki loved it and figured this cat would as well. After a few tense moments, the enormous feline allowed the foreign touch. He closed his eyes and purred for a few moments before he broke contact. He looked back at the other cats, roared, and headed down the stairs. As each cat walked past a stunned Tangus, they stopped in front of Jennifer and offered their own heads for a scratch behind the ears before following their leader.

"Okay, that was weird," Tangus remarked.

"They're adorable," Jennifer exclaimed. "Their fur is so soft and silky smooth. I love wolves, but I want a saber cat as an animal companion. I can't wait for Loki to grow up."

Tangus chuckled. "You can't have him, sweetie. Loki and I..." Tangus stopped talking and headed for the stairs, grabbing Jennifer by the shoulder as he went past her. "Let's go! Mariko won't want to scratch those cats behind their ears! She'll want to kill them!"

Osiris realized from the moment the door opened that the elf staring back at him was connected to the young saber cat he had come out of the mountains to find... which meant the cats had even more reason to cooperate. But he didn't want to waste time with introductions. The scent of the strange creatures below was strong, and their abhorrent nature represented an even more pressing threat to his people. Osiris was eager to go forward. After a 'sniff and greet' with the first elf and a scratch behind the ear from the second, the cats continued their journey down the stairs.

From behind Osiris heard yelling, and though he didn't understand the words, he understood it for what it was, a warning. But who was it for? Him and his brothers? Or someone below? An instant later two arrows, fired in quick succession, flew past him, missing his head by a fraction, though one split an ear. Behind him there was a 'grunt', and then he was bowled over by the dead weight of Moishe crashing down the stairs. Both were unceremoniously deposited on the stone floor at the stair's foot. Cheops and the cat behind him, a young warrior named Kamuzu, rushed to stand over their fallen comrades.

As they roared their defiance, Osiris got up to examine the still body of Moishe. There was plenty of blood, but when Osiris looked, he saw that no arrows had pierced the body. Instead, both had struck just above the eyes and were deflected upwards by Moishe's hard skull. Though there were deep groves in the flesh which exposed part of the skull, Osiris knew Moishe was only unconscious and would survive. If one is to kill a Royal Mountain Saber Cat with a head shot, one better damned well make sure the arrow goes through one of the eyes.

The elf who had fired the arrows was preparing another shot when a second elf, standing behind, forced the shooter's bow down. Then the two elves from above maneuvered past the roaring cats and stood in front of the shooter, using their bodies to shield the cats. An uncertain peace followed.

Kristen walked past Mariko and embraced Tangus. "I love you," she whispered into his ear.

In response, Tangus hugged her tighter. "Till the End of Time," he whispered back.

"I'm sorry," Mariko said. "I thought they were the enemy."

"You couldn't know they weren't," Tangus replied. "They took off before I could warn you. You did the right thing."

Mariko nodded.

By now emotions had quieted. Kristen approached the four cats with her hands extended, palms out. The largest sniffed both palms, nodded its acceptance, then sat and stared at Mariko.

"You need to make friends," Jennifer said. "He needs to smell you."

Mariko cocked her head. "Either that or he wants to eat me."

"His name is Osiris," Tangus said. "He's the leader of the Snow Pride whose home is in the mountains. With him is Cheops, Kamuzu and Moishe, the cat you just shot."

Mariko looked at Tangus. Puzzlement that he knew the names of the cats was clearly registered on her face.

"Remember Mariko," Jennifer said after noticing her friend's confusion. "My father's a master ranger. Communicating with animals is part of what he does."

Mariko kept her eyes in Osiris as she stowed her bow and arrow. Then she approached the cat as Kristen had done.

Osiris went to meet the assassin halfway. Kristen had relieved the pain of his split ear with a healing salve mixture, so he was in a more forgiving mood.

While Mariko and Osiris were getting acquainted, Kristen kneeled next to Moishe and inspected his wounds. Gathering her will, she drew in the power granted by her goddess, Althaya, and healed the cat's head. She looked at his missing eye, the result of an injury long ago, and determined there was nothing she could do for it. Still fragile from her use of the *Bladebarrier Sanctuary* spell, the power used to heal the cat made Kristen dizzy. She started to keel over. But before Tangus could catch her, Moishe, now recovered, leaned forward to lend his support. Kristen, feeling sick, closed her eyes and grabbed the big cat around the neck as she held on for dear life.

Tangus took the weight of his wife from Moishe and helped her sit.

"I'll be all right," Kristen said. "I only need to rest a moment."

Tangus nodded, but he knew his wife was putting on a brave front. She was much more drained then she was letting on. He looked at the four cats. Each was large enough to act as a mount for his wife.

Moishe appeared to understand what Tangus was thinking. He stood and moved closer to the Tangus and Kristen. The ranger scratched the cat behind the ear. He took off his backpack and pulled his heavy blanket out. He then cut two suitable lengths of rope and secured the blanket to Moishe's back, creating a crude saddle.

"No, I'm not going to," Kristen protested.

"You're not strong enough," Tangus answered. "And we can't afford to wait until you have your strength back."

Moishe roared and nudged Kristen.

"He's strong enough," Tangus said. "I promise."

Kristen sighed. She wasn't going to win this battle with her husband. And he was right. If she was going to be any help, she needed to regain her strength. Kristen nodded and let Tangus help her onto the cat's back. Once on, she leaned forward and laid her head on the back of Moishe's neck while grabbing handfuls of fur on each side of the cat. His fur was thick and soft. Tangus used another length of rope to secure Kristen to his makeshift saddle.

"You two done yet," Tangus asked Mariko and Osiris.

"I guess," Mariko replied. She had reached a truce with three of the four cats. Moishe, the cat she'd shot, had been busy helping Kristen. But though she offered her open palm and was accepted, it wasn't as if they were now fast friends. "At least none of these overgrown kitties want to eat me. And they DO NOT care for my bagged Soulreavers!"

"Another reason to like these cats," Jennifer remarked.

"Time to go," Tangus said. "I'll take the lead. Mariko, you stay with Kristen. Jennifer, you're my rear guard."

"And the cats," Jennifer asked.

"Let them do as they please," Tangus responded. "They know better than us the dangers ahead."

"How's that," Mariko inquired.

Tangus answered by tapping his nose.

Osiris walked in front of or next to Tangus when the width of the passages permitted. Cheops was next followed by Kristen on Moishe, and Mariko. Kamuzu stayed with Jennifer.

They had only been traveling for an hour when they ran into bugs. The stench announced the bug presence long before anyone saw them. Of the five that appeared down the corridor, arrows from Tangus and Mariko dropped four while the claws and teeth of Osiris ripped apart the last.

"I've only got about a dozen arrows left," Mariko observed. "If going through their chitin armor doesn't break them, the slime left over when they're dead finish the job."

Tangus nodded. "I know. I wish I had an answer for you."

Suddenly all four cats snarled.

"Are you sure? All I see is a bit of churned up ground."

"Yes, general," Sir Abernathy replied. "The boot prints lead directly to this door. They're mostly covered up by other prints which appear to be large animals of some type. But the boot prints are definitely there underneath." Sir Abernathy pointed to a faint partial indentation in the ground. "Here."

Victoria saw it, but only just barely. Only someone experienced in tracking had the skill to take a few little marks in the ground and recognize the boot prints of the ones they're tracking. "Speculate."

Sir Abernathy crouched down. "Well, the boot prints lead from the palace to this tower here." He then pointed to the east. "The animals… I'd say large cats… came from the east. My first thought was the first group was heading in this direction for whatever reason, saw the cats approaching, and sought refuge here behind this door. It's obvious the cats followed to here."

Victoria tried the door. It was locked. "Do any of the animal tracks leave?"

The knight shook his head. "No. Either they disappeared into thin air…"

"Or they somehow got inside," Victoria said. "Any indication of another entrance… one that's less obvious?"

"No, ma'am." Sir Abernathy stood back up. "Whomever was on the other side of the door decided to open it and let the cats in. The fact that the door has been relocked from the inside tells me that the cats didn't attack but instead were allowed into the tower by whomever."

"How recent?"

"Within the last few hours," Sir Abernathy replied.

Victoria weighed her options. She thought she knew who was inside the tower with the cats. She'd heard stories about a group of elves from the island of InnisRos who'd made the haunted city of Elanesse home. She didn't know the specifics, but all the mercenaries and treasure hunters who'd made a living searching for fortune in the city had been driven out. She also knew the city was the focal point of dragon attacks, and the valley in which it sat had been invaded by Draugen Pesta. None of this could be coincidence… and all of it was very troubling.

"Damn it! I need intelligence!" Victoria exclaimed, frustrated. "I need someone who can take information, put it all together, draw conclusions, and make recommendations. Right now, I'm blind. I need a good spy!"

"You know how the council feels about that," Sir Abernathy said.

"By heart," Victoria replied. "But it's a misrepresentation of the Knight's Code. We need an intelligence service."

After a few seconds of silence, Victoria sighed. "Sir Abernathy let's get the door open. I want you to take a company below and try to make contact. We're on the same side. Defend yourselves if necessary, but don't hurt them. Put yourself in their service. Tell them I'm doing what I can from up here. Hopefully, we can put enough pressure on the creatures on this end to make whatever they're doing down there easier."

"I've no doubt they'll be appreciative of our help," Sir Abernathy observed. "Their …"

"General!"

Everyone turned to looked at the knight who'd called out, then upwards to see what she was pointing at. The clouds were once again extending their strange appendages.

The *Theraesus* queen was satisfied. The atmosphere of this new world fed her eggs, and new batches of drones had started to hatch after only a few hours of incubation. Included in the latest batch of hatchlings were three queens, several males, and three Custodians – a rare guardian warrior capable of using magic. It lived to defend the queens who represented the future of the race. These were the last pieces of the puzzle that would guarantee *Theraesus* dominance over the new world.

"I must keep the offensive," the queen thought. *"I need to buy time for the other queens to escape and to give my Custodians a chance to mature."*

Thousands of *Theraesus* drones poured out of the Pyramid of the Purge and other buildings connected by the labyrinth of tunnels beneath the city. The ones who had broken through their eggshells but an hour before were ravenous.

The Cloud Emperors and the Knights of Astoria just barely withstood the onslaught. It took several hours of heavy fighting to beat the creatures back. The Cloud Emperors, from their perches high in the sky, survived somewhat unscathed. A few of them lost tentacles, but that was the extent of their suffering. It was a different story for the knights.

Almost half the knights had died at the hands of the *Theraesus*. Those still alive were sick from the smell of the putrid mucus left behind by the dead drones. A hastily built funeral pyre burned the bodies of the dead, but the fires gave the living little relief. The remaining knights were forced to gather their horses and retreat out of the city and into the forest, discarding their mucus covered armor as they did so. Though regrouped, Knight-General Fox knew they weren't ready for battle. A few of them were still retching, and everyone looked tired, the strain of combat and illness plain to see in their eyes and on their faces. Even though the healer-knights did their best to aid everyone, it would be at least two or three days before they'd be an effective fighting force again.

Harkum slowly regained consciousness. He'd been dreaming — dreaming that he was being crushed and having a difficult time breathing. As his mind cleared, Harkum came to realize his dream paralleled what was really happening. His entire body was covered by thin strands of a thread-like material. It wasn't sticky or soft like spider's silk but appeared to be closer to metal. He struggled to test its strength and discovered it was extremely strong. As he did this the filaments that held him captive closed tighter and made breathing even more difficult.

The mercenary relaxed and tried to look around, but discovered he was being held too tightly to move his head and could only see in front of him. Other than the slight shimmering light given off by the threads, it was dark and quiet. At some point Harkum lost consciousness again. When he reawakened, nothing about his situation had changed.

Depressed and knowing he was living on borrowed time, Harkum screamed. It was a primal scream — a scream of frustration and anger — a scream of fear. From out of the darkness came a roar in answer. It was close and fearsome. Harkum urinated in his pants. When the source of the roar moved into the little light provided by the thread, the mercenary's bowels released. Then Harkum fainted.

Tangus stepped from around the corner with bow and arrow in hand and pointed at Sir Abernathy's heart. The knight's armor wouldn't stop it at this range. On the other side of Tangus stood Mariko with three arrows notched in her assassins bow. Behind and flanking Tangus and Mariko were three growling Royal Mountain Saber Cats. Further back and in the darkness, Jennifer stood next to Kristen and another cat. Her bow was out as well and trained forward while Kristen was preparing a magical spell should the need for one arise.

Sir Abernathy stopped his column to study the tactical situation he and his knights found themselves in. The ambush site was well thought out… a four-way intersection of tunnels. The knight-leader figured his company of knights could win a pitched battle because the numbers were on his side. But if it came to a fight, he knew he'd not be around to see any victory, nor would a good portion of his knights. What made matters worse, if there was a battle, his adversaries were in a position to split and run down the three tunnels available to them. Giving chase would require he divide his forces. That would be a disaster. Sir Abernathy sheathed his sword and ordered his company to do the same.

Tangus broke the silence. "Astorian knights. I never expected to see you here."

"It's an interesting narrative," Sir Abernathy answered. "But I'm afraid the telling must be held in abeyance. Perhaps over dinner?"

"By the gods he sounds just like Landross," Jennifer said as she walked up to join her father. "Thou art this, prithee that."

Sir Abernathy nodded. "Aye, fair lady. Sir Landross is known as a knight of great repute."

"And not an impolite bone in your body, I'd wager."

"Nay, fair lady. We can become quite bawdry after a couple glasses of wine."

"Two glasses of wine," Jennifer chortled. "It'd take more than that just to…"

Tangus interrupted. "Let's get down to business, shall we? You are?"

The knight bowed. "Please forgive me. Sir Abernathy of the Astorian Knights. I lead a company of knights with orders to place ourselves into your service."

"Orders from who," Tangus asked.

"Knight-General Dame Victoria Fox, the Grand Duchess of Astoria, Defender of the High Reaches…"

Tangus held up his hand. "I've heard of General Fox… and her titles. Is she in the city above?"

Sir Abernathy nodded. "With a thousand knights. The main army headed back, but my lady general had a most curious suspicion regarding the haunted city…"

"Elanesse," Kristen interjected. By now everyone was together, including the saber cats.

"Of course, madam… Elanesse. Anyway, I suppose the strange clouds above the city had something to do with General Fox's decision, as well as the black dragons which were reported to be overflying the city and now lay dead within her confines." Sir Abernathy paused. "But she said it was more a hunch than anything else. So, after we confirmed the Draugen Pesta had left the valley, and there were no signs of the Madeira or Hebron mercenary armies about, everyone, except our thousand, headed back home, satisfied the valley and Havendale were no longer in danger."

"We sure have need of your help," Tangus said, "because I believe the bugs represent a greater threat than even the invasion." He explained what they faced in greater detail. He spoke to his theory that the creatures were like bugs, and like bugs, could multiply in unbelievable numbers. "If our premise is correct, there's only one way to defeat them," Tangus said as he wrapped up his narrative.

"A queen you say," Sir Abernathy remarked as he absorbed everything Tangus had just described.

Kristen nodded. "Think of ants or bees. As long as the queen lives, the nest will never die. It'll continue to perpetuate. And worse, if other queens are born and escape to establish new nests… well, you can see where this is heading and how the entire world is in jeopardy."

Sir Abernathy took a deep breath. "Yes. Yes, indeed. If your assumptions are correct, the battles being fought on the surface are nothing compared to what we shall face down here. And the closer we get to the queen, the worse it'll be. Getting near enough to kill her will certainly be a challenge."

Jennifer snorted. "Turning suicide into nothing more than a challenge! Landross would be proud!"

Mariko rolled her eyes at Jennifer and answered the knight's question, cutting off the rebuke Tangus was no doubt ready to fling his daughter's way. "We have a plan for that. I only have to get within a few hundred yards to kill the queen."

The Astorian knight cocked his head.

"You don't want to know," Mariko remarked.

"But that's not the end of it," Kristen said. "We're also need to find and destroy the egg chambers."

Sir Abernathy looked back at his knights. One hundred Astorian knights is a formidable force, but they'd still be outnumbered ten, twenty, one hundred to one. Yet Tangus remained set upon leading his small ragtag group of eight, if you include the cats, against those same overwhelming odds. By the gods, what courage! Already they'd survived a full onslaught of the bugs. Yet here they were, back for more… still willing to give up their lives for the greater good. This ranger and his companions were as worthy as any knight, or knight-general, and needed their help now more than ever. Putting himself and his men into the service of Tangus per General Fox's orders wouldn't be as hard as he thought. But it must go deeper than that.

At that point Sir Abernathy decided his future. He hoped the rest would join him, but he wouldn't demand it. Each knight must be free to make up his or her own mind, for what he would ask required them to make a life-altering choice. "If you'll excuse me."

"Make it quick," Tangus warned. "The longer we wait, the stronger the bugs get… at least in number."

Sir Abernathy nodded as he turned and walked back up the corridor, gathering his knights around him as best he could in the small space.

"What do you suppose they're discussing," Kristen asked.

"Probably asking themselves if they're crazy enough to join us."

"No Jennifer," Mariko said. "They're with us. Astorian knights never run from battle or danger. It's their greatest strength… and perhaps their greatest weakness."

Sir Abernathy returned to stand in front of Tangus. He withdrew his sword, placed the tip on the floor, kneeled, and placed his forehead against the hilt. All one hundred knights followed his lead and did the same. The sound of their armor echoed throughout the corridors.

"It will be our honor to fight and die at your side… and by your command, now and into perpetuity!" Sir Abernathy said. There was a ritual cadence in the tone of his voice.

Kristen, Jennifer, and Mariko looked around, surprised and unsure. But Tangus knew what Sir Abernathy and his knights were doing. It was the same thing Landross did to enter Father Goram's service. Though it wasn't common for Astorian Knights to switch allegiance from one lord to another, it happened – as Landross could attest – and was acceptable under the Knight's Code. These warriors were his from now until their last breath, provided he accepted them. Tangus was no lord, but as he stood considering the offer, several scenarios ran through his mind. Ultimately, it came down to the one thing Tangus had been worried about from the beginning – the safety of Kristen and Emmy. A small army of Astorian Knights was just what he needed.

Tangus remembered a past discussion he had with Landross regarding the ritual of allegiance change. It fascinated him that knights were allowed to change lords. To him it meant the knight was breaking his sacred bond. But Landross had a different view. There are always new threats, new developments, new obligations. As long as the current lord was agreeable to the change, the Knight's Code was satisfied and there was no breach to a knight's honor. During the course of that conversation, Landross had mentioned the ceremonial requirements, so Tangus knew what was expected. He drew one of his own swords and sliced the palm of his hand, letting the blood flow. He gripped the hilt of Sir Abernathy's sword before stepping back. Sir Abernathy sliced his own palm and gripped the hilt, letting his blood mix with that of Tangus'. He stood and moved behind his new lord.

As a group, the one hundred knights did the same. As each filed past their new lord, Tangus ritually added his blood to the hilt of the sword of each knight. He had to reopen the slit on his palm two more times to keep the blood flowing. After the last warrior, Tangus turned to face them. He didn't give a speech or say anything that was inspiring or prophetic. Tangus never was one for words. He walked through the mass. As he did so, he said "We have a job to do. Sir Abernathy, with me."

Kristen, Jennifer, and Mariko stared, speechless.

"Meet Elanesse's new city guard," Tangus said, "and our very own knight protectors. If I can keep them alive."

They smelled the bugs before they met them. Tangus had been expecting it. He had an idea where the queen was… the floor of the Pyramid of the Purge. It was the ideal place… fortified, huge, and surrounded by several large chambers that would serve well as hatcheries. Bug presence only confirmed his reasoning.

There was only four or five – a small scouting party which the knights dispatched with bow and arrow. Despite the ease in which this threat had been eliminated, each person knew it was only the start of a long and difficult struggle.

And so it went. As they made their way through the tunnels that led to the Pyramid of the Purge, each battle was worse than the previous. But excellent tactics, sprinkled with a smattering of luck, saw them through with only a few minor injuries which Kristen quickly healed. Another problem soon presented itself, however – the stench of the decaying bugs. Sir Abernathy and most of his knights were feeling sick. Kristen determined the mucus-like remains of dead bugs not only reeked but were also noxious… and the confined spaces of the tunnels made it worse. Kristen used magic to keep the air surrounding everyone pure, though it wasn't one hundred percent effective because of the number of people and cats it needed to protect.

Onward they marched. They fought and exterminated bugs over and over again until each were both physically and mentally exhausted. If not for the knights, they'd never had gotten this far. Tangus knew it. Sir Abernathy knew it. Everyone knew it.

During the fighting, the master ranger made several observations. Sir Abernathy excelled in everything he did. There were few weaknesses in his tactics and fighting style, and the two worked well together. It appeared Sir Abernathy would be Tangus' Landross. And the knights, though pledged to him, followed Sir Abernathy's lead. Tangus had little doubt that's why they took the knee.

It also appeared both his wife and daughter had gained cat companions. Moishe never left Kristen's side while Kamuzu always stayed with Jennifer. Tangus didn't think the two cats would follow Osiris back into the mountains even if the pride leader insisted. The ranger approved of both matches – animals enriched lives in so many ways – and he didn't believe Romulus would have a problem with either.

And finally, Tangus decided he needed to talk to Emmy about Mariko. He didn't believe the master assassin would ever be effective as a priestess. Her fighting skills were much too valuable, and she admitted to him and Kristen in private that she'd be clumsy and useless as a priestess. Kristen, who'd been trying to teach Mariko a few simple healing spells, agreed with the assassin's self-assessment. The bottom line, as Tangus saw it, was that Mariko was a square peg being forced into a round hole. Everyone would be much better off if she could apply her own special talents to solving the problems of the day.

The next attack by the bugs came as a surprise and illustrated sometimes even bugs can get lucky… or worse for their victims, use their own calculated tactics.

Knight-General Victoria Fox gathered her remaining knights. The sickness that prevailed throughout her command faded away sooner than the healers expected as the mucus remains of the bugs dried up and turned to dust after only a few hours. The discarded armor, now clean of its affliction, was recovered, and once again donned. Each knight now wore handkerchiefs covered with a mentholated paste made from the leaves of several varieties of forest bushes.

Knight-General Fox was a strong advocate of tactical fluency and threw away standard knight philosophy. She had her knights re-enter the haunted city through not only the main western gate but also through breaks in the walls along the western perimeter. The knights entered on foot and did what they could to blend in with the trees and bushes that had inserted themselves through crumbling walls.

The city was empty.

The bug ambush was simplistic but devastating. The smell, though muted by fresh-air magic, hit them as soon as they turned a corridor corner. There was an intersection in the tunnel fifty yards ahead. Several bugs were marching forward and charged as soon as they saw Tangus and his knights. After a brief struggle, the bugs were mucus puddles on the floor. The knights escaped serious injury.

"I don't care for the looks of that intersection," Sir Abernathy remarked. He and Tangus had moved a few paces ahead. "You don't think the bugs are smart enough to set a trap, do you?"

Tangus shook his head. "I don't know. But I agree it could be a trap, and I don't want to take any chances. If it's an ambush, we need to draw them out."

Sir Abernathy motioned to several of his knights who tiptoed forward and past the two. "They're my 'go to' guys," he told Tangus.

Tangus and Sir Abernathy's instincts were correct. The 'go to' knights sprung a bug ambush. When they got within twenty yards of the intersection, bugs charged from both side corridors. The forward knights withdrew while the main body covered their retreat with bow and arrow. The initial phase of the battle pivoted against the bugs after only a few minutes.

The Custodian stayed in the shadows and watched his drones attack. Behind him were several dozen more drones. The ambush wasn't going well, but that didn't matter. Drones are expendable. The Custodian turned and decapitated two drones with scythe-like claws. Two proboscises snaked out from his mouth and entered each drone body through the open neck. As the Custodian fed on the drone's internal fluids, it gathered strength. His body grew twice its size and glistened with magical power. A black interdimensional doorway opened before him. Without another thought, the Custodian stepped through followed by his drones.

Jennifer, with Kamuzu standing at her side, watched the battle from the rear. She wished she could take part, but the corridor width made that impossible. Without warning Kamuzu turned and roared a challenge. Jennifer sensed the sudden presence of magic behind her. She turned and saw a gigantic bug stepping through a magical doorway accompanied by dozens of regular sized bugs.

With her bow and arrow drawn and ready to shoot, Jennifer fired at the huge bug and hit it in the chest. The arrow ricocheted off the chest and found purchase in an arm. The creature roared in pain but didn't stop. As Kamuzu fought with the normal-sized bugs, Jennifer backed a few paces while firing arrows. Her arrows were hitting, but the creature, protected as it was by an ultra-thick chitin shell, shrugged them off.

With the bug only a few feet away, Jennifer reached back to grab an arrow and found nothing but emptiness in her quiver. Dropping her bow, she pulled her sword. Three arrows flew past Jennifer and hit the creature. Jennifer recognized Mariko's fletching.

"Thank the gods," Jennifer whispered. She wasn't alone.

From the sides several knights squeezed past Jennifer to confront the beast. Most of the knights surrounded it and were taking large chunks of chitin from its body with their great longswords. The rest were helping Kamuzu with the normal-sized bugs. Jennifer, after seeing the knights had things well in control, closed her eyes, took a deep breath, and rested her sword on the floor, buoyed by the knowledge that she was safe for the time being.

Jennifer's relief was short-lived. She heard Mariko yell a warning to her, but in her present state it didn't register. Then she felt pain unlike any she'd ever experienced in her young life.

Mariko did her best to get to Jennifer before the monster bug did, but she was going against the grain as she struggled to push her way through with the knights rushing forward to join the battle up front. She pointed at the beast and yelled. Several knights noticed, reversed course, and hurried past Jennifer to attack the new threat. The knights stopped the charging bug, and their great-swords gouged huge rents in its armor. The smaller bugs were being handled by other knights and would soon be a non-factor. Mariko breathed a sigh of relief because it looked as if Jennifer might be out of danger. But that relief was short lived as a greenish-gray cloud appeared in front of the monster bug. She'd seen that type of cloud before – acid.

The knights dropped to the floor shrieking in pain. Every exposed part of their flesh boiled and burned. Their armor offered little protection and began to melt. Such was the strength of the acid that even those who wore armor protected by magic only gained a few seconds additional reprieve before it too began to dissolve. Jennifer stood near the extreme limit of the acid cloud just before it expired, but that was enough to cause her to scream in pain and fall to the floor.

Mariko approached Jennifer while shooting arrows into the exposed flesh of the bug. The gigantic bug stumbled. Its twin serpent tongues flickered in her direction as it got back up, only to be knocked forward and back to the floor. On its back the saber cat Kamuzu tore through the unguarded flesh of the neck. As the assassin stood protectively over a moaning Jennifer, keeping her attention on the bug, it stopped moving and began to disintegrate. Kamuzu jumped off the corpse and collapsed. Mariko diverted her attention back to Jennifer and cringed. The young ranger was still breathing, but her face was burned beyond recognition. She stepped aside to make room for Kristen and Tangus who had just arrived.

Tangus resisted the urge to turn look away as he cradled his daughter's head in his lap. Time stood still as he listened to each ragged breath mixed with choking sounds as Jennifer tried to breathe. Kamuzu, broken and bleeding, had crawled over to Jennifer and laid his large head on her leg.

Kristen and Mariko removed Jennifer's acid-destroyed outer clothes. The wounds to her exposed flesh were horrid. But of most concern was the damage done to her mouth, throat, and lungs.

"The throat's blistered, but I don't think the acid made it into her lungs," Kristen said in a business-like voice. She had parceled away her emotions… she couldn't allow them to interfere with the healing she needed to do. She gave Tangus a flask of ointment. "This salve will help with the burns. Put it on her face and hands."

As her husband complied, Kristen directed her healing magic into Jennifer. She closed her eyes and followed the magic into the mouth, throat, and lungs to gage the magnitude of the damage. Her ability to do this was unique among healers. It was one of the many different techniques taught to her by Emmy. As she thought, the lungs were only damaged superficially and easy to heal. But the mouth and throat had been more seriously burned.

Kristen directed her magic into the blisters that lined Jennifer's throat, drained them of fluid, and healed the wounds that remained. She then turned her attention to the mouth, healing those blisters as well. The teeth hadn't been injured. Satisfied, she moved to the lungs and fixed what little damage there was. As Kristen moved back out, she inspected what she'd just done to the throat and mouth, made a few minor adjustments, and, content everything had gone as well as could be expected under the circumstances, extinguished her magic, and opened her eyes.

"She's breathing normal," Tangus said. "But her face... and Kristen, the acid has melted her eyes. They're gone."

Kristen inspected the injuries and got back to work. She again brought forth her curative magic and infused it into Jennifer's face and hands, the only flesh exposed to the acid cloud. As part of the healing, Kristen did her best to minimize scaring. Jennifer wouldn't be pretty, but nor would she be ugly. Handsome with character — that's what Kristen could restore.

Jennifer no longer moaned in pain.

"Let her sleep for a few minutes before we move on," Kristen said. "Is there anyone else who needs my care."

Tangus shook his head. "None of the knights in the acid cloud survived. And we've been able to dress the other wounds... except for Kamuzu here."

The cat was still resting his head in Jennifer's lap. There was blood coming out of his nose and ears and he moaned with each breath, the result of several broken ribs. Osiris and Cheops sat a short distance away and observed with keen interest. Moishe had positioned himself behind Kristen, his new mistress.

Kristen didn't hesitate and placed an open hand on Kamuzu's head. Blue healing magic flowed from her hand and into the cat's body, healing broken bones, cauterizing severed blood vessels, and removing the blood clot that was causing the swelling in his brain. The cat sat up and nodded at Kristen but remained next to Jennifer.

"You can't fix her eyes, can you," Tangus said. It wasn't a question. He knew the answer.

Kristen shook her head. "I'm sorry," she said as she tied a clean, silk handkerchief around Jennifer's head, covering the empty eye sockets.

Tangus stood up and motioned for Sir Abernathy. He had pushed his concern for his daughter aside and was now Tangus the warrior and leader. "I don't know what kind of funeral arrangements are made for Astorian knights, but we need to do it quick. The bugs are growing in strength.”

“That big bug used magic to kill my knights,” Sir Abernathy observed. “How are we going to fight that?”

“I don’t know.”

Tangus looked back at his wife and daughter. Kristen, with an arm around Jennifer’s shoulder, was helping her to sit. The two, with four saber cats by their side, were surrounded by knights.

They were in a small chamber just large enough to accommodate their entire number. There was fresh spring water, an air vent to the surface, and no side corridors. After a short discussion with Sir Abernathy, Tangus had sent a small scouting party forward while everyone else waited – and rested.

Tangus joined his wife, daughter, and four very alert saber cats. “Sweetie,” he said as he sat beside Jennifer and put an arm around her shoulder.

Startled by her father’s approach, Jennifer jumped, but settled down and relaxed in Tangus’ embrace.

“What a startling turn of fortune, eh father? Blind as a bat and Kristen calls me ruggedly handsome. Ruggedly handsome! By the gods, my face and hands feel like the bark of an oak tree!”

“Dear, I told you…” Kristen interjected.

“Yes, I know. It’ll take a few days for the inflammation to go away and my burns will heal with minimal scaring. Oh well, at least I won’t be able to see them.”

“It sounds as if you’re giving up,” Tangus said. “You’re better than that.”

Jennifer remained reticent.

Tangus brushed a strand of hair from her face. “You’re a ranger. You don’t need your sight to see things. I’ve taught you since you were a little tyke to feel your surroundings using all your senses, not just your eyes."

"Yeah, just point me in the right direction and I'll shoot an apple off your head," Jennifer remarked with a good bit of sarcasm. Her voice was thick with resentment.

Tangus shrugged. "I think you could. At least I'd trust you enough to let you try."

Jennifer softened. "I'm sorry."

Tangus kissed her on the forehead. "No need. Now get some rest."

Kristen stood when Tangus did. "Stay and rest with us," she said.

Tangus kissed his wife. "I need to talk to Sir Abernathy first. But I promise to come back and get some sleep afterwards."

The scouting party found several hatcheries, at least that's what they thought they were, in deserted caverns. But other than eggs, there was no sign of the bugs.

"Not too surprising," Mariko said. "If they're similar to other insects, those eggs will be that of the drones. Not especially important and probably left to hatch on their own."

"Probably?" Sir Abernathy asked.

Mariko looked at the knight. "Well, it's either that or other drones will return to help at the end of the incubation period."

"We need to destroy those eggs before that happens," Tangus said. He turned to the scouting party leader. "Take us."

There were five interconnected caverns, and each one looked to be the same except for size. Strewn along the floor of each were hundreds of nearly full-sized bugs covered in a thick, translucent membrane. The tops of the eggs were just barely visible above a three-foot-high thick cloud of dirty-white water vapor which covered the floor. A few stalagmites rose from the cavern surface, pierced the low-lying cloud, and met an accompanying stalactite coming from the ceiling, the tips of each touching halfway.

"Well ain't this just great," Tangus said. "I had hoped to burn them and be done with it. But that cloud is way too wet to do that."

Sir Abernathy nodded. "Indeed. We'll just have to dispatch them with our swords."

Tangus shook his head. "That'll take too long. And they're just about full grown, which means it'll probably take more than just a sword thrust to kill each. Besides, how can we be sure we've got all of them. There's no way of knowing what we don't see under the cloud."

Sir Abernathy shrugged. "We'll just have to take our chances."

"No, I believe there's another way," Kristen said as she put Jennifer's hand on the back of Kamuzu and approached her husband and Sir Abernathy. "This water vapor is necessary for the eggs to mature and hatch or else it wouldn't be here. But it's not natural. Somewhere there should be an artificial source generator. Get rid of the generator, get rid of the cloud. Then perhaps these eggs won't hatch."

"Or we can burn them," Tangus said. "Where do we begin? And what will it look like?"

"Look closely at the water vapor, dear. Do you see anything strange about it?"

Tangus squatted to examine the top of the cloud in more detail. "Well I'll be damned!" he exclaimed after a few seconds. "The cloud's moving... billowing... whatever... away from the center of the cavern."

Kristen nodded. "It's subtle, but you can see it. Now follow in the opposite direction and you'll find the source generator."

Tangus, Kristen, and Sir Abernathy waded through the flowing cloud toward the center. The source generator lay against a stalagmite. It was shaped like the other eggs but not as large... and unlike the eggs which were a gray-yellow color, this was green with stripes of red along the outside surface.

Tangus probed the source generator with a scimitar. It was soft and pliant. He looked at Kristen who nodded. Raising the scimitar up and over his head, he brought it down and split the strange egg. It was as if he was cutting a piece of soft fruit, such as a watermelon. The soft tissue inside collapsed and spread out over the cavern floor. The cloud began to dissipate almost at once. As everyone watched, the eggs began to move.

CHAPTER TWENTY-FIVE

Elanesse

"The journey was long and arduous, but the end was like the smell of cherry blossoms on a fresh, clean spring morning. I've never felt so refreshed... so alive!"

-From the Journal of Mariko Takagi

The bugs tried to claw their way through the egg-sacks, but without the moisture from the cloud, the surface of the eggs had hardened and proved to be too strong. If they were to escape, someone would have to break the shell from the outside. Of course no knight would do such a thing. The eggs, now visible, tumbled about for a few minutes before they quieted. Soon, none of them moved.

"Kristen, you're a genius," Tangus exclaimed. "I think you solved our baby bug problem."

"I hope so," Kristen replied. "Still, I almost feel sorry for them."

Sir Abernathy shook his head in disagreement. "Don't feel sorry for them, my lady. I'm sure even as babies they're vicious and deadly creatures. Nay, you did what's right."

"More knight talk," Jennifer whispered to Kamuzu. Then she chuckled. "My hearing's getting better. Aren't I lucky!" she added, her voice dripping with sarcasm.

In each of the other caverns the same device was located and destroyed. And while they had prevented hundreds of bug eggs from hatching, it wouldn't mean a thing if they didn't find and slay the queen. Each of them understood that.

The arrival of 'nursery drones', as Kristen called them, occurred not long after they killed the baby bugs. This new kind of drone looked the same as regular drones, except they had padded, three-fingered hands instead of claws. Another difference was how they used their proboscis. Instead of using it to drink the liquified insides of prey, they used it to inject a chemical soup of nutrients into drone eggs. But those nutrients acted as a powerful, fast-acting poison to elves and saber cats. Two knights died, and Osiris became deathly ill before they learned this lesson.

"Tangus!" Mariko called from behind about an hour after the battle with the nursery drones. "I remember this intersection. I think we're close enough."

Tangus called a halt to the column of knights.

Mariko made her way through the crowded corridor until she was standing with Tangus and Sir Abernathy. "It's time to release our little lovelies."

Tangus nodded while Sir Abernathy, confused, looked at Mariko.

"Tell me, Sir Abernathy, do you know what a Soulreaver is?" Tangus asked.

"Qénsharma!" Sir Abernathy exclaimed. Several of the knights close enough to overhear murmured as they shook their heads. Several of them spit on the floor, an unknightly thing to do, but no doubt deemed justified under the circumstances.

"So, you do know of them," Tangus remarked. "Nasty creatures one and all."

"Not just nasty," Sir Abernathy said. There was hatred in his voice. "But demons from the Abyss."

Mariko nodded. "I've heard Astorian Knights knew their demons. Then you should also know that not every spawn of the Abyss is evil. Cruel, yes, and even nasty as Tangus describes them. But if you consider the nature of the Abyss, what choice do they have? Down there, a chivalrous Soulreaver is a dead Soulreaver."

"But we're not in the Abyss," Sir Abernathy protested. He drew his sword as did his fellow knights. "Only assassins can control and use the Qénsharma," he said. His voice was filled with venom.

Mariko drew both her katanas in response to the threat posed by the knights. She understood the contempt Astorian Knights held for assassins and had hoped her service to Tangus and his family would have dulled their response. Apparently not. And she never expected Sir Abernathy to make the connection between her occupation and the Soulreavers so quickly.

Tangus stepped between the two. "THAT WILL BE ENOUGH!" he bellowed. He waited until the knights were calm enough to listen. "Sir Abernathy, I appreciate your position, but using the Soulreavers to kill our enemies has my full support."

"Do you even know what's left over after a kill?" Sir Abernathy asked. "I don't personally, but I've heard it's... it's..."

"Brutal, unimaginable, blood-curdling, uncivilized, and so forth," Tangus answered. "Yes, I'm aware. I've seen the results."

Sir Abernathy pointed his sword at Mariko. "And she's an assassin! It's a vile, dishonorable profession peopled by vile and despicable individuals."

Mariko, though seething, remained calm. This had to be dealt with swiftly, and she trusted Tangus to do just that.

"So, you'll use your sword to blot out this stain of corruption," Tangus angrily replied. "You, Sir Abernathy, will be judge, jury, and executioner?! You'll kill Mariko and walk away, satisfied you did the right thing... the honorable thing?!"

"Well..."

Tangus continued unabated. "You see, my friend, there's a couple problems with that. First, Mariko isn't going to just drop to her knees and let you have a whack at her. She'll defend herself, and I've seen what she can do with those katanas. Believe me when I tell you she'll kill a dozen of your knights before you could kill her. And just how honorable is all of you against only the one of her, though I suspect my wife, daughter, and the cats would step in to help her. So would I, for that matter."

Tangus, watching closely, waited a few seconds to let that sink in. Sir Abernathy's sword wavered. Tangus pounced.

"As for your second problem… I FORBID IT!"

Everyone in the corridor were astounded by the force of that declaration. The knights bowed their heads. None of them wanted to be reprimanded by their new lord, particularly when the reprimand was so severe. Sir Abernathy nodded and everyone sheathed their swords, including Mariko.

Tangus approved. "That's better. Mariko's proved her worth to me and to those of us who know her time and time again… and I'd wager she has as much honor as you do." Tangus paused. "Sir Abernathy, what's your first name?"

"Shawn, my lord."

"Shawn, knights consider their honor unassailable, an unerring truth that should never be challenged. You bludgeon people with it. You make people feel inferior because they don't live their lives by the same rigid code as you do."

"But we help people," Sir Abernathy complained.

"Sure, you do," Tangus agreed. "The knights do a lot of good. But that's not the point I'm trying to make. Don't let the code make your decisions for you because it doesn't have all the answers. You must make some life and death decisions on your own. You're not the code, Shawn. It's you who defines how the code should work to serve you and others. You must understand that sometimes the code will work against you."

"So I should put aside the code when Qénsharma and assassins are involved?"

Tangus nodded. "In this instance, yeah, that's exactly what I mean. Assassins are a valuable commodity, particularly one who has pledged loyalty to our side. They have many invaluable skills they can use in shadow wars. Even your own hierarchy uses them."

Sir Abernathy shook his head. "Never! That's not how we wage war."

Tangus sighed. "You still don't get it, son. The quickest way to win a war is to not fight it in the first place. What if you can eliminate the enemy king or queen? Or, short of that, place the other side at a disadvantage by knowing what their battle plans are. Even better, assassinate their command leadership. Is it dishonorable if it saves thousands of lives? Lives on both sides? Is it ever dishonorable to prevent war?"

Sir Abernathy was silent.

Tangus continued. "I mean, wouldn't that be the right thing to do?"

"I suppose."

"Okay. So how do you think such things are handled, Shawn?" Tangus asked, though he didn't expect an answer. "There's not a magic wand for it. No... no, it's not that simple. Assassins are recruited and used. Assassins and spies. And like the knight in battle, they use all the tools in their arsenal. Believe me, Shawn, if you're going into battle, you better pray the assassins and spies have had a run at the enemy first."

"You really think..."

"I don't just think, I know your leaders do it," Tangus said. "In fact, I'd go so far as to say they have an obligation to do it."

"So, the code be damned?" Sir Abernathy remarked.

Tangus shrugged his shoulders. "Sometimes. It's up to you to make that distinction. But I suspect the answers you seek... the flexibility I speak of... can be found in the code. It's only a matter of the correct interpretation. When this bug situation is over, I'll take you to InnisRos. You can talk to Sir Landross. Sometimes he acts a bit inflexible where the code's concerned, but most of that's for show. He understands the distinction. Hell, considering the folks he hangs around with, he's married to it."

"I will look forward to that day," Sir Abernathy said.

Tangus turned to Mariko and nodded.

The assassin released the Soulreavers.

"Sir Pellinore, take two or three knights into the palace library and see if you can find any maps of the city," General Fox ordered. "Anything you can find that outlines the underground sewer and water system will be particularly helpful."

The knight lieutenant saluted and hurried off, selecting random knights as he went.

Victoria turned to Sir Basil. "Before we were attacked, did we find any doors leading underground during our initial search?"

Sir Basil nodded and pointed. "In that building just north of that huge obelisk. Several, in fact."

Victoria looked at the building. It was large, three stories tall and who knows how many levels beneath the ground. From the shape and grandeur of its outward facade, even in its current dilapidated state, she had no doubt as to its function. "That's the meeting place of the local parliament. Most cities of import have building's such as this."

"Ahh, so that is where taxes are levied and the local populace gets screwed," Sir Basil remarked.

Victoria ignored the comment. "Those underground entrances probably lead out of the city."

"Escape tunnels?"

Victoria considered Sir Basil's question. "Yes. Sometimes politicians make decisions that, oh, shall we say runs contrary to the people's best interest. They often face uprisings as a consequence. The politicians needed an escape from the 'rabble' until they could restore order. Or, if they've offended the military, an escape to a more permanent relocation. But that's neither here nor there. If the tunnels leave the city, I doubt the bugs are in them. Their queen is here, underneath us, and not out there. This city is too well defended for there to be another answer."

"We still need to check them out," Sir Basil added.

Victoria nodded. "Please see to it."

She watched as Sir Basil carried out her orders. He had a group of knights assembled when she had a thought. She walked over to them.

"Leave your armor," she commanded.

The knights, including Sir Basil, stared at her, wondering if they'd heard correctly.

Victoria swooshed them with her hands. "Go on, take it off."

"But…" Sir Basil began.

Victoria started removing her own armor. "Trust me, your armor is more of an encumbrance underground than an advantage. You'll be quieter, you'll move through narrow corridors easier, and you'll have more freedom to swing your swords and battleaxes. Now let's go."

Sir Basil and most of the other knights nodded and rushed to do as she had directed.

A small group of healers approached Victoria. Unfortunately, the two clerics she had with her, healers capable of using magic, were killed in the earlier engagement. The healers looked exhausted and their robes were filthy. The bottom of each robe had been torn and shorten by two feet. "General," one of them said. "We have what you requested."

Victoria nodded. "So, you found the roots and leaves you needed."

The one who spoke nodded. "Not much searching to it. It was as if the forest just offered them up." He held out a large sack. Each of the healers carried one. "We've used the mint root and mixed it with crushed leaves of peppermint, water mint, lilac, and a smidgen of pennyroyal. There's enough of this paste on these cotton strips to shield everyone from the bug stink."

Victoria accepted a bag and looked inside. "You used strips from your cloaks?"

The healer nodded. "It's all we had for such a large number. Don't worry…. we sanitized them in boiling water before we put the paste on. Just put them over your nose when you smell the bug stink. The paste soaked into the strips will absorb enough of it to prevent you from getting sick."

The knight-general nodded and reached into the sack to grab one. "Please pass these out to everyone. And make sure you keep one for yourselves."

"General," Sir Pellinore called out as he raced to towards Victoria. He was carrying a large, rectangular tome. "I know where the queen can be found!"

Victoria held up her hand to the knights. "Change of plans."

Tangus called a stop to their advance in a large chamber that had a freshwater spring running through it. If his memory was correct, and both Kristen and Mariko agreed it was, they were still about two hours away from the Pyramid of the Purge, which is where they thought the queen bug was.

As the knights, saber cats, and Jennifer were settling in for the welcomed break, Tangus stepped off to one side and motioned for Kristen, Mariko, and Sir Abernathy to join him.

"How much time do you think the Soulreavers will need to find the queen?" Tangus asked Mariko.

Mariko shrugged. "It's hard to say. They'll be traveling along the ceiling, so except for a few occasional stalactites, their movement will be unhindered. Even so… at least a few hours."

"Any chance they'll lose their way?" Kristen asked.

"Probably not," Mariko said as she shook her head. "They have her scent, or whatever they use to find the targeted victim, through the bugs we've fought. Even so, it's impossible to know for sure. I don't claim to understand their physiology. But my past experience with Soulreavers leads me to believe they'll find the bug queen, though I doubt they'll be able to kill her quickly. She's got to be huge."

Tangus turned to Sir Abernathy. He could tell the knight was still having a problem accepting the Soulreavers as allies. "Any questions, Shawn?"

The knight looked at Mariko. "How do they kill?" he asked. His tone was curt. He'd still hadn't warmed up to the assassin.

"From the inside, Sir Abernathy," Mariko replied, unaffected by the knight's hostility. "You saw what they are. They use their form to enter a body orifice. Once inside the victim, they feed on the skin and muscle tissue from the inside out, though I've heard they'll also eat organs if so desired. They're pretty pliable as long as their hungry. One thing they don't eat is the head. They leave that alone because they can't get at the skin through the skull."

Sir Abernathy looked at Mariko in horror. "But that leaves the organs, the inside of a person, unprotected. They expose every nerve while they leave the brain intact to experience the result. Their victims are skinned alive! I can't think of a more brutal death!"

"I couldn't agree with you more," Mariko said.

Sir Abernathy stared.

"There are people who deserve it," Mariko observed as she shrugged off the knights' icy glare. Even though she now walked a new path, she refused to feel guilty. There were far too many people in the world who made people suffer far worse than the Soulreavers.

"How are they going to kill the queen when her skin consists of hardened chitin," Kristen asked.

Tangus breathed a sigh of relief. "Thanks, sweetheart," he whispered to himself. Maybe her question will defuse some of the animosity between Mariko and Sir Abernathy.

Mariko considered. "They'll eat the muscle tissue. I can't imagine the bug queen surviving that. As for the chitin…"

"Chitin's not made of the same material as bone," Sir Abernathy said. It appeared his anger had been set aside, at least for the length of the discussion. "Perhaps the Qénsharma can ingest it."

"Perhaps," Mariko replied. "But it may not be necessary since the Soulreavers are going after the queen. She'll have a large egg sack which won't be protected by chitin. At the very least they can take away her ability to produce more bugs."

"Anything else?" Tangus asked.

"What happens to the Qénsharma once they've eaten?" Sir Abernathy asked.

"They'll hibernate until they're hungry again," Mariko responded. "That can last for as long as two weeks. And before you object, rest assured I'll collect them and keep them from harming anyone else. Granted, the Soulreavers are fiends. But as long as their hunger's fed, they don't represent a threat. In fact, if they accept you, there's little to no danger even if they are hungry."

Sir Abernathy shook his head.

"Don't knock it," Mariko added. "Demons fear the Soulreaver. Evil or not, that gives us an ace in the hole."

"What?"

Mariko sighed. "There's a lot you need to teach this boy, Tangus. Shawn, I'm referring to a card game. It means we'll have the advantage… an unsuspected advantage."

Sir Abernathy nodded. "Against demons. But…"

"Okay, that should cover everything," Tangus said, shutting down any further discussions regarding the merits of using Soulreavers, or Qénsharma, as Sir Abernathy prefers to call them. "Get some sleep. We move out in two hours."

Sir Pellinore set the large tome on the ground. "It's the complete architectural plans for all the public buildings in the city, including the underground systems."

The knight opened the tome and turned pages until he came to the Pyramid of the Purge. Victoria kneeled to take a closer look.

"The actual bottom of this pyramid is several stories down from ground level," the knight explained.

"The Pyramid of the Purge," Victoria read aloud from the book. "Okay. But there's nothing unusual about that. Most pyramids have the same thing."

"It's a perfect place for the queen to hatch her eggs," Sir Pellinore said. "It's large enough. And it has any number of rooms off its sides that could be used to support hatcheries."

Victoria nodded. "As, I suspect, do a lot of the larger buildings."

"No doubt," Sir Pellinore said as he flipped the page to show an overhead view of the floor bottom. "But then I found this." He pointed to a passageway that left the bottom chamber and ran off the page. Sir Pellinore turned to the corresponding page and picked up the tunnel again, using his finger to trace the route to the end.

"Recognize this, general?" Sir Pellinore asked.

Victoria looked over at her officer and nodded. "It's where we found the tracks and where Sir Abernathy took his knights. The tunnel leads back from there to the Pyramid of the Purge."

Sir Pellinore slammed shut the tome. "She's got to be down there," he said with finality.

Victoria stood. "You're right. And that's where Sir Abernathy is headed." She turned and shouted for Sir Basil before returning her attention back to the knight.

"Sir Pellinore," Victoria said to the knight. "Return the tome and join your knights."

The knight saluted.

Victoria watched him leave. "Oh, and Montgomery," she called to the retreating figure. "Excellent work."

Resistance from the bugs became stronger as they approached the queen. That she was where they believed her to be was no longer a point of conjecture. The increasing number of bugs they killed left little doubt. But as they whittled down the bugs, the bugs were having the same effect on the knights… and every knight lost was irreplaceable.

Tangus looked at his people and took stock as he cleaned his swords. They'd just beaten back another bug attack and still hadn't found the remaining hatcheries. Thirty-three knights had lost their lives, and half of those still alive were wounded. Kristen had long ago run out of healing magic and needed a long rest before she had enough strength to use it again. Every one of them were tired, dirty, and hungry. They were running out of arrows to fire at the bugs, and they discovered one consequence of long exposure to bug mucus made steel brittle if it wasn't cleaned promptly. Brittle steel against hard chitin cost several knights their lives.

"How close," a weary Sir Abernathy asked.

Tangus shook his head. "I've only been down here once before… going in the opposite direction. But I think it's close. If memory serves, we'll find several large chambers up ahead. The bottom of the pyramid is just beyond that."

The knight nodded. "If the Qénsharma do their job, we can end this soon."

"Not if any of the young queen's and their male consorts have left the nest," Kristen said.

"We don't even know if there are any," Jennifer said. She held onto a tuft of Kamuzu's neck fur.

"No, darling," Kristen responded. "But we can't afford to take chances. If any queens hatched and escaped, they must be hunted and destroyed."

Both Osiris and Cheops growled from ahead which ended all conversation. Both had been out front scouting. Moishe and Kamuzu took defensive postures in front of their mistresses while everyone peered into the darkness. There was absolute silence broken only by the heavy breathing of anticipation.

From the corridor came the clicking of nails on stone. Osiris and Cheops, running side by side, appeared out of the darkness and stopped in front of Tangus and Sir Abernathy. They both turned to growl at the darkness. It wasn't long before everyone heard what had forced the two saber cats to run. Bugs! Hundreds of bugs clawing their way through the corridor towards them.

"Kristen," Tangus said. He kept his voice calm, but inside, he was worried about what he'd see. Something didn't feel right. As the bugs got closer, it began to sound more like infantry marching in cadence – far different from the normal bug charge which was rag-tagged, disorganized, and fanatical. But the smell left little doubt that these were bugs.

Kristen brought forth a magical ball of light. With a thought she moved it down the dark corridor – one hundred, two hundred, three hundred yards before she stopped it. Marching along the corridor, four across, came the bugs, hidden behind body-sized shields of what appeared to be a kind of excretion.

The Knights of Astoria forced open the double doors which led into the Pyramid of the Purge. They were instantly accosted by bug stink, but the salve in the cotton strips tied around their noses worked as the healers had intended. Several knights threw lit torches down into the belly of the pyramid. Far below the torches were quickly extinguished, but not before the knights saw hundreds of bugs attending a grotesque blob.

Above them, four angled stone walls climbed upwards to meet at the capstone of clear crystal. Not unlike an iceberg, the largest part of the pyramid was below ground. Ringing the four sides of the pyramid beneath them were metal walkways at each level and connected by staircases. Fifty to sixty closed doors ringed each level.

Most of the knights rushed into the pyramid and began their descent while others fired arrows into the darkness below, hoping to hit the queen or kill as many as the bugs as possible. The clash of species was only a few seconds away.

The queen's Custodian realized the danger to its monarch as soon as the knights entered from far above. It ordered bugs to climb on top of her to act as shields while others began the slow process of moving the queen to a nearby overhang. The Custodian heard the sounds of footfalls as the invaders descended the stairs… but didn't act until after the queen had been repositioned out of harm's way. Satisfied, the Custodian looked up and screeched. Hundreds of bugs answered his call and began to climb upwards. But unlike the knights, they didn't need to use the stairs.

The two Soulreavers approached the queen. They were almost completely invisible in the pyramid's darkness as they crawled up the last wall and onto the overhang that covered the queen. They'd have no problem entering the queen, even with the smaller bugs surrounding her.

The queen of the *Theraesus*, though inconvenienced by the sudden move, trusted the Custodian to keep her safe. She never stopped eating the nutrients being fed to her… and she never stopped laying her eggs. *"I feel marvelous!"* she thought.

So intent was she on her happiness, she ignored the brief discomfort she felt when something entered her respiratory system and traveled down her tracheae and deep into her body.

The first two lines of the bugs dropped as the first barrage of arrows hit. Though most of the missiles glanced off the improvised bug shields, enough of them found small gaps to do their work.

"Hold your fire," Tangus called out. The bugs were two hundred and seventy-five yards away and marching forward… but it was slow and deliberate. Tangus had time to plan his next move – whatever that might be. But there was one thing Tangus was sure of. At the rate they used arrows to kill the first couple of rows, they'd run out long before the bugs reached them. And arrows were the one thing they needed if the Soulreavers didn't kill the queen.

"They'll roll over us like an avalanche," Sir Abernathy commented.

"Could be," Tangus replied. "But Kristen has a few magical spells that could turn the tide, though I'd prefer not to rely on those just yet."

"Other than healing, my spells are available and ready," Kristen said. "Even *Bladebarrier Sanctuary*."

Tangus shook his head. "It's too soon to use that again. It'll kill you."

"We've all signed on for that," Kristen replied. "Besides, I don't think we have too many options open to us."

"Damnit, no, Kristen!" Tangus shouted. The one thing that frightened him above everything else was any threat, real or perceived, to Kristen. "I'll send you back if necessary. Emmy can protect you. Elrond, Elanesse… they can protect you if I can't."

The vehemence in Tangus's voice surprised Kristen. She understood his passion. She felt the same for him. But she knew it wasn't his decision to make, and she thought he understood that.

"No, no, no!" Tangus continued. "I'll not lose you!"

Kristen was about to reply when she felt a familiar sensation in her mind. It came and went in an instant, but not before she received a message from her daughter, Emmy. *Father is right, mother. We cannot afford to lose you.*

Though she didn't understand, she trusted her daughter. Kristen looked at Tangus and nodded. Though she had yielded to her husband, the look she gave him promised further discussion.

"Father," Jennifer called.

Tangus waved her away with a hand. "I suspect you'll punish me over this later, Kristen, but there're some things I just can't allow… no, let me rephrase that… things I won't abide. Your safety…"

"Father!"

"What Jennifer!" Tangus snapped as he looked over to her.

"Listen! What do you hear."

Everyone, distracted by the friction between Tangus and Kristen, turned their attention back to their surroundings. Complete silence.

"The bugs have stopped marching," Mariko whispered.

Down the corridor, the magical light Kristen had conjured was extinguished and darkness returned. Tangus moved a few paces forward and stared into the darkness. Barely within earshot he heard a rustling coming from the bugs location. The ranger turned and looked back as the four saber cats began to growl. Something was coming. Something different from the bugs.

"Sweetheart," Tangus said. "Give me a better look."

Kristen knew what her husband wanted. She conjured another ball of light and sent it back down the corridor. She stopped it short of the lone figure moving in the corridor towards them.

"What the hell is that," Sir Abernathy wondered aloud.

The figure looked similar to the bug that had attacked Jennifer and killed several knights, except it was larger. Its smooth chitin shell pulsed with magical power. Its face looked wrinkled and disjointed.

"By the gods, it's wearing a human face," a knight said.

The face-skin of Harkum stared at them as the bug continued to move forward. As it passed the light globe, it reached up, enclosed it in one of its talon-tipped hands and dispelled the magic... though light from the shimmering of magic coming from its chitin encasement still burned through the darkness. It only moved a few more yards before it stopped.

"What's it waiting for," Sir Abernathy asked. "Why aren't the other bugs marching?"

Tangus looked at the bug who was looking at him. "I think I know," he said as he turned and looked at Sir Abernathy and then Kristen. "It's challenging us. Well, one of us."

"You mean like their champion against our champion?" Kristen asked.

"That's foolish," Sir Abernathy observed. "How can we trust mindless beasts?"

"Maybe the ordinary bugs are as you say," Kristen said. "But this one, like the one that attacked Jennifer, uses magic. That takes a high level of intelligence."

"And the human face it's wearing also sends a message," Tangus added. "A message that's intended to intimidate... to frighten... to make us pause. I suspect it's a trophy as well... like worg teeth or ogre ears that's sported on a necklace around a hunter's neck."

"And if one of us kills it?" Mariko asked. "The other bugs are still back there. Won't that send them into a frenzy?"

"Right now he's the biggest threat," Tangus said as he loaded his bow with a magic-tipped arrow.

"Tangus, what are you doing," Kristen asked with trepidation. But she was afraid she already knew. "You can't take that beast on by yourself."

Tangus smiled. "Before I settled on InnisRos, before I met you, I fought against odds worse than this all the time with Elrond, Max, Azriel, and Lester. And never once did we ever play nice... or fair."

Both Kristen and Mariko nodded. Mariko was smiling. Sir Abernathy looked confused, but Tangus knew he'd soon understand.

Tangus turned away and charged the bug, screaming for all he was worth as he ran down the corridor. He fired three arrows in quick succession without stopping. Three more arrows whizzed past his head, close enough to hear as they streaked towards their target. Only Mariko could safely make those shots.

His last arrows spent, Tangus dropped his bow and pulled his scimitars. He'd already covered half the distance between him and the Custodian.

The sudden attack took the Custodian by surprise. He paused as he gathered his will. He would disintegrate the screaming attacker in a blast of fire and earth. But just as the Custodian was ready to release his spell, three arrows hit him. Two bounced off his chitin armor, but the third found an opening and buried itself into his arm. The Custodian screamed in pain and surprise – his spell forgotten. In another instant, three more arrows struck. All three shattered upon impact against his chitin, but as luck would have it, a shard from one of the broken arrows lodged itself deep into one of the Custodian's eyes.

The creature bellowed in pain once again. He tried to pull the shard out of his eye, but it was buried too deeply. In frustration, he repeatedly pounded the wall of the corridor. Each impact of his fist cracked the stone. The Custodian continued to pound the wall. Soon his pain turned into anger... and with the anger came his magic. The magic reinforced each strike. Bits and pieces of wall flew out each time he hit it until it could no longer support the ceiling. Both came crashing down.

Tangus saw that they had hurt the bug. One of his arrows was sticking out of its shoulder and, from the way the bug was gouging at one of its eyes and the pounding on the wall, he assumed at least one of Mariko's arrows had found its mark. Score one for the good guys!

Tangus was close. So close he could almost taste his victory. So close he could envision his magical scimitars slip through chitin and into the bug's innards. And with the big bug dead, maybe the smaller bugs will lose their thirst for combat.

Tangus' luck suddenly took a turn for the worse. A part of the ceiling dislodged and hit him on the head. He dropped to the floor, unconscious. Then the ceiling collapsed.

Knight-General Fox looked down from behind her paste-smeared nose mask. Her knights had fought their way halfway to the bottom of the pyramid. The bugs were in retreat, but Victoria knew it was only a brief respite. They'd be back soon enough.

"How are we," Victoria asked Sir Basil.

"Not too bad considering the number of bugs that attacked," he replied. "These masks the healers put together really work. It's made a big difference."

"Agreed," Victoria said.

The knight continued. "But I got to be honest with you, the number of bugs we're facing is starting to worry me. We're outnumbered at least ten-to-one… and that's just an estimate based upon what I've seen so far. Who knows how many haven't shown themselves?"

Victoria nodded. "The percentages aren't on our side. Understood." She continued to look towards the bottom of the pyramid. "The queen's the key."

A shout came up from below. "Here they come again!"

The queen's Custodian looked at his mistress. Something was wrong. A few minutes ago, she had begun to jerk uncontrollably... and a few seconds ago, she became unresponsive. He believed she was dying. Why or how didn't matter. He knew his duty.

He ordered the bulk of the drones to attack the invaders. With the queen dying, she was no longer important. There are new queens, just hatched, who now required his attention.

Tangus slowly regained consciousness. A scream of pain escaped before he could control it. Both of his legs were buried under stone and crushed.

He reached around in the darkness and found one of his scimitars buried under a layer of dust. He brushed the dirt off and determined it was undamaged. The matching scimitar had also escaped damage. Using the faint magical glow of the blades, he looked around his prison. He lurched his head back as he spied the face of the big bug just inches away. But its lifeless eyes had already glazed over. Tangus took one of his swords and stabbed it. The head rolled a few inches, unattached from the body. The human face it wore lay over to the side, still bloody on the inside. As the ranger watched, the bug head disintegrated. The stink was overwhelming. He retched several times, unsure if it was because of the smell, the concussion he probably had, or the pain from his smashed legs.

Tangus spit vomit out of his mouth and sighed. He knew he was in a precarious position, but he had confidence Kristen would figure out a way to rescue him.

"Hell, maybe she'll even be able to save my legs," he thought just before passing out again.

Kristen dropped to her knees and screamed Tangus's name. She saw no way by which her husband could have survived the tunnel collapse. Her heart was being torn, squeezed, and ripped apart at the same time. She couldn't breathe. She couldn't think. She couldn't feel. It was worse than when Mary McKenna had died.

Jennifer, reacting to the feel and sound of the collapse and Kristen's reaction, realized her father must be underneath it. She grasped the fur of Kamuzu and buried her face into it as she silently grieved.

Sir Abernathy walked to the edge of the collapse and picked up a hand-sized stone. He shook his head and tossed it aside. *"Perhaps we can dig our way through,"* he thought. *"But to do that, we'd uncover Lord Tangus, crushed and dead? Could Lady Kristen survive that sight?"*

"But what choice do we have," Sir Abernathy said aloud as he motioned for his knights to move up and begin the task of moving stone. "The bug queen's on the other side."

Moishe, the one-eyed saber cat who now considered Kristen his mistress, stood guard. But he allowed Mariko to approach, though she did so with caution. She didn't know it yet, but the cat considered Mariko part of his new extended family. Family is not a threat.

The assassin kneeled next to Kristen who had by now completely withdrawn from reality. "Kristen, come back to us," Mariko said. "We need you."

Kristen looked at Mariko, which was encouraging. But as she stared at Mariko, her eyes went from vacant and lifeless to anger. She shook off the hand Mariko had placed on her shoulder. Kristen's rage brought a low growl from Moishe. Then the priestess retreated back into her mind once again.

Sir Abernathy approached and looked at Mariko who shook her head. "We'll do what we can to clear the collapse," he told Mariko. "But it'll take time… if we can do it at all. You've been down here before. Is there any other approach to the pyramid through the tunnels?"

"We're not leaving Tangus buried here!" Mariko barked at the knight.

Sir Abernathy held up his hands. "My Lady, please…"

"I'm sorry," Mariko interrupted. "I shouldn't have snapped at you like that. To answer your question, I don't know. We're following the same route we took when we were going the other way. There are intersections with other tunnels going everywhere, as you've seen. If there's another way around the collapse, finding it could take a long time. We might be better off returning to the surface and getting at them from the top. But I meant what I said. We'll not leave Tangus. So we might as well continue to dig."

"Time, time, time," Sir Abernathy exclaimed. "Not enough time. We've got to get to the queen and her eggs. If any young queen escapes, the entire world is in jeopardy."

"Don't forget the Soulreavers," Mariko reminded. "They may succeed."

Sir Abernathy frowned. "Let's hope they do," he said and then shook his head. "I can't believe I just said that."

"I can find him," Kristen said as she got up and began to walk towards the collapsed stone.

Surprised, Mariko and Sir Abernathy followed. Neither were sure if Kristen was completely sane, but they didn't interfere. Besides, they doubted Moishe would let them. Even Jennifer, now alert and helped by Kamuzu, followed.

The knights working to clear out the collapse stepped aside when Kristen approached. She called to the goddess Althaya to grant her power and brought forth the *Bladebarrier Sanctuary* spell. The whirling knives churned ten feet of stone until only rubble existed. She ended the spell and stepped back.

"Well," Sir Abernathy yelled at his knights. "What are you just standing there for! Get it cleared!"

The Knights of Astoria were locked in a life-and-death struggle with the bugs as they worked their way down the underground levels of the Pyramid of the Purge. At first General Fox believed the bugs would be too much for her knights. But the vaunted knight perseverance served her well. In the beginning they fought the bugs to a standstill, but slowly the tide began to change until the constant flow of bugs started to stall.

Uncharacteristically, the bugs retreated into the tunnels that exited the large bottom chamber of the pyramid. The knights followed, but not into the tunnels. It soon became apparent why the bugs scattered. The bug queen was dead. Victoria studied the lifeless body. The large bulbous egg-laying part of her corpse had disintegrated into a large puddle of mucus. The hard chitin body still remained, but it was disintegrating as well, only slower.

"Do we follow," Sir Pellinore asked. Sir Basil, Victoria's second-in-command, had succumbed to injuries during the bug's second attack.

Victoria shook her head. "No, let's take a break. It appears the main threat is over. Get me a casualty report as soon as you can."

"You understand there could be queen eggs in those tunnels," Sir Pellinore remarked. "Imagine several bug nests like this one, each with a queen laying thousands of eggs which will include even more queens."

"You're such a joy to be around. But you're right. The bugs appear to be a self-perpetuating machine." Victoria sighed. "Get me those numbers as quick as you can. Then we need to discuss our options."

Sir Pellinore saluted.

"And Montgomery, find someone to take over your command," Victoria added. "With Sir Basil gone, I'll need a new second."

The Soulreavers left the carcass of the dead bug queen as quickly as they could. The taste of the creature was disgusting... worse than anything they'd ever eaten in either the Abyss or on Aster. They found a dark and shadowy corner to regurgitate what they'd eaten and recover. For the first time in their long lives they felt sick.

Kristen had just used her *Bladebarrier Sanctuary* spell to break rock for the third time. Her skin had taken on an ashen hue and she couldn't stand without support from Moishe and Mariko. The only reason she believed she was still alive was because she limited each usage to only a couple of minutes... just enough time to carry out the pulverization of the rockfall that kept her from her beloved Tangus.

"You must end this madness," Mariko pleaded. "You'll kill yourself."

Kristen shrugged off Mariko's concern. "I don't care. I need to find him even if it means my death."

"You'd abandon Emmy?" Mariko asked. She knew it was a cruel comment to make, but she needed to say something to shake Kristen from her recklessness. "Tangus is my friend... and in many respects I love him as a brother. But the fate of the world might well rest in our hands. You must stay alive even if Tangus is not. We still have a duty."

Kristen turned to Mariko. There were tears in her eyes. "I'm so tired."

"I found him!" a knight shouted.

Emmy wept. Though she and Kristen were no longer bonded, she still retained the link that all children, regardless of age, had with their mothers… and hers was just as strong for her adoptive mother as it was for her deceased biological mother, Angela. The young goddess felt the raw emotion that emanated from Kristen over the disaster that struck Tangus. And while Emmy could still sense the life force of Tangus, she knew Kristen didn't share her ability to perceive such things.

Emmy understood the path Kristen took to save Tangus posed a grave risk. Even so, Althaya would grant her priestess the power to use *Bladebarrier Sanctuary* despite its dangers. And why shouldn't she? Besides Father Goram, Kristen the priestess had no equal in the service of Althaya. That type of love and devotion demanded the same from Althaya. Emmy had also come to understand that good-aligned gods and goddesses will refuse to hinder free will. But the future of the empath race hung in the balance, and Emmy wasn't about to stand by while that future self-destructed. She'd do anything to keep Kristen alive, even if it were in opposition to Althaya.

Unknown to anyone, the child that grew inside Kristen, fathered by Tangus, represented the empath future. The unborn child will not only be the First Empath, but the first in a whole new generation of empaths. But unlike before, they'll have a goddess to represent them and keep them safe. Even at this early stage in the child's development, Emmy was instructing her in the ways of the empath. Her name was Adonnenniel, which meant rebirth in the ancient elven language, and she was proving to be an exceptional student. In this time of crisis, it was Adonnenniel who had sustained the life-force of

Kristen and prevented the spell she used to find Tangus from killing her. Emmy had found a way around her mother's free will and her stubbornness born from the desperation of the moment. The mother of the empaths, and the First Empath, were safe... for the moment.

Tangus could no longer feel the pain in his legs. He didn't welcome the reprieve, for it told him they were dying. Tangus sighed. He was helpless. Through the magical glow of his swords he could inspect his prison. What he found did nothing to reassure him. The rocks above his head didn't look very stable, which meant he shouldn't try to free himself unless he wanted to risk another collapse. To make matters worse, the stench of the mucus remains of the bug head was making him sick to his stomach and he had a blinding headache.

"Azriel taught me not to panic in tight spaces," he thought as he calmed himself. Who else but a dwarf knew about tight, underground spaces? *"I just wish I didn't have to smell that damn bug."*

Movement caught his attention. A foot-long blind cave centipede was making its way through a small opening in the rocks on the other side of his prison. It walked through the mucus remains of the bug head and towards Tangus. The multi-legged critter made an abrupt turn, meandered to the side, climbed up the wall, and disappeared through the rocks holding him hostage. A few minutes later Tangus heard a muffled shriek of surprise.

"This is it, I'm sure of it," Sir Pellinore said.

"It's collapsed, Montgomery," General Fox observed.

Sir Pellinore brought his torch closer to the wall of rock and then the floor. "Only recently. There are bug signs all around, including some caught in the collapse. Look." Sir Pellinore's torchlight had found drying mucus at the base of the collapse.

"You think Sir Abernathy's on the other side?"

Sir Pellinore nodded. "We know he's down here, so… yeah, I'm fairly sure. In fact, he's probably the one responsible for this."

"General!" a knight called as he ran through the corridor towards them.

Victoria and Sir Pellinore both turned. "Report," Sir Pellinore commanded.

"Dame Jane-Isidore requests your attendance," the knight said after a hasty salute.

"Found more hatcheries?" Victoria asked.

"We're not sure. Unlike the others, this one was unattended."

Sir Pellinore frowned. "No eggs?"

The knight shook his head. "Empty shells," he said.

That wasn't unusual. The bugs literally hatched and reinforced their brethren almost as soon as their eggs were placed in the nursery. The knights, in their efforts to clear out the hatcheries and kill the bugs, had seen it take place.

"And no bugs, madam," the messenger continued.

That drew Victoria's and Sir Pellinore's attention.

General Fox looked closer at the knight. "No bugs, you say. Was there anything else different about this particular hatchery?"

The knight nodded. There was a look of defeat in his eyes. "There's a large air shaft leading to the surface over the hatchery. Dame Jane-Isidore fears these are queens that have hatched and escaped."

Victoria closed her eyes and shook her head in dejection. "Very well. Is there more to report?"

"We think all the bugs are dead. Haven't seen one in a while now."

"The queen dying no doubt had much to do with that," Sir Pellinore commented. "It let the air out of their balloons, so to speak. They probably just couldn't coordinate a defense without her."

The knight nodded. "Yes sir. Dame Jane-Isidore made that same observation."

"At least there's that," Victoria said. "Kill the queen and the bugs are much easier to defeat. All right. Let's go to the hatchery and see if we can figure out how many queens escaped. Montgomery leave a few knights behind to clear away this rubble. Let's see if Sir Abernathy is on the other side as you suggest. And you," Victoria said as she pointed to the messenger. "What's your name?"

"Aidan Hughes, madam," the knight answered.

Victoria nodded. "Get topside. I want to know if anyone spotted the queens flying away, how many, and which direction they were heading."

They reached Tangus. Apart from his legs he was in remarkably good shape considering the circumstances. Tangus had an extraordinary ability to block pain. But when Kristen examined his legs, she didn't know how even he could withstand such agony without passing out or going insane.

Both legs were crushed, mangled, and broken beyond recognition. The bones had been pulverized and the tissue, muscle, blood vessels and ligaments flattened. The weight of the stone had cut off blood circulation… which was the only reason he didn't bleed to death. And though the lack of blood flow saved his life, it also caused the flesh to die.

"What's the verdict?" Tangus asked. Kristen had wanted to put her husband to sleep so she could work but decided she would need his participation if she was to come up with options other than straight removal. They were his legs after all. Instead, she anesthetized him from the waist down with magic.

Kristen took his hand. "It's not good, my love."

"I didn't think so," Tangus replied. "But I'm not surprised. I've been in this business far too long not to recognize things for what they are. And I've seen injuries far less than this kill."

Kristen shook her head. "You'll not die. I've destroyed the infection that was beginning to take hold. There's no more bleeding, and your heart is strong. But I won't lie, you'll never be the same."

"My legs have to come off?"

"That's a high probability," Kristen answered. "But I believe I can save them."

There was a momentary flicker of hope in Tangus's eyes. Kristen felt miserable that she needed to crush it. "But even if I can, you'll be a cripple. They may become strong enough to allow you to walk without a cane, but I don't think you'll ever run… or mount Smoke without help. For the rest of your life your legs will ache when the weather's changing, or you've been on them too long. And the bones will never be strong. There's just too much damage. Just a wrong step, or a slight twist, could break them. Each time that happens they'll become even weaker."

Tangus exhaled. "I've seen people with legs ruined or removed. And in most cases, they look like they've learned to adjust." Tangus reached up with a hand and caressed Kristen's cheek. "Do what you can to save them."

Kristen smiled, bent over, and kissed her beloved. But when she raised back up she was all business. "Sir Abernathy!"

"Madam!"

"I can't wait any longer to work on my husband. Here's what I need you to do." She then barked several orders which the knights obeyed without question.

"You can't cut on him here in all this filth," Jennifer said, anxious.

"She knows what she's doing, sweetheart," Tangus said.

Several knights surrounded Tangus, picked him up, and moved him to the place Kristen had prepared.

"I have to cut open his legs, Jennifer," Kristen said. "There's too much damage to the bones. They're crushed. I need to sculpt them first and then fuse them together. To do that, I must touch them. But before I can begin that, I need to reestablish blood flow before any more tissue dies. That requires intricate healing magic which means I must visually inspect the damage and determine how best to heal it. If not for Emmy showing me this different way to heal, I don't think I could save his legs no matter how hard I tried. Still, they'll always be fragile. But I can at least minimize that."

Jennifer nodded. Mariko sat next to her and held her hand.

"How much time will you need, my lady," Sir Abernathy asked.

"Hours," the priestess replied. "Oh, and Mariko. I need your sharpest dagger."

Mariko snorted has she handed over one. "They're all sharp."

"It's hard to say," Sir Pellinore said as he, General Fox, and several knights looked around one of several hatchery rooms they'd discovered. "But the shell colorings are different."

"Dame Jane-Isidore?" Victoria asked.

"Sir Pellinore's correct. Over in that corner are cobalt-colored shells. Notice they're sitting on a kind of soft, heated material? Bug secretion, I guess. But it's still warm. And next to those are greenish-tinged shells. None are like any of the other shells we've seen in the other hatcheries. Different in not only color, but also size. They're much bigger, particularly the cobalt."

Victoria sighed. She inspected the shells and then looked up the air shaft. She felt the cool, fresh air hit her face and saw the sky far above. It was large enough. She looked at her subordinates.

"It looks like maybe three of the cobalt and... two dozen of the green?" Victoria concluded.

"That sounds about right," Dame Jane-Isidore said.

"Three queens and, what, two dozen males?" Sir Pellinore asked.

Victoria nodded. "Yes. It also means three nests just like this one."

Kristen was in her element – healing. She was exhausted. She needed food and drink. She could use much more sleep. But all that was lost to her as she labored on Tangus's legs. Though as grueling as it was, she felt like whistling a happy little jingle. Tangus was responding much better than she could have hoped. He would still have many challenges ahead, but she now believed his future – their future – was much brighter than she had originally imagined.

"What a crew we'll make," she thought as she snapped together several more veins and arteries. *"Two rangers, one who's crippled and one who's blind. A goddess to be. An assassin who has found religion. A three-legged saber kitten and two full-grown saber cats, one missing an eye. A strange crew indeed! But I love them with all my heart and soul."*

Somewhere in the unoccupied reaches of her mind she heard stones being moved and voices of recognition and welcoming. She realized the knights had broken through and found their brethren on the other side. But the tone of their meeting was oddly somber instead of joyful. Kristen lost interest as she worked on an extraordinarily small and stubborn muscle connection.

✦

EPILOGUE

"For every story end there is a new story beginning."

-Author Unknown

Lessien, looked out over the landscape. It was dark, dirty, and hot – but livable, if only barely. Since their release into the wilds of the Abyss, her main concern had been finding the means to survive. She discovered the sanctuary of a small cave to shelter them from the massive and powerful electrical storms that frequented the area. There was food and water. Neither was tasteful but would keep them alive until help arrived – which Lessien believed in with all her heart – or she could find her own way out. She also discovered that allies were available, but only if one had the gold to bribe them.

The malevolence of the Abyss filled every pore of her body. Demons, monsters, and fiends were there in great numbers. This wasn't unexpected since the Abyss is their domain. That they didn't care about two 'puny' female mortals in their midst came as a surprise, however. Lessien was also shocked to learn that, like the people on her home world, the denizens of the Abyss had their own lives, and the lives of their families, to concern themselves with. While there was a strong contingent of demons who wanted nothing more than the freedom to invade the world of mortals, there were just as many demons who only wanted to live their lives in relative peace. To Lessien's amazement, the inhabitants of the Abyss had built a civilization not so unlike her own on Aster, with cities and towns, a few agricultural areas, and a vast number of grasslands where the realm's primary food source, a huge, strange looking twelve-legged cow-like creature with the claws and stinger of a scorpion – and the disposition to match – was raised, herded, and bartered as any other commodity.

Lessien looked back into the cave at Autumn and shook her head. Her friend had been so brutalized. Being raped by a demon was bad enough. But being impregnated as a result made the situation much worse. Now the only thing Autumn did was stare into space, her eyes unfocused. Lessien feared her friend's mind was permanently damaged, if not destroyed. But that might be a kindness, particularly after the demon child that grew inside her at such an astonishing rate is born. The gods only knew what might result from that dark union. Lessien considered killing the progeny in utero but decided to wait until after the pregnancy before making the final decision. Maybe a child is what Autumn needs to come out of her funk.

"Lesssshion," a gravelly voice called from the entrance of the cave.

Lessien turned to find Verax standing at the cave entrance. Verax was a very minor demon, not so unlike an incompetent thief on her home world, whose loyalty was bought with a gold charm from one of her bracelets. Gold in the Abyss was even more valuable than on her home plane. Verax resembled a snake. He had a longish, slimy body with arms and legs and a flickering, forked tongue. Lessien didn't trust him, but thought he'd do her bidding for the promise of more riches.

"I have food," Verax said.

Lessien nodded and bid him to enter. "Did you get the information I need?"

Verfax shook his head. "Jusssst mention of the *B'nai Elohim* issssh a death sssssentence."

Lessien opened the bag of food and fed Autumn. She had learned to function well with only one hand. "You know our agreement," she said to the demon. "No more gold until I have that intelligence."

"Yessssh, I have not forgotten," Verfax replied. "I cannot bring to you what you need. But I have brought sssssomeone who can."

Lessien stopped and stared at Verfax. "You brought someone here?!" she said as she stood and pulled *Ah-HritVakha* from its scabbard. It's magic, though muted in the Abyss, was still strong enough to kill most demons.

Verfax looked at the ground. The demon looked pathetic and Lessien felt sorry for him. "Sssshe will help."

"Don't be too hard on him," a female voice said from outside the cave entrance. "May I enter?"

"Do I have a choice?" Lessien inquired.

"Not really." The demon who strode towards Lessien was grace and beauty personified. "I've been looking for you. My name is Belladonna."

"And here I thought no one cared," Lessien replied.

The demon smiled. "My father told me not to take you lightly. He said you were a queen on your world, and that you'd be a challenge... providing you survived." Belladonna looked around the cave. "I guess you are. Surviving... that is."

"If you can call this surviving," Lessien retorted.

Belladonna looked back at the mortal queen. "I have to say, if your sharp tongue is a sign of your intelligence, he may be right."

"I'm so glad you approve," Lessien remarked. "Tell me, do I know your father?"

"No, I don't believe so. He's dead now. He was weak. But he knew of you and your mindless friend over there. He put you both here before he was killed by your priest... I believe he calls himself Father Goram... and the demon Nightshade."

"So they killed a major demon," Lessien said to herself. Though the information surprised her, she had learned long ago to hide her feelings and reactions when talking with the enemy... and she knew this exquisite looking demon was just that. "Good for them."

The demon ignored Lessien's hostility. "I've decided to help you leave the Abyss."

"In return for what, Belladonna," Lessien asked. No demon will do something for nothing.

"Perceptive," Belladonna replied. "Nightshade's my sister… though a bit more ambitious. She destroyed everything in her way… including members of her own family… as she sought father's sanction. She wanted a part in father's plan to impress the demon lords… a plan that failed, by the way. But now I hear she's cavorting with the goddess Althaya and has given up her access to the dark powers. I'm curious why she'd surrender her immortality to escape the Abyss. It's not as if she had a hard life here. Was it love? Or did she develop scruples? Can't be a demon with scruples, father used to say. But now that father is gone…" Belladonna paused and shrugged her shoulders. "Anyway, something drove her to that decision. I want to know what it was. But I can't do that from here."

Lessien raised an eyebrow. "As you said, I doubt your life here is hard. Why leave?"

Belladonna considered. "All demons would leave the Abyss if they had but the means. Part of its 'charm' is the never-ending gloom… the endless darkness that weights so heavily on the demon spirit. Even the food is…" Belladonna shook her head. "I want to experience color. I want to experience sunshine… rainfall… different foods… different creatures. I want variety!"

"Your sister didn't have much trouble going from here to there," Lessien observed. "Neither did your father."

Anger flashed across Belladonna's visage. She repressed it quickly. "They found a loophole. A stupid loophole the *B'nai Elohim* have since closed. And they didn't tell me about it! Why wouldn't they tell me about it? I'm as strong as Nightshade… just as powerful. I thought I had a good relationship with father. And…" Belladonna stopped talking. She realized she may have just exposed a weakness – her vanity – and the mortal queen was clever enough to recognized it.

"You were saying?" Lessien prompted with a smirk on her face.

"I was saying you're going to help me like I'm going to help you."

"And how's that?"

"You're going to get me past the *B'nai Elohim*," Belladonna replied.

"I'll allow you to pass, but I can't go with you," Michael said. Nightshade had talked him into making time to discuss their plan to rescue Lessien and Autumn from the Abyss. The leader of the *B'nai Elohim* was cloistered with Father Goram, Nightshade, Landross, Nefertari, and Colonel Tirion behind closed doors at the palace in Taranthi. The Qénsharma had been rounded up without incident, supplies procured, and both Father Goram and Nightshade carried as many magical items as possible to supplement their already significant magical spell-casting abilities. Landross, on the other hand, would rely only upon his magical weapons and armor.

Father Goram shook his head. "No, that's not acceptable. My wife… my wife is hurt, and time is of the essence. The Abyss is a big place."

"Indeed," Michael answered. "But the Abyss isn't like your mortal plane with its worlds and stars dotting the night sky. It's six-hundred-and-sixty-six individual places, like your countries or city-states. There's no sky, no stars, no escape except to this plane. It never ends, never relents, never gives up its secrets. Its denizens accept it as home, yet many would leave if they could. There's good and bad, but in the Abyss, good and bad isn't defined the same as here. It's much more… malleable."

Father Goram looked at Nightshade who was sitting next to him.

"Michael's right. Here the difference between good and evil is a constant. It is what it is, and everyone understands where the line is drawn. In the Abyss we take a more practical view." Nightshade looked at Landross. "The largest component of our… their… morality, if you wish, is the circumstance."

Nightshade held up a hand just as Landross was about to protest. "No objection will change that, Landross. So hold your righteous indignation and accept it."

"Nightshade is correct," Michael said. "And if your Queen Lessien comes to understand that, she just might survive long enough to be rescued."

"And Autumn?" Father Goram asked.

Nightshade gripped the priest's arm.

"Will the queen be able to survive taking…". Father Goram took a deep breath to compose himself. "Will Lessien be able to survive while taking care of my wife?"

"No," Michael said. He was being blunt because he had to be, regardless of the pain it will cause. "Your wife is a weakness. The weak, unless they're fortunate enough to have a strong benefactor, rarely survive. In the Abyss, the queen isn't strong enough to give cover for your wife. Not if she wants to live."

"That's why we need your help," Landross interjected.

Michael shook his head. "The business of keeping demons corralled isn't an easy one," he explained. "I'll help when I can but making sure demons don't escape overrides all other considerations. I'll get you into the part of the Abyss they're in, but for now that's the limit of the help I can offer."

"Some help," Landross grumbled. "Nightshade can do that much!"

"No, I can't. Not any longer," Nightshade replied. "I thought you knew that."

"Peace, Landross," Nefertari said, speaking for the first time. "Is there anything I can do to help? More warriors, perhaps?"

"A large group will only attract unwanted attention," Father Goram said, rejecting the suggestion. "I think we're as ready as we'll ever be."

Michael nodded. "Very well. Follow me."

Nefertari watched from a balcony overlooking the palace courtyard as Michael opened a crack in the earth and led Father Goram, Nightshade and Landross into the Abyss. The steam and smoke that emanated from the crack made it impossible to see details, but she could hear the screams of demons. It made her shiver. The dire wolves Ajax, Razor and Finley had forced themselves onto the same balcony, squeezing Colonel Tirion back into the room. All three wanted to go, but Father Goram would have nothing of it.

A crying baby drew her attention. Colonel Tirion had already taken the child from the wet-nurse and was quieting her when Nefertari walked back into the room from the balcony.

"Miracle's been cranky today," the wet-nurse commented.

"Daeron?" Nefertari asked.

Colonel Tirion shook his head. "She's fine. Just misses you."

The Marine colonel argued early on that Miracle needed a stable family with brothers and sisters and a dog or a cat. But Nefertari had quickly dismissed adopting her out. "She has your Marines. And why would she want a dog or cat when she has a flying boulder," the priestess said with finality.

"I heard that," Maedhros Nénmacil said in her mind at the time. But he was delighted by Nefertari's proclamation and made it his destiny to act the doting uncle.

Nefertari took Miracle and sat in a nearby padded chair. The child had grown since they rescued her from the ruins of Ashakadi, but she was still underweight compared to other children of the same age.

"You'll be crawling soon," Nefertari remarked as she rocked the baby.

"She's already started," Colonel Tirion said as he placed another chair next to Nefertari and sat. When Nefertari looked at him, he shrugged. "You missed it."

"There's been a lot going on the last few days," Nefertari said.

"Tell me about it."

The priestess sighed. "Still, I wish I could have seen it."

The room was quiet. The wet-nurse had retired to the other end of the room, waiting, and the three dire wolves were laying on the balcony sunning themselves.

Colonel Tirion gave Nefertari a few moments peace before he broke the silence. "Father Goram told me to give you this," he said as he pulled a scroll from his belt.

"You've read it I presume," Nefertari said. It wasn't a question.

Colonel Tirion nodded.

"And?"

"He was in contact last night with his daughter on the mainland."

Nefertari nodded. "From Elanesse. I'm aware of the situation with the Draugen Pesta invasion. I thought that was resolved."

Colonel Tirion continued. "It was. But the 'shifts', as Eric the Black calls them, caused by the *Ak-Séregon Stone* has had many serious consequences for our world."

"Yes," Nefertari acknowledged. "Sehanine StarEagle keeps me informed. And I've read the same reports you have."

"Well, his daughter…"

"Her name is Kristen."

Colonel Tirion nodded. "Yes, Kristen. Well she and her husband, along with some Astorian Knights, just battled another shift consequence. Kristen calls them bugs. There's a full description of them in Father Goram's letter. These creatures, or bugs, reproduce like ants or termites with a queen capable of laying thousands of eggs. There was a nest underneath Elanesse which has been destroyed."

"That's good news," Nefertari said. Miracle had fallen asleep which forced them to whisper. "But from the look on your face there's more."

Colonel Tirion unrolled the scroll and held it in front of Nefertari so she could read without disturbing Miracle. "Read towards the end."

When Nefertari had finished, she looked at Colonel Tirion. "You know what this means, Daeron?"

The Marine nodded. "At least three nests to find and destroy."

Nefertari motioned for the wet-nurse to take Miracle. "And if we don't and they hatch more queen eggs, they could dominate the world in short order. I want every pair of eyes on the skies looking to the east. I want what messenger dragons we have left in the air, twenty-four seven, scouting. Let's get the navy out to sea."

"All we have left are frigates," Colonel Tirion mentioned. "None of them are big enough to handle the deep ocean."

"Doesn't matter," Nefertari said. "Get them out at least to the Magnificent Resolve. And I want to convene the full council within the hour."

As Colonel Tirion left the room, followed by the wet-nurse holding a still sleeping Miracle, Nefertari went to the balcony. The dire wolves, alerted by her unease, moved out of the way. Within seconds Maedhros Nénmacil was hovering in the air next to the balcony and conversing with his mistress. There was none of the usual banter, for each understood the nature of this new danger.

"What's going on, father," Daphnia asked her father, Lord Ternborg. "I've never seen this many people in the city." Even atop the huge stallion her father had provided, the child could still pet the head of her wolf, Adimar, for reassurance. They had just entered the Draugen Pesta capital city of St. Petersburg. Apart from the First Phalanx, the king's personal bodyguard, the bulk of the army had already dispersed for a few hours of personal time.

Lord Ternborg wasn't sure if he should tell his daughter that the people she saw were refugees from the east… or that the Hyrokkin had attacked by tunneling under the Eastern Boreskyre Mountains and surprising the defenses meant to stop such an invasion. Lord Ternborg didn't know if he should tell his daughter they weren't strong enough to stop the Hyrokkin because he had led half his army to the west to get her back. And because he had done this, the

Hyrokkin, always one to use any advantage, invaded and were able to established a front along the entire eastern border. The city of Saint Martin in the south had fallen and Saint Dominic to the north had been surrounded and was resisting a siege.

In the end he didn't have to say any of those things to his daughter. They had reached the main gates of the palace and standing just outside of it with a few personal retainers was Sofia. The child slipped down from her horse and ran to the waiting embrace of her mother. Lord Ternborg dismounted as well and approached the two most important people in his life. He noticed that his queen wore the Doom Warrior locket around her neck. The king wrapped his arms around the two and savored the moment, however brief.

It was Daphnia who broke the triangle. "Mother, meet Adimar," she said as she raced to the waiting wolf, reached up and grabbed a tuff of fur on the back of his neck and led him back. Sofia's attendants backed up a step, wary of the wolf's size. Even among giants he was a giant.

Sofia wasn't concerned. She didn't hesitate to pet the wolf. Lord Ternborg, having already come to realize how important the wolf was to Daphnia, and vice versa, stroked the wolf's side. As for Adimar, he sniffed Sofia to get her scent, then sat as he accepted the attention. He'd grown since he met Daphnia, and there was little doubt he will grow to be as big as his father, Fenrisúlfr.

Lord Ternborg drew his wife aside. "You wear the locket openly?" he said.

Sofia bowed her head. "I deceived you when I took it, and for that I offer apologies, my husband." Draugen Pesta's queen looked up into her husband's eyes. "But now I understand its power... enough to realize it shouldn't be left unguarded. So rather than risk its theft, I've decided it best to always keep it in my sight. Besides, other than you, there's only one other who might recognize it, and he's no longer a concern."

Lord Ternborg snorted, "Drugov's always a concern. Unless..." He looked at his wife.

"Three daggers in the neck and chest and stuffed into a latrine," Sofia said. "The carrion eaters have him now." She grabbed the sword-callused hands of her husband. "He was about to call the guards and have me executed. That wasn't going to happen. I don't regret any of it."

Lord Ternborg laughed. "Your prowess with your daggers is legendary. If the fool thought you'd go willingly, he deserved what he got."

"He deserved it for more than just that," Sofia said. "He was never our friend. And as it turned out, later information came to my attention that he was also the one who contacted the Hyrokkin after you left. I knew we had a spy, but I never would have believed it to be him. Right now everyone thinks he's on the run. Do you forgive me for taking the locket, my lord?"

The king kissed his wife on the forehead. "Of course I forgive you. As for the other thing, it sounds like self-defense to me… if it should ever come up, which I doubt. Besides, who can blame you for feeding a spy to the rats. Let's get Daphnia settled back into her room. Then we have a great deal of planning to do."

Sofia nodded. "I've already alerted the war council and have them waiting in the Abramovich Conference Room. Do you want me to be there?"

"Of course! You're my best general!"

The *Freedom Wind* sailed into Grabber Bay after an uneventful trip from InnisRos. The newly formed volcano, Elysium on the Bay, stood in the center. Shipping was forced to go around, but the bay was large enough to accommodate both.

"Beautiful, isn't it," Mr. Krist said. He and Captain Dubois were standing on the quarterdeck and overseeing the operations of the ship as it sailed into the bay.

Captain Dubois nodded. "One of the few positive things that came out of the dark elf invasion," she replied. "Unless it blows."

"There is that." Mr. Krist turned the course of the conversation. "Who do you think is running things now?" They had received a crystal communique during the return journey concerning Lane Dular, the patriarch of the most powerful family on the mainland and their employer. He never fully recovered from the death of his beloved daughter and had committed suicide.

Captain Dubois shook her head. "Hard to say. His wife and daughter are both dead. I suppose there could be some other relative out there who might inherit his wealth, but I don't think Mr. Dular would leave the operations of the company to someone unfamiliar with the business."

Both caught their breath's as they rounded the volcano. In the harbor was the largest ship they'd ever seen… a huge four-masted giant.

"The *Adelaide Gail!*" Captain Dubois whispered. The last time – the only time – she'd been in Lane Dular's office she'd seen a model. She hadn't realized the newest ship in the Dular line had been so close to completion, or such a behemoth. Since the *Freedom Wind* carried no cargo, there were no dock workers to greet them. But the dock wasn't completely empty. A group of officers, including one who wore captain epaulettes on his shoulder, waited as the *Wind's* crew lowered the gangplank.

"I'm your relief, madam," the captain on the dock shouted. "Permission to come aboard!"

"Permission granted," Captain Dubois called. She looked at Mr. Krist. "Looks like I've been replaced. Thomas, please go below and break out a bottle of brandy. We'll be down presently." As her first officer walked away, Captain Dubois added. "And have the bosun's mate oversee the packing of our belongings."

Mr. Krist stopped.

"You do want to come with me, Thomas," Captain Dubois asked. "Correct?"

Mr. Krist turned, looked at his captain, and nodded. "I'll never leave you, Jasmine."

Kyleigh knocked on the door of the Alfheim's newest citizen, the sorcerer Eric the Black. She'd given him quarters in the palace wing that was reserved for important people such as ambassadors and visiting royalty. But she was considering moving him into her own wing of the palace, so he'd be even closer. Their relationship had grown close as they hunted for a way to bring Yury and Eirwen home.

"He's not there," First Councilor Robert Gareathe said as he approached from behind the queen. With him were four of her own guards.

Kyleigh turned. "Following me?"

"More or less," Robert answered. "There's an issue I need to discuss, and guards told me you were heading in this direction. I took a chance."

"And Eric?"

"I saw him earlier in the cafeteria," Robert replied, "distracted as he always is. I managed to get him to tell me he'd be in the Spiral Tower. Something about a new theory that came to him during the night that he wanted to test."

"Thanks," Kyleigh said as she spun around and walked away.

"Kyleigh," Robert called. "Remember. I was looking for you?"

Kyleigh stopped. Robert was handling much of the administration duties of the kingdom, and she felt guilty. But short of war, her priority was getting Yury and Eirwen back if they still lived. They'd given too much to the survival of two worlds to be abandoned.

"I'm sorry," Kyleigh said. "I don't mean to be so preoccupied…"

Robert held up a hand to stop her. "I share your enthusiasm. Yury Petrenko and Eirwen are heroes and I understand not only your dedication to their recovery but also its importance. It's who we are, is it not?"

"Nevertheless, I should make more time to rule," Kyleigh replied. "What do you need?"

Robert sighed. "It's not very pleasant, I'm afraid."

"*Justice…*" Kyleigh heard a whisper in her mind. She looked at her magical and intelligent sword, *Ah-RahnVakha*, the Sword of Rulers, which hung at her side in its scabbard.

"*Justice…*"

Kyleigh grabbed the hilt of the sword. "*JUSTICE!*" it screamed.

"Explain," she ordered.

"Traitors, Kyleigh," Robert replied. "Five who took part in the assassination of King Quarion."

"What!" Kyleigh exclaimed. "But I thought it was only the two brothers who poisoned Argonne!"

Robert shook his head. "They had help. Lots of help as it turns out."

"Why didn't you say something earlier," Kyleigh asked.

"I probably should have, but it seemed like you had plenty of other things on your mind."

Kyleigh frowned. "That's a decision only I should make," she scolded. "Is this the end of it?"

"We don't know," Robert responded. "But we don't think so. In fact, it looks as if the treachery is far more reaching than just Argonne's murder. We believe they're coming after you as well."

"Me?"

Robert nodded. "Since the beginning of your reign, other factions, factions not involved in the original treachery, have sprung up. They don't consider you legitimate. They believe that Argonne was wrong to execute his brothers since they were his only true blood heirs. I learned of this after you left. First it was only rumors. But since the capture and interrogation of the traitors, I believe the rumors are true."

"I wonder if they know about Nefertari," Kyleigh thought. Out loud she said, "What can we do to dissuade these secret factions? Will the executions of those already convicted do it?"

The first councilor crossed his arms and leaned against a wall. "No, I don't think so. They're five hard-core fanatics who believe they're dying for a righteous cause. I'm sure the others in their movement are just as determined. If it weren't so necessary, I'd advise locking them in a hole and throwing away the key. That might be a better deterrent. But they must die. And it must be by your hand. People need to be reminded that you wield *Ah-RahnVakha*, the sword of kings and queens. They must see that the sword accepts you… that it does your bidding. As for those who refuse to accept your legitimacy… we can't take them lightly. They must be hunted down and destroyed. No quarter given."

"Justice…"

Kyleigh exhaled. "This isn't a job for the army," she said as a point of fact. "Do you have any recommendations?"

Robert nodded.

"Justice…"

"There you are," Eric the Black called from down the hall. "I've been looking for you."

Kyleigh, her mind considering the problem at hand, didn't hear Eric at first.

"What's wrong," Eric asked as he drew closer.

The queen looked at the sorcerer and apologized. "Sorry, just a little court intrigue. You have an update?"

"Yury and Eirwen," Eric said. "They're still alive. I don't know where they are yet, but I can confirm they live."

Kyleigh smiled. "That's great news!" she exclaimed. "Show me!"

Eric took her hand and led her down the hallway followed by her guards. Kyleigh looked back at Robert. "Get the execution chamber ready. I'll be there later. And we'll talk about that other thing afterwards."

Robert nodded and walked away in the opposite direction.

"*Justice…*"

"Quit ye sulking, ye great mangy beast!" a voice called from the darkness.

Jörmungander stood up and looked around. He was sitting in a dark cavern, a place he'd found to get away from everything. Everything, that is, except his thoughts. Erika, Solveig, and Max had done everything they could think of to bring him out of the depression brought on by the loss of his close friends, Azriel, and Elbedreth. But their efforts had little effect. Nor were the children of the bat-people, the same ones who so delighted Erika, able to draw him away from his black deliberations. Even the huge living mountain, *Johari*, had tried to no avail.

"I'm hallucinating," Jörmungander said out loud. "Going crazy."

"Ay, I'd say ye be daft."

The young black dragon conjured a magical ball of light to drive out the dark. Next to the entrance stood two sylphs. "Azriel? Elbedreth?"

"Who else, laddie," Azriel said with a smile.

Jörmungander turned into his human form as he rushed the two sylphs. He did his best to wrap his arms around both.

"It's good to see you to," Elbedreth said as she laughed and returned the hug with her glossy sylph arms.

Emmy waited to greet her family as they walked under the protective canopy provided by Elrond and Elanesse. Sir Abernathy and his knights had stayed behind in the city to plan strategy with Knight-General Fox. But the people she'd said goodbye to weren't the same that approached her now. They'd been changed, both physically and emotionally. But she was prepared for that. No one escapes what they'd been through without being altered by it. The physical, mental, and emotional price they paid would either break them or make them stronger, and Emmy wasn't sure where each of her family members stood in that regard.

As Romulus, Sakkara and Kevik greeted Kristen and the one-eyed saber cat Moishe, and as Loki ran around Tangus to show how well he now ran on three legs, Emmy walked to Jennifer, Mariko, and the saber cat, Kamuzu. After introducing herself to the big cat and greeting Mariko, the young goddess cupped Jennifer's face in her hands.

"It's been a long journey, hasn't it, sister," Emmy said.

Jennifer nodded. "Truly. But don't pity me. I'll be all right. My other senses are becoming more acute. And I have Kamuzu here to be my guide."

Emmy reached up on her tiptoes and kissed her sister's forehead. "Of course, you'll be all right… though I wish I could heal you. Your eyes are gone forever."

"I'm not sure I'd want you to even if you could," Jennifer said. "My 'sight' is richer… more vibrant… than when I had eyes. Go see father. He needs your help much more than I."

Emmy hugged Jennifer, Mariko, and petted Kamuzu before turning towards her mother and father. Kristen looked over at her and smiled, but for the moment Romulus and his family had her and Moishe engaged. Tangus had taken a seat on the ground with his back against *Elendrel-Telperiën*, the massive tree that was Elrond. Both of his legs were splinted and bandaged, but Tangus wasn't in pain. Emmy knew her mother would have seen to that. Loki was asleep in his lap, content to be back with his master.

"Father," the child goddess said as she put her arms around Tangus's neck.

Tangus wrapped arms around Emmy and drew her into his embrace with surprising strength. "It's good to see you, little one. There's much to discuss."

Emmy nodded. "I already know much of what's happened and the dangers we still face."

"Aye, the bugs," Tangus replied as he nodded. "A few queens got away."

"Yes," Emmy agreed. "We have to find their nests and destroy them. But it's not only that. This new rise of the Empath we're ushering in will not go unchallenged."

"Another Purge?"

Emmy shook her head. "That evil is gone forever," she replied. There was fire in her eyes and venom in her voice. "And I'm here to make sure it stays that way. So, no, that isn't it."

"Then what threatens the Empath?" Tangus asked. "They're a force for good. I get that people are ofttimes not the most rational of beings, and I understand that fears and superstitions can be a strong motivator and likely drove the Purge's creation. But that's all they were… fantasies."

"And we ended it," Kristen said as she approached with Romulus and Moishe on either side of her. They both seemed to be fine with each other's presence. "Just like we'll end any other threat to the Empath."

Emmy stood and embraced her mother. "It's so good to see you safe," she said. There were tears in her eyes.

Kristen kissed the top of Emmy's head, but said nothing as she basked in the warmth of the child goddess… her daughter by all other accounts.

Emmy withdrew and looked up. Her tears had dried. "You're different," she commented. "I can feel it in your soul." Emmy studied her mother. "You know!" she announced.

Kristen smiled. "That I'm with child? Of course, I know. What woman wouldn't?"

Emmy hugged her mother again, placing her ear against Kristen's belly.

Tangus, with the help of his canes and Romulus, stood on his crippled legs and stumbled the few feet to his family. He then dropped his canes and enclosed his family in a bear hug as he laughed in joy.

Jennifer, being led by Kamuzu, joined in the embrace.

Emmy let her happiness flow outward and into her mother, father, and sisters. "Her name is Adonnenniel, and she is the first of a new line of empaths," the young goddess said.

Kristen withdrew and placed her two hands on her belly. Tangus and Jennifer did the same. "Welcome, Adonnenniel," Tangus said. "Welcome into the DeRango family."

Emmy placed her hands over those of her family to cement the Empath lineage. She looked at Tangus, Kristen, and Jennifer. "DeRango blood flows through the empath race. From this point on your family and the empaths will be forever linked. Your strength, courage, and wisdom will be hers. Her compassion, devotion, and love will be yours. As she champions all that is good, so too will you. Her threats are your threats… her survival is your survival."

"That sounds rather ominous," Mariko said as she walked up to them eating a piece of fruit.

Emmy shrugged. "It's the way of things now. You're also part of this."

"I'm not a DeRango," Mariko replied.

"But you ARE my priestess," Emmy countered.

"And your enforcer," Mariko reminded.

Emmy frowned. "I'm more than capable of defending myself."

"Some things you shouldn't have to concern yourself with," Mariko shot back.

Emmy smiled. "You mean like getting my hands dirty? Deal with the rift-raft? I can be quite cross at times."

Mariko didn't respond. Instead, she crossed her arms and stared at Emmy who finally sighed. "Yes, you can also be my enforcer."

Mariko smiled. "By the way, when were you going to mention the two strangers on the other end of our little refuge here? Elanesse's overly concerned about one who appears to be dying."

"What!" Kristen exclaimed. "Show me!"

"There's nothing either of us can do for him," Emmy said. The tone of her voice stopped Kristen from bolting away. "He knows that. His death has been approaching for a long time. I brought him here for a different purpose."

Kristen looked unconvinced. She wanted to see for herself.

Emmy sighed. "This seems so incredibly impossible, but I assure you it's true." Emmy took Kristen's hand. "Mother, one of those strangers… the one who's dying… is your true father."

Kristen stared at Emmy for a few moments. "Is that what he says?"

Emmy shook her head. "He doesn't know you exist. But he IS your father."

"Emmy…"

"Mother," Emmy interrupted. "I understand your soul as only one who was bonded to another can. You think I wouldn't know? Once I found him it wasn't hard to make the connection."

"Once you found him?" Tangus asked.

Emmy looked away.

"What is it, sweetie," Kristen asked.

When the young goddess looked back at her adoptive parents, there were tears in her eyes. "I have to leave soon. I must if I'm to protect the new empath race."

"Protect the empaths from what?" Kristen questioned. "The Purge is dead and the bugs… well, we'll get them cleared out. What other dangers?"

"I don't know," Emmy admitted.

Kristen frowned. "You don't know?!"

"Honey," Tangus pleaded to his wife.

"I'm sorry, mother, I can't give you an answer," Emmy said. "Only that there will be a threat which must be resolved. It rises from the west, past InnisRos."

"But there's nothing but ocean west of InnisRos," Jennifer said.

"That we know of," Tangus replied to his daughter.

"We'll help!" Kristen said.

Emmy shook her head. "I'll only be taking Mariko."

"But…"

"Mother, you and father must protect Adonnenniel. That is your primary concern. I'll not allow her to be exposed to any kind of danger."

After a few moments of silence Kristen nodded in agreement. "Yes, I understand."

Emmy sighed in relief. "I wanted to give you a… a gift. A gift before I left. Only it didn't turn out very well."

"Take me to him, sweetheart."

Rathal lay on the soft grass at the base of the Tree of Golden Radiance in a semi-conscious state. Kneeling next to him, Rhys used a wet cloth to cool the sorcerer's brow. There wasn't much else he could do to combat the fever that had just recently appeared.

Kristen approached cautiously. It appeared inconceivable that he could be her father, but as she gazed into his sweat-lined face she found she couldn't doubt the obvious.

The person kneeling next to him looked up at her, then back down, several times. "You look just like him," he said.

Kristen kneeled and felt the forehead of the sick man. "He can't sustain this fever for long," she said as she prepared magic healing spells. "What's your name."

"Rhys, healer," he replied. "And this is Rathal Arquen, Master Sorcerer and former Lord Paramount of Havendale."

Kristen raised an eyebrow. "Never heard of him."

"Which is a shame," Rhys said. "Young Emmy says he's your father. And looking at you, I don't doubt her."

"I think he's right, dear," Tangus remarked as he walked up.

Kristen nodded. She closed her eyes and concentrated on her magic. The vivacious, blue glow of healing magic left her hands and leaped into Rathal's body. But a countering glow of yellowish green snuffed out her healing attempt. She tried several different enchantments, but all failed like the first.

Kristen kneeled back, defeated. "There's nothing I can do. It's not a disease of the body, but a disease of his magic."

"I'm sorry, mother," Emmy said. "I know you had to try... but he has the gift of prophecy, and that's fatal. There's no exception... no cure... no chance. It's irrevocable. I didn't know this... before. I wanted to bring your father back into your life. But now... well, you're the gift to him. You're the peace he needs to... to die."

Kristen shifted over and put Rathal's head in her lap. She took the wet rag from Rhys and began wiping his face.

Rathal moaned and opened his eyes. They reflected the same fever that heated and destroyed his body. But for a moment, those same eyes cleared and gazed into Kristen's face.

"Annessa, you came back," he whispered.

"You've always been in my heart." Kristen lied.

Rathal smiled, then quietly, peacefully died.

Kristen cradled Rathal's head and silently wept for the father she'd never met.

Mother Aubria looked across the table at her cloaked, masked visitor. She was annoyed. He arrived as she was coordinating the massive effort to move her thieves' guild back to Taranthi now that the dark elf invasion had ended in victory for InnisRos... and she didn't have the time for a tête-à-tête with a representative from the assassin's guild.

"I'm short on time," Mother Aubria said.

"This won't take long," the assassin said as he reached into his cloak and pulled out a small metal coin which he threw on the table.

"What's that," Mother Aubria asked.

The assassin raised an eyebrow. "You don't recognize your own marker?"

Mother Aubria sighed. "I mean how did you get it?"

"The how isn't important. We wish to cash it in."

Mother Aubria picked the coin up. It was hers, no question. But only she had access to a guild marker.

"Who gave this to you?"

"This came from your son," the assassin remarked.

Mother Aubria nodded. She expected as much. The Shinzo Assassin's Guild wouldn't accept her marker from anyone other than her... or someone of her own flesh and blood. "You've held this for a while. My son's been dead for over a year."

The assassin shrugged.

"Who did my son have killed?"

The assassin started to object but stopped. The information was no longer privileged. The client was dead. "His murderer."

Mother Aubria shook her head. "I don't..." Then it made sense. "So that's what happened! There'd been several attempts on his life, so we knew of the danger. You were his assurance that if something happened, the murderer would be hunted down and punished... and that I'd know who it was."

The assassin nodded.

"You gave me closure. Very well, what do you want?"

The assassin removed the hood of his cloak and his mask.

Mother Aubria gasped. It was Master Yukimura, the leader of the assassin's guild himself. Mother Aubria had never seen him, but all the leaders of the underworld knew he was an albino.

"We want the whereabouts of the assassin Mariko Takagi."

On the main island of the Spiral Islands, Jackson Dade Palanquet rolled over and put an arm across his wife, Rose-Merline. He thought he'd heard knocking on his front door, but decided he'd been dreaming. When the knocking came again, this time louder and more insistent, he decided the real world beckoned him.

"Be right there," he called out as he sat on the edge of the bed.

"What is it, Jackson," Rose-Merline asked sleepily.

Jackson looked around as he scratched his lean, taut belly. "It's still early. Go back to sleep."

His wife rolled over and began to snore softly. Jackson wasn't even sure she had come fully awake. He stood and wrapped himself in an eloquent robe, pillaged booty from long ago, before he walked out the bedroom and closed the door behind him.

Jackson yawned as he opened the front double doors to his residence. Two people stood in the portico. He looked them both up and down. One was a crewman from his ship the *Black Bitch*, though he didn't recall his name, and the other was a young girl of around ten. She was scraggly looking, and Jackson thought she was either a run-away or homeless, though one is usually the other. The crewman removed his hat.

"You're...?"

"Wilkey, captain."

Jackson nodded. "And you're here in the middle of the night with a street urchin because?"

Wilkey twisted his hat in his hands. "May we come in, captain?" the crewman asked.

Jackson sighed and motioned for Wilkey and the child to follow him. "Close the door behind you," he said. "Would you care for coffee?"

Wilkey nodded. "That would be most welcome, captain. I do have a bit of a chill."

Jackson put water on the stove and stoked the fire. "Summer hasn't quite released its hold on us, Wilkey." The nights on the Spiral Islands were still warm.

"It's not that type of chill, captain," Wilkey said.

That drew Jackson's attention. He turned. "Sit. What's your name, little girl?"

"Esther."

"And your last," Jackson prompted.

"I don't know," she said. "I ran away from the orphanage before they told me. Besides, kids like me don't get to have a last name until we're adopted, as if that will ever happen."

Jackson brought two mugs of steaming coffee and a glass of milk.

"I want coffee," Esther said.

The pirate captain looked at the girl. She was far too skinny for her age. "Drink the milk first and then you can have a mug of coffee. And breakfast if you want."

"Thank you for the coffee, captain," Wilkey said.

Jackson nodded. "So why did you leave your post on the *Black Bitch* to come here?"

Wilkey lowered his head and studied his mug. "Begging your pardon, sir, but I received permission from the officer of the deck."

"Good," Jackson said. "So, tell me."

"I saw something," Esther blurted out. "Something like I ain't never seen ever before. They was flying in the sky."

Jackson looked at her.

"I saw them too, captain, from the main mast crow's nest," Wilkey added. "Real up-close like."

Jackson looked between the two. Neither appeared to be lying, and Wilkey looked frightened. "All right," he said. "What did you see?"

"Bugs!" the girl said. "Big, giant bugs!"

The young *Theraesus* queen flew high above the landscape. Behind her were eight males – eight warriors who'd die for her. They'd completed the mating ritual, and even now the queen could feel several thousand eggs growing inside of her, including more queens and Custodians. She'd make a grand nest!

Far below the mountains and foothills gave way to a vast, desolate land. The air darkened with dust and limited her vision. Then the winds picked up speed and bombarded them with small rocks and sand. Understanding that refuge was necessary if they were to survive, the queen led her small contingent upwards hoping that sanctuary would be found above the tempest. They broke through the rolling and dangerous clouds several thousand feet up. Clear blue skies awaited them.

Off in the distance a line of mountains pierced the violent melee of the clouds. Even further away a mountain stood that dwarfed the others. At its base, a vast field of iridescent crystal columns reached aloft to pay homage. It was the king of the mountains.

The further they flew towards the massive mountain, the colder it got. The bodies of the queen and her followers evolved to match the changing environment. Chitin was thinning and falling out while underneath extra layers of fat was being added. Coarse hair, like that of a spider, grew over the places exposed by the lost chitin. By the time they reached the king of the mountains and found refuge within one of its many caves, their appearance had completely changed to allow them to survive in their new environment. Even so, they were still the same bugs with the same objectives.

The young *Theraesus* queen settled into her new nest. The males were cleaning the fur on her new body. When they had finished with that task, they'd prepare hatcheries from the many chambers they'd found.

"And then I can lay eggs," the queen thought. *"Yes, it will be a grand and magnificent nest."*

The last Custodian led the third queen and her male attendants across the Olympus Mountains and into the rich forests and farmlands on their western side. He took them south until he found what looked to be a suitable place to build the third nest. It was a huge, thick forest with large rivers on two sides and isolated enough to give the nest time to grow without interference.

As the *Theraesus* descended into the forest, the Custodian sensed a change taking place within his body. Now it was only a hint – not enough to be a cause for alarm – but enough to give him pause. By the time they had finished building an underground complex of tunnels and chambers, the evolutionary change taking place in each bug had completed itself. Their chitin exoskeletons remained, but coloring changed to a mottled green and brown to match the trees of the forest. Specialized limbs grew out of their bodies with claws which could be used to either climb trees or move dirt. Hollow tubes had grown out of their backs which kept the creatures cooler in the hotter environment.

With few exceptions the Custodian was satisfied… not only with the forest environment but also the changes that had taken place in each of them. It insured their viability. He wanted to visit the other nests to see if physical changes affected them as well, but that would have to wait until this nest had matured, for there were elements of the forest that concerned him… elements that would seek their destruction.

"Danger! Just like our home world," the Custodian thought. *"But unlike our home world, this one has plenty of food."*

AUTHOR'S NOTE

In the world of Dungeons and Dragons – a world I have frequent many times – as well as the majority of fantasy books I've read over the years, magic users (sorcerers and clerics) generally release their magic by a series of words (incantations). This is normally accompanied by hand manipulations, reading from a magical tome, or using a magical item such as a staff. Usually the words themselves are magical and used to focus the energy of the spell just before it's discharged. Since the words are, for the most part, unique to the discipline of either the sorcerer or cleric, I felt they needed to be set apart. To do this, I converted the words or phrases I developed to Latin. (Although I took two years of Latin in high school, my present knowledge of the language is no more than that of someone who's never studied it.) I used translators I found on Google. If you're so inclined, you can use Google or any other search engine to go back to the English translation... though it's not critical to the story. Some mysteries, particularly those of respected sorcerers and clerics, should remain secret.

This is also true of the dark elf language… true in the sense that if you were so inclined, you could use any number of translator mechanisms available on the Internet to determine what's being said. For the language of the dark elves, I used Chinese Mandarin. (I did provide a translator in the story, however, so it's really not necessary to look them up. Unless of course, you think I may be sending secret coded messages to a mysterious foreign entity – or aliens!)

ABOUT THE AUTHOR

Robert E. Balsley, Jr. (1954 -) was born in Sioux City, Iowa. At the age of four his parents moved their family to Cincinnati, Ohio. Upon graduation from high school in 1973, Robert joined the United States Air Force which sent him to Tinker Air Force Base, Oklahoma. Upon his discharge in 1979, he found employment as a civil servant on Tinker until his retirement in 2014. In 2018 Robert and his wife picked up roots and moved from Oklahoma to Burlington, Kentucky, which is just across the Ohio River from Cincinnati.

In 1990 he played his first game of Dungeons and Dragons and was soon writing his own games. From this sprang the ideas which ultimately led to his love of writing and the creation of his current novels. Many of the main characters are based upon actual people who played Dungeons and Dragons with him all those years. This includes personalities, idiosyncrasies, and all those other traits that make friends so endearing… and fictional characters so alive!

Throughout his life he's been an avid reader of science fiction and fantasy. Isaac Asimov, James Bliss, David Eddings, George R.R. Martin, Terry Goodkind, and Robert Heinlein are among his favorite authors.

Robert's also a collector of figures and models such as Star Trek spaceships, WWII airplanes, Dungeons and Dragons miniatures, TV and movie monster figures (particularly Godzilla), and dragons to name a few. It's in this world of mankind's rich imagination that he develops his stories, plots, subplots, heroic and cowardly deeds, laughter, tears (and all the emotions in between) that make tales come alive for the reader… that makes the reader want to "turn the page".